Love and Duty

Judith Henry Wall

LOVE and DUTY

VIKING

VIKING
Published by the Penguin Group
Viking Penguin Inc., 40 West 23rd Street,
New York, New York 10010, U.S.A.
Penguin Books Ltd, 27 Wrights Lane,
London W8 5TZ, England
Penguin Books Australia Ltd, Ringwood,
Victoria, Australia
Penguin Books Canada Ltd, 2801 John Street,
Markham, Ontario, Canada L3R 1B4
Penguin Books (N.Z.) Ltd, 182-190 Wairau Road,
Auckland 10, New Zealand

Penguin Books Ltd, Registered Offices:
Harmondsworth, Middlesex, England

First published in 1988 by Viking Penguin Inc.
Published simultaneously in Canada

Grateful acknowledgment is made for permission to reprint an
excerpt from "God Bless America" by Irving Berlin. © Copyright
1938, 1939 by Irving Berlin. © Copyright renewed 1965, 1966 by
Irving Berlin. © Copyright assigned to Mrs. Ralph J. Bunche, Joe
DiMaggio and Theodore R. Jackson as Trustees of God Bless
America Fund. Reprinted by permission of Irving Berlin Music
Corporation and Chappell International Music Publishers Ltd.

LIBRARY OF CONGRESS CATALOGING IN PUBLICATION DATA
Wall, Judith Henry.
   Love and duty.
   I. Title.
PS3573.A42556L67   1988   813'.54   87-40669
ISBN 0-670-82316-3

Printed in the United States of America by
Arcata Graphics, Fairfield, Pennsylvania
Set in Goudy Old Style

With love to Jim—for the good times.

No book ever happens in isolation. Thanks are in order.

First, to four women in Texas who made pre–World War II New Braunfels come alive for me: Carolyn Karbach Barry, Margaret Pfullman Fields, Anita Hanz Jaroszewski, and Betty Pfueffer Triesch.

To my friend and colleague Joan Atterbury, who serves as my daily sounding board.

And special thanks to my agent, Philippa Brophy, of Sterling Lord Literistic, and my editor, Pamela Dorman, of Viking Penguin, who both deserve enormous credit for making this book happen.

Love and Duty

Prologue

At first Stella thought the man only resembled Charles Lasseter. Her mind denied the possibility. It couldn't really be Charles.

She was having lunch with her sister in the tearoom at Neiman-Marcus. It was a special treat they allowed themselves from time to time—hiring a baby-sitter and riding the bus into downtown Dallas. They would wander through Neiman's, touching the expensive luxuries, then share one of the delightful little lunches that somehow managed to overcome wartime shortages. The lunches, like the rest of the grand old store, were comforting. They made one feel, at least for a time, that the world was not so changed, after all.

The scattering of men in uniform throughout the dining room made it hard to ignore that it was 1944, and America was at war.

Sometimes their cousin Effie joined them. It was nicer when Effie was along. She actually shopped. Some of the salesclerks even knew her by name. But Effie was in Houston this week looking after her husband's business. Her William was in the South Pacific. Stella's and Kate's husbands were in Europe.

Kate continued to chatter away between bites of chicken salad, her voice blending into the genteelly muted tones of the other diners. A woman in black softly played a piano. Gershwin. Porter. The white-jacketed Negro waiters went efficiently about their serving, and an occasional model wearing a sample of the stylish finery to be found on the floors below appeared on the runway in the center of the room. Eisenhower jackets were the latest style. And cocky little hats. Skirts were short. A lot of plaid.

"Let's do something with the children this weekend," her sister was saying. "If it's pretty Sunday, we can take them on a picnic. I'll bring the camera, and we'll take some pictures to send to the guys."

The man across the room *was* Charles, Stella realized slowly, as Kate's words faded into the background noise.

2 ~ Judith Henry Wall

Charles.

Everyone, everything in the large room went out of focus except him.

He was in uniform. He was with someone—a woman. Her back was to Stella. His wife probably. She was talking to him, her head nodding up and down, but he wasn't listening. His gaze was fixed over her shoulder—on Stella.

With a slight nod, he acknowledged her, and Stella tilted her head ever so slightly in return.

She did not know until that moment just how much she still cared. Stella had long ago convinced herself that Charles Lasseter no longer mattered. She was a married woman. She had a child. He should be of no more interest to her than any other old flame. Except he had been her only "old flame"—the only one who really mattered, and they had not parted friends.

There had been other times over the last five years when she had seen a man across a room or across a street and thought for an instant that it was Charles. Her heart would skip a beat, her throat would go dry, then she would realize she was mistaken and the moment would pass. But this had happened less and less frequently—not for at least a year now. She was finally over Charles.

Or was she?

"Are you all right?" Kate asked impatiently.

Stella could tell by her sister's tone that she was repeating the question.

"Yes. I thought I saw someone I knew. But yes, a picnic would be fine."

"If Effie gets back, she can bring Billy," Kate said. "She may stop over in New Braunfels, though—to see her folks. Aunt Hannah's been sick."

New Braunfels. Stella used to tell Charles about back home—about the ranch, her parents, her relatives, even silly things like how she and Kate and Effie waited for the M. K. & T. on summer mornings so they could wave at the engineer. Sometimes they put pennies on the track. She used to dream about taking Charles to New Braunfels, of sitting with him on the front porch in the evening and listening to the katydids, of dancing a polka with him at the dance hall in Gruene, of the two of them rowing across the lake at Landa Park, of listening to a concert from the bandstand in the square.

He was rising, pulling back the woman's chair. Yes, it was his wife. His arm was in a sling. They were coming this way.

Stella felt the inside of her throat swelling. She tried to swallow. So handsome. Still so handsome. Older. Gray at the temples. Rows of ribbons on his chest.

Somehow she managed to get through the next few minutes. She told her face to smile. She couldn't meet his eyes. "Kate, this is an old friend—Charles Lasseter," she said. "He's Blanche Lasseter's nephew—you remember, she was the professor at the university I was so fond of."

He asked how she had been. Just fine, she told him. She had a little girl. Her husband was an Army chaplain—in Italy with the Forty-fifth Division. Charles was in the Corps of Engineers. He and his wife had a little boy.

His arm? Nothing really, he told them, but it had provided him with the opportunity to come home for a while.

So polite. So stilted.

His wife's smile was gracious. Stella had forgotten how elegant she was.

Charles touched Stella ever so lightly on the shoulder before guiding his wife to the elevator with his good arm.

Kate looked at her strangely. "You never said anything about Professor Lasseter having a nephew."

Stella shrugged but said nothing. They finished their meal in silence, pretending to concentrate on the models with their preview of fall fashions. Stella found it difficult to swallow.

She knew he would call. When the phone rang the next morning, Stella knew it would be Charles.

One

The distant whistle heralding the M. K. & T.'s crossing of the Guadalupe River drifted across the clear Texas morning and reached the big white house on the hill—a gaunt house with no shutters and no painted trim. The sky was cloudless and vividly blue; the grass had yellowed from the summer heat. The tracks stretched in two silver stripes, northeast toward San Marcus and southwest toward San Antonio.

Three girls—one in overalls, the other two in ankle-length shifts—burst out the front door, the screen door banging behind them, and raced toward the railroad tracks at the bottom of the hill. Three sets of pigtails—one set blond, one brown, and the other carroty red—bobbed up and down with each step.

In spite of the difference in hair color, the family resemblance among the three was strong, and they were often taken for sisters. But Effie was a cousin. Stella and Kate were sisters.

Stella's hair was brown, parted in the middle, and lay across her head like a sleek, shiny cap. Two silver barrettes caught the hair at the end of her smooth, thick braids.

Her cousin Effie's corn-silk blond hair curled fetchingly about her face, and the ends of her pigtails were tied with crisp pink bows.

And from her sister Kate's rubber-banded red braids, loose strands escaped and flew about her head like an unruly halo. Dressed in overalls and sneakers, Kate easily outdistanced the other two girls and was already perched on the rail fence by the time Stella arrived.

Stella seated herself and watched the dainty Effie skip the last yards, her pretty face flushed from the unaccustomed exercise. Sam, an old black-and-white mongrel, came loping up to join the girls. He put his front paws on Stella's knees, dripping saliva from his great pink tongue onto her dress. Stella hugged him and scratched his ears. Sam was her dog.

"I have pennies," Effie announced breathlessly, and reached into the pocket of her dress.

With a war whoop, Kate leaped from the fence. Stella followed, and Sam barked excitedly, his tail waving frantically. Each girl took a penny to place on the track. Already the ten-o-five's roar could be heard as it climbed the last hill before reaching the edge of the Behrman property. Pennies in place, the girls knelt by the track, and three heads—blond, brown, and red—bent to place an ear on the sun-warmed track and listen to the song of the approaching train.

By the time the train was in view, Stella and Effie had scrambled back to the safety of the fence and were seated on the top rail. Effie squealed at Kate to come. Her voice was almost lost in the roar of the approaching train.

Always the daredevil, Kate waited until a note of hysteria crept into Effie's voice; then, satisfied, she withdrew to the fence, straddling it and bouncing up and down as if she were riding a horse.

Stella thrilled as the train's roar filled the air and the ground shook and trembled beneath her. No matter how many times she sat on the fence and watched a train pass, it never ceased to excite her.

Watching the morning train go by was a ritual of summer they'd performed almost daily as long as Stella could remember. Except for Sundays when the family went into New Braunfels for services at the stately Reformed Protestant Church on Comal Street or on the days the girls drove with one of the uncles or older cousins over to the feed store in nearby village of Gruene, Stella would run after Kate down the long hill to the train track. When Effie was visiting, she would run after them.

The comings and goings of the Missouri, Kansas, and Texas line punctuated the lives of those who lived along its track. Its destinations were the ingredients of daydreams for the young girls. They made up stories about some of the people whose faces they glimpsed through the windows of the train. Someday *they* would ride to far-off places on the M. K. & T., watching the farms and towns and cities roll past. They would wave out the window to children sitting on fences.

The engineer offered a greeting whistle for the benefit of the three girls and their mongrel dog. The girls counted thirty cars, but as usual, it was the dining car that fascinated Stella the most. Glimpses of the white tablecloths, a silver vase on each table with its pink carnation, the white-clad waiters serving the well-dressed diners. Imagine eating a meal in such an elegant setting while watching the world go by.

The lady in the hat, Effie decided, was a Hollywood movie star on her way back to California after an international tour during which two princes and a prime minister fell in love with her. Kate decided that the bald man was an FBI agent following the man at the next table whom he suspected of robbing banks. Stella speculated about the two nuns who had been sitting at the last table. Her father did not approve of Catholicism for Anglos, but Stella was intrigued by the mystery of women who spent their lives wearing black habits, cloistered from the world. The older nun, she decided, had lived among the lepers in Africa and bravely nursed their rotting bodies, offering them spiritual comfort to the end. The older woman was now returning to the mother convent to spend her remaining years in prayer and meditation. The younger nun had been in love with a brave young man who had been killed in the war. Before giving her life to God, the woman had made a pilgrimage to France and placed flowers on his grave. "In Flanders fields the poppies blow/Between the crosses, row on row." Stella closed her eyes and visualized the beautiful young woman kneeling there in the poppies among the endless rows of white crosses, reverently touching that one particular cross with gloved fingers, her blue eyes filling with tears as she said her last farewell to her lost love before returning to the United States and giving the remainder of her life to God.

"Oh, Stella, your story is best," her cousin Effie said with a sigh, her own blue eyes glistening just a little. "So beautiful. You should write it down. Don't you think so, Kate?"

Kate shrugged and scratched her freckled nose. "I don't like sad stories. I'd have the younger nun looking across the aisle and seeing the guy she thought was dead. But the report of his death had been false, and he'd been looking for her ever since. Maybe he'd heard she'd died in a flood or an earthquake. Then right there in the dining car, they found each other. They're probably hugging right now."

"Men can't hug nuns, silly," Effie protested. "If they had found each other, it would be too late. The nun has already taken her sacred vows. No, that would be sadder than having him be dead."

"Don't be dumb, Effie," Kate said matter-of-factly. "Nothing is sadder than dead."

"No," Stella said softly, "the saddest of all would be if no one had ever loved her."

"Well, if anyone ever loves me," Kate announced, hooking her thumbs into her overall straps, "he can come with me on the train. I want to run races all over the world. I'm going to be in the Olympics. I'm going to be the fastest girl in the world. I want to be famous and have reporters meet the train wherever I go."

"I want to be famous too. I'd like to be married to a president or a senator and go around with him when he campaigns from the back of a train," Effie said enthusiastically, her blue eyes sparkling. "I want to go to New York and Hollywood and Niagara Falls on the train. Wouldn't that be romantic?" She sighed and absently twisted a corkscrew curl at the end of her blond braid.

"I'd be happy just to look out the window and learn about the world. Someday," Stella announced resolutely as she scratched Sam's head, "we will be on that train. And not just to go to San Marcos either. Someplace far away. Someday we will." Stella thought of all the places she had read about in books. The family—except for her mother—teased her about reading all the time, but there was so much to learn about. Would she ever go to Hong Kong or Africa? Would she ever see the Northern Lights or the Eiffel Tower? Or would she live and die in Comal County, Texas, like all the other Behrmans?

The girls stared down the track for a while, lost in their daydreams, but for Stella, the two nuns faded away very quickly. She had a wonderful secret. Tomorrow was the last day of German school. For three days a week every summer, New Braunfels' children who were descended from the original German settlers were sent to learn German from Pastor Ludwig Mueller at the Reformed Protestant Church. At the session's end parents were invited for the closing exercises. Stella was to receive the certificate for the best German language skills, and how proud her papa would be.

Kate jumped down first and ran to fetch the flattened coins. Such a miracle! The pennies were now larger in circumference than a fifty-cent piece, with the head of Lincoln still faintly discernible.

One of the Mexican children—Manuel—told the girls that these pennies brought good luck. Manuel was the oldest of the five children of the Mexican couple who lived in the two-room house in back of the barn. He said that putting a penny under a train and thereby giving up the gum or candy it would buy was like buying a candle to burn in church or not eating meat on Friday—a sacrifice. And if it was done with a pure mind, good things would happen to you. Stella had never heard of buying candles to burn at church, but she knew that Catholics didn't eat meat on Friday. It didn't seem either custom had brought much good luck to the Mexicans around New Braunfels, who were all poor laborers and lived with large families in tiny houses behind barns. And Stella wondered if it was wrong to ruin money.

She knew that her father would think so and would lecture them about the Depression, how times were hard and money was dear. No, Frederick Behrman certainly would not approve of wasting money. Pennies added up. Fifteen cents would buy a pound of round steak. And Frederick lived by the frugalness he tried to instill in his daughters. But Stella liked the smashed coins just the same and saved them. They seemed to symbolize a kind of power—not only the power of a train that could so drastically alter something that seemed inalterable but also her own power to instigate such a change.

Stella's collection of flattened coins resided in a small wooden box she kept in her secret place under a floorboard in the storeroom of the cavernous barn. Along with the coins were assorted treasures that brought her pleasure when she took them out and examined them. There was a notebook in which she wrote down things like how it must feel to be a Mexican instead of an Anglo or how badly she wanted to win the certificate at German school. And she copied down poems in her notebooks—she had already filled two of them. She had made up a few poems but suspected they were dumb. In her notebooks, however, she listed mostly facts. Whenever she heard a fact she wanted to remember, she wrote it in the book. A black man named John died at the Alamo. A woman was elected to the Texas senate in 1926; her name was Margie Neal. The Great Wall of China was more than 1,500 miles long. Martha Washington had four children by her first husband but two died in infancy.

And in the box was a small mirror and a tube of Tangee lipstick purchased during a rare burst of courage when no family members were around at Richter's Drugstore in New Braunfels. From time to time, Stella put on the lipstick and rouged her cheeks with it. Then she would stare at herself in the mirror in an attempt to get some feeling for the woman she would someday be—not that any of the grown-up women in her family wore lipstick, but Stella was fascinated by women who did. Makeup could make one look older and glamorous. Sometimes she would unbutton a few buttons of her dress and pull it off her shoulders and unbraid her hair to let it fall over her bare skin. Would she be beautiful? she wondered as she held the mirror away from her in an attempt to get a fuller view.

Would she have alluring, big breasts? Effie was almost two years older than Stella and already she had started her periods. She had budding breasts that caused the fabric in the front of her print dresses to drape in an entirely different fashion from before and had brought sidelong glances from the boys at school. But then Effie would surely have wonderful breasts. Everything about Effie was soft and feminine and pretty. Even her feet were pretty. When she came with Stella to the barn and put on the magical orange lipstick that turned purplish red on lips, Effie looked like the women who stared at them from the covers of magazines in the newsstand at the drugstore.

Eleven months older that Stella, twelve-year-old Kate would have none of her sister's lipstick. Kate was more interested in climbing trees and riding around on Jack, her old gray donkey. Her skinny, boyish figure showed no signs of turning womanly. Stella realized that this suited her sister just fine. Kate hated girl's clothes and seemed determined to remain a tomboy as long as she could get away with it. Stella suspected, however, that Kate's days of freedom were rapidly drawing to an end. If Frederick Behrman had had any idea how far and wide his older daughter roamed by herself or with one of the children from their Mexican family, he would have already put an end to it.

The last object in Stella's treasure box was a picture of Amelia Earhart clipped from New Braunfels' newspaper—a German language publication, *Neu Braunfels Zeitung*. Amelia Earhart had been a passenger in an airplane that flew across the Atlantic—the first woman ever to cross the ocean in an airplane. The caption under the picture said Miss Earhart's goal was to fly across the Atlantic alone, piloting her own airplane. Amelia Earhart was beautiful and brave, a wondrous combination. Stella would have settled for one or the other—beautiful or brave—but to have both embodied in one real-life woman was wonderful. If she accomplished her goal and flew across the ocean by herself, Amelia Earhart would surely be the most special woman in the world. She would prove women could be important—as Joan of Arc and Madame Curie and Queen Elizabeth had done.

Her newest flattened penny safely hidden away in the deep pocket of her shapeless dress, Stella followed her cousin and sister back up the hill to the big, plain ranch house that occupied its crest. It was already hot, and a line of moisture sprouted on her upper lip.

The original frame house had only three rooms when the Behrmans built it after they arrived from Germany in 1845 with the community's first wave of 285 immigrants. But subsequent generations had enlarged the house and added a second floor. The side of the house facing the railroad tracks was saved from starkness by a broad porch that ran across the width of the house. The porch was where family and visitors retired on a summer's evening to cool themselves after the heat of a Texas day. There was no porch on the back side of the house, which greeted visitors who came up the winding gravel lane connecting the farm to Hunter Road. Not even a stoop protected the door into the kitchen, which was how everyone entered the house. Perhaps at one time previous Behrmans planned to bring a drive around to the front and have guests enter through the formal parlor that occupied the northwest corner downstairs. But even the pastor was led through the kitchen before being seated in the parlor. Most of the visitors to the big white ranch house, however, never got past the kitchen but took a seat at the large round table where they were served a meal with the family or coffee and a piece of Anna Behrman's excellent strudel.

A durable tin roof covered the house. Tin roofs predominated in New Braunfels and the surrounding countryside. With typical German practicality, the town's residents opted for a roof that lasted indefinitely and gave them best rates on fire insurance, rather than the more aesthetically pleasing shingle roofs of adjoining towns. New Braunfels was known as the city of tin roofs.

The ranch was sometimes called Rosenheim, or Rosehaven, its name derived from the hardy roses that climbed the front porch railing and the rail fence that ran along the Hunter Road boundary of the property. No one knew how long the roses had been there, but the earliest family pictures—usually of groups standing on the porch steps—proved the roses had been there for a good while, surviving the heat and the wind and droughts of south central Texas.

To the west of the house were the outbuildings—a freshly painted red barn that was considerably larger than the house, a silo, the chicken house, a combination garage and toolshed, a goat shed where the goats were brought for shearing, and a whitewashed Mexican house. East of the main house was a huge garden surrounded by a ten-foot wire fence to keep the deer out.

A lone stately oak shaded the porch side of the house. Stella looked forward to the day when she would push a little brother or sister on the tire swing that hung from its branches. The prospect of a baby brought another smile to her lips. Maybe her father would not get so upset over Kate's behavior when he had a new baby to take his mind off things. Stella knew Papa wanted a son. She'd heard him talk about it with the uncles. He wanted a son to farm the land with him. When Stella asked her mother if she too wanted a son, Anna had said with a shrug, "It has already been decided, so why bother with wishful thinking? I will take what is there and hope for a healthy baby."

Stella and Kate had both been born in their parents' upstairs bedroom. The child their mother was expecting would greet the world for the first time in that room. Stella stared up at the window over the porch and pondered the mystery of birth, a subject much on her mind of late. Anna's swollen belly had precipitated much discussion among the girls. Stella knew about mating and birthing. The breeding of goats and pigs and cows was of prime importance on the ranch. But her mother and father? Stella could not conceive of such a thing. Occasionally Anna and Frederick danced together at the community dances, but other than that, Stella had seldom seen her parents touch each other. Yet the proof that they had mated like the animals was there in the enormous bulge under Anna's smock.

Stella wished her mother weren't quite so pregnant just yet. She knew Anna would not be making the bumpy trip into town for the closing ceremonies tomorrow. Stella wished her mother could be there, but if she had to choose which of her parents should come, it would be her papa. He set great store on preserving the German language among the German community, and he believed in the rewards of hard work.

Anna had come out onto the front porch and seated herself on a straight-backed wooden chair. She was snapping beans from a bushel basket beside her and letting them fall into a bowl she held in her lap. Effie and Stella pulled a backless bench close, and the three girls joined in. Stella's fingers were as nimble and quick as her mother's as she snapped the ends off the freshly picked green beans and broke them into even segments. She knew that some would be cooked fresh for dinner that night, but the rest would be cooked in the big pressure cooker and put up into Mason jars to be stored on shelves in the cellar for the winter.

Effie, too, deftly snapped the beans into the bowl while chattering about the new church dress her mother made for her to wear for her baby brother's christening and of her family's plans for the christening celebration, which would be held in just two days. "Papa says Mama is cooking enough food for an army. He's had the Mexicans paint the fences, and we've beaten all the rugs. I'm glad the christening's in the summer so we can have flowers in the parlor. I love flowers in vases. It's so *genteel.*"

"Genteel" was Effie's new word. She used it constantly. Last month's word was "enamored." Stella like to read books where people used fancy words, but she herself was too bashful to use them.

Kate elected to forgo the bench and sat cross-legged on the floor by the bushel basket. She was as awkward with the beans as the others were deft. Her segments were uneven, and she would often forget to snap off the ends and didn't seem to notice when one of the others retrieved one of her beans from the bowl to correct her oversight. She stared off in the direction of the barn, where the voices of Carlos and Marie's brood could be heard excitedly calling to one another.

"What's going on with the Mexicans?" Kate asked her mother.

"I imagine they're killing chickens," Anna said, her voice flat, tired. "I told Carlos I needed four fryers to cook up for the christening dinner. And yes, you can go help. I'm sure you can wring a rooster's neck better than you can snap a bean."

Anna's gaze followed Kate as her older daughter exited the porch by vaulting over the railing, then leaped over the hedgerow and raced around the corner of the house. Stella already knew the next words that would come out of her mother's mouth. "That girl's going to be the death of me." Anna said it more out of habit than anger. And sometimes Stella thought she detected a note of affectionate pride in her mother's voice as she said it. Kate was not pretty like their cousin Effie. She was not a good student in school like Stella. Kate would rather play ball or run races with boys than flirt with them. What to do about Katherine was a constant topic of discussion among the aunts. But Stella suspected her mother entered into such talks only halfheartedly. Indeed, last Sunday she had heard Anna say to Effie's mother that the girl just marched to her own drummer.

"Well, you better do something to change her tune," Hannah Behrman had clucked. Hannah was an older, plumper version of her pretty daughter, Effie. Although her beauty was fading, her blue eyes, clear skin, and blond hair were still admired. "Katherine will find herself an old maid if she's not careful," Hannah had continued. "No man wants to marry a girl who climbs trees better than she can make a pie. Our Effie and Stella will have no trouble finding nice young men to marry them, but I worry about Kate."

"Being an old maid isn't the end of the world," Anna had said. "Don't forget, that's what everyone said I was for a long time."

That had been a strange revelation for Stella—that her mother had once been considered an old maid. Stella knew from simple arithmetic that her mother had been past thirty by the time she had children, but Stella had never given much thought to her mother's life before marriage and motherhood. Old maids were the passed-over women—it was a state to be avoided. It bothered Stella that her mother once had been a subject of pity.

Stella reached into the bushel basket and pulled out two handfuls of beans. She opened her legs to make a scooped-out place in her skirt and put the unsnapped beans there. As she resumed her snapping, she stared at her mother. Anna's hair was showing the first signs of gray, and a network of crinkly, dry lines radiated from her eyes. Her jaw was very square—like Kate's. But her nose was straight and narrow, and she had wonderfully even, white teeth. Still, she definitely looked older than Aunt Hannah and Aunt Louise. Of course, Frederick was the oldest Behrman brother. It was expected that his wife would also be the oldest.

Stella was aware that her father had been married once before—that there had been another wife who had died giving birth to a baby. The baby died too. A boy. Mother and baby were both buried under a small granite marker in the family plot at the cemetery on Peace Road. Frederick's first wife had been named Anna too. "Anna Marie Behrman," it said on the marker. How strange for a man to have had two wives with the same name. Stella's middle name was Anna. She wondered if she was named in honor of just her mother or of both women, but she had never asked. The first Anna was never discussed.

A small sigh escaped from Anna's lips, and she leaned back in her chair, her eyes closed for an instant. When she opened them, she stared past Effie and Stella, not focusing on anything. She seemed to have forgotten that the two girls were there. She leaned forward and rubbed the small of her back. Another sigh escaped from her lips. "You girls finish the beans. I'm going in the house to rest."

Stella and Effie exchanged puzzled glances. Anna never rested. And it was time to begin preparing the midday meal.

In half an hour, however, Anna was in her kitchen stirring the pot of peas. Effie and Stella set the table and sliced the bread. Frederick drove up in the Ford truck at precisely noon. Stella pumped water at the sink while he washed his face and hands. Effie handed him a towel. "Where's your sister?" he asked Stella.

Anna spared her daughter an answer. "I sent her to help kill the chickens. She's probably plucking the feathers. Run, fetch her, Stella."

Stella ran. The Riveras were at lunch. The unplucked chickens hung by their feet from a hook on the front porch of the Mexican house.

Kate was not in the barn. Neither was her donkey.

Frederick was tight-lipped when Stella slipped into her place at the table. Kate's empty chair stood like an accusation. Stella bowed her head while her father offered his prayer.

"Komm Herr Jesu, sei unser Gast,
Und segne was Du uns bescheret hast."

Then he asked for special blessing on the nephew about to be dedicated to a lifetime of service to the Almighty. He offered thanks for the bounties of the land. Amen.

"Amen," Stella and her mother repeated.

The meal was eaten in silence. Sausage, bread, black-eyed peas, hot potato salad made with bacon and poppy seeds.

Stella and Effie brought the chickens to the back step and started the plucking. At one o'clock, however, Effie's oldest brother, Hiram, came to get the girls in the truck that served during the school year as a school bus to take the older children to town. And sometimes Hiram would drop the younger children by Thornhill School on days it was too cold or stormy for them to ride their donkeys.

Kate had still not returned. Frederick told Hiram to go ahead without her. "The rest of the children should not be late to German school because Kate is irresponsible," he said, his jaw tight.

Kate didn't come home until almost six. She came riding up the hill on Jack with three catfish on a string. Frederick marched her upstairs. Why did Kate do it, Stella wondered, when she knew the razor strap awaited her? Why? Stella had never felt the sting of the razor strap on the back of her own thighs. She would have hated the pain and humiliation, but more than that, she would hate to have displeased her father so much that he was driven to beat her. Frederick all but begged his older daughter to mind him so he did not have to whip her, but Kate seemed to think her freedom was worth any price.

Stella ran across the yard to the barn. Sam crawled out from under the porch and followed her. She didn't want to hear the sound of the strap hitting her sister's skinny, bare thighs. Kate would not cry out, which almost made it worse. Stella knew her sister's cries remained inside of her—her way of punishing her father in return. He would not make her cry.

Carlos was doing the milking. Sam resumed his nap in a corner of a stall. Stella leaned her cheek against the smooth, warm side of the cow. Queeny, this one was called. Stella liked the cows—even Big Bertha who sometimes kicked over the milk pail. In spite of their size, the cows were gentle and harmless. Their soft lowing was a good, comforting sound.

She watched as Carlos's hands deftly worked Queeny's udders and squirted the milk into the galvanized pail. She took comfort in the sights and sounds and smells of the barn. With its high-pitched ceiling and spaciousness, the majestic barn reminded her of church. A sanctuary.

When they were little, she and Kate played in the empty stalls and in the loft among the bales. Now Stella liked to carry a book up to the loft to read. Mother cats went up there to birth their babies. Barn owls built their crude nests in the rafters.

Carlos looked at her, his flat brown face questioning.

"Kate's in trouble for being gone all afternoon without permission," she explained. Carlos nodded. He understood.

As she watched Carlos milk, she tried to calm herself with thoughts of tomorrow. At least Kate had skipped German school today and would not spoil the closing ceremony by being conspicuously absent when the parents visited tomorrow. Stella thought of herself in her pale yellow dress with the lace collar, sitting with the other children in the front pews. There would be the invocations, the recitations, the singing. Each child would be called upon to say a Bible verse in German. Matilda Neiderhaus would sing *"Ein' feste Burg ist unser Gott"* in her impressive soprano. All the children would join in other German hymns. The Berger children would play their accordions. Effie would play the piano.

Then the awards would be given. Perfect attendance awards. Most improvement. Best overall German language student. For that award, Stella's name would be called. She would march, straight-backed, up to the railing and turn to face the audience while Pastor Mueller read the certificate. She would look at her father then. Papa would be smiling at her. That proud smile would make all the endless hours of study worthwhile.

But Kate's name would not be called for anything. Stella doubted her sister could say her assigned Bible verse in German without stumbling.

For a minute Stella was almost glad her sister was getting a spanking. Kate might as well skip school tomorrow, too. She had already ruined Stella's surprise. How could she enjoy being the best when her achievements only served to call attention to her own sister's shortcomings? Stella, the good sister. Kate, the difficult child. Why did she have to feel guilty for being good? Stella thought bitterly.

Being good was what children were supposed to be.

TWO

Kate had realized she would get a spanking for skipping German school, but she had lost the piece of paper with the Bible verse she was supposed to learn in German. That morning she had looked for it in every place she could think of—in pockets, under the bed, behind the bureau, everywhere. She stood in the middle of the room she shared with her sister and looked around at the mess she had made. The bed and the bureau were pulled out from the wall, and the bureau drawers were open, their contents spilling out onto the linoleum floor. Her Bible and German school notebook were open on the bed.

Hands in her overall pockets, Kate stared at herself in the mirror over the bureau and considered her choices. She could be absent tomorrow for the closing day ceremonies. She could go to Pastor Mueller this afternoon on this next-to-last day and admit she had lost the paper and needed another copy. Then he would know she had not been studying it. He would admonish her in front of the others, and he would probably tell Papa. No, he would most certainly tell Papa.

Or she could learn a substitute verse.

Stella's verse was stuck in the frame of the Jesus-at-the-gate picture that hung over the bed. Stella practiced it every night. It was from Proverbs. Stella translated it, explaining to Kate that it was a message to daughters about how favor is deceitful and beauty is vain, but a woman who feared God should be praised, and the work of her hands would bring her praise at the gate.

"What's your verse about?" Stella asked.

"Just dumb stuff, like yours," Kate hedged.

If she had to learn a verse, Kate would have preferred one about fighting battles or vengeance with fiery swords. If she knew German better, she might be able to find such a verse in Papa's big Bible that rested, in a place of honor, on a round table covered with a fringed scarf in the parlor. But most of Kate's German consisted of the phrases that peppered her mama and papa's speech. The written German word was still a mystery. She didn't like learning German. She didn't like German school. And most of all Kate didn't like stern Pastor Mueller. Stella didn't like German school either—not really. She'd admit it when Kate pressured her. All it meant to Stella was another opportunity to make Papa proud of her, but she was so sweet and good when she was there you'd think she adored ruining a summer's afternoon practicing German. Maybe that sweet and good stuff was all right for their cousin Effie; it was hard to imagine Effie being any other way. But sometimes Kate wished her sister had a little more spunk. Kate hoped the new baby was a boy and not another girl who would be good all the time.

Kate had put the room back in order and made a copy of Stella's verse. It was tucked in her pocket when she rode off on Jack to go fishing, her legs wrapped tightly around the donkey's sturdy, round body, her fishing pole in one hand, a can of worms in the other. Kate propped the pole and spent the next-to-last day of German school walking up and down the bank reciting the Bible passage to Jack, who paid little attention and used the time to doze in the shade provided by a clump of willows. Kate said the verse over and over, determined to have it perfect. No one—not the aunts and uncles, not Papa, not Pastor Mueller—was going to find fault. No one was going to shake his head and sigh over "that Katherine." Not this time. She would know it just as well as Stella.

Kate was not without fear on the way home from her fishing expedition. She fully understood that a whipping awaited her, but she had made her choice. It had always been that way—weighing her actions against a whipping. Still, the closer she and Jack got to home, the more perspiration damped her underarms and the dryer her throat became. Papa hit her harder now. Kate realized that he had held himself back when she was younger. But now that she was a big girl of twelve and still didn't mind him, he came down harder with the strap. If she didn't stop forcing him to whip her, Kate knew the day was coming when she would have to cry out in pain.

Kate wasn't going to get married and have babies. She was going to be famous, but if she *were* to get married, she wouldn't let her husband beat their children. She'd beat him up first. Maybe women should try to find small husbands in case they had to fight them. Kate thought of her own mother, who never interfered with the whippings, but Kate could tell by the way Anna held her mouth that she didn't approve.

While Frederick struck her repeatedly with the black leather strap he used to sharpen his razor, Kate tried to think of the words to the verse. Just wait until tomorrow, Kate thought silently, her teeth biting into her lip until she tasted blood. Would he ever be surprised! He thought she didn't know anything.

Kate sat alone in the bedroom until bedtime when Stella timidly opened the door. "Don't talk to me!" Kate barked.

Stella said nothing but put two biscuits and an apple on the bureau. Then she brought a wet cloth for Kate's swollen lip. Kate tried to ignore the food, but she hadn't had anything since breakfast. Silently, she munched on the biscuits. When she bit into the apple, it made a loud crunching sound in the quiet room.

Two dresses hung over the back of the room's one chair. Anna had let the hems down on her daughters' best dresses and tacked a row of rickrack around the telltale line left by the old hems. The dresses were long-sleeved and much too hot for August, but the occasion called for their best Sunday clothes. They would have to wear the dresses to their new cousin's christening too, although they would be allowed to take something cooler to wear in the afternoon after the ceremony.

Effie would have a new dress to wear for the two important occasions, but not Frederick's daughters. He didn't condone unnecessary expenditures in these hard times. Even the camouflaging rickrack wasn't new. Rickrack, lace, buttons, hem tape were all removed from worn-out or outgrown garments before they were either cut up for quilt squares, relegated to the ragbag, or saved for braided rugs. Nothing was thrown away. If the family couldn't use something, it went to the orphanage.

The next day Kate traced the zigzagging trim on her skirt to keep from squirming on the uncushioned church pew. The stiff fabric of her dress made her itch.

They stood while Effie played the national anthem on the piano. She looked very pretty in her blue-and-white gingham. Her blond hair was unbraided and tied back from her face with a blue ribbon. She made only two mistakes that Kate could tell.

Pastor Mueller signaled the students to file to the front of the sanctuary. Kate stared straight ahead while the other children sang the hymns they had learned this summer. She didn't even try to fake the words by silently moving her lips as she had done last summer. She hadn't fooled anyone. Everyone had known she didn't know the words.

Then they were allowed to sit down while Matilda Neiderhaus sang.

Matilda was fourteen and plump. Kate thought her vibrato sounded put-on. Nobody *really* sang like that.

Next the Berger twins played their accordions. They weren't very good, but everyone always enjoyed watching two rosy-cheeked, identical boys play identical instruments. Even Kate had to agree it was cute.

Once again the students filed to the front and arranged themselves in neat rows just in front of the altar steps. Then the recitations began. As a group, they recited the Twenty-third Psalm. Kate stared at the empty choir loft in the back of the sanctuary, her lips closed.

Effie stumbled three times during her recitation, but Pastor Mueller beamed at her the whole time. When she was finished, he praised her perfect attendance, her punctuality, her attentiveness. Effie never whispered during class.

Mary Beth Schleicher never whispered in class either, but the pastor only nodded when she finished her piece. Mary Beth's round, flat face reminded Kate of a baby pig's.

Kate was called before Stella. She felt rather than heard the startled reaction of the pastor and the others when she did not recite verses from the Nineteenth Psalm as Pastor Mueller had announced. Her recitation from Proverbs was letter-perfect.

Her father's mouth was ajar. Kate bobbed a little curtsy in the pastor's direction when she finished. Kate returned to her place, avoiding Stella's eyes. Pastor Mueller cleared his throat when she finished and announced that Stella Behrman would also recite from the thirty-first chapter of Proverbs.

Stella stepped forward and faced the expectant silence of the vaulted sanctuary. Her shiny brown hair hung in smooth, careful braids. Kate stared at her sister's straight little back and waited for the now familiar words to come forward in Stella's clear voice. Stella was good at reciting.

But there was only the silence.

Pastor Mueller looked shocked. So did Papa. Stella had forgotten the words.

Kate felt smug. For once she had done better than her sister. Stella would know at least once in her life how it felt not to do well, not to be the best. *See how it feels,* Kate taunted silently. But Kate realized that she herself was responsible for her sister's humiliation. Stella was so undone by her sister's surprise performance that her mind momentarily balked.

Poor Stella.

The silence in the church was deafening.

Pastor Mueller cleared his throat again and gave Stella the first word. The rest meekly followed in Stella's voice.

The children returned to their seats for the award presentations. Stella averted her eyes when she accepted her award. It was the best one and saved for last. Best overall student in the German language, but Stella hadn't been able to recite her verse without help. Her moment of triumph had been ruined.

Kate was sorry. Maybe Stella needed to be perfect just as Kate needed to run faster than a jackrabbit.

Kate had planned to tell Papa that she learned Stella's verse because she liked it better than her own. But when he asked for an explanation, she said, "Because I lost my verse."

"Do you think you did right?" he asked.

"No, sir. Not because I learned a different verse. It seems to me one verse should do as well as the next. But I didn't know it was going to make Stella forget her words. At first I was glad, and then I was sorry."

Kate wondered if she'd get another whipping. When they got home, she slipped out of the truck and hurried up the stairs. Frederick didn't come after her.

That night, when the lights were out, the sisters lay back to back on top of the sheets, the quilt folded out of the way over the foot of the bed. The curtains had been tied back to admit the stingy breeze. The motor of a lone vehicle could be heard over on Hunter Road. "I'm sorry," Kate whispered. "I thought you acted so good all the time just to make me look bad. I won't think that anymore."

"Good," Stella said.

"I told God I was sorry," Kate said. A sob caught in her throat. She really did feel bad.

Stella turned and put her arms around her older sister. She was crying too. "I get too big for my britches sometimes," she admitted.

"I'll always love you, Stella. You're my sister."

"Yes," Stella said. "Sisters must always love each other. No matter what."

Frederick Behrman had spent fifteen years as a childless widower before marrying the spinster daughter of Wilhelm Theis, a rancher whose land adjoined Frederick's property on the west. Frederick was in his late forties when his two daughters were born.

His older daughter, Katherine Elizabeth, had perplexed him from the day she was born. First there was the red hair. No one in either his family or his present wife's had red hair. His brothers' children all had either blond or brown hair. The red hair made Katherine different from the beginning, and her hazel eyes shone with an inner stubbornness that was the bane of his existence. Sometimes Frederick wondered if his older daughter's mission in life was to cause him displeasure.

What a contrast Kate was to Stella. His younger child was a slender, graceful girl with wide-set gray eyes and soft brown hair. She never gave him a minute's trouble and was studious, helpful, eager to please—a father's delight. Stella was special. Frederick was fond of saying that his Stella was a born lady. Even as a toddler, she had possessed a quiet dignity that Frederick greatly admired. He loved Stella more than any other human being.

Frederick wished he had the easy way with his children that his younger brothers had with theirs. John and Herman both hugged and kissed their children with great frequency—even their grown-up sons. Until she got too big for her father to carry around, Effie's feet never seemed to touch the floor. She was always perched on Herman's arm. He openly adored his beautiful blond daughter with her blue eyes and dimpled smile.

Sometimes Frederick would touch the smooth hair on the top of Stella's head. When she was small, he would take out his pocket handkerchief and dry her tears when she fell out of the tire swing or got pecked by a rooster—something he never did with Kate. Kate never cried. It seemed wrong that the only time he touched Kate was when he was punishing her. But Frederick never hugged or kissed either of the daughters.

Frederick's own father had died when he was seventeen, and his authority as head of the family seemed to require a stern demeanor. He was owned by the land, and the land was a hard taskmaster. Maybe John and Herman had been too young when their father died to remember the hardworking man who labored from dawn to dusk to carve out a life for his family. Their father's work and that of his father before him had built a prosperous, sprawling ranch and a family name that was respected in this German corner of south central Texas, where diligence was much admired.

Frederick's mother had died when he was very young. The mother of John, Herman, and two brothers who had died as infants was one-quarter Irish. Frederick often wondered if it was Mary Behrman's Irish blood that gave his brothers their merry eyes and affectionate ways.

Mary—or Mama Mary as most people called her—lived with John. She was blind now, her world having shrunk to a corner of her daughter-in-law's kitchen where she rocked grandbabies and hummed hymns, her unseeing eyes focused on distant images. Sometimes, however, when Herman or John took their blind mother out on the floor of the huge dance hall by the gristmill over at Gruene and danced the old dances to the music of a German band, Mary's cheeks would grow pink with exertion as she stepped smartly around the floor.

Then Frederick could still see a bit of the young woman with whom his father had returned home one stormy night from a trip to San Antonio. He had said to his eight-year-old son, "Frederick, this is your new mother." Frederick had been kneeling by a crate in the corner of the kitchen, feeding an orphaned goat kid from a pop bottle with a rubber nipple. He stood and stared at the two smiling adults. The kid bleated thinly. To this day, whenever a winter's wind sent sleet against the tin roof of the big white house, Frederick would think of that night in the kitchen, the smiling young woman with ice caught in her golden hair standing there opening her arms to him. Frederick had not accepted her embrace. He always held himself apart from Mary, but Frederick's father spent nine happy years with her. Then he died, and Frederick became the head of the family.

At first Mary had fought her strong-willed stepson for control, insisting she was more fit to run the ranch than a seventeen-year-old boy. But her stepson was much too formidable for her. Frederick had won. Mary cooked for her stepson and kept what was then his house for thirteen more years until her oldest boy, John, married Louise. Still only in her forties, her eyes failing even then, Mama Mary and her younger, unmarried son Herman went to live with John and his bride in their newly built farmhouse just over the hill, a quarter of a mile west of Frederick's house. With his house free of his stepmother's presence, thirty-year-old Frederick then courted and won the first Anna. But she died before their first anniversary.

Frederick, as the oldest son, had inherited the house south of Hunter Road along with half the land. His younger brothers split the remaining half. But in effect, the Behrman ranch was still one property—eighteen hundred acres of rolling ranch land to graze goats and sheep and cattle. The brothers labored together under Frederick's direction. He was still the undisputed head of the family.

John, the middle brother, and his wife, Louise, had two sons. Herman, the youngest of the Behrman brothers, and his wife, Hannah, had—with the birth of their last baby—three sons and their beloved Effie. Only Frederick had no sons.

Frederick's marriage to the second Anna had been arranged in a businesslike fashion. Wilhelm Theis was old and helpless from a stroke. He wanted to see his daughter married before he died, but as each year slipped by, he feared that no man would ever come courting Anna. A plain, sensible woman, Anna found flirting a fool's game and joy only between the covers of books. She told her father that a man would either like her as she was, or she would die a spinster. It was that simple.

But it really wasn't that simple at all. Anna was wise enough to realize that she would have flirted if she had been pretty. Plain girls didn't flirt. They had to hope that some young man too unattractive for the sought-after girls would drift their way—or a sensible, unromantic widower.

Already in middle age, Frederick did not admire tittering or helplessness. He needed a strong woman to bear his children and run his home. He had loved a woman once, and that was enough for a lifetime. He still felt the pain of that love. After all these years it would catch him by surprise when he was driving his tractor or shearing the goats or painting the barn. The sight of that other Anna slowly dying while she struggled to give birth to the baby he had planted in her womb would come unbidden to his mind's eye, leaving Frederick dizzy and ill. In between her pains, that Anna had prayed to God to spare their baby. "Leave my husband with our baby," she beseeched. Before her eyes grew dim, she had looked at Frederick and smiled. "You're a good man. Thank you for loving me. Take good care of our baby."

But the baby had died too.

Their son slept in his mother's arms. Frederick had insisted on burying them that way. He never visited their grave.

Frederick's life had been divided into three distinct segments: before the first Anna, the short and precious time she was his wife, and the time that came after. He never spoke of her, but his concept of heaven was to spend eternity at the first Anna's side.

He lived alone in the big house off Hunter Road. He cleared new land. He invested heavily and successfully in goats, raised for their mohair. The Behrman ranch was one the finest in Comal County. On his forty-sixth birthday he put on his Sunday suit and took to Anna's father a cloth bag of his very good *leberwurst* made of goat and pork liver. He didn't want to die childless. A man should have sons to work the land with him, to carry on after he was gone.

He didn't want to love the woman who bore his children. If he loved her, she might die.

He respected the second Anna. She understood what was being offered and accepted. She too did not want to die childless.

Although no words of marriage were spoken that first awkward evening in the parlor, Anna and her father both understood why Frederick Behrman had come. The two men talked in German about the merits of goats over sheep, of crossing various breeds for better wool, topics Anna knew much better than her father. But she did not enter into the conversation. She served them coffee and peach cobbler covered with heavy cream, then sat quietly darning socks.

After Frederick had left and she had put her father to bed, Anna knelt in front of the cedar chest that stood at the foot of her bed. She took out the layers of linens and blankets. The wedding dress was on the bottom, carefully folded and wrapped in a sheet. She had made it more than ten years before in anticipation of a proposal that never came. Anna stroked the ivory taffeta and fingered the carefully embroidered lace. She would wear it after all. It was like a miracle.

Since she had no mother to help her, her soon-to-be sisters-in-law assisted Anna in wedding preparations. Food was a big part of a German wedding. After so many years of waiting, Anna was determined to have a proper wedding. She was old to be a bride, but her dress was beautiful and her wedding guests would go away with their bellies full.

Two months after Frederick first came to her house, they were married by Pastor Mueller in the front parlor of the house Anna shared with her father. Neighbors, Behrman relatives, and Theis relatives overflowed into the hall and kitchen. Anna tried not to notice that the cuffs on Frederick's suit were frayed. It was the same suit he had worn to court her. Frederick was not a wealthy man, but he could have parted with ten dollars for a new suit in which to be married.

So the second Anna came to Frederick's big, plain house with her invalid father and her books. She owned forty-seven books. Thirty were in German, inherited from her mother. The rest were in English, bought by Anna after her father became powerless. A world history book and a volume of Emily Dickinson poetry were her favorites. She also liked Austen and Poe.

Anna replaced with new the worn linoleum that covered all the floors upstairs and down. To the parlor, she added her mother's hooked rugs, spinet piano, and glockenspiel on its own brass stand. And she brought her own bed. She did not want to sleep in the first Anna's bed. She moved her predecessor's wedding picture from the bedroom wall and put it in the trunk in the attic that held the woman's possessions—her clothes, her Bible, her confirmation certificate, the layette for the baby who had never breathed. Before she closed the trunk lid, Anna stared down at the picture of her predecessor—that first Anna. She had been lovely, with large eyes and a shy, sweet smile. Anna remembered her from school. The girl was five or six years older than Anna and very kind. She had helped the younger children learn their multiplication tables—even the Mexican children.

Anna had no wedding picture of herself to hang in the bare spot by the dresser. The last picture that had been taken of her had been to commemorate her confirmation almost twenty years before. She covered the telltale square of darker paint on the bedroom wall with a picture of the Last Supper that had hung in the stairwell of her old home.

On her wedding night, with her hands at her side, Anna passively waited for Frederick to dispense with her virginity of thirty-four years. "I will try not to hurt you," he said.

"I know," Anna said.

Frederick turned his back to her for a time. Anna was aware of his arm jerking up and down. When he turned back to her, she felt his penis against her hip.

When her father was helpless after his stroke, she had washed his privates. They looked like the scrawny neck and wattle of a dead turkey. But Frederick felt amazingly large and hard. Anna wondered if it would fit inside of her.

He rolled his heavy body on top of her, and with his penis in his hand, he rubbed its tip up and down between her legs. Up and down. Up and down.

"Put your legs around my legs now," he said.

Anna hesitated.

"Come on now. Around my legs. I can't get to you unless you do."

Anna wrapped first one leg and then the other around his thick thighs. Frederick began to push. There was such resistance that Anna wondered if she wasn't made correctly. Maybe he couldn't fit in her.

Frederick stopped pushing and began rubbing her again with the tip—up and down. Anna felt moistness there. Was it from him or her? Frederick began pushing again. This time there was penetration, but he didn't seem satisfied. He wanted more of himself inside of her. He pushed harder, moving back and forth, and suddenly plunged deep inside of her. A sharp, knifelike pain flashed up Anna's belly.

He was pumping very hard now. Frederick's breath came in hard gasps until he emitted a long, animal grunt and was quiet, his heart pounding in his thick chest. She was grateful that he did not say her name. She would not have known which Anna he meant if he had. They did not kiss, but she cradled his head against her bosom for a time.

So this was sex, she thought. A strange act—invasive yet remote. It wasn't much, but then she didn't expect much.

She felt the hair on Frederick's back. He was a very hairy man. His body was thick and muscular. Even his fingers were thick. At one time she would have thought it strange to touch a man, but after caring for her invalid father, she found the male body had lost much of its mystery.

"I will be good to you, Anna," he said.

"I know," she answered back into the darkness of her husband's bedroom. She was not unhappy. Maybe a baby already was growing inside of her.

But there was no baby conceived that night. As the months went by, Frederick wondered if life had played him a cruel joke. He had married to have children. Had he chosen a barren woman?

Anna's father died that winter. Wilhelm's mind wandered at the end. He thought his daughter was his long-dead mother. *"Ich liebe Dich, Mama,"* he said. Anna had never heard her father tell anyone that he loved them before. Frederick never spoke words of love. Was she going to live and die without ever hearing a man tell her that he loved her?

After Wilhelm's death the Theis ranch with its one thousand acres was incorporated into the Behrman lands. Anna suspected that the reason Frederick had asked for her hand rather than that of some other spinster from the German community was that her father's ranch bordered his own. But then Frederick was a pragmatic man. Pragmatism was something Anna understood.

Finally after a year and a month of marriage, Anna found herself pregnant. She could scarcely contain her excitement when she realized her period was a day late. Then two. Then a week. She dared hope. She would wait a month before she told Frederick—just in case. But he knew. He kept careful track of her monthly periods. "I think you may be pregnant," he told her in bed after the lamp was turned off. They talked about personal things only under the protective veil of darkness. Anna was disappointed. She wasn't ready to share her secret with him yet.

Frederick pulled her body to him and stroked her hair. She felt his erection against her leg. Then his lips brushed her forehead, her cheek, and found her mouth. No dry brushing of passionless lips this time. He pushed her lips apart with his tongue, and it entered her own mouth, its thrusting a symbolic prelude. Then his mouth took on a life of its own. He kissed her throat. She did not protest when he removed her gown and kissed her breasts, her pregnant belly. But he always returned to her mouth, devouring it. His hands roved her body, caressing her flesh almost to the point of pain. He was like a man possessed, out of control, not Frederick Behrman at all.

Anna found herself responding. She wanted this to go on and on, but at the same time she wanted him to enter her. She could actually feel her body opening up in preparation.

And when he lowered himself between her legs there was no dry resistance, only welcoming moistness. When Frederick began moving up and down, the most exquisite sensation began building in the inside of Anna's thighs and radiated itself throughout her belly and down her legs. She could not prevent the groan of passion erupting from her lips. The feeling was glorious.

When Frederick fell away from her, he rolled over on his side, his back to her. An embarrassed silence hung over the room.

Then he apologized. "I'm sorry." He did not say for what.

Anna turned away from him and wept silently into her pillow. She understood. It had been a mistake. For a time she had been the first Anna. They had made love like that.

She wished she had never experienced those feelings—carnal feelings. Losing her virginity had been nothing compared to losing her innocence.

She knew Frederick would never lose control again. Her marriage would be forever loveless because her husband preferred the memory of a long dead wife to the physical presence of his living one. Anna was humiliated.

Three

Katherine Elizabeth was born the following spring after a reasonable labor. Frederick looked down at the wet, naked newborn infant being cleaned and dressed on the foot of the bed and wondered how it could be. The first Anna had had red hair—glorious, golden red hair that cascaded over creamy white shoulders. The baby boy who had been born in this very room, who moved but refused to breathe, had had red hair. And now this baby. It didn't make any sense at all.

When the doctor had gone and his sister-in-law Louise put the cleaned and dressed infant in Frederick's arms, he held the angry, crying baby stiffly. This was the child he had wanted so his life would have meaning. He was more confused than ever.

Maybe if the child had been a son. Yes, it was a son he needed. Two or three would be better. It was sons who gave the land meaning.

Stella Anna was born eleven months later. Anna rejoiced that little Kate would have a sister. She had always felt a lack in her own life because she had no sister. And after his initial disappointment over another girl, Frederick allowed himself to love this second daughter.

There were two miscarriages. Then years of no pregnancies. The couplings in the bed that Anna had brought with her to Frederick's house became less and less frequent. When, at age forty-seven, Anna was miraculously again pregnant, Frederick dared to hope one last time.

Anna's labor began the day after the christening of Herman and Hannah's baby—Christian, their third son. Anna and Frederick had gotten home very late from the christening feast. The girls had stayed behind to spend the night with Effie. Anna was restless in the night and rose before dawn.

When Frederick came in from the barn and saw Anna's white, pinched face as she stood by the stove stirring his oatmeal, he knew.

"But it's too soon," he said. His words sounded like an accusation.

Anna turned from him as though he had struck her.

"Are the pains close together?" he asked as he hung his hat on the hook by the door. "Maybe they are false."

She did not answer. The oatmeal bubbled over the top of the pan onto the top of the black stove as Anna sank to the floor, her body doubling in pain.

The taste of fear rose in Frederick's mouth. The last baby, his last chance for a son. This dry, aging woman had no more babies in her. This pregnancy had been a fluke—one last burst of fertility before the change claimed her absolutely. He himself was sixty years old. He'd be lucky to see this child grown—if it lived.

Frederick could not move. For a long moment he simply stood there staring at the burning mess on the top of Anna's immaculate stove. Why hadn't she just stayed in bed this morning? he thought angrily. How stupid for a woman to get up and cook breakfast when she was in labor.

With a sigh, he picked up the pot holder and moved the pan to one side. With a poker, he banked the stove's fire. She must have been planning to do a month's cooking, judging by the size of the fire. He looked around the kitchen and saw the clean tea towels covering loaves of rising bread. It was Monday. Anna always baked the week's bread on Monday.

He knelt beside her and said soothing words. When she was ready, he helped her up the stairs. He eased her out of her dress and into bed.

Another pain wracked her body.

"Is it time for Dr. Hinman to come?" he asked.

Anna bit her lip and nodded. "I'm sorry, Frederick," she said.

"I know. I'll go over to John's and ring for the doctor."

"And tell Louise to come bake the bread," Anna called after him. "Have her tell Hannah to keep the girls over there."

Stella and Kate stayed with their cousin Effie during the birthing. That night a tired Hannah returned home to tell the sisters that they had a brother, but he was tiny and very weak. They were not to go home just yet.

"But he will be all right?" Stella asked.

Hannah poured herself a cup of tea and eased her tired body into a kitchen chair. Effie slid her chair close to her mother's. Hannah slid an arm around her daughter's shoulders.

"Well, will he?" Kate demanded.

Hannah looked from one sister to the other. Good girls. Even Kate. She loved them like her own. Her heart ached for them. The first dealing with death was the worst.

"The doctor says the baby will die," Hannah said.

"Maybe if we pray real hard, he'll be okay," Stella said. Lines of concentration creased her brow.

"Yes, we must pray," Hannah agreed. "We must pray for the strength to abide by God's will."

"Why does God want my brother to die?" Kate said. Tears were spilling over from her hazel eyes and down her freckled cheeks. Her red hair had not seen a comb today and stuck from her braids in angry angles.

"Life doesn't always turn out the way we want, and we're not wise enough to understand," Hannah said. "Perhaps dying now will save him from a greater pain later on. All I know is we cannot question God's will."

"Well, I can!" Kate said, pushing her chair back from the table with such fury that it fell crashing to the floor. "I think God is terrible."

Hannah pushed her own chair back from the table to make room and wordlessly opened her arms. Kate threw herself against her aunt, burying her face against Hannah's neck. Hannah looked over Kate's head at Stella and nodded. Stella fell to her knees at her aunt's feet. Hannah pulled both girls in close to her ample bosom. She kissed the tops of their heads—Stella's smooth and brown, Kate's red and unruly.

Effie squeezed herself into the embrace, and Hannah kissed her own Effie's curly, blond head.

"Maybe he won't die," Effie said. "Is it all right to pray that he won't?"

"Yes, dear," Hannah said. She closed her own eyes and silently prayed for the little mite of a baby born this day. But she added a plea of her own. *If one of our children has to die, let it be the baby. We don't know him yet. I couldn't bear to lose one of these.*

Stella and Kate returned home the next day for the baby's baptism. Ordinarily, baptisms took place in the front of the sanctuary of the church when a child was six or seven months old. But this baby had to be baptized at once—before he died. Stella wept when she saw the pitiful thing in her mother's arms. The curtains were pulled across the window of her parents' bedroom, and a pool of light from a lamp illuminated the pale woman old enough to be a grandmother and her dying son.

The room was lined with the aunts and uncles and older cousins. How strange for so many people to be in the bedroom. The pastor asked the infant's name. He was to be named Henry Wilhelm after Anna's and Frederick's fathers. The baby cried thinly when the minister lifted him from his mother's arms.

"What about godparents?" Anna asked from her pillow.

"There is no need," Frederick said.

"I want Kate and Stella to hold him," Anna said.

So the two sniffling, weeping girls held their tiny brother between them while old Pastor Mueller sprinkled the infant's blue-veined head with holy water and baptized him *"in Namen des Vaters, und des Sohnes, und des heiligen Geistes."* The baby cried weakly. His lips were blue. His little chest heaved with each breath.

The ceremony over, Stella took the baby and put him back beside her mother. She leaned over and kissed his forehead. His skin was so thin, so cool. Kate, with big hiccupping sobs, leaned over and kissed him too.

Effie came next to the bed and kissed the tiny head. The three girls went out into the narrow hall and clung, crying, to one another. The crying made Stella's chest hurt. She didn't want her brother to die. She was going to push him in the tire swing. He was going to make their father smile. It hurt so to know he would die and they would never know him. The baby came out of their mother and would be buried in the ground like the other Anna's baby. The part that was really him—his soul—would go up to heaven. Except he hadn't had a chance to become himself. And he hadn't hugged her neck with little-boy arms or listened to her stories. He hadn't run races with Kate. They would have all loved each other. She loved him already, or at least the dream of who he would be.

"It's not fair," Kate said between sobs. "I just don't understand. He's our brother."

Yes, Stella thought. *He's our brother, and we'll never get another one.* Mixed with the sadness was anger. Kate was right. It wasn't fair. But she didn't have Kate's courage; she wouldn't dare be mad at God.

Stella left Effie and Kate in the hall and went back into the bedroom. Her father was alone in the corner of the room. She went to him and slipped her hand into his. He didn't look at her. Stella understood that he would cry if he looked at her, and he was trying very hard not to cry.

Fathers didn't cry. But he squeezed her hand and let her stand there with him. That was enough.

As they entered adolescence, wedding dresses and weddings became a source of fascination for Effie and Stella. For months before each wedding in the community, they speculated at length about the bride- and groom-to-be, repeating gossip about their courtship, wondering how much they had been alone, if they had kissed at great length or not at all, if she had allowed him to put his hand in the front of her dress and feel her breasts. Word had it that Bessie Kretzer had undressed for William Kling-mann before their wedding and allowed him to see her naked body. Even Kate, who ordinarily spurned such talk, joined in that discussion. Was it immoral for a man to see a woman naked before they married? Effie said no. After all, he would see her soon enough anyway. Husbands got to look at their wives naked if they wanted to. Effie thought it would be all right—if done romantically, with accompanying moonlight and suit-ably reverent responses from the young man. "He must tell her how beautiful she is," Effie insisted, "and he must really love her."

"What if she isn't beautiful?" Stella wondered as she examined her reflection in a cracked mirror that hung on the wall of the attic. She was wearing her mother's wedding veil.

"Well, if he loves her, he will think she is whether she has a good shape or not," Effie said with great authority as she fluffed out the sheer material around Stella's face. Effie, who was now going into New Braunfels each day to attend high school, considered herself much older and wiser than her two cousins. Kate also went into town for school, but she was only a "sub-fish," which was the nickname for the sub-freshman. Stella still attended Thornhill School, where all the Behrman cousins had gone through the sixth grade. In seventh grade the children went to town to complete their education.

"No man is ever going to see me naked," Kate announced from her cross-legged perch atop a wooden truck, "or touch my breasts. I suppose they have to put that thing in you to make you have babies, but I don't see why you can't leave your nightgown on for that."

"I think some women like their husbands to touch them," Stella said, thinking of the married couples she'd observed at dances.

"Of course, they do," Effie said airily as she took her turn with the veil. "And you don't have to be married. Fritz Keller put his arms around me and kissed me, and it was rather pleasant."

Stella and Kate stared at Effie. Kate's mouth fell open. A boy had kissed Effie. Stella looked at Effie's pretty mouth. It was stunning to think that a boy had put his mouth there. And Effie had enjoyed it. Stella could not have been more shocked if Effie had said she'd killed her cat.

"Why?" Kate asked. "Why in the world did you let him do such an icky thing?"

"Because I wanted to see what it was like," Effie said in an affected woman-of-the-world voice. She picked up Anna's ivory wedding dress and held it up in front of her. "I think next time I'll kiss him back. Or maybe I'll kiss Peter Meyer. He's better looking than Fritz."

Suddenly the two years' age difference that separated Stella from her cousin loomed very large. Effie had entered a mysterious other world. Later, as she waited for sleep in the bed she shared with her sister, Stella tried to imagine what it would feel like for a boy to kiss her. She put her fingertips to her lips and kissed them. Then she wrapped her arms about herself, embracing her own body, and tried to pretend that a boy was hugging her. But it was so abstract. Maybe if she thought of one certain boy . . .

But the image she conjured was a faceless one—vague as though seen through layers of gauze. She did not know who he was, but she knew that she would someday love one particular man. It was as though his identity were already established but simply not revealed to her.

When she hugged herself, Stella's arms were his arms. And one hand strayed inside the collar of her gown and moved back and forth over the soft nipples that had budded out from her chest only in the last months. So soft, the skin was there. Stella wondered if a boy would like that wonderful softness. But as her fingers explored, the most incredible thing happened. The nipple on her right breast tightened itself under the fingers. A hard nub arose in its middle. It wasn't soft to the touch any longer. So strange, but the touching felt very good. She forgot about how it would feel to the imagined boy's fingers and thought only about how good the touching felt to her small breast.

She looked over at the sleeping form of her sister to be sure that Kate had not been watching her. Then she hugged her pillow to her chest and waited for sleep.

Stella's periods started before Kate's in spite of the fact that Kate was eleven months older. It had been more than a year since Anna had had her painful, private discussion with her two daughters. "Starting your periods is just part of growing up," Anna insisted. "Women who have periods can get pregnant when they get married." She told Kate and Stella how women care for themselves during this time of the month and assured them that it was all perfectly normal—although Anna's obvious discomfort during the discussion seemed to belie normalcy.

Kate had been so embarrassed she couldn't look at her mother's face while she talked. Kate wanted to tell Anna to stop, that she and Stella had heard it all from Effie. But she was too embarrassed to say anything at all.

"Do you have any questions, Kate? Stella?" Anna asked.

Both girls shook their heads.

Anna sighed her relief. "Very well then. Just come to me as soon as it happens. If you are at school, you tell the teacher that you are ill and ride your donkey on home. Don't wait until the end of the day because your clothes will get soiled."

Kate was not at school when her first period came. It was her year to be confirmed, and she was in New Braunfels attending her weekly confirmation class in the pastor's study. Her belly hurt. When she went to the bathroom after class, there was the blood. Kate stared at it, not understanding. Why should she be bleeding? Then she watched in horrified fascination as a huge, dark droplet of blood hit the water in the toilet and sank out of sight.

Menstruation.

She carefully folded up many layers of toilet paper, making a pad to place in the crotch of her panties.

Frederick was late picking her up. Then he stopped by the blacksmith's to pick up a harrow that was being mended. It wasn't ready yet. Frederick decided to wait. He handed Kate a nickel. "You may go get an ice cream cone while we wait," he told her.

Kate refused the offered coin. "I'm not hungry," she said as she sat first on one hip and then on the other, to keep any telltale signs from the back of her blue chambray skirt.

Miserably she stayed in the truck waiting while her father and two farmers from east of town leaned against the tailgate chatting. Wasn't that something—Jack Sharkey knocking out Schmeling to win the heavy-weight boxing crown? Did Frederick like his Dodge truck as well as he had his old Ford? Sure looked like rain. Been a wet spring, hadn't it?

A bum came up and asked for a handout. He was old—too old to be a bum. Frederick gave the man a nickel. "We even see them out on Hunter Road now," he told the two farmers.

"I shoo them off the place," one man said. The other farmer nodded.

Frederick offered no comment. At Rosehaven the few who took the long walk down to the house were given a sandwich and coffee.

Finally, the harrow loaded in the back, Frederick got in the truck. He looked over at Kate. "Where's your catechism?" he asked.

Kate looked down at her empty lap, then closed her eyes, remembering. She had left the book in the rest room at the church. She'd left her sweater too. She could see them both on the shelf under the mirror.

"I'll get it Sunday," she said.

But already Frederick was driving down Coll Street. "You need to be more careful of your possessions," he said as he turned the corner and parked in front of the church, its stark facade as stern as his own. He turned off the ignition and leaned purposefully against the seat, prepared to wait while his daughter rectified her error.

Kate did not move.

"Well, go in and get your book," he said impatiently.

"I'll get it Sunday," she repeated.

"*Now*, Katherine." He leaned across her and opened the door. "Go," he said, pointing his finger. "And be quick about it. Your mama will have dinner ready, and I still need to stop by Mr. Locke's nursery."

"No," Kate whispered.

"What did you say, young lady?"

"I said no. I'll get it Sunday."

Frederick grabbed her arm. "You will go now, Katherine Elizabeth Behrman, or it will be the razor strap when we get home." He pushed Kate out the door of the truck.

Kate stood facing the truck for a long minute, her hands in fists at her side. Then she squared her shoulders and turned, exposing her shame, which was now quite visible on the back of her skirt.

She marched resolutely up the front walk of the stone church.

"Kate," Frederick called after her. "It's okay. Come back. You can get it Sunday."

Frederick grasped the steering wheel so tightly his knuckles turned white. Poor little girl, he thought in anguish. He had humiliated her. Poor little girl. Why did everything always have to be so much harder for Kate?

"We'll go home now," he said when she got back in the truck.

Kate said nothing.

They drove home in silence. Frederick did not stop at the nursery.

Frederick went to the barn to give the girl's mother a chance to deal with her. He sat on a bale of hay and put his face in his hands. He ached for the daughter he had never quite been able to love. Poor Kate.

After a while Anna came for him. "We can eat now," she said.

"The girl . . . ? Is Kate . . . ?"

"Kate's fine. Supper's on the table."

Four

Stella had joined the four other Behrman cousins at the stone high school at the corner of Mills and Academy streets. Kate was a sophomore, and Effie a junior. Effie's older brothers, Hiram and Jason, had graduated. Chris, her youngest brother, was only three. The other two Behrman cousins attending high school were John and Louise's sons. Carl and Joe took turns driving the truck-turned-schoolbus into town each day. None of the Behrman Mexicans went to high school. Most Mexican children quit after grade school in favor of full-time employment, although like the coloreds, they had their own separate, shabby high school. In New Braunfels no one expected much of the colored children. Even less was expected of the Mexicans.

As a new freshman at the high school, Stella found herself basking in the glory of her pretty cousin's fame. Teachers, other students, even the principal said, "Well, now, so you're Effie Behrman's cousin." No one commented on the fact that she was Kate Behrman's sister, or the cousin of Joe and Carl Behrman.

Effie did not like to arrive at school in a converted truck. She tried to get her father to allow her to drive the family car to town, but Herman said no. The truck was good enough for the other cousins, and it was extravagant to drive two vehicles into town. And what would she do if the car broke down, leaving her stranded on a country road? Herman did, however, allow Effie to learn to drive. She in turn taught Kate and Stella. Effie was allowed to take the family Ford only to nearby Gruene, but the three girl cousins felt very grown-up arriving at the general store in a car instead of astride their donkeys.

Stella was amazed at how easily Effie talked to boys in the school yard or in the halls between classes. She would compliment them on their latest Friday-afternoon accomplishment on the gridiron. She would admire their new haircuts. She would even tell them how handsome they looked today. She would seek their advice about assignments, borrow a pencil, ask about sick grandmothers. And the boys always seemed flattered by her attention. How did Effie have the nerve to talk to boys like that? How did she know what to say?

"Why, you just talk, honey," Effie told Stella. "And smile. That's really important. I think boys are more comfortable when a girl smiles. Otherwise, they're afraid of her."

The notion that boys could be afraid of girls was a new one for Stella, but as she observed male-female behavior at the high school, she realized this was so. Boys and girls were afraid of each other—or at least a little in awe. Except Effie.

Joey Brenner sat by Stella during lunch one day. He was a town boy and had store-bought shirts. He opened up his lunch pail without saying a word, and they ate their respective lunches in silence. The next day the scene was repeated. The third day Joey's voice cracked when he asked her if she would like a cookie. His hand was shaking when he offered her one of his mother's molasses cookies. Stella realized it had taken a great deal of courage for him to speak to her. She remembered Effie's advice about smiling, but Joey never looked at her, so what good would it do to smile? Besides, he was shorter than Stella. But he was the first boy who ever paid any attention to her. She wished it had been one of the other boys but felt rather special that a boy had taken notice of her at all—even a short, shy one.

Unnoticed by the boys except as an oddity, Kate passed her high school years in the company of two girls who had also been her friends at Thornhill School. The three girls were inseparable. They even looked alike—plain, lean, athletically inclined girls who wore unadorned clothing and uncurled hair. Kate, Millie Holzapfe, and Lola Schmidt didn't concern themselves with sewing lace on collars or the bother of curling irons. They never experimented with makeup and privately scorned girls who did. They wondered if it wouldn't have been better to be a boy and talked about it at great length. They didn't want a penis; they just wanted freedom and the opportunity to compete.

"I could even play football as good as a boy," Kate claimed. They were sitting on a hill overlooking the railroad track and enjoying the warm April day, the grass already green and full of yellow dandelions. Dressed in Saturday clothes and hair stuffed in caps, the three could have been mistaken for boys. "I run a whole lot faster than old Teddy Blum. I'd like to score a touchdown and have everyone cheer."

Kate hopped to her feet and did a victory prance into an imaginary end zone.

"Well, I think football is dumb," Lola said. "Why would anyone want to run around tackling and getting hurt?"

Lola's favorite sport was swimming. Her heroine, Helene Madison, had won three gold medals in the 1932 Olympics and currently held fifteen of the possible sixteen free-style records for women. Lola could swim across the lake at Landa Park faster than anyone else—boy or girl. Of course, after she had beaten a couple of boys, the rest refused to swim against her.

While Kate and Millie also admired the accomplishments of Helene Madison, their personal hero was Texas's own Mildred Didrikson, who grew up in Beaumont. The "Babe" had distinguished herself two years earlier in the '32 Olympics as the greatest women's track star ever and now was systematically trying her hand at every other sport, including basketball, swimming, and even boxing.

A distant whistle announced the afternoon train. The track paralleled an empty stretch of Gruene Road. It was where they came to race to the train.

The three girls ran down to the dirt road and waited. When the train grew near, they assumed the ready position. As the train came abreast of them, they took off, head back, knees and arms pumping. Running. It was what Kate did best.

They could run together for a while. Then Millie and Lola would drop back. Kate always ran the longest and fastest. She always earned the brakeman's wave from the caboose.

Sweating and exhausted, Kate walked back to her friends. Someday she would run in real races and not against trains. Someday she would break the tape at the finish line. Someday.

And all three girls loved any physical activity. They liked hiking in the hill country and swimming in the lake at Landa Park. They were the best volleyball players. When they were in grade school, they played softball and kickball with the boys. Now they were deemed to be too old to play with boys. While many other schools in Texas offered girls basketball, the high school at New Braunfels had no gymnasium. Not even the boys had a team. Some of the larger cities had track and field programs through the Amateur Athletic Union. But in New Braunfels, the boys played football, and the girls were in the pep club. There were no other organized sports for boys or girls.

Kate and her two special friends contented themselves with pickup games of basketball, softball, and volleyball. They timed each other, running sprints. Everyone in the high school knew Kate was the most accomplished girl athlete in town. She could outrun, outshoot, outjump, and outhit all the other girls and most of the boys who would dare take her on. And only Lola could swim faster. While not envied by her schoolmates, Kate was acknowledged as incredible.

Kate had knocked the bottom out of a bushel basket and attached it to the side of the barn. She practiced shooting basketballs whenever she had the chance. She wished that New Braunfels had a golf course. When Kate read that the "Babe" was now interested in golf, she predicted, "I bet she'll give Joyce Wethered a run for her money." And everyone knew what a fantastic golfer Joyce Wethered was. She was almost as famous as Bobby Jones and Gene Sarazen. Last summer, when Kate had gone to a Saturday matinee at the New Braunfels movie house with Effie and Stella, she had seen newsreels of Joyce Wethered winning the British Women's title.

"I'm going to be in the newsreels someday," Kate whispered to her sister and cousin.

While Kate earned a reputation as a fast-running tomboy, Stella became known as the "smart Behrman." Not that the other Behrmans were unintelligent, but Stella made straight A's. When she attended the tiny rural school at Thornhill, she made the best grades, and throughout her high school career she was always at the top of her class. She was a library assistant during her study hall hour, which meant she had to do all her lessons in the evening. But she didn't mind. She loved the contact with books that working in the library brought. Even if she didn't have time to read every book in the library, at least she got to touch all of them—to open them, thumb through them, and have a sense of what they were about. She read all the tiny library's history books. Every one. World. European. American. Texas. Comal County. New Braunfels. And she read biographies. Her favorites were about women. Important women fascinated her. It bothered her that there were so few of them.

When she first arrived at high school, Stella tagged along with Kate and her tomboy friends. But soon she began to make a few tentative friends on her own. Her best friend was a girl she knew from church named Beth Schwartz. Beth had attended the tiny rural school at Danville. She was a reader, too. Stella and Beth would sit together at lunch and at church functions. They exchanged books and discussed characters as if they were real. They read indiscriminately. Nancy Drew and the Brontë sisters. Louisa May Alcott and Tolstoy. Biography and beauty tips. They didn't understand Gertrude Stein, but they adored Pearl Buck. They consumed pulp mysteries and westerns. They discussed church-sanctioned readings at great length—did the heathens in China all have to go to hell, even the ones who had never heard of Jesus Christ and therefore couldn't possibly have accepted him as their Savior? The world of the printed page was in many ways more meaningful to them than the one in which they lived.

Stella invested her passion in books. Effie's passion was boys. Kate's was sports. Their school lives were separate, but they were family. They still crept up to the attic from time to time to try on Anna's wedding dress and ponder the mysteries of sex and marriage and birthing. Kate wanted to be bored with such discussions, but she wasn't.

Most of the rural children were expected to go home to their chores right after school and could not participate in any of the after-school activities. The farm children from the east of town, even those of German heritage, were the least accepted. The children of the more progressive ranching population west of town—such as the Behrman clan—were more acceptable but usually unavailable for school functions. The town children considered themselves the most sophisticated. Only Effie was spared the stigma of not being "town." She was the prettiest and therefore the most sought-after—even by the town students.

But at the big dance hall by the mill at Gruene, the lines between country and town did not seem to matter so much. The town and country folks alike drove their cars, trucks, and even a few horse-drawn wagons over the river crossing to the little village with the huge, barnlike dance hall that featured live German music. Couples with young children brought pallets and blankets and bedded them down in the kinderzimmer, a room provided for just such a purpose. The older children played tag in the yard. Old folks sat on the benches that lined the walls and watched the festivities. Teenagers and adults would dance polkas and waltzes far into the night. The men would drink beer, the women and children orange crush.

And in the summer there were dances at the park. The German community loved the music and dances of the old country—even the young people. While the rest of young America was busy with swing, youthful New Braunfels was content to polka.

At the dances the young men paid court to the young ladies. Effie shone at the dances. She would stand in the middle of a semicircle of overgrown boys, many with their hands hanging too far below their sleeves and their "good" pants high-water over their shoes. They would all be vying for her attention. "Oh, my! What's a girl to do?" she would say prettily when all her admirers clamored for her to dance with them.

Sometimes she would do eenie-mienie-minie-mo in an effort to select her next partner. She always managed to end up with someone tall. Effie did not like to dance with short boys.

Kate, Lola, and Millie went to the dances at Gruene but seldom danced with the boys. Like many of the girls, they danced with each other. Kate would not admit it to her two friends, but she sometimes practiced how she would behave if a boy ever did ask her to dance. "Dance? Why, certainly," Kate would say as she nodded into the bureau mirror with an Effie-like smile. She stepped into her invisible companion's arms and they did the polka around the bed. He was amazed at how well she danced. The dancing brought a flush to her cheeks. He wouldn't say she was pretty, but he might like something about the way she looked. Everyone said she had nice teeth. Someday she might have to wear mascara on her pale lashes. Of course, boys might never ask her to dance, but for there to be any chance of it, Kate realized she would have to be more ladylike. And she just wasn't ready to do that yet. Perhaps she never would be. The idea was scary—she would have to give up so much to achieve it.

Stella would sometimes dance with an uncle or cousin; she and her friend Beth were often partners. Boys their own age weren't very interested in dancing, and the older boys who did dance seldom asked Stella or Beth. They were just as intimidated by Stella's scholastic standing as they were by Kate's athletic prowess. The only boys who asked Stella to dance were Joey Brenner and Clark Munsen. They made good grades too.

And Stella and Kate would often dance with each other. Kate's favorite was the Red Wing, which was the fastest dance. "Faster, Stella, faster," Kate would say as she and Stella twirled furiously around the hall.

Effie, of course, seldom danced with girls.

Herman Behrman took pride in his daughter's popularity. He thought Effie was the most special young woman on the face of the earth, and at times it was still difficult for him to believe that he had sired such a wondrous creature.

Like his brothers, Herman was square-faced and sturdily built, with a thick chest and limbs. His hands were those of a man who worked the land—strong, square, thick-fingered, and covered with ugly brown spots from long exposure to the elements. Sometimes he took one of Effie's dainty, unblemished hands in his own and compared them. A miracle, this girl of his.

Next year would be her last year in high school, and Effie's future was much on her father's mind. Herman was neither as stubborn as Frederick nor as quick-witted as John. As a result, he and his wife had formed a more egalitarian marriage. He would not have admitted it to his brothers, but he and Hannah talked things over. She was smarter than he was, and he respected her for it. Often he offered her ideas to his brothers as his own. "What about trying to harvest those native pecans along the creek?" "Our venison sausage won first at the Comal County Fair. Maybe we should make more next year and sell it." Yes, Hannah had a good mind but, unlike some smart women, was not pushy about it. She was perfectly willing to allow her husband to speak for his family. He was a fortunate man.

At his wife's encouragement, Herman had allowed their oldest boy to go to the teachers college over at San Marcos. Hannah admired educated people. She thought Hiram would make a fine schoolteacher. But after one year Hiram had come back to take his place on the farm. Now the boy was twenty-two, and they were going to build him a house down on the creek. He would marry in the fall.

Their second boy, Jason, was a frail boy afflicted with asthma. A bookworm who read even more than Frederick's Stella, Jason had gone to San Marcos for a year and then won a scholarship to the university at Austin. To Hannah's great joy, he was going to study law, a good profession for a boy too sickly to be a rancher. Jason wanted Effie to join him at the university in Austin when she finished high school.

When Jason first brought up the subject, Herman was appalled. Send his Effie away to school? Never.

"If you don't, Papa, she'll get married too young to a rancher and be fat and old by the time she's forty," Jason reasoned.

A university education for a woman seemed unnecessary to Herman, but he knew that Jason was at least partially right. Effie would be married soon. All one had to do was watch the way boys flocked to her like flies to honey to know that. Her dimpled smile was entrancing, her tiny waist and full bosom enticing. Boys would resort to any sort of tomfoolery to evoke her clear, joyous laughter. For along with her beauty and charm, Effie had a zest for life that enchanted all who knew her. Her brothers idolized her. She was her mother's delight. And Herman—well, Effie was the light of life.

"Effie's an intelligent girl," Jason told his father while they stood at a May Day dance in the big hall, renewing a conversation begun the last time Jason had been home. "More and more women are obtaining an education."

"Why?" Herman asked sullenly. "A woman's duty is to be a good wife and mother. She doesn't need an education to do that." He didn't want to talk about it, but Effie's future weighed heavily on his mind. In one more year her high school days would be over. "Surely you don't think she's going to get a job?"

"One never knows," Jason said, adjusting his spectacles, which insisted on sliding down his nose. "Many modern women like to experience a bit of independence before they marry. And after Effie marries—well, who knows? Her husband might become incapacitated like Stubb Keyser and spend his life in a wheelchair. You don't want her to have to take in laundry like Mrs. Keyser. Or Effie might be a widow someday with children to raise on her own. Then what would you have her do? Cook in a restaurant or scrub floors?"

"Of course not," Herman said indignantly. "She would have to come home. I would take care of her."

"After the bad years this country has gone through, you should know that agriculture can fall on very hard times. Farms are being foreclosed everywhere," Jason continued. "We're not as well off as the Landas and the Corephs, but our family has fared better than most. Still, there's no gilt-edged guarantee this will always be so. Fathers aren't always in a position to care for grown children. Besides, you aren't going to live forever."

"We Behrmans have managed to care for our own since we first arrived in this country almost a hundred years ago. When I'm gone, Effie will have her brothers," Herman said pointedly, as he watched the Abrahams boy asking Effie to dance. The lad was visiting his uncle, who owned the mill. Jewish. Herman was uncomfortable about Jews, but they were hardworking people and paid their own way. Still, he wasn't sure he wanted Effie to dance with the boy.

It was then that Jason offered the only argument that made any sense to Herman.

"At the university she will meet the sons of the best families in Texas."

"But they aren't German," Herman said, thinking of his brothers' disapproval if Effie married a man who wasn't German.

"Papa, the day is over when all the Germans in New Braunfels are going to marry only other Germans. It's already happening. There are other respectable, moral people in the world besides Germans. Not every good man is of German stock. Maybe Effie can marry a man who is rich, or will be the next governor of Texas, or will be a great scientist. She won't meet a man like that if she stays in New Braunfels."

Ordinarily, the Behrman brothers discussed family decisions among themselves. But Herman knew Frederick, at least, would be unsympathetic. In his opinion, girls didn't need a university education. For that matter, few men did either. And of course, Effie should marry a German man, his oldest brother would say. What was the matter with the life Herman and Hannah had made for themselves? Wasn't it good enough for their daughter? Frederick would challenge.

Herman had to admit that he and his family did indeed have a good life. Through hard work and frugality the Behrman brothers had done well for themselves. As Jason had pointed out, they were surviving the Depression when others were going under. Their ranches were no longer prosperous but weren't mortgaged, either. And if worse came to worst, a parcel of land could be sold off to pay taxes and meet expenses until the economy got better.

Still, Herman wanted better for his Effie. She should be surrounded by pretty things. She should not have to scrub clothes at a washboard and hang them out in freezing winds or scrub kitchen floors on her knees. It was something that Herman could not explain to Frederick. Of course, there were times when Herman wondered if Frederick, under his stern, unyielding exterior, did not have a really soft spot of his own when it came to Stella. But it was hard to tell with Frederick. The brothers did not talk about matters of the heart.

But regardless of what his older brother might think, as Herman watched his seventeen-year-old daughter being twirled around the floor by first one boy and then another, he knew that none of them was good enough for her. Not one. Effie should be married to a doctor or a lawyer. To a man of means. He did not want her hands to be careworn and red in a few years like those of her mother. Sometimes in the winter Hannah's hands would bleed from cracks in the skin. At night Herman would kiss his wife's poor hands, then rub them with lanolin and wrap them with gauze. He remembered when his Hannah's hands had been as white and soft as Effie's.

The wife of the governor of Texas. Now that was an appealing idea.

And if Effie decided to stay on at the university and earn a degree, she would remain unmarried until she was twenty-two. That was an even more appealing idea. She would stay his little *mädchen* that much longer. And Jason would be there in Austin to look after her for the first two years. Jason said the girls were very closely supervised by house mothers in dormitories and sorority houses. Maybe he'd buy Jason a secondhand car so the two of them could come home more often.

"Such extravagance," Frederick muttered as they walked over the moonlit hill from Hannah and Herman's house. "I don't understand sending a girl to the university in these hard times."

Kate and Stella had run on ahead. Sam was barking a greeting. Anna trudged along behind her husband on the narrow path without comment.

The family had gathered for a dinner to celebrate Effie's graduation. Herman had raised a toast to his daughter and announced that she would join her brother at the university in Austin. Effie's brothers had applauded. So had cousins Carl and Joe. Aunt Hannah beamed. Uncle John and Aunt Louise looked uncertain. Kate and Stella looked at their papa's stern face and said nothing.

Anna too said nothing. But she approved. What else had the frugal brothers labored for all these years if not to give their children opportunities? She wanted a university education for her daughters too. Anna realized, however, that if she spoke in favor of Kate and Stella following their cousin to Austin, Frederick would immediately veto the idea. Such a decision had to come from him, and once he had spoken on a matter, he never altered his position.

In the weeks and months that followed, whenever Frederick commented on the foolishness of educating women, Anna held her tongue and prayed that Effie would in some way distinguish herself at Austin. In a way, her own daughters' future rested on the slim shoulders of their very pretty cousin.

Five

Even as he was living them, Jason had a sense that he might look back on those first days of Effie's college career as the happiest of his life. Having Effie all to himself, playing the role of big brother to the hilt, walking about the beautiful, sprawling campus of spacious lawns and handsome Spanish architecture with his wonderfully pretty sister at his side, introducing her to his friends—it was glorious. He could not sleep at night, so eager was he for the next day of big brotherhood.

Jason knew such exclusiveness would not last. Already overtures of friendship were coming Effie's way from every quarter. She was even receiving invitations to sorority houses in spite of the fact that she had not gone through formal rush week. Jason had wanted her to, but Effie had been frightened of the prospect and protested she was just a country girl who didn't have the clothes for a week of party-going.

Jason was glad now that she hadn't. Effie had had time to become comfortable with being away from home, with being a college student. He could see her relax a little more each day as she discovered her charm worked just as well in Austin as it had in New Braunfels. People responded first to her looks. They *wanted* to like her. And when they discovered she was sincere and sweet, they found her irresistible. Jason was so proud of his sister that he sometimes got tears in his eyes just thinking about it. Of course, one day before long, she would marry and their lives would draw apart. That was as it should be. But he would remember this time as the best.

Effie was everything Jason was not—attractive, healthy, outgoing. Jason's lifelong battle with asthma had robbed him of growth and robustness. He was no taller than Effie. He suspected she weighed more than he did. He wore thick, heavy glasses. But Effie had always treated him with love and affection and always had time for him. She called him her darlin' brother. She would hold his hand when they walked together.

She would sit at his feet and lean her head against his knee while he read to her. He could reach out and touch her soft blond hair.

Though Jason was sure their older brother Hiram cared deeply for Effie, he didn't seem to be smitten as Jason himself was. Five-year-old Christian, of course, was totally in love with his big sister as all five-year-old boys are, but it was too soon to determine how enduring his adoration was.

Hiram, like their cousins Carl and Joe, was more like uncles Frederick and John. They were quiet, solid men not given to outward displays of affection. Of course, Jason had pieced together the story of Uncle Frederick and the first Anna. Apparently there had been a grand passion in Uncle Frederick's life, but that was hard to imagine now, given the stern demeanor of the oldest Behrman brother. Jason wondered how much the present Anna knew about her husband's feelings for her predecessor. Anna seemed so much like Frederick. It was hard to imagine either one of them feeling anything other than responsible love. Jason's feelings for Effie went far beyond responsible brotherly love. With the wisdom acquired from college psychology, he speculated as to whether his love for his sister was a protective mechanism he had created to buffer him from other relationships. Jason knew he would never marry and would join the ranks of other German bachelors in New Braunfels. Jason had not the courage or the health to take a wife and raise a family. He would be a bachelor uncle to his nieces and nephews. He would be a son to his parents. And he would be a brother to Effie.

Effie did not know one Greek house from the other at the university, but she definitely saw the advantages of becoming a part of the system. The Greeks were social and had wonderful parties. Their houses were much nicer than the residence halls. The young men she was finding most attractive in her classes were all fraternity men. And like Jason, Effie understood the real reason she was in Austin was to meet her future husband. She was here so she could marry a man who would improve her station in life.

And she did like Austin. Not just the university, but the city itself—the hustle and bustle of countless cars, trucks, buses; the grandeur of the state capitol building; the department stores, elegant hotels and restaurants, movie palaces. At night the stores were lit with flashing neon lights just like in the movies, only in color—wonderful, gaudy color.

Everyone said Austin was small potatoes compared to the immensity and elegance of Dallas. Effie didn't see how that was possible.

When Effie wandered in and out of the dress shops near the campus, staring at the fashions, touching the fabric, it was like being inside a fashion magazine. The clothes filled her with a longing that made her stomach hurt.

In fact, her most immediate problem was clothes. She would be able to keep up with her studies. And everyone seemed to like her. But she did not have nice clothes. As she began to look past the visibly well-dressed, however, Effie realized she was not alone. Even in the sororities, there were girls attending college with two good dresses, a winter coat, and carefully chosen skirts and blouses. Times were hard. Many parents made great sacrifices just to pay tuition and board. Few could afford fancy clothes on top of that. Effie tried to be clever with accessories. And very quickly she became part of a dorm network with girls her size who traded clothes back and forth.

Jason researched the university's Greek system and suggested she pledge Kappa Kappa Gamma. Their house wasn't fancy, although a new one was to be built. But they weren't as snobby as the Pi Phis. And they weren't all rich like the Thetas. The Kappas had other girls from small towns.

So at Jason's encouragement, Effie became a sorority woman. She met William when the Beta Theta Pi pledge class invited the Kappa pledges to dinner. William wasn't a pledge; he was the pledge trainer— a senior in law. He was over six feet tall and quietly handsome. His brown eyes smiled along with his mouth, which was wide and full and quite wonderful. His hair was the same rich brown as his eyes.

Effie wondered from the first handshake if William wasn't the man she had been waiting for. She suspected strongly that he was, and that made her a little sad. She would have rather met him next year after she had enjoyed college life a bit.

William thought she was pretty. Effie could see that in his eyes. But she was somewhat taken aback when he told her so. "You are very lovely," he said, lingering over a handshake and looking directly in her eyes when he said it.

William was dignified. Effie realized that trait had been missing in the boys back home. William didn't stammer. He didn't hang his head or avert his eyes. He didn't say, "Gosh, you're pretty." He had looked right at her and said, "You are very lovely." Effie was entranced.

When he walked her back to her dorm after dinner, William offered her his arm. That was nice. Effie felt like a lady walking at the side of a gallant gentleman.

They stood in the shadows at one side of the dorm's front door. William took her hand and kissed its palm. Boys had kissed her lips but never her hand. "I plan to court you, Effie Behrman," William said. "I think you are the woman I have been looking for."

Being courted by William Chambers took Effie's breath away. He had grown up in Dallas and was the product of a private high school. He was polished and sophisticated. He had flown in an airplane to Chicago and New York. He had been to Europe. He had read almost as many books as Stella and Jason and knew poetry by heart. He played the clarinet in a jazz group. He wrote beautiful letters Effie knew she would treasure all her life. He had a car, a wonderfully streamlined De Soto Airflow, and Effie felt like a movie star when she rode in his car.

Roses were delivered to Effie's dorm room. There were dinners in expensive restaurants and dancing at nightclubs with cover charges. Effie discovered she liked caviar and champagne. Symphony concerts made her feel like a grand lady, and while she didn't know one great composer from the other, the music reached out and touched her as no other ever had. Effie had to borrow dresses from every girl on the floor to manage the succession of extravagant dates on which William took her.

But it wasn't just the amount of money William lavished on her that Effie appreciated. It was the way he treated her. William adored her just like all the rest. Effie was accustomed to adoration. She was not accustomed to being treated like a fine lady. Effie felt more special than she ever had before in her life.

"I will dedicate my life to your happiness," he promised when he proposed.

"And I to yours," she answered. Yes, William Chambers would have the very best, the most loving wife a man could ever have. Effie had no doubt that being his wife was a job she could do very well. She was a lucky young woman, but William was a most fortunate man.

At Christmas break, William drove her and Jason to New Braunfels in the De Soto.

The family was impressed with Effie's young man. William's father was a city councilman in Dallas and a partner in an old-line Dallas law firm. The Chambers family owned controlling interest in a company that made gas generators and, more recently, gas cooking stoves and gas refrigerators. Their family money was as old as money could be in Texas. Young William would graduate from law school in June. He could even speak passable German. His father was of English heritage, but his mother's family came from Düsseldorf. William had actually been to Germany and visited them. Imagine!

The ring William produced after receiving Herman's blessing was set with diamonds and sapphires. Gems in the middle of the Depression! No one in New Braunfels had ever even seen a ring like that, much less owned one. Herman and Hannah were impressed—and honored—that such a young man should have chosen their Effie.

Frederick watched his niece's fiancé relentlessly, waiting for a flaw in the seemingly perfect young man. Young William's manners were impeccable. At church he joined in all the hymns in a clear baritone without once looking at the hymnal. He commended young Pastor Smitz on his fine sermon and briefly discussed the blasphemy of the German philosopher Hegel. William offered greetings in German to old Pastor Mueller, who was semiretired and now served the congregation as associate pastor.

William fixed the hinges on Hannah's kitchen cabinets and bought her a potted plant at the greenhouse. He sat with old blind Mama Mary in the corner of Louise's kitchen, a fresh audience for her stories. He helped Herman tend the goats and insisted he would come back in the spring and learn how to shear. He seemed to have read every book on Anna's shelves and sat on a stool at her feet discussing Emily Dickinson. Anna seemed quite impressed when he quoted the lines about Death stopping in a carriage. He shot baskets endlessly with Kate even though she always would have only an h or an h-o to his h-o-r-s-e. And he went hunting with cousins Hiram, Joe, and Carl, showing himself to be an accomplished marksman. He climbed into the truck with Uncle John for an all-afternoon tour of Behrman land.

But what impressed Frederick the most was the way the handsome young man treated Effie. William Chambers treated her as though she were a priceless treasure. William was a gentleman. Frederick had never really understood the term before the educated, articulate, and respectful young man from Dallas arrived in their midst.

A gentleman was what Frederick wanted for Stella. No doubt about it.

Reluctantly Frederick was beginning to realize that Stella should go to the university at Austin. His sense of fair play dictated that he would have to allow Katherine to do likewise, even though he had no grand expectations for his older daughter. Kate was too headstrong to make any man a good wife—rancher *or* gentleman.

It never occurred to Frederick to discuss these matters with Anna. He would tell her about it when he had made up his mind.

The summer between Stella's junior and senior year in high school was taken up with preparations for Effie's September first wedding. It was to be a church wedding with a dance following at the big hall at Gruene. Stella and Kate had never been to a church wedding. They were going to be bridesmaids and wear long dresses made of blue tulle.

The newlyweds were to make their home in Dallas, where William would be a junior partner in the family law firm. Effie made several trips to Dallas to visit William's parents and help him select their future home. William, who was engrossed in studying for the state bar, found time to call Effie long-distance every other day and had come to see her twice since summer began. Both times William's cousin, James, accompanied him. James, as mannerly as William, was very kind to Kate, often playing cards with her in the evening and listening attentively as they toured the ranch. She taught him how to milk a cow and shear a goat. "Wait till I tell them about this at the Beta house," he said enthusiastically after he had filled a bucket with fresh, warm milk.

"William says he will die if we aren't married soon," Effie told her cousins proudly early one morning as they baked bread and coffee cake in Anna's big, plain kitchen. It was too hot to bake during the afternoon. Effie had spent the night with Stella and Kate. She was going to Dallas this weekend and wanted to take some home-baked goodies to her future in-laws.

"Don't you worry about the wedding night?" Kate asked shyly.

Stella realized that Kate was actually blushing. Was she thinking of her own future wedding night when she would be made love to by some man? Was she thinking about William Chambers's cousin James?

"Other couples have managed. I'm sure William and I will too," Effie said. "After we get settled in Dallas, you must come to see me all the time. I don't worry about getting married, but I worry about not seeing my cousins. I want us to be best friends all our lives. We must promise always to be best friends."

Stella nodded, then hastily dusted the flour from her hands and raced out to the barn. She came back with a very dusty box. "Look!" she said triumphantly as she pushed a mixing bowl out of the way and put the treasure box on the round kitchen table. The flattened coins, the mirror and Tangee lipstick, the picture of Amelia Earhart, the notebook of girlish writings, and everything else was still inside.

"Remember?" Stella asked merrily, holding up an empty tube of Tangee.

Kate, with flour on her freckled nose, picked up the handful of coins and studied them. "That seems like so long ago. We were kids—now Effie's getting married."

Stella held up the yellow square of newspaper with Amelia Earhart's picture on it. Amelia had gone on to fly the Atlantic solo. A marvelous feat for a woman. Stella had felt proud. And then the brave aviatrix had flown from Honolulu to the United States and across the United States in both directions. She proved women could do more things than people had thought. She proved that women could be brave and have adventures and still be feminine and admired. Amelia Earhart had chosen to be different, and she took risks for her feats of glory.

Effie had chosen the safest course. She would marry a wealthy man who loved her very much.

Kate had vowed to be different.

And Stella herself? She wanted both. She wanted Effie's happiness and Kate's daring. And she wanted the three of them to remain the Behrman girls, as they had all their lives.

Stella replaced the lid on the box. "Put your right hand on top of mine," she instructed her sister and her cousin. "We must swear on the sacred memory of our childhood always to be close to each other, always to be friends, always to come when one of us needs the other two."

And so with their right hands resting solemnly on the top of the scarred wooden box, they bade good-bye to their girlhood and swore on its memory. In the homey comfort of Anna's kitchen, surrounded by the wonderful yeasty, cinnamon aroma of coffee cake, the three cousins clung to one another, fearful that what they had just sworn might be impossible for them to uphold. Life had a way of pulling people apart—even for three cousins who grew up like sisters, Stella realized sadly. Their beloved

Effie didn't belong to her and Kate any longer. She belonged to a man named William who would change her name and her life and give her a new family to replace the one that had nourished and loved her for nineteen years.

It was sad to grow up. Everything changed.

Effie was sitting at the kitchen table letting out a hem when Stella and Kate came rushing through the back door, the screen door slamming behind them.

"Isn't it a pretty day?" Kate said hurriedly. "Let's go sit out on the porch."

"What are you talking about?" Effie said. "It's hot as Hades out there and not much better in here. I made lemonade."

"Yeah, let's take it out on the porch," Kate said, getting three glasses down from the cupboard. Stella chipped off some ice from the block in the icebox.

"What's the matter with her?" Effie asked Stella. "Why this sudden interest in porch sitting?"

"Humor her," Stella said, pulling on Effie's hand. "Bring your mending and come on."

It was hot. A fly buzzed Effie's face unmercifully. She could feel the perspiration running down the inside of her brassiere. She looked at her cousins, sitting side by side on the top step, staring out over the alfalfa field.

"Have we sat on the porch long enough?" she asked.

Kate and Stella shook their heads no.

Effie swatted at the fly. "Well, I have. I'm going inside."

"Sit down," Stella said. "There's a reason."

Kate looked at her watch.

Effie shrugged, sat back down, and picked up the skirt she was hemming. She admired the stitches she had made so far, as she felt the sweat soaking the back of her blouse. This was so stupid. What in the world were those silly girls up to?

"There it is!" Kate yelled, leaping to her feet.

"Where?" Stella asked.

"There. Over the river. Come here, Effie. Right now."

With Stella on one side and Kate on the other, Effie felt herself being pulled down to the end of the yard. Kate had an elbow, Stella a hand. She was still carrying the skirt.

A small airplane was approaching. Imagine that! Here on Hunter Road.

Effie stopped at the fence. The plane was close now. Two men were sitting, one behind the other, in its pair of open cockpits. They were wearing leather aviator helmets and goggles. The man back in the back cockpit was waving furiously.

Stella and Kate were waving back. They were jumping up and down like children, their ponytails bouncing, Kate's a haze of flaming orange in the sunlight, Stella's a flag of rich, shining brown.

"It's William!" Kate screamed. "William! Wave, Effie! Wave!"

"He called us from Dallas," Stella called over the noise of the plane's engine. "He said he'd fly over your house about four and wanted to surprise you. Can you believe it? He's been taking lessons."

The plane dipped its wings in salute, made a wide circle over Uncle Herman's property, then flew toward them again. Stella and Kate took up their waving.

Effie shaded her eyes with one hand and waved the skirt back and forth with the other. That man was her William, but from here he seemed like someone she didn't know at all. Her William wouldn't fly in open-cockpit airplanes. He was studying for the bar.

Flying lessons. But why? What did he need to do that for?

"Wow! My future brother-in-law's going to be a aviator," Kate said, as they watched the plane set a northwest course. "Wow. That's really keen."

Effie wasn't so sure.

Six

Stella and Kate were invited to the Chamberses' Dallas home for a week of prenuptial events honoring Effie and William. Anna and Hannah were to accompany the three girls on the overnight train trip to Dallas. They were to spend a week helping Effie select furniture for her new house and attending parties and showers. Effie's papa and three brothers would come to Dallas at the end of the week for a dinner dance given by William's parents.

Kate wouldn't admit it, but Stella could tell that she was excited over the prospect of seeing William's cousin James again. Never had Kate fussed so much over clothes. She considered cutting her hair short like Effie's. She experimented with makeup, trying to discover a way to minimize her freckles, but she was always careful to take it off before Frederick saw her. Only Effie could calm her. Effie instructed her in the mysteries of rouge and helped her cousins decide which clothes to take to Dallas. Both Kate and Stella would be allowed to buy a new dress in Dallas for the dinner dance. They had to make over their confirmation dresses to wear for other evening occasions. They took the puff out of the sleeves and made the necklines less demure. At Effie's suggestion, they added satin sashes.

"But they still look like made-over confirmation dresses," Kate complained as she held the dress up in front of her and stared at her image in the dresser mirror.

Stella, sitting cross-legged on the bed, had to agree. "But we are who we are, Kate. We are the daughters of a very frugal German goat rancher. I don't think we can pretend to be something different. Effie says everyone will think we are charming if we are just ourselves."

"Well, I'm going to leave my gingham dress and milking stool at home, if you don't mind," Kate said sarcastically.

"What about your donkey?" Stella asked with a giggle. "Maybe we can take the donkeys with us and tie them up in front of the mansion."

The trip to Dallas would be Stella and Kate's first train ride. It would also be their first trip out of Comal County. Hannah and Anna had gone with their husbands once to a wedding in San Antonio, and both had gone to San Marcos several times, but they had never been as far as Dallas.

Effie, with her several trips to Dallas, was practically a world traveler. It amazed Stella how much only a year of college had changed Effie. Oh, she was still the same smiling, fun-loving Effie, but there was a patina of sophistication that hadn't been there before. According to Effie, she had learned far more in her dorm and from her sorority sisters than she had in the classroom. She even smoked cigarettes when her father wasn't around and did so with great aplomb—but, of course, she would give them up when she married. It wasn't seemly for a married woman to smoke. Effie's long hair had been bobbed and hugged her head with fashionable finger waves. She wore her clothes with more flair—the same skirt and blouse from last year but with a scarf draped around her neck and long pearls hanging past her waist. Her nails were painted the same bright red as her lips. Kate was going to attend the university at Austin in the fall. Stella wondered if her sister would change as dramatically as their cousin had.

Effie called her year at college "the best year of her life." She pored over her yearbook with her cousins and pointed out each of her sorority sisters, repeating their escapades a bit wistfully. Stella realized there was a part of Effie that wished she were going back to Austin in the fall instead of assuming her place in society as a married woman. But, as Effie was fond of saying, a man like William Chambers didn't come along every day.

"I was the envy of the girls at the Kappa house when William first came courting," Effie told Stella and Kate, her blue eyes sparkling as she remembered. The three girls had retreated to Effie's front porch in search of a little evening air. The sunset was nice, but the air was heavy with dust and heat. "You should have seen their faces when I came back from taking him home to meet my parents with this ring on my finger," Effie said, holding her hand out in front of her admiringly. "I'm a very fortunate woman to have William."

"Oh, posh," Kate said. "He's damn lucky to have you, and he knows it. You were the catch. I'll bet you were the prettiest girl in Austin, Texas."

"Kate, dearest, what will I do without you?" Effie said as she hugged her cousin, who would never be the prettiest girl in any town.

"Oh, Effie, please don't forget us when you're married to a lawyer in Dallas," Stella implored.

But the sadness over losing her cousin to marriage was replaced with wonder as she rode the train through central Texas and read the names off the railroad station signs—Temple, McGregor, Waco, Hillsboro. And spreading out from the railroad stations were towns to go with the names that had been abstractions before—names in newspaper stories, in her books on Texas history. There was a whole world outside of Comal County. Of course, Stella had known that before, but now she felt it. She wished she had books now to look up each town, to find out why it had been built where it was, to speculate about the secrets that didn't get written in history books. But it was enough for now just to experience Texas firsthand. She'd have her books later.

She was riding on a train—going someplace. She had always wanted to go someplace.

They took a meal in the dining car. "I feel like I'm Alice on the other side of the looking glass. Remember how we used to catch glimpses of the diners on the M. K. & T?" Stella asked Effie and Kate. "And here we are." Stella looked around the moving car, almost expecting to see Clark Gable or Carole Lombard at the next table. Dining cars were romantic.

"Do you suppose we'll ever ride on a dining car with a romantic man like in the movies?" Stella whispered to Kate.

"Fat chance," Kate whispered back.

The porter came to make up their berths. Kate immediately claimed an upper. Stella was glad. She could look out the window from the lower berth.

Early the next morning William met them at the station in his father's Lincoln Town Car. Any doubt the rest of Effie's family had about the wealth of her intended's family was put to rest the instant the large automobile pulled up in front of the Chamberses' Turtle Creek mansion.

"Holy cats!" Kate muttered under her breath when she saw the house. "Quite a house you've got there, Willy, my boy. Do you furnish maps for poor relations so they won't get lost wandering around inside?"

"It's not as big as it looks," William said with a grin. "Do you always say just what you're thinking, Kate?"

"Sure. Why not?" Kate answered with a toss of her red hair.

They were no sooner out of the car than Mr. and Mrs. Chambers were there to greet them. Margaret Chambers offered her welcome in both English and German, and had a special hug for Hannah. "At last I meet the mother of our precious Effie. You cannot imagine how much we adore her. If I had manufactured a bride for my son, she would have been just like your daughter."

"See," Kate whispered to Effie as they helped William carry in the suitcases. "His mother knows. *You* are the prize, and don't you ever forget it."

Effie had been in the Chambers home twice before. But even so, Stella was amazed at how easily her cousin accepted life in the mansion. Effie wasn't embarrassed to let servants wait on her. She wasn't overwhelmed by the palatial surroundings. When she turned her smile on servants and future in-laws, they could not seem to do enough for her.

Stella decided that beauty functioned much like royal blood. It entitled one to homage. Sometimes she wondered if she should envy Effie, but she loved her cousin too much for that.

Kate had scarcely noticed the marvels of a formal dining room, canopied beds, marble fireplaces, and Persian carpets after she saw the swimming pool and tennis court in the backyard. She had been reading about the exploits of Helen Hull Jacobs and Alice Marble and was dying to play tennis, but there were no tennis courts in New Braunfels.

James offered to teach her to play, and Kate spent most of the week on the court. When James or William or Mr. Chambers wouldn't play with her, she spent hours hitting the ball off the wooden backboard. She loved to feel herself improving. The men were amazed at her. With Kate, the term "natural athlete" took on a new meaning. While it was impossible for her to develop their level of skill in just one week, Kate very quickly put together her own game. She played as aggressively as her skill would allow. She wasn't afraid to leap high for shots. She wasn't afraid to sweat.

In the evening Kate would refresh herself by swimming laps in the pool, then with great care transform herself from American sportswoman to "date bait."

For Stella, it was a magic week. She tasted wine for the first time and, under its influence, she allowed herself to be kissed for the first time. Chad, a friend of James's younger brother, did the honors. They were on the Chambers terrace in the dark shadows next to the house. Mountains did not move for Stella. "Your first time?" he asked. Stella nodded. "Well, you're my third," he announced.

After the Friday evening party and a tired Christian had been tucked into bed, the remaining adults gathered in the library for a brandy, and the young people adjourned to the swimming pool. Stella realized that under the curtain of darkness, many of the young people had paired off and disappeared to various dark corners of the huge, landscaped yard. Even Kate and James had vanished. And those left in the pool used water games as a ruse for a great deal of touching.

Stella sat on Chad's shoulders amid wild splashing and tried to unseat a girl from another boy's shoulders. Then Chad trapped her in a corner of the pool. "Let me see your breasts," he whispered. "No one is looking."

Horrified, Stella tried to duck under his arms, but he stopped her. "Come on, Stella. You know you want me to see them. What's the point of having breasts if you can't show them off? Just pull your bathing suit down a bit."

Chad let go of the side of the pool and reached for her bathing suit straps, apparently ready to pull them down himself, and Stella thrashed her way past him to the ladder.

She shrouded her wet body in a large beach towel and sat by herself, willing the erratic pounding of her heart to cease. Later, as she lay under the canopy of the grand bed that was assigned to her and Kate for the week, she wondered how it would have felt to show Chad her breasts. She crept out of bed and went into the bathroom. In front of the mirror, she loosened the ties of her batiste gown and allowed it to expose first one and then the other white breast. She touched them tentatively, watching hard, pointed nubs grow in the middle of her nipples.

Then she covered herself and went back to bed. She was glad Chad had not seen her breasts. She didn't like Chad. She was also glad he was going to Europe with his parents and couldn't come to Effie's wedding.

In the days before the wedding, Behrman relatives from all over Comal County and Chambers relatives from Dallas gathered in New Braunfels for the occasion. It might have been an awkward affair but for Effie. With her laughter, her teasing charm, her constant smile and tireless energy, she was the bridge that brought the two worlds together. She coaxed wealthy Dallas matrons to put on aprons and help the aunts in Hannah's kitchen. She had prosperous central Texas businessmen rolling up their sleeves and playing horseshoes out in the yard with the uncles.

The men discovered they shared political views. The United States should stay out of Europe's squabbles. Roosevelt should quit meddling with the American farm. The Farm Security Act was going to ruin the few prosperous farmers remaining in the country, with all its rules about migrant workers.

Evening meals were taken at dusk on the broad front porches or shaded lawns of various Behrman houses on long tables made of planks and sawhorses. After dinner Kate supervised games for the children and young adults. Kick the can. Dodge ball. Blindman's buff. Hide-and-seek.

When James Chambers showed up with a date, Kate ducked around the back of Effie's house and ran down the path to Rosehaven. She climbed the steps to the attic two at a time and sprawled on the discarded old sofa that had always resided against the railing. The dust made her sneeze.

She sat there for most of the afternoon until Stella found her. "I'm sorry," Stella said.

"Shut up, will you. He's just an old dumb boy. I should have had better sense."

Stella sat down next to Kate on the sofa. "We'll have to go back over to Effie's pretty soon. They're about to set out dinner."

"I'm not hungry."

"We haven't been up here for a long time," Stella said, making a show of looking around her. "Gosh, we used to play up here for hours."

"Did you see her?" Kate asked. "She's pretty. Really pretty."

Stella touched her sister's hand. "You're right. James is a dumb old boy. All that girl has done since she got here is stare at her face in her compact mirror and complain—about the heat, the flies, about having to share a bed with some girl she's never met. Thank goodness she's staying over with Aunt Louise and Uncle John. I'd hate to have to put up with her here. I wouldn't be surprised if someone had to sleep up on this old sofa. Have you ever seen so many out-of-town guests at a wedding?"

"I wish I was pretty," Kate said. Her voice was a whisper.

"You are," Stella said. Her chattering stopped. She didn't know what else to say. But she reached for her sister's hand. Kate tried to pull it away, but Stella wouldn't let go.

The next day Kate gave up on her new hair style, pulled her hair into a ponytail, and began organizing more competitive events than sack races and three-legged races. She proceeded to prove that she could run faster than any cousin, male or female, Behrman or Chambers.

Although her future mother-in-law had offered to buy Effie a fashionable wedding gown in Dallas, Effie had decided to wear the high-necked satin dress in which her mother had been married. Hannah had helped her make the veil. Effie's aunts, Anna and Louise, and her cousins, Stella and Kate, had all helped embroider tiny forget-me-nots down the back of the wondrously sheer fabric.

Mr. Chambers hired a photographer from San Marcos. The bride and her two attendants stood for the photographer on the front steps of Effie's girlhood home. Stella and Kate, in their blue tulle, stood proudly beside their beloved Effie, who was triumphantly beautiful. Stella knew even as the phosphorous flash went off that the resulting picture someday would be one of her most prized possessions. It would record their last moments together as the Behrman girls.

The wedding was simple. Effie, Hannah, and Jason had decorated the church with ivy, crepe myrtle, and boughs of cedar and roses from the front porch at Rosehaven.

At Effie's request, old Pastor Mueller conducted the service—but in English. She didn't want it in German. "The time for that is past," she told her father when he protested.

So in Pastor Mueller's quavering old man's voice, the traditional words were said in English. Love, honor, cherish, cleave only to each other till death do us part. For Effie, there was the additional promise—to obey. She said her vows in a clear voice, a woman's voice.

When she looked at her William, her love was radiantly there for all to see. Tears overflowed from Stella's eyes. She stole a look at Kate. Tears were also trailing down her sister's freckled cheeks.

Why did they cry? Was it a lament for girlhood lost or an acknowledgment of future joys? But marriage was no guarantee of happiness. It was just something people did, like go to school and work and die. People who didn't marry were thought lonely and even tragic. At least marriage sometimes did seem to make people more content than they would be without it. Uncle Herman and Aunt Hannah certainly seemed to belong together. Even Uncle John and Aunt Louise smiled and touched. What about her own parents, Stella wondered, and so many others who seemed to go through life tolerating each other, locked in a duty-bound prison of family and custom?

But Effie was beautiful, and she and William loved each other. There was the hope of a good life together. Effie would manage if anyone could.

The wedding feast was over. The toasts had been made and the wine glasses lifted. "It's time," Hannah told her daughter.

Before she went to her daughter's bedroom to help her change into her traveling clothes, she went into the bathroom and carefully hooked the door. Behind the blankets on the top shelf of the linen closet was the tiny brown vial. She uncorked it and allowed a drop of bright red liquid to pour onto her palm. Hannah nodded, satisfied the solution had not congealed or darkened, and replaced the cork. At first Hannah had tried chicken blood. Then she had tried cutting her own finger and saving some of its blood. But no matter how careful she was to keep air away from it, the blood would clot after a few minutes. She wanted something that would keep its viscosity, and she experimented with several different combinations of food coloring, methiolate, and tomato juice to come up with a solution that pleased her.

Hannah slipped the tiny bottle into her pocket and checked her hair in the mirror. More gray than blond. Once it had been the same color as Effie's. Once she had been a bride just like Effie. Hannah smiled. Poor Herman. What an ordeal their wedding night had been for him! Hannah had never doubted that it was the first time for him. He was mortified that he was not able to accomplish the act for ever so long.

Hannah went down the hall to Effie's room. The boys had always shared a room, but Effie, being the only girl, had had a room to herself. A pretty room. Effie had painted flowers on the walls and made ruffled curtains for the windows and a colorful rag rug for the floor. She had designed and made the colorful quilt on her bed. A clever girl.

Mother and daughter had made Effie's going-away dress, but it was carefully patterned after a dress in a fashion magazine. Hannah thought her daughter looked very smart in the tailored two-piece dress of light-weight blue gabardine. At the waist was a white leather belt above the soft flare of a peplum. The white linen collar was tied with a silk bow. Even the Dallas people would admire Effie in it. This afternoon her daughter had been sweet in her mother's old-fashioned wedding dress. Now she was a sophisticated young woman on her way to a new life. Hannah thought it appropriate that Effie be both women on her wedding day. She would need to be both all of her life in order to make a good marriage.

Effie turned around for her mother's inspection. Hannah adjusted Effie's cloche hat. "You look wonderful. Now let's sit down a minute and talk before you go downstairs."

Effie glanced at the clock on the bedside table. It was late, but her mother took her hand and led her to the bed. Effie sat. Hannah pulled the room's one chair close.

Once seated, Hannah handed her daughter the tiny brown medicine vial.

"What's this?" Effie asked, a puzzled frown on her face. She looked down at the tiny container in her hand and back at her mother's face.

"Something that will pass for blood."

Effie's eyes widened in horror. "But why . . ." Then a flush began in Effie's neck and rose to her cheeks.

"I think you know, dear. Your William thinks he's married the perfect woman. Don't confuse him."

"But this is dishonest," Effie said.

"Then you've already told him?" Hannah asked.

Effie shook her head no.

"Then don't. It will gain nothing and lose you a great deal. Honesty in a marriage must be used sparingly."

"How did you know, Mama?"

"It's not important."

"Does Papa know?"

"Good Lord, no!" Hannah said. "Now, you take that and be clever with it. God made women clever so there could be good marriages. You be shy tonight and wear your gown. Make a great show of spreading a towel to protect the bed, then pull the curtains and turn out the lights. As soon as he's had a glimpse of the evidence, rinse it out. Explain that blood will stain if it's not rinsed out right away in cold water."

Effie looked unsure. Rinsing out a towel was not the sort of activity she had in mind for her wedding night.

"They'll be plenty of time for nudity and passion other nights," Hannah said, patting her daughter's hand. "Wedding nights are something to be gotten through. The nice part comes later."

"Is this why you made my nightgown with a pocket?"

Hannah nodded.

"Oh, Mama, do you hate me? Do you think I'm just a terrible girl? He was so pitiful. He thought no one would ever love him, and he loved me so much. And I was curious. . . ."

Hannah touched a finger to her daughter's lips. "Hush. Some things you don't talk about. And no, I don't think you're a terrible girl. I think you're the sweetest, kindest daughter a woman ever had. It's barbaric to diminish a person's worth over one indiscretion."

"It was more than once," Effie said, her head hanging, her eyes downcast. "I liked it, and I did it again."

Hannah's mouth was ajar. She stared at her daughter for an instant and then began to laugh. "Oh, my dear precious Effie." She threw her head back and rolled it back and forth. Still the laughter came. Tears rolled down Hannah's face.

Hannah reached out and hugged her daughter, and the laughing got mixed up with sobbing.

"I love you so much, Effie Behrman Chambers. And if you have any love at all for your mother, you will live a happy life. Just remember that nothing is worth ruining your life for. Nothing."

"What if William discovers it in my pocket?" Effie said, pulling away from her mother, her mind racing ahead. She stared down at the little bottle no bigger than a tube of lipstick.

"Tell him it's smelling salts. Tell him that your silly old mother insisted you have smelling salts in case you got dizzy on your wedding night."

"Is there enough in here?" Effie said. "It's so tiny."

"There's enough," Hannah said.

At ten o'clock that night the newlyweds got into their beautiful new black Buick sedan with gray plush upholstery, a gift from the groom's parents, and left for their honeymoon. Stella and Kate joined in the procession that chased the bride and groom across the county.

The procession of honking cars and trucks followed the newlyweds past Hunter all the way to the Hays County line. Then the cars slowed. Stella watched the taillights fade into the night.

Only Stella and Kate knew what was left of Effie's wedding night was to be spent at a hotel in San Marcos. Before William, the cousins had shared many secrets, but she doubted Effie would share her wedding night. Stella felt a gulf opening up between herself and her cousin, a gulf that would be bridged only when she herself married.

Thoughts of sex and marriage filled Stella with such a strange mixture of emotions. There was fear almost like her fear of dying, one that comes with not knowing what is on the other side of something, that whatever it was that made her unique would change or cease to exist.

But there was also a longing from someplace deeper and even more primeval than fear. Her body, more and more, spoke to her of this longing to join with a man. In the night it opened her, making Stella feel empty and alone. Her fantasies ran from violent couplings with lustful men to spiritual ceremonies with worshipful ones. Probably she would marry a man who was somewhere in between. Lust seemed to go away after marriage anyway. But would there always be a corner of her mind that wanted the extreme? And did other girls think such horrible thoughts? She wished she could ask Effie.

Effie was clever. Her mother would have been proud. William begged her forgiveness that there had been another woman before tonight. "Oh, Effie, if you only knew how much I wish it were the first time for me also. I just never dreamed it would be so important—that I would someday love a beautiful woman like you. You are so pure and good, and I love you so completely."

William did not question the nightgown. He seemed to respect her for it. Effie was too nervous to worry about her own body's responses. The first night was something to be gotten through, she reminded herself. The next morning she was disappointed when William got out of bed without making love to her. She wanted to follow him into the bathroom and watch him urinate and shave and shower. But she knew better. The second night, in a Victorian hotel on Galveston Island, Effie stood in a shaft of moonlight and removed her nightgown. William knelt in front of her and kissed her belly. The sounds of the ocean came through the open window.

Effie relaxed. She felt as if she had warm honey in her veins. William's fingers were gentle as he reached between her legs and touched her. She sensed the moistness there. He knew where to touch her, and oh, my, it felt good.

He stood and kissed her before lifting her onto the high four-poster bed. He kissed her neck, her shoulders, her breasts. She wanted him to suck on her breasts, but he only kissed them. Another night she would ask him to suck. Bernice Oglethrope said she heard that felt better than sex itself, but Effie doubted that.

William was wonderfully hard and pushing against her belly. She didn't have to pretend to be a virgin tonight. She wrapped her legs around his back and guided him into her. William went wild. Effie had never felt such power. The warm honey in her veins pooled in her belly, in her thighs.

The third night she allowed the waiting moans to erupt from her throat. It was so liberating. She moaned and felt the honey pool, the warmth rolling over her in waves. "Oh, yes," she said over and over. "Oh, yes!"

On the fourth night she touched his erect penis and told him it was beautiful. She wanted to kiss it. She wondered if women ever did that.

As William watched his wife fondling his penis, he knew beyond all doubt that he was married to a woman who would enjoy sex. He was proud of himself. He had been gentle. Her introduction to sex had been carefully choreographed. He had never frightened her or hurt her. He congratulated himself on being such a good husband.

On the fifth night Effie cried out with joy as William brought first one and then a second orgasm. He'd heard that some women faked them. He knew Effie did not. She was in rapture.

When they were finished, Effie arched her head back onto the pillow, stretched her arms in the air and began to laugh. "Oh, Willy, this is so much fun. Do you suppose other people have this much fun?"

Her laughter was contagious. They lay beside each other on sweaty sheets and laughed with delight. William knew that he was the most fortunate man who had ever lived.

Seven

Frederick helped his nephew Jason strap the last of Kate's possessions on the luggage rack on the top of Jason's elderly Ford sedan. Anna, Stella, and Kate hovered nearby. Anna's lips were tighter than usual. Stella and Kate looked as if they were about to cry.

Frederick tugged on the ropes one last time and stepped back from the car. It was time. She was really going.

Over the last few months as the date of Kate's departure approached, he had been filled with doubts over his decision to send his daughters to college. For Kate, it seemed senseless. His older daughter was never going to marry well like her cousin Effie. And perhaps he didn't want Stella marrying some boy from Dallas or Houston and moving away from him. He could not imagine life without Stella's quiet presence, without her soft smiles and gentle humor to balance out the hard, gaunt presence of her mother in his life. Frederick's heart swelled to aching when he thought of days upon days without Stella. But he was sixty-six. An old man. The land had kept him robust all these years, but he could feel age creeping into his bones and into his mind. There were mornings when he understood why men retired to rocking chairs on front porches in the summertime and beside kitchen stoves in the winter—and gave the land over to sons. But he had no sons, and he would labor away as long as he could. He knew no other way.

And while he wanted more than anything else to keep his younger daughter by his side in his declining years, he felt his duty as a father required him to send both daughters away. Their place was no longer here at Rosehaven. The land must be kept Behrman.

Kate hugged her mother and her sister. They were crying—even Anna. Kate turned to her father. "Good-bye, Papa. I'll work hard and learn a lot."

Frederick nodded. "Take care of yourself, Kate. You'll be in our prayers."

They stood awkwardly staring at each other. Father and daughter. The time of parting. Kate was going on to adulthood.

Frederick reached out his hand. They shook hands like two people meeting at church. Formally.

Then he shook hands with Jason. "I'll look after her, Uncle Frederick," Jason promised. Kate was lean and strong; Jason was frail and weak. But men took care of women, and Frederick knew Jason would do his best.

Frederick watched Jason turn the car around and head down the rutted drive until it rounded the cedar grove and disappeared from view. He should have seen Kate off with a hug. Why couldn't he do that?

Ah, well, it was too late now, too late for him and Kate.

Effie, newly returned from her wedding trip, came down from Dallas for sorority rush week with a suitcase full of clothes for Kate to borrow.

Effie had never looked lovelier. Her newly acquired patina of wealth and sophistication did not conceal the old effervescent Effie underneath.

Her sorority sisters clustered around to admire her salon hairdo, her outfit from Neiman-Marcus, her diamond-pavé wedding band.

"Oh, Effie, is it just wonderful being married?" asked Ruth Ann, her former roommate.

"For me it is," Effie said, her dimpled smile the same. "William and I are lucky to have each other."

Effie had come to Austin on the pretext of seeing old friends and helping the Austin alumni with rush week activities. But in reality, like the other cluster of both young and old matrons, she was here looking after the interest of a female relative who was going through rush. Effie feared Kate would go unnoticed if she was not there to remind the Kappa sisters of her cousin's attributes. Every house needed girls like Kate, Effie pointed out. Kate would organize their intramural teams. Kate would plan social activities and direct skits at rush parties. Kate would get the fluffy girls up off the sofa and make them play tug-of-war or have water fights with the Sigma Chi's and other neighboring fraternities. With Kate around, there would be three-legged races at picnics and bobbing for apples at Halloween. Kappa needed Kate.

But Effie didn't go to all this trouble for Kappa. She wasn't particularly devoted to the idea of sisterhood. Her sisters in this life were her two cousins. Effie was doing this for Kate—and indirectly for Stella, who would come the year after. Kate needed Kappa. Without a sorority, Effie feared, Kate would become a dorm mouse—one of those girls who come to the university, go to class, take their meals at the cafeteria, study at the library, then spend the rest of their college life in the confines of a dormitory room.

If Kate was in a sorority, she would be included in social activities. She would go on blind dates. She would have friends other than girls from P.E. class. With Kappa, Kate might have a chance to find a boyfriend.

For Effie did not for one minute believe that in Kate's heart of hearts she really meant all that nonsense about never getting married. Every girl wanted to get married. Kate was just afraid to admit it—even to herself. As long as she claimed she wasn't interested, if it didn't happen, she was protected.

Rush week began with open house. Kate felt awkward in her French heels and Effie's ruffled dress. Her name tag read Katherine Behrman. Braunfels was spelled "Braunsfel."

"Now where in the world is New Braunsfel, Katherine?" asked Cynthia, a Kappa Alpha Theta from Lufkin. Kate was seated on a velvet sofa in the elegantly decorated living room of the Theta house. Cynthia was perched prettily on the coffee table in front of Kate.

"It's sixty miles southwest of here," Kate explained.

"Really. I've never heard of it. What does your father do?"

"He's a rancher. We raise Angora goats for their wool."

"Goats? How quaint. Margaret, Katherine's father raises goats. Katherine, this is Margaret Thompson. Her father is president of a big ol' bank over in Fort Worth. And this is Missy Bullock from Corpus. She's a cheerleader for the football team."

"What do you want to major in, Katherine?" Missy asked, perching on the arm of the sofa, a cigarette in her hand. Her nails were long and red. She looked very sophisticated.

"Physical education," Kate answered.

"Oh, well, then you must meet our Billie Jo Reagan," Margaret said, waving over a mannish-looking girl with a Dutch-boy haircut. "Billie Jo's a P.E. major. Her grandmother was one of the founders of our chapter."

Once Billie Jo had arrived and sat beside Kate on the sofa, Cynthia, Margaret, and Missy drifted away to turn their charm on more likely prospects. Kate asked Billie Jo where the rest room was and spared the girl the trouble of small talk with someone who wouldn't be invited back to the Theta house for tomorrow's party.

But thanks to Effie, Kate was invited back to the Kappa house the next day and each subsequent day. At week's end she was issued a bid to pledge Kappa Kappa Gamma sorority. Kate wasn't sure it was what she wanted to do, but it would be insulting to Effie not to accept. And there was comfort in knowing she would belong someplace. The University of Texas surely wasn't New Braunfels. So she curled her hair and put on one of Effie's dresses in preparation for the preferential party that would show Kappa was her first choice. That was a joke. No one else had even asked her back. The girl who had shared the room with her went home in tears the second day of rush after being cut by her dead mother's sorority. Since then Kate had sat alone in the room waiting until it was time to go to the Kappa house again.

Kate stared at herself in the mirror. She looked like Kate, the rancher's daughter, dressed up in her wealthy cousin's dress. She tried a bit more powder on her freckles. Effie kept telling her they would fade if Kate'd stayed out of the sun. But Kate loved the sunshine. Where would she run if it wasn't in the sunshine? She loved the sunshine on her face, her arms, her legs as she ran down country roads, seeing if she could run faster than she had the day before. She loved the feel of her lungs expanding, her muscles straining, her breathing coming harder and harder as she pushed herself to the limit. She'd die if she couldn't run in the sunshine.

What she most looked forward to at the university was having access to a real track, to a gymnasium and swimming pool, to tennis courts and a golf course. Why were all the things that gave her most satisfaction frowned on by others? Kate was happiest when she was competing—against others or against herself. She found joy in being fast and strong and agile. And she wasn't going to give up sunshine to fade her freckles no matter what Effie said. But they were unattractive, Kate had to admit.

She tried some of the foundation Effie had given her. She wished her cousin were here to put on her makeup. It always looked better when Effie did it. But the rushees were allowed no visitors once rush had begun. The only time she had seen Effie all week was at the Kappa house.

Kate rubbed the makeup across her nose and cheeks. It did help some. The freckles blended in a bit. She applied it to her forehead and chin. Then she put mascara on her pale lashes and lipstick on her lips. She had to admit she looked better—not quite like herself, but better.

Kate sighed and picked up a silly little beaded purse and a pair of white gloves that one didn't have to wear but at least had to carry.

But she could not bring herself to squeal and weep like the other new pledges when they were welcomed by their new Kappa sisters. Effie pinned on her light blue and dark blue pledge ribbons and gave her a corsage. Kate gave Effie a hug. "Thanks, Cuz. I know you went to a lot of trouble for me."

"No more than you would have done for me if the tables had been turned. Enjoy it, Kate. You don't have to give body and soul like these other girls. Just take out what is good and soft-pedal the rest."

As Kate looked around at all those excited, silly girls, she wished she had the nerve to forgo sorority life. But she suspected that Effie was right. If she didn't pledge, she would be lonely. And Effie assured her that there would be other Kappas who were interested in more than parties and boys. Kate wished Stella were here with her, and she wished Effie weren't married. At least she had good old cousin Jason. He was a good pal and would keep her company. He tired very easily and couldn't do anything athletic. But he knew his way around, and they liked each other.

Effie was right. Kate did find kindred Kappas to be friends with and others she liked in her freshman dorm. And Kate went around with Jason a lot. He walked her to her classes until she learned her way around. He would sit on the sidelines and watch her play tennis, run, or swim her laps, practice on the driving range at the golf course. In the evenings they went to hear the university chorus or the symphony.

And there was an occasional movie. But movies were a luxury. After seeing Greta Garbo in *Anna Karenina*, Kate sighed over her cherry Coke and asked, "Don't you think she's the most beautiful woman in the entire world?"

Jason shook his head and absently pushed his glasses back up his nose. "No. I think Effie is the most beautiful woman in the world."

Kate regarded her frail-looking cousin as he stared into space. Poor Jason.

Or maybe loving Effie suited him just fine. Loving from afar was certainly safe. Not loving at all was the safest.

If she were a boy, she'd probably love Effie as more than just a cousin,

Kate realized. Effie was everything a girl should be. How could boys help falling in love with her?

As Kate became more involved in campus life, she had less time for Jason. She felt a little guilty about it, but Jason assured her it was okay. He needed to spend more time with his studies anyway if he was going to pass the bar.

In October Kate and the other girls in her Kappa pledge class began formal blind dates, which paired off each girl with a boy from a fraternity pledge class. The girls would advance one step at a time down the curving stairway while a boy stepped forward from the line in the entry hall and claimed his date on the bottom step. The respective pledge trainers stood on either side of the bottom step and took care of introductions. When the pairing was completed, they would all go to the fraternity house for a party. Kate was often the life of the party. She joked with the boys and sometimes took them on in arm wrestling or dart throwing. In the Beta house front yard, she proved she could broad-jump farther than any boy there. Kate knew she was going about this dating business all wrong. The girls who got invited out didn't arm wrestle, and they stayed out of the sun if they had freckles.

When formal blind dates ended, no boy had asked Kate out on a real date. But it didn't matter. She was busy, becoming faster and stronger. Her chances of becoming a famous athlete would be much better if she didn't bother with romance and marriage. Marriage meant cooking and children and having to stay home all the time. Athletes had to train.

Roosevelt was reelected by a landslide. The Spaniards were fighting a civil war. The nation had a horrid fascination with the Bruno Hauptman trial. People were flying the Atlantic in a German dirigible. But somehow news of the outside world was greeted with detachment on the university campus. It lost much of its impact when filtered through the students' cloistered existence. Collegiate was their world.

Kate was no different in that respect. She seldom read a newspaper. Golf was her latest passion, occupying huge chunks of her time. Her long game was fantastic, but she needed to work on her short game. She put in long hours practicing putting and her chip shot. And she never neglected her running. Her times in both the 100- and 200-meters were good. She just might get to the Olympics someday if she got herself into a good Amateur Athletic Union program and the hands of a good coach.

Kate competed in the fall A.A.U. meet that was held at the university track. It was her first experience with sanctioned competition. She'd trained for only a few weeks with the local A.A.U. organization and knew she probably had no business entering the meet, but she allowed the coach to put her name in for the sprints.

She was so nervous the night before the meet that she threw up twice. She tossed and turned in her bed, unable to sleep. What if she wasn't really a good athlete, after all? She was better than anyone in New Braunfels, but that was just a backwoods town. Girls didn't go in for sports there. Kate had never faced real competition.

The 100-meter trials were first. Kate was in the first of two heats. She methodically stretched all her leg and hip muscles. She tried to blank out her nervousness. What if she came in last? What if everyone wondered what that rank beginner was doing at the meet?

Calm down, old girl, Kate told herself. This was just a local meet, just other runners like herself trying to find out if they had anything. Fewer than a hundred spectators were scattered about the stands. Other trials for field events were being held simultaneously with the running events. It wasn't as if the world were holding its breath waiting for her performance.

Only 100 meters. About as far from the kitchen door back home to the first goat shed. Nothing. Just run full out. It was too short for strategy. Just get ahead and stay there.

"Take your mark."

Under fourteen seconds, Kate thought. *Please.* Just respectable. She could do faster than that, but she'd settle for respectable.

"Get set."

Get off fast, she cautioned herself. *You can lose it with a bad start no matter how well you run.*

"Go!"

Adrenaline flowed. Energy burst through her muscles and sinews. Two other runners burst off the start ahead of her. Damn.

Push! Harder.

Kate pulled out ahead.

Show them. Show them all.

She was going to do it! She was going to break the tape. She was a runner. Kate, the runner. Kate, the athlete.

Head back, she felt the tape across her chest. Just like the pictures of the Babe and Helen Stephens, who had won two gold medals in last summer's Olympics.

Kate slowed and jogged on down the track to cool down. There was applause from the stands and from people lining the track. Kate looked at their faces. Smiles. Applause and smiles for her. She waved in acknowledgment.

Victory. God, it felt good.

Her coach came running up to shake her hand. "Good show," he said. "You ran a 12.5."

12.5 seconds. More than respectable.

Kate won the finals in the 100. By then several hundred spectators occupied the wooden bleachers. The applause was punctuated with cheers, and there were hugs from team members.

She set a meet record in the time heat for the 200 meters. Twenty-eight seconds flat. Pretty damned good for an unproven runner. Her coach was pleased. This time he said, "Damned good show. You're a runner, girl."

Yes, Kate thought. *A runner. That's who I am.*

Kate liked winning. She liked it a lot. She liked the write-up in the Austin paper the next day: NEW BRAUNFELS GIRL SETS RECORD. She sent a clipping home and one to Effie.

Stella wrote back enthusiastic congratulations. "I'm so proud! I took the newspaper clipping to school. Everyone was so impressed. The *Austin* newspaper! I can hardly wait until I can see you race in person. I'll jump up and down and tell everyone around me, 'That's my sister. Kate Behrman of New Braunfels.' "

Effie ordered flowers to be delivered to her during the Monday night dinner at the Kappa house. Everyone clapped. Kate could feel herself blushing.

Frederick offered no comment on her victory in his weekly letter. Anna's note at the bottom of the page told only of Aunt Hannah's cold and two orphaned goat kids she was having to bottle-feed. But the letter was addressed in Anna's back-slanting script. And there was a twig with three leaves enclosed in the letter. Kate recognized the waxy leaves of the cherry laurel bush that grew at the southwest corner of the house. Laurel for victory.

Thanks, Mama.

The sports reporter from the school paper came to the dorm to interview her. Garrett Gardner from Belton kept saying, "Gosh, that's really good for a girl." His own sport was swimming, and he was on the university swimming team. And he was an avid baseball fan. His heroes were the Cardinals' Gas House Gang. He couldn't believe that Kate knew the batting averages—lifetime and season—for Dizzy Dean, Pepper Martin, and just about any other player he could name.

"Why don't you come to the swimming meet on Saturday? Maybe we can get a Coke afterwards."

Kate promised she'd try to come. She had lots of homework, and her cousin was coming by to help her study. "I'll sure try, though," she promised.

Kate went to the swimming meet. Garrett swam freestyle and butterfly. He didn't place.

Before the meet, Kate thought she might hang around for that Coke. But afterwards she went on home. What if they had a Coke and then Garrett asked her out for a real date? Kate didn't want to be tested. She was afraid she might say yes, and then she might start thinking about him all the time as she had with James Chambers. She didn't want a boy to get that important again. Other things in her life were more important. She was a runner now. She was on the archery team, and she was going to compete in intramural tennis, golf, basketball, and volleyball. Life was exciting. She couldn't let a boy become more important than everything else. If that happened, it meant her carefully ordered world was a sham. It meant she wasn't doing what she wanted to do, after all—but only what was left over for her to do.

Yet as she walked home from the pool, Kate felt kind of let down. By evening she fell into a real funk. When Jason called to ask if she wanted to go to a free dance at the Union, she barked back, "Now, why in the world would I want to go to a dumb dance with my cousin?"

She called him back later and apologized.

It was always like that when she met a new boy. She didn't want to go out, but when he didn't ask her, she would at first feel relieved, then she would be sad with the kind of sadness that was as vague as a melancholy cloud of gray fog.

Then, somehow, she was having an affair. With a zoology professor.

·   ·   ·

At age fifty-five, Frank Billingsly could not believe his good fortune at having found the young redheaded coed with the long brown legs and firm, high breasts who would come so willingly and so often to the plaid-covered sofa in his professorial office.

The sofa had once resided in the living room of his Elm Street home. His office had inherited it when the children were deemed old enough to risk an investment in new living room furniture. The sofa still bore the stains of a variety of spills, from baby cereal to airplane glue. It still smelled vaguely of soured milk. And there were the later stains of love-making, although no one but Frank recognized them as such, so well they blended with the other stains and the dirty, faded plaid.

Kate was not the first coed to come to his office sofa. The first time, the young woman had approached him. Frank was in his tenth year of teaching, long enough for weariness to have set in, to find himself dreading the start of each new semester, each classroom of new faces to connect with names, each new grade book to be filled. An unimaginative researcher, a mediocre teacher, Frank Billingsly was beginning to realize that the rest of his life meant more and more semesters piled on top of semesters, more of the same until one day he would retire, be honored at a tea, and shuffle off into that period between retirement and death that academia has labeled "emeritus." He would be allowed to keep his office, though all he would do in it was open the mail he collected when he came to the department office once a week for that purpose, emptying his mailbox of journals he no longer read, calls for papers he would no longer write, announcements of professional meetings he would no longer attend. Gradually, his name would be culled from mailing lists, and there would be no mail. He would stop coming to the campus except at Christmas for the annual departmental party and in the spring for the retirement tea. The door to his office would remain firmly locked until his death would bring about a reopening for a bright new faculty member who would scarcely give a thought to the old codger for whom the shelf-lined room was his professional home for forty or more years. The young professor would not stop to think that the office's previous occupant had once been young, had once been excited to be beginning his academic career, had once longed for eager young scholars to seek out his knowledge, had once thought his life would somehow make a difference.

Frank's first affair had been with Precious. Precious, he came to find out, was the girl's actual name. Imagine someone naming a child that!

What if she had been fat and unlovely? But Precious Patten from Houston was quite ripe and golden and lovely—and quite stupid. She seduced him in order to pass Zoo I. He gave her an A.

After that, he was wise enough to keep grades out of his "little flings." He realized it was not necessary to barter grades to attract coeds to his sofa. Of course, Frank had been fairly handsome when he was younger. Dark hair. No belly. No red veins on his nose. But that aside, he understood that some young women just seemed to have a penchant for professors. A colleague of Frank's had once said jokingly that some women just couldn't resist priests, professors, and physicians. Or maybe the man hadn't been joking. Frank was no psychologist, but he had some vague notion that the young women were seeking love and approval from an authority figure. Or maybe they were thumbing their noses at authority figures. Whatever. He knew that he was using them, but they put some degree of anticipation back into the deadly routine of his life. They gave him something to think about when he dutifully made love to his wife, who was dull but quite comfortable and dear. Edith had long since ceased to excite him.

But Frank was no longer handsome. He had assumed his sofa days were over until Kate had come to explain she would miss the first test because of an archery meet.

"So you're an archer," he said.

"Yes," she said with a defiant tilt to her square jaw, as though preparing for a disparaging retort. "And a sprinter on an A.A.U. track team—actually I'm a natural distance runner, but they don't let girls do distances 'cause they think we're too delicate. And I play intramural basketball, golf, and volleyball. I'd swim if I had time. I'm not bad at tennis either."

Frank adored golf. It helped keep him from drinking and was currently the only passion in his life. They discussed golf for almost an hour. Frank told her how he admired Patty Berg and Babe Didrikson. Kate was pitifully eager to talk. She was a very bright girl, and now that he was accustomed to her face, he found her rather appealing. If she curled that wonderfully outrageous hair and used a little mascara on her pale lashes, she would look better. Her eyes were wide and a hazy sea-green. When he put his hand on her thigh, she jumped. "You have the loveliest legs I've ever seen, my dear. I noticed them the first day of class. You have no idea how hard it has been to keep my mind on my lecturing with you sitting out there with your beautiful legs crossed—so feminine, so alluring."

He pulled her skirt up over her thighs and realized she really did have beautiful legs. He knelt on the floor in front of her and kissed first one brown, muscular thigh and then the other. "Lovely. So lovely," he murmured. "You are so lovely."

When he looked up at her face, she had tears in her eyes. He understood. No one had ever called her lovely before. He told her again. Her eyes. Her teeth. She was so firm and young and strong. Frank realized he wasn't lying. She was lovely is her own special way. Her firm breasts. Her smooth throat. Her flesh. God, her flesh! It was fresh and salty and sweet smelling.

Kate was sobbing now, and Frank kept talking and admiring and touching. "You can't imagine how much I want you. I've never wanted anyone like I want you. Give me your hand. See, feel how hard you have made me. It would be the most beautiful thing I could possibly think of if I could just kiss your breasts."

Kate was overwhelmed with a desire to please him. A man wanted her—really wanted her. He knelt on the floor in front of her and begged to love her. The physical proof of his desire strained against his trousers. A small wet spot appeared beside his fly.

She hadn't thought a man would ever become physically aroused over her. And there was such a reverence in the way he touched her skin and kissed her throat.

Kate felt honored.

But she didn't want him taking her clothes off. How did she dare stop him, though? He was a *professor*. He was older. And wiser. And he seemed to think it was perfectly normal and natural.

Somehow, where all this was heading didn't really hit home until he dropped his trousers to reveal a very erect and very red penis. Kate looked away, horrified. This had gone entirely too far. Her blouse was unbuttoned. He had touched her breasts and suckled at them like a baby. She couldn't believe how lovely that felt. But now he was pulling at her underpants, rolling them off her hips. He couldn't do that. He meant to put that ugly thing inside of her.

He never stopped talking. He never stopped saying that her nipples were perfect, that her flesh smelled sweeter than flowers, that her skin was the smoothest thing he'd ever felt, that he was desperate, that she was driving him out of his mind with desire. Her heart was racing. She was sweating.

And suddenly he was on top of her, pushing. Pushing hard. He pulled first one of her legs and then the other around onto his back.

"No," Kate protested. "I don't want you to do that. Please, no."

"Oh, my dearest, darling Kate, I can't stop. Please forgive me. I can't stop. Oh, you're so wonderful, so sweet, so dear. Oh, God, Kate!"

And he pushed very hard.

Kate gasped. He was hurting her.

"Oh," he moaned. "Oh, my dear God."

He was inside of her. Kate was stunned. There was pain, but mostly there was shock.

He moved up and down. Faster and faster.

It was over very quickly. Kate felt only a rush of wetness.

"Oh, that was so sweet," Frank said as he became dead weight on top of her. "Oh, sweet Jesus. You are the sweetest girl ever. No one ever made me come that fast. So sweet. I'll make it up to you, Kate. I'll teach you how to want it as much as I do. We'll have wonderful times together."

Awkwardly, they got themselves unwound and into sitting positions. Frank gave her his pocket handkerchief to put between her legs. He turned over the middle sofa pillow. Kate had been a virgin.

And so it had begun. Frank did not mind her less-than-pretty face. Kate did not seem to realize that his sexual prowess was on the wane, and she denied him nothing. She allowed forbidden pleasures—things Frank would never have dreamed of suggesting to his wife of almost thirty years. Kate was lithe and eager. Kate's sighs were aphrodisiac.

Frank often told Kate how lovely she was. He never used the word "beautiful" because that was too specific a word. She wouldn't have believed him. But lovely could mean something else, and Kate did have something else. He told her she was an extraordinary woman, that their time together meant a great deal to him. He was not insincere, but he understood the rules of the game. He did not discuss or even think of the future. He carefully avoided the word "love." An affair did not mean love. And he made very sure there was no pregnancy.

With Kate, however, it was love. She could not live with the sordidness of what they were doing unless she believed they were doing it with love. For Kate, their clandestine couplings were not so much physically fulfilling as continuing proof that a man loved her. She repeatedly gave herself to him. For her, it was a gift. The satisfaction came in denying him nothing. Having a man want her so made Kate feel more special than she ever had before in her life, even more special than when she broke the meet record in the two hundred meters. She would even give up her dream of becoming a famous athlete if Professor Billingsly would marry her and allow her to have his baby and care for him in his declining years. She kept her dream to herself for three semesters, waiting for the day that he would tell her he was leaving his wife and wanted her to marry him. But he never said those words. Finally, after a year and half of clandestine meetings—sometimes even at Frank's house when his wife had gone to visit her sister in Kerrville—Kate shared her dream with him. They were in his office on the sofa. His trousers and white cotton boxer shorts were on the floor. The shorts had been ironed. Frank was still wearing a shirt and tie and socks. Kate's skirt was around her waist. Her underwear resided beside his.

Frank pulled on his shorts and trousers, then sadly kissed Kate's tears. "I'll never forget you," he promised as he buckled up. And he wouldn't. Kate had been the last and the best.

Frank felt very old as he shuffled out to his worn brown Hudson and drove home to his wife, who greeted him with an affectionate peck on his cheek and served him a dinner of chicken and dumplings. By the time he had finished a piece of her fine blueberry cobbler served warm with a scoop of vanilla ice cream, Frank felt better—even a little relieved.

Kate wept all the way back to her dorm. Then she dried her eyes and went to dinner with her roommate. She ate the roast and potatoes, but she could not manage the pecan pie. She cried silently into her pillow that night and each subsequent night for a week.

Then she was too numb to cry. She simply went to bed and went to sleep. While her grief was genuine, Kate, too, eventually felt relief. It was over. Really over. Each passing day had a purifying effect, and she liked herself a little better. She didn't have to lie anymore about where she was going and what she was doing. The horrible distance she had felt between herself and the other coeds, between herself and her sister, who had joined her at the university as a freshman, diminished. It was almost like getting her virginity back—like getting herself back. But not quite. For Kate had found passion. Then one day she realized it wasn't Frank she missed. It was the passion. His passion. She liked having a man want her. She wondered if she could ever want a man in the same way.

By the end of the semester, Kate had put enough emotional distance between herself and Professor Frank Billingsly to realize that if he had left his wife and married her, it would have been a disaster. Kate felt quite foolish and was glad she had never confided in anyone about her professor. An old man like that! With a paunch and a drinking problem. And she was a serious athlete. There was no place for marriage and husbands and babies in her life—at least not for a long, long time. But her heart still skipped a beat whenever she walked by the zoo building.

And even at age nineteen, there was the fear that no young, desirable man would have her—that if there were to be other men in her life, they might have to be other portly, middle-aged ones who were also afraid. For the first time, Kate found herself wishing more than just in passing that she had been born pretty rather than coordinated. She would like to explore her sexuality with someone her own age, someone with health and vigor, someone who didn't have a wife sitting at home.

But the girls who got young healthy men all seemed to be pretty.

Kate looked in the mirror and wept.

Her golf game suffered. Not for long, however. Kate was a competitor. The only thing that even compared with winning a golf tournament was having a man want you. Kate wanted to be loved.

Eight

Books. Stella hadn't known there were so many books in the whole state of Texas.

She wandered up and down the rows of shelves, from floor to floor of the university library, stopping to pull out a book, to hold it, see its title, its copyright date. Some old. Some new. Books about everything. Precisely organized. A wonderful, organized world of orderly knowledge.

Stella felt as if she were in a temple. A sanctified place. She even liked the way it smelled. Like old books and floor wax.

In the second-floor humanities section, a librarian asked if she could help Stella find something.

"Oh, I just want to be here. Is it okay?"

The librarian smiled and nodded. "Are you a freshman?"

"Yes. My high school had a very small library. I can't believe . . ." Stella's voice trailed off. She looked around her. The books went on and on.

"Do you understand the Dewey Decimal System?" the woman asked.

"Oh, yes," Stella said. "I was a student aide in the library at New Braunfels and helped our librarian install the new system."

"Well, it works just the same way here, only on a grander scale."

Yes. Grander. The librarian left Stella to her wandering.

Stella spent hours during her first weeks on campus just roaming through the stacks. She held worn books in her hands and had a sense of being part of a continuum of knowledge-seekers, joining those who came before with those who would come after. She felt honored and determined to do well. And afraid. Her life was being changed.

Her English composition professor assigned a paper on capital punishment. Pro or con.

Stella thought of her father's strong views on the subject and wrote pro. She found wonderful essays in the library justifying with fervor society's right to take a life for a life, for treason or other crimes society deemed heinous. She had great thinkers and God on her side. An eye for an eye. She wrote with feeling, using quotes liberally. She wound her way to an impassioned conclusion.

"How many of you wrote pro papers using Biblical references to reinforce your thesis?" Professor Granger asked his class on the day the papers were due.

Stella joined those who raised their hands.

"How many of you who wrote con papers using Biblical references?" the professor asked.

Another batch of hands went in the air.

Professor Granger, a tall, spare man with thick glasses, allowed himself a sardonic smile.

"Those of you who used Biblical arguments will rewrite the papers using logic. To say something is an edict of God is not logical. It's like a small child insisting something is true because his father said so. His father may or may not be correct, but the child must learn to think for himself, to arrive at his own truths. The same is true of religion. Our respective religions may or may not be true, but we must logically arrive at truth. The value of that we have seen here this morning. Half of you have discovered God is on the side of capital punishment. The other half of you found that He is against it. Religion has failed us in arriving at an answer, has it not?"

Stella was stunned. What would Frederick Behrman say if he knew he was paying for his daughter to sit in the classroom of a man who discredited religion and God? She felt she should disagree with the professor, but she could think of nothing to say. She thought of the many times her father found answers in the big German Bible in the parlor. Could he have found contradictory answers if he had searched for them? How was one to know the truth?

Logic.

Stella rewrote. Her conclusion was still impassioned. Capital punishment was surely the only effective deterrent to some crimes. "What else but the fear of a similar fate can prevent a person with murder in his heart from pulling the trigger or plunging the knife in an innocent victim's chest?"

Professor Granger made the next assignment as he collected their papers. Write a paper taking the opposite side from the first one. At the bottom of the paper they were to write a few sentences explaining what they had gained from the project. Grades would be based on both papers and progress made in the student's ability to write and think logically.

Stella went again to the library. She ignored the essay writers this time and studied reports of statisticians. She found countries that had the death penalty did not have a lower instance for the crime of murder than states that did not. It was not a deterrent, after all.

Her conclusion was subdued.

At the bottom of the last page, Stella wrote:

I know that you want us to write that we have learned there is no absolute truth, that the world is not black and white, that we must never be comfortable with simple answers, that truth for one person might be another person's falsehood, that our quest for truth must be based on fact and not faith. But acknowledging that is very difficult. I feel like I'm disobeying my father and God.

The professor's comment on her paper was: "Someday your father will die. And what if you discover there is no God? Who will think for you then?"

He gave her an A-minus.

Several members of the class drifted over to the student union after class. They drank coffee and talked.

"I feel like everything has changed," Stella said. "The old world of absolutes was a lot more comfortable."

"The coed from New Braunfels has just lost her innocence," said Willard, a pudgy boy from Dallas whose glasses were hinged with a safety pin.

"Well, it's sure not high school," offered Mary Ann, a tall, plain girl from Belton.

"I think he's dead wrong," Benjamin said. He was a pale, scholarly-looking boy from Austin. "You can't just turn your back on the Bible and religion. My God, that's blasphemous."

"Says who?" Willard challenged.

"You can't totally discount faith," Mary Ann offered.

Stella told them what Professor Granger had written on her paper. "What if you discover there is no God?" Imagine.

"Now, you've got to admit that's blasphemous," Benjamin insisted.

Willard would admit nothing. He gathered up his books and headed for his chem lab. Mary Ann left to meet her boyfriend.

Stella hated for the discussion to end. She found herself smiling on the way back to the dorm. It had been a good day.

Every morning when Stella left the freshman dorm and walked across the beautiful campus with its distinctive Spanish renaissance architecture on her way to her first class and heard the chimes from the newly completed tower on the Main Building, she felt anew the wonder that she was here at all—a student at a university.

She was a different person here. She wondered if she'd ever quite get used to being on her own, to not being accountable to her father about almost every facet of her life. Who was the real Stella Behrman—the free girl in Austin or the good daughter in New Braunfels? It was confusing. But with each day that went by, freedom expanded within her. She smiled at other young faces. She got back papers with good marks. Her confidence grew. She could do almost anything. She would work and study and earn degrees and be someone other than Frederick Behrman's daughter. She would be a scholar and have a career. Such thoughts brought feelings of both disloyalty and excitement. She was a real person, but a person who would probably never be completely free of the bonds of her past. Maybe that was as it should be.

While Stella went through periods of genuine homesickness, on the balance she found she relished not having to ask her father's permission every time she went someplace. At the community dances in New Braunfels, he had always been there watching her. The few times a boy had invited her to accompany him to an Honor Society Banquet or the Senior Banquet, her father had driven them both ways. It was so strange to be with other young people in a social setting without her father being near at hand.

And Stella had an allowance she could spend as she chose. True, the allowance was meager, but if she wanted to spend it frivolously, she had only herself to answer to. She put off having her black oxfords repaired so she could buy lipstick and mascara. She decided to brush her teeth with soap to avoid spending money on toothpaste, using the money she saved to buy rouge. She could wear all the mascara and rouge she wanted without Frederick's ordering her to go upstairs and wash her face, and she could put a touch of eau de cologne behind her ears. Frederick disapproved of women perfuming themselves. At Austin even some of the men were scented.

Yes, freedom was heady and a little frightening. But it was the knowledge that excited her the most. She was in awe of her professors and hung on their every word. At least once a week some scholar of importance delivered a lecture. An astronomer who had discovered one of Jupiter's moons. A biographer of Stephen Austin. An explorer who accompanied the second Byrd expedition to the South Pole. Stella joined the literary society and the history club.

Like many Americans, she experienced a vague discomfort when she read about Hitler's violation of the Treaty of Versailles. Already the size of his army was estimated at six hundred thousand men. His troops hovered at the borders of France. But the United States was neutral, and the greedy German with the funny moustache seemed a million miles away from UT's sprawling campus. Surely nothing could threaten the timeless world of academe.

Stella had pledged Kappa Kappa Gamma because Kate was a member and because Effie had come once again to Austin, bringing pretty dresses and gloves for a cousin to wear for rush.

It was exciting—all the kissing and hugging at the last party. Kate pinned the blue ribbons on Stella's dress. "Welcome, little sister," she said with a kiss.

Girls whose names Stella didn't remember gave her flowers and welcoming hugs. Stella had felt wanted. It was very nice.

"The only reason I'm a Kappa is because of Effie. They pledged me because Effie asked them to," Kate later said matter-of-factly. She was sprawled across the top of her narrow bed in the room she shared with a girl from Houston. Pictures of Clark Gable and Spencer Tracy decorated the wall over her roommate's bed. Over Kate's bed were pictures of Dizzy Dean and Pepper Martin—and, of course, Babe Didrikson.

"I've been a good member for the Kappas though," Kate said. "I represented them in both the singles and doubles of the Greek Ping Pong Tournament and won, of course. I put together the skits at this year's rush parties. And I do sports, and that makes them feel like they have a well-rounded membership. But they would have wanted you even if you weren't a legacy," Kate explained. "You were valedictorian of your high school class, and you're pretty."

Stella opened her mouth to protest.

Kate held up a hand to stop Stella's next words. "Please spare me the 'beautiful big eyes, the pretty mouth, the straight nose' bit. And my hair is *not* auburn. It's carrot red. My eyes are not green; they are plain ol' hazel. My freckles are not wholesome; they're a plague. Of course, I might have been all right even with the hair and freckles, except the jaw is just too square. Beauty, I've decided, is a matter of millimeters. If the proportions are off just a fraction of an inch, you go through life as one of the plain. It could be worse, however. There is grotesque."

Stella regarded her sister. Kate's greenish eyes were larger than Effie's. Her teeth could have been used in a toothpaste advertisement. And when the sunlight shone on her hair, it was like gold. Kate glowed with good health and vitality. And her jaw—well, she always looked determined. It suited her. Stella couldn't imagine her sister any other way. "I think you're beautiful," Stella told her sister.

"I know you do," Kate said. "Thanks."

Stella had looked forward to being with Kate again. It had been so strange the last year living alone with her parents in the big old ranch house. Some days Stella felt as elderly as her parents—as if they were three old people living out their days among their goats and responsibilities. But now that she too was a UT coed, Stella found her relationship with her sister was not as she had imagined it would be. They did not go every place together. They were not the inseparable Behrman sisters. Kate had made her own life at the university and obviously expected her younger sister to do likewise. Kate seemed to be busy all the time. Some days Stella saw her sister only at meals at the dorm cafeteria or on chapter nights at the Kappa house.

Stella was not as outgoing as Kate and was more studious than the majority of her sorority sisters. Without a legacy's almost automatic entree into Greek life, Stella realized she would have never gone through rush or pledged a sorority. And indeed, the elitism of the Greek system bothered her. But sorority life brought social contacts and a comfortable feeling of belonging. Although a larger house was under construction, only seniors now lived in the two-story frame house on Rio Grande Street. But the house served as a meeting place for the Kappa sisters. The pledges came there each afternoon for study hall, and there were teas, parties, and the twice-weekly required dinners. In spite of Kate's words to the contrary, Stella knew the membership had found her too quiet and reserved for their tastes, and she had been pledged primarily as a courtesy to her cousin and sister. But Kate had found her niche in the sorority and on the campus, and Stella was determined also to find hers.

Stella did not fit into Kate's athletic world, and she feared she would never be able to achieve the carefree sophistication of a "sorority girl." Smoking made her sick to her stomach. It took only one hangover to convince her to limit her drinking. She felt conspicuous when the tried to imitate Effie's flair with clothing.

Not all the Kappas were stereotypical sorority girls, and Stella found within the sisterhood a small group of kindred spirits—young women who took their studies seriously, who participated in and enjoyed chapter activities but never felt quite at ease with the sorority girl persona, which on the Texas campus meant young women of breeding and intelligence for whom college was more a time of life than an educational opportunity.

"They're all here to get husbands," Kate claimed defiantly.

Cleata Jo Bradley, Stella's best Kappa friend, agreed with Kate. Cleata Jo's father was a political science professor, and she had lived in Austin all her life. She often came to Stella's room in between classes rather than walk the mile and a half home. Cleata Jo was petite and vivacious. She was also very bright.

"Yeah. No one really cares if a girl learns anything but social graces," Cleata Jo said. She sat cross-legged on the floor, her sociology notes spread out around her. "My mother asks me every day if I've met any nice boys. My folks hope I'll meet someone soon and get married so they won't have to send me back next year. My dad wants me to marry a doctor so I won't always have to pinch pennies like my mom has always had to do."

"It works both ways," Stella pointed out, allowing her English literature book to slide onto the bed. She adjusted the pillow behind her head. "The boys are expected to find their future wife while they're here."

"But not until they're seniors or in graduate school and have prepared themselves for a profession," Kate said between bites of an apple. She sat backwards on Stella's desk chair, her arms resting on its back. "Then they find themselves some wide-eyed freshman coed. Look at Effie and William. Boys don't want a girl who's been around for a few years and gotten serious about her studies."

"Effie and William love each other," Stella defended. "And lots of women go on to earn degrees."

"Pish posh," Kate said. "The only ones who earn degrees are the fat ones who might never get a man and had better find a way to take care of themselves, or the girls who start going with a boy their same age and hang around until he graduates."

"Are you girls going to graduate?" Cleata Jo asked.

"Damned right!" Kate said, sitting up ramrod straight. "I'm a new breed of woman. I think for myself. I don't need a man to take care of me. No, sir. And if I ever do marry, it will only be after I'm so successful and famous that everyone knows I'm marrying because I want to and not because I have to."

"But how can you be so sure? Don't you ever have any doubts?" Stella asked her sister.

"Nope," Kate said. "Not a one. I'd rather be important than married."

"What about you, Stella?" Cleata Jo asked. "Do you want to graduate?"

"Yes, and I think I want to go to graduate school. I'd like to become a professor and stay here at the university forever. It's so orderly. I've always liked the beginning of a new school term, with clean new notebooks and new classes and new books. You get to start fresh with each term—a clean slate. It would be nice to live my whole life like that—getting fresh starts, always learning something new and being around people who like to learn."

"Then why do you defend all this dumb boy-girl stuff that goes on here?" Kate demanded.

"Because it's a part of life," Stella said with a shrug. "I'd like to have a boyfriend someday—and get married and have a family."

"You can't do both graduate school and marriage," Cleata Jo said.

"Why not?" Stella asked.

"Boy, are you dumb!" Kate said. "No man wants a wife more educated than he is."

"Then I'll marry a professor," Stella said defensively.

"I know lots of professors' wives," Cleata Jo said, "including my mother. None of them teaches. They go to a lot of teas."

Stella realized that any knowledge women acquired at college was simply a part of their packaging. The sort of men they were seeking to attract expected their wives to have some knowledge of literature, music, history, and the arts. In Texas a foreign language was not considered important, but if you studied one, it should be French or German—never

Spanish. Only Mexicans spoke Spanish in Texas. Most Kappas majored in letters or fine arts. They would make fine wives for the next generation of Texas bankers, oilmen, physicians, attorneys, and businessmen. Stella wasn't sure where she fit in—part of her shared Kate's resentment, yet she understood Cleata Jo's acceptance. And there was a part of her that longed to be the right man's wife. Yet why did wifehood have to require putting aside her own yearnings and ambitions?

Strange how she and her sister seemed to stand apart from most of the other girls—Kate especially. Kate was so adamant about never marrying. Was it the dour image of marriage that had been held up to them by their parents? Yet Stella wondered what sort of life Frederick and Anna would have had if they had never married. They didn't have passion or joy, but they had a family. And they weren't alone.

Stella sensed that she would marry just like everyone else. It was more a question of who and when than if.

The best part of sorority life for Stella was the dinners, when everyone would gather in the big dining room. The trials and triumphs of each day could be shared with the Kappa sisters over dinner. The members wore their gold Kappa keys proudly pinned over their heart. The pledges had long since replaced their ribbons with the triangular blue pledge pin.

At the end of the meal the Kappa sisters sang traditional Greek songs. "Violets" for the girls going with boys from the Sig Alph house. Hoagy Carmichael's wonderful "Sweetheart of Sigma Chi." "Marching Along in Beta Theta Pi," and other fraternity songs. Pledges were required to learn one song for each fraternity. And of course, there were the Kappa songs. "I Love You Truly, K-K-G," sung in close harmony was Stella's favorite. And other songs lauding their sisterhood and its symbols—the owl, the key, the blue and blue, the fleur-de-lis. She would learn the meaning of these mystical symbols when she was initiated. Now she just accepted them. The blending of young female voices was quite beautiful. It was indeed a time of sisterhood. They all felt it. Stella could tell by the looks on their faces. Gradually she lost her feelings of being an outsider. It was better to be here among these young women than not to be here.

Stella soaked up knowledge like a sponge. She never had enough time to study and would sit up far into the night reading English literature, government, biology, philosophy, French. She loved it all. Learning was the best there was. She studied to learn, not just to make good grades— something that was hard for many of her sorority sisters and dormmates to understand.

Like Kate before her, Stella participated in the formal blind dates with fraternity pledge classes. And she went out on several arranged double dates with various sorority sisters and one of their boyfriends' fraternity brothers. They would cross the bridge over the Colorado River to dance to the nickelodeons at one of the popular hangouts or to go to the movies. But it was late October before any of these blind dates called to ask her out on their own.

A business major from Fort Worth named George Sandlin asked Stella to accompany him to the Saturday night dance at Gregory Gymnasium. She wore a blue taffeta dress that Effie had sent her. "See if this fits you," Effie's note said. "It's too tight in the waist for me. I'd better stop eating my own cooking." Stella doubted that the dress was too tight on Effie, but she was grateful to her cousin for supplying her with such a nice party dress.

The Saturday night dances were referred to as "Germans," and Stella was at first disappointed to discover the music was popular and in no way resembled that played at the German dances in Gruene. Still, it was fun to dance to "Dipsy Doodle," "Harbor Lights," "The Continental," and other current favorites.

George was a member of Sigma Alpha Epsilon fraternity. "All the Sandlin men have been Sig Alphs," he informed Stella as they sat on the bleachers and sipped Cokes, watching the dancers. George was reasonably good-looking in a pale, thin way. He wore tweed jackets and smoked a pipe. Stella thought he looked like a British gentleman. He was majoring in business administration to prepare himself for entering the family business when he graduated.

When Stella inquired about the nature of his father's business, George announced, "Coffins. Sandlin Brothers Coffins. We're the largest coffin manufacturer in the Southwest. We ship all the way to Albuquerque."

The following week George asked Stella to Sunday dinner at the Sig Alph house. And the week after, they attended a tea dance featuring the music of Henry Busse and his orchestra. After three dates they were considered regulars. George put his arm around her in the movies. They held hands while walking to class. And they ended their evenings with dry kisses in the front seat of his Chevrolet coupe before he walked her up to her dorm. They did not kiss at the door. Kappas did not kiss in public.

"I'll call you tomorrow," George would say, usually specifying a time. Sometimes he didn't call when he said he would, but Stella felt the need to be at her dorm at the appointed hour—just in case.

Stella was not greatly concerned about the lack of passion in her and George's relationship. The main thing, she had discovered, was to have a boyfriend. It made her feel more comfortable living among girls who rushed up and down the hall on Friday and Saturday evenings, exchanging clothes, trying each other's makeup, and preparing themselves for their date. No longer did she stay in her room and study or go to a movie with a girlfriend on Saturday nights. When George came to call for her, when she walked out the front door of her dorm with a boy at her side, she felt very proud.

As she lay in her narrow dorm bed at night, however, it was difficult to put George's face into her fantasies. But she convinced herself that would come in time. She supposed that she and George would someday have a lovely wedding in the parlor of her home in New Braunfels—the church was too formal for Stella's taste. She supposed it would be George who kissed her bare neck and shoulders and told her she was beautiful. He would touch her breasts and kiss her deeply with his tongue. They would pledge their undying love. They would be like Clark Gable and Carole Lombard—beautifully in love, sighing as they looked into each other's eyes, laughing over private jokes, always touching, kissing, embracing. Stella's fantasies of George seldom went below the waist, nor did they deal with what life would be like after her breasts were touched on her wedding night. She had other fantasies, but try as she might, an image of George refused to star itself in these. This fantasy man's face was still in shadows.

As Christmas vacation approached, Stella found she was ready for a break in courtship. It was not without stress. George would get irritated if she missed one of his phone calls, and he resented the nights when she insisted she must study for an exam rather than go out with him. "Instead of constantly trying to please Papa, now you've got Mr. Sandlin," Kate chided.

Kate's words had the sting of truth, but to Stella, that seemed to be the way of the world. She found herself wondering if Kate held herself apart from the world of flirtation and dating because she had strength of character or because she was still gun-shy after being rejected by William Chambers' cousin James.

Stella realized she was counting the days until she could return to her family and the New Braunfels countryside—and take a vacation from the constant worry about missed phone calls, chipped nail polish, and trying to avoid evoking the now-familiar irritated tone in George's voice.

Once home, she wore old clothes and helped her mother with the baking and her father with the chores. She boxed some *lebkuchen*—traditional Christmas cookies—and mailed them to George. She went with Frederick to cut the Christmas tree. Stella took extra pains decorating the house, hanging garlands of greenery over the doors and windows, making wreaths, and spending hours stringing tinted popcorn for the tree. When it came time to decorate the tree, each ornament she took from the wicker storage chest seemed to evoke a memory of other Christmases. Never had there been a Christmas without the white angel at the top of the tree. The angel's wings were crumpled and her painted features scratched, but you couldn't tell when she was enthroned on the topmost branch. Stella wondered how many more times the four of them would come together like this, how many more Christmases she would be among the Behrman clan as they gathered in one of their homes to pray over the laden table and share their Christmas feast of baked ham, piles of venison sausages, pheasant, sweet and sour pork, sweet rice, homemade noodles, sweet potatoes, winter squash, home-canned green beans and beets, spiced peaches with pork. And for desert, bread pudding with brandy sauce, mincemeat pie, plates of *lebkuchen*, and aniseed cookies.

All three Behrman wives spent much of the week before Christmas in their respective kitchens preparing food for the holidays. The smells from Anna Behrman's kitchen had never been more enticing. If Stella wasn't actually helping her mother, she was usually sitting on the tall kitchen stool watching her. Suddenly it seemed important to know how her mother made strudel and stollen and bread pudding. Someday she would have a kitchen of her own. Anna passed along her secrets, but asked, "Why do you get a college education if you are going to spend your life in a kitchen like your mother?"

The question surprised Stella. "Do you think that women with college degrees don't have to cook?" she asked her mother.

Anna shrugged and continued to shell walnuts for the stollen.

Late on Christmas Eve Frederick and his two daughters sat at the kitchen table for the Santa Claus ritual. Every Christmas it was the same, held over from the days when Stella and Kate were little and full of wonder about the upcoming visit of Santa. Anna would disappear, suddenly needing to fetch something upstairs or take something down to the Mexican house. Then there would be a face glimpsed at the kitchen window. "Ah, did you see him?" Frederick would say. "Santa was peeking at the window. You girls best run off to bed or else he will pass this house right on by." And early the next morning they would slide the doors open to the parlor, and there would be a fully decorated Christmas tree—complete with burning candles—that hadn't been there the night before—the work of Santa for sure.

This Christmas, after Santa had dutifully been glimpsed at the window, Anna joined them. Arm in arm, they went into the parlor. Stella and Kate lit the candles on the tree. They gathered around the piano while Anna, accompanied by Kate on the glockenspiel with its wonderful bell-like tones, played the German hymns that meant Christmas to their family. They began with the favorite—"*Stille Nacht, Heilige Nacht, Alles schlaft, Einsam wacht.*" Stella felt as though she were singing in a choir with all those who had come before them, those hardy folks who had dared brave this rugged new land of Texas and make a life here but had hung on to the traditions of their homeland to soften their loneliness. She was a part of that. It was a part of her.

Kate spent much of her Christmas vacation running up and down section line roads in gray knit athletic clothing. She feared losing her conditioning. Frederick had suggested she spend more time in the kitchen helping her mother with the holiday cooking. Kate responded by going out on the porch and doing push-ups. After that, the two warily kept their distance.

Effie and William came from Dallas the day after Christmas to spend four days with her relatives. Effie was recuperating from a November bout with influenza, and William hovered over her like a mother hen. Obviously, he had lost none of his adoration for Effie. Stella found it quite amazing the way he jumped up to get her unasked-for cups of tea or was constantly tucking an afghan around her legs, telling her she was beautiful at least once an hour. Effie would graciously and without the slightest bit of embarrassment allow him to wait on her and help her up and down stairs. She would smile her wonderful dimpled smile and tell him that she was the most fortunate woman in the world to have a husband as kind as he. William would beam as if he had just been given an award. Effie insisted she was strong enough to bake William's favorite pie for Sunday dinner. "Nobody can make an apple pie like Effie," he announced proudly after the first bite.

Stella had never known a man to be as considerate of women as William was. She was shocked the first time she saw him fetch something for Effie. Such behavior was not what she was accustomed to seeing between men and women. Stella's father and her uncles were themselves waited upon. Yet William even insisted on carrying his mother-in-law's heavy laundry basket out to the clothesline. Stella had never seen a man carry a laundry basket. She was charmed, but she found herself wishing William wasn't always around. Effie's four days passed without the three cousins having any time alone. Maybe her mother and aunts had no one to carry their own laundry baskets, but they had some time to themselves. Their husbands weren't always hovering. The thing Stella had most looked forward to about Christmas vacation was being with Effie and telling her about George, but only over farewells did Stella finally have a chance to ask, "Are you all right—really all right? You're still glad you got married?"

Effie smiled. She was still a little pale and had not regained the weight lost during her illness. But her smile was the same. Stella basked in its warmth.

"Of course I'm all right, my sweet Stella," Effie said with a hug. She kissed Stella, then held her at arm's length. Her blue eyes sparkled and her chin took an upward tilt. "I will always be all right. And of course I'm glad I got married. What a silly question! Everyone gets married, and William is a perfect husband. I do miss you and Kate, but maybe you'll marry men who live in Dallas, and we'll all be together again. Wouldn't that be fun?"

Stella nodded. "I have a boyfriend," she said shyly. "He's from Fort Worth."

William returned and helped Effie into her coat. "I'm so happy for you," she said as she hugged Stella. "Write me all about it, you hear."

As Stella watched Effie and William drive off in their luxurious black Buick with handsome chrome headlamps, she felt angry. Christmas had come and gone without her and Kate and Effie having a real talk. Effie belonged to her and Kate too. But in her heart, Stella knew that Effie's first allegiance was now to her husband. And although Effie loved William, that allegiance had nothing to do with love.

Kate went back to Austin the day after Effie left. Classes did not start for a week, but she was planning on entering the state amateur tennis tournament in the spring and wanted to use some of her vacation time to work on her tennis game. Frederick did not protest her early departure.

When Stella returned to Austin in January, George seemed different. She kept forgetting to listen to his long explanations of United States foreign policy and his plans for the coffin business when he took it over. Had he always been that boring? Had he always run his tongue over his lower lip after every few words? she wondered.

But he was her boyfriend. She wore a Sig Alph drop on a chain around her neck. They would get pinned next year, and the year after engaged. It was all decided. It was nice to have a boyfriend. Girls who didn't have one were pitied by their more fortunate Kappa sisters.

Stella took George to New Braunfels during the Easter break. A newly pregnant Effie was the center of the family's attention. William treated Effie as if she were made of priceless crystal. Herman would get misty-eyed whenever he looked at his beautiful, expectant daughter, and at church on Easter Sunday he sang the hymns out with even more gusto than usual. Aunt Louise spoke of Effie's "Madonna glow," and indeed, Stella had never seen her cousin look lovelier. Everyone spoke of the baby as if it would certainly be a boy—except Kate. "I hope my niece looks like her mother, is as smart as her Aunt Stella, and can run as fast as me."

Stella was grateful that Effie's pregnancy diverted the limelight from her and George. But still, the scrutinizing gaze of her father fell on George with great frequency. George did not eat processed meat and refused to eat Frederick's homemade German sausage. George did not drink beer, preferring instead "fine" Scotch—he had brought his own bottle. George didn't polka and made no attempt to learn how. "I hadn't realized how *German* your family was," George said as they returned from the special Good Friday church service conducted in German. Stella could feel George's growing distance every time German phrases were used among family members. George and Frederick clashed over Roosevelt's farm policy. George informed Frederick that *good* Americans supported their President. "He's our President, not our God," Frederick said dryly.

George said little on their bus ride back to Austin. Kate and Stella were full of Effie's pregnancy and gossiped about the family for most of the trip.

Stella didn't hear from George for several days. Finally he called to invite her to Sunday guest meal at the Sig Alph house. He was busy the next week writing a term paper, then had a sore throat and missed the Kappa Spring Dance.

They met for a Coke at the union twice, then suddenly it was the end of the semester and time to prepare for finals. George called to wish her a happy summer and promised to write.

When Kate and Stella arrived home, Anna told them Effie had lost her baby.

"When?" Kate asked.

"Two days ago, but she just called her mama this morning. She's already home from the hospital. Effie's a sensible girl and won't let this get her down."

Anna thought of the disappointment of her own miscarriages, but she'd been old and her husband was waiting for a son. Effie was in the bloom of youth, and her husband would love her even if she never got pregnant again.

"You two girls go write your cousin and unpack your trunks while the banana nut bread is baking. Then we'll have coffee, and you can tell me about your examinations and all that learning. I'm glad you're home. We missed you."

"She's all right?" Stella asked. "She can have other babies?"

"Effie's fine," Anna said. "She told her mama that you two weren't to worry. She wants you to come to Dallas when Herman and Hannah drive over next week."

Kate and Stella stood dumbly staring while Anna chopped nuts. "Go," Anna said. "Effie's fine."

Anna liked the sound of their muffled voices and their footsteps overhead. There wasn't much talking in this old house when the girls were gone.

George Sandlin wrote one time—to explain that he was transferring to Texas Christian University in the fall so he would be closer to home and could take more of a role in the family business. He would not be returning to Austin in the fall. Stella never heard from him again.

She was somewhat disappointed to find her heart unbroken. The tragic heroine role was not one she was comfortable with, and as Kate pointed out, "Any man worth his salt wouldn't let a girl's father drive him away." That helped—that and the knowledge that she wanted to marry a man her father respected.

Nine

Stella first saw Charles Lasseter standing in the hallway of Garrison Hall, a three-story limestone and brick building that housed the history department. The hallway was crowded with students, searching for their classrooms on this first day of classes for the fall semester. But Stella noticed Charles at once. He glanced in her direction, then returned his attention to the woman he was talking to. He was not a student—and not a professor. He was older than the students but not so old as to be professorial, and his clothes weren't graduate-assistant shabby. He wore a gray suit of good cut. Clearly, he was a visitor to the halls of academe.

His eyes were brown and the skin crinkled nicely at their corners when he smiled at his companion. He was leaning against the wall outside Room 110—the classroom Stella was supposed to be going into. But she went instead to the water fountain to give her purpose, then without knowing quite why, pretended to study the bulletin board outside the history department office while watching the man. The woman he was talking to said something that amused him. His laugh was quite wonderful. He had a fine mouth and teeth. In fact, all of him was fine. He was handsome, but so were many of the other men in the busy hallway. But Stella found this man more appealing somehow.

His dark hair was the same shade of brown as his eyes. It was thick and wavy. He was blessed with good cheekbones and a strong jaw, with broad shoulders and slim hips. But all that was incidental. It was his manner that held her attention.

He touched the arm of the woman in a gesture that conveyed genuine affection. She was older than he was. Stella was certain the woman was a professor—probably the professor of the history class that was about to have its first meeting inside Room 110. A nondescript woman of inde-terminable middle age with a frizzy permanent, she wore sensible brown shoes and a shapeless brown suit. She liked the man she was talking to very much.

A former student perhaps? Or her son?

The woman professor looked at her watch.

No, Stella protested silently. Don't make him go just yet.

He leaned down and kissed the woman's cheek. She patted his arm and entered her classroom.

The man was walking in Stella's direction. She should have looked back at the bulletin board, but she didn't. Instead, she allowed their eyes to meet. He smiled a small smile and nodded. Stella nodded back.

He walked on past and out the back door of the building.

The hall emptied quickly. Stella stared at the door from which he had exited for a few seconds before realizing she was now the lone occupant of the hallway.

The door to Room 110 was closed. Timidly Stella opened it and slipped into the last row of American History 101, an introductory survey.

The professor had written her name on the blackboard. Dr. Blanche Lasseter.

Stella took a seat in the back of the room and stared at the name on the blackboard. Professor Lasseter asked her a question. The only reason Stella knew she was being addressed was that the professor was looking directly at her and seemed to be waiting for an answer.

"I'm sorry. I wasn't listening," Stella admitted, feeling a wash of heat over her cheeks and neck.

"Obviously," Professor Lasseter said sarcastically. "If you daydream in my class, you do so at your own risk. Twenty percent of your grade will be based on classroom recitation."

At the end of September, Neville Chamberlain returned to London promising "peace for our time" after signing the Munich Agreement, which forced Czechoslovakia to give up the Sudetenland.

The issue was debated in Professor Lasseter's classroom. Of course the Munich Agreement was morally wrong, the students contended, but wasn't peace worth the price? Hitler promised the Sudetenland was his last territorial claim in Europe.

"So Hitler has been appeased?" Blanche Lasseter asked her students. "He will make no more demands?" She made her class uncomfortable.

The most popular songs that fall were "Flat Foot Floogie with a Floy Floy" and "Jeepers Creepers." Wayne King was booked for a November dance in the union ballroom. And the Lambeth Walk was all the rage on the dance floor. It was hard to think of Europe's problems when dancing the Lambeth Walk.

But enrollment in R.O.T.C. was up.

For her term paper in Professor Lasseter's class, Stella wrote on "Pioneer Women." She put more into the project than into any other paper she had ever prepared. Winning her lone female professor's respect was important to her. But the paper was returned marked C. The comment scrawled across the bottom of the last page read, "A romanticized accounting that only hints at the truth. See me in my office during posted hours."

Stella had never made a C in her life.

The following afternoon she went to Garrison Hall. The door was open to Professor Lasseter's office, a book-lined cell full of many years' worth of clutter. Journals were stacked as high as the windowsill. A picture of Susan B. Anthony hung on the wall over her desk. The glass was cracked.

Stella tapped on the door frame. Professor Lasseter waved her to a chair.

"So, Miss Behrman, have you ever talked to a pioneer woman?" Professor Lasseter said without preamble.

"Why, no," Stella answered.

"Why not?" the older woman asked. "I'm sure if you inquired you could find several women right here in Austin who arrived in covered wagons, who buried children on the prairie, who broke sod and grew crops, who butchered the mule so their family wouldn't starve."

"I've always prepared term papers from books and journals," Stella said stiffly. "I used *scholarly* sources."

"Scholarly sources are fine as far as they go," Professor Lasseter said. "They offer one man's overview of events. But oral history is richer, and it's been my experience that women's history is usually left out of the books or is romanticized garbage like the stuff you parroted back in your paper. 'Nobly served her family.' 'Courageously followed her husband westward.' What drivel. You left out the agony. You overlooked the suffering. You didn't deal with the isolation and loneliness. You glossed over the danger. You eliminated her tragedies. You forgot to bury her babies. I doubt very seriously if any one of those women watching the dirt being thrown into her child's grave thought noble thoughts about the opening of the West. The only reason I didn't give you a D was that you at least recognized women as having played a role in the nation's history. And you didn't write about Dolley Madison. My God, I'm tired of reading about Dolley Madison saving that damned picture."

Stella clutched her notebook to her breast, not knowing in the least how to respond to this strange woman with frizzy hair, whose jacket sleeves were as frayed as the male professors'. Stella didn't dare tell the woman that she had seriously considered a paper on Abigail Adams.

"Now, if you'd like to rewrite the paper, I will revise your grade. Here are the names of three Austin women who can fill in your blank spots."

"Professor Lasseter, I really don't think this is fair," Stella finally managed to say. "When you assigned a term paper, you did not indicate that other than the normal sort of preparation was expected. I doubt very seriously if any of the other students used 'oral histories.' "

"Well, I didn't say you couldn't," she retorted with a shrug. "Students *are* allowed to think for themselves. Frankly, I expect more out of some students than I do others. And I promised the class on the first day to teach you American history. I never promised to treat all students the same. The sooner you stop expecting identical treatment in life, the better off you will be. In my book, fairness is to treat people as individuals."

Professor Lasseter handed Stella a piece of paper with three names and addresses. She returned her attention to an open journal on her desk. Stella had been dismissed.

He was in the hall, leaning against the wall just outside Professor Lasseter's office, obviously waiting for her to finish with Stella. It was the same brown-eyed man who had been talking to the professor the first day of the semester. He wore an amused look on his face.

With a conspiratorial wink, he held a finger up to his lips. "Shhh," he whispered and took Stella's arm.

Startled, Stella allowed herself to be led down the corridor in silence. At the end of the hall, he stopped and let go of her arm. "Wow!" he said with a grin. "The old girl really let you have it with both barrels, didn't she? I think I'm morally obligated to buy you a cup of coffee after listening to my own aunt crucify you. The union okay?"

Stella nodded dumbly.

"Let me hold your things while you button up. It's chilly out there."

Stella handed him her notebook and purse, then obediently buttoned her coat. "Is Professor Lasseter expecting you?" Stella asked.

"Sometime this afternoon. She'll never know I took one of her students to coffee first," he said as he handed back her possessions. "Charles Lasseter, at your service." He extended his hand.

"Stella Behrman," she said placing a hand in his. She was glad she hadn't put her gloves on.

"Aunt Blanche has a terrible tendency to pick on the students she likes," he said, holding the door open for her.

"She obviously adores me," Stella said dryly.

Charles Lasseter laughed. It was the nicest laugh Stella had ever heard.

There was indeed a chill in the air. Autumn leaves blew briskly across the sidewalk. The carillon in the Main Building tower played "The Battle Hymn of the Republic." A pair of squirrels played tag on the lawn. Students put their hands in their pockets and their heads down and hurried into or away from the wind. It was a wonderful day. If she hadn't been walking with Charles Lasseter, Stella would have skipped a few steps. But then, the reason she felt like skipping was because he was at her side.

Stella discovered history under the exacting, often biting tutelage of Blanche Lasseter.

She had interviewed the three women whose names Professor Lasseter had given her. They were old, lonely women who had outlived their husbands, their siblings, their friends. They could not believe that someone wanted them to talk and actually would listen to their stories. They had pioneered, they supposed, although none of them really thought of themselves that way. They had followed restless men west. Their lives had been hard and unglamorous. One of the women chewed tobacco and spit into a rusty coffee can. Her husband had been a "scoundrel who got himself shot in a poker game and left her with six brats to raise by herself on a piece of land not fit to pee on." The second had lost four of her children to typhoid. She showed Stella two teacups—one cracked—and a saucer, the only possessions she still retained from her life in Providence, where the ladies made social calls wearing white gloves and drank tea from china cups. The third had left the St. Louis orphanage where she had been raised on her sixteenth birthday and found her husband the next day by answering an ad in the newspaper. They married and headed west on the same day. She had grown cotton and raised their three children while her husband went on to California to pan for gold in '89. He came back in 1910 when oil was found under the sod of their homestead. The couple now lived in a thirty-room mansion. She showed Stella their original one-room cabin that still stood behind the mansion, a shrine to their roots and their success.

Stella's second paper on pioneer women was called "Plows, Funerals, and China Cups: Three Pioneer Women of Texas." It earned her a B and another note commanding her to drop by the office.

Stella felt a stab of disappointment when no handsome nephew was in evidence in the corridor of Garrison Hall. She thought constantly about Charles Lasseter. Constantly. She had replayed every minute of their time together over and over. He was an architect in Dallas. He had grown up here in Austin—his aunt had all but raised him. His eyes smiled along with his mouth when he looked at Stella. Brown. Wonderfully warm brown eyes. It was his smiling eyes she liked best. That and the fact that he insisted she talk about herself. He kept asking her questions about *her* life, her studies, her goals. He wanted to know about her family, about her upbringing. How different he was from George Sandlin!

Her goals? Stella hardly knew how to answer that. She wanted the same thing that all girls her age wanted—find a man to fall in love with, get married, have children. Except that she also wanted to learn things, maybe teach, maybe continue her education after graduation. Do *something*. Maybe. "Finish school," she answered. "Teach awhile. See what happens."

Instead of one cup of coffee, they had lingered over several, with doughnuts. They sat there all afternoon. The nickelodeon played "Over the Rainbow" and "I'll Never Smile Again." Stella missed her English literature class. It was the first class she had missed in three semesters of college.

She hadn't been nervous. They talked like two adults—like two equals. It was the first such conversation she had ever had with a man. She told him about riding her donkey to the country school, about German school and the brother who died. She told that she missed Effie and worried about Kate. She even told him that she'd never seen her parents kiss.

And in turn, he told her of summers he spent with his aunt in her cottage on Galveston Island, how he'd wanted to be an artist but wasn't talented enough, of the houses he built and the ones he only dreamed of building, of his father who died young and his invalid mother who died while he was in college.

Stella liked the way he looked. She liked the dark, curly hairs on the back of his hands, the strength of his jaw, his well-defined brow. He had a good mouth—generous, with even teeth. And he liked the look of her. She could see it in his eyes. But more than that, he liked *her*. He smiled with pleasure or frowned thoughtfully at the things she said. He listened to her, *really* listened. Stella felt giddy with delight. Her skin tingled. She felt beautiful.

She wondered what it would be like to touch him. His mouth. She would like to reach out and touch his mouth. She didn't want their time together ever to end.

But finally it did. He looked at his watch. "I've kept you too long." Stella wanted to tell him that she would sit here with him all evening, all night, forever. But that would be silly. And Kate would wonder where in the world she was. It was Monday. That meant dinner and chapter meeting at the Kappa house.

He walked with her to the dorm, then solemnly shook her hand. "It's been a very special afternoon, Stella Anna Behrman. I will never forget it—or you. Be happy. Go to graduate school. Don't sell yourself short."

She watched him walk away from her. She would never forget him either. She felt happy and sad at the same time. Would she see him again?

She ran up the dorm steps two a time. Kate was waiting for her. "Cripes, Stella," Kate chided. "I was about ready to go without you. Where have you been?"

If it had been Effie, Stella would have explained.

Stella didn't eat much that night. She kept forgetting to put the food in her mouth. The house mother asked if she had an upset stomach.

After chapter meeting Stella challenged Kate to a race back to the dorm.

"You're kidding," Kate said.

"No, I'm not. I want to run."

Kate won, of course. But the running had felt good.

She ran because Charles Lasseter talked to her all afternoon. She ran because he had smiling eyes, broad shoulders, and was a man and not a boy. She ran because it was physical, and she craved something physical.

That night she sat cross-legged on her bed and touched her right hand with her left, attempting to recreate in her mind the touch of Charles Lasseter.

She started a letter to Effie, thinking she would say something about the man she met today. But she couldn't think of anything to write. The man's presence in her life was too tentative. Too fragile. Writing about it might make it go away.

For one month she had dreamed of seeing him again, of walking down the hall and seeing him there by his aunt's office. She never entered Garrison Hall without looking down that corridor to see if he was there by Professor Lasseter's office. But he never was.

"Come in, Miss Behrman," Blanche said, stretching back in her chair and putting her hands behind her head. She was wearing her brown suit. Her other suit was navy. "Well, your second attempt was an improvement."

"It was fantastic," Stella said boldly. "Why did I only get a B?"

"I told you. I expect more out of some students. It was nice, but why did you rely only on your interviews? Some of their dates and facts were incorrect. You should have used the background material from your first paper. I want you to enroll in my Texas history class next semester."

"I'm an American lit major. I wasn't planning on taking more history," Stella said.

Blanche shrugged. "Fine. I want you to read your paper at the next meeting of the Faculty Women's Association. It's on the fifth. In the second-floor meeting room at the Student Union. Eight o'clock."

"Shouldn't you select an A paper for them to read?" Stella asked. "I mean, won't they think it strange when a student reads from a paper with a big red B on the front page?"

"Just leave the title page at home if it bothers you," Blanche said.

Stella gave up. Obviously she was not going to get Dr. Lasseter to adjust the grade on the paper.

Stella was already in the doorway before Blanche said, "Come to my house for dinner before the meeting. Six o'clock will be fine. Here's the address."

She handed Stella a piece of paper.

Stella stammered a surprised, "Thank you," and left.

No one was in the hallway.

She looked down at the address. A professor had invited her to dinner. How extraordinary.

Blanche Lasseter's house was shabby but with a genteel quaintness—a cottage left over from another era. It was furnished with her mother's Victorian furniture and worn Oriental carpets. And Blanche wasn't wearing one of her two suits. Instead, she had on a print dress than fell softly about her matronly figure. Her graying hair was still frizzy, but there was a touch of rouge on her cheeks. She didn't look so formidable. "I inherited this house and my little summer house on Galveston Island from my mother's family," Blanche explained. "My brother died young, and I was a disappointment. My parents never understood a woman who lived alone by choice."

"I'm not sure I do either," Stella said.

Blanche wandered over to a graceful spinet piano. "This was my mother's," she said, caressing the wood. "She played extremely well. She was a very intelligent, talented woman who put up with a tyrant of a husband all her life. He was a failure at everything, and the more he failed, the meaner he became. But she was a good wife to him. A saint. I always hoped he would die first so my mother could have some years of peace, but he didn't. Such a wonderful woman. She was always there for me, fussing over me when I was sick, brushing my hair in the evening before I went to bed, reading over my school papers. I had a birthday the other day. No one has baked me a cake since Mama died, and I always feel a little sorry for myself on birthdays. But that's neither here nor there. Why I didn't marry. Well, I made up my mind very early that I would find a way to earn a living so that if no nice man came along, I wouldn't get married. I wasn't going to marry a man who wasn't nice just to be married. Teaching and nursing were about the only dependable professional areas open to women when I was young, and I don't like sick people. So it was teaching."

"And no nice man ever came along?" Stella asked, wondering if she was being impertinent, but curious enough to ask anyway. And Blanche seemed willing to talk.

"There was one man, not when I was young—but later when I was well past thirty and already labeled a spinster." Blanche's expression softened. Stella could almost catch a glimpse of the younger, more vulnerable woman she once had been. "He was a fine man," Blanche continued, "and I was sorely tempted. But by then I was used to running my own life, and when I thought of having to answer to another human being—even a nice one—I just couldn't do it. We were lovers for several years, but eventually he found a woman who fussed over him. I think even the best of men expect considerations that I wasn't willing to give. When I was younger maybe. But not by then."

Stella digested this as best she could, but her mind hung up on the lover part. Her professor had just admitted to having had a lover. Incredible.

"What about children?" Stella asked as she accepted a glass of sherry. "Wouldn't you have liked to have children?"

"Yes," Blanche admitted. "Very much. I paid a big price for independence, but I own myself. As I look back over my life, I think it was an even trade. Children for independence, but not without regret. My nephew Charles has softened the disappointment, however. He accepted my gruff attempts at mothering over the years. I couldn't stand his mother, but I never let her know because I was afraid she would stop letting him come to visit me. For years he and I spent every summer on Galveston Island. I was sorry to see him grown."

There was a seascape over the fireplace. The artist had captured a wild and restless sea full of movement and mystery. Nature was awesome, the painting said, the ocean humbling. The initials in the corner read "C.L."

"Did your nephew paint that picture?" Stella asked, immediately wishing she could recall her words. Blanche did not know that Stella had met her nephew, that she knew what his initials were.

"Why, yes," Blanche said. "It shows the view from the porch of my cottage. You can just make out the causeway. On clear days you can see it quite well. He painted it when he was nineteen. I think he did a nice job. The clouds are very good."

The two women stared at the painting. Or rather Stella stared at the painting. She could feel Blanche's speculative gaze on her face.

"So Charles told you he used to paint?" Blanche said. "He told me he took you to coffee after I gave you a hard time over your paper. What did you think of him?"

Stella hesitated. Her first inclination was to minimize. But instead she said, "He was different. He didn't treat me like I was a child, and he listened to what I said. I liked him a lot."

Blanche nodded. "Come, let's have dinner. I've made a Lebanese dish I learned during my travels. It's a hell of a lot of trouble, but I'm aiming all my guns in your direction."

"Why?" Stella asked.

"I want you to change your major."

From her vantage point in the dining room, Stella could see Charles Lasseter's seascape.

"He's engaged, my dear," Blanche said softly after they had eaten. The table was cleared and coffee poured from a silver service. "Her father paid for his education. Charles's father died when he was a boy, and his mother was never well—or at least she thought she wasn't. I helped them all I could. Charles went to work as a draftsman for Marisa's father when he was a teenager. The old man recognized quality. He sent him to college. Paid for everything. He even took care of the tremendous expenses associated with his mother's final illness. Even hypochondriacs get sick and die, it seems. Charles is obligated."

"Does he love . . . Marisa?"

"I think so. She's lovely. Plays the flute. Fragile. The kind of woman men want to protect."

"I wish he had mentioned it," Stella said, looking at her half-full cup of coffee.

"Charles thought you were a charming, bright girl, Stella. He said he practically had to sit on his hands to keep from touching you. He said your hair was so sleek and shiny, your eyes were gray like the sea on a stormy day, your hands were graceful. By the time he realized he should be telling you he was engaged, he knew it would spoil the afternoon. And he truly enjoyed the afternoon."

"I see," Stella said stiffly.

She tucked away the knowledge that Charles Lasseter belonged to another woman and didn't take it out again until later that night after she had read her paper to the faculty women's group—which seemed to go well enough—and was safely in bed, her back turned to her roommate's side of the room, her pillow clutched to her bosom.

For one month the man in her fantasies had had a face. She had whispered into her pillow that she loved him. Her fantasies went below the waist.

Stella felt cheated and hurt.

Life doesn't always turn out the way we want. Stella remembered Aunt Hannah telling her and Kate that after their brother died.

Stella had hurt then too.

Memories surfaced of tiny Henry Wilhelm, whom she had held only once. He would have been almost eight years old now. She hadn't wanted him to die. With all her heart, she wanted that baby to live and be her little brother. Hank. She would have called him Hank. She would have been a good sister. She would have loved him well.

And Charles Lasseter? Would she have loved him well?

Ten

William Chambers hated sitting at a desk lawyering all day. He was more interested in rushing home to Effie in the evenings than in staying late and making a success of himself. He cared more about Effie than being a successful attorney.

And he cared more about flying than being a successful attorney. He really liked to fly and did so every weekend. He could soar when he was in an airplane and when he was with his wife.

William had gone to law school to please his father. After all those years of study and preparation, he still found law tedious and dry. He had hoped when the cases represented real people and situations rather than hypothetical ones that law would come alive for him. It didn't. When William used to sit in class at law school and watch the minutes on the clock tick by, he assumed clock watching would be a thing of the past when he became a real attorney. But he still checked the time with great frequency, and then mentally calculated the time remaining before he could maneuver an exit.

He would hurry out of the office like a boy escaping from school. Often he made a quick stop on the way home to buy Effie flowers. Sometimes he brought home a special bottle of wine to have with one of their romantic candlelight dinners. He even got brave enough to shop for wonderful French lingerie. Effie had a beautiful body and liked him to look at her. She would wear the deliciously naughty scraps of lace, teasing him with her movements, with her eyes, with her laughter, their "fashion shows" providing a wonderful prelude to sex. He loved the feel of her body in silk underthings. He loved the look of a lacy strap falling from one of her white shoulders, her nipples showing through sheer fabric, her pubic hair curling around the edges of tiny panties.

But oddly enough, the sight of her in an apron fixing him dinner was quite satisfying too. It felt like God was in his heaven and all was right with the world when he walked in the back door and Effie smiled at him from the kitchen sink, when she turned and opened her arms to him.

Yes, he adored his Effie. And flying.

For Effie, adoration was nothing new. Her greatest talent was instinctively knowing how to respond to people, to make them like her. She could turn her charm on anyone, from cabdrivers to clergymen, from servants to in-laws, from the oldest to the youngest and obtain desired results. Effie did not abuse her charm. She gave in order to receive, but she sincerely liked people—all sorts of people. She understood that cabdrivers drove away happier because of her interest in their problems and families. She knew her colored maid found more joy in her work because she was doing it for Miss Effie.

Effie enjoyed doing things for people. She took old ladies from the church out to do their shopping. An accomplished seamstress, she made beautiful handmade gifts for birthdays and Christmas. She could now afford to buy expensive gifts, but she knew a gift of herself was more precious to the recipient. For her first Christmas with her new husband's family, she had made Margaret Chambers a white silk bed jacket with embroidered flowers on its collar. For her father-in-law, she had made a wonderful plaid bathrobe of the softest wool with the plaids perfectly matched at the seams and the flat-fell seams straight enough to win a prize at the Comal County fair. She made a second perfect bathrobe in a different plaid for William, but in the right pocket of her husband's gift was a written promise for the pie of his choice every Sunday for the coming year, and in the other pocket was a promise of bedroom delights every night forever. At a sit-down dinner for thirty in the Chambers home on New Year's Eve, Mary and Bill Chambers brought out the Christmas gifts from their charming daughter-in-law to be passed around and admired by Dallas's rich and powerful. Effie was a treasure. Everyone could see that.

Every Sunday morning Effie would clear away the breakfast dishes and bake William his pie. While it was baking, she dressed for church. William always wanted apple. Effie did make a fine apple pie. And she understood that a man feels better about himself when his wife ties on an apron and makes him a pie. If her William had been President of the United States, she would have still gone into the White House kitchen and baked him apple pies.

And in their bed at night she found pleasure in pleasing him. He was constantly delighted with her. She liked to plan their lovemaking during the day while she ran her errands and did her housework. She would decide if she wanted to be sweet or seductive, queen or serving girl, virgin or whore. William could not tell her enough times how beautiful she was, how desirable she was, how much she excited him, how much he loved her. Effie liked his words as much as his lovemaking. Maybe more. She planned to be his darlin' Effie forever.

When she miscarried her first pregnancy, Effie briefly considered being theatrical about it but decided that was silly. There would be other pregnancies. She insisted on going home from the hospital the next day. "I'm not sick," she told her doctor. "Why should I be in a hospital?"

"You're right," he said with an approving nod. "Just take it easy for a few days. You'll be fine."

"Of course, I will," Effie said.

Her sweet William needed much consoling, however. "We'll have a baby," she promised, offering him one of her very best smiles. "You'll see. Now, be a lamb and bring me a cup of tea, then come sit here on the bed beside me and tell me about your new client. Did he really embezzle all that money? Is he really related to the governor?"

She stayed in bed for two days, allowing William to hover a bit. But after two days, she moved her daytime station to the living room sofa.

By week's end she went to a meeting for next fall's Junior League provisionals. One week out of circulation was enough for a miscarriage.

Their growing circle of friends sent flowers and discussed her bravery among themselves. Effie was much admired.

Kate and Stella both wrote letters. Kate's was awkward. "I'm so sorry for your trouble," she said, "but sometimes these things are for the best. Let me know if there's anything I can do. I miss you terribly. I wish we were kids again, riding the donkeys to Gruene for penny candy."

Stella's letter said, "I know you will always wonder about the baby who might have been. I'm sure he or she would have been much loved. How could it have missed with such wonderful parents? Take care of yourself. Kate and I will come up with your folks next week. I'm glad you are my cousin."

After she read the letters, Effie cried. They were the only tears she allowed herself. Life was happy, not sad. And soon she would be pregnant again.

Stella enrolled in two of Blanche Lasseter's history classes the second semester of her sophomore year. The following semester, she officially changed her major to history. She eagerly accepted Blanche's offer to become her research assistant for a project on Texas women's history, which Blanche had undertaken for the state historical society. The idea that women had been a part of history excited Stella. They didn't lead armies or run governments, but in their way they were just as important as the men. Blanche taught her that, and Stella was grateful. With empathy and pride, Stella read the journals and the letters those early Texas women had left behind. The university library archives and those of the state historical society were full of such material—mostly unread. Stella felt a sense of excitement each time she and Blanche opened a storage box or file for the first time.

"Look at this," Blanche said excitedly, as she opened a black-and-white ledger book she had removed from an archive storage box marked "Ethan Stromb." The lined paper of the book was full of drawings. This women had not written her story, she had sketched it. The pencil drawings documented life on a poor ranch in Martin County. A primitive kitchen. The butter churn. A pot hung over the fire. Clothes hanging on a fence. Chickens roosting. A cow being milked by a boy. The same boy standing at the door with a gun in one hand and a dead rabbit in the other. A man—Ethan Stromb?—reading the Bible, saddling a horse, plowing a field. A little girl leaning on a crutch. A china teapot. Quilt designs. A sketch of a dress with full sleeves and princess waist. And landscapes full of nothing but horizon and an occasional cow.

Stella held the book reverently. What a hard, lonely life the woman had lived. And there were no pictures of the woman herself. She was faceless, anonymous, and talented. She could have done other art besides poignant pencil drawings on lined paper, but she never had the chance, not in Martin County in the 1880s. Had her life been wasted or vital?

"It makes me cry," Stella said, wiping her eyes.

"Yes," Blanche agreed. "I hope she got to make that dress."

Other women's lives weren't so isolated. They ran newspapers, stage lines, livery stables, cattle ranches, hotels, schools. Often they carried on alone after husbands died.

The women coped with disease, death, poverty, fear, marauding Indians. Some gloried God. Others cursed the forces that brought them such a hard life. And they remembered with longing their other life— before they came west with their man. Stella learned how they did laundry, made soap, slaughtered pigs, made sausage, stitched up wounds, practiced birth control, and laid out their dead babies for burial.

Sometimes Stella and Blanche spent gratifying hours organizing their research in the cluttered study of Blanche's cottage. They drank countless cups of tea while poring over their notes. Stella ate with Blanche more than she ate at the dorm cafeteria. Blanche gave Stella a key to the house so she could work anytime.

Her growing friendship with the eccentric history professor was both satisfying and disturbing to Stella. A woman who lived alone by choice was hard for Stella to understand. The better she knew Blanche, the more Stella comprehended the extent of the stigma under which Blanche lived and the courage a woman had to have to thumb her nose at society. Whenever students mentioned Professor Lasseter in their conversations, some disparaging reference was always made to her marital status. The term "old maid" almost seemed to have been incorporated into her name. It was assumed that no man had ever asked for her hand. No woman was unmarried by choice.

"She could have married," Stella defended. "She had a chance to marry but chose not to."

The others in the classroom scoffed. "You can't tell me any man ever asked her to marry him," a girl said.

"Not if you paid him," a boy added.

Then someone went, "Sh," and Blanche came marching into the room for the day's lecture.

Blanche would chastise Stella for defending her. "Don't you see, my dear, that you are saying that a woman is somehow defective who didn't have at least one man at one time in her life who wanted to marry her? But then you believe that, don't you?"

"I'm not sure," Stella said honestly.

"Is a woman's measure of worth through her desirability as a wife?" Blanche asked. "Can't it be through her work, through her achievements?"

"But haven't you been lonely?" Stella asked.

Blanche looked past Stella, her eyes staring out the window of her cluttered study, but unfocused, as though looking inside herself rather than out.

"Yes. There have been times when I have been so lonely I thought I would die from it," Blanche confessed. "But I think subjugating myself to a man's career, a man's schedule, a man's sex drive, a man's comfort— I think that my spirit would not have survived."

"I'd like to be a scholar like you," Stella said carefully. "I think I'm happiest when I'm searching for answers in a stack of old books, letters, diaries, manuscripts, transcripts—whatever. I especially love the old photographs, the oral histories. The women's history project—it's like a part of me, like a cake I've baked, only a hundred times more fulfilling. But I want to have a man love me, and I want to have children. I want to teach my daughter to cook as my mother taught me. I want to fill their stockings with surprises at Christmastime. I want grandchildren when I'm old."

"And what if you can't have both a family and a scholarly life?" Blanche asked.

"Then I would get married," Stella said without hesitation.

Blanche hugged this slim, intelligent girl who was the best student among all she had ever taught—her most talented protégée. She rested her cheek for a minute against Stella's smooth brown head. Did Stella have any idea how much she loved her? Blanche wondered. "Of course, you want to get married," Blanche said. "You will make a splendid wife for the most fortunate of men. But choose wisely, my dear. Find one who is inspired by your brilliance and not afraid of it."

"I'm not brilliant," Stella said. "I'm just curious. Why would that bother a man as long as I was a good wife and mother?"

Blanche cleared away the teacups and did not respond.

Stella accepted dates from the young men who asked her out. She knew they found her attractive and pleasant enough. She did enjoy dancing— especially when a band came to Gregory Hall or the Texas Union for one of the Saturday night "Germans." But her dates also found her reserved. She did not rebuff their kisses, but she did not respond with much enthusiasm. Either they did not call back after a few dates, or they would start reminding Stella of George Sandlin, and she would be "busy" when they invited her out.

"I've been out with him three times, and he's never even asked what my major is," she told Kate after refusing a date with a law student from

Wichita Falls. "And three evenings of hearing about his political aspi-
rations is enough." Stella never quite got over the feeling of being honored
when a man asked her out, but she had learned to be discerning. Not
just anyone would do—not just yet anyway. She'd see if someone special
came along before she settled for less.

Kate did not have dates. Although she pretended that it didn't matter
to her, Stella wondered if in spite of Kate's passion for athletics, her sister
was really no different under the skin from the rest of the women at the
Kappa house. Maybe she just didn't know it yet. All the Kappa sisters—
some more blatantly than others—were searching for the man they would
marry. The lucky girls got to pick. The less fortunate took what came
along. And some, like Kate, didn't seem to have a prayer. Stella ached
for her sister. Once when one of Stella's dates asked her to bring along
a date for his friend, she coerced Kate into going. The following Monday,
when Kate's date called to ask Stella out, he seemed quite puzzled at her
anger.

Blanche invited Stella to spend a few weeks at the end of the second
semester with her at her beloved Galveston Island cottage. Stella felt a
great curiosity about the place that had been so much a part of Blanche
and her nephew's lives. Stella was at Blanche's house for cake and tea
when the call came from Charles.

"Of course, I'm fine," Blanche told him, beaming as she listened to
his voice. "Just because I'm old doesn't mean I'm not still healthy as a
horse. How's Marisa?" she asked.

Blanche tapped her fingers on the table while Charles answered her
question, her face expressionless, her eyes on Stella.

"It sounds like a lovely party. I'm sure Marisa entertains beautifully.
And I hope she gets to feeling better before the wedding."

Blanche listened again.

"All the way to New York for a wedding dress!" she responded,
making a face at Stella. "My goodness! It should really be special. Well,
if Marisa and her mother are going to be gone for a while, why don't you
come down to Galveston and spend a few days with me at the cottage?
Stella Behrman will be there. You remember Stella, don't you?"

Blanche paused, listening, smiling. "Yes, she is lovely. And no, I
really didn't think you would forget her. Well, it's settled then. I'm going
to enjoy having my two favorite young people there at the same time to
boss around. Yes. I'll like that very much."

Stella busied herself clearing the tea things away. Blanche offered an affectionate good-bye to Charles and hung up the receiver. Stella could not meet Blanche's gaze.

"Say something, Stella," Blanche demanded after a few minutes of silence.

"I can't."

"Are you angry at me?"

Stella shook her head and carried the tray out to the kitchen.

When they arrived at Galveston, Stella helped Blanche clear away the dust and cobwebs of her strange "stick house," built on stilts to protect it from the hurricane-driven waves that inundated the island every few years. Together, they laid in provisions. They moved the radio into the kitchen to hear the continuing news from Europe. Italy had overrun Albania. Germany had taken the remainder of Czechoslovakia in March with Hitler proclaiming that Czechoslovakia had "ceased to exist." And now he had taken someplace called Memel from Lithuania. Blanche predicted the United States eventually would be sucked into a war.

But on Galveston Island it was a happy time for the two women. Together, they scrubbed and cooked. Stella made a kettle of vegetable-barley soup and baked German coffee cakes. Charles was scheduled to arrive the end of the week.

In the evenings they would walk on the beach. "Charles loves this place as much as I do," Blanche said. "Once when he was a boy, he told me he felt more like himself when he was here. I'll leave it to him when I die. He's never brought Marisa here. I doubt it would suit her."

The day before Charles was to arrive, a telegram from Anna was delivered to Stella. Frederick was in the hospital. A stroke.

Kate, Anna, the brothers, their wives were all gathered around Frederick's hospital bed. Stella stood in the doorway looking around the small room. It was a deathwatch, she thought in panic, like when her infant brother died.

She walked to the bed. A strange sight—her father flat in a bed. He had never been sick before. The only occasions Stella had ever seen her father in a bed were at night if she went to her parents' room to say good night. He would be propped up with his pillow against the high wooden headboard as he read the newspaper or a magazine. Anna would be reading a book. Frederick was always up in the morning by the time Stella woke up.

Frederick had always been so robust, his thick body strong. Now he looked smaller, diminished, under the white sheet. His skin was ashen. His eyelashes fluttered when Stella leaned over to kiss his cheek. The two sides of his face did not match.

"I love you, Papa," Stella said, choking back tears.

"Mein braves Mädchen," he mumbled, his speech slurred as he called her his good girl.

Kate took her sister out in the corridor. "My God, Kate," Stella said. "He looks awful."

"I know. I think I knew I'd see him dead in a coffin someday, but I never thought I'd see him helpless and sick."

"Will he . . .?" Stella could not bring herself to say the word.

"The doctor doesn't think so. He's encouraged that his speech is only slurred. And his right side is greatly weakened but not paralyzed. But he's not going to be shearing any goats for a long time, maybe never."

The two sisters were silent a minute, trying to visualize an invalid Frederick.

"Mama says the three of us can manage," Kate continued. "God, Stella, I don't want to get buried out there on that ranch chasing a bunch of goats around."

"Let's not worry about that yet. Maybe by the end of the summer he'll be better."

They looked at each other. "I'm scared, Stella," Kate said.

Stella nodded. Scared.

There were footsteps hurrying down the hall behind her, coming in their direction. Kate was looking over Stella's shoulder.

From the way her sister's face lit up, Stella knew the footsteps belonged to Effie.

Effie, radiant, like a ray of sunshine and hope and love, came swooping down on them, hugging them as closely as her pregnant belly would allow. She was almost eight months along and shouldn't have come. But she had—to be with them.

How can anything bad happen if Effie is here? Stella thought.

Her beloved Effie and Kate. As long as she had Effie and Kate, she could endure anything.

It was a strange time. Frederick, who had always been the dominant force of the ranch and in the lives of those who called it home, was now inactive and withdrawn. Anna, who had with passivity followed her husband's dictates and quietly served her family, now ran the ranch. And disturbing news continued to reach out from the radio and the newspapers. The world was going crazy. Hitler occupied Bohemia and Moravia. He placed Slovakia under "protection." Bit by bit, he was gobbling up Europe. Appeasement was not working. Stella thought of Blanche. She had known it would not.

With no fanfare and with quiet efficiency, Anna Behrman took control of the ranch and her husband's care. She felt as though her life had gone full circle, from caring for her invalid father to caring for an invalid husband, from one old and helpless man to another. She had a bed installed for Frederick by the window in the parlor, since the stairs were impossible for him. She bought a bedpan and extra sheets.

Stella had assumed that her mother would consult her father on ranch management. But she did not. When a hired Mexican laborer resisted her authority, she fired him. When Frederick's brothers told the laborers to cut the alfalfa, Anna told Herman and John it wasn't ready yet, and *she* would tell the Mexicans when. The brothers went away, shaking their heads, not quite knowing what to do about Anna but reluctant to discuss the problem with Frederick, who had just not been himself since his stroke. Anna worked Kate and Stella and the Mexicans from morning until night. The animals had to be fed. The corn had to be cultivated. The alfalfa cut, baled, and stored in the barn. Goats sheared. Cows milked. The garden hoed and mulched. Caterpillars picked off the tomato vines. Vegetables picked and canned. The weekly laundry, ironing, baking, cleaning, errands to be done. Repairs to fences, roofs, equipment. An invalid man to be cared for. It was endless. At night they sat with Frederick in the parlor. He would occasionally insist on reading a Biblical passage to them from the old German Bible. Other times he studied the Bible or the newspaper in silence. The three women did mending or played cards. The radio was like a member of the family. They listened to Burns and Allen, Jack Benny—and to the news, always the news.

Kate still found time to take her daily run, but Stella knew her sister longed for a golf course, a tennis court, a gymnasium.

Frederick improved. His speech was almost normal. The right side of his face no longer drooped. But his right leg and arm remained weak. It was apparent that he would never again be robust. Gradually, however, he began to shuffle around, to get in Anna's way. He still had to use the bedpan, since it was impossible for him to manage the stairs to the bathroom. But by the end of July, with great effort, he could get himself upstairs. The bed was taken down from the parlor. Frederick spent most of his days on the broad front porch surveying the small kingdom he once ruled.

On the first day of August he announced that Stella and Kate were needed on the ranch permanently. "You've had enough education. Now you stay home and help your parents."

Later, after Frederick had gone to bed, Anna stuffed a darning egg in one of Frederick's socks and began to repair a hole in the toe. "You will return to Austin," she told her daughters without looking up. "You will finish your college degrees."

Kate and Stella exchanged glances. "But Papa . . ." Kate began.

"I say that you will go. I'll take care of your papa." When Anna went to bed, Frederick was propped up against the headboard, his arms folded across his chest.

"I heard what you told those girls. They *will not* return to Austin."

"Yes, they will," Anna said, turning her back to him as she pulled her dress over her head.

"They are needed here," Frederick said.

Anna slipped on her cotton gown and turned to face him. "Have you raised two daughters to be farm laborers?" she demanded. "If that is the case, why did you send them up to Austin in the first place?"

"Money is too dear. It's ridiculous to spend money on education for girls. Neither one even has a boyfriend. I'm wasting my money."

"What is it you are saving this money for, old man?"

"It should be spent on the land."

"The land! You have lived your whole life putting the land first. The land be damned. Your daughters will finish their college education or you can cook your own food and do your own laundry for the rest of your life. I will never lift a finger around this house again if you don't allow our daughters to finish their education."

"I don't need you. The girls will be here."

"Yes, daughters do stay and take care of old fathers while the rest of the world passes them by. I remember changing the sheets on my father's bed after he soiled them while other girls went to dances. I remember washing the filth from his naked, old body. Which daughter do you want to do that for you after your next stroke—Stella or Kate?"

Anna opened the window wider. So hot and so still. Not a leaf was stirring. Frederick had decided that electric fans were an unnecessary luxury—that people had done without such contraptions since day one. "The same could once have been said about tractors and flush toilets," she had told him. But still they had no fan. Saturday, when she went into town, she was going to buy one.

She turned out the light and settled herself beneath a sheet. Frederick remained sitting.

"I don't understand," he said in the darkness.

"Everything changes. Be glad you're still alive."

"Why?"

"Because the sun comes up, and the birds sing. If you're lucky, you'll live to see your grandchildren."

"Will you take care of me?" he asked.

"If need be," Anna said.

"You promise not to die first?"

"I'm thirteen years younger than you. I'd say chances are that you'll die first."

"Anna?"

"Yes."

"You've been a good wife."

"And you've been a good husband. Go to sleep now."

To Anna's amazement, Frederick touched her shoulder. That was all. Just a touch. They had not touched in years.

"Do you ever think about the baby that died?" he asked.

Anna wondered which baby he was thinking about. Hers or the other Anna's.

"Hardly ever. I think about my living children."

Eleven

How upside down the world had become—their mother openly defying their father. True, Anna was doing so to benefit her daughters, but Stella did not feel grateful. As much as Stella wanted to go back to Austin and to her studies and Blanche, to the possibility of seeing Charles again, she was uncomfortable with Frederick's fall from power. It did not seem fair for a man to lose both his health and his authority. She hurt for him. In all her life, she had never gone against his wishes, and now, more than ever, he needed for her to be his good girl. It was with an oppressive feeling of guilt that she began to pack her trunk at summer's end.

Stella realized she was waiting for Frederick to come swooping into their bedroom, to demand to know what she and Kate were doing, to put an end to their defiance. Kate would leave anyway. Stella was not sure what she would do.

But Frederick said nothing.

Their last evening at home they listened to the radio in the parlor. Hitler's troops had invaded Poland. The family looked at one another. What did it all mean?

Would the nation from which their ancestors sprang once again be at war with America? Frederick and his brothers had been too old for war in 1917, but other New Braunfels men had fought and died for the United States. It had been a difficult time, however, for a community that in 1917 still used the German language in its schools and churches. And now was it going to happen all over again? Would they once again be made to feel secretly ashamed of their origins? Already it seemed to Stella that German was spoken less in town even than the year before.

When Stella and Kate told their father good-bye, he looked from one to the other. "When are you girls going to get married? A man wants his daughters married before he dies. Your cousin Effie has a fine husband. My brother knows his daughter will be cared for."

"I'll take care of myself, Papa," Kate said.

Frederick snorted.

On September third Great Britain and France declared war on Germany. That evening, their suitcases still unpacked in their rooms, the girls of the Kappa house clustered around the radio in the living room for President Roosevelt's fireside chat. The Kappas' beautiful new house was not completely finished, and the living room was almost bare of furniture. The walls were only half papered. People sat on the floor or leaned against the wall. Stella had a sense of an entire nation clustered around its radios, waiting for comfort from its President. Many boyfriends were present, their young faces serious, but there was a hint of eagerness in the way their bodies leaned forward to listen to history being made. It was a frightening time, but exciting. They listened while the President said, "This nation will remain a neutral nation, but I cannot ask that every American remain neutral in thought as well."

On September fifth the country officially proclaimed its neutrality, but even so, enrollment in the university's ROTC program soared to new highs. The young men looked quite dashing in their uniforms and high boots.

Blanche was not in her office at Garrison Hall. She did not answer the telephone at her home. Classes were starting the following Monday. Surely Blanche had returned from Galveston. Her phone must have been disconnected for the summer and was still not in service. Stella borrowed her roommate's bicycle and peddled over to Blanche's house, but the small bungalow was still shuttered and empty. Puzzled, she went to the history department office to find out when Professor Lasseter was expected back from Galveston. It was only four-thirty, but the door was locked.

When Stella got back to the Kappa house, there was a message for her to call Charles Lasseter at a Galveston telephone number.

Stella stared at the piece of paper, her heart quickening. Charles Lasseter. Why? He was married now.

Then it dawned on her. He was calling about Blanche.

Stella's hand shook as she dialed the number. It was a hospital. "Lasseter? Are you family?"

"No. I'm a friend. Is Mr. Lasseter there?"

It seemed like a long time before Charles was on the phone.

"Blanche had a heart attack, Stella. The doctor doesn't expect her to live. I thought you should know. She loves you like a daughter. Did you know that?"

"Yes," Stella said. "Is there time for me to get there?"

"I'm not sure. Do you have a way?"

"I'll come on the bus."

Stella sat for a long time on the chair in the hall by the second-floor telephone, her hand still on the receiver. Blanche dying. Blanche not being here this semester or ever again. But what about their project? Who would be her mentor? Blanche shouldn't die. She still had years of teaching left to give.

The phone rang. Stella jumped.

"Kappa Kappa Gamma," she answered automatically.

Stella went first to find the girl wanted on the phone, then to find Kate and explain where she was going. Kate was playing cards in the second-floor lounge. She followed Stella down to her new room. There was space for everyone to live in the new house.

"Gee, that's tough," Kate said sympathetically when Stella explained.

"Yes. She was a very special friend."

"Yeah. I know. You sure were with her a lot."

Kate had been jealous of the time she spent with Blanche, Stella realized. Year before last, Kate had never seemed to have time for Stella. Last year Stella hadn't had much time for Kate. Maybe this year would be different. That would be nice. It was Kate's last year.

How strange to think that something good might come out of Blanche's dying.

Stella didn't go down to dinner. She packed a bag and waited until it was time to go.

When Kate came whooping into the room, she jumped.

"Effie's had her baby!" Kate said, grabbing Stella's hands and pulling her to her feet. Kate was hopping up and down. Stella had never seen her so excited.

"William just called," Kate said. "A boy. Effie had a boy. She says for us to come to Dallas right away. Effie's a mother."

Kate began a mad twirling around the room, pulling Stella with her. Around and around, her red hair bouncing up and down, tears streaming down her cheeks.

"Effie's had a baby," she said again and again.

Stella laughed with her, twirled with her, but she felt detached. She had to deal with Blanche's death before she could celebrate the birth of her cousin's son.

Kate finally stopped and flopped on the bed. She looked at Stella's overnight bag sitting on the desk. "You can't go to Galveston now. We have to go see Effie and her baby."

Stella shook her head. "You go on. I'll meet you there after I go to Galveston."

Kate looked crestfallen. "I can't believe you're saying this. Effie is *family*. She'll be crushed."

"Then please try to explain to her that this is a duty I feel very strongly to a woman who's been a good friend. Please."

"You're spoiling this for me and for Effie," Kate said. "The three of us should be together at a time like this. Cripes, Stella, you're the one who thinks women should have babies. And now you won't even go see *Effie's* baby boy!"

"I'll meet you in Dallas," Stella said again and picked up her purse and overnight bag. "I'll get there as soon as I can—as soon as my friend *dies.*"

On the bus Stella stared at her reflection in the dark window and hoped Effie would understand. Thank God, Effie wasn't one to hold grudges.

What a day. Birth and death. How strange.

Stella felt sorry for herself. When she should be thinking about Blanche, Stella found herself feeling sorry that she'd have to manage two more years of college without her mentor and friend.

Stella took a cab from the bus station. She and Charles had agreed to that on the phone. He shouldn't leave Blanche's bedside.

It was midmorning when Stella walked in the front door of the hospital. A woman at the front desk directed her down the hall to Room 116.

Charles was sitting beside the bed. The woman in it was old, with an open mouth and no teeth. She looked dead.

Charles stood. Stella looked more closely at the woman in the bed. It was Blanche. And she was breathing.

Stella looked at Charles.

"She's in a coma," he explained.

"Will she wake up?" Stella said.

"No. I'm sorry. She knew you were coming, though. At first she was angry with me. She said I shouldn't put you through that, but then I could tell that the thought of seeing you one last time pleased her. When she could manage, she talked about you. You were very much on her mind. She wondered if she had done you any favors by showing you the world of thought. She wanted me to tell you to finish school, to get your degree, to go to graduate school if you can."

"Did she suffer?" Stella asked, looking down at Blanche's all but lifeless form. Stella closed Blanche's mouth for her. Blanche wouldn't like people to see her without her dentures. But her mouth fell open again, exposing gums as toothless as an infant's.

"Yes. She had a lot of pain. I was glad when the coma came."

"I wish I could have told her good-bye. Did she really talk about me at the end—when she knew she was dying? On the way down here I thought about what you told me on the phone—that she loved me like a daughter. And I realized I loved her too. I'd just never thought of that word in conjunction with Blanche. But I did love her. I wish I could have told her."

Stella sank into the chair that Charles had vacated. She took Blanche's hand. The skin was dry and wrinkled, like used tissue paper.

Dear Blanche. She should have collapsed and died at the end of a brilliant lecture. This was so undignified for such a remarkable human being.

Childless, brilliant, eccentric, kind Blanche. Blanche, who was in the process of teaching Stella to think. Would the job be forever unfinished? Sometimes when Stella was with Blanche, she almost believed that she could have a life inside *and* outside a kitchen. And Blanche was her link with Charles. But most of all, Blanche was Blanche. Special. A good and caring friend. The world would not be the same without her.

Stella brought the old dry hand to her lips. "I love you, Blanche Lasseter. Thank you for everything."

Then she cried. She put her head down on the side of the bed and wept. She still wasn't sure whom she was crying for—herself or Blanche, maybe for them both. It was over for them, and they could have had so much more.

She felt Charles's hand on her back. She lifted her head and looked up at him. "I'm so sorry—for her, for us."

Charles knelt beside Stella and took her in his arms. He was crying too. Stella clung to him.

They waited together throughout the day.

At Blanche's request, there would be no funeral, Charles told her. Blanche's body would be cremated. "I'll scatter her ashes in the ocean in front of her cottage. That's what she wanted."

Stella had never known of anyone being cremated. It seemed unnatural. The thought of it made her uncomfortable. But Blanche's ashes being scattered in the ocean off Galveston seemed appropriate.

Midafternoon, Stella walked down to Rexall Drug and bought two tuna fish sandwiches and two Cokes.

She and Charles sat out in the hall and did their best with the sandwiches. It was hard to eat. Blanche was dying in the next room, but Stella was dizzy with hunger. She chewed rather than ate. She left the crusts. She didn't think they would go down.

Blanche died at 7:15 that evening. It was very undramatic. She was alive one breath, and then there wasn't another. She simply ceased to live.

Charles called the nurse, who pulled the sheet up over Blanche's face. "I'll have a doctor come pronounce her," the woman said. "There's no need for you to stay."

Back home in New Braunfels, there would have been people, food, the minister. It seemed so strange for death not to be an occasion.

They drove in Charles's car to the hotel. Stella was exhausted. Her head even nodded a bit during the short ride.

At the hotel Charles went to the desk and got her a room. They walked up to the third floor. The carpet on the stairs was faded floral and threadbare.

Charles unlocked her door and handed her the key.

"I don't want to be alone," Stella said. "I know you're married, and I know it's improper to ask, but would you just be with me for a while? I don't mean that you should . . ." She paused, embarrassed.

"I understand," Charles said. "You get ready for bed. I'll come back in twenty minutes."

Stella put on her gown and robe and brushed her teeth. She had never been so tired in her life. Shouldn't she be wide-awake and unable to sleep? Blanche had died. Stella looked at her watch. For only one hour and twenty minutes, Blanche had been dead. Stella had just lost the best friend outside of her family that she had ever had.

Charles had taken off his jacket and tie.

He sat on the side of the bed and stroked her arm. It felt very nice. Stella started to cry. "I'm really going to miss her. I know you will too."

Charles pulled her to a sitting position. She cried against his shoulder while he gently rubbed her back.

"I'm so tired," she said.

"Sh. Just relax."

Very soon, she felt him lower her back onto the pillow. Her eyes were closed, but she held out her hand. She wanted him to hold her hand until she went to sleep.

His hand slipped into hers. "I want you to come lock the door after me now," he said.

"Do you have to leave?"

"Yes. I have to."

Stella followed him to the door. Before he opened it, he took her in his arms and held her for a long time. Stella leaned into his embrace. He felt so solid. She could smell the starch in his shirt, the soap on his skin.

If he wanted to stay the night, she would let him. Should she tell him? He could hold her and do whatever. Anything. Make love. Yes. Make love. She wished she weren't so tired. It was hard to think.

He was talking now. "If things hadn't been so arranged, if I hadn't been so obligated. Oh, Stella, dearest Stella, I wish I didn't think about you all the time. I wish I could forget you."

Then he left her.

Stella fell across her bed. She wished she could forget him too. She suspected that she never would. This had been the saddest day of her life.

He took her to the bus station early the next morning. They had coffee and a doughnut in the small café across the street.

"I'm sorry that what brought us together again was Blanche's death," Charles said. "I've thought of you so often."

"Yes," Stella said, leaning her head against the high wooden back of the booth.

"I was very disappointed when I got to Galveston and you weren't there," he said. "How's your father?"

"Better, but he'll never be the same. It's beautiful at Galveston, isn't it?"

"Yes. I've come to think of that little rundown cottage as my center on this earth. Blanche left it to me, and I plan to keep it always. She wanted the two of us to be there with her this summer. I wish we could have done that. I'd like to have that memory. I'd thought of showing you my secret places on the island, of walking with you on the beach. Over the years, Blanche and I often built a fire on the beach at night and roasted wieners or marshmallows. Blanche had a hand organ she played rather badly. Her favorite song was 'A Perfect Day.' She'd play that sitting by the ocean. I thought of you in the firelight. I wanted to see your face in the firelight."

"Don't," Stella said. "Please."

The bus pulled into the bus station. Charles walked her out. There was a brief hug at the bus door.

Only three people got on. The bus left almost at once. When Stella looked back, Charles was still standing there.

It was almost dark before she finally arrived at the hospital in Dallas.

Her first stop was the nursery, where she joined the senior Chamberses, William, Uncle Herman, Aunt Hannah, and Kate at the viewing window. Stella stared through the glass at the funny little dumpling of a baby who would now be a part of her life. Kate chattered away about what sports Billy would play. Herman kept wiping the tears from his eyes. His little Effie's baby. Hannah looked exhausted. William looked strained.

"The baby's all right, isn't he?" Stella whispered to Kate as they walked down the hall toward Effie's private room.

"Yeah, but Effie had a real long labor. I think they all got pretty worried. William said it just went on and on."

"Is *Effie* all right?" Stella asked.

Kate nodded.

Stella walked into Effie's room, expecting her cousin to be wan and pale. But she was radiant. If ever a human being glowed, Effie was glowing at that moment. Her hair was tied back with a ribbon, her lips a rosy pink, her satin robe a lovely aqua.

"My poor Stella," Effie said, opening her arms. "I'm so sorry about your friend, and I know how sad you must be. But it's all right to be sad and happy at the same time. Did you see Billy? Can you be happy now for me and our wonderful baby?"

"Oh, Effie, how could anyone be sad around you?" Stella said. "Of course, I'm happy. I'm so happy I'm going to cry."

"Me too," Effie said. "I waited for you before I cried. Come over here, Kate honey. The three of us are going to have a wonderful, happy cry."

In November Charles called on Stella at the Kappa house. He brought the seascape that had hung over Blanche's fireplace. He wore a beige suit and a striped tie. He looked beautiful.

"She wanted you to have the painting," Charles explained.

Stella led him to the sorority house's now elegant living room with its heavy draperies and thick carpet newly in place. A grand piano occupied one corner. They sat side by side on a brocade sofa opposite the marble fireplace.

"Thank you for bringing the painting," Stella said. "But shouldn't your wife have it?"

Charles smiled. "She has several already. That's all I ever painted—the sea. Once I tried a beautiful woman, but she eluded me."

The clock on the mantel ticked too loudly in the quiet room. Stella did not know what to say to him, but she didn't want him to leave. She thought of his arms around her in Galveston. It had seemed normal then. Now they did not touch.

She stared at the gold band on his finger. Had he been wearing that in Galveston?

"How are your classes?" he asked.

"All right, I guess. It's hard to care about things as much without Blanche. I used to discuss everything with her. She knew so much. It's hard to believe that all that knowledge just vanished when she stopped living."

"A lot of that knowledge now lives inside your head."

"Not nearly enough. I was just beginning to feel like a scholar. But without her—I just don't know."

"You don't have all her knowledge in your head, but you carry her legacy," Charles said. "Someday you'll teach others to think like scholars. You must do that, Stella."

"That's a lovely thought. I have the inquiring mind, but I'm not sure I have the courage."

Charles looked at his watch. "I really need to be starting back, and I'm sure you have studying to do."

"Thank you for coming. Whenever I look at the painting, I'll think of Blanche—and of you."

But still they sat there, staring at the empty fireplace, neither one rising, neither one making the motions of parting. Upstairs there were muffled footsteps of girls rushing up and down the hallway. From deep in the house a radio played "You Must Have Been a Beautiful Baby."

Charles reached over and took her hand from her lap.

"Dearest Stella, I want to come back here from time to time. I won't say anything to upset you. I just want to sit here with you for a while, to see that you're all right."

Stella nodded.

Together, they rose.

Charles took her gently in his arms and stroked her hair. Her head rested against his shoulder.

She wanted to tell him she loved him, and she mustn't.

His lips were against her forehead. She lifted her face, and his lips brushed hers.

Then he stepped away from her, his hands holding both of hers. "You are very lovely," he said. "And very special. I think of you more than you know."

Stella didn't trust herself to talk. She was afraid she would cry.

She walked with him to the door. This time his lips touched her cheek and lingered. His breath was warm on her skin.

Stella climbed slowly up the curving stairway. He was coming back to see her. He thought about her.

He wore a gold band on his finger.

Twelve

Warsaw fell. Russia invaded Finland. A few daring young men left the university to enlist in the Royal Air Force. One such adventurer was the sweetheart of Stella's roommate. She and Maggie Michaelson shared a room in the Kappa house. Maggie was from McGregor and had loved Johnny Prince since her grade school days. She cried at night and wrote voluminous letters to him by day. A picture of her handsome RAF pilot appeared on the desk. Almost overnight Maggie became a romantic heroine. Packages and letters bearing postage stamps with the King's image began to arrive. Maggie wore a tiny Union Jack in the lapel of her coat. But she was flunking her classes. She could not concentrate and panicked every time she was called to the phone.

The bad news did not arrive by telephone, however. In March a tall graying man arrived at the house asking for Maggie. They talked for a few minutes in the living room. The Kappas learned later that the man was her Johnny's father come to inform Maggie that his son had been shot down over the North Sea.

After Mr. Prince left, Maggie went upstairs to bed. Two days later she was still there. She wouldn't speak or eat. She wouldn't tell Stella what was wrong.

The second afternoon Stella called Maggie's parents in McGregor.

Mr. and Mrs. Michaelson arrived that night to take their daughter home. By then the word was out. Johnny Prince was dead. Maggie used to say that all she wanted out of life was to marry Johnny and have his babies. Now she would never be Mrs. Johnny Prince. There would be no babies.

Bathrobe-clad girls with stricken faces lined the second-floor hallway as the Michaelsons half-carried their daughter between them. Mrs. Michaelson was crying. Mr. Michaelson was trying not to. Maggie looked horrible. Her hair was matted. A huge pimple had grown on her nose. She smelled like she had wet the bed. She didn't respond to her sorority sister's farewells, to their words of sorrow. There was nothing glamorous or romantic about the devastated young woman they saw being helped along by her frightened parents.

The next week Maggie's mother wrote to tell Stella she could keep Maggie's bicycle. Maggie wasn't coming back to Austin. She had committed suicide.

The women of the Kappa Kappa house wore black ribbons under their key-shaped pins for the rest of the term. The war had become a grim reality.

It was Kate's last year in Austin. While not the academic star that her sister was, and in spite of the fact that her studies took second place to sports, she would graduate right on schedule.

Other than table tennis, archery, and a halfhearted effort at a golf team, there was little opportunity at the university for women to compete in meaningful athletic competition, so Kate found other opportunities. She continued to compete in A.A.U. track. She was good but had reluctantly concluded that she didn't have what it took to be world class in the sprints, and there were no distance events in the Olympics for women—not even the 800 meters. It had been run in the '28 Olympics and dropped. Kate figured she could probably do the mile about as fast as any woman alive, but there was no way to find out. It was generally believed that women did not have the stamina for distances.

And basketball. High schools took women's basketball more seriously than colleges. Kate went off campus to play in a city league for a local dry cleaning plant. She was the best player in town.

And she entered her first golf tournament to be held at Austin's Riverside Country Club course, one Kate had played several times with various women whose husbands were members and who had taken an interest in her career. In fact, it was at their encouragement that she entered the tournament.

Just because there were no professional ranks for women didn't mean that there were no ambitious amateurs. Kate was impressed with the level of competition among the better women golfers in Austin. They were sportswomen who had married well and had the money and time to devote their lives to competitive golf, and if there was anything Kate relished, it was competition. Competition provided the passion in her life.

Kate was a powerful golfer, and she had the stamina to practice long hours and play two rounds in one day if her class and study schedule permitted. Her long game was terrific. With her driver she could hit the ball 220 yards—unheard of for a woman. She practiced her short game constantly. Her chipping improved. Her putting was inconsistent. Sometimes she was brilliant. Other times she three-putted. The teaching pro at the country club helped her a great deal, giving her free lessons when he wasn't booked and taking her out to play practice rounds early in the morning before the course opened. When she had the opportunity to play later in the day, it always seemed strange to play out of dry instead of dew-soaked grass.

It had been the pro who first suggested Kate enter the Austin Ladies Golf Association Texas Open. The women of the club took up the cause— even the club A-flight champion. "You're good, Kate," said Heather Henderson, a fiftyish sportswoman with a lean body and skin tanned brown as leather. "I've worked at this game for twenty-five years, and after less than four years of playing, you're better than I am. I just hope you don't marry an Austin man. I'd like to be club champion for a few more years."

Thirty-seven women came from Houston, Waco, Beaumont, San Antonio, Dallas, Fort Worth, Abilene, Lubbock, Amarillo. Several Austin women also entered. All were married women. All but Kate were entered under married names. Mrs. Carter Wilson. Mrs. Douglas Hightower.

The drawing was held, and Kate was paired against the Fort Worth County Club champion in the match-play competition. The woman had played to the semifinals of last year's state tournament. They were put in a foursome with a woman from Dallas and one from San Antonio.

It was Kate's first experience with a gallery. She was nervous. This was a real tournament, not just another round of golf.

She pulled her drive off the first tee. A par four. She was short of the green on her second shot. She hit a long chip that left her a fifteen-foot putt. Not bad. She could two-putt and be only one over par on the hole—or she could get lucky and one-putt.

Her first putt was on line, but she left it eighteen inches short. People were watching. Too casually, Kate played the putt like a tap-in— and missed.

Kate walked over to the edge of the green to compose herself before she putted out. Damn. Stupid. Just plain stupid. Talent was only half the battle. The rest was concentration. She knew that. She wiped the sweat from her forehead and turned to watch her opponent, Mrs. Anderson Cartwright Hodges of Fort Worth, putt out for par.

Kate concentrated. The second hole was a par three. She was on in one and two-putted. Better. She tied Mrs. Hodges.

The Fort Worth golfer, however, won holes three, four, and five. Kate was down four after only five holes. The Dallas player, Mrs. Wolverton, was easily handling Mrs. Wigington of San Antonio.

Kate went one over on the long par four number six. Mrs. Hodges hit into the lake. She recovered nicely with her second shot but went two over for the hole. Kate had won a hole—finally.

She tied Mrs. Hodges on number seven—another par three.

The par-five eighth hole, the course's longest, had a fairway that doglegged to the right. The green was hidden from the tee by a towering grove of cottonwoods.

The hole offered an intriguing choice for better male golfers. They could take the safer, dogleg route and have a clear approach shot to the green. Or they could attempt a long, high, blind shot over the cottonwoods. It was a risky shot at best and one seldom attempted in tournament play. If a player didn't clear the trees, it fell into the thick grove that offered impossible underbrush and terrain. And if the ball cleared the trees, there were five large sand traps on the near side of the green just waiting to gobble it up.

Ladies played the dogleg.

The few people who had been following the foursome had drifted away and strolled over to watch more interesting groupings. Only two spectators, the four caddies, and two tournament officials were there to witness Kate's next shot.

Mrs. Wolverton had the honors and hit her tee shot first—a nice shot that landed about 150 yards down the fairway. Mrs. Wigington landed in short rough to the right of the fairway.

Kate was next. The caddie handed over her driver. Kate remembered the country club pro telling her she could hit a driver longer than any woman he had ever seen or heard of—even longer than Babe.

Kate didn't even consider the safety of the fairway. What did she have to lose at this point? She carefully teed up her ball high for lift. Taking her time, Kate adjusted her hands on the grip of the driver and lined up with her intended line of flight. For additional lift, she played the ball forward in her stance.

Her driver connected with a wonderfully solid *whump*.

The ball sailed high, higher. There was never any doubt that it would clear the trees. A thing of beauty.

One of the caddies whistled his admiration. Another one said, "Well, I'll be damned . . ." The other two looked at each other in disbelief.

The two-woman gallery applauded furiously.

Kate turned to one of the tournament officials, a seasoned Austin golfer who had played several rounds with Kate. The woman winked at Kate.

Mrs. Hodges looked stunned. So did the other two players. Over the trees. Women didn't try shots like that, much less make them.

Mrs. Hodges stepped up to the tee. She lined up her shot—then suffered an apparent moment of indecision. She altered her alignment and swung.

Her ball disappeared into the treetops. The sound of the ball hitting wood was loud in the still air.

Kate almost felt sorry for her opponent. Mrs. Hodges was going to have the devil of a time playing out of those trees.

Before her caddie picked up her bag, he patted her driver. "Secret weapon," he said with a grin.

Kate grinned back. "Yeah, but what about those bunkers? I'm not out of the woods on this hole yet."

Mrs. Hodges, her caddie, and one of the officials headed for the trees. Kate and her caddie started down the path along the fairway with the others. They waited while the other two women made their second shots. As they rounded the curve, they heard Mrs. Hodges's ball hitting another tree.

And there on the green, less than three feet from the cup, was Kate's ball.

The caddie stopped in his tracks and stared, open-mouthed. Then with his free hand he took off his hat to Kate. "I wouldn't believe it if I hadn't seen it with my own eyes," he said. "I hope I get to carry your clubs tomorrow."

"Provided I'm still playing."

"How can you even think of making a shot like that in a losing round?"

With great deliberation Kate made her putt.

Three under par!

She wanted to jump up and down. She wanted to hug her caddie.

A double eagle on the notorious Number Eight! But all she could allow herself was a small, "Wow!"

The two women spectators, however, applauded with wild enthusiasm. One took off in a trot toward a group of spectators on the adjoining hole. As she approached them, her arms began waving for attention. A double eagle! She could hardly wait to report what she had witnessed.

Soon the gallery following Kate's foursome began to grow.

The secret weapon served Kate well. Her opponent was intimidated into a mediocre game. After nine holes Kate was down two.

The round ended on the sixteenth hole when it became mathematically impossible for Mrs. Hodges to win. Mrs. Wolverton had already dispensed with Mrs. Wigington on the fourteenth.

Kate shook Mrs. Hodges's hand. "Thanks. It was a good round," she said.

The woman accepted Kate's outstretched hand. "Good luck," she said, struggling to be gracious. She turned to walk away, then hesitated and turned back to face Kate. "Mrs. Zaharias and her husband are pushing for a professional tour for women. I never supported the notion until today, but now I hope they succeed. I don't want to have to play against the likes of you again. Women like you are a breed apart."

Kate had to stop and think a moment. Mrs. Zaharias? Then she remembered. That was Babe Didrikson's name now. Babe Zaharias. She lived in California and grew roses. But she still played golf better than any other woman in the world. Mrs. Hodges had just put her in a league with Babe! But "a breed apart." Was that a compliment or a jab?

Kate played effortlessly, brilliantly, in the second and third rounds. The following weekend, play continued with the field pared down to eight. Kate sailed into the semifinal round. The gallery was much larger now. There had been articles about Kate in the Austin paper. The dark horse from New Braunfels. How did a girl who grew up on a goat ranch ever learn to play golf like that? It was unbelievable that a woman could hit a golf ball so far.

At least two hundred people followed Kate and the other tournament survivor for the final round. Mrs. Hodges was there. The club pro. Several of her physical education professors. And Stella and Effie—God bless 'em.

Kate and the veteran player from Houston traded the lead back and forth. Kate won the long holes, the Houston player the short ones. They were tied at the end of nine. And at the end of eighteen.

The finals went into sudden death. The gallery raced back to the first hole to get a good spot.

Kate had honors. She wiped the sweat from her hands and changed into a dry glove. When the caddie handed Kate the driver, the gallery burst into spontaneous applause. Kate lifted her now-famous driver over her head and smiled.

She stepped up to the tee and drove to the apron of the green on the par-four hole. The applause was incredible. Stella and Effie jumped up and down.

With an easy birdie, Kate won the hole and the tournament. Stella and Effie rushed up to hug her. Mrs. Hodges and the club pro joined in. Kate was delirious with joy. Winning. Was there anything sweeter?

Photographers took her picture with the sterling silver punch bowl that served as the trophy.

She floated on a sea of euphoria for a few days, then got back to serious practicing. But for what?

Her victory made her restless. What now? she asked herself. Of course, she would continute to enter nearby tournaments. But she planned to be really good. She yearned for more than local play. She couldn't afford to travel about the state or to regional and national competition. She thought of Mrs. Hodges's words about a professional tour. If there was one, Kate had no doubt that would become her goal in life—to earn her living on the golf course. She wanted to become one of the best woman golfers in the country and be paid for proving it.

Kate sometimes played with men on the university's golf team. Some of them joined in her lament that the university didn't take women's golf seriously. But when she beat one of the team's better players, he refused to shake her hand and called her a bull-dyke.

Kate wasn't sure what that meant. Her dictionary did not include the word. She asked "Bunky" Brown, her best friend on the men's team, the meaning of bull-dyke. He didn't want to tell her at first, then he told her to try "Lesbian" in her dictionary. They meant the same thing. When Kate found the second word, she realized Lesbian must have another meaning in addition to "a native of ancient Lesbos."

Finally Bunky explained the words to her. Kate felt as if a bomb had exploded inside her. Just because she played golf as well as a man, did people assume she was a pervert of some sort—not a real woman?

"Do you think I'm a . . . bull-dyke?" she asked Bunky.

"Hell no, Kate," Bunky said with a reassuring slap on her back.

"Then go to bed with me," Kate said.

Bunky regarded her for a long minute. "Kate, honey, I just don't think I can get it up for any girl who hits a five iron farther than I can."

Why had God played this awful trick on her? Kate wondered. What she did best were things athletic. Pushing her body to the limit. Yet to be successful at womanhood, she apparently was expected to turn her back on her talent.

Her own father disapproved of her. Effie had always told her that muscles and sweat weren't the way to make a man admire her. "You catch a man with sugar, not sweat," Effie insisted. And Kate would claim that catching a man wasn't important to her.

But what about James Chambers? Kate asked herself. What about Professor Billingsly? She might be able to look back now and realize that she was better off without them, but at the time she had wanted their love. Couldn't a man love a woman who ran faster than he did? Why did women have to seem weak to be lovable? Women weren't weak. Her mother and aunts certainly weren't.

She looked longingly at Bunky. He wasn't handsome. His ears and teeth stuck out. He often sprayed spit when he talked. He'd probably have a hard time getting a date with most girls. But Kate would have gone to bed with him.

She wanted to beg him. But instead, she left him sitting on the front steps of the Kappa house and raced across the lawn. She hurdled the hedge and set a course for the track. Damn him. Damn them all. Men were pitiful. They were the weak ones with their fragile egos.

She was who she was. And men could just go to hell.

Kate entered the state tennis tournament. She won the women's singles, and she and her partners won the women's and the mixed doubles. Kate competed in A.A.U. track and won state in the 100 meter. She ran on a 400-meter relay team that came in second. She won golf tournaments at San Antonio and Waco.

A page in the 1940 University of Texas yearbook was dedicated to Kate. A large picture of her swinging a golf club was surrounded by smaller pictures of her with a tennis racket, taking a hurdle, aiming her bow, making a racing dive into a pool. She was heralded as the greatest woman athlete ever to attend the University of Texas. Her list of achievements was impressive. She was compared to another outstanding woman athlete from Texas, and the text on the page concluded with the words, "Look out, Babe. Kate Behrman is on her way."

William invested his passion in two things—Effie and flying. He had been practicing law less than two years when he approached his father about commercial aviation. Of course, he would continue with the family law firm, but he would also like a little company of his own on the side.

"Commercial aviation? Now?" Bill Chambers challenged.

"Why not? Surely you agree that aviation is a growth industry," William countered. They were sitting on the terrace having a beer after a round of tennis on the senior Chambers's backyard court. Effie and her mother-in-law had gone to a Sunday afternoon tea. Margaret Chambers was continuing her campaign to establish Effie in Dallas society.

"Of course, it is," Bill Chambers said. "But I think you are being unrealistic in your approach. I can understand your wanting to become involved in aviation. If I were a young man, I might be looking that way myself. And I'll give you financial backing, but only if you take into consideration that the primary role of aviation before very much longer is going to be winning a war."

William ran his hands through his hair in exasperation and regarded his father. Still handsome, the elder Chambers was beginning to show his age. William had no trouble besting his father in tennis now. "I don't accept the inevitability of war. And even if I did, I don't think I want to invest in it."

"Take my word for it—it's inevitable," his father said. "I do the corporate taxes for much of big business in this city, and what I see is just a reflection of what is going on all over the entire country. The powers that be in this nation are preparing for war. Their dollars are going into industries that will be crucial to a war effort."

"You may be right, Dad," William acknowledged. "But if you are, this whole discussion is needless. I'll be off flying planes over Nazi Germany and not running an airline in Texas."

Bill leaned forward and put his hand on his son's arm. "Get in on the ground floor, son, and you won't have to go. If you're training pilots for the military, you'll be exempt from service. Your mother and I . . ."

Bill hesitated. His face was very close. He squeezed William's arm. "You're our only child, son. We don't want you to fight in a war."

"You fought in the last one," William reminded his father.

"Yes. And the whole time I kept telling myself that at least my son would never have to go to war."

"If my country is at war," William said softly, "I don't want an exemption. I would do my part."

"But that's what I'm telling you, boy. In the long run you could help America a hell of a lot more by running a company that trained pilots for the military."

"Maybe so," William said. "But a man has to live with himself. Would you really want your son staying home while the sons of your friends went off to fight?"

Bill Chambers's shoulders sagged. "I think an only son has a special responsibility to his parents. If anything happened to you, it would kill your mother. And what about that lovely wife of yours? And little Billy? Don't you want to live out your life with your wife and family?"

"More than anything."

"Yes, but you also want to march off to war," Bill said, his voice too loud. The colored maid stuck her head out the kitchen door to see if she was being summoned. Bill waved her away. "God, it's a disease of young men," he continued vehemently. "You don't understand until you get there, and then it's too late."

William watched his father take a long draft of his beer. Bill replaced the glass on the table and regarded his son. "I'll give you the backing to buy that airline, but I'm telling you that the government will buy up all the civilian craft when war is declared. The military will control the airways. Only those supporting the war effort will have a role. Buy the damned company if that's what you want, and hire good people to run it. You go off and be a hero, but at least you'll have a prosperous business to come back to—if you survive. Texas Central has the hangars, the mechanics, office space. You can convert a corner of a hangar to a classroom. This country is going to need twenty thousand or more military pilots, and the primary training will be done by civilians. Without pilots, there very well may be no America for you to come home to. A hell of a lot of this next war will be fought in the air and from the air. The role of Texas Central over the next years—if *it* is to survive—will be in the war effort, not flying freight and passengers from McAllen to McGregor."

"Maybe you're wrong, Dad," William said, but he sensed his dad was right. If there was a war, it would be in great part a war of the air, and the prospect was exciting beyond belief. Two solitary men in the rarefied air high above the earth dueling to the death for an ideal. Like the knights of old. War at its purest. Everyone else pared away, with only bravery and skill and death remaining. And the winner would be proclaimed a hero. William would like coming home to his wife a hero.

William bought his airline—Texas Central—and all but gave up his law practice. He followed his father's advice and opened the Texas Central Flight College. He had three De Havillands and six good pilots to fly daily passenger routes from Dallas to a scattering of Texas towns. Braniff and TWA covered the larger markets, but there was a need for air service to secondary markets. And he also hired a staff of four flying instructors and acquired half a dozen World War I Jennys, purchased for three hundred dollars apiece, and rebuilt them to use for primary trainers in his flight school. Soon he added three Ford Tri-motors and two more Jennys to his fleet. He rented an additional Love Field hangar from the city of Dallas and hired additional mechanics. Texas Central was a going concern. William felt at home with aviation.

William's growing enchantment with Texas Central meant he was gone from home more than Effie would have liked, especially now that they were parents.

He wanted her to be a part of his other love. He knew of no other way to combat her jealousy. Dear Effie. Of course, he loved her more than anything else in the world. Effie was a woman among women. But he felt a need to prove himself in the world. He wanted to be worthy of having a wife like her. He started inviting Effie to come with him on his flights, to travel Texas with him, as he opened up new opportunities for the small airline.

At first Effie refused. She was angry. She wanted her husband at her side at a growing list of social engagements.

The popular and attractive young couple were much in demand in Dallas society, and Effie was earning a reputation as a talented fund-raiser for various philanthropic causes. It was hard for Dallas businessmen to say no to William Chambers's pretty little wife when she came asking for their donations or selling tickets to benefit galas.

Effie even considered asking William to prove his love for her and give up his airline to go back to practicing law, especially when it became

apparent that her husband was not going to be in town for the Black and White Ball to benefit the symphony. She wondered how many other important social events she would be forced to miss because William was out of town.

"I want him to be a lawyer, not an aviator," she told her mother during their weekly phone call.

"Effie, you might be able to get William to give up Texas Central, but that is one battle you would lose by winning," Hannah cautioned.

"But I don't like him being gone so much. I don't like him liking Texas Central so much."

"Men are what they do, child. Your father is a rancher. William owns an airline."

"But that makes women less important," Effie said peevishly.

Effie knew, however, that her mother was right. William was Texas Central, and it was him. He was obsessed with his new enterprise. If she made an issue of his absences, it would only cause a rift between them, for in the end, she sensed, he would pursue this new career anyway.

Effie sent her regrets for the Black and White Ball, left the baby with her in-laws, and flew with William to Houston. It was her first flight. Prepared to play the role of a martyr, she was certain she would be frightened—that the experience would be an ordeal.

But it was extraordinary to look at the world from this new perspective. How beautiful and orderly everything looked from the air. How quickly they arrived. And just imagine—being able to travel to Houston and back the same day. Incredible. She began to understand William's enthusiasm. Air travel *was* the coming thing, and William was clever to be getting in on the ground floor of intrastate air travel. Soon every town of any size at all in Texas would have an airfield. Even towns like Brownsville and Kerrville would have airports. And instead of being part of his father's law firm, William would have a business of his own. That was good for a man, she rationalized. It was better to have a husband who was excited about life rather than one who dragged himself to the office day after day in order to fulfill his obligations. Effie began traveling often with William and sometimes even took little Billy along. She started listening when William talked about the business, and she asked questions. She even made carefully worded suggestions. And she told her husband well in advance when it was extremely important to her for them both to attend a social event. He usually honored her requests.

Little Billy was an unqualified joy. Effie loved being Billy's mother. She loved the way his precious little face lit up in the morning when she went in to get him from his bed.

"How's Mama's little baby boy?" she said. When he put out his little chubby arms to be picked up, her heart turned over. She would feed him and bathe him, then lie with him on her unmade bed and nibble on his little pink toes and bury her face against his plump, sweet-smelling flesh.

With his fingers in his mouth, Billy gurgled contentedly, then touched his mother's face with his wet fingers.

"You love your mother, don't you, Billy boy? And she certainly loves you. We're awfully lucky to have each other, you know."

She took his chunky little hands and did patty-cake, and he laughed his delight. Such a silly little laugh. Such a silly little toothless mouth.

Effie already wondered about having another baby. If having one baby was this satisfying, what about two? But William was against it. He had been frightened by Billy's birth. Effie remembered well the fear in his face. It had made her afraid.

But she did adore her little Billy boy. Their relationship was so uncomplicated. He needed her absolutely. He loved her absolutely. In a way, her relationship with Billy was more physical, more intimate, more passionate than the one she had with William. She was as obsessed with being a good mother as William was with his new company, but she knew she must not let that obsession detract from her first obligation—that of being William's wife. With or without Texas Central, Effie was determined to remain the good and adored wife. In the long run, she knew she was more important to William than his company. And children grew up and didn't need mothers anymore, but husbands were for life. The more children a woman had, the less time she had for her husband, and the less of a wife she became.

Billy shrieked with laughter when Effie blew into his round little tummy. She squeezed the plump flesh of his thighs and kissed the unbelievable softness of a tiny earlobe.

"Just you wait until Stella and Kate see you," Effie told her enchanting baby. "They won't believe how you've grown and all your new tricks."

I'm a very fortunate woman, Effie thought.

Not only did she love her William and her Billy, she enjoyed her growing social role. She enjoyed being Mrs. William Chambers. Yes, her life was perfect. She planned to keep it that way.

The day after Christmas she and William made their holiday trek to New Braunfels with their six-month-old baby boy.

Billy drew Kate and Stella like a magnet. They could not get enough of Effie's baby. They were constantly touching and kissing him. He was always being carried around by one or the other of his mother's cousins. Billy patty-caked and smiled on cue. He adored peek-a-boo. He laughed at their antics. They laughed at his. He was endlessly fascinating to them.

"I can hardly wait until you're older, Billy Boy," Kate said. "Old Kate here is going to teach you to throw a baseball and swim like hell and run like the wind."

Kate almost wished she didn't like Billy so much. She had to admit that Effie was lucky to be the mother of this wonderful baby. Kate had never had any trouble manufacturing a case against marriage. All she had to do was look at her own parents. But motherhood? She begrudgingly admitted that motherhood was a different story. But mothers couldn't be world-class athletes, she reminded herself. And some kids were real brats.

When Stella sat beside Effie and watched her cousin hold her baby in her arms and place her swollen breast in his mouth to nurse, Stella felt a stirring in her own breasts. She felt almost as if she had milk there for a baby.

Thirteen

Charles had designed a house for a wealthy Austin couple, and he periodically would drive down from Dallas to check on its progress. He would call Stella the night before.

Stella almost wished he wouldn't call first. She could not sleep for thinking about the next day—about seeing him.

The smile on his face when she came down the front stairs of the Kappa house was almost more than she could bear.

If the weather permitted, they took long walks through the residential area adjoining the campus, often ending up at the union for coffee and doughnuts. Other times they sat on the sofa in the sorority house living room. Each time he came, Stella would feel awkard at first, but his questions about her classes and stories of his work put her at ease. And it would be like that first afternoon they had spent together all over again. Other than her sister, her cousin, and Blanche, Stella had never shared herself so much with another human being. And it was different with Charles because he was a man. She and Charles talked about everything. He seemed as curious about her past, her experiences, her opinions as she was about his. They discussed books, movies, politics, her studies, and, of course, the war news.

"Blanche said the United States would be sucked into it, that we are heading for another world war," Stella said. "Belgium was a neutral just like we are. And look what's happening to them. Hitler's dropping his bombs on them along with Holland and France. He's a monster."

"Yes," Charles said. "I hoped Blanche was wrong, but I think it's only a matter of time."

"Will you go?" Stella asked.

"Yes," Charles said. "I've been in the Reserves since college. I have no illusions about war, but if there is one, I imagine most able-bodied men will be called upon to do their duty."

In April Charles came in the late afternoon and took her for an early dinner. They went to a small Italian restaurant on the edge of town, complete with red-and-white tablecloths, breadsticks in a glass by the candle in a Chianti bottle, and an accordion player. The candlelight and the wine made an intimate glow about their table. Their knees touched under the table. This is how it would be if we were lovers, if we were married, Stella thought. After dinner, as they sat in his car in front of the Kappa house, their good-bye was strained. To part seemed wrong. Stella allowed herself to cling to him as they embraced. She wanted him to kiss her. She *needed* him to kiss her with an ache that made her stomach contract, but she understood. Kissing would make what they were doing something else. As it was, he was an older man looking in on a young friend, fulfilling a promise to his beloved, dead aunt. She felt his lips against her hair. He liked her hair. He often told her how he admired its rich sheen. He whispered her name.

Charles's visits became the landmarks of Stella's life. She felt a distance now from campus life. Sorority functions, the dances, the frantic gaiety no longer had any appeal for her. She studied diligently and waited for Charles's next visit. She dreaded the separation that summer would bring. Would she really have to go the whole summer without seeing him? And what would happen next fall? The house he had designed was nearing completion.

In May he took her to see the house. It was perched on a wooded hill overlooking the river and was constructed of rough wood and glass. Contemporary and clean. Elegant in its simplicity. Charles admired Frank Lloyd Wright. Stella had never seen a house like it outside of a magazine.

He told Stella he was designing a similar house to build in Dallas for himself and his wife.

And he told her his wife was pregnant. Marisa. He called her by name.

They were standing on a wooden deck that jutted out over the hillside. All about them the trees were bursting forth with their fresh foliage. The wind teased at Charles's thick brown hair. The sunlight made him squint, and there was a network of lines radiating from the corners of his brown eyes, a glimpse at an older Charles. Would she know him then—when he was older and a father? Stella hated Marisa for being pregnant with his child, and she hated him for making Marisa that way. Marisa and Charles made love.

But of course they made love. They were married. They belonged to each other and would soon be a family. Marisa had Charles's baby inside her, and Stella felt empty.

She looked away. Charles put his hand on her shoulder. "I know you'll be a wonderful father," she said.

"I hope so. Very much. I missed having a father, and I want to give this child everything I didn't have."

He loved this child-to-be already. Stella could tell. He wanted it very much.

Stella didn't trust herself to say anything further. She turned and went back through the nearly completed house. It smelled of sawdust and fresh paint—the smells of a new beginning. Her steps echoed on the bare wooden floors.

A baby. She should be pleased for them. Charles deserved a baby. Stella was sure his wife wanted one very much, but all she felt was despair.

A baby pushed him even further away from her.

Charles caught her arm before she opened the unvarnished front door.

"Maybe I shouldn't say this," he said. "Maybe it will only make things worse, but I've been in love with you since that day at the union. I told Blanche that same evening how much I admired you, how meeting you had filled me with doubts, how very different you were from Marisa. I told her that I had been with you only one afternoon, but I felt as if I had loved you for a long, long time. She told me I had a choice between love and duty. I took duty. On my wedding day Blanche said I was either a fool or noble. She wasn't sure which. She said people like you and me had a chance for a different sort of marriage—one that would allow us to grow and be happy, but she understood why I had to marry Marisa. I don't think I could have lived with myself if I'd run out on Marisa after all her father had done for my mother and me, after all the promises I'd made to her—since she was a girl. She had grown up expecting to marry me. I felt so obligated."

Stella's chest hurt. She couldn't speak. He was touching her hair.

"You are so dear to me, Stella. I'm happiest when I'm with you. There ought to be some way to make things right, but there isn't. And now there's the baby."

What did he want her to say? Stella wondered. Was he asking for her blessing? She didn't have it to give.

"I want you to know the afternoons I've spent with you this past spring have been the best times of my life."

Stella managed a nod. For her too.

She knew he was going to kiss her. A kiss of farewell. Their only kiss.

His lips brushed her lips, then her eyes, her cheeks, her throat, her hair. A sob erupted from Stella's throat. And then his mouth was covering hers. They clung to each other, their kiss touching the surface of the passion that would never be.

Finally Stella could stand it no more. She broke away and ran to the car. Charles followed in a few minutes. When he was out on the highway and didn't need to shift gears, he reached for her hand. They did not speak until he parked in front of the Kappa house. She was late for dinner, but what did it matter? What did anything matter?

"You won't come in the fall?" Stella asked.

"I don't think I can. I'm not strong enough . . ." His voice trailed off.

He'd have his baby to love, Stella thought. And his wife. What would she have?

But already she knew. There would be babies for her someday too. And a dutiful love for a good man. Maybe unrequited love was just something one had to go through, like childhood diseases or puberty.

Charles touched her cheek gently with one finger. Stella realized he was wiping away a tear. She leaned her face into his cupped hand and kissed his palm.

He took her in his arms and held her for a time. His lips brushed her forehead, but he didn't kiss her again.

Stella let herself out of the car and went up the front steps without looking back.

"But I want to play basketball," Kate said.

"Then take the job with the insurance company that sponsors the team," Effie said. "Goodness, Kate, I don't see what all the fuss is about."

"It's a secretarial job, Effie," Stella explained. "It's not the sort of job Kate would enjoy. But if she uses her physical education degree and takes a job teaching P.E. in some school, she could probably coach basketball, though she probably wouldn't have the chance to play it herself. If she takes a job with a company that sponsors a woman's team, she can play. All the time. The company teams get taken all over the state—all over the region if they're good enough. The really good ones go to a national tournament."

Kate's head bobbed up and down in agreement. "Yeah, I could play *real* ball for a change and not that sissy intramural stuff I've been playing at Austin. Some teams like Sun Oil and Employers Casualty have even gone to nationals," Kate said longingly. "The players get a shot at A.A.U. All-America honors. I'd like that. I'd like to be All-America."

Stella and Effie observed a moment of silence while Kate indulged herself in her private dream. The three women sat in the modern kitchen of Effie's Dallas home. Such a contrast to the kitchens back home, Stella thought, as she recalled the black wood-burning stoves and galvanized metal sinks. Back home the sturdy kitchen tables were made of wood. Aunt Louise still had a pump by her sink. And the kitchens in New Braunfels were functional—not pretty like Effie's. Hers looked like something out of a magazine. She had a fine new gas stove and a Servel gas refrigerator. Wallpaper patterned with little Dutch boys and girls decorated the walls. Blue-and-white gingham curtains billowed at the open windows. Effie's kitchen table was glass-topped wrought iron. Ivy in a yellow pot sat in its center.

But the aromas were just like home—freshly perked coffee and pumpkin bread baking in the oven—Aunt Hannah's recipe. And there was a familiarity about women drinking coffee at a kitchen table. Stella was reminded of the times her two aunts and her mother had sat like this at a kitchen table, drinking their coffee, sharing their lives and their strength. She thought of the times she had sat at Blanche's kitchen table in Austin drinking tea instead of coffee, exchanging ideas, planning their projects. She remembered the isolation and loneliness of the pioneer women whose diaries and letters she had read. That was why their lives were sad—because they were devoid of other women. Stella understood that the camaraderie of the kitchen table was very important in women's lives, and she was grateful a long succession of such times stretched in front of her. The thought was comforting.

"What do you think I should do, Billy Boy?" Kate asked Effie's son, who was busy smearing applesauce over the tray of his high chair.

Billy regarded his mother's cousin, then with great seriousness issued forth a series of unintelligible syllables complete with inflection. When he finished, he cocked his head to one side as though waiting for a response.

"There you are, Kate," Stella said with a grin. "There's your answer. Now, if you could just understand it."

Stella reached out and touched one of Billy's sticky cheeks. "You're really something, kid," she said.

Billy sat up straight, picked up his heretofore unused spoon and waved it like a royal scepter. He was a small prince holding court from his high chair throne. At one year, Billy was plump and fair. Stella thought he was the most beautiful being on the face of the earth. And fascinating. Every time she saw him, Billy was more full of himself, more into things, more curious, more fun.

Billy put his arms out to Stella. Kate grabbed a dishcloth and wiped the applesauce off his hands, and Stella lifted him out of the high chair and onto her lap.

"I just love having you two around," Effie said as she watched her cousins fuss with her baby. "It's like a vacation."

Stella put her cheek against Billy's silky head and thought how special times like this were—the three of them together again, her and Kate and Effie. And now Billy too. Dear little Billy, who felt so good on her lap, who smelled like a baby.

But it wasn't the same as before. There was always a time limit imposed on their visits. Always there was the feeling that they had more to share than could be accomplished. Gone was the seemingly timeless expanse of childhood, when each day took up where the other one left off, when it felt as if nothing would ever change.

Effie was wearing a ruffled cotton dress the same cornflower blue as her eyes. A starched white apron covered the front of the dress, and a blue ribbon held her blond hair in a ponytail. Motherhood and marriage had done nothing to diminish her. At twenty-two, she had lost none of her fresh prettiness. William was fond of telling people he was married to the prettiest little gal in all Texas. Stella agreed with him.

Kate was dressed in a sporty white blouse and a plaid skirt. She wore bobby socks and saddle oxfords. Sporting a new permanent wave, her hair was a halo of carrot-colored curls. The style was becoming to her, softening her features and lifting her hair away from her wide, clear brow. Dear Kate. The restless energy that could find its outlet only in athletic endeavor was still so much a part of her. Stella knew her father had hoped Kate would outgrow sports. He never had understood that his oldest daughter's athletic talent was her special gift. Without it, she would have had no way to shine, but to Frederick, Kate was a rebellious girl who refused to grow up.

Stella wondered if their papa was not, at least in part, correct. Perhaps Kate was only putting off the inevitable. Sooner or later women married or became society's castoff spinsters. Would that ever change? she wondered. Blanche had predicted it would—someday. Stella wasn't so sure.

Billy wiggled off Stella's lap and crawled over to Rosie, the saintly cocker spaniel who loved this baby in spite of his endless fascination with her ears.

Effie went to her gleaming white stove for the coffeepot and refilled the three cups. Creamed-colored Spode with yellow buttercups. China cups in the kitchen. At home they used earthenware mugs.

"Are you happy, Effie?" Stella asked, surprising herself that the thought had erupted into a question.

"Well, now, why wouldn't I be?" Effie asked, her eyebrows arching.

Why indeed? Stella wondered. Effie had married into a wealthy family, lived in an elegant home, had a maid three afternoons a week to clean house and care for Billy while Miss Effie went out to her teas and meetings. She was beloved by a fine man, had a beautiful baby, and was doing very well in Dallas society. She was already a member of Junior League; her picture had appeared twice in the society pages of the Dallas *Morning News*.

"I just want to know," Stella said. "You seem happy, but if you had to do it all over again, would you drop out of college and marry William?"

"Oh, yes," Effie said firmly. "William is everything I want in a husband."

"But is marriage everything you wanted it to be?" Kate demanded, taking up Stella's line of questioning. "There's such a conspiracy of silence with you married women. All of you are forever encouraging other women to get married, but no one gets up and gives testimonials in behalf of the institution."

"You want a testimonial?" Effie asked, a frown bringing two vertical lines between her carefully tweezed brows.

"Yeah. As a matter of fact, I do," said Kate, whose eyebrows could have stood a little tweezing.

"All right," Effie said, sitting up straighter in her chair, her eyes serious as they looked from one cousin to the other. "First of all, there's Billy. I think it's natural and right that women be mothers, and I wouldn't want to have a child out of wedlock—for its sake and mine."

Kate and Stella nodded. Yes, one should be married to have children. Stella looked over at Billy. He had curled up next to his cocker spaniel, put his fingers in his mouth, and fallen asleep. Rosie acknowledged Stella's look with a thump of her tail, but she did not raise her head. Stella understood. It might disturb the baby.

"Second," Effie continued, "ever since I was a little girl, I thought how nice it would be to have my own home. And it is. I like fixing it up and making it pretty. Sometimes, when I'm all cleaned up in the evening waiting for William to come home, I like to walk through and admire *my* house. I wake up in the night and think of ways to make it prettier, of new flowers to plant in the yard, of different ways to arrange the furniture, the next walls to paper. After three years I still feel like I'm playing house," she admitted with a girlish shrug.

Effie paused and looked around her kitchen. Her head nodded as though agreeing with herself. It was a nice house. She had made it pretty. Then she returned her attention to her cousins. Stella sensed that Effie was just getting warmed up to her subject.

Effie twisted her wedding set on her finger, then held out her hand to admire the pair of handsome rings. "I like the respect that being William's wife brings me. The Chambers name is important in Dallas. It brought me a place in society, and I like that. I guess marriage always gets you a place in some sort of society, whether it's church-circle stuff like in a New Braunfels or Junior League in Dallas. Isn't that funny—a girl from a New Braunfels goat ranch in Dallas society? But I feel like it's where I belong. I love the luncheons, the teas, the receptions, the balls, the benefits, the symphony, the ballet. Imagine me at the ballet or symphony! But I love the music. I love dressing up in an evening dress and looking pretty, and William is so proud of me. He says he feels ten feet tall when he walks in someplace with me on his arm. I like that. I don't know about you girls, but I need a man to make me feel good about myself. When I was little, I had my dear papa. I'd march into church holding his hand, looking pretty in my Sunday best and feeling so good to be beside him. When Papa was pleased with me, I felt good. Now I have William. I would feel like I was incomplete if I didn't have my

William—if I wasn't a married woman. I think the most beautiful sound in the world is hearing his car pulling into the driveway in the evening— my husband coming home to me. My hair's combed, and I have on a fresh dress. Billy's clean and fed. Dinner's cooking on the stove. The table is set. William walks in the door and hugs me. It's a good feeling to please the man you love."

"And you love William?" Stella asked.

"With all my heart," Effie said with a small, shy smile. "And with more than my heart. Even after three years it seems so deliciously naughty to have sex. Most of the time I like William to make love to me. It's always nice, but some of the time it's fantastic. I wear pretty nightgowns. We play little games—not so much now that we have Billy. But marriage is more fun than I thought it would be. My mama and papa loved each other, but I don't think they had much fun. Aunt Louise and Uncle John didn't have fun. And your mama and papa—they look like that painting of the unsmiling farmer with the pitchfork standing by his unsmiling wife. Maybe William and I are just lucky."

"So you're happy?" Kate persisted.

"Yes," Effie said, a pensiveness in her voice. She looked over at her baby. "I would be completely happy if it weren't for that stupid war over in Europe. I'm so afraid. With William being a pilot, if he had to go, he'd probably end up flying those awful deathtrap fighter planes. I'm happy—except when I'm afraid. That's the bad part about loving a man and having a good life with him. It makes you afraid of something changing it. Now, why all this third degree? Are you trying to decide if you should get married or not, Kate? Stella? If the man is as wonderful as William, then, of course, you should."

"And if he's not as wonderful?" Kate challenged. "There aren't many Williams around."

"Then a girl has to take the best she can get," Effie said with complete conviction. "It's better to be married than not to be married."

"Surely it's better to be happy unmarried than unhappily married," Kate insisted.

"I don't believe there is such a thing as being happily unmarried," Effie said. "And even if a woman doesn't like her husband, at least she'll have children."

"I suppose children would be nice," Kate acknowledged, "but are they worth the price? Come on, Effie, what's the worst part about being married? There's got to be something worse than being afraid of the war," she prodded. "There has to be something about it you can't abide. I just don't believe it's all that rosy."

The cocker spaniel's tail thumped at the mention of her name. Billy stirred and took a couple of sucks on his fingers.

Effie absently ran a finger around the top of her coffee cup. "Oh, I get jealous sometimes—of his business, of his life away from this house. William has two lives. I have only one. I used to think he only worked to make a place in the world for his family, to take care of us, but I think men work for more than money. I wonder sometimes which life is more important to him. He loves flying and his airline an awful lot."

"I want a life outside of a kitchen," Kate said. "I guess all this is what makes you happy, Effie, but I want more."

"Then you should have more," Effie said, reaching over to pat Kate's hand. "But I don't think you can have it both ways, Kate. You can't be an athlete or a career woman and have a family too. What if you don't marry in order to become a great athlete, then realize you made a mistake and you're too old for any man to want you?"

"Men don't have to give up their dreams to marry and have kids. It's not fair for women to be expected to," Kate said, thrusting her square jaw out defiantly.

"Kate," Effie said patiently, "someone has to be the mother. Men can't do that."

"And that explains everything, I suppose," Kate challenged.

"Yes," Effie said, tilting her head to one side, considering. "Yes, I think it does."

Such a contrast—those two, Stella thought. Accommodating Effie and rebellious Kate. She herself was someplace in the middle. She too longed for a life outside the kitchen—not on the playing field of athletic competition but in the world of academe. But more than that, she longed for a life with a man who would never be hers, a man married to someone else. If giving up every other dream she had ever had would change that, Stella would do so without hesitation. Maybe she was more like Effie than she realized.

Stella thought of Blanche again. It did seem that women had to choose one way or the other, and the world was not particularly kind to women who chose not to live their lives as their mothers had done before them.

If only Blanche were still alive, Stella thought. She wanted Blanche still to be in her little Austin home, ready to talk, ready to listen. Sometimes she thought of reaching out to Anna, of trying to form an adult relationship with the quiet, private woman who was her mother. She wondered what Anna Behrman really wanted for her daughters. But Anna had always kept her thoughts to herself.

"I'd like to go to graduate school," Stella told Effie and Kate. "But sometimes I wonder what's the point. You don't need a graduate degree to change diapers."

"What are you going to do about a job, Kate?" Effie asked. "I'm sure you'll meet nice men whether you teach school or work for the insurance company. But you've got to stop challenging men to run races with you or take them on in a game of one on one. Men don't like women to beat them."

Kate got up, took a stance and drove an imaginary golf ball out the window over the sink. "Someday I'd like to find a man who falls in love with me the minute I outdrive him on the golf course or because he can't return my sensational serve. For me, that would be the perfect man."

"That's the silliest thing I ever heard of," Effie said in her best schoolmarmish tone. "I keep telling you, women win men with sugar not with sweat."

"I think what Kate means," Stella offered, "is that it would be dishonest for her to pretend to be like you when she's not, Effie. Sugar is becoming to you. For Kate it would be a lie."

"Women have always lied to men when it's necessary," Effie said, stacking the Spode teacups and saucers and carrying them to the sink. She turned and glared at Stella. "I worry about your sister," she said as though Kate were not there in the room with them. "I worry about her a lot. I don't want her to be an old maid. That's a whole lot worse than being a little dishonest. Your papa worries about her. And you do too, Stella. I know you do. I'd think both you girls would want your papa to see you safely married before he dies."

Effie took the pumpkin bread from the oven and set it on the windowsill to cool, then went over to her sleeping baby and picked him up. She cooed softly to him as she carried him off to bed for his nap, leaving Kate and Stella uncomfortably alone in her pretty kitchen.

"Sounds like you and Effie have been discussing me," Kate said as she got up and went to turn off a dripping faucet. "Do you worry about me, Stella? Do you think I should forget about sports and concentrate on getting myself married?"

"I just want you to be happy," Stella said defensively.

"And marriage will make me happy?"

"It seems to be making Effie happy."

"But what about Mama and Papa?" Kate challenged. "Not much happiness there."

"I think they have been better off together than they would be apart. I think loneliness would be the worst sort of unhappiness."

"What about that woman professor you liked so much? Would Professor Lasseter have agreed with you?"

Stella stared at the glossy ivy leaves. Effie must have waxed them with something to make them that shiny. "Funny, I was just thinking about her," she answered. "I'm not sure what Blanche really thought," Stella admitted. "I never was able to decide if she was rationalizing, or if some women would be better off unmarried than married. Maybe it's like religion. Most people embrace a religion because the alternative is painted so grimly. But it does seem that when people fall in love, they want to do something about it. And marriage is the logical something."

"Maybe I'll never fall in love and therefore be spared," Kate said, once again practicing her golf swing.

Fourteen

Kate's first love was golf. But in 1940 golf for women was largely a country club sport. Women outside of country clubs had no one to play with, no competition. And a woman needed a wealthy husband to provide her entry into a country club.

It seemed to Kate that basketball offered her the best opportunity to compete at a meaningful level. While girls did not play basketball in Comal County, Kate was aware of the tremendous popularity high school girls' basketball enjoyed throughout the twenties and thirties. In spite of the efforts of Mrs. Herbert Hoover and her Women's Division of the National Amateur Athletic Federation, which advocated that the weaker sex should be demure and take its exercise out of the public eye, large crowds turned out to watch high school girls play. Mrs. Hoover was convinced the real attraction for male spectators was the sight of all those young women cavorting about in bloomers, but many people, including such sportswriters as Frank G. Menke and Grantland Rice, found women's basketball a fast, exciting game. Kate read their words with great interest. She attended games whenever she had the chance. She even saw Babe Didrikson play in an exhibition game in Austin. The crowd gave her a standing ovation. Kate cheered herself hoarse.

Kate's collegiate basketball at the University of Texas had been limited to intramural competition. And while there were exhibition teams, no meaningful professional level for women's basketball—or any other sport—existed. But the industrial leagues flourished. Throughout the nation, companies fielded teams made of female employees who were usually hired for their basketball prowess rather than their typing skills. Some of the best women basketball players were heavily recruited and received handsome salaries from their sponsoring company. Their travel to A.A.U. games was subsidized. Their teams were closely followed on the sports pages of the nation's newspapers.

And playing basketball in the industrial leagues offered Kate the best opportunity for meaningful athletic competition. The Lone Star Insurance Company of Dallas was keen on building a first-rate women's team. It had seen that the success of such teams as Kansas City Life, Sun Oil, and Employers Casualty brought their respective companies much publicity and goodwill. The teams provided a valuable public relations tool.

Lone Star Insurance also offered a track and field program, which was very attractive to Kate. She felt that if she had good coaching and trained hard, she might have a chance in four years to make the 1944 Olympics women's track and field team. She remembered well how Babe Didrikson catapulted to fame after her incredible performance in the 1932 Olympics.

So Kate put her newly earned college diploma in the dresser drawer of her and Stella's bedroom in New Braunfels and accepted Lone Star's offer as a well-paid file clerk who would also play forward on the Lady Star's basketball team, and she moved to Dallas. She took a room near the SMU campus not far from Effie's house. Lone Star had an agreement with SMU, which allowed its teams to use the university's track facility for its athletes and its gym on weekends. Kate's room was spacious, with three windows along one wall and a tiny kitchen in one corner. Kate brought a quilt from New Braunfels for the bed in its cozy alcove. She did not bring her baseball pictures for the walls. She bought a picture of a lighthouse and some ivy in a pot for the table in front of the lumpy sofa.

Kate dodged Effie's attempts at matchmaking, offering instead to baby-sit for her nephew Billy while his parents went off to their social functions. Kate was crazy about Billy. She wasn't sure what she would do without Billy, Effie, and William. They were her only hedge against loneliness. She missed Stella, and after a year of counting the days until she could move out of the Kappa house and have a place of her own, she found she hated coming home to her empty room. It was a shock after the hustle and bustle of a sorority house. She started asking around for a woman at work to move in with her. Kate wished that Effie would ask her to come live with her little family. But she understood. A cousin in the house would take away from Effie and William's privacy. Kate wished William would go off and set aviation records for a couple of years so she could move in with his wife and son.

Kate's already lean, brown body grew even leaner and browner as she trained for the upcoming season. And Dallas's fine municipal golf courses drew her like a magnet. She played every opportunity she could. In August 1940 Kate entered and won the Dallas Women's Golf Association tournament. Stella brought their mother up from New Braunfels to watch the final round. Frederick had declined the invitation. Byron Nelson, the Fort Worth golfer who had won the U.S. Open the year before, presented Kate with her trophy. Stella, Anna, Effie, and William holding little Billy all watched proudly. A group picture of them appeared in the New Braunfels newspaper.

After the presentation Byron Nelson and his tall young friend, Jimmy Morris—another pro on the tour—joined Kate and her family for a drink in the clubhouse.

"You're quite a golfer," Jimmy told Kate. "I kept wishing I had a motion picture camera to take pictures of your swing."

Kate couldn't look at Effie. Kate was afraid she'd get a foolish grin on her face. She knew exactly what her cousin was thinking. A man who'd admire her for her athletic prowess—could Jimmy Morris be that man?

Jimmy invited Kate to assist Byron and him with a clinic for the country club's ladies' golf association the following weekend. She discovered that Jimmy wasn't married. That he had a fantastic sense of humor. That he was fun to be with.

"I've always liked women with red hair and freckles," Jimmy claimed. "They never act stuck-up. And they don't talk like little girls. I never did understand why so many grown-up women talk in little-girl voices."

"They talk that way because most men think it's cute," Kate explained. "Daddy's little girl and all that."

"Well, this is one man who isn't interested in being a daddy to his lady friends."

"What are you interested in being?"

"Oh, I see myself as a combination Clark Gable–Humphrey Bogart sort of guy," he said with an endearing grin. "You know—dashing, handsome, Don Juanish."

Jimmy was a bear of a man, an unlikely-looking golfer. He had a round face and unruly blond hair. He was pleasant looking, but Clark Gable–Humphrey Bogart he was not. Whether or not he was a Don Juan, Kate couldn't say. His lopsided grin just looked friendly, not seductive.

He invited her to meet him for a Sunday afternoon round of tennis at a park near her apartment house. She beat him 4–6, 7–5, 6–1.

"Ran out of steam, didn't you?" Kate called as she trotted toward the net after slamming the winning shot home.

"Please excuse me if I don't leap over the net and congratulate the winner," he said. "But I'm just going to limp over to yonder bench and contemplate the loss of my self-esteem. We men don't take too well to being beaten by a woman. I'll probably be impotent from this day forward."

Kate liked him.

She thought about Jimmy a lot. Crazy things, like what he would think of her little apartment, if he'd ever been to New Braunfels, whether he'd ever milked a cow, if he would like Billy.

She went to Fort Worth the next weekend to watch Jimmy compete in the Fort Worth Open. He finished fifth.

When Kate finished second in 100 meters hurdles in the Fort Worth Invitational, Jimmy was in the stands. She rode with him back to Dallas. When he walked her to the door, she knew he was going to kiss her. Her heart was pounding so hard in her chest it hurt.

"I like you, Kate Behrman," he said, pulling her into his arms. He covered her cheeks and mouth with soft little kisses. Kate's lips parted.

Then his mouth was covering hers. His tongue was deep in her mouth. Kate had forgotten it could feel so nice. Or maybe it hadn't felt this nice before.

When he stopped, she protested. "Oh, do it again, please."

They stood in the tiny dark alcove by the door to her room and kissed for a long time. Kate didn't care if she ever went inside. This man really wanted to kiss her. He was a nice man other women would like to go out with. He liked being with her. He'd driven all the way to Fort Worth to watch her run today. He'd cheered for her. She had heard him in the stands. "Come on, Kate! You can do it!" That's probably why she hadn't won—because she was so aware of him watching—but she wouldn't trade his being there for a victory.

"He thinks I run like a gazelle," Kate told Effie the next day.

"Well, honey, if that's what makes your heart go pitter-patter, I think it's wonderful. You two going to get married?"

"Good grief, Effie, I've only known him for a month."

"I knew I was going to marry William the first moment I laid eyes on him," Effie said. "And soon. I didn't want any other girl to get him first."

Stella returned to Austin for her senior year. She gave herself over completely to scholarly pursuits. She lived in the Kappa house but kept apart from much of sorority life. She overheard a new freshmen referring to her as the one down at the end of the hall who always had her nose in a book. "Oh, yeah. The nun," another freshman acknowledged.

With only half a heart, Stella entered into sorority activities. The invitations for dates—blind or otherwise—came infrequently now. Coeds who lasted to their senior year were expected to be engaged or at least pinned and proudly wearing a fraternity pin firmly linked with a bit of gold chain to their sorority pin. Stella's Kappa key, when she bothered to wear it, was unchained. She never put it on without thinking of the black ribbon she'd worn under it last spring—for Maggie, who died for love.

What would it be like to love that much, Stella wondered, to want not to go on living without someone? Maybe she wasn't as in love with Charles as she thought she was. Charles was lost to her, but she still wanted to live and experience life, even though it would be with someone else. Juliet she wasn't.

Throughout the entire year, every time Stella was called to the telephone, her heart would jump. Her hand would tremble as she picked up the receiver, but Charles Lasseter never called.

Stella's scholarship did not go unnoticed. While no faculty member stepped into Blanche's mentor role, the now all-male faculty of the UT Department of History gave Stella Behrman high marks. Stella often had the feeling, however, that they resented her scholarship. She was not invited to join the department's honorary fraternity whose members were selected for "achievement and a devotion to historic inquiry." She usually was not invited to special discussion groups with visiting scholars and had to content herself with their public lectures. When her senior paper on the Ku Klux Klan in Texas was judged the year's best, Stella wondered if it would have earned the honor if the papers had been submitted with names on their cover sheets instead of anonymous numbers assigned by the departmental secretary. Her undeniable straight-A average and senior paper honors brought her the Department of History's award as their outstanding senior. Stella was aware, however, that they would have rather given their award to a male student, to someone who would go to graduate school and distinguish himself and their department. No one expected a reasonably attractive girl to go to graduate school. Serious scholarship in a woman was not particularly admired—unless the woman was homely.

Stella graduated magna cum laude. As with Kate's graduation last year, the family gathered for her graduation ceremonies that were held outside on the terrace area in front of Old Main. Effie and William left Billy with William's parents and drove over from Dallas. Aunt Hannah and Uncle Herman came with cousins Jason and Chris. Cousin Hiram and wife had a sick baby and didn't come. Aunt Louise and Uncle John came with cousins Carl and Joe. Carl and Joe had slicked down their hair. They looked uncomfortable in suits and oxford shoes. Except at church, they wore overalls and work boots.

The band played "Pomp and Circumstance" for the processional. Stella felt very special in her cap and gown. How privileged she was to be a college graduate! Governor Coke Stevenson told the graduates their degree obligated them to do something meaningful with their lives and for the great state that was their home.

As they walked back to the car after the ceremonies, Anna fell in step between Kate and Stella. "I'm very proud," she said, "that both of my daughters are college graduates."

"But, Mama, I'm not sure what it means—to be a college graduate," Stella said.

"It means you did more than your mother. If you're lucky, your daughters will do more than you."

"More what?" Kate challenged.

"Just more," Anna said. "The what is for them to decide."

Frederick would not even discuss graduate school. He was adamant. Instead he made arrangements for Stella to teach school in New Braunfels at the high school.

Stella tucked her dream of a graduate degree away for the time being. She would save her money and do graduate study in the summers. And after she had a master's degree, perhaps she could get an appointment as a paid graduate teaching assistant and work on her doctorate. Someday maybe she could be a professor—like Blanche. There were only two passions in her life. One was unattainable. But she would be a scholar. She would have knowledge.

She did not accept the job in New Braunfels. Instead, she found a job at Memorial High School in Dallas. "I can't come back here to live," she explained to her mother. "I would be afraid. . . ." Of what? she asked herself. Then she looked at her mother—the drab, unsmiling woman who had borne and raised her. Was *that* what she was afraid of—of being like her mother?

Anna nodded. "I understand," she said.

Stella wondered how much she understood.

"But Papa—he will be so angry with me," Stella said.

"Yes, he will," Anna said without looking up from her mending. If Anna was sitting down, she was either mending, darning, or snapping beans. Only at night in bed did she allow her hands to be idle. That was when she read her books. Over and over. The same old worn books. She must know them by heart now. "And disappointed," she added. "You are your papa's 'good girl,' and good girls do what their papas say."

"Do *you* think I should come here to live?" Stella asked.

Anna put her mending in her lap. Stella had drawn the footstool over to her mother's chair and sat at her feet. Anna looked down into her daughter's face.

"I'm not sure it makes any difference where you live," she said. Her lips were chapped. The skin on her face was dry and wrinkled—so many wrinkles. "But it *might* matter, so I suppose you should live someplace else."

"But, Mama, surely you don't think that life in Dallas would be like it is here," Stella said with a wave of her hand to indicate this house, the ranch, the countryside and town beyond.

"What do I know? I'm just an old country woman."

As the physically largest of the touring pros, Jimmy Morris attracted a lot of attention. He towered over his colleagues, and his grin and constant kidding repartee endeared him to the galleries at tournaments.

Raised in Fort Worth, where his uncle had managed the country club, Jimmy had always played golf. For him, there wasn't anything else. He had come perilously close to marriage twice in his twenty-five years. The first time he grew fearful when Sandy, his fianceé, started trying to pin him down about how long he planned to chase around playing golf and when he would be ready to settle down and take a really fine job in her daddy's cement company. The second woman insisted on going with him to all his tournaments. Susie took lessons and expected to play with him when he wasn't actually involved in tournament play. By himself, Jimmy could play a round of golf in a little less than two hours. With Susie along, it took four. She got thirsty. She had to go to the bathroom. She lost balls. She found her way into every trap. She squealed when she hit a good shot. She said, "Well, Jimmy!" in an accusing tone every time she hit a bad one, as though he were somehow involved in her deficiency. And she took incredible liberties with the rules. Mulligans were a way of life for Susie. Still, the two women had had their good points too. Susie was gorgeous, and Sandy was a good sport about all his kidding. He missed having a woman in his life.

Kate Behrman was the only woman Jimmy had ever met who understood about golf, about competition and training and dedication and ambition. She played by rules and adhered to golf etiquette. Kate wasn't pretty, but she was a smart sportswoman.

Their kissing sessions became a nightly occurrence—first in his car and then on her sofa. He liked her mouth. She didn't rebuff him when he began touching her body. An athlete's body. He liked that. Firm and strong. High, taut breasts. Long, muscular legs. First he felt through her clothes. Then he unbuttoned and unzipped. Her flesh was smooth and lovely. She smelled wonderful. When he managed to get his mouth on her breasts, he couldn't get enough. He loved breasts. Kate held hers high for him so he could get more. "Oh, yes," she whispered. He grabbed a sweet young breast between both his hands and kneaded at it while he sucked. She shivered with pleasure.

He wanted her. She wasn't pretty, but he wanted her anyway. He was very much aware of the bed in the alcove with its colorful quilt. Soon.

But he went slowly with her. Each night he went a little further. It was a delightful game. He thought about it all day—the next step with Kate.

"I want to see you naked," he said after two weeks. "All of you."

"And when I'm naked, will you make love to me?"

"If you want me to."

"I'm not pretty," she said, her fingers trailing to her cheeks, her hair. "I wish I were pretty like my cousin Effie."

"Your cousin Effie can't drive a golf ball two hundred yards."

"Two-twenty. You know what I mean."

"Yes, I know what you mean. Maybe you aren't pretty like your cousin, but you're you. You look like Kate Behrman, and I like Kate Behrman. She's a terrific kisser and more fun to be with than any other woman I've ever known—on and off the links. Now, let me undress you. Let me kiss you all over. Has any man ever done that, Kate—kissed you all over?"

"Yes."

Her reply startled him. "And made love to you?" he asked.

He felt her nod. He was sorry. He had thought he would be the first.

He came too soon. Almost at once.

They lay together on her bed. He held her and stroked her back. She cried a bit.

Then he kissed her all over. Tenderly.

The second time he lasted a long time. Her legs were strong around his back. She touched him with her sweetness, with her desire to please him, but he had a feeling her orgasm was faked.

The next time they made love, he was certain. She didn't have orgasms. He wanted to change that for her.

She told him about her professor. He told her about Sandy and Susie.

When the Lady Stars' season began, Jimmy was in the stands. Kate could hear him cheering every time she made a shot. His tour was over. He played golf every day the weather allowed, followed Kate's track and basketball career, and made love to her every chance they got.

"Don't try so hard, honey," he would tell her. They were usually in her bed in her apartment. Her bed sheets were cleaner. Jimmy didn't do much laundry. "Just relax. I'm not going to come this time. I don't want to. We'll just do it until we're tired. I love the way it feels to be inside of you. You're the best, baby. Your body is so tight and firm."

And one night it happened. He gently teased her body for the longest time, caressing her breasts, sucking on them endlessly, kissing her deeply. She really liked kissing. That's how he knew she would eventually make her way to an orgasm. Only a sensual woman could be so crazy about kissing.

While he kissed her, he fondled. She pushed against his hand, her body asking for his fingers to fill the emptiness. She was open and wet.

She moaned as he teased her, using his fingers only to touch, not to penetrate. Her breathing became faster and faster until she was almost panting.

"Please, I want you in me," Kate said. "Please. I feel like I have to have you."

She melted around him. Her moans were like an aphrodisiac to him, but he held back. He gave her plenty of time. She didn't know just where she was heading yet. She needed time to find the way.

Then her whole body changed. She grabbed at him and buried her face against his neck. Her sounds changed to one long moan. Then she went limp, going with it, sailing bravely into new territory. He was proud of her, proud of himself. He actually got tears in his eyes, but he said nothing. It would be like an invasion of privacy if he did. Then she'd know that he knew the other times were a lie.

Jimmy wasn't sure if he actually loved Kate, but she was a great gal and knew as much about athletics as he did. She was a walking encyclopedia of career highs and world records. When they bought a newspaper, they argued over who got to read the sports page first. He'd rather spend time with her than with anyone else.

Jimmy realized he would probably get married sooner or later, and there were surely advantages to having a plain wife when you were on the road a lot of the time. And the idea of having a nice place to come home to was starting to appeal to him. His apartment was disaster. It smelled like a locker room because of all the unwashed clothing piled in corners and scattered about over unswept floors. After a long trip he hated to come home to a kitchen that had no food in the cupboards and only souring milk and moldy bread in the refrigerator. He missed his mother's cooking. He'd like to have someone manage his laundry. His utilities kept getting turned off because he forgot to pay his bills. He kept promising himself he'd do better, but his resolve never seemed to last. He didn't know where to begin. He wasn't sure just how one cleaned a toilet. He seemed to either shrink clothes or run the colors when he did laundry. When he asked his mother about laundry, she told him it was time he got married. There was always something more important to occupy his time than cleaning and laundry—even if it was just taking a nap. He briefly considered moving back home with his parents, but he had always thought it peculiar for grown men to live with their parents no matter how good a cook their mother was. No, he needed to have a home of his own and a wife to run it and his life. He needed a wife who understood and was sympathetic to the sort of life he led.

The idea of having Kate's steady income from Lone Star to fall back on was also attractive. It might take him a few years to get into big money as a touring pro.

Kate had her life. He had his. They could help each other without getting into each other's way. Kate sure wouldn't be whining around for him to quit the tour and work for her daddy's company.

And he liked to make love to her, more all the time. Jimmy was surprised to realize that he was jealous now when he thought of that old zoology professor she'd had the affair with.

But most of all, Jimmy missed her when they were apart. It was not the grand passion he had envisioned, but maybe getting married was just something you did when being unmarried was no longer tolerable.

Kate had no illusions. She knew Jimmy Morris wasn't in love with her. Not really. She knew he was spoiled and sloppy. But he was there in the stands cheering when she made buckets. He bragged about her track times. He didn't pout when she hit a better shot than he did on the golf course. "Hell, Kate," he'd say, grinning that crazy grin of his. "How'd you do that?" She made an adjustment in his grip that helped his swing.

They analyzed each other's golf swings by the hour, and they had wonderful sex. Kate understood now what all the shouting was about.

Kate's resolve not to marry weakened. She thought of Effie's advice to take the best man you could get. She wondered if Jimmy was that man. What if the next beau after Jimmy didn't want her to do sports? What if he was one of those men who maintained that "horses sweat, men perspire, and ladies glow?" What if there was no man after Jimmy? Kate suspected she wouldn't have too many chances to escape the specter of spinsterhood—if that was what she wanted to do. Sex was important. She'd miss it. Besides, when she wasn't with Jimmy, she missed him. Really missed him. A life without him sounded damned lonely.

With Jimmy, it seemed as though she could have her cake and eat it too. She wouldn't have to be an old maid, and she could keep on playing her beloved basketball. Married women had run in the Olympics. And golf? Golf was a game designed for married women. They needed a husband to pay their way to tournaments. Even Babe Didrikson Zaharias. Someday maybe there would be a professional tour for women, but with war on the horizon, Kate doubted it would come along soon enough to do her any good.

There was no formal proposal. They simply slid from one stage to the next, to "if we ever got married" to "when we get married." And it seemed stupid for them to pay rent on two places when they slept together every night they were both in town.

Thanksgiving Day 1941, Kate and Jimmy had a family wedding in the parlor at New Braunfels. Kate wore her mother's wedding dress. Anna and the aunts outdid themselves with the Thanksgiving dinner, which did double duty as a wedding feast. Jimmy declared he had never seen so much food in his life. Frederick was less gruff than usual. He refused to buy a new suit for the occasion, however, and his old one swallowed his shrunken body.

Effie, William, Stella, and little Billy drove from Dallas. Jimmy's parents and his sister and her family rode the train from Fort Worth. The house was full of cousins, aunts, uncles.

Kate found herself almost resenting the fuss. She fully realized that her relatives had wondered if she would ever get herself a man. Aunt Louise and Aunt Hannah dabbed their eyes during the ceremony, so pleased were they that their niece had been spared being an old maid. Kate realized that in their eyes the wedding ceremony was her salvation, her induction into the sisterhood of chosen women. A part of Kate still wished she had found the guts to buck the system. But she hadn't. And at the wedding dinner, when her father gave her and her bridegroom his blessing and lifted his glass in toast to "my daughter Katherine—may she find happiness at the end of her races," and actually offered her an awkward hug, Kate could not stop the tears from filling her eyes. Finally, she had pleased her papa.

Then Jimmy stood and raised his glass. "To my wife, Kate. Let's be good to each other, honey. Let's have a good life."

For their wedding trip, Jimmy went with Kate to Kansas City for an A.A.U. regional tournament. Lone Star won. Kate scored a sensational eighteen points in the finals. A story on the sports page of the Kansas City Star was headlined "Kate Morris Attack Carries Lady Stars." The accompanying story labeled "the newly married Mrs. Jimmy Morris (formerly Kate Behrman)" as a real comer. "Unless a little bundle from heaven ends her career, Mrs. Morris should be on her way to national honors."

Kate stared at the words. Kate Morris. Always she had dreamed of headlines lauding Kate Behrman. It didn't mean as much for someone named Kate Morris to be lauded.

When they returned to Dallas, Kate moved into Jimmy's apartment. Her place was cleaner but far too small for their joint possessions. She had a busy week with her work and training schedule, but she was determined to make inroads in the apartment's filth and disarray. Jimmy helped when he was around, but he had to be told what to do. "You know what dirt looks like, don't you?" Kate challenged. He would grin and say, "Only women see dirt."

Kate tossed a scrub brush at him. "Well, prepare to be educated in the fine art of toilet cleaning and floor scrubbing. And this, my lad, is a clothes hanger. It was designed so that civilized people can keep their clothes off the floor. I suggest you start using them for your clothing, or you will awaken in the morning with clothes hangers wrapped around your neck. Start hanging."

"And I thought they were for roasting marshmallows," Jimmy said as he scooped up an armload of clothes. "What *will* they think of next?"

By the following Sunday she had caught up on the laundry, the bathroom was respectable, and there was food in the kitchen. Sunday afternoon she planned to wash and iron the living room curtains, but Jimmy lured her to the clean sheets of their bed. They were making love when a newscaster interrupted the mood music on the radio. Frank Sinatra had been singing "How High the Moon."

"Wait, Jimmy. Listen," Kate said.

Naked, clinging to each other, they learned that the United States had a naval base in Hawaii at someplace called Pearl Harbor. The Japanese had just bombed it.

"God damn," Jimmy said. "If we go to war, they'll probably cancel the tour."

The doorbell rang just as Effie took the roast out of the oven. Her in-laws were arriving for Sunday dinner. They were always punctual.

"Billy and I will get it," William called.

Effie paused to survey the table in the dining room as she headed for the living room to greet the senior Chamberses. Her beautiful new hooked rug was perfect on the polished wooden floors. The potted poinsettia made a colorful centerpiece. Her crystal was spotless. The silver was polished. The china elegant. The lace tablecloth snowy white. Nice.

She knew something was wrong as soon as she walked into the living room. Her in-laws and husband were clustered about the console radio. Mary Chambers was holding her grandson, her eyes wide and frightened. "We stopped for gas," Bill Chambers was saying. "The man at the gas station had just heard it on the radio."

William was adjusting the dial. He found a station. Effie listened with horror. It had happened. There was going to be a war.

She looked at her husband. His hands were clutching the sides of the radio as he bent over it. His whole body was tuned into it.

He would be the first to go. She had done everything just right, but her husband would leave her and their child and go tomorrow if they would let him.

Effie looked around her beautiful living room and felt her snug world crumbling.

No. She would not let that happen. Wars didn't last forever.

She took her baby from her mother-in-law's arms and stood by her husband. William released his grip on the radio and put an arm around her waist.

Stella was grading papers. Her roommate, church hat askew, eyes wild, came bursting into their small apartment. "My God, Stella! The Japanese have bombed Hawaii. There's going to be a war!"

Yes, of course, Stella thought. The United States will go to war. In Asia. Then Europe. Another world war. She thought of Blanche.

And Charles. He would go to war.

It was all so inevitable. She felt helpless and afraid. Suddenly she wanted to go home—to New Braunfels, to Rosehaven, to see her mama and papa. But all she could do was call them. Tomorrow morning she needed to be in her classroom, war or not.

She could not get through. She tried into the night, but the lines were tied up. All America was calling home, it seemed.

Fifteen

John and Louise's boys—Joe and Carl—were among the first to enlist in Comal County. Anna sent Stella a copy of the newspaper with their cousins pictured on the front page among the group of the county's first volunteers. Of Herman and Hannah's two older boys, Anna wrote, "Jason tried to enlist, but they wouldn't take him because of his asthma. Hiram will probably not go since he's the father of two small children and needed at home to run the ranch. For the first time in my life, I'm grateful I have no sons. There would be no joy in my heart to see my children marching off to war."

Stella stared at the picture of her cousins, at their open, eager faces, at their uplifted hands taking the oath. Joe had taught his girl cousins to drive the truck and shear a goat. Carl had sat up with Stella and Frederick in the barn the night her old donkey died. She remembered Carl and Joe looking awkward in their Sunday best, singing the church hymns in toneless voices. They were men now—unmarried bachelor ranchers, their passion invested in the land. They were thick, sturdy men—like the uncles. Hardy German stock—going off to fight the nation from which those first settlers of New Braunfels came. Stella prayed they would return to work the land again. It was difficult to imagine them anyplace but at the ranch. That such solid men as Joe and Carl were volunteering to go off to war amazed Stella. For them, the decision surely must be born of patriotism; they were not adventurers. Did they feel more obligated to go because of their Germanness, because they must prove their hearts were American?

She hoped they would not suffer because their name was Behrman, but suspected they would. Even at the high school where she taught, students quizzed her about her name and became distant and even disrespectful when she explained.

Stella touched the grainy, newspaper faces of her cousins with her fingertip. Their first furlough home, she vowed she would go to see them.

And Charles.

Women had been having thoughts like this since the world began, Stella realized, feeling they must see their men one last time before they marched off to war just in case they never came marching home again.

She had lived in Dallas for six months now, ever aware that Charles Lasseter lived there, too. She looked for him everywhere, even though she knew he wouldn't be riding buses or frequent her neighborhood grocery store. She had even seen his house. It was near Effie's in the Mockingbird Lane area by SMU—not the house he had dreamed of building but a substantial, older home with the look of old money. His wife's family home, Stella assumed.

Stella awoke every morning wondering if today would be the day their paths crossed. She went to sleep every night wondering if it would be the day that followed. She sensed they would meet again—someday. What would happen when they met she did not know. She had no vision past the moment when recognition would dawn in his eyes.

But now there was the war. Stella remembered that day in Austin, when they toured the house he had designed. Charles had said if there was a war, he would go. She could no longer trust to inevitability. She couldn't wait any longer to see him.

She called his office. The woman asked who was calling. Stella hung up without answering. It was two days later before she had enough nerve to try again.

"This is Stella Behrman. I'm an old friend."

And before she expected it, his voice was on the phone, the same warm voice as before.

"Hello, old friend."

"Hello, Charles. How are you?"

"Well. And you?"

"Fine. Just fine. I live in Dallas now."

"Oh?"

"I teach school. History, at Memorial High School. I'm a good teacher, I think."

"I'm sure you are. One of these days I need to go through Blanche's history books and give you some of them. I haven't had time to deal with her books and papers yet. They're all boxed in the attic." He sounded formal, stiff. It occurred to Stella that he might not be alone. "Living in Dallas," he continued. "That's hard to believe."

"Yes. My sister lives here too. And my cousin."

"Well, now that we live in the same city, I hope to see something of you from time to time."

Stella closed her eyes and took a deep breath. She felt as if she were about to dive into a pond without knowing how deep the water was. She would either break her neck on the bottom or experience the thrill of plunging deep into the cool, murky depths. "That's why I called," she said. "I'd like to see you."

There was a pause. Stella's heart stopped beating.

"Fine," he said cautiously. "How about dinner? Let me see." He spoke to someone in the room. His secretary probably—checking his schedule. Stella could not make out his murmurings. Then he was back on the line. "Thursday evening okay?"

"Yes."

"Tell me your address, and I'll pick you up at eight."

It was done. Stella fell back limply in her chair. She stared at the picture of her family that resided on the desk by the telephone, the four of them standing on the porch. Effie had taken it four years ago—before Frederick had had his stroke. Her father would not approve of what she had just done. He had not raised the sort of daughter who would pursue a married man.

Then she buried her face in her hands and cried.

When the tears had passed, she made a list of all the things she had to do between now and Thursday.

Her roommate had moved back home to Belton. For the first time Stella was grateful to be living alone. She looked around at her tiny apartment. What would he think of it? She had furnished it mostly with pieces from attics back home. Cousins Jason and Hiram had helped her move the furniture over in Uncle Herman's truck, then she'd refinished and repaired it all. It looked nice, kind of quaint, rather like the living room in Blanche's Austin cottage.

After school the next day she rushed to Sanger Brothers department store and bought a new dress. It was a two-piece blue-and-white print with a peplum on the jacket. She didn't know how she would pay her rent the first of the month, but right now the dress was more important. On Wednesday she had her hair cut. Wednesday evening, she cleaned and rearranged the furniture, then carefully gave herself a manicure and pedicure. She practiced opening the door and greeting Charles graciously.

She rehearsed the small talk she would make while mixing him a cocktail. When she went to bed, she could not sleep.

But when he arrived, Charles turned down her offered cocktail. It was just as well. Stella knew her hands would shake.

He was slimmer. His face was different—not so much older as more thoughtful. His smile was sincere. He took her face in his hands and lightly kissed her mouth. "You are lovely," he said. Stella knew he meant it.

She had thought they would linger awhile in her immaculate apartment. She had visualized him sitting on her love seat while she sat in the rocker. They would talk, get used to each other. It would be Blanche they talked about. Dear Blanche would help them over the awkwardness.

But he picked up her coat from the back of the rocker and held it for her to slip her arms into. He waited beside her in the hall while she fished the key out of her purse and locked the door.

A gray Buick was parked at the curb. There was a woman in the front seat. Charles opened the door, and the woman smiled out at them. "Stella, this is my wife, Marisa," Charles said.

Marisa moved to the middle of the seat and Stella found herself sitting next to Charles's wife.

"At long last we meet," Marisa said in the charming Old South accent of highborn Texas women. Her coat had a deep fur collar. "Charles's dear Aunt Blanche was so devoted to you. She spoke of you so fondly— 'the crown jewel of her teaching career.' Charles and I are so grateful that you allowed her to end her life and career on a positive note."

How had this happened? Stella felt disoriented. When she was little, she used to get turned around on the bed, and when she got up in the dark, the door wasn't where it was supposed to be. She felt that way now.

Charles's wife's skin was flawless. No pores. Stella never understood skin like that. How did it breathe? The woman's hair was parted in the middle and pulled sleekly back on her head. No bangs. She had the sort of face that stood up to such severity. A perfect oval framed by the fur collar of her coat. Perfect features. Perfect teeth behind a careful smile— the countess smiling benignly at the peasant girl.

They went to an elegant restaurant with crystal chandeliers, a woman playing a harp from the corner, and discreet, white-coated waiters. Stella had never been anyplace so grand, but the evening was a nightmare. She felt as though her face were made of wood. It was difficult to talk, to answer the polite questions from Charles's wife while he looked on. They had a son. They had plans for a new home. Charles would design it. It would be similar to a house he had designed in Austin. That house had received wide acclaim and appeared in many magazines.

Between the entree and dessert, Stella visited the ladies' room. She stared at the face in the mirror for a long, hard moment, then splashed some water on her less-than-perfect skin and returned to the table. With more aplomb than she'd known she had, Stella told of her dreadful headache. Charles would not hear of her taking a taxi and called for their check.

Stella called Charles at his office the next day. Would he please stop by on his way home from work?

Charles hesitated, then said, "Yes, maybe that would be a good idea."

This time Stella made no preparations. She came home from school and sat numbly in her rocking chair, waiting for the rest of the afternoon to pass.

When she opened the door to his knock, she had no words of greeting. They stood looking at each other in the middle of the tiny room.

"Marisa was in the office when you called," he said.

"If she hadn't been, would you have come alone?" Stella asked.

"I'm not sure," Charles answered, then with a resigned shake of his head, said, "Yes, I guess I would have. It's best that it happened the way it did, though. Marisa is my wife. I don't want to have secrets from her."

"And you'll tell her you came here this evening?" Stella challenged. Her voice sounded almost ruthless.

"Maybe. I don't know yet."

He was sitting on the love seat now, but it wasn't as Stella had imagined it before. He was uncomfortable. There was no cocktail in his hand.

Stella sat in the rocker and began rocking back and forth. She was outside herself, watching—wondering what would happen next.

"I think about you every day," she said.

He nodded. "And I you. But, Stella, it's no good."

"Why?"

"I'm married to a very fine woman who doesn't deserve a cheating husband. I have a little boy."

"And the father-in-law who bought you for his daughter would not be amused," Stella said, knowing how ugly her words would sound but saying them anyway.

"My father-in-law is dead." Charles leaned forward and took her hand. She stopped rocking.

"Stella, stop this. If you want me to say I want you—yes, I want you. I've been in agony since you called. And yes, I think of you every day. Maybe every hour. But some things are just not meant to be. The part of me that is married to Marisa is not sorry. I'm sure you will marry a man who'll make you happy. Sometimes you'll be sad things didn't turn out another way, but for the most part you'll be happy. I do love my wife, Stella. Perhaps it's a love born of responsibility and her very real need to be my wife, but it is real."

"So there will be nothing."

Charles's eyes were tormented.

"I will always stay married to Marisa. I am committed to her and our marriage and our child. Andy has special problems." Charles shrugged helplessly.

"When you think about me, do you think about my body? Have you ever thought about making love to me?"

Charles closed his eyes and moaned. "Stella, Stella. Of course, I have. But you've got to understand. I could never marry you. It's wrong for me to think of you that way. I can't be a cad—not with you. Someday you will find the right man. You don't want me in your past."

"What did you think about after I called?"

He stared at her. Stella thought he wasn't going to answer.

"I thought about your shining hair," he said slowly. "I thought about your beautiful mouth, your white throat, your slim hips. I thought of how it felt when I kissed you that one time. God, only that once."

"Help me, Charles," Stella said, looking down at her lap, at his hand covering hers. "I don't know how to seduce you. Tell me what to do to make you want me. Should I take my clothes off?"

Stella rose abruptly from her chair and frantically began unbuttoning her blouse. Charles stood and grabbed her hands.

"Stella, no. Don't."

"Help me. Tell me what to do," Stella whispered. "Please. I want you to make love to me. I'm so afraid you never will. What if I go through my whole life with you never making love to me?"

"Are you a virgin?" He was whispering too.

"I love you," she said. "Please, I love you."

"Are you?"

"Yes," she said hopefully. "I want you to be the first, the only man ever. How could it be anyone but you? I've always known it would have to be you."

But he turned away from her. His voice was low, hoarse.

"It wouldn't be right. I have no right to deprive your future husband of your virginity. That is a gift you should give to him. I don't want you to have to explain me away. I've always been an honorable man. . . ."

Stella's hands went to her unbuttoned blouse. Her face burned with the tight sting of rejection.

Charles embraced her awkwardly. "Forgive me, Stella, but I can't turn you into that kind of woman," he said. His cheek was against her hair. "I couldn't live with myself if I did."

Then he was at the door.

The dream was over. Really over.

"You care more about the 'rights' of some nameless man than you care about me," she told him hurriedly, before he opened the door and was gone. "It's my body! Are you saying that you'd make love to me if I weren't *virtuous*? Is that what you mean? Damn you, Charles Lasseter. Damn you to hell!"

The door opened and closed.

Charles was gone.

The assistant principal of the school where Stella taught was not as honorable as Charles. He dispensed with her virginity and his pent-up lust in half-a-dozen quick thrusts.

After she had let him out of her apartment and locked the door after him, she went back to her room and stared at the bloody towel in the middle of her bed. How ugly it looked.

She took a long, very hot shower and scrubbed herself until her skin felt raw.

Stella assumed she would not be able to sleep, but she did— dreamlessly.

The assistant principal was quite hostile when Stella refused all his future invitations. She applied for a transfer to another school but was told she had to finish out the academic year at Memorial.

Gordon Kendall was the assistant pastor of the Morningside Methodist Church, which the Chambers family had attended for three generations. Effie first saw him when he performed the funeral service for one of the senior partners from her father-in-law's law firm. She knew at once that her search was over.

Stella resisted.

"No, I don't want you to arrange a date for me with a minister," she told Effie peevishly when her cousin brought it up for the third time. "In fact, I don't want a date with anyone right now. I like teaching. I still want to go back to graduate school. And I'm certainly not interested in a clergyman."

"He's young and progressive," Effie insisted. "Methodist ministers aren't like old Pastor Mueller. And Reverend Kendall is good-looking and charming. I want you to meet him."

One simply did not say no to Effie. Stella agreed only to accompany Effie to church. Effie came by for her in the Buick. Of course, Effie picked the early service, as the assistant pastor, Gordon Kendall, usually preached at the early service.

Stella found herself sitting next to Effie in the second pew. The Reverend Mr. Kendall was handsome. His white surplice accentuated his tanned skin. His wavy hair was darker than Charles's. His was a thoughtful face; his eyebrows lifted when he asked a question, his forehead creasing into three distinct lines.

But a clergyman. Stella wondered at the audacity of any man who stepped into the pulpit and spoke for God. When she was a little girl and wanted to make the supreme declaration, she would announce, "My father says . . ." It was the same with ministers. God says this or that. They had Biblical quotes to back them up. There was no comeback. Fathers and God were above logic.

"These are difficult times," Reverend Kendall said. "God tells us not to kill. He tells us to turn the other cheek, but our country is threatened. Our beloved American way of life is in jeopardy. Is it possible to be both patriotic and Christian during a time of war?" he asked his parishioners. "How do we obey God's commandments when we take up arms?"

The sanctuary fell into a hushed silence.

"I suppose most wars have been fought with both sides believing that God was on their side. Men on opposing sides have marched into battle singing the same battle hymns. But wars are not the doing of God. Wars belong to men."

Gordon Kendall spoke of his own personal dilemma—of seeing cousins and friends enlist, of wondering if he too should join the war effort even though thoughts of war were an anathema to him. "But I'm an American just as you are Americans. No matter what our vocation, our ethnic background, our religion, we are all Americans in this time of need. We do not have it in us to allow evil men to destroy precious freedom, to threaten our beloved nation.

"We have not chosen this war. It was chosen for us. I don't know if this is a moral or immoral war. Maybe all wars are immoral. There are no easy answers, and the best words I can offer you in closing are those of Irish poet Valentine Blacker. 'Put your trust in God, my boys, and keep your powder dry!'

"Sometimes, my friends, the only course is to trust God and sin bravely."

Reverend Kendall stepped down from the pulpit and took his seat in the thronelike chair beside the altar.

The quiet lingered a moment longer until the organist began playing the final hymn. "God Bless America, Land that I love, Stand beside her and guide her Thru the night with a light from above." Tears stung Stella's eyes as she sang. She knew she was not alone. She felt one with her cousin Effie, with a church full of people she had never seen before this morning, and with a young minister who didn't claim to have all the answers. They were Americans.

Effie was right. Gordon Kendall was not like Pastor Mueller. He may have been speaking from the pulpit, but he was also speaking from the heart. His God seemed more approachable than the God of Frederick Behrman and Pastor Mueller.

Stella was glad she had come.

She knew without asking that Reverend Kendall had been invited to Effie's Sunday dinner. Effie chattered on the way back from church, but Stella only half listened. What would he be like without vestments? Would he seem more like a normal man?

The senior Chamberses also came for dinner, smiling benevolently at Effie's matchmaking.

The dinner conversation turned to William. He was completing his officer's training at Fort Sam Houston in San Antonio and hoped to go to Florida for pilot training in May. "He's afraid they'll make him an instructor," Effie said. "I wish they would, but he wants to fly in combat."

Bill and Margaret Chambers looked down at their plates. Combat. William was their only child. Margaret began fussing with her grandson. "Here, Billy. Eat your peas. They'll make you big and strong."

Stella let the others do most of the talking during the meal. She felt strangely subdued and very much aware of Gordon Kendall's glances in her direction. He was not wearing a clerical collar, which pleased her.

After dinner Effie shooed Stella out of the kitchen. "Why don't you and Reverend Kendall take Billy and Rosie for a walk? Billy's coat's on the hook by the back door."

With the dog running ahead and the small boy between them, they walked to the park near Effie's house and took turns pushing Billy on the swing.

"I liked your sermon," Stella told him. "I thought you dealt honestly with a very difficult subject."

"But I had no real solution," he protested. "That bothered me."

"Really? That's what I thought was so good about it. I've never known a minister who admitted not having all the answers. It gave you credibility."

Billy was content to dig in the sandbox with a stick. The two adults sat at a picnic table. Rosie had chased a squirrel up a tree and was waiting excitedly for it to come down the way it had gone up. The trees were budding. The air was fresh with the promise of spring.

They talked. She told him about New Braunfels, about her job. Gordon was from Tyler. His father and grandfather had also been Methodist ministers. "I grew up knowing the one thing I would never be was a minister. Sometimes even now I'm not sure. Maybe I'm like a man who studies psychiatry to understand his own problems. I wonder about that— if I didn't become a minister so I'd feel more secure about God myself."

"Are you?" Stella asked.

"I'm more convinced about the role of the church in society. And yes, I see God in people's faces. So I guess I am, but not in the ways I thought I would be. I suppose I'm still searching for more dramatic answers. I'd like to find a more black-and-white world. In my heart I want old-time religion and values, and my own life will always reflect that. Intellectually, though, I understand the need for change and flexibility."

"Do you talk this openly to everyone?" Stella asked.

"No. I think you're the first woman I've talked to like this. Now you talk. What about you?"

He smiled. He had a good smile. He liked her. Effie had known that he would, or she wouldn't have manufactured this day.

And Stella had to admit that she liked him; Effie had known that too.

"My father has always been unquestioningly secure in his faith," Stella told him. "My mother simply accepts—religion and life."

"And yourself?"

"I have a lot of questions. Most of them I've simply filed away and never expect to have answers to."

She wouldn't make a very good minister's wife, Stella thought to herself. It was going to be difficult for her. Maybe she was more like her mother than she realized, for as she sat there warming her face in the gift of March sunshine, Stella accepted her future. Charles was lost to her. She had to do something. Her father had refused to send her to graduate school, and graduate teaching appointments usually went to those who had already earned a master's degree and were working toward a Ph.D. Postgraduate fellowships in history went to men. And maybe she didn't have the courage to be an academician, to be different like Blanche. It would be much easier to go the other way.

And little Billy was so adorable.

Rosie had given up on the squirrel and flopped down beside the sandbox. Billy was solemnly sprinkling handfuls of sand across his dog's back. He was hunkered down on sturdy little legs, his fine hair making a halo in the sunlight.

Stella wanted a baby. It was as real a yearning as anything she had ever felt. There were other yearnings too, but the sight of a baby pulled at her and filled her with longing.

The man beside her would choose her and give her babies. Had it already been written someplace? Stella almost wished she had never gone to the university, never opened all those books that only made her want to open more. Just as her father had gone into the fields like his fathers before him, and her mother had gone into a kitchen, Stella would follow the deep ruts in the road.

Sixteen

S tella's first real date with Gordon was to a church dinner honoring a returning missionary. Stella was not sure she believed in missionaries. The tall, gaunt man and his drab, silent wife, on furlough from their mission in Ethiopia, shook hands with church members as they filed into the large basement meeting hall. The ladies hurried over to add their covered dishes to the already laden serving tables. Stella had made an oatmeal cake with broiler icing—her mother's recipe. She felt curious eyes turned upon her. The Reverend Kendall's woman friend.

He smoothly introduced her to dozens of people. "My friend, Stella Behrman," he called her. Sometimes he would explain that she was Mrs. William Chambers's cousin. Or that she was from New Braunfels but now was teaching school in Dallas. Gordon knew everyone's name, the names of their children. He asked about ailing grandmothers and about sons in the military.

Stella was embarrassed to be seated at the head table between the senior minister's wife and Gordon. She self-consciously ate her food and then listened while the missionary described his work in Africa. He showed them items crafted by the natives. His wife was encouraged to say "a few words."

"I'm grateful to be doing God's work in a heathen land," the woman said hurriedly and reclaimed her seat.

The missionary presented the minister's wife with a tiny giraffe carved from elephant's ivory. And he gave Stella a basket woven by a native man who had no arms and used his feet instead. Stella was sure the missionary thought she was Gordon's wife.

Her hand brushed against Gordon's as he admired the basket. Stella drew back. She had not wanted his touch. Not yet.

.   .   .

In the days that followed, their courtship flowed with a naturalness that Stella found comforting. She and Gordon were young and beautiful. Everyplace they went, people smiled at them. Only Kate didn't approve. A *minister*.

Gordon asked Stella if she had ever been in love. They were taking an evening walk in the neighborhood near Stella's apartment, where they inevitably ended up at the corner drugstore for a Coke.

"Yes," she said honestly. "He was an architect, the nephew of a dear friend, but he married someone else."

Stella had promised herself she would be honest with Gordon. But she lied when Gordon asked, "Do you still love him?"

"No. I seldom think of him. It's over. Have you ever been in love?"

"No, not really," Gordon answered.

Stella knew the conversation was intended to clear away the past and make room for the words of love that would soon be spoken. She wished he would reach over and take her hand. She knew Gordon was displeased with her, that he wished she'd waited until he came along before loving anyone.

Stella wondered if the day would ever come that she didn't think of Charles Lasseter. She loved him and she hated him. If he suddenly appeared in front of her and said, "Come with me, Stella," she would have gone.

Gordon kissed her that night for the first time. Stella found that she needed to be kissed. His arms felt strong around her, his lips at first soft and then demanding on her mouth.

He stopped kissing her too soon. But he wanted to tell her that he admired her dignity, her intelligence, her sweetness. "You're a born lady, Stella," he told her.

That's what her papa used to say.

"You sound like you expect to marry him," Kate challenged.

"I do—if he asks me," Stella admitted.

"Creepers, you don't want to marry a minister! God, what a dull life," Kate said, making a face. "Church dinners. Living in a parsonage. Everyone knowing your business. Jesus, Stella, are you sure you can handle that?"

"If it's the price I have to pay to be Gordon's wife, then I guess I'll have to."

Kate gave an exasperated sigh and stared down at her plate of half-eaten food. "I'm not hungry," she said, and pushed her chair from the table. They were sitting in the tiny kitchen of Stella's apartment. Stella had made macaroni and cheese and fixed a salad. Later, they were going to a matinee of Greer Garson in Mrs. Miniver. Jimmy was playing in a tournament in Little Rock.

"Why does it matter so much to you?" Stella asked.

"Ministers' wives can't do anything, Stella. Don't you see that? They can't even laugh."

"That's not so."

"Oh, yeah? Tell me one thing you two have laughed about."

Stella tried to deny Kate's words. Of course, she and Gordon laughed, but she couldn't remember anything specific.

"Why can't you be happy for me—like Effie is?"

"Effie thinks a woman isn't a woman unless she has a husband. Is that what you think, Stella? Is that why you suddenly have to get married to the first man who's courted you since that coffin maker's son? Afraid it's your last chance to be a real woman?"

"You're the pot calling the kettle black. Why did you marry Jimmy? And I've gone out with other men. Lots of them. I just didn't like any of them." Stella was angry. Kate was supposed to be happy for her.

"A minister's wife," Kate continued unrelentingly. "Holier than thou. The ultimate goody-goody. Suffering is noble. Plain hair. No makeup."

"Shut up, Kate," Stella said. "I happen to love and respect Gordon. I would be honored to be his wife."

"I'll bet Reverend Kendall won't want you to go to graduate school. Ministers' wives just listen. They don't need to know anything. Their husband speaks for God."

"You're being hateful," Stella accused.

Kate sighed as she picked up her dishes and carried them to the sink.

"Do you love him?" Kate challenged.

"Do you love Jimmy?" Stella countered.

"Yes, I do," Kate said. "He's fun. He doesn't try to change me. I'm happier than I was without him."

"I love Gordon," Stella said. "I'm not *in love* with him, but I love him. Does that make any sense?"

Kate nodded grudgingly. "More intellectual than heartfelt."

"He's a good man," Stella said. "He'll never leave me. He'll never hurt me. I want to have children."

Lone Star Insurance Company was dropping its women's athletic program for "the duration." Rumor had it that the men's pro golf tour for next year would be canceled, and fewer people were interested in golf lessons these days. Jimmy was trying to decide if he should go ahead and enlist or wait to be drafted. "Everything is so up in the air. One minute you think your life will be one way, and then suddenly it's different," Kate told Stella and Effie.

In April, after only one month of "keeping company," Gordon drove with Stella one afternoon to Morningside Methodist. Puzzled, Stella followed him inside. Such an opulent sanctuary—plush carpet, brilliant stained-glass windows, cushioned pews—so unlike the New Braunfels' austere Reformed Protestant.

Gordon led her to the first pew and there in the hushed silence with the agonized eyes of Christ regarding them from his towering crucifix, Gordon proposed. His chin trembled. That moved Stella more than his words. She was loved. She would marry this man of God and bear his children and make him happy. She felt at peace.

And if she did not feel the unfathomable passion for Gordon that she had for Charles, it was probably for the best. Such emotions got in the way of true love. She understood that now. Thoughts of making love to Gordon brought tears of tenderness to her eyes. That was surely better than the tumultuous confusion Charles had caused her.

"I'm not a virgin," she confessed before agreeing to be his wife.

Gordon looked stunned. His hold on her hand weakened. Then with great resolve, he took her to the communion rail in front of the altar. They knelt together. At his bidding Stella prayed for forgiveness, but it was not God's forgiveness she wanted, only Gordon's understanding. What had happened before she met him had nothing to do with them. Stella thought of Charles's words—"You don't want me in your past." But he was there. She had given away her virginity not to him but because of him.

With Gordon's modest engagement ring on her finger, Stella received a special sort of deference from the parishioners. She was the chosen of a man of God. This reflected glory made her feel special and uncomfortable at the same time.

She would have gone to bed with Gordon before their wedding, and she told him so. But he thought it best that they waited until they were married. Some things were best saved for the sanctity of marriage, and anyway, she might get pregnant. So Stella contented herself with long sessions of kissing and touching. It was awkward on her small love seat. She preferred the sofa in his garage apartment next door to the parsonage, but he was uncomfortable with her being there after dark.

So it was on her love seat that she unbuttoned her blouse for him, and he knelt in front of her and tenderly kissed her breasts. Stella liked it very much—she wanted to be naked for him and have him touch her everywhere, but she was too shy to ask.

She preferred their long kisses to some of their discussions. Sometimes, even though he asked her opinion, she knew he really didn't want to hear it. He thought Virginia Woolf irrelevant. He was opposed to the formation of the Women's Army Corps. Oddly enough, when they were with other people, he urged her to speak out, to offer historical perspectives; then he seemed quite proud of her.

Stella appreciated his attentiveness. He saw her every day, brought her small gifts—magazines, a flower, a French pastry. He complimented her on her appearance and asked her about her day. He rubbed her neck and fixed her cups of tea when she was tired.

She traveled with Gordon to Tyler in the eastern part of the state to meet his widowed father. She had never been east of Dallas and loved seeing the wooded, rolling countryside and Tyler's famous rose farms. The senior Reverend Kendall gave them his blessing and instructed them on the responsibility of marriage. Stella was certain his words were the same he used when giving his required, pastor's-study talks to engaged couples before he joined them in matrimony. His house had a musty odor about it. No wife aired out its rooms. When Stella went into the kitchen to fix coffee, she discovered the kitchen cupboards were a jumble of pans, dishes, and canned goods in no discernible order.

The weekend before Easter Stella and Gordon drove to New Braunfels. Anna opened the screen door and came out to welcome them. As Stella opened the car door she was greeted by the warm, yeasty, cinnamon aroma of her mother's special coffee cake.

Frederick was seated at the kitchen table. With great effort he got to his feet and shook hands with his daughter's intended. Then they drank coffee from heavy white mugs and ate the freshly baked coffee cake with butter melted on its gooey topping. Gordon ate a second piece and said, with a chuckle, that it was *sinfully* good. Stella laughed obediently. Anna said little while Frederick quizzed Gordon about his plans for the future, his beliefs, his interpretation of Biblical passages, his feelings about the war. Had his family ever farmed? Stella wished there was some way to spare Gordon from Frederick, but he endured her father's inquisition with patient good humor.

The next day Stella showed Gordon the town—the same tour on which she had always imagined taking Charles. She was not without regret.

Gordon understood that she needed him to see it all. He asked questions. They had lunch in the dining room at the Faust Hotel. They drove around the courthouse square with its bandstand, past the high school and through Landa Park. Stella showed him the site of the first open-air church service held after the settlers arrived in March 1845. She loved this quaint little town. It would always mean home to her.

That evening they went dancing at Gruene with Cousin Hiram and his wife, who was pregnant and just beginning to show. And on Sunday Gordon met the rest of the relatives when they gathered at the house after church. The women congregated in the kitchen, the men in the parlor. Gordon expressed amazement at all the food. He ate some of every dish and sang its praises, singling out Aunt Louise's meat balls, Aunt Hannah's hot potato salad, and Anna's persimmon pudding. Stella was proud of him.

Frederick had run out of questions for Gordon. He could not fault the man his answers. But still . . .

Looking over the top of his glasses, Frederick regarded his beloved Stella's intended. A minister. Gordon was intelligent and ambitious. He would probably have an important church someday. Methodist. Methodists weren't so bad, Frederick supposed. He should be pleased, but he wasn't. This man wasn't like Effie's William. Gordon Kendall did not adore Stella. Maybe he loved her in his way, but he didn't adore her.

And while he stared at the young minister from Dallas, Frederick understood at last what it was he had wanted for Stella. It had nothing to do with how important the man she married was, or even how successful he was as long as he had his pride and worked hard. But Frederick wished that Stella could be loved the way he himself had loved the first Anna.

Frederick grabbed the arms of his chair with old, gnarled hands as the memory of that love came flooding back. The memory of his darling Anna watching for him out her kitchen window. Of her arms coming sweetly around his neck. Of her smile across the table. Of the way she would suddenly grab his hand and cover it with kisses. Of her breath warm on his neck as she tucked her body next to his before sleeping. Stella could love a man that way. But not Gordon Kendall.

Frederick, however, knew he had no choice but to keep his misgivings to himself. He was old and ill, and he should be grateful to see her married before he died.

Frederick could feel the nearness of death. He was tired of life. After all these years to grow accustomed to the idea, it still bothered him that he had no son to whom he could leave his land. He had worked the land all his life, helping his father in the fields from the time he could lift a hoe, always knowing that someday the land would belong to him and to his brothers. A man should have a son.

The ranch, Frederick had long ago decided, would be divided between his two brothers, both of whom had fine sons. That way the land would continue to be Behrman land. He would leave his daughters and his wife trust funds, but men should keep the land. His girls had husbands to provide for them and had no need of a ranch. Anna could stay in the big white house until she died. His brothers would look after her.

Now with Stella's future assured, Frederick could almost feel himself letting go. He searched his Bible for answers about heaven. Which of his wives would he have into eternity? If he wasn't with the first Anna, it would not be heaven. He was beginning to doubt heaven anyway. Strange, after all those unquestioning years.

But oddly enough, the possibility of death as a black void wasn't particularly distressing. He just didn't think about it. Instead, more and more, he allowed his thoughts to thread backward—to Anna. To him, still, that name belonged to only one woman.

Frederick had the new Mexican boy move his rocking chair onto the front porch. He rocked away his days now. Dozing and rocking. If he searched for it, there was a place between dozing and wakefulness in which he found her waiting for him. She was still young, still loved him after all these years. She didn't know he was old.

Anna went out to the porch one July evening—two weeks before

Stella's wedding—to help Frederick in to dinner. She'd made chicken soup with homemade noodles.

He was slumped over in his chair. She knew he was dead without touching him.

Anna sat down on the front step and stared out at the sunset. The insects had already begun their evening chorus. A train whistle sounded in the distance.

How many years? Twenty-five. No, for twenty-six years she'd lived here with this old man. He'd seemed old when she married him, and now he was dead. He'd never loved her, but without him she would not have been a mother. For that, she was thankful. Her life would have been nothing without Stella and Kate.

She was a widow now. She wouldn't miss Frederick himself, but taking care of him had given her life focus. His passing would leave a void.

She went inside to call her daughters. And the brothers. There was much to do.

Frederick was already laid out in the parlor when Stella, Kate, and Effie arrived. Effie went to the kitchen, and the other relatives filed out, leaving the two sisters alone with their mother and the body of their father.

"He didn't suffer," Anna said as she hugged her daughters. She was wearing her black funeral dress.

A vase of roses sat on the small round table beside the Bible. Their scent was sweet. The blinds were pulled, and the room's two lamps were on.

Timidly, hand in hand, Kate and Stella approached the open coffin. The old, still man inside looked so wrinkled next to the smooth satin lining.

"Oh, Papa," Kate sobbed as she stared down at him, "I love you."

Kate and Stella hugged each other for comfort. "I never once said that to him when he was alive," Kate said. "But he never told me either. Do you think he loved me, Stella?"

"My God, Kate, he was your father. Of course, he loved you," Stella said.

"He loved you the most. Didn't he, Mama? He loved Stella more than anyone." Her words were more a statement of fact than an accusation.

"Yes," Anna acknowledged. "But then she loved him back. Tit for tat."

Yes, she had loved him very much, Stella thought, as she looked down at the lifeless body that had been her father. He was her papa. She was his *mein braves Madchen*, his good girl.

She bent over and kissed his cold, dead cheek. "Sleep well, Papa."

Then she cried, clinging to her sister. Effie came into the room and cried with them.

Stella and Gordon talked of postponing their wedding, but she had already moved her things into Gordon's apartment and had been staying with Effie. "Get married," Anna said. "Your father wanted that for you."

They decided to have a parlor wedding rather than hold it in the Reformed Protestant Church as planned. Gordon's father would still officiate. Strange—Stella hadn't wanted a church wedding in the first place, but Gordon had thought it appropriate. Because her papa died, she got to be married in the parlor like Kate, as she'd wanted. And like her sister, Stella wore their mother's lovely wedding dress. She became a wife in the same room where her father's dead body had lain. And long ago that of the tiny brother. And before she was born, the other Anna and her baby. Papa had read to them from his Bible in this room. It was the room of Christmas trees, ministers' visits, and birthday presents, all the celebrations of life and death.

Her grief made it impossible for her to enjoy their week-long honeymoon in Galveston. Gordon was patient and understanding. He held her when she cried. She was numb. The sex seemed mechanical; even the kissing did not move her.

But she liked waking in the night and having someone sleeping beside her. It reminded her of growing up, sleeping beside Kate. And she liked Gordon to hold her and stroke her hair and her back. She wished it didn't always have to lead to sex. When the sex began, it seemed oddly impersonal, as though Gordon retreated from her.

Could their mother stay on alone at the ranch? Both Stella and Kate were unsure. Of course, Anna had always been competent, but she was not a young woman. But then, she wasn't that old—only sixty. She had been thirteen years younger than Frederick.

Perhaps it was the idea of any woman living alone on a ranch that was distressing. Of course, the uncles would help if Anna would let them, and she had Mexicans to tend to the goat herd.

But Anna shooed the uncles from the place and contested Frederick's will, claiming it denied her and her daughters their rightful inheritance. They, not Herman and John, should own the farm. Fully one-third of the land had come from Anna's father. It was wrong for Frederick to give it away. She would run the ranch herself, and when she died, Anna wanted her daughters to be women of property whether they ever lived on the ranch again or not, whether they had husbands or not. *It was their right.*

But old Wilhelm Theis had deeded the land to Frederick at the time of Frederick's marriage to his daughter. And Frederick had not actually disinherited his wife and daughters. He had provided for them in the will with trust funds to be administered by his younger brother Herman, who was more comfortable with financial matters than the middle brother John. Legally, Frederick had been within his rights to leave his property to his brothers.

After the court hearing, Anna went home. Without removing her Sunday coat and hat, she climbed the steep stairs to the attic and took her wedding dress from the oversized cedar chest.

Clutching the dress in her arms, she stood and looked around the dimly lit room under the eaves of the old house. All about her were dust-covered mementos of her life in this house—a crib, high chair, rolled-up scraps of linoleum, leftover rolls of wallpaper, a broken kitchen stool, a dresser with a cracked mirror, a thronelike chair that once sat in the parlor of her father's house, her father's shaving stand, trunks of forgotten clothes, the stained mattress that served as her father's deathbed, a basket of toys, the carved chest that held the possessions of the other Anna.

Kate and Stella drove up in time to see their mother stuff the ivory satin and lace dress into the incinerator by the chicken house and ignite it.

"You had no right," Kate said, staring at the burning dress. "Stella and I were married in that dress too."

"Don't you try to tell me what my rights are," Anna snapped. "How can you worry about that dress when your father has disinherited you? He didn't leave his own daughters his land because he wanted to 'keep it in the family.' They let us get married to them in pretty dresses, but we don't really matter."

Stella watched the flames eat away at the sacred garment. How many times had she and Effie and Kate opened the big wooden chest and stroked the folds of shiny, smooth satin and admired the intricate workmanship of the lace? To their young eyes, it seemed a dress fit for a queen—or at least for the one day in a woman's life when she was queen. Stella had always known she would marry in her mother's wedding dress. She recalled how her maturing figure began filling the bodice as she changed from girl to woman. The three of them would take turns putting on the dress and staring at themselves in the cracked mirror of an abandoned dressing table. She had seen her sister marry in that dress and had been married in it herself just weeks before. The dress had been symbolic for Stella of the hope of marriage, of all her best expectations for wifehood, of being honored and loved and cherished by the man who would share his life with her.

Stella would rather have seen her mother burn the big German Bible. Did that burning dress mean that all those years Anna and her father had shared, sleeping in the same bed, raising their daughters—had all those years been a sham? Hadn't they loved each other? Maybe marriage wasn't about love at all.

The next day Kate and Stella watched helplessly while Anna began packing her belongings. "The house belongs to Herman and John," Anna said. "Since I'm not in the family, I don't want to live on *Behrman* property."

Anna wanted to buy a small house in town. She found one on Bridge Street with room for a garden and a few chickens in the backyard. Herman, as trustee, had to give his approval for the purchase of the house. At first Herman was unwilling. He did not understand why Anna could not stay on at Rosehaven as Frederick's will had specified, but Hannah, in the "do as I say or else" voice she usually saved for the children, told her husband to approve the transaction. Herman wasn't exactly sure what the "or else" would have been, but he decided it wouldn't be too costly to the estate for Anna to buy the little house. When it was sold after her death, it would probably turn a profit.

Herman and Hannah's boy, Hiram, and his young family would move into Frederick's house. At last, when Stella realized the big old house would no longer be there for her to go home to, she had to admit her anger. Her father had taken away her birthright. Maybe she or Kate never would have lived in that house on that land, but it would have been *theirs*. They would have had something to pass on to their children. Through her anger and disillusionment, however, Stella wondered if her father had simply been acknowledging in his last will and testament what was already so. Family lines were for men. Women went namelessly from one family to another but belonged to neither. Not really.

"I'll never set foot in that house again," Kate declared, her hair the color of flames in the sunlight as they closed the back door, the final cleaning complete, the house ready for its next occupants.

"Never say never," Stella said automatically—one of her mother's pet phrases. The older she got, the more like her mother she became. Her father had lived in a world of absolutes. Anna was more practical.

Seventeen

Gordon and Stella lived in Dallas for only six weeks, then moved to Galveston. He had accepted a church post in the picturesque island city known for its Victorian architecture and turn-of-the-century charm. Gordon had visited the Bayside Memorial Methodist Church and its elders during their honeymoon, and the parishioners had been impressed with the earnest young man and his dignified young wife. Stella was charmed by the historic city and by the Victorian parsonage with its gingerbread trim, curving stairway, and polished woodwork. She threw herself into the task of making the parsonage their home. It was heady to have her own house. Using the furniture from her Dallas apartment and what she had claimed from Rosehaven, she arranged the rooms. She refinished furniture, made curtains and slipcovers, varnished floors, painted some walls and wallpapered others.

With satisfaction, Stella would walk through her house, her fingers lovingly trailing along the polished wood of the banister, straightening pictures that needed no straightening, smoothing already smooth bedcovers, aligning books in the bookcases, rearranging knickknacks on their shelves, fluffing cushions, refolding the towels on their racks, setting the table in the dining room, polishing silver—and dusting. She usually had a dustcloth in her hand. She never tired of cleaning, waxing, polishing. If one could be in love with a house, Stella was in love with the charming old parsonage on Galveston Island. Her husband became an extension of the house. She cared for him and his needs as carefully as she cared for the floors and furniture.

Stella found herself resenting interruptions in her housekeeping, but a minister's wife was expected to go to circle meetings and teas and covered-dish luncheons and evening socials. She fretted too much over what to make for the covered-dish affairs, for she had discovered that everyone made it a point to check out what the new minister's wife had brought. But people were kind to their young minister and his wife. Gordon seemed quite pleased with Stella. She was, after all, a perfect wife. His underwear was neatly folded in his drawer. His meals were beautifully prepared and punctually served. His home was immaculate. Stella was sweet and affectionate in bed. She never told him no. He was a very fortunate man.

Stella did not miss her teaching job, and it was only occasionally that she pulled out a history book from the shelf and thought of academe. Only once had she driven out to Blanche's cottage. Its shutters were closed, and weeds were growing up through the boards in the front porch. Stella sat on the steps and remembered what it had been like to have a scholarly life.

And she thought of Charles, of the days they were supposed to share here on this isolated beach. He had wanted to walk with her on the beach and see her face in the firelight.

She had tried to hate Charles after he rejected her. She would have done anything for him, and he'd pushed her away. But she would not allow a lost love—or thwarted ambitions—to ruin her life. She would not be the foolish old woman in *Great Expectations*. The greatest immorality was to allow something to ruin your life. Effie believed a person could choose happiness over unhappiness, and the Effies of the world could do that. For Stella, it was more a matter of not being unhappy.

Stella trained herself not to think of Charles. At first that was difficult, but now she was pregnant. It was less difficult to tuck his memory safely away with a baby nestled deep inside her. Charles's seascape hung over the sideboard in the dining room, but after all, it had once belonged to a former professor, she explained to Gordon. "Blanche Lasseter left it to me. It was painted by her nephew and used to hang over her fireplace." It would be foolish not to use it, Stella had decided; it was just what the room needed. At first she thought of Charles every time she looked at the painting, then one day as she was dusting the frame, Stella realized she no longer thought of him every time she walked by the picture. In fact, she seldom thought of him at all.

Gordon had mixed feelings about her pregnancy. "Of course, I'm thrilled, but with times so uncertain, I just think it might have been better if we'd waited."

Times may have been uncertain, but Stella wasn't uncertain at all about wanting a baby. For her, marriage and babies went together.

One by one, Gordon heard about members of his divinity class from SMU enlisting. Older ministers were coming out of retirement to free the younger ones for the chaplain corps.

And after less than six months in Galveston, Gordon told Stella over dinner one evening that he had volunteered. She looked around the dining room that she had so lovingly painted a soft rose beige, at the floors she had varnished, the table she had refinished, the draperies she had made. She had already bought paint for the nursery and fabric for its curtains. And now she would have to give it all up. It would be given to Gordon's replacement at the church.

Stella put her face in her hands and wept. When Gordon came and knelt by her chair and soothed her, she realized he thought she was crying because he would be going to war. Stella felt so ashamed.

Later, when Gordon asked if it would be hard for her to leave the house on which she had labored so hard, all Stella said was, "It's only a house."

Never again, she thought, would she allow herself to care so deeply about a house. None of them would ever be hers—not really. She had learned her lesson.

Gordon was sent almost at once to the Army's chaplain school at Harvard University. Effie and Jason came to Galveston to help her move. Stella had decided to move back to Dallas to be near Kate and Effie. It was January and very cold. The wind bit at her legs as she carried things into her duplex apartment.

Kate, who was five months pregnant, organized Stella's new kitchen for her, putting down shelf paper and stacking the dishes and pans away.

Like Stella and Effie, Kate was also alone now. Jimmy had seen the draft coming and enlisted. He had heard that those who enlisted got better assignments. He requested San Antonio but got London. At least his request for Special Services had been honored, however, and he wasn't in a fighting outfit. He parlayed his country club experiences into an assignment running an NCO club in London. He wasn't much of a letter writer. His letters, when they did come, sometimes mentioned big-name performers who came to entertain the soldiers. And he wrote of the Blitz, although many such portions of his photocopied V-mail letters were blacked out by military censors.

And Effie's William, after serving six months as a naval flight instructor in Norman, Oklahoma, was now flying Hellcats in the South

Pacific—from the decks of the carrier *Enterprise*. William wrote almost daily, his letters arriving dozens at once in tied-together bundles. He wrote of the daily life on the aircraft carrier, his "missions" mentioned only in passing.

After completing the chaplain school, Gordon was assigned to minister the citizen soldiers of the Forty-fifth Division at Pine Camp, New York, in March 1943. He would rather have been assigned to Texas' Thirty-sixth Division, but they didn't need another Methodist. Composed mostly of National Guard units from Oklahoma but with units from other southwestern states, the Forty-fifth had been mobilized in August 1940 as part of a preparedness movement on the part of the military. Nicknamed the Thunderbirds because of its Indian insignia, the division had undergone more than a year of intensive training. Before it joined the war in Europe, its ranks had been swelled by recruits from all over the nation. The sixteen division chaplains included a Lutheran from Colorado, a Catholic priest from New Mexico, and a Methodist from Texas—Gordon.

After New York the Forty-fifth had additional training in Maryland and Virginia before being sent to Algeria for staging their entry into Europe. Gordon's last letter from Africa said, "Everyone is curious to see what the citizen soldiers can do—including the citizen soldiers themselves. Such a mixture of emotions I see—from incapacitating fear to steel-nerved determination to meet the enemy and inflict harm. Soon the waiting will be over." Gordon knew better than to speculate about the division's destination or dates. The censors would only black out such remarks.

Stella settled into a life of waiting for the photocopied V-mail letters from her husband and watching her pregnant belly swell. If she hadn't been pregnant, she would have gone back to teaching, but the Dallas school system was firm in its maternity policy. Teachers could not teach more than three months into their pregnancy, and they could not return until six months after their babies were born.

In May Anna came from New Braunfels to await the birth of Kate's baby. Stella was bothered by her sister's appearance. Kate had gained a lot of weight. Her pregnant belly was not so remarkable looking, but the sight of Kate with less-than-lean arms and legs and buttocks was. Even her face was fuller. She had the beginnings of a double chin. But surely her sister would return to her former athletic self after her baby was born.

Stella spent her days and evenings at Kate's apartment. It was the most peaceful time Stella could ever remember, with few chores and no men to look after. She took long afternoon walks with Kate and Anna. In the evenings after dinner, the three women would sit around the radio, stitching baby clothes. Strange that they had peace in the midst of a war. So many of America's men were living in fear and dying, while she and her sister and mother told family stories and speculated about the babies soon to be born. Europe's women suffered along with their children while the three of them enjoyed Anna's chicken and dumplings. It didn't seem fair.

"Our time may come," Anna said. "If they start dropping bombs on American cities, you girls and your babies will have to come live with me in my little house in New Braunfels."

Kate and Stella agreed. They would do that when and if the United States was invaded. No one would drop bombs on New Braunfels.

Stella touched her pregnant belly protectively. Stella had seen the newsreels showing the bombing in London. She looked out the window of Kate's living room. Would such scenes be repeated in Dallas, Texas?

Stella, Effie, and Kate helped each other install the required blackout shades in their windows. They read the procedures for air raids that were published in the *Morning News*. They kept a supply of water in glass jugs and stocked up on canned goods—just in case.

Finally, one week after her due date, Kate was in labor. Effie drove them all to the hospital. "A baby. Jesus Christ, I'm having a baby!" Kate said, between pains.

"Don't take the Lord's name in vain," Anna commanded automatically.

"It's not in vain," Kate said. "I'm quite serious about this. Oh, my God!"

Stella was frightened. Suppose Kate had her baby before they got to the hospital. Stella put her hand on her own belly, vowing that when her time came, she would leave for the hospital with the first pains.

There had been no need to hurry, however. Kate's son did not arrive until the next day. She had labored through the night. Stella was horrified. Kate screamed hysterically. Couldn't something be done, Stella asked repeatedly, but the nurses who went in and out in their silent shoes didn't seem concerned. Anna and Effie were sympathetic but not alarmed. But Stella was certain Kate's labor couldn't be normal. Kate was tough. She hadn't even cried when she'd fallen out of the loft and broken her arm.

The bone had even poked through the skin. She wouldn't be screaming now unless the pain was unbearable.

"You go on to the waiting room," Anna finally told Stella. "There's no need for you to sit here. It's just upsetting you."

Stella went gratefully. She seated herself in the magazine-strewn room and tried to calm herself.

When she was finally summoned to her sister's side, Kate was smiling. The sunlight was streaming through the window. "Hug me, Sis," she said, opening her arms to Stella. "I'm a mommy."

"Are you okay?" Stella asked.

"Yeah, I guess so," Kate said. "It was pretty grim, wasn't it?"

Stella nodded.

"You'd think someone would have warned us," Kate said. "I feel like I was a victim of some sort of conspiracy of silence."

Stella spent much of her time with her sister and baby Mark, less with her cousin. Effie was assuming more and more responsibility in running her husband's small airline during his absence. At first Effie had gone to the office to answer the phone and help keep things running smoothly, but the man William had left in charge was drafted just two months short of the safety of his thirty-fifth birthday.

"Well, that leaves you and me," Effie told her father-in-law.

Bill Chambers had all but retired from the law firm and now devoted his days to golf. Reluctantly, he started meeting Effie each day at the offices of Texas Central. "Well, I never thought my wifely duties would extend to the office," Effie said from behind the now-tidy desk in William's old office. "But I know how much Texas Central means to William. It would just break his heart to have all he had worked for crumble."

Bill admired Effie's determination that her husband come home to a viable business, and he supposed he'd have to get involved. He could hardly expect Effie to run things by herself. At least it was winter, and he wouldn't be missing too much golf—at least for now. Maybe he could find a replacement for the manager by spring. But a good man was hard to find these days. So many were in the service.

Bill's first surprise came when he discovered how much Effie already knew about the business. "Well, a man likes to talk about his work," Effie said nonchalantly when Bill asked her why. "I asked lots of questions.

He gave me good answers. And I read over a lot of the correspondence. He liked doing his paperwork at night, and I typed things for him. I'm a better letter writer than he is."

And she admitted that since William had left, she had been coming into the office a lot. She did not share the same degree of confidence in the manager her husband had left in charge and often dropped by to review contracts, work schedules, financial statements. "He didn't much like it," she admitted, "but he didn't have the authority to keep me away. And I didn't have the authority to put a stop to his incompetency. Such a sloppy man. He didn't pay attention to details. He hired people who were just as sloppy as he was."

Automatically Effie straightened a stack of folders. She was wearing a light gray suit. Her white blouse had a large soft bow at the throat. A silly but altogether fetching little feathered hat sat on her blond curls.

"He might have managed but for one thing," Effie continued. "His worst crime was he refused to hire women mechanics and pilots. And with the men all getting drafted, the business was starting to founder. I think we would have had to step in eventually. His getting drafted was a blessing for Texas Central."

"Effie, honey, it can't be as bad as all that," Bill said. "After all, William wouldn't have left him in charge if he wasn't up to the task."

"William left in such an all-fired hurry, he would have left little Billy in charge of Texas Central if it meant he could get off to his war faster."

"Now, Effie, William felt it was his patriotic duty to go."

"Yes, I know. Now, you want specifics, I suppose, of what is amiss around here?"

Bill nodded, wondering what she was so worked up about. Probably she didn't like the color of the paint on the office walls.

"Well, three planes are out of commission and have been for weeks. The flight instructors are stretched too thin. The students are having a hard time getting in their flight hours for licensing. And several government contracts were turned back because the company couldn't meet government requirements in our training program. I don't want that ever to happen again. It's not good for the war effort and not good for Texas Central."

Bill lit a cigar and regarded his daughter-in-law through the resulting smoke. Maybe he could get back to the golf course sooner than he thought.

"But what if there aren't any qualified women out there?" he asked, knowing somehow that Effie would have an answer.

"We'll train them," Effie said without hesitating. "I want at least thirty more pilots for starters. I don't want planes on the ground any longer than necessary. I think with tight scheduling and the additional pilots, we can increase the number of students next term—and shorten the term from twelve weeks to ten weeks. I'd rather have all women than continue using old men who have no business at the controls of a plane, much less teaching. I'll have to let some of the present pilots go, and I want to hire at least fifty more mechanics."

"Fifty!" Bill said, sitting up straighter in his chair. "You don't need fifty more mechanics to keep a couple dozen planes flying."

"I need them to rebuild engines. I bought a whole warehouse full of used engines and parts from the government. For a song. We'll rebuild them and sell them back for a lovely profit."

Bill shook his head in wonder. Amazing. Pretty little thing like that. There she sat in her little feathered hat sounding like she'd run a business all her life. His son's business was in good hands, and Bill was relieved. The hands at the reins wouldn't have to be his. Would he ever have something to tell Margaret when he got home tonight! He couldn't wait.

"What do you want me to do?" Bill asked.

"You know people down at City Hall," Effie said. "See what you can do about renting additional hangar space here at Love Field—for all those engines and mechanics."

Bill saluted. "Right. What else?"

"Call on the military adjutant for Dallas. Let him know we'll be ready for more training contracts and planes. I think it's best if you handle all the contacts with the military. They'll feel more comfortable with a man in charge at Texas Central."

"You just tell me what to say, and I'll say it," Bill said. "What else?"

"I need to rent another building close by. A large house would do nicely. In good repair. No drafts."

"Are you going to move the offices?" Bill asked.

"No, I'm going to start a nursery school. All those women who will be working for us need to have someplace to leave their children."

Bill laid his cigar in the ashtray and offered Effie his hand across the desk. "I just want to shake the hand of my new boss."

"Why, Bill Chambers, I'm not your boss. I'm just helping out till that son of yours gets back."

"Shake my hand, Effie," Bill commanded.

Effie shrugged and accepted her father-in-law's handshake. "We'll do this together," she reminded him.

"I'll do whatever you say," Bill said.

Effie kept him busy in the weeks to follow, but Bill did her bidding willingly. He knew that come summer, he'd be back on the golf course.

"You're really quite incredible," Bill informed Effie as they walked back toward the offices after making their daily rounds of the facility. In flat shoes and slacks, Effie strode along beside him with ease, a clipboard tucked under her arm. She wore slacks now so that her overall-clad female employees would feel more comfortable around her. It seemed to work. Women greeted her wherever they went. They all called her Effie, and Effie seemed to know everyone by name.

After only three months Effie had worked wonders. Texas Central was a thriving company with more than two hundred employees. They had almost one hundred flight students and would double that number shortly when fifty more PT-19s arrived. They were going to make a fortune with the engine-rebuilding operation.

"Oh, I'm not incredible at all," Effie said. "It's the times. Everyone pitches in and works hard, and running a business isn't much different from putting on a bazaar or organizing a charity benefit gala. You have to get good people and pay attention to details."

Bill wondered if she had any idea how cute she looked in those slacks. Women in slacks. They were everywhere. He didn't much like it, but then most of them just looked like they were wearing men's clothes. Not Effie, though. Her fanny was unmistakably female.

Why did he still have such a hard time believing that any woman who looked like her could be so efficient and bright? He was going to miss these days with her, but the weather was getting nice. It was time for him to get back to golf. Bill had always liked Effie. Everyone liked Effie. But now he admired her, and he would forever have a very large soft spot in his heart for this special blond woman who was married to his son.

Effie's four-year-old Billy often spent his days in the Texas Central nursery school. His mother and some of the other mothers would come over and have lunch with their children. He took his nap on the sofa in her office and often accompanied her on visits to the hangars. Sometimes she would take him along when she flew to Houston or Oklahoma City on business trips.

Like the other males in Effie's life, Billy openly adored his mother, lavishing her with bouquets of dandelions and childish drawings that decorated her office.

And her bachelor brother Jason still adored her. He often spent weekends with them, doting on Billy and caring for his nephew while Effie put in weekend hours at Texas Central. Sometimes when Effie wasn't too busy, she cooked for them. Otherwise, Jason cooked. Effie's meals were wonderful. His were basic. They would eat in the dining room— just the three of them—Billy, Effie, and Jason. Then Jason would help Effie with the dishes. He would read to Billy and help Effie tuck him in for the night. Then it would be just the two of them, sipping wine, talking, or listening to the radio. When they went upstairs to bed, she would kiss him at her bedroom door and say, "Good night, darlin' Jason. I love you." On Sundays they would go to church and out to dinner at a cafeteria. Sometimes they took Billy to the zoo or swimming at the senior Chamberses'. Jason knew Effie missed her husband, but it was so lovely being with her and Billy like that. So lovely. Jason would hate for it to end.

Effie and Billy had dinner once a week with William's parents. And they often had dinner with Stella and Kate. The three cousins would cook simple meals together and linger over coffee.

Stella enjoyed these times so much she felt guilty. She and Effie and Kate were allowed them because the world was at war. When the men came home, such times would end. Sometimes she missed Gordon so much it made her sick to her stomach. Other times she didn't miss him at all.

Kate's baby was a sweet blond child, quieter than Billy had been. Kate was certain Mark already showed promise of great athletic talent. "Just look at how well he holds his head up," she would exclaim. "And look at the way he pushes with those legs."

Mark slept in a crib next to Kate's bed. "I like him there so I can hear him breathing," Kate explained. "It makes me nervous for him to be in the next room. Sometimes I wake up and just sit there staring at him. My baby. I wonder what's happened to me. I never wanted kids, and now I can't imagine a life without Mark."

"No regrets?" Stella asked.

"Oh, yes. I have regrets," Kate admitted. "I hate what pregnancy did to my body. I dream of competing again but wonder if I ever will. I don't want to give my life completely over to kids, yet at the same time I want another baby in the worst way."

Stella was still the lady in waiting, her pregnancy approaching its last trimester. Her modest duplex apartment was just two blocks from the Southern Methodist University campus. She planned to enroll in a couple of courses after her baby was born. Kate had offered to baby-sit. But Gordon, in his letters, advised her against getting involved in anything that would take her away from her responsibilities as a mother. Stella considered rebelling against her husband's wishes but decided that it would not be right to do something and not tell him. And she could not bring herself to write a letter saying that she planned to defy him.

She learned to drive in Dallas traffic instead. That took some getting used to after the quiet of New Braunfels and Galveston, but she enjoyed the independence of being able to drive wherever she pleased in Gordon's old brown Pontiac. She hoarded her gasoline ration coupons carefully and talked Kate out of hers. When she had enough, she allowed herself day-long excursions to towns in central Texas. She liked the local museums in little towns like Waxahachie and Cleburne and the art and natural history museums of Dallas and Fort Worth. Each community had its own rodeo, and there were antique car shows, square dance festivals, country fairs, and quilting demonstrations. Kate went with her until Mark was born. Stella didn't go as much after that unless Jason would accompany her. Stella did not mention these trips in her letters to Gordon.

She wondered if she would lose this newly found freedom when Gordon returned, and she worried that when he came home he would wonder how she'd put all those miles on his car. She hoped he would assume she drove to New Braunfels, but actually, in order to save their precious gas coupons, she and Kate usually took the bus when they went to see their mother. When the uncles' mother—old, blind Mama Mary, who had rocked in the corner of Aunt Louise's kitchen for more than forty years—died in her sleep, Bill Chambers drove them to the funeral. One of the few times Stella did drive to New Braunfels, she lost a hubcap. It was impossible to buy a replacement; all metal went to the war effort. Stella fretted for days about whether to write to Gordon about it. How could he be angry? It was just one of those things. But she didn't mention it. Maybe by the time he came home, she would have found a replacement.

Gordon's letters often disturbed Stella. At times they did not seem to have been written by the same self-assured man she had married. He wrote of being thankful for her pregnancy during their time of separation. Stella wondered what he meant. And he wrote of his difficulty in dealing with her "past." While he respected her right to privacy, he felt she would be a happier woman and their marriage would be stronger if she confided in him. Why was he waiting until now to ask such things? Stella wondered. When they were together, nothing of the sort was ever discussed. She ignored the first such letter, but Gordon wrote repeatedly about it. "This is a festering sore between us. You need to excise the past and heal it."

Stella crumpled the letter and threw it against the wall.

That evening she sat staring at a blank page, trying to think how to deal with Gordon's request. The Andrews Sisters were singing "I'll Be Seeing You in All the Old Familiar Places" on the radio. Stella longed to scribble, "How dare you?" angrily across the page. He had no right to chastise her for something that had happened before they'd ever met. But her husband was alone and preparing for war. She could not possibly understand the torment he was going through.

She wrote:

> I love you and you only. Anything that happened to either one of us before we met has nothing to do with our marriage. I will not write of past history in a letter, but if—when you return from the war—you still feel the need to discuss the events of *both* our lives before we met, I will do so then. Please do not write to me of this matter again. Surely you have other thoughts of your loving wife than ugly ones. Can't you share some of these?
>
> I feel very well. The doctor estimates our baby will be born in less than a month. I regret we are not together at this special time in our lives.
>
> Keep the faith, my darling, in me, in yourself, in our marriage, and in God.

In this letter Stella did not put any of the trivial events of her daily life that usually filled her letters. The message of this letter would carry more weight if it stood alone.

In her next letter she would tell him about her telephone conversation with his father, about the afghan she was crocheting for the baby, about the broadcaster interviewing Effie on the radio about Texas Central Flight College.

Stella found that living alone had its compensations and was glad she had declined offers from both Effie and Kate to live with them while their husbands were gone. While still obsessively neat, she did not go overboard decorating her small apartment. She had stored many of Gordon's and her possessions at his father's house in Tyler, and the apartment's spartan feeling rather pleased her. The seascape hung over the sofa in the living room.

Stella planted a victory garden in her half of the backyard. She bought a cookbook full of recipes for wartime shortages. She sweetened recipes with honey. She used meat substitutes. She tried mixing her coffee with chicory or ground-up lentils and decided she would just drink less coffee. She made mock-hamburger patties with chopped vegetables and experimented with eggless cakes. She tried using margarine, carefully kneading in the accompanying yellow food coloring so it would look like butter, but it didn't taste like butter. She learned to eat her toast dry. Log Cabin syrup, when available, no longer came in those wonderful little tin cabins. She wished she'd saved one.

Stella envied Effie's involvement with Texas Central. Effie's life was so busy and vital. What she did was important to the war effort, and Anna and the aunts, along with cousin Hiram's wife, regularly took the bus to San Antonio to do volunteer work in the military hospital and in the soldiers' canteens. Many women were taking jobs for the first time in their lives—assembly-line jobs in a local factory—to take the place of the fighting men. Stella wished she could do something important for the war. Her life seemed so useless. She and Kate had to content themselves with buying stamps toward war bonds and dutifully straining and saving cooking grease, which was used in the manufacture of explosives, and saving scrap metal—mostly flattened tin cans from which steel could be reclaimed. She would have felt un-American throwing away a tin can.

Stella wondered what would happen after the war. Would the women all return to their homes? Effie claimed that was what she was going to do.

Kate supplemented her government allotment by typing term papers for SMU students and baby-sitting in her home three days a week for two-year-old twin girls whose mother had taken a factory job. As an officer's wife, Stella's allotment was sufficient for her simple needs. The income from their trust funds went unspent.

Stella walked and read a great deal. Religiously, she kept up with the war news, locating battles on the large world map she hung in her hallway. She renewed her old habit of reading far into the night. She ate simply and left the radio on all the time. She seldom went to church.

Like all women with a loved one at war, Kate, Effie, and Stella had acquired a terror of telegrams. Once the postman rang Kate's doorbell to collect on a postage-due letter. Kate saw a gray-haired man in a blue uniform and got hysterical. A bomb had fallen on Jimmy. He was dead.

The postman kept saying, "It's not a telegram. See, it's not a telegram."

Effie had more to fear than bombs. Pilots were the most vulnerable. When people learned her husband was a pilot, they looked solicitous. "Oh, you poor dear," they would say. The newsreels showed footage of only Japanese and German planes going down. Effie wondered if similar footage of American planes going down was being shown in Japanese and German theaters. While the audience cheered, Effie thought of William being trapped like that, of his burning aircraft plunging to the ground. She wondered how the German or Japanese wives were notified about the deaths of their husbands.

More than anything else, Effie wanted her William back safe and sound. Her love for him was strong and true. She missed him at her table and in her bed. Since that fall day in 1936 when she first met him at the Beta house, all she had ever wanted to be was William Chambers's wife. That was as true today as it was then. And when he first confessed in a letter that he had wanted to be a hero, but now all he wanted was to come home to her, Effie forgave him for so eagerly going off to war and leaving her behind. As she read his letters so full of love and yearning and disenchantment, she knew William would come home hers more than ever.

But if William did not return, she would grieve sincerely and then get on with her life. For Effie, doing otherwise would have seemed immoral. Life was to live, to enjoy. But oh, how she wanted her William back to enjoy it with! She stopped listening to radio music when she was alone. It wasn't so bad when she was with Stella and Kate, but when she was alone, every song made her think of William and made her realize how much she missed him. She would lose her train of thought and waste time feeling sad and lonely. Sometimes at night the missing got so bad she had to cry in her pillow, and Effie didn't like to cry.

Stella knew that while chaplains were safer than frontline troops, they had no special immunity to mortars or land mines or bombs. But except for momentary fear that clutched her when the doorbell rang unexpectedly, Stella believed that Gordon would return to her. Perhaps it was irrational, but now it almost seemed that their life together had been preordained.

Eighteen

Frances Anna Kendall arrived on May 13, 1943. Before going to the hospital, Stella, with her sister and cousin, heard on the radio that the last of the Axis forces in Africa had surrendered. The North African campaign had been won, but the price in lives had been unbelievable. And in the South Pacific the tide at last seemed to be turning. In March the Allies had defeated a Japanese naval force in the Bismarck Sea off the coast of New Guinea.

"Maybe this means we're on the downhill stretch of this damned war," Effie said. "I'm ready to get William home. It seems they send the *Enterprise* into every battle that comes along."

"Don't count on it," Kate offered. "I think it's only the first step up the mountain. Now the other fronts will just get more concentrated. Jimmy writes that the bombing in London is unbelievable. Are you having another pain, Stella? I think it's time we go. Effie will get Mama at the bus station, and they can meet us at the hospital."

Effie was more slender now than she had ever been. She still had on the tailored suit she had worn to a business appointment. Her blond hair was in a chignon. She looked smart and self-assured.

Kate, however, had never lost the weight she had gained during her pregnancy. Her red hair was cropped sensibly short, and her face was void of makeup. Stella had never seen her sister looking less attractive. Kate had changed. She seldom mentioned golf. All she talked about was her baby and motherhood, and she loved her Mark with the same fierceness she had once invested in athletics. But her golf clubs still leaned against the wall in the corner of her bedroom. And her trophies, along with Jimmy's, were carefully shined and displayed on the bookshelf, first in the living room of her apartment and then in the small two-story house that she had rented before Billy was born.

All the restless energy she did not channel into Mark she had spent "fixing up" the house. Kate haunted used-furniture stores for pieces to refinish. She put up chintz curtains, braided an oval rug for the dining room. She painted and papered and was constantly planning her next project. "Old Jimmy's really going to be surprised," Kate commented as she showed off her latest triumph—Jimmy's favorite easy chair reupholstered in a soft gray-and-yellow plaid. Stella knew he would indeed be surprised. The woman Jimmy had married was not this domestic. She played basketball, golf, tennis and ran in races. Stella wondered what Jimmy would really think. But then what man would not like a lovely home and a well-tended son?

On the way to the hospital, Stella asked Kate, "Do you think you'll have another baby?"

"Hope so. Nine months after old Jimmy boy gets back would suit me just fine."

"But your delivery was such an ordeal. Don't you dread going through that again?"

"I suppose. Yeah, it was awful. But honestly, Stella, I remember how I acted so I know it must have hurt a lot, but I don't remember the pain itself. Isn't that funny? I guess it's a good thing, or no one would ever have a second kid."

"But if you keep having children, when will you do anything for yourself?" Stella asked, wondering how much her words would apply to her own life.

"Yeah," Kate said. "I think about that a lot. But motherhood is so seductive. No one has ever needed or loved me like Mark. I feel like I'm a snowball on a downhill roll. Maybe there's no going back. Maybe I'm destined to raise athletes rather than be one." Stella gasped. "Another pain?" Kate asked. "Well, hang on, kid. The hospital's just around the corner."

Nothing in Stella's past experience—not even witnessing her sister's torment—prepared her for the agony of labor. It was an endless nightmare of humiliation and bone-grinding pain.

She could not think past the pain she was enduring. *Please God, make it end.* But the medication she had been given made her sleep between the pains, robbing her of any sensation of time. Her mother would tell her that she had slept two minutes, but all that accomplished was making the pains seem virtually continuous to Stella.

The pains became something to live through, not something that would produce a baby. Her body was being torn apart from within. If someone had offered to make the pregnancy vanish, she would have accepted instantly. Anything to end it.

Stella grabbed at her mother's bony hand and screamed. *I can't believe I'm screaming. This is a hospital. I'm probably disturbing sick people.* But the screaming came. She could no more stop it than the pains.

Anna bathed her forehead with a cool cloth. The drugged sleep took her once again.

But then, immediately, a new pain exploded inside of her.

She grabbed for her mama's hand.

No more babies. I'll never have another baby. Gordon should be here, damn him. He'll never understand how awful this has been. I'd die before I'd let him make me pregnant again. I hate him for not being here.

Her last thought as the anesthetist finally put the mask over her face and brought her blessed oblivion was how much she hated her husband.

When a nurse placed a clean, beautiful baby in her arms, it was hard to relate the tiny infant to the agony of the night before.

Her daughter.

And then Stella understood that the pain had been worth it. Already its memory was receding. Stella felt smug and special—a mother. She was a miracle, this baby girl with perfect hands and feet, with features that already attracted the attention of admiring nurses.

She wrote Gordon triumphantly:

> A girl! You're the father of the most beautiful little girl ever born in the state of Texas. She loves you already and promises to be a real daddy's girl when you get home to us.
>
> She weighed in at seven pounds even and is nineteen inches long. Her hair is dark now, and her eyes deep blue— but that could change. She has her daddy's brow line and her mother's mouth.
>
> I had no idea giving birth was so full of pain. It was very difficult for me, but I suppose no more difficult than women have always endured and always will. And as soon as our daughter was in my arms, I knew the pain was unimportant when measured against the gift.
>
> I kiss our child for you. Stay safe for us.

When Effie, Kate, or her mother wheeled Stella down the hall to the nursery viewing window, it took only a few visits for her to realize just how many visitors singled Frances out. "Look at that beautiful baby!" they would say, pointing through the glass. "A little girl. Isn't she lovely?" "Beautiful" and "lovely" when other babies were "cute" and "sweet." Stella stared at her baby and wondered if "cute" wouldn't be better.

Stella read in the paper on July eleventh that the Thunderbirds had landed in Sicily the day before. Gordon's war had begun.

She stood in front of her map and stared at Sicily. The football at the toe of the boot. A name out of a geography book. Mountains and Mafia. And now her husband.

Stella threw herself into motherhood with the same enthusiasm with which she had decorated the parsonage in Galveston. Her life revolved around the sleeping and feeding schedule of her baby. Frances was healthy as well as beautiful. Stella was enchanted with the child she had borne, if a little in awe of her. She photographed Frances almost weekly for the benefit of the baby's absent father, and she would sometimes have Effie or Kate photograph mother and daughter together.

Gordon's letters continued to disturb Stella. After almost four months of continuous fighting in Sicily, the Forty-fifth had landed at Anzio and was now battling their way up Italy's boot to Rome. His letters were sometimes written from behind frontlines where he went to visit the troops.

> The mortar shells are exploding less than a mile from here. I gave Communion this morning to a boy from Hunter—says he knew your dad. I'm going to rotate back through the staging area next week so they can bring a Catholic chaplain up for a while.
>
> The pictures of you and the baby are wonderful. Seeing you slim again fills me with desire. I so wish that I were there to love you and keep you from temptation.

Stella stared at the letter's closing words. Being slim again made her want her husband to be desirous. More than ever before in her life, she was aware of her sexual self. Frequently she thought about sex during the day. She fantasized each night how it would be when Gordon came home and made love to her. They would be more passionate after their long separation, more creative. She would have orgasms, again and again.

But the phrase "keep you from temptation" made her angry. With righteous indignation, she wrote and told him so.

> You have no right to cast innuendos. I too am full of desire, but only for you. And I resent your thinking otherwise. Do you honestly think I'm lusting after other men while my husband is off at war, while I nurse our baby at my breast?
>
> More and more, I read about the brave soldiers of the Thunderbird Division. I know that bravery comes at a terrible price and that your days and nights are filled with more fear and death and sorrow than I can possibly imagine. On the surface, life for us back home seems strangely normal. Our cities are intact. We have shortages, but we don't go hungry. But please know that in our minds and hearts is a constant prayer for our men at war. And you, my darling, are with me every minute of every day. Your doubting makes me sad.

Gordon pulled back the tent flap and entered the station hospital. It was near the town of Capua, in the mountains northeast of Naples.

"Oh, God, am I glad to see a chaplain," a fatigues-clad nurse said by way of greeting. Gordon wondered absently if the woman was pretty. In her present haggard state it was hard to tell.

"We've got a Catholic boy dying over there behind the curtain. He's been asking for a priest. And there's a new amputee in six and an attempted suicide in eleven."

Gordon automatically turned and walked toward the corner where a curtain was hung to allow for privacy in dying.

He smelled the putridness before he pulled back the curtain. His stomach did an involuntary spasm, and the taste of bile rose in his mouth. He swallowed hard, willed his stomach to calmness, and stepped inside.

What greeted Gordon behind the curtain was grotesque. Burns. The worst death. It came slower to burn victims. They lingered, conscious, while their fluids drained from their skinless bodies, while bacteria attacked the exposed flesh and turned it into cesspools of pus.

The boy was almost totally wrapped in gauze and covered with a yellow ointment that smelled of sulfur. But overriding the sulfuric smell was the disgustingly sweet smell of the thick green pus oozing through the gauze. The sulfuric antibiotic ointment had been ineffective in curtailing the infection. With burns this bad, it always was.

The smell drove Gordon back from the bed. He took a deep breath to control his nausea and offered a "my son" to the dying boy. The boy's eyes were swollen shut. One cheek was covered with a thick gauze pad.

"I'm not a priest," Gordon explained, "but I am a chaplain. Do you know Father Gonzales?"

The soldier whispered yes with dry, cracked lips.

"I'm putting a crucifix blessed by Father Gonzales in your hands. And I will tell him that I have been here with you, and he will say the rites. I'm sorry, son, but this is the best we can do. If they are willing, I have Father Gonzales's permission to give Catholic soldiers Communion. Do you want Communion?"

The boy kissed the cross and nodded. "Yes," he said in his barely audible voice.

Gordon opened his case containing his bedside Communion set and other religious paraphernalia and took out one of two pint flasks of wine. "The wine and wafers have been consecrated by Father Gonzales," he said as he poured some wine into the small silver chalice. Actually he couldn't remember which flask contained the consecrated wine. He might have used it for those Lutheran boys yesterday. The Lutherans were very particular. Not all of them would take Communion from a Methodist, but these lads had been willing. They wanted him to sign their Communion card. Foolishness. A Communion card in a war. Like little Sunday school boys needing proof they'd been good.

Gordon dipped a wafer into the wine and put it in the dying boy's mouth. "Eat and drink this in remembrance of Me," he said.

The boy was lucid. He said his confession in a gasping voice. Every time one of his buddies got shot he had been glad it was them and not him. Their wounds, their dying made him feel guilty. Was that why this had happened to him?

"I beat up a girl once," he said, pausing between every two or three words to gasp for breath. "I thought she was my girl, and then I found out she was going out with another guy. I waited for her down the street from her house and beat her up."

There were other sins. But the boy—Frank from Indiana—kept coming back to the girl he beat up. In spite of his increasingly labored breathing, he talked on. He did not confess killing any Germans. Maybe he hadn't. Maybe it wasn't a sin.

Gordon said the words of comfort, trying to be the priest the dying boy needed. Other times he became a surrogate rabbi, handing out little capsules called mezuzahs that contained a tiny scroll inscribed with Biblical passages in Hebrew. And Gordon baptized soldiers any way they wanted it—immersion or sprinkling. He said the words they wanted to hear. Some of the chaplains were purists, but not Gordon. No longer. The carefully drawn denomination lines with which he had been raised did not exist for him here. And if those lines didn't exist, perhaps the whole idea of religion was false. He wondered about that a lot. What would happen if rites of extreme unction were never performed for a Catholic? What about the Jewish kid from Colorado he had watched die? Did that boy sink immediately into hell because he didn't believe Christ was his savior? And what about the ones with no religion at all? Gordon wasn't sure about heaven, but any residual feeling he had left for hell had vanished. Hell was here. What other punishment could God dream up for this boy on the bed?

Gordon continued to go through all the motions. It brought comfort to those who had none. It was not the time to rethink theology, he kept telling himself. He was not himself.

The death and destruction overwhelmed him. He dreaded writing letters of condolence home to parents and wives. The letters sounded so insincere. Assurances that death meant something when he didn't really believe it. The patriotic words flowed better. He was having trouble with God, but he did believe in the war. Hitler had to be stopped. America and democracy were worth saving. Gordon loved America and her sons, and he would do for them what he could. And that meant going through the motions. Bringing comfort. Easing the comings and goings.

So he preached his announced services at encampments and his impromptu sermons in the field. Boys knelt in the mud to receive his blessings, as if he had them to give. Gordon was just as afraid as they were. He had always known he was a coward. The reason he'd joined the Army was that he had been more afraid of being criticized for not going than he had been of going. Ministers were exempt from the draft, but he hadn't had the courage to stay out of it.

The boy on the bed lifted a gauzed-wrapped hand and placed it on

Gordon's arm. Gordon immediately recoiled. "You won't leave me?" Frank asked.

"No. I'll be here," Gordon promised.

"When you write my parents, don't tell 'em it was like this. Okay?" Gordon agreed.

"They live at 2090 Kent Road in Evansville, Indiana. Mr. and Mrs. Paul Murphy." Gordon fished in his pocket for his notebook. He repeated the name and address.

"Yeah," the boy said between gasps. "Write them, please. Tell them I love them. That I wish I could go home. Oh, God! I want to go home! I don't want to die! Please, God, I don't want to die!"

His breathing was reduced to shallow flutters. He didn't try to talk anymore. Gordon waited. He desperately wanted to leave. But he had promised, and a man should not have to die alone.

Gradually the fluttering breaths were replaced by deep gasps that got further and further apart. Then after a long pause, the fluttering breaths started again. The cycle repeated itself maybe a dozen times. Then came the pause, only this time Gordon realized it was over. He watched the body relax, give up. The boy's parchment lips fell back from his teeth. The look of final surrender. Death. How many times had he been its unwilling witness! And each time Gordon had to fight down the feeling of relief that it was over. He was glad this boy had been selected for a ghastly death and not himself. Gordon shared the boy's same terrible sin.

"Well, thank God, that's over," the nurse said from behind Gordon. "Or maybe I should say damn the Old Buzzard to hell for letting shit like this go on."

Gordon stared at the nurse. How did she dare such blasphemy?

He decided she was pretty. He looked at the back of her neck as she bent over the dead boy, checking for a pulse—how could she stand to touch him? Her neck was very white. Wisps of brown hair escaped from a random arrangement of bobby pins. The wisps floated softly over that smooth white skin. Gordon's hand lifted a few inches from his side, wanting so much to touch the smooth skin of a woman.

There was a tiny mole just above her collar. He wanted to put his lips on that mole.

Oh, God, Gordon thought, what had he come to, standing here with his silver crosses on his collar, lusting after a woman in the presence of hideous death!

Only seconds earlier he could not wait to escape from this stifling corner with its piteous, sticking remains. Now he was rooted to the wooden flooring. His penis stirred painfully inside his olive-drab undershorts.

The nurse unhooked the IVs. She had lingered for a moment, touching the unburned left cheek. Her hands were red and raw. Her fingernails clipped short. No rings. Her wrists were dainty. Gordon knew his fingers could circle them easily. At his side, his forefinger and thumb formed a circle. She pulled a sheet up over the already putrid corpse and turned to face Gordon. Her eyes were damp, the tip of her nose red. How extraordinary that she still could do that. Gordon used to cry. Maybe she hadn't been here long enough not to cry.

The nurse started to speak, but something in his face stopped her words. She looked at him for a long moment, then quite deliberately her eyes traveled to his swollen crotch.

"Oh, brother," she said and threw back the curtains. "I need two orderlies and a stretcher back here," she called to a nurse in the front of the tent.

Gordon looked down at the small circle of telltale wetness on the front of his uniform trousers. He walked briskly from the tent, carrying his case of religious paraphernalia awkwardly in front of him.

It was in June 1944 that Stella saw Charles Lasseter again, there in the tearoom at Neiman-Marcus.

The next morning Stella was still in bed when the phone rang. She was neither asleep nor awake, but rather suspended, waiting. When the phone rang, she didn't even jump. The ringing woke Francie. Stella lifted her year-old daughter from her crib before hurrying into the hall to answer the phone.

"Stella?"

It was Charles. Of course.

Francie fussed to be put down. Stella let her child slide to the floor. "Yes," she said.

"This is Charles Lasseter."

"I know."

"I have to go back tomorrow. I'd like to see you. Could we have lunch?"

Francie clung to Stella's nightgown, whining. Her diaper was wet.

She wanted to be fed. Stella reached around the corner and pulled a box of crackers from the kitchen cupboard. One wasn't enough. Francie fussed until offered a second, then she sat on the floor at Stella's bare feet with a cracker in each hand.

The receiver was wet in Stella's palm.

"Stella?"

"Where?"

Stella went by Effie's to borrow her navy suit with the red piping. Effie was still in Houston. Stella hugged Billy absently, then explained to the housekeeper what she wanted.

When she dropped Francie at Kate's house, Kate—still in her bathrobe, holding eighteen-month-old Mark against her hip—gave her a questioning look. "My, you look nice."

"I should be back by midafternoon," Stella said, because she had to say something.

"Are you going to meet that man we saw yesterday at Neiman's?"

"He's an old friend."

"Yeah? Will his wife be with him today?"

"I don't know," Stella said. "Maybe not."

"I think you know not. Don't go, Stella. You're asking for trouble."

"No, I'm not, Kate. Trust me."

Stella arrived at the Adolphus first. She was already seated in the dining room when Charles arrived. She watched his face change when he caught sight of her.

He was in uniform. He carried his hat in his left hand. His right arm hung in its sling. He wore the castle insignia of the Corps of Engineers on his lapels. Stella hadn't noticed that yesterday. He took her hand.

"Hello, Stella."

"Charles."

"You're even more beautiful than before. But I knew you'd be. I knew if I ever saw you again you'd be more beautiful."

Stella didn't know how to respond so she didn't.

He accepted a menu from the waiter but didn't open it. Instead he continued to look at her.

"I've never stopped thinking about you," he said. "Are you happy?"

"Happy? I worry about my husband, but other than that I suppose so. I like being a mother. Sometimes I long to be back on a college campus, but that's not the real world."

"And what is the real world?"

"For me—my husband, my baby, my kitchen, my garden. And you— what is your real world?"

"I have several. The war. It's pretty damned real, although it tends to recede a bit while I'm back here in Dallas. And there's my profession and my family. And there's you."

"Me? How can I be part of your life?"

"Perhaps because you have come to represent . . ." He stopped and held out his hand. Stella paused, then slowly put her hand in his. "For me," he continued, "you're all those vague longings, all those might- have-beens, all those if-onlys that I suspect everyone has—" He broke off, as the waiter hovered. Were they ready to order?

Flustered, Stella withdrew her hand and opened the menu. She had forgotten they were supposed to eat. The words on the menu swam around in front of her.

Stella closed the menu. "Please, just order me something light. Soup and a salad would be fine."

When the waiter had departed, Stella asked, "Could we just do small talk now and save the serious stuff for later? I'm awfully nervous."

He smiled. "Sure. Tell me about your child. A daughter?"

Francie was intimidating even as a baby, she explained. Sometimes Stella wished her daughter were sweet instead of beautiful. She showed him a photograph of her enchanting child with incredibly long lashes around large eyes that stared boldly at the camera.

Charles's boy wasn't normal. Down's syndrome. They were afraid to have other children. "In a way I think I love Andy more because he's like he is. He needs us so. And he loves so absolutely. Marisa is great with him. Really incredible. I can't tell you how I admire her."

Stella told him about Kate and Effie. Her sister, who at one time had wanted to be the next Babe Didrikson, was getting fat. Her cousin Effie was incredibly busy running her husband's business, but in spite of this was still the most contented person Stella had ever known.

Charles wanted to design hospitals and schools. He didn't want to do any more houses for rich people or pretentious office buildings, but he knew he would.

"What about graduate school?" Charles asked. "When are you going to earn a Ph.D. and teach?"

Stella shrugged. "I'd still like to."

"Does your husband want you to?"

"I don't know," Stella said. "We've never really discussed it."

Charles was silent. He stared down at his plate.

Finally, over coffee, Charles said the words that had been hanging there, waiting to be spoken.

"I know I have no right to ask, but do you think we might see each other after the war?"

"Since I'm no longer a virgin," Stella challenged. At last she'd had her moment of vindication. But it was not as she'd thought it would be. She almost wished she hadn't said the words.

"I guess I deserved that," he said. "Part of me has been sorry about that ever since. But I was right. It was the most right thing I've ever done. If you hadn't come today, I promised myself I'd never try to see you again, but you came. I think we could have something together, Stella—something that has nothing to do with your husband or my wife. We could have a small corner of our lives just for us. I want that very much."

Stella glazed into the eloquent brown eyes of Charles Lasseter and wanted to say yes. She wouldn't even have to say anything. Just a nod of her head would do.

"I don't think it works that way," Stella said slowly, her voice low. "I guess I came here today because I still have feelings for you. I probably always will. But I don't think either one of us could live with the kind of deceit you're talking about. I think I finally understand the dilemma you faced that horrible night when I tried to get you to make love to me. Now I too have a marriage and a family I'm committed to. Our time has passed. No, that's not right. There never was a time for us, Charles."

She was glad she had said her piece before he took her hand again. She could not have said it if he had been touching her.

"I'll call you after the war," he said.

"No," she said, staring down at his hand. His right hand. The wedding band was on the other one.

She felt his gaze on her downturned face. She lifted her chin and looked back. He nodded. He would not call her.

"I need to sit here awhile longer," she said. "You go first."

He brought her hands to his lips. Tears burned in Stella's eyes.

"Go," she said. "Please."

She watched him wind his way through the tables. He looked back over his shoulder at her one last time.

Stella lifted her chin slightly in acknowledgment. Then he was gone.

After a while she placed her crumpled napkin on the table and left. When she walked out onto Commerce Street, she stood there blinking at the bright sunshine and trying to remember where she was supposed to go now. The car in the lot. Then pick up Francie at Kate's.

She had done the right thing. Of that she had no doubt. Why was there no joy in it? Or even a sense of righteousness? Why was there only heaviness in her heart?

Charles walked aimlessly up and down the streets of downtown Dallas. What was love all about? Why couldn't people love the person they were with or be with the person they loved? And why was love so damned important to him? Other men seemed to do just fine with wars or ambition.

But he loved Marisa, Charles reminded himself. What he felt for Stella was different. *The vague longings, the might-have-beens, the if-onlys.* If he died this minute, he would want it to be in Stella's arms.

He stopped and leaned against the side of a building. God, he was weary.

"Hey, mister, are you okay?"

A teenaged boy was looking at him with concern.

"Sure, son. I'm just a little tired."

"War injury?" the boy asked, staring at the sling.

"Just a small one," Gordon said. He looked around. He was lost. The boy was still looking at him.

"Would you mind finding me a cab?" Charles asked. "I need to get home."

The boy raced off to help a serviceman. When he returned, he wouldn't take Charles's offered dollar.

In the cab Charles leaned back and closed his eyes.

Aunt Blanche had told him he would have a different sort of marriage if he married Stella Behrman. Charles had thought at the time she was speaking out of concern for his happiness. Later, he wondered if it weren't Stella she was thinking about. Blanche thought Stella could continue her studies if she married Charles.

Because he had not married her, Stella was locked in a traditional marriage. She'd never even told her husband what *she* wanted out of life. Charles felt ill.

Marisa didn't want to go to graduate school. But then life had presented her with a cause that she embraced with open arms—Andy and the education of the mentally handicapped.

Charles asked her that night—just to make sure.

"Would you like to go to graduate school?"

"Charles, you've asked me that before! Do you think I seem uneducated?"

"Of course not. I just don't want ever to stand in your way."

"My way of what?"

Nineteen

Jimmy had never enjoyed his fellow man more than during his years in London. War, he decided, brought out the best in people—and in life. Even as he was living them, he knew his war years would be the best years of his life. War was better than golf.

Yet how could that be—with the horror of the Blitz an almost nightly occurrence, with lives routinely being lost and ruined, with families returning home after the bombings to discover they had no home, with each day having the distinct possibility of being one's last?

But along with the horror and the fear, there were the good times. Oh, such good times.

There were nights in the pubs—Jimmy's favorite was near Edward Square. He enjoyed the NCO club he managed, but he liked the pubs best. To the pubs came American soldiers and sailors and marines. There was the British military. And Canadian, Indian, South African, even a few Russians. There were the British civilians—old men and women. Most of the children had been sent out to the countryside. It was an unnatural mixture of adult humanity that came together in wartime London, but out of it a camaraderie flourished. Maybe there would be no tomorrow, but there was tonight with singing and talk, with dry sandwiches of hard bread and even harder cheese washed down with dark ale, with laughter and melancholia. People who before the war would have not rubbed shoulders at a bar did so now. In the pubs, class and ethnic lines dimmed. There were stories to be told. Every man was Jimmy's friend. Every woman was his darling. Every day a gift. Every night a joy.

Jimmy bought a harmonica, renewed his boyhood skills, and became an accompanist for the barroom singing. And in the bomb shelters he would pull the harmonica from his pocket and play, sometimes in total darkness. "Danny Boy." "I'll Take You Home Again, Kathleen." "Dixie." "Billy Boy." "Basin Street." "The Eyes of Texas." His high school alma mater. Anything—all strung together in a continuous medley to his unseen audience. No one ever clapped, but no one ever asked him to stop.

Maybe it was the living of life on the brink that enhanced its flavor. Each experience, each sensation was felt more acutely. He'd never bothered much with sunsets before, but now they spoke to Jimmy with eloquence. The greasy diesel smell of London streets and the accented voices of its people gave him a heightened sense of place—along with the ancient buildings, the historic Thames with its wonderful bridges. The Tower. Buckingham Palace. Kensington Gardens. Piccadilly Circus. Fish and chips wrapped in newspaper. Feisty pigeons sitting on your head in Trafalgar Square. Sassy cockney barmaids. And at night total darkness—a great city under complete blackout. It wasn't Texas.

The sounds of the air-raid siren filled him with electricity. He was afraid, but even the fear was exciting. Never had Jimmy felt so alive and in touch with his own feelings. He missed his parents more than his wife. He missed golf not at all. Maybe he'd feel different if he'd been injured or even had a close call—if he'd had one of those life-passing-in-front-of-your-eyes moments, if he'd seen death looking at *him*. But while death was often very close, it had never stared at him personally. And maybe he'd feel different if he had to kill, but Jimmy ran a club. He didn't even have a weapon. Even before he met Linda, he sometimes guiltily wished the war could go on forever.

He met Linda while taking shelter in a subway during an air raid only a few months after he came to London. At first she offered only one-word answers to his inquiries. Her tone said to leave her alone, but as the hours wore on, they talked.

She was from East Looe. In Cornwall, by the sea. Yes, there was a West Looe. At his probing her disembodied voice described for him the white houses and cobblestone streets, the rock walls lining the lanes, the harbor, her father's pharmacy, her mother's kitchen.

Jimmy told her about Texas bluebonnets in spring and the state's oil well forests. He told her about summer trips to Padre Island and American hamburgers—with mustard, onions, and pickles, the only true way. He explained the difference between American football and British soccer.

They agreed that FDR and Churchill were the greatest men alive today. Mark Twain was wonderful. And Nat King Cole.

Occasionally the lights came dimly on for a time, and he could see that she was young and blond as Kate's cousing Effie and that she was pregnant. He found her pregnant state oddly disappointing, although he wasn't sure why. He wasn't looking for a wartime sweetie. But he had liked her soft voice.

When, finally, the all-clear sounded and feet began shuffling toward the stairs and the blacked-out streets beyond, Jimmy extended his hand to her. "Well, good luck to you now." He indicated the suitcase on which she had been sitting. "Going home to East Looe? It would be safer there."

The woman offered no comment.

Jimmy watched her pick up her battered suitcase and start up the stairs. Let her go, he told himself. He had no need of pregnant women.

But he followed her. It was starting to rain. She had no umbrella. She turned first to the right, then hesitated and started across the deserted, dark street. Jimmy fell into step beside her.

"You don't have anyplace to go, do you?"

She said nothing and kept walking.

"Look, I've got a room not far from here—with a hot plate. I can offer you a cup of tea and some biscuits. I don't imagine there'll be any more trains tonight for Cornwall."

She slowed and turned. "A cup of tea?"

Jimmy took her arm. She was a skinny little thing. "Come on, dearie. I suspect you're dead on your feet and haven't eaten for God knows how long. My name's James but everyone calls me Jimmy."

"I'm Linda," she said, allowing herself to be led along.

Jimmy closed the blackout curtains covering his room's one window before turning on the lamp. He turned to look at his visitor. She had great, dark circles under her eyes. Hazel eyes, mostly green—like Kate's. The woman's pale hair had no sheen and was in need of washing. Her neck and arms were scrawny. Her pregnant belly looked like it must surely be strapped on to her otherwise-wasted body. She wore no wedding band.

She stood in the middle of his room. Jimmy hastily cleared the pile of clothes from the room's one chair and tossed them into a corner.

Linda tried to be delicate about the biscuits, breaking off small bites at a time, but Jimmy could see that she was very hungry. Her hands shook as she carried each bit to her mouth, and her eyes closed as she chewed. He wished he had something else to offer her. She held his one mug with both hands like a child and drank the tea. He poured her a second cup.

When she finished, she rose to her feet and picked up her suitcase. "I thank you for your hospitality," she said formally.

"And where might you be going?" Jimmy asked, thinking how British he was starting to sound. Texas seemed so far away.

"Someplace," she said.

"You can stay here tonight. I'll treat you to a train ticket to East Looe tomorrow."

"But I don't know you."

"Linda, my wife is also pregnant—with our first child. I'd hate to think of Kate out on the streets on a rainy night with no place to go. Let me help you. If it makes you uncomfortable for me to be here, I'll go bunk with a buddy."

Linda stepped backwards and tried to sink back into the chair, but she missed. Before Jimmy could grab her, she fell onto the floor, knocking the chair on its side.

She made no effort to get up but started to cry soundlessly, her skinny shoulders shaking.

Gently, Jimmy pulled her to her feet and led her to the bed. He swept a pile of magazines and newspapers to the floor and waited for the girl to lie down. She stood looking down at the bed, indecision written on her face. Gently, Jimmy pushed her to the bed. "I'm sorry about the sheets," he said. "They're not very clean."

He took her shoes from her feet. The holes in the soles had been covered with cardboard inserts. Her stockings were neatly darned but soiled. She drew her legs up and tried to hide her feet under her skirt.

"Your old man run out on you?" Jimmy asked.

"I never had an old man," she said defiantly. "It was just some boy in a uniform. Soon as I started showing, the tailor I worked for fired me. His wife said it wasn't proper. And yesterday my landlady gave me the boot 'cause I couldn't pay my rent."

"Why don't you try to get some sleep? We'll see about getting you back to your mom and dad tomorrow."

"You're very nice," Linda said. "I think your Kate's a lucky lady, and you don't need to leave. I'll scoot over to one side. I really don't think you're of a mind to ravish me. And if you did, I'd probably sleep right through it."

Jimmy pulled the covers back for Linda. He stretched out on top of the spread. They both slept in their clothes.

Linda looked even worse in the morning light. Jimmy suspected she was anemic. No one had skin that pale. Even her lips were colorless. He fixed her more tea and went down to the NCO club to pilfer some bacon and an egg or two. And some bread and cheese for her to eat on the train.

After he had fed her a hearty breakfast, he said, "Now, about West Looe."

"East," Linda corrected.

"Now, about East Looe, shall we go see about getting you back there?"

Linda shook her head no. "I can't," she said. Her voice was so soft Jimmy leaned his head close to hear her.

"I can't face going back to Cornwall. My pop's a deacon. My mum's big on respectability. My sister's properly married. I would disgrace them."

"But they wouldn't want you here alone like this—pregnant. I think you should at least give them a chance," Jimmy said. Jesus, he thought, if she didn't go home, what the hell was he supposed to do with her?

Linda stayed on in Jimmy's room for a week, sleeping with her back to him on the lumpy mattress of his brass bed, fixing him tea on his hot plate and gratefully accepting the food he brought her. She folded all his clothes and put them on the shelves. She changed the sheets on his bed and swept things out a bit. It was nice to have the room clean for a change.

In the evening Jimmy would sit with her while she ate, then comb his hair and head out for his evening at the pub or go back to the club if there was a USO show or other special event.

At week's end his landlady told him the girl had to leave.

Jimmy bought Linda borrowed respectability in the form of a gold-plated ring and moved her out of London to a village south of Gloucester, far enough away so she would be safe from the bombing. He found her a room with a retired bricklayer and his wife—Mr. and Mrs. Wiggins, who assumed without asking that Linda was his wife—as did the local doctor who examined Linda and ordered Jimmy to fatten her up. He predicted the baby would come in six weeks.

The bricklayer's wife promised to look after her. Jimmy kissed Linda on the cheek and headed back to London, glad to have solved his problem. He had missed his privacy.

But when the late-night radiogram came informing him that he was the father of a baby boy named Mark, he wished Linda were still there to share his pleasure with him. If he had someone to tell, it would seem more real. He sat alone for a long time, thinking what it meant to have a little boy named Mark. On an impulse, he knelt by the bed and folded his hands. He hadn't said a formal prayer in a long time, but it felt good to say the Lord's Prayer and offer thanks to the God of his childhood for his baby's safe arrival.

He went to see Linda two weeks later, taking a box full of food from the club—a leg of lamb, sugar, flour, cans of green beans. Mrs. Wiggins was beside herself over all that food. Linda looked better. Her hair wasn't quite so dank, and a touch of rouge added color to her cheeks. Jimmy spent the afternoon. He and Linda went walking in the town. "My wife had a baby," he told her. "A boy."

"Oh, Jimmy, that's so lovely." She grabbed his hand and kissed it. Jimmy was startled when tears sprang to the corners of his eyes.

That evening they sat down to a really fine roast lamb dinner.

When he returned next, Linda had a tiny infant at her side. Jimmy realized the beaming Mrs. Wiggins was waiting for a proper response from the new father.

Jimmy picked up the alarmingly tiny creature and did his best to coo a bit. It was a boy. Edwin.

When the baby was a month old, Linda took a position as the chemist's assistant at the local pharmacy, leaving her baby with Mrs. Wiggins, who was delighted to have an infant to rock on her spare lap. The Wigginses' only daughter and her two children lived in Australia. They hadn't seen them since 1939.

Linda would come home at noon to nurse little Eddie. In the evening she would sit on the rocking chair in the corner of the kitchen and nurse her child while Mrs. Wiggins fixed supper and Mr. Wiggins read his paper. It was nice.

Jimmy did not come again until the baby was almost two months old. "Your hair's starting to shine," he told Linda. And she wasn't as skinny as he'd thought she'd be, but he didn't tell her that.

She looked up at him and smiled. Her eyes shone too.

Mrs. Wiggins fixed them a picnic lunch and shooed them out of the house. In Jimmy's borrowed jeep, they drove out into the countryside. It was a lovely day, with high fluffy clouds and gentle breezes to tease the soft curls about Linda's face. The sunlight warmed them. The birds and flowers didn't know there was a war.

Linda seemed more shy than before. She'd blush when she looked

Judith Henry Wall

at him. "I've been thinking about you lots," she finally told him. "You're a nice man. I owe you a great deal."

"You don't owe me anything," Jimmy said. He touched her hand.

Linda's voice was soft. "I know you'll go home after the war."

"You don't owe me anything," Jimmy repeated. "I won't come back here if you think that."

She nodded. "I think I'd like for you to kiss me now."

They made love at twilight, Jimmy's jacket spread on the grass in a small grove near a country churchyard. Her body was slight, so different from Kate's, childlike. Their lovemaking was not passionate—just sweet. Very, very sweet. Jimmy was overwhelmed with the need to be gentle and kind to her. Poor kid. She felt so vulnerable there underneath him. Her breath was warm against his neck. Her sighs were so soft, so real. For an instant Jimmy forgot her name. Then he said it out loud. "Linda." Over and over again, he said it as he came inside of her.

Back at the Wigginses', Jimmy stayed the night, waiting until she fed her baby and tucked him away in his crib, then loving her again. Again her sighs were soft against his ear. He tried to remember—did Kate sigh like that? The feel of Linda's arms and legs about his body was firm and natural and good. In spite of the difference in their size, they fit together really fine. She was dainty and feminine. It made him feel all the more manly. He could feel her changing, tensing, then going limp about him. The sighs became moans. "Come in me, Jimmy. Please." He felt like he was exploding.

When he woke up the next morning, the baby was between them. Linda was asleep. The baby looked at Jimmy with solemn brown eyes. Jimmy wondered about his father—a man with brown eyes. "Hi there, partner," he whispered, and gave Eddie a finger to grasp.

Jimmy came almost every weekend after that. In the evenings Linda would go with him to the local pub and laugh and sing with him. Soon the townfolk knew him by name and called out requests for him to play on his harmonica. Linda had a lovely low voice. Everyone stopped to listen when she sang "When the Lights Go on Again All Over the World." Her notes were true and pure. When the pub closed at eleven o'clock, Jimmy and Linda—feeling slightly and pleasantly drunk—would walk home arm in arm talking in low whispers along the sleeping, dark streets, teasing each other with images of the lovemaking that was to come. The nursing of her baby was a part of their nighttime ritual. Jimmy found the sight quite tender and moving, but at the same time arousing. When he too licked and nursed at her breasts, Linda moaned her approval.

By this time, the Wigginses had learned that Linda and Jimmy were not married, that Eddie was the son of an anonymous father. Mrs. Wiggins insisted Linda write to her parents and tell of her plight. "They deserve to know about their grandson," she persisted. Linda never received an answer to her letter, but she really hadn't expected one. Her parents and older sister were tight-lipped, unforgiving people who believed life was a condition to be suffered. They did not approve of makeup, modern music, alcoholic spirits, or fun. And they certainly would not approve of babies born out of wedlock. Without telling Linda, Mrs. Wiggins wrote a second letter—just in case Linda's had gotten lost. She described the darling baby and the nice young man Linda was keeping company with—an American from Texas. "I wouldn't be a bit surprised if your daughter won't be moving to Texas after the war. I do hope you allow her to make her peace with you before then." Mrs. Wiggins did not know Jimmy was married.

When Linda learned how infrequently Jimmy had been writing to his wife, she got a pad and pencil from a drawer in Mrs. Wiggins's sideboard. "Kate will know something is wrong if you never write. I won't have you burning any bridges, Jimmy Morris."

"But I hate to write letters," he protested.

So Linda made it easy for him. She dictated and Jimmy wrote. It became a weekly event. She would even jot down things during the week that Jimmy might include in his Sunday afternoon letters—observations about British life, questions he should ask about his new son, plans of what he would do after the war, descriptions of the USO shows. Linda felt a bond with this woman in Texas who was married to Jimmy. She demanded to see Kate's picture. Jimmy started bringing Kate's letters for Linda to read. She felt she knew Kate and her boy, Mark. They seemed like very nice people, as well as Kate's sister, Stella, and her cousin, Effie. "I know you won't understand this," she told Jimmy, "but I wish I could meet Kate someday."

As Eddie grew into a precocious toddler, Jimmy became more and more involved with the brown-eyed little boy. The kid was really cute, and he clapped his hands and laughed when Jimmy came for a visit. Jimmy liked to give Eddie his baths. Such a funny little body. Eddie would tuck his hands between his legs and fondle himself. "Feels good, doesn't it, buddy," Jimmy said, splashing the good-natured baby. Eddie would reward Jimmy with a silly-sounding laugh. Jimmy enjoyed sharing all Eddie's "firsts" with Linda—Eddie tasting sweets for the first time, Eddie pulling up for the first time, Eddie seeing a kitten for the first time. Jimmy couldn't believe how exciting it was when Eddie took his first steps. They all cheered—Linda, Jimmy, Mr. and Mrs. Wiggins. Eddie was so startled he started to cry.

Later that day, while Eddie napped, Linda helped Jimmy with his weekly letter to Kate. "I regret all the things I am missing in my son's life," she dictated. "I never got to see him take his first steps or be with him when he experienced all the sights and sounds and tastes of the world for the first time. I hope to make it up to him someday."

Jimmy stopped writing and stared at Linda. "That's right. I have missed all that. I never realized how important it was until Eddie, but I feel more like Eddie's father than my own kid's."

For now, Linda and Eddie were his little family. When Jimmy thought of Kate and Mark, it was with guilt, so he tried to do so as infrequently as possible. What was going to happen after the war was never discussed. Jimmy didn't know himself.

Linda knew, however. She was grateful to the tall, easygoing American who had saved her life. She never told Jimmy how close she had been to throwing herself in front of a train or jumping from a bridge. She had been at the bottom, and he had pulled her out of the hole. She certainly was not going to repay him by insisting he stay with her rather than return to his beloved Texas. Linda was wise enough to know that England after the war would not hold the same appeal for Jimmy that life there now offered. And Linda knew that she herself would not be so dear to him in Texas. She represented a time in his life that was destined to pass. She understood that the day would come when he would regret throwing away his rightful place in the bosom of his American family, that although he didn't think about his son as much as he did about Eddie, deep in his heart he really did not want to turn his back on Mark—or Kate. And more than anything else—more even than she wanted Jimmy—Linda wanted an orderly, secure life for herself and Eddie. After Jimmy had gone, she planned to play by society's rules. She wanted a proper British husband who would not have divided loyalties and who would never regret marrying her.

So when the time came, she was the strong one. "Don't you dare forget me, Jimmy Morris. And don't you dare ever tell your wife! I don't want to be responsible for a good woman's pain."

Leaving Linda was the hardest thing Jimmy had ever done, but in spite of his protestations, he feared that she was perhaps right. The only way he found the strength to deal with their final farewell, however, was to tell her that if it didn't feel right back home, he was coming back. "I mean that, Linda. In a month or so, you're probably going to look up, and there I'll be. We'll buy a pub and make a brother and sister for Eddie." Linda nodded and kissed him one last time.

When he first arrived aboard the *Enterprise*, Naval Lieutenant William Chambers felt like royalty. He was a pilot aboard the Navy's most important and legendary carrier, the one the Japanese were already referring to as "that damned ship," the one that more than any other vessel represented the pride of the United States Navy. Providentially, she had been two hundred miles out to sea and missed by mere hours the tragic fate of her many sister ships at Pearl Harbor. She would still be around at the war's end; of that her men were certain. Of all the ships on the line, the gallant lady carried an unequaled mystique and was well on her way to chalking up the greatest battle record in naval history. Already, after the battles at Midway and Guadalcanal, the *Enterprise* was responsible for the sinking of dozens of ships and the downing of hundreds of planes.

It took William a while to understand that the special deference with which pilots were treated was like that given to the sacrificial virgin before she was tossed into the volcano's mouth.

Until then he had been a little cocky, wore his cap at a rakish angle, strode with a slight swagger in his walk, just as pilots were expected to do. The pilots were always onstage.

William came aboard in late October with a group replacing pilots lost in the Battle of Guadalcanal, during which the ship had suffered her first hit.

In the two and a half years to follow, William tasted fear many times. From the cockpit of his Hellcat Fighter plane, he was forced to look on the face of his enemy as he bore down on the Japanese Zeros. Young faces. Human faces. He relived their deaths in his sweaty, suffocating nightmares. But still, life went on, more leisurely for the pilots than for the others with shipboard jobs. William trained for "field days," held on the 275-foot flight deck. His best event was the 220-yard dash. There were the hazings of the newcomers every time the equator was crossed. On the hangar deck, there were boxing matches, amateur shows, an occasional USO show, movies. Once during a Saturday-night western, a bugle sounded. Within seconds the area was cleared as the men scrambled to their battle stations. Minutes later they sheepishly returned to the film after an announcement over the public address system informed them that the bugle call was for the movie's cavalry charge.

Mail transfers to the ship were the biggest events of all. William would reverently carry Effie's bundle of letters to the privacy of his bunk. He would sort them, putting them in chronological order, and then read them straight through. And then he would reread them in the days that followed. Sometimes with a particularly sweet or lustful letter, he literally wore it out at the creases and would have to tape it together with cellophane tape.

It was during the landing at the Gilberts that William crossed an imaginary line and felt his own mortality. His was the second crash of the day. He had not yet taken off when the first occurred. The cockpit of that Hellcat had been almost shot away. The right wing was on fire. William was the first to the plane. He scrambled up on the left wing, and with one arm thrown across his face to protect it from the heat, he grabbed blindly. An arm. Two arms. William yanked, but the pilot's body did not budge. William pulled with all his might and suddenly the body jerked free, heaving William backwards off the wing onto the deck. The body fell on top of him. William rolled away and stared in horror at the gory corpse. Simpson from Baton Rouge, Louisiana. Half his face was gone. Bloody brain tissue was exposed. A gurgling fountain of blood was spurting from his chest. His right hand and forearm were missing. William stared down in fascinated horror, waiting for Simpson's hand to pop itself out of the stump. Jesus. The blood. His brain. Christ Jesus.

Fire units were aiming sprays of water at the burning craft. Soon it would be dragged by asbestos-clad seamen to the edge of the flight deck and dumped in the ocean. But what about Simpson's hand? Two seamen had grabbed the dead pilot and were dragging him off the flight deck. Someone else was pulling William to his feet. But when he looked back at the burning craft, for an instant his body tensed. Shouldn't he go retrieve Simpson's hand?

But two people were pulling on him now. Half dragging him. As soon as they cleared the area, another plane took off. When the two men let him go, William fell to his knees and vomited.

One of the sailors knelt beside him. "You okay now?"

William nodded. "Just give me a minute."

"Your plane's up next."

When William crawled into his cockpit, he looked back. Two medics were carrying Simpson away on a stretcher. His dumped plane had already sunk.

William's craft took a hit in the nose within five minutes of leaving the ship. His oil pressure dropped quickly. For a time, he thought he was going to have to ditch, but suddenly the flight deck loomed in front of him. He knew it was coming up too fast, but when the flagman gave him a wave-off, the vestiges of control had vanished from his craft. He couldn't keep his nose up. He was going to miss the hook. "I'm dead," William screamed. He clutched the unresponsive controls as the plane hit hard, then flopped completely over. Immediately a wall of flames enveloped him.

But William was still alive when he woke up in the ship's infirmary. That confused him. Somehow he had suffered only minor scrapes and burns. He remembered nothing of his rescue. He felt sure that if he went to look, his charred body would still be in that plane. He kept staring at his bandaged hands. Did they really belong to him? Were they both all there under those bandages?

The next day an orderly helped him up to the flight deck for the funeral of fifteen seamen and one pilot minus his hand. He watched their bodies given over to the deep. Within an instant the sharks would be there feeding. William didn't want to be eaten by sharks. He wanted to go home. He read Effie's letters over and over as though searching for some clue, some great truth that would guarantee his return to her arms. Once he said aloud in the cave of his bunk, "I'll die if I can't see Effie again." How stupid, he thought. The only thing that would keep him from Effie was if he was already dead.

After his crash William went through several bad weeks. His burns healed, but he cried at everything. He had no appetite. When he tried to read a book or magazine, he kept losing his place. He forgot to watch the movies he went to. He crawled into his bunk at every opportunity, lying on his side, his hands tucked between his knees. He left his reading light on all the time. He didn't think he could get back into one of those Hellcats ever again. What if he never saw Effie again? For the first time, William realized how real a possibility that was.

"You want me to get you transferred?" the doctor asked him, sitting at his metal desk in his metal-walled office in the middle of the cold, gray metal structure that was their ship. "I'm going to have to send you back to duty or get you shipped back to Pearl for psychiatric help."

"Death or dishonor?" William said sarcastically.

"There's no dishonor in needing a shrink to straighten you out," the doctor said. "It's stupid not to if that's what it's going to take. But nonflying pilots have no place on an aircraft carrier."

William flew. His pride would not let him do otherwise. He flew timidly at first. Then automatically. Every time he went up, he expected to die. Every time he returned home safely he was more frightened than before. Every time he survived meant the odds were just that much closer to catching up with him.

No longer was he the cocky aviator. He sought out the company of other grim-faced pilots, who like himself had become fatalists in order to cope. When the end came, death would come as no surprise.

The surprise for William was that he lived.

In May a bomb-laden Zero broke out of the clouds and smashed into the flight deck. The *Enterprise*'s wounds were too great to continue, and she was ordered home. William finished out the war on another carrier, the *Essex*. He was shipped home aboard a disabled destroyer, the *Douglas H. Fox*.

On that glorious fall afternoon, when the *Fox* steamed into San Francisco Bay, William knew Effie would be waiting for him on the dock. He had no letter saying she planned to be there. He just knew, just as he knew the sun would be shining when he saw her again.

Would she even recognize him? He hardly knew his own face in the mirror anymore. He was graying and gaunt. He no longer woke up in the mornings with an erection. He doubted he would be able to make love to her right away, but that would be all right. With Effie, everything would be all right. All he wanted out of life was to live quietly with her for the rest of his days. *Please God. If I have to go to hell for the killing, let me have some time with Effie first.*

He pushed his way through the press of men at the rails. There were thousands of people on the dock—a solid wall of thousands of cheering, waving people. American flags waving everywhere. Streamers flying. A band was playing "The Stars and Stripes Forever."

Out of all those thousands of people, he spotted Effie right away. She was waving a white handkerchief. A silly little hat perched atop her glorious blond hair. William had never seen anything more beautiful in his life than Effie on the pier in San Francisco. He climbed on the railing and called her name. He waved frantically until at last, just as the last yards of black, oily water closed, she saw him. Her lips formed his name.

William's chest swelled with the pain of absolute joy. The war was over.

Twenty

Gordon's nightmares were as often about Stella as they were about the war. In a safe bunk or in a foxhole behind insecure lines, if he slept, it was the same. Stella with a man, with men. But it was so stupid. Stella wouldn't do that.

As he trudged and bounced his way up Italy's boot with the Thunderbirds, he compared every woman he saw to Stella—fatter, thinner, taller, shorter. When he found a point of similarity, he would stare. A woman's nose. Gray eyes. A mannerism. The size of her breasts.

Stella's nose was the perfect size and shape for her face, but he was intrigued by the boldness of larger noses. His wife's gray eyes with their fringe of long, dark lashes and graceful browline were the most beautiful eyes he had ever seen, but he liked the dark eyes and heavy brows of Italian women he saw in the villages. He considered Stella's breasts perfect, but he was attracted to full bosoms, even those of older women, and found himself wondering what it would be like to bury his face between such breasts, to come between them.

What he admired most about Stella was her dignity, her ladylike manner. Yet he was fascinated by the ribald language and humor of the military nurses and Signal Corps WACS.

He realized the only thing preventing him from seeking comfort with one of the American or British nurses was the small silver crosses on his uniform collar. He could not bring himself to slip so far from grace as to remove them for such a purpose, and he could not defile what they stood for by wearing them when he went to commit adultery. Why was he like this? He hadn't thought about sex this much back home. It had had its place, and it didn't go spilling over into the rest of his life. Now he even had sexual thoughts during sermons. If only the war would end!

Each day Gordon wondered if he would be able to say any more blessings to any more young men trudging off to battle, to kill, to be killed. Would he be able to attend the bedside of mutilated and frightened men? And the dyings. How many more deaths would he have to attend? Prayer became difficult; frightened, Gordon began avoiding it. He felt like such a hypocrite, preaching his little canned sermons up and down the front, although no one seemed to notice a lack of sincerity on his part. When his mouth opened, the words flowed, even with shells exploding all around. His fear came mostly in the night, sometimes spent in an above-ground "foxhole" manufactured from small boulders, when soil was too rocky and hard for digging. In the daytime he had grown numb to fear. He was awarded a medal. While he was praying with a platoon on a mountain path outside an Italian town named Venafro, mortar fire erupted. He dragged several wounded men to safety behind a rocky outcropping and applied a couple of tourniquets—all done automatically, the type of thing people do instinctively whether for an injured animal or a man. In fact, one of the casualties was a mule, one of many used to haul supplies up mountain paths too winding even for jeep travel. Gordon had taken a sidearm from one of the wounded men and shot the screaming animal between the eyes. Two men died in spite of his efforts—died because they had stopped to listen to his prayers. The medal was an embarrassment. Gordon didn't write home about it. The only thing that kept him sane was the knowledge that he must return home to Stella a whole man. More than anything else, he wanted to go home to Stella. The six months with her in Galveston had been the best in his life. She represented an orderly life with a clean bed and polished floors. Stella was soft, smooth arms coming willingly around his neck. With his wife, he could be a man without guilt.

The baby Gordon had never seen wasn't real for him yet. His daughter. Interesting, but not important. It was Stella who was in his mind and gut. He wished she were stout and plain. He wished she were locked in a cell. He would rather have her dead than with another man. Men looked at her every day and thought thoughts about her. He couldn't stand it. She had been with another man once. He hated her for that.

Gordon masturbated almost daily, sometimes two or three times, furtively in the daytime, but at night he made it last, building and receding, again and again, his mind taking him away. At first with Stella, then with one of the nurses. Or an Italian woman from one of the villages. For many nights it was a young nun he saw at an orphanage. Sometimes in his fantasies the young private who assisted him with services in the base camp would be watching. It was glorious until Gordon ejaculated into a wad of toilet tissue or a towel with spasms that were painful and disgusted him. Often he wept. And he said his wife's name into the duffel bag he used as a pillow.

After seeing Charles again, Stella was afraid to have fantasies. Charles might be in them. But she was lonely and restless. Pregnancy had changed her. Her body meant more to her now, and she was more in tune with its feel and responses. More than at any other time in her life, she was aware of her own sexuality. When her body ached for fulfillment, she carefully choreographed a fantasy of her husband's homecoming. Time and again, dozens of variations. What she would be wearing when he got off the train. How they would kiss. What they would say. How he would react when they undressed. The touching. The excitement. The passion. Stella thought of the words Gordon would say. How she needed to hear the words of his need, of his love.

Her most explicit thoughts came in the middle of the night. She would awaken to them. Gordon would be there kissing her with his whole mouth, really kissing her, not dry pecks with pursed lips on her cheeks and lips and neck, but with his tongue. Wet, soulful kisses. Before they were married, he had kissed her like that, but he stopped after they married. Why? she wondered. Why did he withhold that from her? But in her fantasies he adored her mouth. He couldn't get enough of her mouth. He kissed her endlessly.

Stella's hands became Gordon's hands—at her waist, her lovely waist, the swell of her hips. She was proud of being as slim now as before. The feel of her own body excited her all the more. *He* touched her breasts, cupping and kneading, turning her nipples hard and pointed. Yes, like that. She liked that. She wanted him to like her breasts, to be fascinated by them, to want to touch them for himself.

Her longing and her ministrations to her body would make her milk flow—just as when she heard Francie cry to be fed. Stella rubbed the wetness from her breasts over her skin. If Gordon were here, would he want to taste her milk?

Stella's leaking nipples reminded her of the wetness that sometimes leaked out of Gordon's penis when he became excited. She wanted to excite him as much as he would excite her, to make him explode with wanting her.

Before Stella had experienced only occasional, fleeting orgasms, but after Gordon left, she had learned to bring herself to climax, but she always felt sad afterwards—more lonely and empty than ever, promising herself she wouldn't do that anymore. Sometimes though, a tension came out of no place and drove her to frenzy. She wanted her husband to return from the war and give her climaxes. Then she could feel the closeness of his arms, his flesh against her flesh, their living, breathing bodies as one. She would feel contented and fulfilled afterwards.

When thoughts of Charles did stray into her mind, they were not sexually explicit. Just fleeting recollections of shared moments. And sometimes she thought of touching his mouth. When such thoughts came abruptly, at odd times, her fingertips would tingle. Her eyes would close. She could see her fingers tracing the outer line of his lips, along that delicate, defining ridge, then across the soft fullness of his lower lip. But her child would whimper. The clerk would hand her a package. Or Kate would say, "A penny for your thoughts." And Stella would come back into herself.

On her wall map she had followed her husband's progress up the boot of Italy, the landing in France, and then the advance into Germany itself. She watched the horror of newsreels and read every account of the war in the newspapers. When the news came on the radio, she stopped what she was doing and listened. She prayed for his safe return even though she was no longer sure there was any difference between praying and hoping.

Kate had no need of a map to keep track of her husband. Jimmy spent the war in London. While death fell from the skies almost daily in London, Kate did not feel the concern for him she knew Effie and Stella were feeling for their husbands. Somehow, it was hard to be too worried about the safety of someone planning USO shows and providing booze for off-hour servicemen.

At first Jimmy's letters had been so infrequent that at one point Kate put in an inquiry about him through the Red Cross. But for the past year his letters had arrived almost weekly—really nice letters that let Kate know her husband was thinking of his wife and child back home. She would be glad to get the war behind them, so they could get on with their life. If motherhood was to be her lot, then Kate was ready to have more babies and move into a house with a backyard. Mark would need a basketball hoop and a jungle gym. Of course, these past years with just Effie and Stella and their children had been nice. She would miss their times together. For when the men returned, they would once again resume their married lives.

Effie had no reservations about her William's return. She was more than ready to have a husband to fuss over. She felt less wonderful when he was not there to make her feel wonderful. And she missed William—*really* missed him. She had become quite proficient at managing the external facets of her life. But inside she was empty without him.

She sensed from his letters that he was going to need her love and care when he returned. And that was what she did best.

Stella had just returned with Francie from the park when she heard the news on the radio. Victory in Europe. At last. Asia would follow. Stella called Kate. No answer. She dialed Effie's number.

Kate answered. "We've been trying to call you. Come. Right now."

The three women hugged each other and wept in Effie's kitchen as their children stared at them with solemn, frightened eyes. Effie got a bottle of wine from the pantry and poured three juice glasses full. Kate put on an Andrews Sisters' record. The three cousins made a conga line around the dining room table, Kate's red ponytail bouncing up and down, Effie's blond curls dancing about her head. Stella remembered them in pigtails. *We're women now*, she thought, *with children and husbands coming home from war. How did that happen?*

The children caught their enthusiasm and began imitating their mothers' incredible antics. They danced and giggled and climbed on the furniture. A lamp was broken. Three little faces turned, expecting the worst. Effie only laughed. Amazing.

The war in Europe was over. The war in the Pacific was on its last legs. They had arrived at the end of the long tunnel.

Sometimes it had seemed as though war were a permanent fixture in their lives, but it had ended. Effie started singing "When Johnny Comes Marching Home Again." Kate joined in, changing the "Johnny" to

"Jimmy." They sang it again each with their own husband's name. And again, this time with tears on their cheeks as they heard the melancholy note in the Civil War tune: "Hurrah! Hurrah! The men will cheer, and the boys will shout. The ladies they will all come out." But the men who marched off to war would not be the same ones who came home. Life would not automatically put itself back as it was before.

Stella thought of Gordon's strange letters and shivered.

They listened to another news broadcast. It wasn't a mistake. The war in Europe was really over. Edward R. Murrow himself told them from London. And Harry Truman from the nation's capital.

Finally they fed the children and put them to bed. They had coffee first at the kitchen table and planned their respective hero's welcome. The cooking and cleaning. New lingerie. Kate would diet. Stella wanted a different hair style. Effie would have William's office at Texas Central redecorated in honor of his return. She would have a new sign made for the side of the building and a perfect accounting of the state of his business ready for him. And she had collected a drawer full of husband-pleasin' recipes.

Effie got a second bottle of wine. She led her cousins into the living room and this time poured the wine into crystal glasses. They listened to yet another news broadcast, relishing every word. Over. They couldn't hear it enough times. Kate put on a stack of records: "Sentimental Journey," "Comin' in on a Wing and a Prayer," "The Last Time I Saw Paris," "I'll Be Seeing You in All the Old Familiar Places," "The White Cliffs of Dover," "Swinging on a Star." Kate sprawled on the floor. Effie curled up on the sofa. Stella was in the easy chair with her feet on the ottoman. Each song evoked a different set of emotions.

Kate's and Stella's husbands had survived and would be coming home to them. *Just hang on a little longer, my darling William,* Effie thought. *It will be over in the Pacific soon. Please come home to me.*

Stella closed her eyes and offered a prayer of thanksgiving. *This is the happiest day of my life,* she thought.

And Kate thought how the past three years had been a timeless limbo. Everything had been put on hold. Now it was time to face the rest of her life.

She wondered if Jimmy felt any reservations. Was he glad they would soon be together?

.　　　.　　　.

Japan surrendered on August fourteenth.

Effie closed the door of her Texas Central office and wept. *We made it, William.*

She reached for the telephone to call Stella and Kate. Already the champagne corks were popping in the outer office. They were prepared for the celebration.

She and her cousins would have dinner together. "I'm so thankful that William's coming home," Stella said tearfully. "I hope you and William have at least fifty more years of making each other happy. You two do that very well."

Kate said, "If any woman deserved her husband back, it's you. You've been the best wife a man could ever have. William's thinking about you this minute, Effie. He's so happy."

"I know," Effie said. "I know."

She called her in-laws. "My boy's coming home," Margaret said over and over. "I'm proud of my boy, and I'm proud of you," Bill said. "We're so lucky, Effie. Our William is coming home to us."

And she called home—to New Braunfels. Jason answered the phone.

"You've heard?" she asked through her tears.

"Yes. Thank God."

"I'll have him back, Jason. I'm so happy I could die. And just 'cause William's home, you don't stop coming. Billy and I would miss you too much."

Effie talked to her parents, then dried her tears and went out to join her employees. The secretaries had cleared off the desks and put out the paper cups and bottles. The mechanics came streaming in from the hangar, and employees came from adjacent airport offices. More paper cups of bubbly were poured. Effie sent out for more champagne. "Cases and cases," she said.

Telephone books were torn up for confetti. Everyone was kissing and hugging. Effie joined in. God, how good it felt to kiss a man again, she thought as a mechanic named Jess took liberties with the boss.

Effie lifted her cup for a toast. No one noticed, so she climbed up on a desk. Finally the room grew quiet.

Effie raised her cup again. "Here's to William Chambers, who fought a war for all of us. He's an American hero, and I'm very lucky to be his wife. Here's to all our heroes."

"Hear! Hear!" voices called out. Paper cups were raised.

Effie drained hers, then smiled through her tears at the assemblage. "And if I'm late to work in the morning, it's because I'm having a hard time finding the sexiest nightgown in Dallas to buy for my hero's homecoming."

The cheering was deafening.

Effie pulled two of the secretaries up on the desk with her. She had to put her mouth right up to their ears to make them understand what she wanted.

The three women put their arms around each waist and began to sing. "God Bless America, Land that I love."

Those around the desk joined in, and quickly the entire room was singing and crying and singing it again. Home, sweet home. Their America. It was over. Freedom and America had prevailed.

But at what a price, Effie thought as she battled her way through the wild traffic to meet her cousins. The whole city had taken to the streets or was leaning from the windows of buildings. The honking was incessant. Toilet paper streamers flew from every building. There wouldn't be a phone book left in Dallas tomorrow.

Edward R. Murrow said on the radio last night that, worldwide, an estimated thirty-five million people had died because of the war. It was beyond comprehension.

But William was alive. Kate had said he was thinking about her. Effie could feel it. She could feel his jubilation at this very moment, knowing he would be coming home to her.

Effie left seven-year-old Billy with his grandparents and flew to San Francisco, arriving the day before the *Essex* was scheduled to arrive. Alone in her hotel room, she willed herself to sleep the night before in spite of her excitement. It was absolutely necessary that she be at her best tomorrow.

And she was. Effie, at twenty-seven, had never looked better in her life. Maturity and self-assurance only enhanced her rosy prettiness. The outfit she would wear to the dock had been hanging in her closet for three months, the result of half-a-dozen shopping forays. It had to be perfect. And it was—a smart suit of pale green that fit her to a "T," its padded shoulders accentuating her slim waist and hips, sexy without seeming to be. Her hat was a frivolous bit of fluff set on glorious shoulder-length blond hair. Her gloves and shoes were white kid. She would be the prettiest woman there. Absolutely. William would be so proud.

She fretted about lipstick. With her fair coloring, she looked better in lipstick—a bright pink. But when William kissed her, it would smear. And she had planned on that kiss for so long. If only by the end of the war someone had invented a lipstick that didn't smear.

Effie finally decided to wear lipstick but have a handkerchief all ready in hand to repair the damage. Yes, a lace handkerchief. She could wave it prettily at her husband standing at the rail of the docking ship.

The photograph of Effie waving her lace handkerchief made the wire service. Someone at the Dallas *Morning News* recognized the pretty blonde as Mrs. William Chambers, Jr., and ran the picture thus captioned on the front page. It was also picked up by *The New York Times* and *Newsweek*.

William had the photograph framed in a handsome pewter frame and hung on the wall of his reclaimed office. Effie had managed Texas Central in his absence. Very well. Over the war years the business had prospered beyond anything he could have imagined. Effie had run a business that employed more than two hundred people. Texas Central Flight College had given more than nine hundred military cadets their primary flight training. The company had rebuilt more than a thousand airplane engines. Its profits had increased twentyfold. The employees, from janitors to pilots, were uniform in their praise of his "little woman." The company had grown and prospered partly because of the war, but William realized that most of the credit had to go to careful management. Effie had taken his fledgling company and made a fortune. William was grateful. And resentful.

It amazed William to see Effie as an authority figure, but when she walked through the Texas Central offices and hangars, it was obvious that she was the boss. An approachable one. Employees stopped her to ask questions at every turning. And Effie had answers. Effie made decisions.

"I think you should continue with Texas Central," William told her. His sense of fairness dictated that he make the offer. "A vice president in charge of management. You deserve it, Effie. My God, you've done a terrific job."

"Me? A vice president? Heavens no," Effie told her husband with a lilting laugh. "The war's over. It's time to make Texas Central back into an airline. Passenger service for the state of Texas just like you always wanted. It's a buyers' market for military transport planes. We've got the people to renovate them for passenger service. Routes are wide open. But all that's for you to do. I'll just stay on until you're used to things. Of course, we'll always talk in the evenings like before, but I won't come to the office anymore. It's time I get back to being a wife."

When William protested, Effie was firm.

William realized he was relieved at her answer—profoundly so. He wanted his wife in his home and not in his office. He was the luckiest man on earth to have such a wife as Effie. And God, it was good to be home. He had wanted to go to war, but now he couldn't remember why. He never wanted to go back again.

William never told war stories. He never spoke of the war in any way. And he knew he would never again pilot a plane.

With some of the money his company had made in his absence, he installed Effie in a palatial Turtle Creek home. More than ever, William openly adored his pretty little wife. In return for the adoration, Effie gave parties and laughed and made his world a lovely place. And she still made the best apple pie in the state of Texas.

Kate had been a lean size eight when the war started. She had spread to a generous size fourteen by war's end. Effie said she was a "bit plump," but "plump" was a pretty word. Kate did not feel pretty.

With the prospect of her husband's return looming over her head, she did something she hadn't done in a long time. Kate took off her clothes and looked at her naked body in the mirror—really looked. She hated what she saw. How could this have happened? Of all the things she had feared in her life, getting fat was not one of them. She was an athlete, and athletes didn't get fat.

But the body in the mirror wasn't going to be running any races or shooting any baskets. She hadn't hit a tennis or golf ball since she got pregnant with Mark. It didn't make any sense at all. What she had liked most about herself she had let slip away.

Kate ran her hands over her waistless figure. She cupped her hands under sagging breasts and lifted them to their former position on her chest. She stared at her wide hips with the V of wiry red pubic hair at their center. Her belly was so covered with stretch marks it looked like a worn-out girdle. No one had ever told her that nursing would ruin her breasts, and she'd never heard of stretch marks until she had them. Even her bladder wasn't the same. She still had to get up in the night to go to the bathroom at least twice—sometimes three times—like when she was pregnant. And when she sneezed, she got the crotch of her panties wet. She looked like a cow. Like a peasant. Like a matron.

Certainly not like an athlete. She never talked anymore about what she had once been. It was an embarrassment.

Stella and Effie both got their figures back after they had babies. Why hadn't she? Kate was certain their breasts didn't sag, and a stretch mark would never mar Effie's flesh. Stella's maybe, but never Effie's.

Kate doubted if an athletic body still existed under her now matronly one. It was not just covered up. It was gone. She wondered if her body was making sure she could never again devote herself to anything except motherhood. Or was the fat providing her with an excuse? If she was fat, she'd never have to find out if she was world-class. She already knew she couldn't be in track. She wasn't that good a sprinter, and women still didn't run distances. And basketball was a young woman's game. She loved tennis, but tennis players needed to start in the cradle. She'd never picked up a racket until she'd graduated from high school.

Golf had been her hope. She'd seen the Babe play. Glenna Collet Vare. Patty Berg. Could she ever be *that* good? There had been talk of starting a women's professional tour when the war was over. Kate still dreamed of winning tournaments, being famous. You didn't have to be a kid to play golf. You didn't even have to be skinny. Of course, you couldn't be fat either. And you had to be dedicated. Practice, practice, practice. A good teacher. Wanting it more than anything else. Kate knew how it was done. She could get her game back if she really worked at it and wanted it badly enough. She could be written up in sports pages. She could tour with other women professionals. They could be pioneers together.

Kate assumed her golf stance and swung. Her naked breasts swung back and forth like two pendulums. *Whap!* The ball sailed down the fairway. The gallery cheered. That Kate Morris. Wasn't she something! A real comeback story.

God, how she wanted that!

Kate dropped to her knees. She sat back on her heels and covered her disgusting nakedness with crossed arms. What had happened to Kate Behrman, the girl who swore she would never marry? What happened to the girl who could run up and down the roads of Comal County for hours without stopping? If she wasn't Kate the athlete, who was she?

She didn't want to cry. She hated feeling sorry for herself, but she couldn't help herself. Her head rolled forward, and Kate sobbed. Who in the hell was she?

She didn't hear the door open, but suddenly there was a small hand on her bare shoulder. A child's voice said, "Mommy?"

Blindly Kate pulled Mark's small, sturdy body against her soft, flaccid one. Still on her knees, still naked, she rocked him back and forth. Mark, whom she loved above all else, defined her. She was a mother.

And once a mother, there was no going back.

Before she opened her eyes the next morning, Kate remembered what day it was. Every night before she went to sleep, she promised herself she'd start her diet the next day.

But today she really was going to start. She had to. Jimmy would be home soon. Today was the first day of her diet.

"It's time to fish or cut bait, old girl," she told herself.

Mark stirred next to her and snuggled up against her body. Most nights he still crawled into bed with her. Sometimes she knew when he came; other times she just woke up and he was there.

But tonight Mark would have to stay the whole night in his own bed. He had to learn. His father would be home soon.

Kate had read in a magazine that it was necessary to cut back five thousand calories a week just to lose one pound. But she needed to lose more than a pound a week. What if Jimmy came home next month? Next week?

He must never see her looking like this. Never.

It was the hardest thing she had ever done, but Kate managed to starve herself down over the next two months to a reasonably attractive size twelve. She could no longer kid herself, however. Food had become very important to her, as important as not being fat. It was a constant battle that would have to be fought over and over every single day of her life.

Fat didn't interfere with motherhood, however. Mark didn't care if she was fat. He seemed to like cuddling up against his soft mommy.

Her son Mark was three years old and his mother's pride. A fine, tall boy who did indeed seem to run and jump and throw the ball with greater adeptness than the average three-year-old. He would be athletic. Kate just knew he would.

Since Mark's birth Kate had feared polio more than the war. She knew in her heart that she could face something happening to Jimmy, but if anything ever happened to Mark, she would die. Every childish cough or fever threw her into a panic. Mark was her life. Her joy.

Once, when Mark had been dreadfully ill with whooping cough, Kate had sat beside her son's bed and bartered with God. A future child if He had to take one. Just spare Mark. Even as she prayed, Kate knew she would love her future children as much as she loved Mark, but he was here. He was now.

Effie had tried to convince Kate she should go to meet her husband's ship as Effie herself had done when William came home. "You and Jimmy could have a second honeymoon in New York—just the two of you," Effie encouraged her cousin.

But Kate could not bring herself to leave Mark even for a second honeymoon, so she met her husband's train in Dallas with Mark at her side. When she saw that Jimmy had a paunch hanging over the belt of his khaki trousers, she smiled. They embraced and laughed and cried and hugged Mark between them. "I think we both ate our way through the war," she said, patting his belly affectionately.

"Ah, Katie, how I missed you, girl," he said in a voice that had lost much of its Texas drawl. And then he kissed her, really kissed her.

In the car, as Kate drove them home, Jimmy pulled his son onto his lap. Mark looked a little overwhelmed by the mythical father who had finally come home, but he answered Jimmy's questions solemnly and well. No, he didn't have a girlfriend. Yes, he liked his cousins. No, he didn't know how to play golf. Yes, he would like to learn. Yes, he had been a good boy. No, he didn't like Brussels sprouts. Yes, his mother was a good cook. And Mark added on his own, "I have a gerbil. His name's Byron Nelson." Jimmy's laugh was deeper now. Maybe it was the belly. Kate was pleased at how good he was with Mark. He had a natural way with children, it seemed.

Jimmy walked into the front door carrying his son and stared at the huge welcoming banner Kate had hung across the entry hall. There were crepe-paper streamers hanging from the ceiling and balloons from the light fixtures. "God, Kate, I'm so glad to be home," he said with tears in his eyes.

By the time they had tucked Mark into bed and eaten their candle-light supper complete with champagne, the fatigue from his long journey was beginning to take its toll on Jimmy. He stretched and yawned. Then he looked at Kate and winked. "Ready to give the old man a real welcome home?" he asked.

Arm in arm, he and Kate walked down the hallway. They looked in on their sleeping son, then self-consciously undressed their now-fuller bodies. Kate locked the bedroom door before she slipped into bed. She hoped Mark wouldn't wake up. What would he think if he came to get into bed with her and found the door locked?

Jimmy pulled her to him and buried his face in her hair. "I missed you, girl," he said, his voice playfully gruff. "You can't imagine how lonely I've been."

And Kate knew at that moment he had not been faithful to her. She heard it in his voice. Regret. At least he felt bad about it. But how did she feel? Kate was wise enough, however, to tuck the revelation away to deal with later. Maybe it didn't matter too much.

Their lovemaking was strong and natural. Kate didn't try to have an orgasm. That would come later. Right now she just wanted to relish the feel of being in her husband's arms again. Whatever had happened over there, it was good to have him back. Kate wondered if their lovemaking would make her pregnant. She hoped so. She wanted another baby.

The next day was Sunday. Effie had dinner. Her brother Jason drove from New Braunfels with her parents and youngest brother, Chris. The oldest brother, Hiram, arrived with his wife and two children. Cousin Joe had arrived home from France the month before and came with his parents and Anna. Cousin Carl was wounded and still in a hospital in England. Margaret and Bill Chambers were there, of course, as were Jimmy's parents and sister. Gordon's father and uncle came from Tyler. They all came to welcome Jimmy and William home from war.

Gordon's welcome would have to come later. The Army had asked some of its chaplains to stay in Europe to help the International Red Cross and World Church with the formation of camps for displaced persons. Gordon and other American chaplains volunteered to help local clergy across Europe in providing religious services and assist in administering the clearinghouse process by which separated families could locate one another.

The aunts brought food to the welcome home celebration. Fresh sausage. Baked chicken and dressing. Baked ham. Homemade egg noodles. Streusel. Hiram's wife brought angel food cake, pickled watermelon rinds, goat cheese, and a chocolate cake. Effie had been cooking for days. Homemade bread, home-canned strawberry preserves, meat pie, bread pudding, fruit salad served with whipped cream, *blitskuchen*—a fruit torte. Never had there been such a feast. Effie wouldn't hear of a buffet. They had to sit together at one table, so she put both leaves in her table and added a card table on one end that stuck out into the living room. Two overlapping white tablecloths made the arrangement into one table. Red, white, and blue carnations arranged with little American flags formed the centerpiece. Kate took pictures first of the table empty and then again with all assembled. Stella had Kate sit down and took a picture with her in it. Everyone raised their glasses twice in a toast to the men returning from war—to Joe and Jimmy and William.

Herman asked the blessing in German, but he finished in English with a "God bless America."

"God bless America," Effie repeated. Then they all said it together. "God bless America."

Gordon should be here, Stella thought, feeling cheated by his absence. She was trying to understand why it was necessary for him to volunteer to stay on in Europe for a few more months but was finding it difficult. Her husband was a better Christian than she was. She wanted him here at her side. She wondered how many more times these dear people would all come together like this. Already her father was gone. Her mother was old. The aunts and uncles and Gordon's father were old. Her cousin Jason was frail and had the look of a man who could die young.

"Don't you fret, honey," Effie said later, sliding her arm around her Stella's waist. "We'll celebrate all over again when Gordon comes home."

Stella kissed Effie's cheek. Dear Effie. But shortly her cousin slipped away from her and went back to her husband.

Twenty-one

Gordon did not return to Texas until January 1946. By that time cousin Carl had died—not of his wounds in England but of hepatitis in the hospital at Fort Sam. The war was over, but Carl died anyway, his body arriving home in New Braunfels in a flag-draped casket riding in a boxcar. The family gathered to meet the train at the Landa Park station, to sit at the funeral home, to attend the service at the church on Comal Street, to drive solemnly out to the cemetery at the end of Common Street and lay him to rest among generations of Behrman dead and among the Hasenbecks, Zunkers, Pfeuffers, Waldschmidts, Hofheinzes, and others, some of whom had come over with the first immigrants. Stella took a rose from one of Carl's floral tributes and placed it on her father's grave. "I miss you, Papa," she whispered, touching the granite marker with her gloved fingers. She stood and stared at the tombstone of his first wife and baby. "Anna Marie Behrman, beloved wife of Frederick, and their infant son, Hans Joseph." Beside her grave marker was a smaller one for her other brother, Henry Wilhelm. Stella wondered if it bothered her mother that her husband and son were buried next to another woman.

The family journeyed back to the cemetery that evening, after neighbors had served them dinner. Still in their funeral clothes, they made a circle around the raw, fresh grave and said their private good-byes to the solid, good man who had been taken from them. Joe stood by his parents, his face wet with his tears, his nose red and running. As long as Stella could remember, it had been Joe and Carl—the brothers. John and Louise looked smaller, frailer. Their boy was dead. Louise sank to her knees and kissed the earth mounded over her firstborn. Embarrassed, John pulled his wife to her feet. The fresh dirt clung to her skirt and stockings.

Stella cried over her cousin and thought of Charles. Was he still alive? So many had died. But surely, if he had been killed, she would have read about it in the Morning News' "Today's Army-Navy Casualty List." She read the paper every day.

In April 1945 Dachau was liberated by the Forty-fifth Division. As a chaplain, Gordon was among the first to enter the death camp when the gates were opened. He was one of the first to witness the horror therein. More than a thousand corpses were stacked like wood, waiting for disposal. Outside the camp walls hundreds more naked, rotting bodies stacked four and five deep on flatcars were still parked on the rail spur where they had been waiting for disposal in Dachau's two ovens. The sweet, putrid smell of rotting death hung in the air. There was no escaping it. The smells gagged Gordon—as did the sight of festering sores and gangrenous flesh on the living. For the more than 30,000 survivors were often as grotesque as the dead, with bodies bloated from starvation, bodies mutilated from war and experimentation, bodies covered with their own filth. Gaping sockets empty of eyes were commonplace. As he toured the camp, Gordon even saw faces without noses, without ears, without lower jaws.

But the greatest horror was that human beings were capable of such evil. Gordon felt irrevocably tainted. Nothing could be more evil than what had transpired here.

He could not stay in this place. How could he work here when he gagged at the sight of the people he was supposed to help? How could he dare offer spiritual comfort to people who had been living in hell? How could they have any spirit left?

But when the chaplain's corps asked for volunteers, Gordon stayed on. And no matter how desperately he wanted to, he could not turn his back on Dachau. If he did, he would have felt no better than the Germans who created such camps. If only he had never seen Dachau, it would not be his responsibility. But there was no going back.

So Gordon gradually became oblivious to the smells. He learned to avert his eyes and not look directly at some things. Destroyed faces bothered him the most, so he looked past them, around them, over them. He thought of men of the cloth who in former times went among the lepers. Those missionaries saw the humanity of the lepers along with the horror of their disease. Gordon searched for humanity in the faces of Dachau. And when he saw it, it tore at his heart and made the horror worse. For they were indeed human beings, and therefore what they had suffered was beyond belief.

He asked himself daily how long the Lord required his presence here. When would it be all right for him to leave? How would he know when he'd been here long enough? He prayed for a sign. Would he ever stop feeling guilty because he had flesh on his bones, because he was alive?

But surely there would be some reward in all this. Maybe he would leave Dachau feeling noble. If he did penance for his diminished faith, maybe it would return to him. Perhaps he would lose his fear of going home.

His thoughts of Stella had become even more tortured. The night-mares of her with other men continued to haunt him. With them, she was doing things he had never done with her. How could he face her with such thoughts in his mind?

Yes, he had to get back his faith in God and in Stella. Or find another solution.

Gordon wondered about suicide. Death beckoned all around him. Ghastly, ugly, putrid death—yet somehow seductive. An end to doubts. An end to self-loathing.

Dachau became his world. The camp had been quarantined. Four station hospitals complete with medical personnel moved into the compound, and the gates were reclosed, leaving the doctors and nurses to deal with the typhus epidemic and the malnutrition and a greater concentration of disease than they had thought could possibly exist in one place. Gordon and other volunteers stayed with them on the inside to begin the cataloguing of the prisoners. It was inside the walls of Dachau that Gordon met Micah.

One day the boy was just there—walking at his side. It was a warm, sunny day in June. The smells in the air were of spring. The rotting corpses had been taken away and buried in great trenches.

At first Gordon thought Micah was a girl. The child was delicate and had enormous black eyes framed by the longest lashes Gordon had ever seen. Thick, dark hair fell across a high, white brow. A slightly pointed chin gave the youngster a lovely heart-shaped face, and the child's mouth had soft, full lips like a woman's. But Gordon took a second look. The child walked like a boy. There was soft down above his upper lip.

The boy was older than his size would indicate. Twelve maybe. Or thirteen. His head appeared too large for his small, fleshless body. Primitive numbers were tattooed on a wrist not much bigger than a baby's. With a shock, Gordon realized the child had no thumbs. His hands had a grotesque birdlike appearance. Why in the world had they chopped off his thumbs? But then none of it made sense. None of it.

Gordon never knew why Micah had selected him, but from that day forward, the Methodist chaplain had a small Jewish shadow.

Gordon scrubbed the lice from Micah's head and painted his impetigo lesions with iodine. He got the boy clean clothes from the Red Cross boxes. He had him immunized against typhoid and gave him K rations. Micah took to hanging around the large room where Gordon worked with its disarray of desks, file cabinets, and tireless men—mostly American and British chaplains—who attempted to locate families and find places to relocate the survivors of Dachau. Gordon started giving the boy chores—sweeping, taking out trash, fetching coffee.

In the evenings Micah followed Gordon to his room in the building that had once housed German guards. The boy would polish Gordon's shoes, brush mud from the cuffs of his trousers, and straighten the clutter in the cell-like room, his maimed hands making peculiar compensating movements as they went about their tasks. The boy refused to leave at night. At first he slept in the hallway, curled up outside Gordon's door. He would smile and look up at Gordon with those compelling black eyes. After a few nights Gordon gave him a blanket, and Micah took up residence on the floor beside Gordon's cot. Two days later Gordon obtained a spare mattress to go with the blanket.

Micah grabbed Gordon's hand and kissed it. And looked up at him. Those eyes. Gordon had an uncomfortable feeling that Micah had planned all along that he would sleep beside Gordon's bed on a clean mattress with a clean blanket.

Micah's lips curled in a smile. They were strikingly dark against his pale skin—almost as though they were rouged, even outlined in a slightly darker shade. The fuzz above his upper lip was already darker than it had been two weeks ago. Micah was perched between childhood and puberty, a mystical time in a boy's life when the forces within him battle for power.

The lad was bright and learning English with amazing ease. He apparently had no family with whom to be reunited. Soon Gordon let him do filing in the international office. And the boy worked at teaching himself how to type, devising his own method for hands with no thumbs.

As Micah's skin took on a healthier color, he developed a habit of running the tip of his tongue along his protruding lower lip before he spoke. The gesture held a strange fascination for Gordon. He began to anticipate it.

Gordon learned that Micah's Jewish father and gentile mother had both been killed in a pogrom before the war. He had been taken in by his mother's brother, who moved his family from Bonn to a small village outside Solingen, where everyone assumed Micah was a son of the family. But one night in December 1944 the police came and took away the unaccounted-for child, some bureaucrat having made the connection between an extra child and a Jewish brother-in-law. Later in Dachau a former neighbor of the family told Micah that the rest—his aunt and uncle and their children—had been taken away the next day. Gordon made inquiries but was unable to locate the family. They had never returned to the house near Solingen, local officials informed him. The house was still standing.

Often when Gordon bent over the table in his room, reading or working, Micah came up behind him and rubbed his neck with the heels of his maimed hands. Gordon would moan his appreciation as his muscles relaxed. How nice it was to be touched again. Nobody had touched him in more than a casual way for a long time. Years.

Sometimes Micah played little jokes on Gordon. Shoestrings tied together. Military brass carefully pinned on Gordon's bathrobe. Hidden toothbrushes or combs for Gordon to find under his pillow or in his folded undershorts.

Gordon began investigating the possibility of taking Micah home with him. He wasn't sure just what he would do with the Jewish lad in Texas, but he hated the thought of leaving Micah behind. He would miss him, and besides, Gordon owed the boy a great deal. Micah kept him from going crazy. The boy's presence had calmed him and taken the edge from his loneliness. Stella could mother him, or maybe he could go to live with her cousin Hiram and his family on the ranch.

One night Gordon awoke with a start to find Micah kneeling beside the cot, his slim fingers rubbing Gordon's temples. "You have bad sleep," Micah said.

Gordon sensed this was so. His heart was pounding. The bedclothes were soaked with sweat. Yes. He remembered. He was on his way home, but the troopship sank. People were drowning all around him. Gordon was caught in the vortex of a whirlpool. Around and around. No hope of breaking free.

Gordon threw back the damp sheet and struggled out of his sweat-soaked underwear. Naked, he fell back on the bed. The pillow was damp. He pushed it onto the floor and slipped back toward sleep. At first, he wasn't sure what he was feeling, so soft was Micah's touch. Then Gordon's eyes flew open. Micah was once again kneeling beside the bed. He was rubbing the heel of his right hand softly—ever so softly—up and down Gordon's penis. Feather-light touches.

Gordon raised up on his elbows and stared. Micah's left hand trailed down to Gordon's testicles and fondled them. His right hand continued to caress Gordon's penis.

Micah leaned forward. His face was very close to the head of the penis, which had the beginnings of an erection.

Suddenly Gordon knew why Micah was still alive, why he had not been gassed and his body burned in the ovens. He had done this before. He knew exactly what to do.

Gordon's penis jerked to full erection.

That mouth—that unbelievable mouth—was so near. The full lips parted. They would surround Gordon's erect penis. Gordon would come in that mouth.

It was the most beautiful mouth Gordon had ever seen, but he knew where it led. Micah's beautiful mouth was the gate to hell.

Gordon groaned. "No," he protested, pushing the boy's face away.

"No?" Micah questioned, looking up at Gordon. His eyes were luminous in the moonlight from the open window. They almost glowed. Micah began massaging the penis between both of his outspread hands. Its bulging head showed between two thumbless hands.

"Oh, God," Gordon said. His voice was hoarse. He remembered the biblical term. An abomination.

Micah leaned closer, very close. The tip of Micah's tongue touched the milky wetness on the tip.

Gordon wanted to scream. But he was paralyzed. He could no longer speak. He couldn't scream. He couldn't move. His mind was in a frenzy, turning over and over on itself. He had never consciously had sexual thoughts about boys. He wasn't one of those. He had a wife. He had fathered a daughter. He wasn't. But the Devil had looked inside of him and was offering him the ultimate sexual act. Micah's mouth would be warm and soft. It would feel better than anything that anyone had ever felt since the world began. It would suck his soul right out of his body.

Never had Gordon wanted anything more than he wanted to come in that Jewish boy's mouth. But if there was a Devil, there might be a God.

With a mighty shudder, Gordon let out a roar. "Abomination!" His fist flailed out and knocked away Micah's face, slamming the boy against the wall.

Lights went on in the next building. The walls seemed to reverberate with Gordon's voice. The door slammed behind the fleeing boy.

Gordon rolled over on himself and buried his face in his pillow. He sobbed his wife's name over and over.

The next morning he told the ranking chaplain that he was applying for his discharge. He wanted to leave Dachau as soon as possible. Today.

The bird colonel looked at Gordon strangely. Gordon could feel the gaze of the other men from across the room. They had heard him last night. How much did they know about that boy? Maybe they all knew what Micah was and had assumed Gordon did too. They probably thought that Gordon let the boy come to his room at night for . . .

No. He wasn't one of those. He hadn't done that, Gordon wanted to yell at them.

But he had wanted to. He would have to carry that knowledge with him forever. For a horrible moment he had wanted it more than anything else.

The colonel nodded. He would not stand in the way of Gordon's leaving. The war was over. Gordon's enlistment was up. He'd see that the orders were cut.

Gordon stayed in his room the following day and into the next. It took that long to prepare his papers and arrange transportation.

He was weak with hunger the next afternoon. It took all his strength to throw his duffel bag in the back of a truck and crawl in after it. When the truck pulled away from the gates of Dachau, Gordon allowed himself to breathe. He was going home to Stella. Only Stella could make him whole.

It wasn't Stella, however, who met Gordon at the train station in Dallas. It was Kate. He hardly recognized her. She was matronly. And pregnant.

"Oh, Gordon," she said, her eyes full of tears, "Francie's in the hospital!"

Kate rushed him to Parkland Hospital, where the daughter he had never seen lay gravely ill with meningitis. An exhausted Stella greeted her returning husband at the bedside of their unconscious child.

"Oh, Gordon," she said and rushed into his arms.

Gordon was in a daze. Stella's unwashed hair smelled sour. He wanted to push her away and look at her. She was slender, but was she still pretty? He allowed her to cling to him. He looked at the child he had seen only in photographs. She looked very ill. Francie. He wondered if she was going to die. Would it be his fault if his child died? God, he was so tired.

For three days three-year-old Francie hovered at the edge of death. Much of the time Stella's mother and sister and cousin Effie were also there with her, but Stella refused to leave her child's bedside.

It was almost a week before Stella agreed to leave the hospital. She and Gordon would be alone at last—after they dropped Anna Behrman at the bus station to catch an evening bus back to New Braunfels. Now that her granddaughter was better, Anna wanted to get home to her garden, her laying hens, and her two yellow cats.

Stella automatically headed for the driver's side of the car. Gordon reached out his hand for the keys. Stella hesitated, then handed them to him.

The bus was late. They waited on the wooden benches with Anna. The talk was mostly of Gordon's trip home and Francie's illness. Finally the bus was ready to depart.

Stella watched the bus pull away and turned to her husband. "Welcome home, my darling."

"Come on, let's get you something to eat and go home."

The stopped at a cafeteria. Dinner was awkward. Finally, at Stella's probing, Gordon told her something about the refugee camps. But he seemed reluctant to talk about what he had left behind, why he had come home so suddenly. So they speculated about where his next church would be.

"Sometimes I'm not sure I want to stay in the ministry," he confessed. Stella was surprised. But she knew as long as Gordon's father was alive, he would remain a clergyman.

Stella made a valiant effort to eat her steak and baked potato, but the bites seemed to stick in her throat. Her eyes kept filling with tears. She could not make the transference from mother to wife. Her thoughts were still with her sick child. Maybe she should have waited one more night before leaving the hospital. Francie was still so weak. But Kate was there with her. It was Kate who had insisted that it was time for Stella to devote some of her time to her husband.

Stella knew her sister was right. But as she and Gordon drove home, Stella felt more nervous than she had on her wedding night. She felt an overwhelming desire to put her face in her hands and weep. The last ten days had been a nightmare. Poor Gordon. What a mess he had come home to. Francie's illness had interrupted her preparations for his home-coming. All those things she was saving until the last minute—having her hair cut, manicuring her nails, cleaning the stove and refrigerator, shopping, cooking. Only half the windows were washed. She'd cleaned the closets and cupboards, thank goodness, and the slipcovers were washed and the rugs cleaned. But she still hadn't emptied out drawers for Gordon in the chest of drawers. No cake had been baked. No cookies were in the jar. The kitchen floor wasn't waxed. The car was cluttered with Frances's toys, the windows sticky with her fingerprints. It should have been washed and waxed. The oil should have been changed. It was still missing a hubcap. The new bed sheets she had bought were still in the box. And her emotions were weeks in arrears.

Stella did most of the talking on the way home, pointing to the new buildings going up in the city's skyline, talking about how the city had grown, would grow. A real boom was predicted. Gordon offered no comment.

Gordon pulled Stella to him as soon as they walked in the front door. She had thought he would look around first to see the place where she and Francie had spent the war. And she would fix him coffee. There would be time. But he was clutching at her. Stella felt panic swelling in her. She wasn't ready.

"I haven't had a real bath in ten days," Stella protested.

Gordon showered first, then Stella ruthlessly scrubbed her body and then shaved her legs and underarms. Maybe she should have just sponged off. She was terribly aware of her husband waiting for her in the bedroom that had been hers alone for three years. After three years should she have insisted on a bath? But she needed the time to shift gears from worried mother to welcoming wife. She needed more time than this. She sat in the tub of hot water until it became tepid and her skin turned to goose flesh. Her stomach hurt with nervousness as she stepped from the tub and dried her shivering body. She regretted every bite of her dinner.

Stella wiped the moisture from the mirror and stared at the reflection of the slender, naked woman. She didn't look like someone about to have sex. Her eyes had dark circles under them, and her shoulders sagged. Stella covered herself with a robe and squared her shoulders. There was a new nightgown in a bureau drawer. It was black, sheer and lacy, but it seemed silly to put it on and immediately take it off. She had envisioned wearing it while they drank a toast of champagne by a moonlit window.

Gordon was waiting for her in bed, his lower half covered by a sheet. Self-consciously, Stella turned off the light and slipped off her robe.

The feel of his nude skin next to hers was a shock. They kissed for a very long time, before Gordon began exploring her body with his hands. It all felt so alien to Stella. And his penis was soft. That made her really afraid. What if he couldn't have sex? What if they couldn't get this over with?

Stella touched him tentatively, then began to try to massage him to erection.

They kissed some more and ground their bodies together frantically. Stella felt responsible for Gordon's lack of response. "I'm so tired—and so worried about Francie," she told him. "Tomorrow night will be better. Or in the morning. Just kiss me now and hold me. God, how I've wanted you to hold me! It's been so long."

But he continued to rub himself against her belly and leg until the phone rang. It was an apologetic Kate calling from the hospital. "Honey, I'm sorry, but Francie refuses to settle down. She's really crying hard. The nurses say they'll have to sedate her if she doesn't calm down."

"I'll be right there," Stella said.

"No," Kate said, her voice carefully neutral. "You stay home and get some sleep. It's Gordon she wants. Francie is crying for her daddy."

Gordon dressed and went to the hospital alone. When he had gone, Stella allowed herself to cry into her pillow. Underneath her disappointment over Gordon's ruined homecoming was an ugly feeling. Jealousy. Her daughter wanted Gordon, a man she did not even know, to be with her. Francie had asked for her father and not for the mother who alone had loved and cared for her since she was born.

When Gordon entered the hospital room, Francie opened her smooth, little-girl arms to him and whimpered as he sat on the bed and held her against his chest, rocking her back and forth in a motion that came instinctively. Her hair was damp with perspiration. Gordon smoothed it from her forehead and kissed the smooth skin there. She smelled warm and sweet and innocent.

For the next two days and nights, Gordon kept the bedside vigil at the hospital, although Francie was rosy and almost well. It was hard to believe she had ever been sick. Children are like that, the doctor explained. They get well almost as quickly as they get sick.

Stella had her hair cut and put the new sheets on the bed. They were blue-and-white striped—really pretty. She packed away Gordon's uniforms in mothballs. She cleaned the oven and shopped for groceries. She baked a chocolate cake and oatmeal cookies. She fried chicken and made potato salad. During her visits at the hospital she felt like an outsider.

The next time Gordon and Stella tried to make love, Francie was home—in the next room of the tiny and very quiet apartment.

Stella wore the nightgown. She and Gordon drank a toast to their future. Gordon said she was beautiful. He did not carry her off to bed. Stella followed him into the small room.

Stella was uncomfortable. What if Francie heard them? It was a new and unnatural experience for them both—to be intimate while a child slept in the next room. Stella listened for sounds on the other side of the wall and could not become aroused. She thought of all those nights when she had lain alone in this bed afire with longing, when out of desperation she had touched her own body. Where were those feelings now? Why could she no longer feel them now that her husband was at her side?

She pretended desire. She hoped her kisses seemed passionate. She hoped her tiny moans seemed sincere.

Gordon seemed to be going through some sort of ritual, touching first one breast and then the other, thrusting his fingers in her vagina, sucking on her nipples. He would touch himself to check his progress and have her masturbate him. But his penis stayed limp in her hand. Then the whole sequence would be repeated. He sucked too hard on her nipples. It was painful. He changed from two fingers to three as he thrust at her vagina. The thrusting grew more desperate, too rough. She wanted to pull away.

And still his penis refused to respond.

Stella tried again to manipulate him to an erection. Please, she thought, as she concentrated on the flaccid penis. Please. He needed it to feel right about himself. Stella felt a sick desperation. What would happen to them? Gordon would hate her. He would hate himself.

What had happened to him over there that had done this to him. God only knows what horrors he had experienced. Only she could make it right for him.

She knelt at his feet as Gordon sat weeping on the side of the bed. She whispered of her love. She kissed his palms and each fingertip. She kissed his chest, lingering over his nipples. She buried her face against his belly, compassion painfully swelling in her chest and throat.

She would help him. She would make everything all right. This man was her beloved husband returned from war. She was his wife. She would do anything to make him happy.

Gordon was frightened. Really frightened. The implications of not having an erection overwhelmed him. His life hung in the balance.

He watched Stella kneel beside him. Could he let her do that? Stella was a good woman. His wife. But his mind refused to examine reasons.

All he had to do was think of that boy, and it would happen.

Gordon allowed his wife's warm mouth to nurse him into desire, but when he was sure of his erection, he pulled her into the bed beside him and quickly pushed himself into her vagina. Relief spread throughout his body as he reclaimed his wife. Stella, who made him a man.

Afterward Gordon stared into the darkness. How had she known to do that to him?

Francie insisted her father fix her breakfast the next morning. Two things became apparent to Stella as she watched father and daughter together. Gordon adored Francie, and Francie knew it.

Twenty-two

W hat a beautiful little girl," the cashier exclaimed.
Francie was perched on Gordon's arm, her plump little arm circling his neck. Her dress was pink-and-white striped with a white collar and carefully ironed ruffles around the hem and the sleeves. Gordon turned and regarded his daughter, then kissed her cheek. As many times as he heard it, he never tired of the words. Frances *was* beautiful. Her hair framed her face in dark ringlets. Her dark eyes were not only bright and unusually large, but framed with a set of incredibly thick black lashes. Her upper lip protruded over her lower lip in a way that was both innocent and provocative. Gordon was certain there had never been a more beautiful child.

Gordon found himself disliking people who failed to comment on Francie's beauty. Parishioners especially.

Gordon thanked the cashier for her compliment and paid for his purchases. She called to another woman in the back of the drugstore. "Ethel, come up here and look at this precious child."

Ethel hurried up to touch Francie's hair and pat her arm. "What a little angel. How old are you, honey?" She watched as Francie held up three fingers. "Three years old! What a pretty girl you are. Just look at those eyes and that pretty little mouth. Isn't she something?"

The cashier nodded. "You'll have to beat the boys away with a stick someday," she told Gordon.

Gordon thought about that sometimes—of those boys who would come around someday. Already he disliked them. They wouldn't be good enough for Francie, but he didn't worry much about that distant day. Right now he was the man in her life. She loved her daddy more than anyone else.

Gordon couldn't believe how quickly his daughter had become the brightest light in his life. He looked over at her sitting in her car seat like a young princess on her throne. "You Daddy's girl?" he asked. Francie smiled and nodded. Yes, she was her daddy's girl. Francie was a constant source of joy, and Gordon's love for her was so pure and uncomplicated. He never wondered what Francie thought of him. He knew. He never saw doubt in her eyes, never wondered if she secretly had ever loved another daddy more. He did not have to prove anything to Francie.

Gordon ignored Stella's pleas that he was spoiling the child. He rocked her to sleep every night. When her daddy was at the table, Francie refused to eat unless he fed her. "She's old enough to feed herself," Stella protested. But Gordon liked indulging her. He liked the way she squealed with delight when he got home and she came running to him with her arms out, knowing he would pick her up and hug her.

His enchantment with fatherhood helped to ease his disenchantment with the ministry. Every day the burden of finding answers for a congregation of people became more difficult. Their faith seemed stronger than his, and he resented them for it. They should be telling him how to believe in a God who allowed a Dachau in this world. Yet he liked the deference that being a clergyman brought him. He liked the special category into which he and his family were automatically placed. The chosen of God. The women of the congregation—from the oldest to the youngest—especially wanted his attention, his handshake, his smile. He read books and journal articles that justified the church as a social institution. Organized religion was valid in preserving social order. It was worthy of support no matter what one's personal convictions—or lack of them.

Gordon wasn't sure if he should continue in the ministry, but he did know that he wanted more children. Soon. Fatherhood was the most satisfying part of his life, and he had missed most of Stella's first pregnancy. He would like to experience a pregnant wife at his side. What a fine feeling that must be for a man.

When Gordon stepped into the pulpit of Christ the King Methodist Church in Arlington, a community midway between Dallas and Fort Worth, he moved his family into a rundown parsonage located next door to the church. With some paint and repairs, the house could be made nice, but as Stella toured the house for the first time, she knew she wouldn't bother. They would not be there very long. Gordon either wanted a big, important church or a new direction. Arlington was an interim step. He was ambitious for bigger and better things. Gordon was considering many options, but Stella realized there was one thing of which her husband was certain. He wanted to be an important man someday.

When Stella read the announcement of his appointment in Arlington's weekly newspaper, she learned for the first time of Gordon's Distinguished Service Cross awarded for bravery in combat. Why had he told the newspaper something he had never told her?

Stella cleaned the house and arranged the furniture. She used what curtains she already had. She hung the seascape over the sideboard in the dining room. Francie's room was down the hall from the master bedroom, with the guest room in between. That was good. Sex would have a better chance.

By the time the appointment came from Westminster Methodist in Fort Worth, Stella was pregnant with their second child. With this pregnancy, there was morning sickness. Gordon was solicitous. He hovered during those first awful months and helped around the house.

"Oh, Gordon, I'll be all right," Stella said when he brought a plate with crackers and a sectioned orange. She had discovered that crackers eaten dry with no liquid helped prevent morning sickness. "Just take care of feeding Francie. It's the sight of food this early that bothers me the most."

"Francie has eaten. As soon as I get her dressed, I'll bring her in here. I've told her she will have to color quietly until you feel like getting up. Be sure to eat the crackers first before you have the orange. I was reading that diet the doctor gave you, and you aren't getting enough citrus fruit."

Gordon adjusted the pillow behind her and kissed her cheek. "And don't worry about cooking," he said. "Mrs. Brammer is bringing over dinner tonight. You remember her—she teaches the young adult Sunday school class. She says she was like this with her second pregnancy."

Stella nodded and nibbled her crackers. Why did she feel so grateful to him? He was her husband and should take care of her when she was pregnant and sick. But that's how she felt—grateful and a little guilty because she was neglecting the house and Francie.

Even though it put the household budget in the red, Gordon hired a woman to come in one morning a week until Stella felt better. Actually, as Stella pointed out from time to time, there was other money besides Gordon's salary. There was income from the trust fund that her father had left her. They had never touched a cent of it because Gordon refused to use that money. It wasn't necessary. He could support his family. They'd save the trust for their children.

Gordon came home to lunch when he could. He took Francie off on late-afternoon excursions so Stella could rest before he helped her prepare a simple dinner. When Stella began to feel better, he discouraged her from doing too much too soon. Stella realized he had enjoyed having her dependent on him.

Westminster operated a day school for grades kindergarten through eight. Gordon took great interest in the operation of the school. He found his responsibilities there more to his liking than the church itself.

The Westminster parsonage was in better condition than the one in Arlington, but it was an unadorned, serious house that was saved from severity by an abundance of tall, arched windows. Gordon's study was across the entry hall from the living room. The seascape hung on a landing of the wide, uncarpeted stairway.

Their two sons were born in rapid order. Brian first, and thirteen months later, Tom. Brian was as beautiful as Francie. Tom was plain from the day he was born, favoring the squat, thick Behrman males.

Three children. How amazing. A beautiful five-year-old daughter. A pair of baby boys. Stella was proud and tired. Always tired. Sometimes she felt like she was being buried alive in laundry and formula and hungry children. She was responsible for what her family ate and wore. She was responsible for their cleanliness, health, and entertainment. When Gordon had to put on his robe and go downstairs to the utility room to look for clean underwear, Stella was apologetic. "I'm so sorry. I'll get it put up this morning." But there were as many dirty clothes in the hamper as there were clean ones to be folded. There was a basket of wet clothes waiting to be hung out on the line in the backyard. And another basket of ironing to be done. Gordon's shirts. Francie's dresses. It was so endless.

But in spite of her growing family, or perhaps because of it, Stella wanted very much to be a part of the church-run school that her husband administered. She could teach history. Just one or two classes a day while Francie went to afternoon kindergarten and the boys napped.

Gordon resisted the idea.

"You can teach Sunday school, Stella, but I don't think it would look right for you to leave small children and go to work. It would look like I wasn't doing enough to provide for this family."

Stella didn't quite understand how Gordon had gained so much control over her life. Perhaps fatherhood and the paternalistic nature of his ministerial career made Gordon authoritarian. But what made her accept it? She felt the personalities of her parents being superimposed on herself and her husband. She was a passive Anna to Gordon's stern Frederick. Stella squared her shoulders and fought off feelings of inevitability.

"I don't have to be paid," she insisted. "Tell everyone I'm volunteering. Just one class. I not only need to do this, Gordon, I believe it is my right."

Gordon frowned. But after cautioning Stella about neglecting her duties as a minister's wife and her duties at home, Gordon announced from his pulpit one Sunday that Mrs. Kendall would be teaching Texas history to the eighth graders—as an unpaid volunteer—using her God-given talents to serve the congregation.

Gordon looked down at his wife. She nodded and smiled at him from the front pew. She looked lovely. Somehow her simple department-store suit and single strand of imitation pearls managed to look elegant. Just the right amount of makeup enhanced her gray eyes. Her dark hair was shiny and smooth, her lipstick a soft pink. Her earrings were small gold knots, her black pumps plain but carefully shined. Her hands were folded in her lap, her gold wedding set her only rings. An impenetrable aura of poise surrounded her. He wanted more from her than a smile, but what did he expect—thrown kisses during a church service? Stella wasn't the type to throw kisses anyway. She would hug him later and tell him thank you, her soft mouth again curving in a smile, but Gordon would still feel cheated.

Gordon realized that his wife was a bright woman and might at times desire more intellectual stimulation out of life than was provided by home and family, but having a wife who worked diminished a man. Even though Stella was not going to be working for money, her teaching job implied that she needed more out of life than was offered by wifehood and motherhood. Gordon wanted very much for Stella to be satisfied as his wife. He wished Stella were more like her cousin Effie. He wished she would fuss over him. He wished she adored him. If Stella adored him, he would feel better about so many things, but he was never quite sure what she thought of him. Did she really admire his sermons as she said she did? In their bedroom at night did she really want him to make love to her?

Stella was acutely aware of Gordon's reluctance over her teaching, and she felt uncomfortable in her victory. But she went ahead with her preparations.

She bought an old rolltop desk at a secondhand furniture store and had it moved to the parsonage's oversized utility room. She oiled the desk's dry wood and mended its broken drawers. She lined her reference books along the broad top. She put her empty lesson plan book and a supply of paper and pencils inside. In the file drawers she organized her collections of newspaper and magazine clippings on Texas history and present-day happenings that were history in the making. In other drawers she stored her college notebooks.

She saved a few drawers for household papers and bills, but most of the desk was hers only. The desk drew her like a magnet. Dozens of times during the day she would go out to the utility room to admire it there between the Maytag and the white metal cabinet that held laundry supplies. Her desk. She did not share it with anyone. Francie was fascinated with the assortment of drawers, some of which were no more than a few inches wide. Gordon suggested Stella designate one drawer as Francie's. Stella didn't like the idea, but somehow it seemed selfish not to. Francie would kneel on the chair in front of the open desk "working" with her pencils and notebook. Stella put an end to sharing when Francie colored the pages of Stella's copy of Mary Austin Holley's *Texas Diary*, a treasure left over from the days when Stella haunted used bookstores in Austin with Blanche Lasseter. After that, she always kept the desk locked to keep Francie and Brian out. Tom wasn't getting into things—yet. Stella built a shelf above the desk to get her books out of reach of adventurous children who climbed on the Maytag. She kept her most treasured books locked inside the desk's ample interior.

Stella supposed it was pitiful that having her own desk meant so much to her. She remembered with a tinge of longing the privacy she had enjoyed while Gordon was overseas. Until Francie was born, she had lived alone for the first time in her life—and probably the last. Now she shared a house and bed and closet space with her family. And the medicine cabinet and a chest of drawers. And her bed. Seldom was she in bed alone. If Gordon wasn't there, one or more of the children were. There was no place in the house that was just for her. Gordon had a study opposite the living room and an office at the church that were both inviolate. Stella supposed that most women had proprietary feelings about their kitchen, but the kitchen was the most communal room in the house. She worked there a great deal, but it wasn't *her* room. The desk by the washing machine, however, was hers. Her only privacy was in that desk. Just to have a ruler and scissors and string locked dependably away where she wouldn't always have to search for them was satisfying.

She hired a woman to come in right after lunch while the boys took their naps. She hurried to the school with Francie, dropped her daughter off at her kindergarten class, and climbed the stairs to her borrowed classroom. Usually she got home before the boys woke up—Tom cried if she wasn't there. Then she would give the boys a snack, and with Tom in the baby buggy and Brian poking along at her side, the fat new puppy sometimes following, they would walk to school and meet Francie. It was difficult to find time to prepare her lesson plans and grade papers. The puppy resisted housebreaking as much as Brian did toilet training. Gordon expected his meals on time. Francie's starched and ruffled dresses took forever to iron, and Francie never seemed to be able to wear them more than one day. "I like to look pretty," Francie explained. "Wrinkles are ugly. The teacher always says how nice I look."

Teaching made Stella's life difficult, but it was better than not doing it.

She thought of jotting a note to Charles to tell him she was teaching history again, that it made her think of Blanche, that she had three children now. But she didn't. Let sleeping dogs lie.

But she thought of him often. He was there in her heart—no longer an ache, but a part of her nevertheless. Sometimes she wondered what it would have been like if she had agreed to his calling her after the war.

Stella seldom actually had the chance to sit in front of her wonderful desk. Her reading and class preparation was usually combined with other things—often with being at the park or at the kitchen table while her children ate, played games, colored. She wanted to be innovative in the classroom. She wanted to be brilliant. But there were days when she was still reading the assigned chapter as her students filed into the room.

Other days, however, she would have somehow found the time to prepare special lectures offering those wonderful behind-the-scenes looks at history that had so illuminated her time in Blanche Lasseter's classroom. Stella loved the look on her students' faces when they began listening to her as they would to someone telling a fascinating story. They forgot they didn't like history. They asked questions. They wanted more.

To prepare her lectures, Stella used her old college textbooks and notebooks. Some of the notebooks were filled with Blanche Lasseter's words. How those notebooks made it all come back! Stella stared at the words and could actually remember them coming out of Blanche's mouth. What a time that had been! Each day had been different and exciting. Even the examinations were wonderful. Stella had loved the preparation, the feeling of walking to class on exam day and knowing she was ready, that she would do well. Best of all, she had liked the research and writing. It was good to work hard on a paper and finish it. You could hold a finished paper in your hands. So much of what she did now was temporary. The floor she scrubbed got dirty again. The food she prepared got eaten. The laundry was all to do again. The only time Gordon noticed her work was when it *wasn't* done. But those college papers she had written stayed done. Blanche used to talk about getting their project on Texas women's history published when they finished it. Published. Permanent. In a book. On a shelf in a library. What a dream that had been! But Blanche had died.

Stella wondered if she would ever get back there—to the world of academe. Such a satisfying world. She still thought of graduate school, but perhaps she was yearning for a return to a way of life as much as she was yearning for knowledge. What else was there for her to yearn for, though? She wasn't sure why she needed something else when she had three healthy children and a good husband. And having a time in her life when she could do something like that—something so blatantly for herself—seemed remote indeed. Right now she was pleased to be teaching just one class even if she didn't have the dignity of a salary. The feeling she had after a really fine class session was euphoric.

Chicken pox provided the first problem with Stella's teaching arrangements. Then she had to miss several days when Brian broke his arm. When all three children were quarantined with whooping cough, Gordon hired a graduate student from Texas Christian University to take over the class. Stella told herself that her disappointment was disproportionate. After all, it was only one class. She really didn't have the time anyway, but it was with regret that she returned her history books and her notebooks to her desk, which now seemed foolish sitting there in the laundry room by the Maytag.

Not that she found motherhood lacking. Quite the contrary. Stella found that she was fiercely maternal. And motherhood provided moments of wonderful contentment.

At night she brought a book with her into the bathroom and sat on the toilet lid, supervising bath time. But she seldom got much reading done. She was easily distracted by the sight of three little bodies lined up naked and healthy in the big, footed bathtub—the sight of her children taking a bath was often more enchanting than the Texas War for Independence or the biography of the indomitable Sam Houston.

Francie tickled Tom and made him laugh. He had a funny little hiccupping laugh that made his older brother and sister laugh in turn. Brian poured a cupful of water over Tom's head, leaving him sputtering. He looked at his mommy to see if he should cry. Stella smiled a big-eyed smile to show him it was okay. Tom picked up the metal cup and returned the favor. Soon all three of them were pouring water over each other's heads. Stella put a towel on the floor to sop up their splashing.

"When's Tom's little wienie going to look like Brian's?" Francie asked.

"It's a penis," Stella corrected. "He has so much baby fat now that it kind of gets lost up there, but when he's not so chubby, his penis will look like Brian's."

"I'm glad girls don't have penises," Francie said. "Aren't you, mommy? They're silly-looking."

"If I were a boy, I'd want one," Stella said. "But since I'm a girl, I'm glad I don't have one."

Brian was busy soaping Tom's back. Francie soaped his front. Tom rubbed his hands over his torso, obviously enjoying the silky feeling of his soapy body.

"Baby Tom's clean," Francie said in her best big-sister voice.

"Baby Tom clean," Tom obligingly repeated.

"*I'm* not a baby," Brian said, drawing himself up to his full sitting height. "When you're three, you're not a baby."

Gordon thought it inappropriate that Stella still let seven-year-old Francie bathe with her brothers, and she supposed she'd have to end it soon. But she'd miss these times. She liked kneeling by the tub and joining in the soaping. She liked the feel of her children's young, supple flesh under her hands.

Sometimes when she buried her face against their necks and drank in the sweetness of their smell, Stella's eyes stung with tears. She couldn't touch them enough or kiss them enough. Their hair, their feet, their calves, their bottoms. She was in love with her children's bodies. She was in love with being a mother. She would do anything for her children.

Francie grew more bossy with each year, but her brothers didn't seem to mind. Often she would sit between them on the front-porch glider and read to them from her schoolbooks in her best grown-up voice. Tom would take his fingers out of his mouth and point at the correct picture in response to her schoolmarmish questions. Brian actually recognized words.

Stella took many photographs of her children, and even when she didn't have a camera in her hand, she had a feeling that she wanted to record each moment in her mind, to take out in a distant time and savor its sweetness. The puppy sharing plump baby Tom's zwieback. The ever-curious Brian hunkered down on the front lawn staring in wonder at an ant caravan. Francie's pride at her first piano recital. Tom and Brian curled up together like two puppies taking their afternoon nap. A laughing child being carried high on his father's shoulders.

Still, Stella never became accustomed to her children's mindless chatter and sometimes grew impatient with their endless questions. Francie, at times, seemed to take pleasure in tormenting her brothers. Stella worried that Tom would always feel inferior to his more beautiful and brighter siblings. She resented the constant demands of motherhood. It was a never-ending, messy, noisy, tiresome job. But her love for her children was unconditional. They did not have to be perfect or even special. Mother love made Stella more vulnerable than anything ever had or would. It made her heart leap every time the tires of a braking car squealed in front of the house. It brought the cold fingers of fear around her heart when she felt a feverish forehead, when a child complained of aching legs. Their hurts were hers ten times over.

During endless days of mothering, Stella would look forward to her husband's nightly homecoming, to having another adult in the house. But Gordon, who spent his days talking to people and discussing their problems, was not interested in more adult conversation when he arrived home. He'd ask Stella, "How was your day?" but he seldom waited for a response. Stella automatically answered, "Fine," as she leaned her cheek into his kiss, her hands continuing to chop, roll, stir, wash, whatever. "How was yours?" Gordon often gave her a perfunctory listing of the people he had seen, the business he had conducted on behalf of the school and church. Then he went upstairs to take off his coat and tie.

After dinner Gordon romped with the boys and cuddled with his Francie until the children went up to bed. Then Gordon read his newspaper—his favorite time of day, he often said. He read the newspaper from front to back, including the want ads. Stella would talk to him, babbling on about her day, what she had heard on the radio, what cute things the children had said, what awful things the children had done. Gordon only half-listened, nodding absently and saying, "Uh-huh," just as Stella herself often did with the children. She often had the feeling that her talking annoyed him, but she couldn't stop the flow of words. She had such a need to talk to an adult—even one who didn't really listen. Yet he wanted her there with him. "Where are you going?" he asked if she got up. "Sit here for a while. The dishes can wait." Stella didn't understand. Should she feel diminished or important?

But her family was her life, and she enjoyed doing things for them. She took special pleasure in fussing over birthdays and holidays. Christmas, with all its planning and secret missions, was best of all. Was there anything nicer on the earth than a family decorating a Christmas tree together, with Christmas carols playing on the radio, with cookies and stollen and coffee cakes all made from Anna's wonderful family recipes baking in the oven and filling the house with the smells of Stella's childhood?

Her children and her husband filled her life. Only at times did she puzzle over how much they filled it. When she had a moment to herself, she read. Gradually, she found herself giving up on history and biography and turning to women's magazines and current novels. Effie always had a novel or two that Stella "simply must read." Stella didn't seem to have the concentration or inclination for anything else, and even some of the novels didn't get finished. Something in the book would make her think of Charles. It would slide into her lap, and her mind would wander. In a book people often got their heart's delight. More often than not obstacles were surmounted, or spouses conveniently died or went away. But life was not a book, and Stella didn't want Gordon to die. She wanted to raise her children with her husband at her side. She and Gordon would grow old together. Charles was no more real than the novels. And her husband was a worthy man.

Stella wished they lived in Dallas near Effie and Kate. She was often jealous because her sister and cousin got to see each other more frequently that she got to see either of them. Fort Worth was more than an hour's drive from Dallas. And Gordon didn't like her to use the car for long periods of time. A parishioner might need him. He might have to go to the hospital or call on a newly bereaved family. The bus was difficult with three children. A bus ride to her sister's or cousin's was almost a half-day trip. She would have lunch and visit awhile, then need to return home to fix dinner. It hardly seemed worth the effort. More often than not, Effie and Kate drove over to see her.

Stella felt left out. Effie and Kate's children played together. Their husbands didn't seem to mind if they hired baby-sitters and went to town for lunches and shopping. Of course, they weren't married to ministers. William was rich, and Jimmy was comfortable. And Jimmy didn't seem to mind if Kate used her trust money.

When the three women did get together, they talked of their husbands and of relatives back home. Effie was undauntedly happy. Her darling William was good to her—but who wouldn't be good to Effie, Stella and Kate agreed. Kate was pleased that Jimmy was a wonderful family man. He was tired of his job but enjoyed yard work and tinkering around their new home. He wanted a daughter. "Men all want a Daddy's girl, don't they?" Kate observed. And Gordon? He was restless and irritable. Stella worried about him.

Sometimes the three women would ponder. What if they had married someone else? What if Effie had stayed in school? What if Kate had put off motherhood and competed longer? What if Stella had gone back to New Braunfels and taught as her papa had wanted her to do?

Gordon's father died Easter Sunday, 1950. Gordon had already left for church when the phone call came from Gordon's uncle. Stella called her mother to come take care of the children. Then she called her cousin Jason to ask him to drive Anna to Fort Worth. She waited until after the service to tell Gordon. "Did he suffer?" Gordon asked.

"No. He died in his sleep," Stella said. Tom was fussing. She picked him up. He'd messed his pants. "Oh, Tom, bad boy. Why didn't you ask to use the potty? Brian, go find your sister. We need to go home now."

"I'll go change Tom," she said. Gordon wrinkled his nose at the smell. "When are you going to get that child trained?"

"I'll hurry," Stella said.

The rest of the family had already gone to the car when Stella returned from the rest room with Tom.

"Are you all right?" she asked Gordon as she got in the car. "Do you want me to drive?"

"No. I'm all right. Brian, stop roughhousing with your sister in the car." He sat with his hands on the steering wheel. "It's hard to believe," he said softly. "Hard to believe."

Stella fed the children and packed up the Easter ham and chocolate cake to take to Tyler. She and Gordon left as soon as her mother arrived.

The funeral was on Tuesday. Jimmy and Kate came with Effie and William. Every seat in the sanctuary was full, and several people stood in the back.

Gordon eulogized his father, beginning with a question. "What is a father?" He wound childhood reminiscences of his father with his own personal experiences with fatherhood. His father had been stern but loving. When he finished his remarks, Gordon walked over to the open casket and looked down. He leaned over to kiss his dead father's brow before the funeral director stepped forward and closed the casket. Gordon joined the pallbearers in carrying the casket down the aisle. His eyes were dry.

In Stella's arms that night, he asked in the darkness, "Why can't I cry?"

"Tears aren't always necessary," Stella said.

"He didn't love me," Gordon said. "My mother caught me and another little boy touching each other's penises when I was six. I don't think either one of them ever loved me after that."

"Oh, Gordon, that's ridiculous. I can't believe you said that. All children do things like that. It doesn't mean anything."

Gordon didn't try to tell her about the look on his parents' faces when he asked if could watch the neighbor's dog give birth. He didn't tell of the time his father caught him masturbating into the pages of a girlie magazine. Of his mother's disgust one morning when she discovered the sticky wetness on his sheets. He was more careful after that.

"No, it didn't mean anything, but my parents thought it did. Or maybe they were just looking for an excuse. Maybe my presence was an embarrassment to them. It proved they had been carnal at least once, didn't it? Parenthood was difficult for them. It's hard to raise kids without touching them, but they gave it their best. I didn't cry when my mother died either."

"But you loved her," Stella said softly.

"God, yes. I would have done anything for her. I just wish she had loved me. I wish my father had loved me."

Then he sobbed.

"You're such a good father," Stella told him soothingly as she stroked his back. "You're not like your father at all."

"Make love to me, Stella," Gordon whispered. "I need you."

"Of course," Stella said. She massaged his soft penis into erection.

It took a long time tonight. Her hand grew weary until finally he reached for her. But her nightgown was still on. He wanted it off. By the time she was naked in his arms, his erection had faded. Stella used her other hand to massage him back to firmness.

Her parents hadn't touched her either, Stella thought later in the darkness, but they had wanted to. They just didn't know how.

The wetness trickling from her vagina bothered her. Stella went into the bathroom and dried herself. She put her nightgown back on before she got into bed.

Gordon proved to be an excellent administrator. Under his leadership both Westminster's congregation and academy grew. The sanctuary was enlarged. A high school was added to the academy. Gordon took graduate classes in school administration two nights a week at TCU.

When the Korean War broke out, Gordon went into his study and closed the door. Another war. He stared at the photograph of his family in its brass frame. Did God expect him to go to war again? But hadn't he done enough in Europe? Why did he still feel that he owed someone something? Why did the memory of Dachau make him feel he must suffer other horrors? He was older now. Thirty-eight. Would his age make him braver and more secure in his faith? What could this war teach him about himself?

But Gordon knew he did not have the courage to find out. If Jesus Christ himself had appeared in front of his desk and asked him to go, Gordon was not sure he could.

Stella tapped on the door to tell him dinner was ready.

"You and the children go ahead," he called.

He buried his face in his hands. War. Godless war.

K rations. Mud. Shells bursting. Mines exploding. Death. Dachau. The smells. And Micah.

Gordon worked with the Fort Worth Ministerial Alliance to organize vigils of Prayers for Peace. He was tireless in his efforts and was awarded a commendation from the alliance. They ran his picture on the front page of the Fort Worth *Star Telegram*.

Twenty-three

Jimmy did not try to resume his career as a touring golf professional; instead he became the assistant pro at the Dallas Golf and Country Club. He traded in Mark's first set of golf clubs for a set that fit his present height. Mark often played a round of golf with his father on Sunday afternoons. "I think the boy has real potential," Jimmy would tell Kate eagerly. "If he ever makes the pro tour, I'll retire and be his caddie."

"Do caddies earn enough to make house payments?" Kate snapped, feeling left out of this image of Jimmy caddying for their son, the professional golfer. But she wanted it too—the thrill of seeing her children succeed. She thought Mark's best shot was in baseball, however. Pitching. He was good. She dreamed of a college scholarship and a major league career for him.

When the Korean War broke out, Jimmy considered reenlisting. After four years of teaching rich men how to improve their golf swing, he had come to regard his war years ever more fondly. But Korea wasn't England. His time in London had been fantastic. He still missed the pubs with the camaraderie, the singing, the dancing, the flirting—all made so special by not knowing what tomorrow would bring. It was terrible and glorious. The best and the worst. And the sweetest. Linda had been that. Jimmy doubted he would ever again live so fully. War in Asia could never be like that. So he accepted an offer as a salesman with a sporting goods manufacturer and discovered he had a natural flare for selling.

Jimmy traveled a great deal, calling on high school and college coaches and athletic directors. With the growing interest in weight training for football players and other athletes, he helped high schools and colleges establish weight programs and equip weight rooms. As the company grew, he earned promotions, higher salaries, and fine commissions. But he knew he would never be invited to serve on the board. He was their best salesman and wasn't paid to think. Good ol' back-slapping

Jimmy Morris with the big grin, hearty handshake, and stories about his golfing days when he'd played with the greats.

After a few years, however, he found himself spending a lot of time in his parked car, psyching himself up to go inside the next coach's office, to make a presentation before yet another school board. He grew weary of hearty. His tales of Byron Nelson, Ralph Guldahl, Gene Sarazen, and others made him remember the time when he had aspired to greatness himself. He became bored with athletic equipment, with coaches and physical fitness experts. His own body grew soft while he explained about his company's surefire systems. His smile was starting to feel painted-on.

While Anna's trust fund had been for life, under the conditions of Frederick's will, his daughters' trusts dissolved when they reached age thirty. Kate used the principal on her trust to make a substantial down payment on a fine new Tudor-style house in Grand Prairie on a half acre of land. The monthly payments would be impressive, but Jimmy was doing well—well enough to have a swimming pool put in the backyard as well as a racquetball court that doubled for half-court basketball. Kate was thrilled with her new house. She took an almost sensual pleasure in its surfaces and obsessively spent as much time as her children would allow waxing, vacuuming, polishing.

If only Papa were still alive, Kate often thought. How she would have liked to show him her fine house. His darling Stella lived in an old parsonage, but Kate lived in a grand house with a swimming pool.

The house was a good place to raise her family. At first she was able to keep her stomach reasonably flat by swimming endless laps in the pool, but her third pregnancy made her tired. She napped more than she swam.

Like each of her two previous pregnancies, her third added ten pounds to her figure. She had become the plump mother of three sons. Her wardrobe consisted of flowing tops to be worn untucked over skirts or pants. She preferred pants. Often she wore one of Jimmy's shirts over jeans.

As Kate's second and third sons entered her life, her days on the links—and the courts, both tennis and basketball—seemed more and more remote. Her clubs grew dusty in the garage. It was Jimmy who instructed Mark in the intricacies of the game.

But Kate dreamed of golf.

In her dreams she still swung the club in a perfect arc and watched the ball sail down the fairway. In her dreams she heard the solid *whump* as the clubhead hit the ball. She chipped to within inches of the cup. She blasted out of sand traps. She was magnificent from the rough. She leaned over balls, concentrating before executing dramatic putts from the apron. And people were watching. Always people were watching. Women and men. Clapping. Sometimes cheering. Even the men thought she was incredible.

Kate didn't tell anyone about her dreams. Not even Jimmy. She wondered what other women dreamed about.

She asked Effie and Stella. They had returned from Christmas shopping. A bone-chilling wind had swept unmercifully through the tall canyons of downtown Dallas. Effie fixed spiced tea.

Effie's hair was windblown and her cheeks still red. She looked like a girl.

When the wind blew Stella's hair, it always settled itself back smoothly onto her head, a rich, sleek curtain of brown that stopped just below her collar. Stella never looked ruffled, never acted that way either.

Effie said she often dreamed about their New Braunfels days—being a girl again and having chickens and goats and living with her mama and papa. "And other things," she admitted. "Usually nonsense. Time gets messed up. Dear cousin Carl will be helping our children ride on my old donkey."

"I dream of Papa a lot," Stella said, cradling her warm cup between her hands. "And Blanche Lasseter and Carl. The beloved dead. It's so strange how they can be alive in dreams. And I dream sometimes that I can fly like a bird. Silly things . . ."

Stella stopped talking and looked down at her hands. A small shudder went through her torso. Kate noticed. *My God*, Kate thought, *Stella dreams about a man*. It was that man she had lunch with during the war. Blanche Lasseter's nephew. Kate remembered very well the look on Stella's face the day he stopped at their table in Neiman's.

Kate felt a wave of anger toward her sister. Stella was stupid. What was the point in harboring an old love? What was the point in being discontent? Of course, Kate herself dreamed about an old love of sorts, but golf wasn't a man. Golf didn't make her vulnerable.

Did Effie dream about men too? Probably. But Effie could handle it.

"So what do you dream about, Kate?" Effie asked.

"Oh, same as you guys," she answered with shrug. "Things from before mixed up with the present. Or my kids frolicking in a field of wildflowers with Sam, that old black-and-white dog we used to have. Sometimes I dream I'm climbing stairs that just keep going up and up, and I never make it to the top."

Kate followed the emerging women's professional golf tour. She read of Babe Didrikson Zaharias's victories. She watched other women become celebrities. Patty Berg. Betsy Rawls. Louise Suggs. Their clubs hadn't grown dusty in garages. They had been practicing during the war. And now they won money—not the fantastic amounts of money that men won—but suddenly women as professional athletes were respected. Babe wasn't making money by putting on golf exhibitions or being the only woman on a men's exhibition basketball team. She was a competing professional.

Then suddenly Babe had cancer. Kate wrote her a letter and sent it to the hospital in Beaumont. "You don't remember me, I'm sure. We met only a few times before the war. But you have been my hero since I was a girl. When you won those medals at the Olympics, you made me proud to be a girl."

When Babe died, Kate cried.

Kate's trophy collection went from the family room to an upstairs hallway. Finally she moved it to the attic. The fact that she had once been a very promising athlete was now an embarrassment, considering her far-from-athletic body. She seldom swam laps now. Her once-slim body assumed the matronly proportions she feared would be hers for the rest of her life.

The trophy case didn't remain in the attic very long, however. She had it refinished and reinstalled in the family room to provide space for the next generation of athletic trophies.

The announcement in the University of Texas alumni magazine of the death of Frank Billingsly, professor emeritus of zoology, almost went unnoticed by Kate. Then her eyes returned to the name.

Frank Billingsly. God, that was a hundred years ago. She hadn't thought about him in years. He must have been ancient. It was embarrassing to remember what a stupid little twit she had been to go screw the zoo prof. But he had wanted her so much. That's what she remembered most. She remembered how grateful he had been to be allowed to touch her body and make love to her, how his sweet words of praise brought tears to her eyes. Of course, she realized now she hadn't really been in love with the aging professor. It was just a predictable schoolgirl crush. Lonely coed. Horny old professor out to lay anything young.

Little League was the most intense part of Kate's life. She participated in the Kappa alumnae group and other ladies' groups only when they didn't interfere with her Mark's ball games. With year-old Freddy sitting in the stroller or napping in the back of the station wagon, and five-year-old Jeffie playing in the dirt or swinging at a nearby playground, Kate would station herself in her lawn chair, a thermos of lemonade at her side, a sack of cookies presumably for Freddy and Jeff. Mark pitched or played shortstop. Jimmy joined her whenever he was in town, and side by side they would watch their athletically precocious son. Kate preferred to watch the game alone, however. She didn't like it when Jimmy came or another mother pulled up a chair and sat beside her, although she enjoyed the after-game camaraderie among the parents—especially when they praised Mark. During the game, though, Kate needed to concentrate. She held her breath with each pitch. Her heart pounded furiously every time Mark came to bat. Kate liked the team to win, but how Mark performed was infinitely more important.

She prayed. *Please God, let him throw a strike. Please God, let him get at least a base hit. Don't let him make the final out. Please.*

Often Mark would look over at her from the pitcher's mound after a strike. She would give him the thumbs-up sign.

The euphoria Kate felt from a well-pitched game, a sensational play, a home run lasted for days. At dinner she and Mark would replay the game's high points for Jimmy's benefit.

Next year their number-two son would be on a Little League T-ball team. Jeff could throw a ball better than his friends, and Kate thought Jeff might be an even better basketball player. He was already taller than Mark had been at five. She taught Jeff to dribble and had a six-foot-high basket hoop installed beside the driveway next to the regulation one.

Jeff had red hair. When Mark was blessed with his father's wavy blond hair, Kate had been grateful. During her second pregnancy, she had known the baby growing within her had carrot-colored locks. Jimmy thought his redheaded, freckled-faced son was adorable—"straight out of a Norman Rockwell painting on the cover of *Collier's*"—but Kate wouldn't have wished her hair and freckles on anyone, most of all, one of her children. Yet she felt a special bond with little Jeffie because of it.

Her baby, Freddy, was another blond. It was too early to tell about his athletic prowess. And now, at age thirty-two, she was pregnant again. She and Jimmy decided to try one last time for a daughter. When she had broached the subject of having another baby, Jimmy had said from his side of the bed, "Sure. We're still young. I make enough money. I think kids are the best part of life for both of us." And they made love. Warmly, affectionately, making-a-baby kind of love with words of commitment. A good life. Good kids. How lucky they were. Always. Forever.

Kate thought from time to time how she used to say she was never going to marry and have children. Children were her life now. She didn't look back. She couldn't regret abandoning her dream of gold medals, of being a famous female athlete. That would be like regretting her children. Maybe it would have been possible to have been a mother and a competing athlete, but Kate didn't see how. At least for her. She was a full-time, station-wagon-driving mother. She seldom had a tube of lipstick in her purse, but she was never without Kleenex, Band-Aids, baby aspirin, and zwieback teething biscuits.

Grand Prairie was halfway between Dallas, where Effie lived in her elegant Turtle Creek mansion, and Fort Worth, where Stella lived in the Westminster parsonage. Kate's big house with its wonderful pool and yard became a favorite summertime gathering place for the cousins of both generations. Sometimes they came on weekends and included the men in backyard cookouts and swimming. But more often than not, it would be a weekday happening with just women and children. Effie would come from Dallas with Billy to spend the afternoon. Stella would come from Fort Worth with Francie, Brian, and Tom.

For Mark's tenth birthday they gathered for the day. Jimmy took the afternoon off to drive to New Braunfels to pick up his mother-in-law. All the daddies would be coming for dinner, and afterwards everyone was going to attend Mark's ball game.

At fourteen, Effie's Billy was a gangling lad with braces. Not an early-maturing boy, his chest was still thin, and only a trace of fuzz decorated his upper lip. Billy was good-natured and seemed equally at ease playing hide-and-seek with his younger cousins as in the company of his older relatives. He treated Effie more like a date than his mother, always waiting on her and asking her if she needed anything. And Effie, ever appreciative, would smile and kiss his cheek or touch his hand.

"You run along and keep Francie and Mark from arguing," Effie said.

She watched her son lope across the yard, her smile pensive, her expression soft. "I think it's time that boy gets himself a girlfriend, but I'm going to miss my sweet boy when he does."

"He does love his mother," Kate agreed. "How's his batting average?"

"I'm not sure," Effie answered. "He's not as interested this year, and I think this will be his last year for baseball. He thinks he may want to go to a music camp over in Arkansas next year. Says he's going to get serious about his French horn. Of course, what he's really smitten with is everything that has anything to do with aviation. He's already talking about taking flying lessons when he's old enough, but his father won't hear of it."

Francie came to sit with the women, her expression sullen. "I don't see why I have to spend my day with those stupid boys."

"Next time why don't you bring a friend?" Kate said. "It sure took us a long time to get another girl cousin, didn't it, honey?"

Francie nodded, but her expression indicated that a baby female cousin was inconsequential.

"Why don't you go and look in that sack on the dining room table? There just might be a new Nancy Drew mystery in there for a bored girl cousin."

Francie's face lit up. "Thanks, Aunt Kate. That's great."

"That's thoughtful of you, Kate," Stella said, as she watched Francie hurry into the house.

Kate shrugged. She was glad she had thought of it. It was something Effie would have done.

"Did you notice that Francie's getting a waist?" Stella asked. "I think she's going to mature early. We've already had some little talks, but she acts so bored."

"Remember when poor Mama talked to us?" Kate asked. "It was really painful for her."

"Yes," Stella said. "She never said why women bled every month. She only gave instructions about what to do about it. It's hard to believe that she and Papa ever had sex."

"I'd hear my parents at night," Effie said. "They'd moan and groan, and the headboard of their bed would hit against the wall. Once when I was a little girl, I asked them about it, and Mama said it was a game she and Papa sometimes played late at night. As I recall, they also played the game on Sunday afternoon. 'You children go out and play. Your mama and I are going to have our Sabbath rest.' "

Stella went in the kitchen to get the coffee while Kate stacked up the paper plates from their hot dog lunch and Effie dished up three servings of the peach cobbler she had brought. The kids could have theirs later. Right now, the mothers just wanted to sit and relax.

Kate felt a tinge of irritation when Effie handed her a piece of cobbler noticeably smaller than the ones she had dished up for herself and Stella. Effie would never give up. Kate was sure that before the day was over her cousin would be telling about some new wonderful diet that helped this friend or the other lose weight.

"When can we swim, Aunt Kate?" Tom asked, his words muffled by his fingers in his mouth. Tom, at four, had never completely lost his baby fat. He was a plump, serious little boy who forever kept the three fingers of his left hand in his mouth. His father was always getting onto him about it. Kate thought Gordon was too stern with Tom.

"You can swim in one hour, honey," Kate said, grabbing her nephew's little fat face and kissing his nose. "Your food has to digest first."

Tom nodded solemnly and wandered over to watch his brother play basketball with the cousins.

Brian and Mark had taken on Billy and Jeff in a basketball game. They yelled for Tom to get out of the way.

Jeff's hair was brilliantly orange in the sunlight. It made him stand out. At six, he was tall and agile for his age. Kate wondered if he would be an even better athlete than Mark.

Kate got a set of box toy trucks from the garage and put Tom to work with little Freddy building roads in the huge sandbox that Jimmy had built. "You have to be the big boy," she told Tom, "and teach your cousin Freddy how to build roads in the sand."

Kate's baby, four-month-old Sara, was asleep on a pallet under the elm tree. Sara's curly hair was a pretty strawberry blond that seemed to be a blending of her mother's and her father's hair color. Kate hoped it stayed that way and didn't turn carroty, and she hoped the freckles stayed away. "Did I have freckles when I was a baby?" Kate had asked her mother. Anna couldn't remember.

Kate had thought it would be easy to slip another baby into their lives, but she had to admit she was spread pretty thin these days. She was tired all the time and never seemed to get everything done. She wished she had more time to decorate her house and work in the yard. She liked her house. Jimmy had suggested she wean this baby early. She was considering it.

"Sometimes I still can't believe I really have four children," Kate said as she sank into her lawn chair.

"You're the most fantastic mother of four ever," Stella announced as she arrived with the coffee. "I can't believe Sara is already four months old. It seems like she was born last week. I don't know why time is in such a hurry. I want them all to stay children forever."

"Sara is beautiful," Effie said, looking over at the sleeping child under the tree. "Such a dainty little thing. And Lord, that hair! Prettiest hair I've ever seen."

Kate beamed. "Yeah. Her daddy thinks she's pretty special too."

"Jimmy said you're playing golf again," Stella said. "I don't know how you find the time."

Kate nodded and took a bite of the cobbler. "My God, Effie, this cobbler's fantastic."

Kate didn't want to talk about the golf. It was too soon. No, she didn't have the time—or the energy. She was exhausted to the point of dropping after just nine holes, but she couldn't just keep on having babies. She'd promised herself all during this last pregnancy that she would play golf again. She didn't know how she felt about it yet, though. Any of it. Hiring a baby-sitter so she could play. How awfully she hit the ball. How fantastic it felt when she wasn't awful. What it was she wanted out of golf. She had not played for almost a dozen years. Not a stroke. And she wasn't sure why. She wasn't even sure why she didn't say no this year when they called from the country club about her joining the ladies' golf association. She would have quit if any of them had said anything about her former athletic accomplishments, but no one said a word. No one knew.

Kate sipped her coffee and half listened to Effie and Stella discussing what to do about Aunt Hannah's cataracts. The covered patio was nice. The extension on the roof was worth the money. It would be too hot to sit out here without it. Kate wondered what time Jimmy would arrive with Mama. What would have happened if she had used a five iron on that second shot on the fifth hole?

How peaceful it was.

Then Kate sat up straight and put down her cup. It was too peaceful. Tom and Freddy were still in the sandbox. Sara was still asleep under the tree. But the handball court was deserted. Where had the boys gone? Small hairs stood up on the back of Kate's neck. But the gate to the pool enclosure was securely locked. She relaxed.

Sometimes she forgot how big they were all getting. The big boys would look after Jeff and Brian.

There was no sound coming from inside the house. Maybe they were in the front yard.

"Aunt Kate," Francie called from the back door, "the boys have crawled out on the roof."

"Jesus Christ," Kate said under her breath. "I caught Mark and Jeff up there last week and told them I'd tan their hides good if they ever did that again."

Stella put down her cup, alarm on her face. Effie raced out in the yard and stood with her hand shielding her eyes. "Billy Chambers, you get those boys down from there. You hear me. Right now."

Kate heard the tumbling, the out-of-control sliding, then a second of nothing. The crash was almost directly over her head as a child's body hit the patio roof, then slid down over the edge. Before Jeff hit the patio's brick apron, Kate knew it was him. She could tell by the red hair.

She screamed.

"Don't move him," Stella yelled. "He's landed on his back."

Kate knelt beside the still form of her child, fear turning her insides to liquid. She wanted to pick him up, to press him against her heart, but she only touched his face.

In that instant she remembered how she had once asked God never to take Mark from her, how she prayed that if she ever had to lose a child please not to let it be Mark.

What if God was collecting on her bargain?

"I'll call the ambulance," Effie said, racing into the house.

Stella knelt beside her sister. "He's breathing," she said.

"Oh, Stella, what if he dies?"

"I don't think he'll die, honey. His breathing seems okay, but he landed on his back. I just hope it's not broken."

A fearful image flashed across Kate's mind. A crippled child. Oh, no. That would be worse than death.

But instantly she took the thought back. She wanted Jeff to live at whatever cost. She'd be crippled for him. Don't let her baby die or be crippled. *I'll do anything,* Kate promised. *I'll never want anything for myself again if you'll please not let anything bad happen to my children, not my children. Not Jeff or Mark or Freddy or Sara. When I had just Mark, I didn't think it would be possible ever to love anyone else that much, but I love them all. I love them more than anything else. More than Jimmy. More than my sister or cousin or mother. More than golf. More than being skinny again. Please.*

Jeff was still unconscious when the ambulance arrived in the hospital, but in the examining room his red eyelashes fluttered open.

"Mom?"

"I'm here, honey. You know what happened, you little turkey? What in the world were you doing on the roof?"

"Mom, I can't feel anything."

"What do you mean, Jeff?"

"My body feels like it's gone away."

Kate had to fight the black fog that enveloped her. She had to stay awake. She had to face this. She was Jeff's mother.

It wasn't Jeff's back that was broken. It was his neck.

He was taken to surgery. When Kate and Jimmy next saw their son, grotesque scalp tongs had been mounted to the sides of his skull and fastened to hanging weights that immobilized his neck and pulled it straight and taut.

The doctor said the paralysis could be temporary, the result of tissue swelling around the nerves. It was too soon to tell. All they could do now was wait.

All through the night Kate sat by her sedated son's bed and prayed constantly. She cursed God. She threatened. She demanded. And she made her bargains. Jimmy sat at her side, ashen-faced.

Gordon and William stayed out at Kate and Jimmy's house to watch the children. A neighbor took Sara. Effie, Stella, and Anna stayed with Jimmy and Kate at the hospital through the night.

"Pray with me, please." Kate begged. "Let's all kneel and pray." She pulled Jimmy down beside her.

Stella knelt. Precious little Jeff, who had hair like his mommy's, her dear sister Kate. Jeff, a sweet boy who liked "Kukla, Fran, and Ollie" almost to obsession, who liked peanut butter on toast, who liked her to tell him stories about when his mommy was a little girl.

Anna would not kneel. "I'll make my peace in my own way," she said.

"Please, Mama. It's important to me."

"What difference does it make if I kneel?"

"I don't want to do anything wrong. I don't want to make God mad."

Anna sighed and forced her old knees into the required position. "This is foolishness, Kate."

"The Lord's Prayer, Mama."

Anna said the prayer in German. So many times she had said these words over the years—with faith and without. She wanted Jeff to be all right. He was a dear little boy. But if there was a God and if He wanted Jeff to be all right, He wouldn't need prayers to help Him make up His mind. And if there was a God, why had He sent Jeff tumbling off the roof, anyway? But the words to the prayer rolled off her tongue. They were familiar and comfortable.

Effie wept softly and said out loud, "Oh, dear God in heaven, help our darling Jeff. And help his mommy and daddy to be strong. We love little Jeffie very much. He's a good boy. Please let him run and play again with all his cousins."

Then Effie found a nurse and asked for a breast pump for her cousin. Kate dutifully pumped out her milk for Effie to take to Sara.

The next morning Stella and Effie insisted Kate go home for a while to shower and nurse Sara and change clothes. Milk had leaked from her breasts throughout the night, and the front of her blouse was wet. She smelled of sweat and sour milk. "You'll feel so much better, honey," Effie assured her. "Jeff's asleep. We'll hurry back, then Jimmy can go home for a while."

In less than two hours Kate was back at the hospital. She knew as soon as she walked in Jeff's room. Jimmy looked as though he had just seen an angel of the Lord. Jeff was awake. "I can feel my toes, Mommy."

Kate allowed the soft, warm blanket of unconsciousness to overtake her. Her knees buckled, and she sank to the floor.

·　　　·　　　·

For one month Jeff's head was held immobile by the medieval-looking contraption mounted to his skull. Their boy was a good soldier, better than they themselves could have been, Jimmy and Kate both agreed. They were proud of him and weak with relief. Sometimes they would look at each other across Jeff's bed and have to turn away, so grim were the shared thoughts of what could have been. Kate felt permanently altered. She had faced the worst and come back from it, but she sensed the fearful vulnerability that she would feel for the rest of her life.

When at last they were allowed to take him home, Jeff was to have two more months of total inactivity. The contraption was removed from his head, but Kate almost longed for its protective presence. Every time Jeff moved his head, Kate cringed.

But he was all right. Everything was going to be all right. Gradually the fearfulness receded, and Kate went about her nursing chores euphorically. Jeff would be well. He would walk.

"He'll even do sports again," she told Jimmy. "You wait and see."

"God, Kate, you're sick. Is that why you had children—so they can go out there and perform for you like precocious seals?"

"You like it too, Jimmy Morris. I watch you at those ball games. 'A chip off the old block.' And the boys like you to like it. So cut out the crap and go put Jeff on the bedpan."

Kate kept her promise to God and put her golf clubs in the attic. Maybe it wasn't necessary. Maybe it was stupid to think God gave a damn, but she wouldn't take the risk.

Twenty-four

Kate and Stella took Effie out for a steak at the Cattlemen's Restaurant in honor of their cousin's thirty-fifth birthday. After dinner they went to see *From Here to Eternity* with Burt Lancaster and Deborah Kerr, then went back to Effie's to spend the night, something they did when one of the husbands was away. They wouldn't have considered such a thing with a husband in the house. They didn't even talk on the phone to each other in the evenings when their husbands were at home.

Finally Stella had her own car and with the toll road completed connecting Fort Worth, Grand Prairie, and Dallas, the cousins were able to spend more time together.

The three cousins put on their bathrobes and sprawled across the big bed in Effie's bedroom. Effie and Stella traded back rubs. Kate didn't like to be rubbed, so she brought in the portable record player from Billy's bedroom and kept the music playing and the wine glasses full—and at Effie's insistence read an excerpt from Alfred Kinsey's new book, *Sexual Behavior in the Human Female.*

Kinsey claimed to have discovered there was no such thing as vaginal orgasm. Effie said he was wrong. "I feel it up inside of me, don't you, Stella?"

"Yes, I guess I do," Stella admitted, feeling a small flash of yearning at the thought.

"I've decided sex isn't as important as everyone makes it out to be," Kate announced, finishing off a second glass of Uncle Herman's home-made apple wine.

"It looked pretty important in that movie," Stella said dryly. "Deborah and Burt sure seemed to be enjoying themselves on the beach."

"That's different," Kate said.

"Why?" Effie demanded.

" 'Cause it's the beginning. In the beginning there's always lust. Then sex becomes dutiful. Duty and lust don't go together."

"Oh, Kate, it doesn't have to be that way," Effie said. "I think it's fun to wear pretty lingerie and get William all excited. That excites me."

"Wouldn't that be a joke if I put on 'pretty lingerie,' " Kate said, indicating her stout body.

At thirty-four, Kate's athletic figure was a thing of the past, but curiously, her face was more girllike. The ponytail of her high school days had returned. The makeup of young womanhood had been left behind. Her extra pounds made for smooth, round cheeks, and the hours spent at her children's athletic events left her arms and face as tan and freckled as they had been in her youth. But somehow it wasn't the girlhood face that Stella remembered. Blanche Lasseter used to say that people got more like themselves the older they became. But not Kate. Something in her had been lost. The present-day Kate seemed less defined than the gutsy tomboy who defied a stern father to ride her donkey off on adventures of her own making.

"Lingerie comes in all sizes," Effie insisted, "and besides, you've still got a good shape. There's just more of it than you need."

Effie was as pretty as ever, Stella thought. Truly. More stylish. Thinner. But her dimpled smile and laughing blue eyes had never lost their sincerity and charm. She was a master at manufacturing her own happiness and pulling others along with her.

Effie is good for us, Stella thought. Their cousin absolutely refused to look at the down side of anything. Kate, on the other hand, left Stella vaguely depressed. There was something frantic about Kate. She had transferred her fierce competitiveness to the shoulders of her children. Now they bore their mother's burden.

"Did I tell you Mark's team made the playoffs? He's batting .305," Kate said, closing the Kinsey book.

"Wait just a minute there," Effie said, her fingers skillfully massaging the small of Stella's back, Stella murmuring appreciatively. "We're not through talking about sex."

"You may not be, but I am," Kate said, shifting her weight uncomfortably.

"We used to talk about sex more when we were kids," Effie said.

"When you're young, you think about it more," Kate said.

"Nonsense," Effie said, giving Stella a slap on her rump to signal the end of the rub. "I think about sex all the time. What about you, Stella?"

Stella pulled her nightgown up over her shoulders and slipped on her robe. "I think about it sometimes," she said, feeling cornered. Sometimes her most frequent thoughts concerning sex were how to avoid it. When Gordon insisted, she would concentrate on the ceiling shadows.

But other times, she was aware of an aching need that went far beyond the sexual, and then she would initiate lovemaking—usually after a prerequisite two glasses of wine. These sessions would be extremely physical and impersonal, she and Gordon each lost in their private fantasies. Stella would have intense, lengthy orgasms that left her momentarily satisfied but ultimately more empty than before.

"Actually, I guess I think about sex a lot," she admitted, "and sometimes it's wonderful, and sometimes not so wonderful. I keep feeling like I forgot something I was supposed to remember, or lost something I meant to find. Oh, hell. I don't know. Sex isn't the end-all."

"Oh, Stella, honey," Effie said, becoming serious. "Don't expect so much, and you won't be disappointed. Just relax and have a good time. That's what sex is all about—having a good time with someone you care about. Sharing your bodies and laughing and teasing and feeling damned good."

Effie jumped from the bed and grabbed a pillow. She danced around the room to the strains of Kay Starr singing "Wheel of Fortune."

"Maybe you both should have an affair to liven up your lives," she announced as she and the pillow executed a dramatic dip.

"My God, Effie!" Kate said, her body jerking upright in the chair, the book sliding to the floor with a loud thump. "You aren't having an affair, are you?"

Effie stroked her cousin's cheek. "Me? An affair? Heavens, no," Effie said, her eyebrows lifting over wonderfully blue eyes as she looked down at Kate. "William is all the man I'll ever want and need. Now, let's go make your mother's coffee cake."

"At this hour?" Stella asked. "It's after midnight."

"Sure. You can sleep late tomorrow. There're no kids or husband around for you to worry about. You can be just as decadent as your cousin Effie. I bought cream and yeast and pecans and butter. Come on. I've really been having an attack lately for Aunt Anna's coffee cake."

.   .   .

In the summer of 1953 Gordon left his ministerial post in Fort Worth and moved his family to Johnstown to accept the presidency of United Wesleyan College, a Methodist school with four thousand students and a traditional, wooded campus.

Once, Gordon had thought he wanted to be a bishop in the Methodist church, but as he grew disenchanted with the ministry, that goal faded along with his desire to continue serving as the pastor of a congregation. Still, he had grown accustomed to the deference paid to him because of his profession, of people leaping to their feet when he entered a room, of people listening when he spoke, of his opinion automatically carrying weight and value.

Stella did not like being a minister's wife. She never complained, but Gordon knew she resented the constant restrictions placed on their lives. Other women could wear shorts when they worked in the yard, but not a minister's wife. She couldn't say "damn" when she stubbed her toe. Every decision had to be based on his position—whether Francie could have her ears pierced, if Brian really had to go to Sunday school when he was afraid of the teacher, if Tom could name his kitten Satan because it was black as sin.

And now, instead of a congregation of hundreds to check up on the family's propriety, there would be a town of twenty-five thousand. The college was very important to Johnstown, and its president was automatically one of the city's leading citizens. His world would grow beyond the bounds imposed by a single church and its day school. Gordon was excited.

Gordon realized that Stella and his children would continue to be subjects of scrutiny, but surely being the wife or children of an important man would more than compensate? He hoped that they were proud. Especially Stella. If only she would be a proud wife instead of a quietly dutiful one.

The seascape disappeared during the move to Johnstown. Stella called the moving company. The secretary insisted there had been no oil painting on the inventory. Stella called the secretary at the Westminster Methodist Church to ask if the painting had been left in the parsonage.

"Why, Mrs. Kendall, that painting sold in our white elephant sale last week. Pastor Kendall brought it in."

Stella thanked the woman and explained that she'd forgotten about the sale.

Gordon was in the garage organizing his tools. *He's handsomer than he used to be*, Stella thought. Or was it just that he carried himself better?

"Why did you give the painting away?" she asked.

"I never liked it."

"It was mine, Gordon. You should have asked."

"Was it important to you?" he asked. His tone was challenging.

"Yes. It was left to me by a dear friend. You had no right."

Stella wanted to say more. But she knew it would accomplish nothing. The painting was gone, and her instincts told her to let it drop.

Francie was suddenly ten years old. Incredible. Stella was almost thirty-three.

Still spry at seventy-one, Anna came for Francie's tenth birthday party. She had crocheted an afghan for her granddaughter. Effie and Kate had driven down together the day before. They had spent the night in Salado and eaten at the Stage Coach Inn. "You should have tasted those hush puppies, Stella," Effie said as they carried in the bags. Stella offered no comment. Her sister and her cousin talked on the phone or saw each other almost every day.

Stella was now a three-hour drive from Dallas. Once again she felt left out of the day-to-day sharing with her sister and cousin. But Gordon was excited about his new job. A college president. She was happy for him. He needed her to be pleased.

Francie was exquisitely beautiful in her ruffled birthday dress of pale pink organza. Stella watched her daughter blow out her candles and marveled. Her daughter was the most beautiful human being she had ever seen. Cousin Effie was the prettiest, but pretty was different from un-questionable beauty. Stella worried that her daughter's perfection might somehow have dehumanized her. At ten, Francie was already cool and poised and accepted homage as her due. For her adoring father there were hugs and kisses, but she now treated her mother with polite distance. For her brothers, there were moments of cold disdain even though Brian—who went to morning kindergarten—and Tom ran to meet her each day when she came home from school and never seemed to mind when she shortchanged them on sticks of gum and pieces of candy.

As Francie grew older, Stella began to feel like her daughter's hand-maiden. She dutifully brushed Francie's hair or picked up after her. Francie did not hang up her clothes. Even if she undressed by a clothes hamper, she dropped her clothing on the floor. Whenever Stella chastised her, Francie ran to her father. "She's only a child, Stella," Gordon would gently reprimand his wife. When Stella reminded him that she had been doing farm chores for years by the time she was Francie's age, Gordon would ask, "Don't you want better than that for our children?"

One day she answered Gordon's question. "No, I don't think I do," she told him. She regarded him in the mirror of her dressing table. He was getting undressed and was wearing only his baggy undershorts and socks. "I had a good childhood. We were a family and everyone did his share."

"Francie's not a country girl, Stella." Foolishly he hopped about on one foot, taking off his sock. Why didn't he sit on the bed? Stella wondered.

"That's her loss," Stella said. "Pulling caterpillars off tomato plants might have taught her a little humility."

Gordon let out an exasperated sigh and stomped off into the bath-room in his baggy shorts and just one sock. Stella let out a sigh of her own.

The quaint little college prospered under Gordon's leadership. Stella fulfilled her role as president's wife with a graciousness that pleased her husband. With quiet efficiency she ran the colonial-style president's home overlooking a spacious parkway. With six white columns across the front, the house reminded her of a smaller version of Tara from *Gone With the Wind*. She used to envy people who lived in such houses. The house was undeniably lovely but too grand for comfort. Somehow its grandeur made their furniture looked shabby, and Stella bought a new living room set to use in the formal room. She forbade Brian and Tom access to it except on special occasions—when they had clean hands and no food.

While he never formally left the ministry, Gordon's life had taken a new direction. He knew he would never return to the pulpit. He enjoyed the prestige that his new position as college president brought him. He began to take an interest in civic affairs and local politics. He was named chairman of the Williamson County Allan Shivers for Governor Committee. He went to the state Democratic convention. He started shaking hands with the expansiveness of a politician—reaching out, pumping, smiling, asking personal questions. Gone was the close ministerial handshake clasping someone's hand in both his.

He was much admired in the community. So was Stella. But then, how could anyone find fault with Stella? She was a perfect lady. Gordon looked at the wives of men like Lyndon Johnson, John Connally, and Price Daniels. They seemed very proud of their husbands and to take pleasure in the role they played.

Gordon wondered if he could ever be like those men. And would Stella step into their wives' shoes out of pleasure or duty?

Johnstown was only seventy miles from New Braunfels, and Stella and the children often drove over to see her mother. Anna fixed lunch. Sometimes they would weed the garden or visit with the aunts. Anna kept the children if Stella wanted to visit the cemetery.

"Sometimes I worry that I don't love Francie enough," Stella confided to her mother one day. The boys were inside watching television. Francie hadn't come along; she was spending the day with a girlfriend. Stella was helping Anna put out rows of onions and radishes in her mother's backyard garden.

Stella wiped her brow with the back of her hand and waited for Anna's reply.

"What's enough?" Anna asked, sitting back on her heels.

"As much as I do the boys," Stella said, pushing the trowel into the rain-soaked earth. It was a good day for planting. Anna's chickens clucked contentedly as they scratched for worms in the damp ground.

"Maybe they're more lovable," her mother offered.

"Did you always love me and Kate the same?" Stella stole a sideways glance at Anna. Her face was impassive, as always.

" 'Course not. Sometimes Kate was too ornery to love, and you were too self-righteous."

"I was not!" Stella said indignantly.

Anna shrugged. "Finish that row, then let's have tea. My old knees have had enough for today. I'll finish up tomorrow."

They sat on Anna's porch. The larger of the yellow cats jumped into Stella's lap.

"Do you think it's awful that I don't love Francie as much as the boys?" Stella couldn't let it drop.

"It's natural," Anna said. "They need you more. Francie has her daddy. Maybe someday Francie will need you too."

"You don't understand," Stella insisted. "Sometimes when she's mean to the boys and cool to me, I want to shake her and tell her what a little bitch she is. My own daughter!"

"Maybe you should."

"Should what?"

"Shake her and tell her what a bitch she is."

Stella thought about that on the way home. Gordon would be horrified. He would demand that she apologize to Francie and promise never to do it again. Suddenly she hated her husband and her daughter. Only not really. She really loved Gordon and Francie. She'd worried about them when they were late getting home. She'd be devastated if anything happened to them. And if anything ever happened to one of the boys . . .

Stella could not complete the thought. Her stomach knotted. A bad taste rose in her throat.

She looked at her watch and increased the pressure on the accelerator. She should have left something out to thaw this morning. What in the world would she fix for dinner? She hoped she would beat Gordon home. He hated to come home to an empty house.

Tom and Brian delighted in pleasing their mother. They hugged her neck with great strong hugs and planted sticky kisses on her cheek. Tom, especially, liked to help her cook and hovered about her in the kitchen. He begged to be allowed to set the table or stir cake batter.

Francie nicknamed Tom "The Toad." Stella forbade the name, but even Gordon used it sometimes. Tom had almost no neck. His little body was square and thick, his hair straight and unimaginative. His round hazel eyes were forever looking to Stella's face to discover if something was funny or sad, if he had behaved properly or poorly.

Brian provided the male counterpart to Francie's beauty—almost. Total self-assuredness went with Francie's kind of beauty. Brian was serious and cried over dead birds and goldfish. He wouldn't step on spiders. He was afraid of the dark. Gordon thought it best that he learn to sleep without a light on, so Brian usually crept into bed with his younger brother. Sometimes Stella thought Gordon was too stern with his sons. Strange, when he was so permissive with Francie. But the boys respected and loved him. A word of praise from their father brought looks of unabashed pride to their faces.

Stella's days were taken up with children's activities, teas, alumni functions, fund-raising dinners for the college. She was leader of Francie's Girl Scout troop and helped one afternoon a week at Brian's kindergarten. She participated in the women's activities at the Methodist church. She greeted visiting dignitaries at the college and feted retiring faculty.

Stella was often at Gordon's side in receiving lines. President and Mrs. Gordon Kendall. Gordon was so good at it. His smile was genuine because he was doing exactly what he wanted to do—what he did best. He met people well. They responded to his dignified good looks, to his firm handshake, to his questions. Sincere questions. He really liked finding out about them. People were flattered that he remembered their names, when he met them in Austin, that they had made a contribution to the Development Fund.

"Miss Jackson, this is my wife. Stella, Miss Jackson's family arrived in Johnstown fifty-five years ago in a covered wagon. Her father owned the hotel and the newspaper. Miss Jackson is interested in our music department."

Stella understood. Gordon thought Miss Jackson was a potential contributor to the new recital hall.

"Have you seen the plans for the recital hall we hope to begin next year?" Stella asked. "Would you like me to have Dean Frazer show them to you?"

Too blatant, Stella thought as Miss Jackson ignored the bait and moved on down the line, shaking hands with the president of the alumni association. Stella put on her smile for the next guest.

The oldest living alumni of the school. "Mr. Weaver has never missed a Wesleyan homecoming," Gordon told her. "His five children have all graduated here."

A professor emeritus of history. "Our Dr. Washburn had a career as a circus acrobat before he decided to become a scholar. Dr. Washburn is donating his library to the school."

How did Gordon do it? Stella wondered. She wouldn't remember the names of any of these people fifteen minutes from now. United Wesleyan was lucky to have him. Stella wondered how long he'd stay.

Almost weekly the president's home was the site of some event. A tea or reception, a dinner party or a faculty smoker.

The sit-down dinners at the president's house were the most difficult for Stella to manage. She hired help for the evening, but she was constantly going back and forth between the kitchen and the dining room, and then excusing herself to go upstairs and check on the children. The children always seemed to select these evenings to have their worst arguments, to vomit in their beds, to stop up the toilet trying to flush away the gravel from a goldfish bowl.

Her hectic schedule left her little time to think. She was usually exhausted when she fell into bed at night. Stella thought it best that way. Busy hands were happy hands. Aunt Hannah used to say that all the time. And Aunt Hannah was happy. So was Hannah's daughter, Effie.

A crate addressed to Stella was delivered at the stately home of the college president. The return address bore the name of Charles Lasseter. Stella sat on the bottom step of the stairway and stared. Why, after all this time? What could he be sending her?

Finally she got a screwdriver and pried the lid off. The crate contained Blanche's books. An accompanying note read that Charles and his wife were moving to a new home. He decided to send the books to Stella rather than move them. He knew his aunt would want Stella to have them rather than have them continue to sit in boxes in an attic and never be used. "I think of you often. I hope you are happy and well. Always, Charles."

A safe note. One that a husband could read.

He thought of her often.

Stella slipped the note in the pocket of her blouse and drew it out several times during the day. She studied each loop of the handwriting. His fingers had touched this sheet of stationery. She imagined him sitting at a desk, writing it, thinking of her. How did he look now? How would she look to him? What would she like to be wearing if she were to see him again?

And how had he known where she was living? He had not called after the war, but then she had told him not to.

Stella realized she was angry with him for doing as she had asked.

Gordon suggested donating the books to the college library. "Surely you don't want those old, outdated books. I can't imagine why that man would have sent them to you," he said, looking at the return address. Lasseter and Cochran Architectural Design, Inc.

Gordon reached into the crate and picked up one of the books. He held it by two fingers as though it were contaminated. He put it down and picked up another. The inside of the book slipped from the cover and fell back in the box.

But Stella did keep them. She gave other books to the library and made room for Blanche's. They drew her like a magnet. She started missing teas.

Thoughts of graduate school once again began to creep into her head. Was it knowledge she longed for or just *something*? United Wesleyan College had no graduate courses, but Austin was only thirty miles away.

The next fall Tom entered first grade and Stella entered the University of Texas graduate school, working toward a master's degree in history. She did not ask Gordon's permission. He offered no comment, but she sensed his disapproval. Poor Gordon. She never seemed to be quite the wife he wanted and needed.

Stella allowed herself two afternoons a week in Austin. She loved the drives to Austin. When she got out of her car and started across the campus, she felt as if she were being transformed. She took great breaths of air. Her step lightened. God, she loved being here. The campus was the same. So beautiful. The Main Building with its impressive tower. The Texas Union. Garrison Hall. She never walked into Garrison Hall without thinking of Charles standing by Blanche's door.

Stella liked the anonymity of her classes. No one knew she was a college president's wife with three children. She was just the name on the roll. Stella B. Kendall.

The lectures were stimulating, the seminars lively. She devoured the assigned readings. She wrote her papers in spurts of white-hot fury. She dreamed of completing her master's degree and someday earning her Ph.D. It would take years, but that was okay. She had a goal—one that belonged just to her. That was the something that had been lacking in her life— a goal. Thoughts of research and teaching filled her mind. Maybe she could get a faculty position at United Wesleyan someday. Or at nearby Trinity University in San Antonio. She would finish the research project that she and Blanche had started all those years ago.

Stella was careful to fulfill all her responsibilities at home. It was important that Gordon find no fault with her. She cooked more elaborate meals than before. Clean underwear was always carefully folded in the drawers. She began attending teas again and never begged out of anything because she was too tired or had to study—not cooking or college functions or the children's activities or sex. She usually did her studying early in the morning before anyone was up.

Gordon grew more accepting. He even asked her about her classes. She was careful not to be too enthusiastic. "I enjoy them," she would say. "They get the cobwebs out of my brain."

Stella had a feeling for the future. She had motherhood *and* graduate school. At last she was happier than she had been in a long time.

Twenty-five

Stella was sitting on the back porch snapping green beans. Buster, the brown mongrel, had followed her outside and found himself a patch of sunshine.

She heard the gate creak. Francie was coming home, her overnight bag swinging at her side. The sunlight captured the sheen of her chestnut hair. She wearing white shorts that enhanced the tan on her legs. The outlines of her newly purchased first bra showed under the thin fabric of her T-shirt. Her periods would start soon, Stella thought. How beautiful she was, this daughter of hers.

Francie's maturing body was arresting. She shouldn't wear such short shorts, Stella thought. Those white ones would have to go.

Her daughter's skin was flawless, with not a sign of the pimples and blackheads that were beginning to plague her friends. Her lower lip was fuller than her upper, giving her a pouting, almost seductive look—even as a toddler, she had had that look. And when she smiled, she dazzled. Her teeth were perfect, her eyes large and vividly green.

Young and luscious and beautiful. The look of Francie made Stella feel old. Her own skin had never been that smooth, and now it was aging. Freckles had appeared on the back of her hands, a coarseness to the skin on her neck, radiating lines from the corners of her eyes. Francie's hair was fuller and a richer color than hers had ever been, and now Stella's was sprouting its first gray hairs. She pulled them out.

"How was the slumber party?" Stella asked.

"Really neat," Francie said as she plopped down beside her mother. "Boys kept ringing the doorbell and running away. Mrs. Thompson got mad. She went running out on the porch in a really dumb-looking poison-green bathrobe with her hair pinned up in little wads of toilet paper and yelled that she would call the police if they came back again."

"Did they?"

"No, but they called on the phone all night. I don't think Cindy can have another slumber party for a while. The boys up?"

Stella nodded. "They're watching the Saturday morning cartoons."

"Cindy's cat has kittens. I thought I'd take them over to see them." Francie picked up a handful of green beans and started snapping.

"What a good idea," Stella said.

Mother and daughter sat for a while, side by side on the step, snapping beans. It was nice—like back home. Stella felt a rush of love for the child whom she loved the least.

Later Stella watched out the open kitchen window as Francie, with a brother clinging to each hand, headed toward Cindy's house and the new kittens. Francie was playing big sister, instructing the boys that they mustn't pick the kittens up, that they could only touch them very carefully. "They don't have their eyes open yet. They just came out of their mother day before yesterday."

"Are they blind?" Brian asked.

Francie could be so sweet, Stella thought, but only the day before, she had made Tom cry by telling him he was so stupid that he was going to flunk kindergarten. Tom wasn't sure what flunk meant, but he was sensitive about the word "stupid." He'd heard it almost daily from his sister. He couldn't color in the lines. He couldn't skip. He couldn't remember his telephone number. He couldn't count the squares on the Chutes and Ladder game correctly so Francie wouldn't play with him. "Stupid, stupid, stupid," she would taunt. "Like a dumb old toad." And Tom would cry on cue. But today she was being nice to him. And Tom would instantly forgive her for being mean and hug her neck and tell her he loved her.

Brian was more impervious to Francie's taunts, so she didn't waste many on him. He had learned to challenge her and offer taunts of his own. She was stuck-up. She lied to boys on the telephone. But today Brian loved Francie, too. Stella wondered if there was film in the camera. She'd take their picture when they came back, holding hands like that. Big sister being nice to her brothers.

They were growing up so fast. Brian was going to be long-legged like Francie. Tom was squat and plump. He was affectionate like Brian. So dear. Wonderful, sweet little boys who cuddled and hugged and kissed their mother.

Stella worried that Gordon didn't seem to enjoy Tom as much as he did Brian. Brian could play catch. He was learning to play chess. He was in the top reading group in his first-grade class. He shook hands when he was introduced to a grown-up. Tom still sucked his fingers.

Gordon was just as foolish about Francie as ever. He still held her on his lap and called her Princess. He still nuzzled her neck and made her squeal. "Give your daddy a big kiss," Gordon would say. Francie kissed him on the mouth. And on his eyes, his neck, his cheek. She stuck her tongue in his ear and made him squirm and laugh. "My turn," he said. Stella had to look away. Francie was too aware of her body, of her mane of wonderful hair. She shouldn't be sitting on her father's lap. Gordon shouldn't touch her so much. Or maybe it was perfectly all right. Stella wasn't sure. Would the day come when she shouldn't touch her boys?

As Stella's first semester in graduate school drew to a close, Gordon began talking of having another child. Stella made a joke out of it at first, saying they were getting too close to grandparenting age to consider another baby. Their three children were all in school now. Francie would soon be in junior high. Surely he didn't want to do babyhood all over again.

But Gordon was serious. Very serious. A chill crept into Stella's bones.

"I feel fortunate to have a husband who's as devoted to his family as you are," Stella told him. "But a fourth child? That makes me tired to think about it, Gordon. I can't. I really can't."

"I think we were happiest when the boys were babies, Stella. In fact, I know we were. Babies are good for a family."

Stella was not willing to give up her hope of another degree and deal with babyhood again. She just couldn't. She tried to explain to Gordon how important her studies were to her. "I'd like to have a teaching career someday—when the children don't need me anymore."

"We're still young," Gordon insisted. "You'll have plenty of time later on for earning degrees. Your family needs you now."

"I need me too," Stella said. "Don't I count?"

"I miss having a baby in the family," Gordon said, taking her hands and kissing each palm in turn. They were on the sofa in his study. His territory. Stella always felt as if she were being called into the principal's office when he asked her please to step in there for a minute.

"Please," he continued. "This means so much to me. Another baby would be good for us."

"I don't want to hear any more of this, Gordon!" There was a crash in the kitchen. Something had broken. Francie and Brian were arguing. Stella hurried off to mediate.

Often the discussions took place in bed under a protective veil of darkness. No matter what she said, Stella always seemed to be put on the defensive.

"You're obsessed with thoughts of another child," she accused in an attempt to turn the tables.

"And you're obsessed with not having another child," he retorted from his side of the bed.

Stella stared at the shadows on the ceiling. Why did he make her feel guilty? Was she being selfish? Did her denial of this potential fourth child diminish her as a mother?

But another baby. The very thought made her weary.

Gordon began to court her. He took her out to dinner and brought her a bouquet of daisies, then a rose. Then pearls with a diamond clasp. Stella was stunned. The only jewelry he had ever bought her before was her wedding ring and a watch on their tenth anniversary.

His attempts to get her pregnant took on a seductive nature. He wanted her almost every night, and he resented her slipping into the bathroom for her diaphragm. "I've always hated that thing," he said. "It's so greasy."

"Then you use a rubber," Stella said. "I don't intend to get pregnant, Gordon. I mean it. I don't want another baby."

"But I do," he insisted. "And I think in your heart you do too. You are just caught up in a short-term goal. What is more important, Stella, a child or a graduate degree? Are you a mother or a graduate student?"

So that's it, Stella realized. Her school. Her goals. What was he afraid of? she wondered, but she didn't ask. She doubted he knew. Gordon sincerely thought that he wanted another child.

Francie and the boys started asking for a little brother or sister. "Damn you, Gordon," she whispered. "How dare you put them up to that!" She wanted to yell the words, but the children would hear.

Stella was homeroom mother for Brian's second-grade class. She forgot to go to the second-grade Christmas party. Her mind had been on a research paper—women law enforcement officers since statehood. "I'll be right there," she said when the teacher called, and she raced out the door. She stopped at a bakery to buy the cookies she was supposed to have baked, then raced next door to buy sacks of candy instead of the traditional individual favors. Brian was very quiet on the way home. Poor baby, Stella thought. How terrible that must have been for him, everyone wanting to know when his mother was going to arrive with their party. There was no Kool-Aid. No hand-decorated little felt stockings filled with candy. Bakery cookies.

Francie told on Stella at dinner. "Mommy forgot the Christmas party for Brian's room," she informed her father.

Gordon said nothing.

Stella continued to protect herself carefully when they had sex on the "dangerous days." But often, if they hadn't had sex at night, in the early hours of the morning Gordon would be there, waking her, his erection hard against her leg. Stella would try to think. She was so groggy. Did she need her diaphragm? What day of her cycle was this? Sex was so impersonal at that hour. No words. Quick strong strokes fulfilling her husband's early morning fantasy. Nothing was expected of her except to receive him, to be a receptacle for his coming. His orgasms were more intense at these times. Then he would offer a thank you. A kiss. And he would roll over and sink immediately into a deep sleep. Stella would be awake then. Sometimes she got up to study after drying the wetness between her legs.

When she was one day late with her period, she did not allow herself to worry. Usually she was regular, but not always. One day was certainly not a cause for alarm—unless one of those middle-of-the-night sessions had been ill-timed. The next day she kept going into the bathroom to check. She concentrated on her uterus. *It's time. Let go.*

On the third day she promised herself she wouldn't worry until tomorrow. She had never been four days late with her period unless she was pregnant.

The fourth morning she awoke early and crept into the bathroom. Gordon was snoring softly in the bed. If she didn't start today, it would be true. She urinated, then sitting there on the toilet, took a deep breath and rubbed tissue across her genitalia. No blood. No blood at all. Stella wrapped toilet paper around her finger and stuck it up inside of herself. Her vagina was bloodless.

Stella stared at the moist, unstained paper as though looking at it long enough would make a streak of bloody mucus appear there.

"No, damn it," she whispered. She reinserted her finger in her vagina, poking it cruelly inside of herself. Maybe higher up.

Nothing.

She felt as if she were being sucked down into a pit of quicksand. Stella bent forward and rested her head on her knees. The dog was scratching at the bathroom door, telling her it was time for her to let him outside.

Stella lifted her head and called, "Gordon, let the dog out."

She and the dog waited.

"Gordon!"

The dog resumed his scratching.

Stella ignored it and put her head back on her knees. She hated her body for betraying her. She hated being a woman. She did not want to be the vehicle for another human being to grow within. At age thirty-six, she did not want to be the handmaiden for another baby. She was weary of selflessness. She did not want another infant to suckle her breast. She couldn't make any more milk. She was dry. She could not nurture anymore.

Stella didn't tell anyone for weeks. Finally Effie guessed.

"Have you thought of an abortion?"

Stella could not believe that Effie had said that word out loud. The sin of sins.

"Yes," she admitted, her voice barely audible. Her face burned with shame.

"Gordon doesn't have to know. Or Kate," Effie said. "God, no. Not Kate. She's gotten so righteous about motherhood. For years she's been after me to have another baby. Says it's unnatural for a woman to have only one child."

"Why *did* you have only one?" Stella asked.

"Fear, I guess. I loved Billy and William so much. Life felt good. I was afraid I couldn't love other children as much as I loved William and Billy—and myself. I love myself too. I like being happy. I looked at Kate getting fat and at both of you getting weary." Effie shrugged. "Maybe I'm wrong. But William and Billy and I are going to Europe next summer. I am not going to have another baby, and you don't have to either."

Effie put her hand over Stella's. She had beautiful rings. Her nails were manicured. Stella wore only her simple wedding band. Her nails were clipped short. The skin was rough and red, and the veins stood out. Her mother's hands. "I can arrange it for you, honey," Effie said. "No one will ever know but you and me."

Stella wondered why Effie knew of such things, but she did not ask. Effie seemed somehow diminished, somehow less wonderful for sitting here at her kitchen table speaking of such things. Effie had on an off-white wool dress. She looked slim and elegant. Imagine—white. Stella couldn't have worn such a dress. The boys would touch her once and get it dirty.

Stella carefully considered Effie's offer over the next few days. Could she do that? If she'd never had children, maybe so. But somehow, in some hard-to-understand way, the fact that she was already a mother stood in her way. Mothers shouldn't erase children—or would-be children. At least this particular mother probably couldn't live with herself if she did. No matter how hard she tried to convince herself, Stella knew she couldn't go through with an abortion. Her decision wasn't a moral one or even very emotional. It was more one of accepting things as they were. The best she could do was guiltily hope for a miscarriage.

She told her husband the baby he wanted was on the way. She couldn't keep it a secret anymore. She was becoming too sick to hide it. This was not going to be an easy pregnancy. She was too old for that.

Gordon put his face against her bosom and wept. "Oh, God, Stella. Thank you. Thank you."

Stella was sick every morning, suffered from almost continuous headaches, and was forever exhausted. When she fell asleep at the wheel of her car on the way back from Austin, she ran off the road, bending the axle of her station wagon and bruising the ribs above her pregnant belly. At first she thought Gordon's concern touching, but she found herself wondering if his concern was for her or for her wonderful pregnancy. Then she felt guilty. Of course, he was concerned about her. Gordon would be lost without her. He needed her more than the children did. She dropped out of her spring-semester classes, too exhausted to continue.

Gordon started helping her around the house. And he told the housekeeper to come in three mornings a week instead of two. He touched Stella more now and often told her that he loved her. "I love you, too, Gordon," she would parrot back. And she did. She really did love Gordon. He was her husband. Their lives were woven together like cloth. Love was just different from what she'd thought it would be.

"Come on, Stella," Gordon pleaded. "Just for a short time—to greet the dignitaries. And you don't have to stay for the banquet or attend any of the meetings tomorrow if you don't feel like it. Go home and take a nap before you get dressed. Maybe a little glass of wine would perk you up."

"Gordon, I look awful and feel worse. Can't you just tell people I'm pregnant and don't feel well?"

Stella did not feel up to attending the reception. Her feet were swollen, her eyes puffy. She knew she would get dizzy if forced to stand up for too long in the receiving line.

"You don't look awful, Stella." Gordon got up from his desk and came to sit beside her on the leather sofa of his presidential office. He took her hand and stroked it. "I'm always proud to have you at my side— especially pregnant with our child."

"Does it really mean so much to you that I come?" she asked reluctantly.

Apparently, it did, and Stella went home to wash her pitiful hair. But even clean, it wouldn't shine, and in spite of her best efforts, it still looked unstyled. The sides refused to match, and it wanted to part un- attractively in the middle of her head. Finally she gave up and pulled it back in a knot that made her look like an aging schoolmarm. By then it was too late for a nap. Stella put on her one dressy maternity outfit, a navy faille with a pleated front and a lacy collar that made the dress look as if it had been designed as a choir robe. Stella removed the collar and stuffed her feet into a pair of navy pumps. Studying her reflection in the mirror, Stella decided she now looked like a pregnant, aging schoolmarm. She added the pearls Gordon had given her when he was trying to con- vince her they needed this last pregnancy. They helped some, but not much. She reattached the collar and left the pearls.

With a sigh, she decided that was the best she could do and went downstairs to see about the children's dinner before meeting Gordon. She hadn't hired a sitter. They'd have to stay alone. Francie claimed she was too old for a sitter, but she talked on the phone and never paid any attention to her brothers. But Stella knew she wouldn't be gone long. All she wanted to do was put in an appearance at the reception, then come home and put her feet up.

This pregnancy had been more difficult than her other three. She had gained far too much weight, yet anemia was a problem. Her hair lost its luster and thinned. She avoided looking at herself in the mirror as much as possible. The doctor assured her that her problems were tem- porary, but Stella wondered. Was this some sort of turning point in her life? Would this pregnancy mark the end of youthfulness and beginning of middle age? She hated feeling unattractive even more than she hated the physical discomforts.

But she would stand at Gordon's side in the receiving line feeling tired and ugly. It was better to do that than to suffer his displeasure.

Gordon had grand plans for the college he administered. He understood well how success built on success—for the school and for his personal ambitions.

He had simultaneously launched a United Wesleyan College Campaign for Academic Excellence and his Second Century Building Program for the school. Both plans were well received by the college's governing board. Fund-raising activities began to take up much of Gordon's time.

Careful thought went into selecting a steering committee to oversee the first phase of Gordon's master plan. It was to be composed of community leaders, influential alumni, builders, architects, members of the state Methodist hierarchy, industrialists, and financiers. This committee would be instrumental in implementing both the drive for academic advancement and the campus building program.

Gordon decided to bring his carefully selected committee together for the first time during a weekend of meetings, social activities, campus tours, and a homecoming football game. The initial brainstorming for a master plan would begin during the weekend. Stella had helped Gordon plan the event, which was to begin with a Friday-night reception and banquet in the college gymnasium. The governor, legislators, the bishop, and many other dignitaries were sent beautiful, embossed invitations.

Standing by her husband in the receiving line, Stella began to realize just how political Gordon had become. Governor Shivers actually came and was obviously paying court to Gordon. And Senator Lyndon Johnson, made even taller by his expensive cowboy boots, told Stella with a conspiratorial wink that her husband was a "real comer." Stella could not believe that the governor, a United States senator, a congressman, and four state legislators had actually traveled to little Johnstown for their event. But as she watched them with Gordon, she realized they were more interested in her husband than his plans for the college.

Stella shook hands and smiled. Her back was killing her. "Do you think I can go now?" she finally asked Gordon. "I think most of the people have arrived."

"Just a little longer," he said. "Why don't you sit down for a minute? I'll get you a cup of coffee."

She sank into a nearby chair and realized she could have gone to sleep right in the middle of all those milling people. All she wanted to do was go home and crawl into bed. Would this baby ever come? She felt as if she had been pregnant forever.

Gordon was talking to Senator Johnson, her coffee forgotten. Stella caught his eyes. "I'm leaving," her lips mouthed.

Gordon frowned and shook his head.

Grabbing the edge of a table, Stella pulled herself up and headed unsteadily for the gymnasium foyer to pick up her coat. As she slipped her arms into the sleeves, the outside door opened, and a solitary late-arriving guest entered.

It was Charles Lasseter.

"Hello, Stella," he said.

Stella clutched at the lapels of her coat and stared.

Charles? But why? What was he doing here?

Then she remembered how she looked.

It was too much. The shock, the exhaustion. Tears ran down her cheeks. Her knees went soft, and she leaned against the wall for support.

Charles quickly stepped close and grabbed her arm. "It's nice to see my presence still has some effect on you," he said gently.

Stella closed her eyes and shook her head slowly back and forth. "I can't believe you're seeing me looking like this." She looked down at the navy faille belly her coat would not cover. "Why are you here?"

His hand caressed her arm through her coat. "I was invited. I hoped it was your idea, but obviously it wasn't. I'm sorry if my being here is upsetting."

Charles had been invited, yet his name had not appeared on the official guest list. Gordon had not said a word about it. If he had, he knew she wouldn't come tonight. Her husband had wanted her here so Charles Lasseter could see her eight and a half months pregnant and uglier than she had ever been in her life.

"No. I didn't have anything to do with the invitation," Stella said. "If I'd arranged to see you again, it would have been at a time when I was unpregnant, slender, and wearing one of my rich cousin's most wonderful outfits."

"Would you ever have done that—arranged to see me?" he asked.

She didn't know whether to turn and run or bury her face against his neck. "I don't know. I've thought about it." Her voice was a whisper.

Charles's hand moved up her arm to her neck. His fingers were soft on the skin of her throat.

"You didn't call me after the war," she said. "I know I said not to, but I sometimes I wished that you had anyway. I might have seen you if you'd called. I don't know. I never really got past thinking what it would be like to pick up the phone and hear your voice. And I never go into the tearoom at Neiman's without looking around to see if there's a handsome uniformed man from my past. Of course, I know the uniform's in mothballs. . . ."

His eyes were so dark and beautiful. Lines radiated from their corners now. Like hers. He was older but just as handsome. No, handsomer. Seeing his mature, chiseled face made her want to cry. Their lives were floating by, and he had lived years without her seeing him.

"In my mind, I've called you a thousand times," he said. "I've even dialed your number. Twice I even waited to hear you say hello, but I was afraid your husband was standing there beside you. I didn't want to interfere in your life."

Stella touched his mouth. She said his name softly. "Charles. Dearest Charles."

He kissed her fingertips, softly, his lips lingering. Softly. Stella closed her eyes.

"If you ever need me . . . ," he whispered.

Stella opened her eyes. "Need you for what?"

"I don't know. I think about you every day. For seventeen years I've thought of you every day."

Stella nodded. "Yes. I think about you, too." Her voice was thick.

"When will I see you again?" Charles asked.

"I don't know. Maybe never. No, maybe sometime. Take care of yourself."

He led her out the door for a private embrace in the shadows, her belly hard between them. He took her face between his hands and kissed her again. Not softly this time, but with passion and yearning.

"I love you, Stella," he said. "I always have and I always will."

Stella knew she was going to be ill, and probably before she could get herself home. But through the nausea and the anger, she kept hearing Charles's voice saying those words. "I love you, Stella. I always have and I always will."

She choked back the hideous taste of bile as she opened the front door of her house. The boys were watching television—"The Donna Reed Show." Francie was upstairs in her room.

"Pop some popcorn," Brian pleaded. "Please."

"I can't, honey. I'm sick. Maybe Francie will."

She heard the disapproving silence behind her. Sick again. Mothers weren't supposed to get sick.

Clumsily, she climbed the stairs and went into the bathroom to vomit.

After she had rinsed off her face and dropped her dress to the floor, she fell across the bed.

In her bed she thought of all the things she would say to Gordon. How dare he do that to her—inviting Charles here like that without even telling her! Was that why he got her pregnant, so Charles Lasseter could see her looking used-up and ugly and *owned?* Pregnant—the ultimate mark of ownership. Was that why she was going to have to raise another child? What ugly thoughts had Gordon been harboring all these years? Those letters he had written during the war—always implying that she was not capable of being faithful. The words came flooding back.

Stella rolled heavily out of bed and unpacked the box of letters from the bottom of the cedar chest. She read them again. And again. By the time Gordon came home, she had worked herself into a rage. The horrified look on her husband's face pleased her. He had never seen her really angry before. Good, old sweet-tempered Stella. She wadded up a letter and threw it at him. Then another. Then she picked up the box and threw them all. The wooden box hit the wall with a thud. Letters flew everywhere. In between the news of his life and telling her that he loved and missed her were the lectures, the veiled accusations. Why had she saved them? But then, wives always save the letters their husbands write them from a war.

Without a word, Gordon picked up the letters one by one and replaced them in the box. Stella sat on the side of the bed in her no-longer-white maternity slip and watched him.

When he was finished, he put the box on the bureau and hung up her dress. Then he came to sit by her.

"I'm sorry, Stella. It was wrong of me to invite him here without telling you. Very wrong."

Stella listened to his voice, droning on, explaining.

He shouldn't have surprised her like that. It had been an afterthought—having Charles Lasseter come. He had been advised to add another architect to the committee. Lasseter's name had been mentioned. No, that's not true, he admitted. Gordon had brought his name up himself.

"It had nothing to do with my desire for another child. My God, Stella, how can you think that? You know how much I love my family."

"But you wanted him to see me like this," Stella whispered vehemently. If they had been alone in the house, she would have screamed.

"Yes, damn it." Gordon said, his voice too loud. "Yes. I wanted him to see you pregnant with my baby inside of you. My *fourth* baby."

"Why?" Stella's shoulders slumped. "Help me understand."

Gordon grabbed her hands. "You said you loved him before. 'An architect from Dallas'—you told me that once. 'The nephew of a dear friend.' And then the way you've carted around that damned picture you inherited from that woman professor. A picture signed 'C.L.' *He* painted that picture. I hated you for bringing it into our home."

"So you got rid of it?" Stella asked.

"Yes, damn it. I didn't want a picture in my house painted by him." He was squeezing her hands—hurting her.

"Sometimes when you get distant, I know you're thinking about him. I worry about losing you. I wouldn't be anything without you, Stella. I need you. Don't you know that? I shouldn't have invited him—I'm sorry. But I wanted to see your face when you saw him. Then I would have known. I saw a chance to find the answer to the question that's been eating at me for years, but now I don't know. Please, please tell me that you don't love him."

"For God's sake, why didn't you just ask me?" Stella demanded.

"I don't know. I wanted to. I was afraid of your answer."

He slipped to the floor, kneeling in front of her and burying his face against her swollen belly. Stella put her arms around him and rocked him back and forth like a baby. The child kicked inside of her. She could hear Francie and Brian arguing downstairs. Francie was accusing him of listening in on her phone call. The shower was running. Tom—he was using up all the hot water. There was a cobweb in the corner of the ceiling. She would have to put a clean cloth over a broom and sweep it down. If you didn't use a cloth, the broom soiled the ceiling. Her mother used to do that—put a cloth over a broom to knock down cobwebs. So long ago.

Her gaze traveled from the cobweb to the grouping of family pictures. Gordon's parents. Her parents. Her and Gordon's wedding picture. Baby pictures of their children. Family pictures of the five of them. Three generations of pictures. Soon another child would join the gallery. And someday Gordon's and her grandchildren would be framed and put alongside them.

Her husband was trying to tell her how tortured he had been all these years. How long now? Almost fourteen years they had been husband and wife. Stella felt numb.

Automatically she kissed his hair. He still had a full head of hair. Interesting how few ministers went bald. Did God reward their piousness with hair? Of course, he was no longer a practicing minister, but he was still the Reverend Kendall. Stella mumbled comforting words: The baby would be dear. She was flattered by his jealousy. She knew it was just because he loved her. And she loved him. Only him. Charles was just an old friend from long ago—the nephew of dear Professor Blanche.

"But you made love with him," Gordon said, looking at her with a tearstained face.

"No. I never had sex with Charles." She had thought about it a thousand times, but husbands didn't need to know things like that.

"Then who?" Gordon didn't believe her.

Does this really make any difference? Stella thought. She had three children by the man kneeling in front of her. A fourth lived inside her. Their lives were so interwoven it would be impossible to separate them— like Siamese twins who shared the same vital organs. Ultimately, it wasn't a question of what happened before the joining. The facts had outlived their relevancy. Losing her virginity to that now-faceless man had happened long ago, and she herself never gave it a thought. But she had given Charles Lasseter her thoughts over the years, and even though it wasn't Charles, it should have been him she made love to that very first time in her life. It should have been him on the nights thereafter. But it didn't work out that way, and the way her life had evolved was hardly tragic. If she had married Charles, there would have been children, a house, problems, joys. Maybe it would have been some better, but perhaps not much. She would have known, however.

Now she would never know what it would have been like to be Charles's wife, to bear his children instead of Gordon's. But Charles's children would not have been Francie, Brian, Tom, and this one yet to be born. Wishing she had been Charles's wife instead of Gordon's was like erasing her own children. There was no point in looking back. It made her head spin in endless circles. She didn't like it. She made it stop.

Stella's voice was calm as she explained away the mystery of her virginity. She realized she was using the same tone she used when the children were upset. "You don't know him. His name would mean nothing to you. A schoolteacher. And he's dead. Do you understand me, Gordon? That man is dead. Now, please, let's bury him and forget about it. I don't want ever to speak of this matter again. Ever. Do you understand? Not ever."

"Do you swear?" he asked. "Will you kneel here beside me and swear by Almighty God that you're telling the truth?"

"Good grief, Gordon. Is that really necessary?" But Stella looked at his face. Yes. It was necessary.

With a sigh, she lowered her heavy body to the floor. She knelt beside her husband and swore before a God who had grown vague and indifferent.

"I swear to Almighty God that I never had sex with Charles Lasseter. I swear the only man I've ever had sex with other than my husband is long dead. I swear that I never loved that man. I swear that it was only that one time. I swear I will always be faithful to my husband."

Stella started to pull herself back up to the bed. Gordon put a restraining hand on her arm. "Do you love Charles Lasseter?"

Stella sank back onto her knees and refolded her hands on the edge of the bed. She closed her eyes. "I swear to God that I don't love Charles Lasseter. I never loved him. I love only my husband. Only Gordon."

Gordon helped her onto the bed. She was too tired to remove her bathrobe. Gordon gently eased her out of it. He massaged her swollen feet and covered her with a quilt made generations ago in New Braunfels by some other wife.

Without opening her eyes, Stella said, "Never again, Gordon."

When he did not respond, she opened her eyes and looked at him. "Never again," she repeated. "Do you promise me you will never bring this matter up again? Do *you* swear by Almighty God that this is the end of it?"

He nodded, then turned out the light and left her.

Blessed darkness blanketed her. She heard him going down the stairs.

Francie demanded that he punish Tom for using all the hot water. "I had to wash my hair in cold water," she said in a wounded voice to her father. Stella could not hear Gordon's reply.

Soon the smell of popping corn drifted up to the darkened room.

She wondered for the first time in years about the assistant principal to whom she had presented her virginity. A smile played across her lips when she realized she couldn't even remember his first name. She had thrust her virginity on a Mr. Henderson to get back at Charles. And Charles never even knew. How foolish it all seemed. Virginity was so inconsequential. How had it gotten to be so important? And love?

Stella had forgotten what love was. Or maybe she had never known. Right now she didn't *love* anyone—not Gordon, not Charles, not those children downstairs, not the infant in her belly, not herself. Right now what she loved was being in this bed all by herself.

Stella wondered if Mr. Henderson was really dead. Did he remember *her* first name?

Twenty-six

D o you love the girl?" William asked his son.

"I don't know. I thought I did when . . ." Billy hesitated, not meeting his father's gaze.

"But you're willing to enter into a marriage with her even though you aren't sure you love her, even though you're only seventeen years old."

"Well, what else can I do?" Billy sat on the living room sofa, his hands dangling between his knees, his shoulders drooping.

William left his chair and came to sit beside his son. "Does she want to marry you?" he asked.

"Yes, sir."

"Is she a nice girl?"

"Yes, sir."

"Do you want her in your bed every night for the rest of your life? Do you want her to be with you every morning when you wake up? Do you want her face over your dinner table, her embrace to welcome you home from work in the evening? Do you feel like you are the most blessed of all men because this woman loves you?"

"You're talking about you and Mom, aren't you?" Billy asked, looking sideways at his father.

"I'm talking about your mother and me and you and this girl. More than anything else, I want you to have the good life that I've had. And make no mistake about it, Bill Chambers, you are looking at a happy man because I married the right woman. A man's wife is the difference between joy and just plodding through the days until the end. My heart still beats a little faster when I come up the walk toward the front door just knowing that inside the house is the woman I love. During the war when I was in the South Pacific and thinking every time I went up in one of those Hellcats that I'd never come back to Dallas and Effie and my baby boy, I really got things in perspective, son. I hated war more than anything else, but war taught me how much I love my home and family. I knew that if I ever was allowed to come back here I'd never leave again and that I'd never do anything to threaten this life. I don't flirt with other women. I don't drink and drive. I don't fly planes anymore. I want to live every day that I'm entitled to with your mother."

His father had tears in his eyes. Billy was embarrassed. "But Marsha's pregnant, Dad. I made her pregnant."

"I know. And you will feel bad about that for the rest of your life, but it doesn't have to ruin your life. Your mother always says that nothing is worth ruining your life over, and I suspect she's right."

Billy was crying now. "But what can I do? Will you help me, Dad? I'm so scared. I don't love her like you love Mom. I'd never seen a woman naked, and we just . . .'"

William reached and pulled his son to him. He held him close. His father was a tall, lanky man. Billy was smaller, more like his mother. He curled up inside his father's embrace and was grateful for his bigness. He buried his face against his father's shoulders. His sobs were muffled against the soft wool of William's sweater.

"I'll go and see her father," William said. "Maybe she doesn't really want a baby. Maybe she'd rather have her way paid to college. If she does want to have the baby, we'll see that she has plenty of money to live well and take good care of it. We'll work out something."

"Can they make me marry her?" Billy sobbed. "Marsha says it's the law."

"No. They can't make you." William said soothingly. He stroked his son's head as he had done when Billy was a child.

"What if they want a lot of money?" Billy said, pulling away and staring at his father.

"I'll give it to them," William said calmly. "I'd give them every cent I have if that's what it takes. It's worth that much to me for my son at least to have a chance to be really happy."

"I'm sorry, Dad. I'm so sorry. So sorry. So sorry."

"We all do things we're sorry about. It's part of life. The sin is if we don't learn from it."

Billy wondered what in the world his father could have ever done to be sorry about. The war maybe. Killing people. Today was the first time Billy could ever remember his father talking about the war. Billy knew from long experience that World War II was not discussed at their table, in their house.

Billy had always felt guilty because he loved his mother more than his father. His mother was the most wonderful, beautiful, funny, kind, happy person in the world. His dad was just a nice, quiet man who was always around.

But at this moment Billy realized he loved his father a hell of a lot.

"Does Mom have to know?" Billy asked into his father's sweater.

"I'm not sure. Let's wait to decide that until we see what Marsha's father says."

His father was somehow going to make it all right. Billy felt his body relaxing. Just as he used to fix broken toys and make order out of chaotic homework assignments, his father was going to fix things. Billy was grateful to sink back into the role of child. But grateful as he was, he knew that it would be one of the last times. It was time he became an adult. The idea made him sad. It felt very nice here in his father's arms.

William never told Effie the pregnancy that could have become their first grandchild ended in a very expensive abortion. He made sure the girl had the best, and she would go to the college of her choice driving a new car. She would have an income for the next five years. But the girl had cried. William knew that she would have rather had it the other way. He cried too. The fetus they were flushing away was a piece of him and Effie and their son. Marsha allowed him to hug her before he left her house. "I wish Billy had loved me," she said.

William had a hard time driving home. He wanted to go back and tell her not to do it. But Marsha and his Billy had more right to their lives than a mass of cells that had potential, but only that. Still . . .

"How was your day?" William asked after he kissed her.

William always asked how her day had been and usually listened to her answer.

Effie told him about her committee meeting—the Kappa Kappa Gamma alumni group was raising money for the burn unit at Parkland Hospital. She recited as much gossip as he was interested in. They carried their usual Tom Collinses out onto the patio. The sprinkler threw water in graceful arches across the backyard. The crepe myrtle bushes were in full bloom—pink and white and red ones. William liked crepe myrtle. It was so dependable. Rosie, the ancient cocker, scratched on the screen door, and William got up to let her out. She waddled out to join them.

"Now's your turn," she said. "How did the board meeting go?" She scooted her chair closer to his—so their knees touched. William smiled. He liked that.

"Phil Starling and Stan Bishop are dead-set against the commuter airline idea. They said businessmen like to get out of town overnight. They don't want to fly back home the same day."

"I'm sure that's true of many businessmen," Effie said, "but time is money for others. I think you've come up with a dynamite idea. Why don't you suggest a six-month trial run between Houston and Dallas? Cheap flights. No first-class. No amenities. No assigned seating. On in Dallas at eight in the morning. Have meeting and lunch in Houston and back in Dallas by early evening? Or vice versa. I think it will open up an entire new phase for commercial aviation in this part of the country. Didn't you say it was working well on the East Coast?"

"Yes. But Phil says Texans are different from Easterners. Texans don't like to hurry. And maybe we're just too spread out down here and proud of it. Maybe Texans don't want their state shrunk by commuter flights. And we'd have to add additional planes and personnel. I don't think I can get the board to go along with it."

"Why can't you drop the New Mexico flights? You said they were only marginally profitable. Concentrate on Texas, Oklahoma, and Louisiana—where the oilies are."

Effie went inside to check on her casserole. William followed her. "Smells good," he said.

"Mexican chicken," Effie said, "and fresh green beans. Why don't you pour us a glass of wine?"

"Do you ever miss it?" William asked as he turned the corkscrew.

"Miss what?" Effie asked as she sliced the tomatoes Jason had brought from their mother's garden.

"Texas Central. Being there. Being a part of it."

"I am a part of it," Effie said. "You keep me in touch. I appreciate that, William. A lot of men wouldn't talk about their business with their wives."

"A lot of men aren't married to a woman as sweet as Effie Chambers who lets her husband bore her with shop talk to help him unwind."

William looked over at Effie bending over to get the casserole out of the oven. "And not many men are married to a woman with a fanny as cute as that one. What are you doing later, pretty lady?"

Effie grinned at him over her shoulder. "Well, just what did you have in mind?"

Ruth Alice Kendall was born December 5, 1955, the same day a seamstress was arrested in Alabama for refusing to relinquish her seat to a white man. Stella was thirty-six. Gordon was forty-one.

Effie and Kate were there the next morning, smiling, saying all the right words of congratulation, but it wasn't the same as before. They knew it. Stella knew it.

Effie's coat had a mink collar that looked marvelous with her hair. Kate was wearing a navy pea coat that probably belonged to Mark.

"I think this little girl will be very special to you," Effie said.

"Why do you say that?" Stella asked.

"She's a Behrman, honey. Through and through. She will always stand by you."

Effie was right. Ruth Alice was a Behrman. She wasn't a pretty baby. She reminded Stella of Kate.

Gordon started calling the baby Ruthie from his side of the nursery viewing window. The designation stuck.

So here was the baby he had wanted. Plain little thing, she was. He was the father of two boys and two girls—a perfect family.

Gordon's reputation as an administrator and a man on the way up parlayed him into the state committeeman slot for the Democratic party. He went to Austin once a month. Sometimes more often. He came back pumped-up. He would follow Stella about the kitchen telling her about it. Important people. Decisions. Luncheons at the governor's mansion.

John Connally, a member of Senator Johnson's high command, came to the house one night courting Gordon's support at the National Convention. Johnson was to receive a favorite-son nomination for President. The senator wanted the Texas delegation's pledge to vote for him on every ballot.

Connally's job was to maneuver delegates away from labor-liberals. Gordon assured Connally that Johnson would have his support until the senator himself released the delegation's vote. Connally stayed all evening. Stella fed the children early and served dinner to the two men.

They retired to Gordon's study. The smell of cigar smoke drifted under the closed doors.

"I'm going to run for the Texas Railroad Commission in two years," Gordon told Stella later. She was in bed. He was wandering about the bedroom, aimlessly opening drawers and leaving a trail of clothing. "Johnson will support me."

So we move again, Stella thought. *Austin. How lovely.*

The Texas Railroad Commission, its name left over from other times, was a triumvirate of anonymous men who regulated the state's all-powerful oil and gas industry. Stella understood that the commission post was a steppingstone, a place for men hand-picked by the establishment who might be given the opportunity for something more attractive later on— provided they played ball. And it was very important to have men who played ball on the Texas Railroad Commission. Texas floated on a sea of oil. In Texas oil made the wheels go around.

Powerful as it was, the commission attracted little attention in elections. The campaigning was low-key. Since Gordon was known as a Johnson man, his election was virtually automatic.

In January 1959, United Wesleyan had a round of functions to bid their president farewell and send him off to the state capital. Gordon had done a good job for them. The school had never known such activity, such prosperity. Gordon was a born fund-raiser. Stella had seen Gordon grow more confident as president of the school, surer of his ability to charm, and he was more inclined to delegate. That had been hard for him, but gradually he had begun to leave academics to the deans and concentrate his efforts on fund-raising and public relations.

United Wesleyan was grateful. The new recital hall was named Kendall Hall in his honor. His bust was unveiled in the foyer at a ceremony attended by the entire faculty and by Johnstown's community leaders.

Stella's trust had ended the year before, and she told Gordon she wanted to use it to buy a home in Austin. He insisted the money should be invested for their children, but with less conviction than before. A nice, solid home in a good neighborhood would be image-enhancing.

They bought a home on Atterbury Lane, a tree-lined street in one of Austin's older and most pleasant quadrants, and for the first time in her marriage, Stella was not living in an institution-owned house.

Stella liked her new house. Two stories, white and roomy with a broad front porch, it reminded her of the unpretentious New Braunfels house in which she had grown up. Gordon couldn't understand why she wouldn't remodel the large old-fashioned kitchen, but its wooden floors and countertops pleased her. From the window over the sink, she could watch the seasons come to a pair of handsome elms. There were even squirrels. She added her own stove and refrigerator. She searched through at least a dozen secondhand furniture and antique stores before she found a round oak table to put in the kitchen's center. In a corner she put her rolltop desk and a tall, glass-fronted bookcase. Many of her books were on the shelves in Gordon's study, but the most special ones lived in the corner of her kitchen.

Once again Stella entered graduate school—just one class in the fall semester, while Ruthie went to morning play school at the Methodist church. The following semester Stella traded baby-sitting with a woman she had met on campus and was able to enroll in two classes. With her studies, four children, and a large house to manage, Stella was constantly busy, but at least she didn't have to go to teas. She studied in the evenings now, after she put Ruthie to bed, usually while Gordon watched television or read. Stella learned to tune out the noise. He was more amenable if she was at least in the same room with him.

Would she have been happier, Stella wondered, as the wife of a dawn-to-dusk goat rancher in New Braunfels? Would she have been happier if a certain man had never wanted to take her to coffee at the Texas Union one day so many years ago? For Stella still thought of Charles.

The only thing pretty about Ruthie was a rather remarkable pair of widely spaced, intelligent eyes that seemed too wise for her years. People had a difficult time comprehending that this child was truly the sister of the dazzlingly beautiful Francie, who was busy breaking the hearts of an astonishing number of young men both at her high school and from the university. Stella wouldn't let Francie go to fraternity parties, however. "There'll be time enough for that next year." Gordon supported Stella on this one. He didn't trust college boys with his daughter. Francie pouted, but Gordon didn't give in.

He still adored his Francie. He seemed awkward and ill at ease with his younger daughter. He patted Ruthie's head and turned away from her serious little face. At Stella's urging, he would sometimes hold Ruthie on his lap and read to her but never with the cozy, intimate affection he had shared with Francie. Stella pitied the child she had not wanted and tried hard to give Ruthie attention and love. When Stella looked into the child's solemn eyes, she felt a pang of guilt, and she was so bored with feeling guilty.

It pleased Stella to be living in Austin. She appreciated the anonymity it brought to her life after her previous fishbowl existence. She could wear shorts in her yard and slacks to the supermarket. On the campus she was just another student—older, but not the only nontraditional student. But Stella knew it would not last. Her husband was being groomed for a higher position, something he longed for very much. Stella was fascinated by the politics of Texas's past. Present-day state politics annoyed her. How could anyone know what it all had meant until years put it in perspective?

Stella had wondered why William would come to see her without Effie. In all the years she had known him, Stella couldn't remember ever seeing Effie's tall, gentle husband without his vivacious wife at his side. Dear William, who still so adored his Effie. It was always there for the world to see, written across his face, in his eyes as he watched her sparkle.

She took William into Gordon's study, where the children and television wouldn't bother them, and she listened while William apologized for the interruption and explained that he was dying.

Stunned, Stella sat, staring at him, feeling her mouth open but unable to close it.

Dying? But their generation was too young to die. They hadn't finished burying the previous one.

"You are the first person I've told," William said. They were sitting on the sofa in Gordon's study. The sounds of the television drifted in from the living room. Joe Friday's voice on "Dragnet."

Stella had seen dying before. William didn't look as if he were dying. Not yet. Cancer of the prostate, he had told her. Metastasized. He had driven to Austin just to tell Stella. Six months at the most. But he was a good man. He shouldn't die until he was old, until he'd seen his grandchildren, until he'd buried his parents.

Stella did not say the usual things. She didn't ask him if he was sure, if he'd gotten second and third opinions. He wouldn't be sitting here in her home announcing his upcoming death if he wasn't sure.

And she didn't tell him about the miracles of modern science, about how there is always hope. She reached out for his hand and sat there quietly with him for a time, her eyes filling with tears. "William, dearest William. You've been a wonderful husband for Effie," she said. "She loves you very much. We all love you. I'm . . ." She hesitated. To say she was sorry seemed so inadequate, but she said it anyway. "I'm sorry." The tears spilled over.

William nodded. Yes, Effie loved him. "She's been my life," he said.

"And you haven't told her? Why have you told me first?" Stella wanted to know. She needed to blow her nose. She had no handkerchief, no tissue near at hand. She sniffled.

"Because you're strong," William said.

"I am?"

William laughed. "Of course you are. Everyone knows you're the strongest person in the family. Effie will need someone to lean on when I'm gone. Billy's so young—only twenty-two, and he'll have his hands full learning the business. I want you to promise me that you and Gordon will look after her. I need to know that."

Did he really believe that? Stella marveled. Effie had run Texas Central single-handedly during the war. In the years that followed, she had raised hundreds of thousands of dollars for the Dallas symphony and other causes. She entertained often and well in her and William's elegant, efficiently run home. Effie could do anything. Yet William thought of his wife as helpless.

And William thought of Stella as strong. How had he gotten such a notion? She just put one foot in front of the other and coped as well as she could. Strong?

She couldn't talk him into staying for dinner. He apologized again for coming without calling. "I was on the highway and saw the sign to Austin and knew you were the one I needed to talk to."

Stella cried again as they embraced. She heard herself telling him once more that she was sorry. "I'll help in any way I can," she said, feeling unbearably inadequate.

"I know," he said. "I'm glad Effie has such a wonderful family."

As Stella watched William walk down her front walk, she realized he had shrunk. He didn't lift his feet when he walked. Dying. He was only forty-six. She thought of the dashing aviator he had once been. She remembered even before then, the handsome young gentleman Effie brought home from college. Always a gentleman. That William had been full of dreams and grand ambition. Now he shuffled down the walk to his final days. He wouldn't tell Effie until he had to. He wasn't ready to be her dying husband just yet.

Stella suspected that Effie already knew. Effie would be the best wife a dying man could have.

Stella went inside to start dinner. Even now, when she had just found out that Effie's dear William was dying, there was dinner to cook. She put on her apron but stood in the middle of her kitchen unable to think of what to do first. She went out into the backyard for a few minutes and sat in the shade on the glider. William. He was so good. He loved Effie so much. The next months were going to be very sad. For such a long time now, there had been Effie and William. They belonged to-gether, and soon Effie would be alone. Stella's chest hurt as the tears welled up again.

A crash and the sounds of fighting came from the living room. Tom was calling for her. Stella wiped her eyes on her apron and went inside.

For a time they all played a little game that everything was all right with William. Stella told no one, but at the celebration of Herman and Hannah Behrman's fiftieth wedding anniversary, there were concerned whispers behind William's back. He was too thin. He didn't pitch horseshoes on the lawn with the other men, and his appetite was poor, but he managed the day fairly well. Stella kept him supplied with cups of tea laced with whiskey.

Kate and Stella had come to New Braunfels with Effie three days before to help their cousin prepare for her parents' special day. The women spent most of their time in the kitchen. Effie tried to shoo her mother out, saying she wasn't to do the work for her own golden wedding. "Nonsense," Hannah said. "I'll cook for my funeral if I know ahead of time." William rested a lot, supposedly recovering from a bout with flu. Effie frequently checked on him. Sometimes she would look out the window and a shudder would pass through her body. *She knows*, Stella thought. *William hasn't told her yet, but she's guessed.*

Stella longed to embrace Effie, to tell her she also knew, that her heart hurt for her dear cousin and her darling William. But the time for that was after the golden wedding celebration.

Four generations gathered to celebrate the event at Herman and Hannah's big farmhouse. Even Anna came. It was the first time she had set foot in their house since she had moved from Behrman land.

Anna sat in a rocking chair on the front porch and held her youngest grandchild. Ruthie and Anna. Somehow they were alike. Plain, serious. Even as a five-year-old, Ruthie—like her grandmother—didn't appear to expect much out of life.

Jimmy and Kate arrived from Grand Prairie with their four children. Mark was a senior in high school and had already signed a letter of intent to play baseball for Texas A & M. Twelve-year-old Jeff had completely recovered from his neck injury and played junior high basketball and baseball. He still looked like a Norman Rockwell character with his red hair and freckles. Freddy, blond and slender, was a carbon copy of his brother Mark. He was in the sixth grade and ran track. Daughter Sara was a petite fourth grader and training as a gymnast. She was a self-contained child and held herself apart from her rambunctious and noisy older brothers, who were always wrestling with one another, playing catch, or challenging one another to one more race.

Effie and William's son Billy was the photographer for the day. Now a senior at the university, he was still much the devoted son to his parents, but Effie reported he had a new girlfriend. "I think it's serious," Effie said. "William's absolutely crazy about her. And she is a dear, sweet little thing." Effie looked over at William in his chair. "I think it'd be nice if Billy got married sometime soon."

Billy, with his usual boyish enthusiasm, took pictures of every possible grouping of relatives. Stella wondered if he knew about his father. She didn't think so. He looked too happy.

The various offspring of Effie's two married brothers, Hiram and Chris, joined in the games Kate organized. Hiram and his family still lived in the big old ranch house where Stella and Kate had grown up. Effie's youngest brother, Chris, taught agriculture at New Braunfels High School. Her older brother Jason, always asthmatic and frail, had given up the practice of law and moved back home with his parents. Jason drove each day to San Marcos to teach history at the college there. Uncle John and Aunt Louise came with son Joe, who at age forty had finally taken a wife. Joe's son was named Carl after his dead brother.

The only cousin missing was Francie. She had been invited to go to New Orleans with the family of her best friend. They were going to go to the French Quarter, then cruise the gulf for four days aboard a relative's yacht. When Stella insisted that her daughter attend her aunt and uncle's golden wedding celebration instead, Gordon had intervened. "You're only young once," he told Stella. "Herman and Hannah will understand."

Anna brought the old glockenspiel that had once stood on a brass stand in the parlor of Rosehaven. After the last dish was finally washed and the last callers had paid their respects for the day, the family all gathered on the wide front porch and in lawn chairs on the grass. Anna placed the glockenspiel in Kate's lap. "Oh, Mama," Kate protested, "it's been years." But everyone insisted. Tentatively at first, then with more authority, Kate played and they sang. "Bicycle Built for Two." "Down by the Old Mill Stream." "Yes, We Have No Bananas." "Show Me the Way to Go Home." And the hymns—once through in German, then in English for the younger generations. The moon rose over the treetops. The night train whistled in the distance.

Later Jimmy lit the bonfire that he and his boys had laid between the house and the barn, and they roasted marshmallows and sang a few more songs. Goats clustered at the fence and watched. Ruthie fed them marshmallows.

The celebration ended when Effie had everyone join hands in a large circle around the bonfire, thirty-one of them. Old faces, young faces, in-between faces, all glowing in the firelight. Effie started the words to "Jacob's Ladder," its haunting melody filling the air as they circled the fire and sang. "We are climbing Jacob's ladder, soldiers of the cross. Every round goes higher, higher, soldiers of the cross. If you love Him, why not serve Him, soldiers of the cross?" Uncle Herman's rich baritone led all the rest.

When the last notes died, Effie stepped forward. "I know the toasts have all been made," she said, "and so many good words have been spoken today, but before we all scatter again and return to our homes, my brothers and I want to thank you for being here to honor our parents on their golden wedding day. And I want to remind you all how blessed we are to have each other. We are joined by blood and marriage. A family. God bless you all, and thank you, Mama and Papa, for being our mama and papa."

That night, in the same bedroom where Effie had slept as a girl, William told her they would never have a golden wedding. Or even their silver. They clung to each other into the night and wept.

"We've had so much love," William said, "so much more than most.

We must remember that. I don't want to feel bitter or angry. I just want to live what days I have left in love with you."

The week after the celebration, William began a series of hospital stays that came at closer and closer intervals. Effie never left his side. She fed him when his therapy made him too weak to feed himself. She read to him. She slept on a cot by his bed.

The pretending was over. They had no future, so Effie and William talked of the past, reliving their years together, recalling moments grand and small that had been special, had made them happy or sad—but mostly happy. They went through family albums together. Almost every sentence seemed to begin with "Remember when . . ."

Family gatherings were awkward now. They all knew about his illness, about its prognosis. No one knew quite how to treat William, quite what to say. He looked skeletal. He and Effie started keeping mostly to themselves. It was better that way.

William stopped the therapy. No more injections. No more radiation. Enough.

Effie made custards and mashed potatoes. She searched through her cookbooks for foods that would be easy for him to digest. She was determined to keep him alive as long as she could. She didn't want to be cheated of a single day with her William.

"No man ever had a wife like you," William told her. He understood that it had been Effie who had made their marriage work. She had made her life fit into his. She had done it well.

"I'm the luckiest woman in the world," Effie responded.

When it came time for him to go to the hospital again, William sent Effie on an errand—some papers at the office he wanted to work on at the hospital. With Effie gone, William went into his study and with an antique Colt .45 shot first Rosie, the ancient and incontinent old cocker spaniel whom Effie didn't have the heart to put to sleep, then lay down on the floor beside the dead dog and put one hand on her still chest. Such a good old dog. Billy used to fall asleep on the floor curled up with Rosie. Little baby Billy. Rosie's tail would thump on the kitchen floor as William bent over and picked Billy up to carry him off to bed. Effie would follow and pull off Billy's little shoes and tuck him in. They would stand arm in arm looking down at their sleeping child. William

put the barrel in his mouth and without hesitation pulled the trigger.
It was his final gift to Effie—to end it.

When Effie got home, she was greeted by such quiet. She called for
William. In panic she raced upstairs to the bedroom. Then back downstairs. It was then that she noticed the note thumbtacked to the study
door:

My darling Effie,

The door is locked. I don't want you to come inside. Call
Jimmy to come take care of things. I've put you through enough
with this illness. It is time to end it. And Rosie too. It was
time for us to be off. I love you more than I can ever say. Thank
you, my darling, for honoring me all these years with your
presence and your love and the gift of our beloved son.

If there is a hereafter, you will find me waiting there for you.
If not, farewell. Be happy. That's what you do best. Don't let
this interfere with that.

My love forever,
William

Effie read the note. Reread it. She pounded on the door, calling
desperately for her husband. She screamed out her denial into the silent
house. Then there seemed to be nothing to do but call her cousin's
husband as William had instructed.

Jimmy's secretary informed her that Mr. Morris was in a meeting.
"This is a family emergency," Effie said, her voice shaking.

"Effie?" Jimmy's concerned voice was on the line. "What's
happened?"

Effie didn't think she could say the words.

"Effie, are you there? What the hell's the matter?"

"Please come over, Jimmy. William is dead."

She hung up the phone and stared numbly at nothing. When Kate
arrived with Jimmy, Effie collapsed in her cousin's arms. "Where's Stella?"
she asked.

"She's on her way," Kate said. Kate understood that Effie needed
the three of them to grieve together.

Effie would not take the tranquilizers their family doctor thrust on her. She listened politely to their minister's platitudes. She insisted on making all the funeral arrangements herself. She sorted through William's personal possessions and business papers. He had left everything in order for her, with a list of who was to receive many of his personal possessions. The Colt .45 was to go to the weapons collection at the museum at the University of Texas.

Effie and her son buried Rosie in the backyard and William in his family's plot. The family all gathered once again, their ranks expanded by the Chambers cousins, uncles, and aunts. Mrs. Chambers was dead. Mr. Chambers looked as though he didn't quite understand what was going on. Everyone from Texas Central came and told Effie and Billy what a fine boss William Chambers had been. Story after story of his "helping out" surfaced. A good man.

Births and deaths, Stella thought as she stood beside William's open grave, not listening to the rites, sweating in a dark suit too hot for the brilliant Texas sun. Her life was punctuated by an endless series of family births and deaths.

Twenty-seven

Effie cried herself to sleep at night.

She had loved her husband. He was a dear, good man who had treated her well. There would never be another William, but almost from the moment she read his farewell note, Effie knew there would be another husband. She would eventually put grief aside and look for him.

"I need to be a wife," she explained to Stella and Kate. "I feel incomplete without a husband to look after."

But first there was Texas Central to look after. Billy wanted to go to law school like his father and grandfather and Uncle Jason. And he was in love. At this point in his life he was more interested in his upcoming marriage than he was in running his dead father's business.

"Why don't you take over Texas Central?" Billy asked his mother.

"Me!" Effie protested. "My goodness, Billy. I couldn't do that."

"Why not? You ran it during the war. Did a damned good job, I hear. Trained all those pilots and started the shop to rebuild airplane engines. I hear some of the employees talking about it, and they say you were pretty incredible."

"But that was during the war. Things just kind of happened during the war. The company's changed, and times have changed. Texas Central doesn't train pilots or rebuild engines. It's a public company with a board of directors now. Back when I was helping out, it was just me and your Grandpa Chambers."

"Mother, I know for a fact that you still read the minutes of the board meetings religiously. I've heard you and Dad discuss the business over your evening coffee for years. I've heard you make those subtle little suggestions of yours that always ended up seeming like Dad's idea in the first place. Don't you tell me you don't know anything about Texas Central. I think you know it inside out and backwards—a hell of lot more than I do."

"Billy Chambers, don't you say things like that. Your daddy just liked to use me for a sounding board. It's part of a wife's job to be interested in her husband's business and listen while he works through his decisions, but don't you think for one minute that it was anything more than that. It's your place to run that company. Now, if you need me to help you in any way, I will, but *you're* the president of Texas Central. I think you owe it to your father to try to follow in his footsteps."

So a "III" was added to the name on the president's door and to the company letterhead. William Edward Chambers III. But Billy went off to law school and usually came to the company offices only for monthly board meetings. William's old desk remained uncluttered and virtually unused. Effie "helped out" at the office. She used a desk in the large, open clerical area that was populated by secretaries and managers. At her son's insistence, she accepted the title of Executive Director—a vague title that didn't necessarily interfere with the vice-presidential areas, a title of which she could make what she wanted.

The airline had fewer Dallas-based employees than during World War II when they ran the flight school. But now the airline had ticketing and service personnel in all the cities on their routes. And the investment in planes was far greater. The days of flying converted military transports were over.

Some of the personnel she had hired during the war were still with the company. None of the female pilots had stayed, but two women mechanics were still working, and many of the clerical staff dated back to the days when Effie had kept them going during the war.

Effie always wore suits to the office. She didn't insist that everyone call her by her first name, as she had during the war. Times were different. It had been more exciting during the war. People had worked so well together. Now there were unions and grievance committees.

A group of female employees approached her at the end of her second week.

"Our legs get so cold when we go back and forth between the buildings. Hangar four is a long walk, and the maintenance people are always using the electric carts."

"Why don't you wear slacks on cold days?" Effie said. "We always did during the war." She'd have to stop calling it *the* war, she reminded herself. There'd been Korea in between, and that Vietnam thing was looking more like a war all the time.

The women exchanged glances. Effie took the bait. "Is there some reason why you don't wear slacks?"

"The dress code," a payroll clerk said. She was the woman who went around to the hangars and maintenance shops collecting time cards.

"Dress code? You mean there's a rule against slacks? I see. Have you discussed this with Mr. Fuller?" she asked.

The women nodded.

Martin Fuller was the vice-president of internal affairs—not a brilliant man, but a solid administrator.

Effie waited until a cold, blustery day. She wore a full skirt of wool challis and a chic leather jacket.

She invited Fuller to accompany her on her twice-weekly rounds of the facilities. Fuller put on his overcoat and pulled it closed across his decided paunch.

Every time Effie stepped out a door, her skirt went flying. And she shivered. "My poor legs are freezing. You men don't know how fortunate you are with your sensible clothes. I've surely learned my lesson today. From now on, the chilly days I make my rounds, I'm going to cover up my poor legs."

Another gust caught her skirt. Her blue satin slip was trimmed with a wide band of beautiful ecru-colored lace.

"You don't object to slacks, do you?" she asked. "I've noticed none of the women wear them. There isn't some sort of rule against them, is there?"

"As a matter of fact, we do require skirts for any women in the front office. Skirts are more in keeping with a public office."

"Well, then, I guess I'll just have to freeze," Effie said with a decided shiver. "I hope I don't catch pneumonia."

She waited until the next cold day before asking Fuller to go with her again. "Why do you bother with these *rounds?*" Fuller asked, his breath condensing into a white cloud. "None of the other executives take the time away from their desks to stroll about the hangars."

"I learned during the war—World War II—that it's good for morale," Effie explained, careful to keep her voice sweet. "Billy and I think it's a good idea that employees in the outer buildings not feel they're working in isolation. And I want to go beyond the Dallas employees. I'm planning to visit two or three of our cities every month. I see things when I go around. I see work schedules that need tightening—or more flexibility.

I see hangars without Coke machines. Dirty rest rooms. I see ticket counters in out-of-the-way locations at airports—we need to see that the Oklahoma City Airport Authority knows that our counter has got to be moved at the first opportunity. I hear Mid-Continent is dropping Oklahoma City—we should request their slot. But anyway, I see people doing excellent jobs who need commendation and people doing shoddy jobs who need to be reprimanded."

"Are you telling me I haven't being doing my job?" Fuller was bristling.

"Oh, Martin, don't you go and get all huffy. You do a fine job. My word, you and William were together *before* the war. He always knew he could count on you. You just have more important things to do than worry about Coke machines and dirty rest rooms. I'm just trying to help out, and I have more time than you do for poking around. Can you walk a little faster? My poor legs are absolutely freezing."

When they arrived at the next hangar, Effie raced over to stand in front of a floor heater. She stuck a leg out for Fuller's inspection. Even through her stockings, it was plain to see that the skin on her legs was beet red with the cold.

"Why don't you just change the rule yourself?" he asked.

"If you think the dress code should be changed, that's up to you," Effie said with a small pout.

Fuller called for an electric cart for their return trip. When they arrived at the front office, Effie smiled her best smile and thanked him for accompanying her. "And, Martin, if you do change the dress code, make sure it's worded so that women won't start showing up in blue jeans."

"Why don't you just write it?"

"Why, Martin, I wouldn't think of it. If you don't sincerely believe that the women are suffering because of the no-slacks rule, Billy and I wouldn't expect you to change it one little bit."

"Inclement weather only," Fuller said gruffly.

"That's fair," Effie said. She smiled again.

The company's public relations director was waiting at her desk. Henry Grimm. He was, too. Effie never understood why such a sourpuss had gone into public relations. William had been with Grimm's older brother in the war. He'd watched his plane go down. William gave Grimm the job out of loyalty, but Effie felt no loyalty toward him. The job he'd done for the company in the past was adequate, she supposed, but concepts were changing, and he wasn't. And she didn't think he had shown the proper respect for William. Grimm had actually introduced her to his wife as "the old man's wife."

As she approached her desk, Grimm started waving a memo at her. Effie knew without looking that it was one she had written to him yesterday.

"Coupons!" Grimm said, throwing his hands in the air in a gesture of masculine exasperation. "You mean like housewives cut out of newspapers to save a few pennies on margarine and cereal?"

"Something like that," Effie said, seating herself behind her desk and folding her hands in front of her. "People love to save money. Billy and I think it'd be a wonderful advertising ploy. We could offer discount coupons as a reward to people who fly with us regularly. We could offer coupons to perk up lagging runs. We could have coupons for people over sixty-five, for people willing to fly at slack times."

"We'd be the laughingstock of the industry," Grimm insisted. He was upset. He always got red in the face when he got upset. And the long lock of hair he slicked across his balding head had fallen across his forehead. "It's undignified," Grimm was saying. "It cheapens the airline."

"We aren't TWA or American, Henry. We're just a local airline, hopping our way across Texas and its neighbors. We don't have to be dignified, and I seem to recall that you were the one who wanted the ticket agents to wear shorts and high heels. Now *that's* undignified."

"I refuse to have anything to do with coupons," Grimm said, throwing the memo across the desk.

"Fine. I'd like Miss Rodrigez to research the idea and work up a proposal."

"Miss Rodrigez is my girl. She does what I say for her to do."

"I've reassigned her—temporarily, of course. She's a bright young woman, and she has a public relations degree from UT. I think she should be given a chance at more than clerical work."

"She's an uppity Mexican who's damned lucky to have a desk job. Most of 'em clean bathrooms."

"I saw you trying to get her into the stockroom the other day," Effie said, her voice low, flat. "I don't think there are desks in the stockroom."

Grimm's jaw dropped. "Are you trying to run me off from this job?"

"I'm not sure," Effie said honestly. "My husband had high regard for your brother and felt a loyalty to you because of him. I will defer judgment for the time being. Of course, if you'd like to resign, I'm sure my son would accept your resignation. But if I ever catch you so much as winking at one of the female employees, *I* will fire you on the spot."

Effie resigned from the board of directors at the symphony but tried to keep up with her other activities as best she could. There was a husband waiting for her out there someplace, and she didn't want to miss finding him by never going anyplace social.

There were no candidates for marriage on the Texas Central all-male board of directors. They all had wives. A ten-year board member, Albert Fitzsimmons of Texas Bank and Trust, announced to Effie that he had been in love with her for years and offered to get a divorce and marry her. But Effie kissed him lightly on the cheek and told him in her best southern drawl not to be an old fool. "Your sweet Betty Jane is a darlin' wife. My goodness, what are you thinkin' about, Albert? She would be devastated—and those three beautiful daughters. You would be too, you silly boy."

Effie dated. A great number of Dallas hostesses knew a widower or divorced male they wanted to pair off with Effie. Some of Effie's well-meaning women friends even called bachelor brothers and uncles who lived in other cities and insisted they come to Dallas for the next social event in order to meet the charming Effie Chambers.

Effie was very particular, however, about her dates. No playboys. No born-again Christians. No man who had been divorced twice or whose last wife had been twenty years his junior. Usually she went out with a man only one time. It took only one date for her to know that the man was not the one she wanted for her next husband, and Effie wasn't interested in going out with men just for the sake of going out. She had no need to play the field, to make conquests, to have sexual escapades. She would have escapades with her next husband.

Unfortunately, most of the men she went out with wanted to take her out again. Some even proposed before the end of the evening.

"You've got to stop being so sweet and Effie-like," Kate told her. "Of course, they fall in love with you when you smile that dimpled smile and listen to them like they were saying something important."

"Kate," Jimmy said with a laugh, "that's like telling the sun not to be sunny."

Kate felt a pang of jealousy. Jimmy admired Effie. All men admired Effie. It was a foregone conclusion. Kate had no admirers. If she hadn't loved her cousin so much, she wouldn't like her.

Effie was busier than she had ever been in her life. Texas Central took more and more of her time. She wondered what she was going to do with the company when she married again. It would be hard to find time to bake pies and fuss over a man when she had to go to work every day. She wished Billy took more of an interest in the company, but maybe that would come in time.

And she did enjoy doing a good job as executive director. She was a born organizer, whether dealing with gala benefits or company business, and she had good instincts about people. William had been a little too trusting and had made some poor decisions about the people he hired. Effie had definite ideas before she walked into the head office the day after William's funeral about who would stay, who would be let go, and who would be put on probation.

And William had let the charter-passenger end of the business go downhill in favor of regularly scheduled flights. Effie personally made calls on the head of every major corporation in Dallas and explained their newly expanded services.

She even eased out one member of the board of directors—old Lester Franklin whose hearing problems and cantankerous ways were disruptive to the board meetings. He left thinking it was his idea. Effie invited Jimmy Morris to be on the board. Her brother-in-law was a realist.

Effie was at a Special Olympics organizational meeting in the Adolphus Hotel ballroom when she met a lovely man named Charles Lasseter.

But he was wearing a wedding ring. Effie gave him a regular smile.

"You're Stella Behrman's cousin, aren't you?" he asked.

There was something about the way he asked that alerted Effie. She let him talk—about his aunt, about when he'd met Stella years ago in Austin, how they hadn't been together in Galveston because Stella's father had had a stroke, how she used to talk about her cousin Effie and her sister Kate.

"Have you always been in love with Stella?" Effie asked.

Charles looked startled. His eyes misted over. He looked away, embarrassed. "Does it show that much?"

"Yes," Effie said softly. "You'd better not talk about her anymore."

"Tell her you saw me. Tell her I still think about her every day. Always." There was desperation in the way he said it.

Effie shook his hand and watched him wind his way back to his wife's side in the receiving line. Effie recognized her from the Ballet Society—an exquisite-looking woman, like a *Vogue* model.

Effie felt sad. She should have known. Suddenly she understood her cousin Stella a whole lot better.

It was later that same evening that Effie met Pete. As she looked back over that evening she wondered if her conversation with Charles had made her all the more alert to possibilities, a little bit more intent on her quest. She didn't want to be sad. She wanted to be with someone she loved and who loved her in return.

And except for his height, Pete would have been easy to overlook. He appeared to be one of those plain, gangly men who didn't wear their clothes well and always looked awkward, whether they elected to stand or sit or lean against the wall. Effie watched Pete do all three—and try to mingle. His haircut was all wrong. And he was thin.

There was a man who needed a wife.

Pete saw her coming. She was weaving her way through the crowd and heading directly for him.

But he didn't know her. He didn't know anyone who looked like that. My God, what a beautiful woman! Men turned to look at her. She had blond, shoulder-length hair pulled back on one side to reveal a diamond earring. She was wearing a white dress that swished about her legs as she walked.

She stopped in front of him and held out her hand. Her eyes were the purest blue. "I'm Effie Chambers," she said.

"Pete Peterson," he said, taking her cool, slim hand.

"Isn't that redundant?" she asked.

"Well, actually it's *Frank* Peterson. But everyone has called me Pete as long as I can remember. Now if anyone calls me Frank, I have to remind myself they're talking to me."

"What happened to your wife?"

"How do you know that something happened to her?"

"No man with a wife would have ever shown up at this function wearing a brown tie with his navy suit."

Pete looked down at his tie. It had a spot on it. "She's dead. For two years."

"I'm sorry," Effie said. And she was. The sadness in Frank "Pete" Peterson's eyes was sincere. She liked a man who had loved his wife.

"How long were you married?" she asked.

"Almost thirty years."

"Are you a born-again Christian?"

Pete looked puzzled. "I've been a Presbyterian all my life. Are you an evangelist or something?"

"Heavens, no," Effie said. Then she smiled at him—her very best smile. "And now I wonder if you'd like to have a drink with me."

Pete felt like he had just been knighted.

They went into the hotel bar and stayed for three hours. Pete couldn't remember ever talking to a woman for three hours. He told Effie he had played basketball at Texas A & M in the early thirties. And about the painful crush he'd had on his high school English teacher. He'd never told that to anyone before.

Effie told him about New Braunfels—about her brothers and cousins and mama and papa, about growing up happy.

The next morning, as Pete fixed breakfast in his cluttered kitchen, the phone rang. He expected a patient. It was Effie Chambers. "Last night, when you said you were going to call me, did you mean it?"

"Of course, I did," Pete stammered. He couldn't believe it was she. "I had a wonderful time last night. Really wonderful."

"When were you going to call me?"

"I thought about it a lot late last night—whether it would be more proper to wait a few days or if I should call today."

"What did you decide?"

"I haven't yet. I'm not sure what's appropriate. I really want to do the right thing."

"Well, I'm sure you will. I had a wonderful time too."

Frank Peterson was a physician. He was tall like William. That pleased Effie. She liked being the "little woman" to a man's tallness.

After her phone call Effie spent the day considering the possibility of seducing him into an immediate marriage but decided instead to allow him to court her. She was dying to cook dinner for him, but she would wait. They would do restaurants before she made him a pie. But she could hardly wait to bake that pie. Lord, how she'd missed fussing over a man.

Their first date was to the Texas-Oklahoma football game at the Cotton Bowl. Always held in Dallas rather than the respective campuses in Austin and Norman, the college football game was one of the most colorful in the country. Commerce Street was closed in downtown Dallas the night before the game to accommodate the river of fans that filled the street, carrying their beer in six-packs, getting into fights, forming impromptu pep rallies, singing "The Eyes of Texas" and "Boomer Sooner."

The next afternoon at the Cotton Bowl the stands were half Texas orange and half Oklahoma red. The bands had their own contest, each trying to outplay the other.

Effie had a new dress for the occasion—a cream-colored linen she wore with a burnt-orange scarf as a show of colors. Pete, a Texas A & M graduate, confessed he always cheered against the Longhorns, but he'd make an exception today in her honor.

The only scoring until late in the second half was a Texas field goal. With less than three minutes in the half, the Longhorns elected to pass on a third and four from their 41-yard line. The pass was apparently incomplete, but interference was called on the Sooners.

"Oklahoma was robbed," Pete said as Texas stormed into the end zone on the next play.

"I thought you were on my side," Effie said.

"Right. Great officiating," Pete corrected.

Late in the third quarter, Oklahoma finally came to life and was threatening inside the Texas 20-yard line when Effie noticed a man coming up the steps. He was big, balding, and staggering. He tripped and fell flat against the stairs a few rows down from where she and Pete were sitting. At first she dismissed the man as a drunk. But the look on his face as he tried to get to his feet was one of fear.

Effie put her hand on Pete's arm. "Pete, that man. Something's the matter."

The cheering was deafening. The Sooners were at the goal line. All around them, Longhorn fans were on their feet, screaming, "Defense! Defense!"

At first Pete didn't understand her. She pointed.

Effie could feel Pete's body become tense under her hand in the second before he slipped past her and the two teenagers standing next to her.

Effie watched Pete kneel at the fallen man's side. There was pandemonium all around him as he leaned over the man and spoke into his ear. Pete put his own ear close to the man's lips to hear his reply.

Pete yelled to one of the teenagers for help.

Effie followed as the young man helped Pete half drag the stricken man the last few steps to the causeway.

The man went limp at the top step. His skin was gray. His eyes rolled back.

They stretched him out on the concrete. Pete's fingers were searching for a pulse at the man's throat.

"Find a policeman!" Pete yelled at the teenager. "Tell him we need a crash cart immediately. Possible heart attack."

"Can I help?" Effie asked.

But already Pete was pushing on the man's chest with the heels of his hands. Hard. Rhythmically.

A woman in red knelt beside him. "I'm a nurse anesthetist," she said.

"Check his airway," Pete instructed, without breaking his rhythm.

The nurse pulled the man's head back, exposing a fleshy throat, and began to administer mouth-to-mouth resuscitation, while Pete continued pushing at his chest. Sweat poured from Pete's forehead. Circles of wetness appeared under his arms.

That man's dying, Effie thought in horror. Right in the middle of a football game.

A policeman arrived with a uniformed nurse. She had a stethoscope in her pocket.

"Are you a doctor?" she asked.

"Where's the crash cart?" Pete asked, never breaking his rhythm.

"Sorry," she said, kneeling beside Pete. "We don't have one. Just first aid. There's an ambulance on the way."

"Jesus Christ!" Pete said. "Eighty thousand people on a hot day at a football game and no emergency provisions."

A plump woman in an orange pantsuit came running up, and with one look at the unconscious man, she began screaming. Effie knew without asking that it was his wife.

Effie reached for her, instinctively putting her arms around the woman. "The man with him is a doctor," she explained.

"I'm losing my airway," the nurse anesthetist said. "I need an endotracheal tube."

The uniformed nurse shook her head no.

"Oh, my God," the two kneeling women said almost in unison as vomit erupted from the man's mouth and ran down both sides of his face, his chin, onto the concrete floor. The sickening odor filled the air.

The two nurses and Pete struggled to get the man turned over. "I think he's aspirated it," the nurse anesthetist was saying. "We'll never get an airway back without a tube."

On all fours, Pete was almost face down on the concrete, using his finger to clear out the man's mouth and throat.

"I knew we shouldn't have come," the man's wife was saying as she clung to Effie. "I knew it. He had open heart surgery six weeks ago. A bypass. He's never missed one of these games in thirty-seven years. Oh, God, I knew we shouldn't have come."

Hot dog vendors continued to hawk their wares all around the man on the pavement. The bands were playing their respective fight songs at the same time. People were on their feet, cheering, as the game continued on the field.

It should all stop, Effie thought. How can this be going on when a man is dying?

Two ambulance attendants with a stretcher came hurrying up. "Am I glad to see you guys," Pete said, standing. "We had him going, but he's aspirated vomitus. No airway."

"You'd better go tell them about your husband's bypass," Effie told the woman. "They'll let you ride with him to the hospital."

Pete was wiping his hands on his handkerchief. "I'll be right back as soon as I wash my hands," he told Effie. "Find out what's happening down on the field for me."

Down on the field? Effie leaned weakly against a pillar. He wanted to know about the football game.

She was still standing there when Pete came hurrying out of the rest room. He looked at her quizzically.

"Will he die?" she asked.

"Yes. I imagine he already has."

"How can you still care about a ball game after what just happened?"

"Not watching the ball game won't bring that man back, Effie."

"Well, I can't do it," she said. "I'm too upset. That was horrible, Pete."

"Yeah, it was. I plan to write some pretty scathing letters to the Cotton Bowl officials about their responsibility to the public, and I'll bring the matter up before county medical. But right now I want to know what all that yelling was about. Did Oklahoma score?"

"I haven't the faintest idea," Effie said.

"Well, then, let's go find out," he said, holding out his hand.

"I don't feel right. It seems inappropriate to cheer when a man just died."

"People are dying everywhere, Effie. I see it in my business all the time, and it's usually 'inappropriate.' But I believe in life. I came here with you today to celebrate being alive. I think you came for the same reason. We could be home living out our lives as the grieving widowed, but we aren't, are we?"

Effie allowed him to direct her back to her seat. The two teenagers caught him up on what had been happening. Carpenter had fumbled away OU's scoring opportunity. The Longhorns were threatening. But it was all so meaningless, Effie thought. She began to shake.

Pete put his arm around her. "I'm sorry, Effie. I shouldn't have insisted we stay. Come on. I'll take you home."

"No. I'm all right. Just leave your arm there for a while."

"You sure?"

Effie nodded. "You know, you were pretty spectacular up there," Effie said, tilting her head toward the concourse behind them.

Pete's grin was boyish. "Thanks."

"And I think you just gave me a lesson in my own philosophy of life. It just needs a while to sink in."

Texas won 24 to 0. The Sooners weren't what they used to be.

Pete took Effie home and promised to return for her at seven. He had reservations at the Chaparrel Club.

Effie had a brandy and soaked in the tub. By seven she was in black sequins. When Pete arrived, he let out a low whistle of appreciation.

Effie did a little pirouette. The back of the dress was wonderfully bare.

"My, my, my," he said. "You are one fantastic-looking lady."

"And you, Dr. Peterson, look rather elegant." His haircut was good. He was wearing a carefully tailored charcoal-gray suit with an ivory-colored shirt. His tie was striped in muted shades of gray, peach, beige, and green. "What happened to the brown tie?" she asked.

"I don't need it tonight."

"Explain, please."

"It let women know I'm available. It's harder for a man, you know. But women see that awful brown tie with a navy suit and a detergent-gray shirt, and they know I couldn't possibly have a wife."

"How many times have you used that ruse before?"

"A few," he admitted, "but never with such fine results as the other night. I had been wishing I'd never let my friends talk me into coming. I'd been up most of the night before. I was tired. My back hurt. When I looked up and saw you heading my way, I felt like a gawking sixteen-year-old."

Pete had reserved a window table. They looked out at the lights of Dallas and sipped their cocktails.

"I think I should tell you that I really loved my husband," Effie said, "and I will continue to love his memory. I don't ever want to forget him."

Pete nodded. "I loved my wife too. She was a great lady. But two years are long enough. I'm lonely."

"Are you going to court me?"

Pete shook his head and smiled. "You're direct, aren't you?"

"Well, we aren't a couple of kids. I don't want to waste the good years I have left. I don't like limbo."

"Yes, Effie, I'm going to court you. I will retire the brown tie. I want us to have a wonderful courtship."

"I make a fantastic apple pie," she announced.

"I'm sure you do lots of things well," he said.

"Yes, I do," she said, and blushed.

She didn't go to bed with him that night. She would have, but he didn't push for it.

The next night they picked up a six-pack of Lone Star beer and a mushroom-and-extra-cheese pizza and watched a rerun of *Casablanca* on television. "Would you have let her go?" Effie asked when the movie ended.

"I don't know. It was war. He was trying to do the right thing."

It wasn't the answer that Effie wanted, but she forgave him when he told her how he hadn't slept last night thinking of her, wanting her.

"I think I'm in love with you, Effie. Already. I knew it would come to that, but my God, so fast."

The kissing was wonderful. He understood about breasts. Effie adored having hers fondled and could hardly wait to bare them for him.

She had thought they would make love in the guest room. She was hesitant to take him to the bed she had shared with William. But she forgot. Without thinking, she had led him to her bedroom.

She stared at the bed. Tears filled her eyes.

Pete held her and whispered into her hair. "It's okay. I understand. I think the first time should be in a nice neutral hotel with no ghosts hovering. Right?"

Effie nodded, grateful. *This* was a very nice man.

Pete wasn't on call the following weekend, and they went to San Antonio. Effie felt shy. Pete was nervous. "We're like two kids," he acknowledged.

"My mama once told me the first time was just something to get through," Effie said.

Pete smiled. "I think she's right. Let's do it so we can get to seconds. You use the bathroom first. Would you like some of this wine?"

When they finally got through the logistics of getting themselves naked and into bed, Effie warmed. How nice it was to be naked in a man's arms, Pete's arms. He kissed her for a long time before the touching began. By then she was ready for it.

His penis was longer than William's but not so thick. He moaned his appreciation as she moved her hand up and down its length.

"Please don't be upset if I don't come the first time," she said as he entered her.

"Just don't pretend," he said. "Ever."

Pete was more vocal than William had been. He told her how warm and wet and wonderful she felt, how beautiful her body was, how much he wanted her, how he wanted to be the only man for her for the rest of her life, did it feel all right to her, did she want another way, was he hurting her. Effie found it distracting. She couldn't have her own thoughts for all of his.

Finally she claimed his mouth, hushing him, and allowed her body to relax. No, she wasn't going to come, but it felt lovely to have him in her, moving, joining, climbing toward his climax. And she hadn't come the first time with William all those years ago.

She released his mouth as his groans erupted with his orgasm. He said her name.

Effie was relieved to have it done. Now she could go forward. And she absolutely refused to be sad. William was dead. He would have wanted her to get on with her life. Pete wasn't William, but he was a perfectly lovely man whom she was going to love and take care of. She'd need to do something about all that talking during sex, but that shouldn't be too much of a problem.

Effie cradled Pete's head against her bosom and wondered if he was good for another round this evening or if she would have to wait until morning for seconds. Her stupid body waited until he was done to become aroused, but she would enjoy the delicious sense of anticipation while she waited for him to be ready.

The following week Pete proposed. "I changed my mind about a long courtship. I suppose I can live without you," he said, "but I really don't want to try."

They were married in Kate's living room. Gordon officiated. Effie wore blue.

When they left on their Bermuda honeymoon, Effie had filled half a suitcase with wonderful new lingerie, including a lacy black teddy and an ivory satin nightgown that would have made Marilyn Monroe proud.

Pete was beside himself as she paraded around the room in her teddy. Never had he seen such a sight outside of a magazine. She swished her hips and allowed the strap to fall off her shoulder seductively as she looked over her shoulder at him and rolled her eyes.

Feeling delightfully foolish, Pete insisted on drinking champagne from her slipper. And her navel. They got hysterical over that. He'd never had laughter during lovemaking.

Pete loved Effie's teasing, her body in satin, her delight of sensual pleasures. He rose to the occasion time and again. "God, I never knew I was such a stud," he admitted.

"Stick with me, baby," Effie said in her best Mae West voice, "and anything's possible."

Pete believed her.

Effie's life continued much as before—Texas Central, the few organizations and charities in which she was still active, her same bridge foursome, almost the same circle of friends. Pete moved into her Turtle Creek home, and they mingled possessions, friends, and families.

Effie often thought of her beloved William, the husband of her youth. Reminders of him were everywhere. Usually the thoughts were just in passing—an affectionate acknowledgment of the good life they had shared together. Occasionally thoughts of William would fill her up, and she would get sad, need to go off by herself and weep. William, dearest

William, how she had loved him. Few women have ever been loved as well as she was loved by William. But after a while she would dry her tears, fix her face, and go back to her life.

Pete had a busy practice in internal medicine. Effie decided to continue with Texas Central in spite of her marriage—at least until Billy finished law school. The company was running smoothly. She had added routes back into New Mexico and was looking to Kansas for next year. She had added six new Lear jets to the charter fleet.

Stella marveled at how Effie grew more glamorous with the years. In her mid-forties, the rosy prettiness of her youth began to fade, but she compensated with style. She even learned to live with the gray hairs that were now mixed with the blond. On Effie, it looked wonderful.

Effie's son married—not the sweet little girl from Houston that his father had like so much, but Barbara, a bright, young newspaper reporter from Dallas. Billy was still boyish and always seemed more in love with his mother than with his wife.

Dr. Pete could not believe his good fortune over such a wife as Effie. He loved the busyness of their life together, along with her good humor and her good cooking. She was incredible. Absolutely incredible. She even liked sex. A woman among women. The wife every man dreams of.

Pete had reached that inevitable male plateau when a man realized that making a lot of money wasn't as important as he had once thought. Pete had grown tired of walking into the endless examining rooms and hospital rooms to listen to the next set of complaints. He had thought medicine would be noble, but ultimately it was just a job, and the job consisted mostly of listening to people complain. But now at the end of the day, he could go home to Effie. She seldom complained. He was grateful to the splendid woman who had rescued him from the boredom of middle life.

Twenty-eight

Stella and Gordon attended Lyndon Johnson's watch party at the historic Driskill Hotel in downtown Austin. Johnson always had his watch parties there. He had been instrumental in saving the grand old hotel from urban renewal.

And now Johnson and Lady Bird greeted friends and political colleagues as they waited for the official word that he had been elected vice president of the United States.

Lady Bird did not photograph well, and each time Stella saw her, she was struck anew by how really pretty the woman actually was. In person, the nose didn't matter; the eyes and smile were more important. And if her Texas charm was overdone, Stella had the feeling that under the syrup was a sincere person. Lady Bird wore white chiffon. All her evening clothes looked like pretty nightgowns.

Stella never saw Lyndon Johnson without being surprised at how tall he was. He looked strange in a standard tuxedo and patent-leather shoes. She had never seen him in anything other than western-cut suits and expensive boots. Stella didn't like Lyndon Johnson, though in many ways he had been good for the state. His smiling, good-ole-boy persona had brought him to national status, but to Stella he still exemplified Texas's establishment politics.

"Ah, Gordon, I see that little woman of yours is as pretty as ever," Johnson said before kissing Stella's cheek. He always said that—always in the third person.

Gordon beamed. Gordon enjoyed his association with Johnson and appreciated the man's power. It was Johnson who had invited him to run for the Texas Railroad Commission, and Johnson was still telling people that Gordon Kendall was a comer. Governor Price Daniels had picked up on the expression. Kendall, the comer.

Stella would not have been surprised if Gordon started wearing boots and a big hat. She was glad he didn't.

Gordon was busy and happy, full of hope. He was serving as a visiting professor at the university, teaching philosophy of religion. He liked the mentor role. It was like being back in the pulpit. He took his teaching seriously, and while Stella studied in the evenings, he prepared his lectures, often interrupting her to try out a new tack.

And Gordon took his membership on the railroad commission very seriously. He went to his office at the state capitol daily, read every report with care. He kept up with the oil industry and traveled around the state visiting the fields and offices of the independents and majors. He apprised himself of all legislation, state and national, that affected the industry. He audited a course at the university on the politics of the oil-rich Middle East. But ultimately he was not really a part of the decision-making process. The votes on the three-man commission were usually unanimous and usually preordained.

Stella knew that if Gordon was indeed a comer, it was because he would never cross those who put him in power. She understood that Gordon was allowed to ride the coattails of the likes of John Connally, Price Daniels, Dollar Bill Blakely, and Sam Rayburn because he was not a threat. "A loyal Democrat," Gordon basically did as he was told. He embraced the conservative establishment politics of an Anglo rule that answered only to the vested interests in banking, oil, land development, law, the merchant houses, and the press. More subtly perhaps than in years past, the Texas Democrats still embraced antilabor laws and a segregationist philosophy. Gordon was a better man than that, but he seldom looked behind the facade.

Sometimes, though, he worried about the future of the state. "Texas needs to divest," he told Stella. She agreed. It was unhealthy to be so dependent on one industry. Her study of history had taught her that everything was cyclic. She gave Gordon historic precedents for his thesis. Spices. Slaves. Coal. Gold. Empires. Nothing stayed the same. What was precious one day could be devalued the next. Whale oil used to light the world. How strange for Gordon to really listen to her. Almighty Texas would someday be humbled if foresighted people didn't exert some influence.

But Stella didn't see her husband in that role. She wished Gordon had stayed in higher education administration. He had done a good job at United Wesleyan. When he started getting restless and wanting to move on, she had encouraged him to apply for a vice presidential opening at the University of Texas. Vice president of university affairs—the public relations and fund-raising area. Gordon's forte.

But the glamour of politics lured him. He wanted to be ever more important. Gordon waited in anticipation for the day when he would be told what office he should seek next. Something more visible. Stella wondered if the call would ever come. Were they holding a carrot in front of his nose to keep him in line? Of course, he was a good campaigner. He met people well. He spoke well. She watched him now as he mingled with the crowd in the Driskill ballroom, shaking hands, smiling, knowing who they were, why they were important. He grew more handsome each year. Tan, slim, graying, distinguished, but with a sincere smile. Gordon *was* sincere in his concern for people, but Stella feared the corrupting aspect of politics. Already her husband was owned.

Gordon sensed she was watching him. He looked over at her and winked. Stella smiled and walked over to join him.

"You really are as pretty as ever," he said.

"Why, Gordon, thank you. You're not so bad looking yourself. As a matter of fact, I was just thinking that you're the handsomest man in the room."

Stella felt pleased. It had been a long time since he told her she was pretty. She felt a silly urge to run off to the powder room and check the mirror to see if it was true.

The presidential election was close. But the Kennedy–Johnson ticket defeated Nixon and Lodge.

When Nixon finally conceded, Gordon whooped like a schoolboy. The band played "Deep in the Heart of Texas." Lady Bird and Lyndon waved and kissed; Linda Bird and Lucy hugged their parents. Lyndon spread his arms wide, both hands showing the victory V.

Tom dropped the ball.

There was a stunned silence in the stands. It should have been the last out. The game would have been over and the Eagles would have been league champs.

But the rules of Austin's Little League program said you had to play every boy. The Eagles' coach, an insurance company executive whose boy played catcher, had almost forgotten about the Kendall kid down at the end of the bench. Momentarily the coach considered disregarding the participation rule and not playing Tom, but that would have been risky. The scorekeeper or the opposing coach might notice. Or the kid's parents might say something. And he certainly didn't want to invalidate the game. The team's next stop was the playoffs for Austin city champs. The Eagles were ahead 9–6.

"You'll go in for Jimerson in the next inning," he told Tom.

When her brother came to bat, Ruthie crossed all her fingers and her legs. But Tom struck out.

Was it really necessary to go through this every summer? Stella wondered. No matter how much batting practice Gordon put Tom through, no matter how many times he hit the ball when his father or brother pitched to him in the park, he still struck out in an actual ball game. Gordon insisted Tom could do it. Brian could. His cousins Mark and Jeff could. Even little cousin Freddy could.

Tom wanted to. He wanted to please his father. The few times he had managed to get himself on base—usually on a fielder's error and after an unnecessary slide into first base—Tom would look over at his father. "Did you see that?" his eager expression asked. Gordon would nod and give his younger boy the thumbs-up sign.

After the third out, Tom grabbed his glove and went racing out to left field. Stella prayed no balls would be hit to him. Please.

The Braves' first baseman got a base hit. Batter number two was the league's home-run king. He was walked. The third batter bunted unsuccessfully, and the pitcher made an easy throw to first. The next batter popped up. Stella breathed a sigh of relief when it went to center field. Easy out. But the next batter hit a line drive into right field. And suddenly the bases were loaded.

The boy who stepped up to bat was small, plump—Tom's counterpart on the Braves in for his mandatory inning and not the boy the coach would have chosen to be at bat at this crucial moment when his team was down three in the bottom half of the ninth with two outs and the bases loaded. As the two men sitting in front of Stella decided, the Braves' coach was probably wishing he had put the kid in early in the game and gotten it over with. Damned rules that made you play the bench warmers even in a championship game, the shortstop's father commented to the father of the home-run king. Stella's skin bristled. At that moment she hated the two men. Gordon pretended he didn't hear, but Brian looked at his mother and winced.

The batter hit a high, easy pop fly. To left field. There was no sun in Tom's eyes. He had plenty of time.

Stella had a sick feeling in the pit of her stomach. Tom simply wasn't cut out to be a hero. She knew he would miss it.

But he didn't. For an instant he had the ball safely in his glove. The Eagles supporters started to breathe a collective sigh when the ball slid on through the glove onto the ground and rolled behind him.

Stella watched in horror as Tom spun around. He stumbled and fell. Scrambling to his feet, he picked up the ball, fumbled with it for an interminable minute, reared back and threw.

To first base.

The home-run king's father muttered an angry, "Jesus Christ!"

The batter had long since rounded first base. The first baseman had raced up the baseline to back up the catcher at home plate. There was no one at first base to catch the ball.

The shortstop raced like mad, grabbed the still rolling ball, and tossed toward home. There was still time to get the batter. The other three runners had already scored.

The catcher collided with the first baseman. The fourth runner scored.

The Braves were league champs.

The Eagles coach gave a valiant attempt in his post-game wrap-up to cover for Tom. He called attention to earlier errors. But everyone knew. Tom Kendall had lost the game for them.

"I'm sorry," Stella told her weeping son, wanting desperately to hug him. Later. A hug from his mother would only add to his humiliation.

"Tough luck," Brian told his brother. "Well, at least your team finished better than mine." Brian looked at his mother imploringly. *What can we do to make it better for him?* he asked silently.

"I still love you," Ruthie said, grabbing Tom's hand and marching along beside her devastated brother.

But Tom shook his sister's hand away and ran to the station wagon.

Gordon waited until he got in the car before exploding. "Why in the hell did you drop that ball?"

"He didn't do it on purpose, Daddy," Ruthie said. She was crying now, too.

"Ditto," Stella agreed angrily.

Gordon shot her a hostile look.

"I don't want Tom to play baseball next summer," Stella said with forced calm in her voice. "He's better at other things."

"He's the best musician in the family," came Brian's voice from the backseat.

Stella turned in her seat to offer Brian a grateful look. Brian was sitting in the backseat with Ruthie, with Tom behind them in the cargo section, his face buried against doubled-up knees.

"He could play baseball too—if he tried," Gordon shot back.

"You may be right, but I disagree," Stella said with more diplomacy than she felt. "I'd think he would be happier if he didn't have to play."

Stop, Stella told herself. This should not be discussed in front of the children. Gordon was not in control of himself, and maybe she wasn't either. But she hurt so for her child—her slightly plump, slightly effeminate younger son who never seemed to earn his father's approval. Baseball was unnecessary.

"Kate's kids play ball," Gordon said. "It's good for kids to play ball."

"Not all of them. It's only good for them if they want to."

"For the boy's own good, he shouldn't be allowed to quit," Gordon challenged.

"Discretion is often the better part of valor," Stella answered.

"You want a sissy for a son?" Gordon whispered out of the side of his mouth.

Stella said no more. They had gone too far. The silence in the car was painful as they drove home.

Dinner was spared more of the same stony silence by the added presence of two high school friends of Francie's. The three girls had been practicing for the senior play—*Meet Corliss Archer*. Francie had the part of Corliss. The three were full of gossip and kept filling in their conversation with lines from the play, seemingly oblivious to the silence around them. After a few minutes, however, Francie commented, "I take it that Tom's team lost his ball game. Well, cheer up, folks. It's not the end of the world, and as they say, there's always next year. You get any hits, Tom?"

Stella threw Gordon a look threatening him to silence.

"Naw," Tom said, without looking up from his plate of uneaten food.

After dinner Gordon took Tom out in the backyard. Stella was doing the dishes. She could see them from the open kitchen window. She could hear them over the squeaking of the glider.

"I'm sorry, son. I know you didn't mean to drop the ball. I shouldn't have been so hard on you. It was just a tough break. If you want to play baseball next summer, I'll help you, and maybe you can go to the baseball camp out at the university this summer. Your cousin Jeff's going to go with a couple of his buddies from Grand Prairie. But if you'd rather not play any more baseball, it's okay with me."

"I'd rather not."

"Okay. What sport would you like to try next?"

"If it's all right with you, Dad, I think I'd rather not do sports. I'm going to play in the band next year when I go to junior high," he added hopefully. Was band an acceptable substitute? his tone asked.

Gordon hesitated too long. "That's great, son. I always wished I had learned to play an instrument. I'll look forward to seeing you play at half-times and concerts. Yeah, that's really great."

The crickets seemed to turn up their volume to fill in the silence. Father and son pushed back and forth, the old glider protesting the lack of grease on its runners.

"Want to go get a root beer?" Gordon asked.

"Sure. I'll get the others."

"No. Just you and me. Maybe we could play a few games on the pinball machine."

Later Stella rolled over in the bed and took Gordon in her arms.

"Why do I do that?" he asked, burying his face against her hair. "Why do I do everything wrong when it comes to Tom? Francie and Brian are so easy. With Tom, I never know how to handle things."

Stella waited for him to say something about Ruthie. He didn't.

"I look pretty good, don't I?" Ruthie asked as she scrutinized her reflection in the mirror over Francie's dresser.

Francie added a couple more squirts of hair spray, putting the finishing touches on Ruthie's hair, which Francie had curled in honor of her little sister's first day of first grade.

"You look wonderful," Francie assured her.

Francie's gaze met her mother's over Ruthie's freshly curled head. There was pity in her eyes. Stella retied the bow at the collar of her younger daughter's new plaid blouse, the blouse Ruthie had fallen in love with because it was almost like one of Francie's. Ruthie's hair looked nice, the curls softening her jaw line. No, Ruthie would never be beautiful. To Francie, that seemed a tragic flaw.

"I like your haired curled, pumpkin," Francie said. "You want me to give you a permanent?"

"Would you?" Ruthie continued to stare at her reflection. "You think I'd look better?"

"Not *better*, necessarily. Just different—in a nice way," Francie said.

After breakfast Francie and Ruthie joined their brothers on the front steps while their mother took her annual first-day-of-school pictures, first each child alone and then lined up, oldest to the youngest. Brian towered over the rest. Francie and Tom were almost the same height. Ruthie looked like the afterthought that she was. The pictures would be placed in the family album under the caption "First Day of School—1962."

Brian was a high school freshman. He'd always been an A student.

Tom was a year behind. He made more C's than B's.

The following week Francie would begin her studies at the university. She had been a B-student in high school. And yearbook queen.

When Stella kissed her youngest child good-bye at the door of her first-grade classroom, it was with a special pang of sadness. Her last child had started school. A landmark day. Stella loved this plain little girl with eyes that looked as though they had seen life before.

Tom and Ruthie—her plain children. Stella hurt for them. The world would not be as kind a place for them as it was for Francie and Brian, who were loved for their beauty. Francie's and Brian's features were in perfect proportion. Acne never blemished their clear skin. Fat didn't collect around their middles or across their rumps. Their hair was thick and lustrous. They looked wonderful, so everyone assumed they were. And Brian was. Francie had her moments—like this morning when she did Ruthie's hair. But Ruthie and Tom were tender and dear. Tom was musical—not a virtuoso, but he played his clarinet competently and with feeling. And Ruthie was probably the smartest of the four, even smarter than Brian, Stella had decided. Certainly more analytical—even going on age six. Brian wanted to know everything. He *absorbed*; his prowess lay in retaining all he heard and read. Ruthie questioned. If the teaching was right, Ruthie would adore school.

Her youngest child off to school—Stella felt as if she also were ready for the first day of the first grade. It was a new beginning for her too. She would miss that time at home with just Ruthie, but as Stella walked home, she sniffed away a mother's tears and found herself smiling. Even laughing. She had some freedom. Finally. Some time to herself. Incredible.

Francie adored college. Following in the footsteps of her mother and Aunt Kate and Effie, she pledged Kappa Kappa Gamma sorority. She was named a yearbook beauty her freshman year. By her sophomore year she already had a sizable collection of adoring young men who begged Francie to accept their fraternity pins and undying love. If a boy hadn't asked her to accept his pin or ring or heart by their third or fourth date, Francie was irritated. But as soon as a boy proposed, she dropped him. It was a wonderful game with her. In the front of her notebook she wrote down the names of all the boys who had proposed to her. Some of them were darling boys, but none was rich enough or special enough for Francie. Besides, she didn't want to get married for a long time. She had other things to do first.

One of the young men who laid his love at Francie's feet was Carter Bonifield, Jr.

Carter, or "Junior" as he was known, was the son of a former University of Texas football great. The senior Bonifield was known as "Dub," a nickname of obscure origin. He had been an All-American back for the Longhorns in 1937 and had often been compared to TCU's great Davey O'Brien, who won the Heisman Trophy in '38. Many still called the pair the two greatest backs ever to come out of the state of Texas.

Following in his father's footsteps, Junior made All Southwest Conference as a sophomore and junior. Sportswriters agreed the Longhorns' talented fullback was headed for All-America honors his senior year. Media coverage of Junior's exploits always mentioned he was Dub Bonifield's son. They recalled Dub's gridiron exploits. Dub dragged out all his own press clippings and combined them into a father-son scrapbook.

The senior Bonifield was a Midland, Texas, oilman. The license plates on Dub's white Cadillac Fleetwood bore his old football number. The Cadillac sported a golden oil well as a hood ornament and two red telephones. Dub's handmade cowboy boots had oil wells tooled into the leather. Dub's wife, Mary Sue, had been a runner-up in the 1940 Miss Texas Pageant, and wore a diamond-encrusted gold oil well on a chain—a gift from Dub.

Junior had been raised to play football. Like a registered steer being prepared for auction, Junior was fed and cared for with one goal in mind—to play football for the University of Texas Longhorns.

Francie Kendall almost put an end to that goal. From the time Junior first saw her at the Kappa spring formal toward the end of his sophomore year, he was smitten. She was spectacular in gold lamé. He was at the party as the date of Francie's sorority "big sister," with whom Junior politely danced all evening and would never ask out again. The next morning, as Francie knew he would, Junior called.

As a date, Junior got mixed reviews. He was well-known on campus, and his family had tremendous wealth—but no class. Junior himself was even embarrassed by his parents' excesses, by his overdiamonded, over-teased, overendowed mother and his father with his two-carat diamond pinkie ring and a diamond wristwatch.

But during the following year, Francie went out with Junior from time to time. She liked walking into a restaurant and having all heads turn. Junior was a local hero. Everyone, it seemed, recognized the sandy-haired football hero from Midland. "Hi, Junior," men would call out, some adding a conspiratorial wink at Francie.

Junior's major was art. Everyone thought that was quite peculiar. No one could remember an art major who played varsity football. It was a source of embarrassment to Dub, who considered artistic endeavors to be "sissy." Junior's mother was secretly proud of her talented son. Mary Sue also painted. She had taken art during her two years at UT. She still took lessons, and her watercolors of flowers and Texas sunsets sometimes got honorable mention at the local art shows. Once she was awarded a second-place ribbon. She treasured that ribbon as much as her Miss Texas trophy.

When Junior asked Francie to marry him, she declined. They were sitting in his Buick convertible on a hill overlooking Lake Austin. She had let him touch her breasts. Francie adored driving a guy crazy, then giving him a little touch as a reward.

But when he started talking about marriage and making babies, Francie removed his hand from her right breast and put it in his lap. She rebuttoned her blouse before responding.

"I enjoy going out with a football player, but I'd never go steady with one," she informed Junior. "And I'd certainly never marry one."

Actually Francie liked Junior as well as any the young men she dated, but she considered herself too sophisticated for football. And for beauty contests. Yearbook queen was all right. That honor came to her. But she wasn't going to seek out titles. She wasn't going to parade up and down a runway like a horse at auction. Francie was majoring in drama. She was going to be an actress.

The day after Francie's refusal, Junior quit the team. Dub and Mary Sue came at once from Midland in the white Cadillac bringing with them Junior's minister and high school football coach—all very hush-hush. Junior had to be protected from the press while they got him straightened out.

When Junior tearfully told of his love for Francie, Dub left the others with Junior in his room at the athletic dorm and drove his Cadillac at high speed to the Kendall residence. "Francie's at the Kappa house," Stella told the agitated man standing on her front porch, who introduced himself as "Junior Bonifield's daddy."

"Can I help you with something?" Stella asked. "Is Junior all right?"

"Oh, yes, ma'am. Me and the missus are in town and thought we'd like to take your pretty little Francie out to dinner. That boy of ours is quite taken with her."

Stella watched the white Cadillac backing out of the driveway. She winced as the car went over the curb and flattened a spreading cedar shrub.

Francie was attending a rush committee meeting in the study hall. When she was informed that Junior Bonifield's father wanted to see her, she excused herself and went to freshen her makeup before greeting Dub and leading him to the sorority house's formal living room. Dub had met Francie only once—after the Arkansas game. Then, as now, he felt himself intimidated by the cool beauty and poise of the young woman. She was really something, he had to admit. *Really* something. Ice water in her veins. He knew the type. Insatiable. They'd pussy-whip a man to death, but oh, what a way to go! He wondered if Junior had fucked her yet. Man, that would really be something to get into the pants of a filly like that, Dub thought with a flash of mixed desire and jealousy.

"Do you know that Junior has quit the team?" Dub asked.

Her lifted eyebrows told him she did not know.

"He quit because you said you won't marry a football player," Dub accused. "Did you tell my boy that?"

"Yes," Francie said. "But I never said I'd marry him if he wasn't a football player. I won't."

"Now, see here, missy," Dub started to protest indignantly, but as Francie took one sweeping look at his boots, at his three-hundred-dollar western-cut suit, his diamond watch and rings, and his sideburns, Dub hesitated. He felt his ears turning red. With a look, Francie Kendall had managed to reduce him to a West Texas clodhopper. He had on twenty-thousand-dollars' worth of jewelry, and the sorority girl was not impressed.

"I want my boy to play football, Miss Kendall," Dub said in an uncharacteristically humble voice. "It's what he does best. He has a good chance of being named All-America his senior year, and he could get a pro draft. His whole future depends on him staying with the Longhorns."

"Junior tells me he wants to paint," Francie said, studying her fingernails in a gesture that indicated she really didn't care if Junior Bonifield played football or not.

"Now, you tell me, Miss Kendall, do you think Junior has more of a future ahead of him as a football player or a fuc . . . —or as an artist."

Francie raised her cool gaze to meet Dub's imploring one. "I suppose you're right," she said.

"If there's anything you want . . ." Dub began.

"What do you mean?" Francie said, her eyebrows shooting upward.

"Junior says you want to go to New York and be an actress. It gets cold in New York, and you'd look mighty fine in a fur coat. A beautiful full-length mink. You'd be the toast of the town."

Francie puffed up, ready to let forth with her indignation, but her own reflection in the gold-framed mirror over the mantel stopped her. She stared at herself. Dub knew she was visualizing how she would look in that coat. He relaxed. The distance between them had just been reduced. They both wanted something.

"You would really buy me a mink coat if I persuaded Junior to continue playing football?" Francie asked.

"Well, I'd like to do something to show my gratitude for saving my boy's future."

"I want to pick it out," Francie said, "then put it in cold storage until I go to New York. My parents would not understand."

Dub nodded again, then fished around in his pocket and extracted a solid-gold case of business cards. Clumsily he took out a card and handed it to her. "Send the bill here," he said. "Mark the envelope personal."

The logo of Dub's company was a gold oil well with horns—longhorns.

He watched Francie tuck the card in the pocket of her navy blazer.

She extended him a smooth white hand. "Nice to have seen you again, Mr. Bonifield. Junior will be at practice tomorrow."

"I'd like him to be All-America," Dub said.

"Yes," Francie agreed. "I'll see that he gives it his best."

Dub watched her cross the elegant entry hall and ascend the curving carpeted stairway. He realized he was sweating. Poor Junior. He'd do it all for the love of a woman who'd break his heart. But Junior didn't yet understand about glory. He would someday, however. Glory would last longer than Francie Kendall's perfect tits and tight ass.

God damn, she'd really be something in a mink.

Francie wasn't the only Kendall studying at the University of Texas. Stella took only one or two classes a semester, and during the semesters of Tom's mononucleosis and her mother's final illness, she had to drop her classes. The semester after Anna died, Stella lost heart and did not even enroll. She'd never be able to complete her research and get a thesis written, she despaired. She'd be better off finding contentment with a garden and cats as her mother had done. But she went back the following semester. She needed it.

Anna had begged to be allowed to die at home. She had never been hospitalized and didn't care to be now.

"To me, this little house and garden are the dearest places on earth," Anna explained. "For twenty years I've been here, caring for my cats and chickens. I've had twenty summers with my own vegetable garden. I've been content here."

Stella and Kate alternated weeks in New Braunfels. When the end came, they were both there. And Effie, along with her mother and Aunt Louise.

Anna was eighty-one.

The doctor had promised a coma, but Anna was conscious to the end. Her breathing was labored, and it was very difficult for her to talk. But she managed to say her farewell.

"I love you," she said. "Be good to each other."

And she was gone.

Through her tears, Kate said, "That's the first time she ever said that."

"Said what, dear?" Effie asked.

"I love you."

"But we always knew she did," Stella said, "in her way."

At Anna's request, they buried her in the Theis family plot, leaving Frederick alone for eternity with the first Anna.

On their way home from the funeral, the radio music was interrupted. The President had been shot in Dallas. He was reported to be gravely wounded. Eight-year-old Ruthie began to cry. Stella held her close. The other three children listened to their father's reassurances. The announcer had said the President was still alive, Gordon reminded them. They had taken him to Parkland Hospital. Maybe he would live.

When the station wagon pulled into the driveway on Atterbury Lane, they all rushed inside to the television set and watched together as the grisly truth become apparent.

Gordon wept openly. Gordon admired Kennedy above all men.

That evening he sent a telegram to Lyndon Johnson.

OUR NATION IS FORTUNATE TO HAVE A MAN SUCH AS YOURSELF TO TAKE THE REINS AT THIS DARK HOUR. STELLA'S AND MY PRAYERS ARE WITH YOU AND LADY BIRD.

Twenty-nine

S tella finished the course work for her master's degree during Francie's junior year at the University. She took the following year to complete the research and write her master's thesis on the pioneer women of Texas. She was able to use much of the research done years ago with Blanche.

Stella stole moments here and there, working at her rolltop desk until the oven timer went off, while the clothes were washing, until Ruthie had to be picked up at Brownies, until it was time to get dressed to go out with Gordon to a political rally, a reception, sometimes a movie.

And finally the day actually came when she sat at her desk and typed "The End."

She stared at the words. She had really done it. Incredible.

Stella took the last page out of the typewriter and put in another. On it she wrote, "Dedicated to the memory of Professor Blanche Lasseter, my mentor and friend."

Then she started dinner.

Stella couldn't turn loose of her thesis for a while. She kept reading it, retyping pages, but at last it was time to get copies to her committee.

The defense of her thesis was more difficult than she had expected. Actually, it turned into not so much a defense of her thesis *per se*, but a defense of the concept of women's history. Three professors in suits and ties sat across the conference table from Stella and challenged her.

"I think my thesis documents the historical contributions of women in the settlement of this state," Stella said carefully. "Most historians have chosen to include only the male half of Texas history. Frontier Texas in their texts sounds exclusively like a man's world. Yet women rode horses and bumping wagons and even walked to Texas just like their menfolk. And if you think they didn't hunt wild animals for food and kill marauding Indians, you should read the diaries in the university's archives. Frontier life in most cases was a true partnership. Women suffered the same hardships, died the same deaths from Indians and disease.

'Women's work' included, in addition to the housework, the care of the poultry, the dairy—included the milking, making butter and cheese, care of the livestock, gardening, sewing, mending, making candles and soap, educating children, feeding hired hands, even working in the fields. The successful operation of a frontier farm or ranch depended in great part on women's efforts. And this same male-female partnership existed in other areas of frontier life. Cottage industries. Newspaper publishing. Care of the sick. Most missionary work was done by husband-and-wife teams. Why shouldn't present-day students—male and female—be taught the contributions of women? Even if history is limited to the study of power and exploration, as many historians would have it, even then the role of women has been omitted. If one is to believe many American history books, the only female playing a significant role in the opening of the west was Sacagawea. I want my daughters *and* and my sons to know this isn't so."

One professor said, "Brava." The second member of the committee shuffled papers. The committee head asked her a question about methodology.

They grilled her for two hours. Her voice grew hoarse until at last they asked her to leave the room.

Stella waited on a bench in the hallway for an hour—the accused waiting for the jury to come to a verdict. Obviously there was dissension.

But finally the three men filed out into the hall. Each shook her hand. "Congratulations, Mrs. Kendall," the committee head said. "Your thesis has been approved."

Stella was relieved and proud. In spite of births and deaths and the eternal laundry, she had done it. She had completed the work for a master's degree. A copy of her thesis was handsomely bound and sent to the University of Texas Library. She would even be in the card catalog. Stella couldn't stay away from her own bound copy. She kept picking it up and touching it, carrying it around from room to room.

The foreword of her thesis—a tribute to the women of Texas past—appeared in *Texas Monthly*. A condensed version of the thesis was printed in the journal of the state historical society. She sent copies of the journal to Effie and Kate—and to Charles Lasseter.

Charles called.

It was extraordinary to pick up the phone and have it be him. As soon as he said her name, she knew who it was.

"Can you talk?" he asked. He was tense.

"Yes," she answered. "I'm alone."

"Thank you," he said. "Blanche would have been proud, and I'm honored that you sent me a copy. It's a beautiful piece of work."

"I can't believe I'm talking to you on the telephone," Stella said.

"I know. I can't believe it either. May I call you again sometime?"

"I don't know. Probably not. But talk to me now. I'm happy that you called. Very happy. Are you all right? Your boy? Your wife? How many gray hairs do you have? Are you fat?"

Charles laughed. And then they really talked. First they discussed the thesis. He had actually read it. Gordon had not yet found the time.

"I know your family is proud," Charles said.

"Proud? Oh, I don't think so. They're probably just hoping to have homemade desserts again."

On into the afternoon they talked. Stella switched ears. Brian came in, got his pitcher's mitt, and left. Ruthie fixed herself an after-school snack out in the kitchen. Tom took the stairs two at a time, and soon the sound of his clarinet came from his room.

And still they talked.

His son was in a special home for retarded adults. The residents learned what they could and worked at simple trades. Andy wove place mats and sanded furniture to prepare it for refinishing. Someone else did the refinishing. Yes, the school was in Dallas. He came home on weekends. Marisa was executive secretary of the state organization for parents of Down's syndrome children. Dallas was exploding with new buildings. Everyone wanted mirrored facades these days. Every new building looked the same. Charles was burned out as a practicing architect. He thought he might like to teach.

"Me too," Stella said. "I still want to get my Ph.D. and teach."

She told him about her children, about her mother dying, about Effie and Kate. Yes, Effie had told her they had met. Stella would be a graduate teaching assistant in the fall and begin work on her Ph.D. "I'll earn a grand total of two hundred dollars a month, but I'm excited. I'll be teaching. I'll be part of a faculty. I'll be working toward a future."

"You'll be a terrific teacher. Someday, after that Ph.D., when you are Professor Stella Kendall, may I come see you in Garrison Hall just as I used to come see Aunt Blanche?"

"I'd like that," Stella said. A new fantasy to add to her repertoire. Charles coming to see her in Garrison Hall. Maybe she'd even have Blanche's old office. They'd go for coffee in the union.

It was a magic time. An hour spread into two, but finally Stella knew Francie would be home soon. Or Gordon. They would sense she wasn't talking to Kate or Effie or some woman friend. And she needed to start dinner. She needed to have something cooking before Gordon arrived. There were still wet clothes in the washer and a pile of freshly done laundry on the bed yet to be put away.

"You need to go, don't you?" Charles asked.

"Yes. Duty calls."

"I hate to hang up," he said. "There's more I wish I could say."

"I know. Take care of yourself. Be happy."

"You are ever in my thoughts, Stella. I dream of things I shouldn't dream."

Stella sat with her hand on the receiver after she had hung it up.

"Charles." She whispered his name. "Beloved Charles."

Then with a sigh, she hurried to the kitchen. She turned on the oven and put a pot of water on to boil without yet knowing just what she was going to cook. She emptied the dishwasher and set the table. When Gordon walked into her kitchen and kissed her on the cheek, everything seemed normal.

Francie had the Margot Channing role in the university drama department's spring production of *The Three Faces of Eve*. Gordon was transfixed by her performance. Her beauty. Her stage presence.

At intermission he heard two professorial types referring to her performance as amateurish. Gordon could feel his blood pressure soaring. He wanted to turn around and say something ugly. Francie was incredible. What clods they were not to see it.

"She's really good, isn't she?" he said when Stella returned from the rest room.

"Oh, Gordon, I wouldn't say *really* good. I think the whole cast is doing a nice job for a university production. Francie does show a lot of promise. If this is what she really wants to do, if she works hard and will be amenable to coaching, she might have a chance. Up to now, I think she's been getting along on looks and poise."

"My God, Stella, can't you say better than that about your own daughter?"

"Being a parent doesn't have to mean a total loss of objectivity," Stella said. "I'm very proud of Francie, but I'm not going to kid myself into thinking she's going to waltz on up to New York and be an overnight sensation."

Gordon left her standing there and went to buy a Coke. He didn't even ask if Stella wanted one. She didn't deserve it. She was jealous of her own daughter. She'd never loved Francie—not really. Francie was *his* daughter.

The boys and Ruthie went home after the performance, but Stella and Gordon stayed for the cast party to congratulate their daughter.

Francie came bursting into the room, the last of the cast to appear. There was applause. Francie offered a charming curtsy to her admirers and threw kisses with both hands.

She spotted her father almost at once and bounded into his arms. "Oh, Daddy, what did you think?"

"I think you're the next Sarah Bernhardt. You were *fantastic!*"

Francie kissed him on both cheeks and then on his mouth. She leaned back on the circle of his arms. "I was, wasn't I?" Her smile was coquettish.

Her thick chestnut hair was upswept loosely on her head. She had the slender white neck of a princess. Her eyes glowed. Her waist was small under her father's hands. She was the most beautiful human being he had ever seen. And tonight, in her triumph, she was dazzling. Gordon swelled with pride. His little girl. And just look at her. Turning on all her charm for her daddy.

"I love you, honey."

"I love you too, Daddy. I love you the best."

Stella watched them from across the room. Lovers. They looked like two lovers, and she wasn't even jealous. Not anymore.

Stella heard the boys come in. She called out a greeting from the kitchen, adding, "There's still some chocolate cake from Sunday or leftover meat loaf for sandwiches."

She heard footsteps on the stairway but no acknowledgment from either boy. She walked into the entry hall and called up the steps. "Brian? Tom?" Their elderly mongrel dog briefly looked up at her from the living room sofa, then went back to his nap. "Get down, Buster," she ordered automatically.

"Yeah, we'll be down in a minute," Tom called.

Something in his voice made Stella go upstairs.

Brian was sitting on the toilet lid. Tom was bending over him, wiping blood from his brother's face with a washcloth.

Stella gasped. Brian's cut, raw face turned in her direction. He offered a sheepish grin and said, "Yeah, but you should've seen the other guy."

"Are you okay?" Stella asked, trying to sound calm. She took the washcloth from Tom and examined Brian's wounds. His lower lip and his left eye were already starting to swell. His right cheek looked as though the skin had been scraped off with rough sandpaper, and his nose was askew. Stella felt sick. His face, his beautiful face. "You're not dizzy? Did you get knocked out?"

"Naw. Nothing like that. But he was kind of a big guy and connected on a lot of punches."

"Brian whipped him," Tom said proudly.

"I'm not sure that's anything to brag about. Brian, you're a mess. You're going to have to have stitches in the cut over your eye, and I wouldn't be surprised if your nose is broken. Your left eye is turning black. Tom, go get some ice for his nose. I'll get him cleaned up, and we'll take him to the doctor."

Gently Stella sponged away at the caked blood.

"The rest of you okay? Ribs? Stomach? You don't feel faint, do you?"

"I'm okay, Mom. Really."

"You want to tell me what happened?"

"Just a fight. It was no big deal," Brian said, wincing as Stella touched his nose. "Tom and I went to the gym after school to shoot some baskets. This guy decided to pick a fight."

"The other boy. Who was it?"

"Robby McPherson. You don't know him."

"Is he going to be all right?" Stella asked. Obviously, there was something Brian wasn't telling her. "Did the school authorities get involved?"

"The principal said Robby had it coming," Tom said, reentering the bathroom with an ice tray. "He called Robby's dad and told him so."

"I think you'd better tell Brian's mom about it," Stella said, standing back and looking first from one boy to the other. "You're going to have to explain about this when your father gets home. You might as well practice on me."

Brian slumped over on the toilet lid, his hands dangling between his knees. Tom was leaning against the wash basin.

"Robby called me a fag," Tom said, his lip trembling, tears welling in his eyes—gray eyes, like Stella's own. "He tried to pull my jeans down, said he was going to see if I had one."

The pain she felt for Brian was nothing to the agony that now grabbed at her chest. She closed her eyes, seeing it all, seeing Tom with his soft body and quiet ways being humiliated by a bully named Robby. In front of people.

"Oh, Tom, I'm so sorry," Stella said, putting her arms around her younger son. Brian towered over his mother, but, at sixteen, Tom was no taller than Stella. He didn't resist her embrace, and he put his head on her shoulder. Stella smoothed his hair and fought back tears. She would do anything to keep her children from pain. Suffer it for them. But that was impossible. Why did the world pick on Tom? Gentle Tom, who took spiders outside and turned them loose rather than step on them.

Gordon was home when they returned from the doctor's office. Brian had a dramatically large bandage covering his right eye. His left eye was decidedly black, his nose red and swelling. His raw left cheek was an angry red. And his lower lip was puffed out to twice its normal size.

"Well?" Gordon asked collectively of the three of them.

"It was just a kids' fight at the high school," Stella said, tying on her apron.

Gordon looked sternly at his older son. "You know we don't approve of fighting in this family, Brian."

"Yes, sir." Brian hung his head. The repentant son.

"What was it all about? Who was the other boy? I think I should call his father."

"No," Brian said quickly, raising his wounded face. "Let it drop. We went to the gym to shoot some baskets. The guy called me a queer, so I decked him. And he decked me back. The principal lectured me about fighting, but he as much as said the kid had it coming."

Stella exchanged glances with Tom. Tom's mouth fell slightly ajar as though he were going to say something but didn't.

Gordon's posture, his entire attitude changed. "Called *you* a queer! Now, that's what I call stupid. What in the world possessed the boy to say such a thing?"

"Ah, he was just picking a fight. He knows I'm not a fag, but he was mad about something else. His girl had a crush on me last year."

Gordon seemed to accept the story. He was visibly upset at someone calling Brian queer. But the obvious stupidity of such an accusation soothed him.

Gordon went upstairs to hang up his coat and tie and get ready for dinner.

Silence fell over the kitchen. Stella had never been more proud of a child than she was of Brian at that minute. He had done a noble thing, but they couldn't even discuss it.

"Well, guess I'd better fix dinner. Do you think you can eat anything, Brian? How about if I fix you a milk shake?"

Tom set the table and went to find Ruthie. Stella hurriedly put together a simple meal. Macaroni and cheese. Canned green beans. Sliced tomatoes. Store-bought cookies.

Gordon had a meeting. Leaving Ruthie and Francie to do the dishes, Stella took her iced tea and went out into the backyard to sit on the glider. It was a beautiful evening, one of those nights when the Big and Little Dippers jumped out importantly. The hair on her forehead was damp with perspiration. The small breeze was welcome. Stella turned her face to it appreciatively.

She looked in the window. Ruthie was at the kitchen sink. Francie was passing back and forth behind her sister, bringing dishes from the table. Soon Francie would vanish, leaving Ruthie to finish up whatever remained while she talked on the phone or got ready for a date.

Stella thought of her four children—three were more kind than selfish. Francie was more selfish than kind. Stella's love for Francie was dutiful. Her love for the other three went to her core, but perhaps without Francie she never would have truly appreciated the good in Ruthie and Brian and Tom.

Motherhood—it was her joy and her curse. It was what she felt most deeply and what had kept her from experiencing other things.

Now, at least, she had her studies, her hope of teaching. She would be awarded her master's degree in two weeks at the university's commencement exercises, the same commencement at which Francie would graduate with a bachelor's degree in drama.

Earning a Ph.D. would probably take forever, but it was a goal. She needed that. Stella had already received some recognition for her work on the history of Texas's women. But the amount of research required for her dissertation was intimidating. Many of her archival sources were here in Austin. However, there were other sources throughout Texas in museums, libraries, country historical society files. An enormous task, but a wonderful one. She would travel the width and breadth of this state. She would compile into one fabric the threads of so many women's lives. She would read their diaries and letters, their family histories. She would interview their descendants. Occasionally she could interview the women themselves—old women who had little notion that they had lived history. In some instances she would be able to read newspaper accounts of their accomplishments, but usually not. Women's accomplishments didn't make the newspapers.

She would be an expert. An authority. She would publish and lecture. *Dr.* Stella Kendall. Heady stuff.

And she would teach. She would direct academic careers just as Blanche Lasseter had once directed hers. She would be the living legacy of Blanche Lasseter. Someday.

But for now the thought of returning to the campus next fall as a faculty member—even the most junior of faculty, teaching only freshmen survey classes—was as exciting as her first pregnancy. Twenty-two of her forty-five years had been spent mothering. Now she had embarked on a different course, one that had nothing to do with her children or her husband. The past had been for others. The future would be for herself.

Gordon was late. Stella had already gone to bed when he came home. She heard him slam the door. "Everyone wake up," he called, his voice exuberant. "Come down here. I've got big news."

Stella grabbed her robe.

"What's up?" she heard Tom call.

Ruthie came out of her room, sleepy-eyed. Her nightgown bore a likeness of the Beatles. Paul, George, Ringo, and John did not conceal the outlines of two erupting nipples.

Tom had on undershorts and a terry-cloth robe that hung open, revealing a smooth, hairless chest. An earphone dangled from the tiny radio in his hand.

Brian looked awful, a study in discolored and swollen flesh. He wore a pair of gray gym shorts with an orange Longhorn logo and came down the stairs with an ice bag pressed over his nose.

Francie was still dressed from her date. "Dress" jeans, a jade-green silk blouse, red belt and shoes, a gold chain at her throat.

Gordon was waiting for them at the bottom of the stairs. Beaming. Excited. He ushered them into the seldom-used formal living room. Stella helped him switch on lamps.

"What's up?" Tom asked again.

Gordon stood with his back to the fireplace, grinning, rocking back and forth on his heels. He was bursting with his news, but held back, obviously relishing the moment. He looked around at them. His family.

Then he said it. "I'm going to run for Congress."

Silence blanketed the room for a minute while his words sank in.

Brian reacted first, throwing his ice bag in the air and emitting the best war whoop he could manage with his injured mouth.

Francie rushed to her father and hugged him. "Oh, Daddy! That's wonderful. Wonderful!" Tears filled her eyes.

Reaching around his clinging daughter, Gordon extended a hand to Tom. Then Tom joined in the embrace. "That's great, Dad. Really great."

Gordon pulled away to reach for Ruthie. She fairly flew in his arms. "Oh, Daddy, are you going to be the most famous man in Texas?"

Suddenly they had all joined hands and began skipping around Stella, chanting "Congressman Kendall. Congressman Kendall."

Stella felt as though she were standing in the corner of her living room, watching them. She'd never seen this family so happy, so united. Francie wasn't dignified. Tom and Ruthie were holding their father's hands. Brian's face looked terrible, but his joy showed through. They were dancing around her. Like a children's game. She was their captive.

Congress. Washington, D.C. She didn't want that. What about next year? What about her job? What about her Ph.D.? But one didn't give up becoming a congressman for the sake of a wife's two-hundred-dollar-a-month job. Stella felt as though she were shrinking.

Finally the children fell exhausted on the floor, across the sofa. Only Gordon and Stella remained standing in the center of the room.

Gordon was waiting. His face was flushed. He needed her approval. He needed her to be proud.

That's what she told him. "I'm very proud. You'll make a wonderful congressman." Then she joined in the laughter. She popped popcorn, and they all drank toasts with Hires root beer. Stella listened to their speculating, their plans. Yes, they would all have to work hard. This was to be a family project. Rallies. Yard signs. Canvasing. Television commercials.

Stella thought of those television commercials, with the candidate surrounded by his well-scrubbed, eager family. *These are my children—my lovely wife, Stella.*

Gordon described for them in detail how the meeting had gone, what each kingmaker had said. The incumbent was retiring. The man handpicked to replace him had died last week of a heart attack. It had been decided that Gordon should resign his state position and make the race. One of the President's staff had been at the meeting. Gordon had the support of Lyndon Johnson himself. Francie, Brian, Tom, Ruthie—they all looked at their father with awe. He was important. It made them feel good to have an important father. Very good.

Finally Gordon decided it was time to adjourn. "Tomorrow will be a big day. So many people we need to tell." Everybody hugged one another again.

Gordon was full of himself and his passion. He needed Stella to return his ardor, to share his excitement. She set her body on automatic pilot and stepped outside. When his passion was spent, Gordon asked, "I know this graduate assistant business was important to you, Stella. It seems unfair for you to have to give it up. Maybe you can continue with your research at one of the universities in the Washington area. Georgetown or George Washington. They're good schools."

"Not for Texas history," Stella said.

Gordon was silent for a minute. "Are you unhappy about this, Stella?"

"I wish there were some way we could both have what we need and want, but I guess it isn't going to work out that way."

"I'm sure there'll be lots to keep you busy in Washington," Gordon said lamely.

"I'm sure there will," Stella said from her pillow in the darkness. She reached for his hand. "It's all right, Gordon. Really it is."

"Isn't being the wife of a congressman more important than being a graduate assistant at UT?"

"I suppose. It will just take me some time to readjust. The children are thrilled. It will be good for our whole family."

Gordon talked and talked. Stella stopped listening, stopped thinking. She even stopped murmuring agreement, but still he talked. And then he wanted her again. He came a second time, something he had not done in years.

Then he could sleep.

Maybe he'll lose, Stella thought as she listened to his deep, easy breathing. But could she hope for that? Never had she seen her husband so excited, wanting something so much. And the children. They all wanted it.

He would win. Of course, he would win. Lyndon Johnson himself had already decided it. The machine would roll him into a victory. He had selected Gordon Kendall, a youthful, handsome ordained Methodist minister who had elected to do God's work through public service, who would do God's work by blindly following the dictates of those who put him in office. A family man. A distinguished career in education. A wartime chaplain who won the nation's second highest medal for bravery under fire. A man naïve enough to do as he was told and rationalize the rest away.

The next morning Stella dialed the number of Charles Lasseter's Dallas architectural firm. When the secretary answered, Stella hung up. What was she doing? she asked herself. What did she expect from Charles?

Maybe just to feel she mattered to someone—just for herself. Stella Behrman Kendall. She needed to hear the delight in his voice when she said his name.

When the phone bill came, she quickly paid it and destroyed the evidence of a very short, seventeen-cent phone call to a damning Dallas number.

But she would talk to Charles again. He had read her thesis. Stella doubted if Gordon would ever take the time.

Kate and Effie came to fix graduation dinner. They insisted that Stella stay out of the kitchen. After all, the day was honoring her as much as Francie. Imagine. A master's degree. It was a lovely family day. Dressed in their caps and gowns, Stella and her daughter stood on the front porch while Gordon and Effie and Kate snapped their pictures. And they called a neighbor to come over and take the whole clan together, clustered around Francie and Stella.

Stella felt a little foolish. It was a day she had dreamed of for years, and now that it was here, it didn't mean what she'd thought it was going to mean. In academe, a master's degree was not an end unto itself. It was only a steppingstone to a Ph.D., and she was left stranded in the middle of the stream.

Thirty

With Lyndon Johnson's crushing defeat of Barry Goldwater in the 1964 presidential race, it was clear sailing for Texas Democrats in the 1966 congressional contests.

Francie staged Gordon's watch party in the ballroom of the Austin Hilton. By ten o'clock victory was apparent. Gordon stepped to the podium with his family lined up behind him. Junior Bonifield stood off to the right along with Kate, Jimmy, and their four children, next to Effie, Dr. Pete, and Billy. Gordon's eighty-year-old minister uncle and assorted cousins stood off to the left.

Huge banners decorated the walls with the words "Kendall for Congress" and Gordon's picture—earnest, confident, handsome. The brassy six-piece band played "The Eyes of Texas" and "Dixie." At a nod from Francie, a string was pulled, releasing hundreds of red, white, and blue balloons.

The ballroom was full. Dozens of the campaign placards proclaiming "Kendall for Congress" waved frantically. His supporters knew why he had come before them. Victory was theirs.

The band took up the Longhorns' fight song. Hands clapped in cadence.

Gordon stepped back to embrace Stella and then each of his children. He returned to the podium and held up his arms in a halfhearted plea for silence. The cheering increased. Whistles. Applause. The band repeated the fight song. The placards were thrust up and down. Flash bulbs and balloons popped. Gordon pulled Stella up beside him, and the roar increased. With one arm firmly around her waist, he waved to the crowd. It was his moment. Stella looked at her husband's face. He was intoxicated. It was everything he had dreamed of and more. His happiness was contagious. She pulled his face toward hers and kissed. "Congratulations, my darling."

Gordon's speech was perfect. Humble but confident. Grateful but aggressive. He thanked all the appropriate people. He spoke of the greatness of their state and district. His references to the Almighty were tasteful and appropriate. His years in the pulpit served him well.

Gordon concluded by reading a telegram that had been delivered to him from the White House.

"CONGRATULATIONS TO A GREAT TEXAN WHO WILL CONTINUE TO SERVE HIS FELLOW CITIZENS WITH VIGOR AND BRAVERY. I AM GRATEFUL THAT A MAN OF GOD SUCH AS YOURSELF WILL BE REPRESENTING THE TWENTY-FOURTH DISTRICT IN OUR NATION'S CAPITAL AND LOOK FORWARD TO WORKING CLOSELY WITH YOU ON PROGRAMS TO BENEFIT OUR BELOVED UNITED STATES OF AMERICA AND THE GREAT STATE OF TEXAS. SINCERELY, PRESIDENT LYNDON B. JOHNSON."

The cheers were deafening. Gordon and Stella waved. The children stepped forward to join their parents. Francie kissed her father.

"What do you think, Stella girl?" he said, putting his mouth close to her ear so she could hear him over the din.

"I'm proud of you and our family and proud to be your wife." She meant it.

And it was what Gordon wanted to hear. He had made Stella proud. He had made her the wife of a congressman.

They all had. The campaign, more than any other undertaking in their family's history had been a joint undertaking. Francie seemed totally caught up in the idea of Gordon's going to Congress. She told her parents that she would wait to move to New York until they moved to the nation's capital.

They would, of course, keep their Austin home. The boys could live there. Brian was a freshman at UT. Tom wanted to finish high school in Austin.

After their father announced for the District Twenty-four race, Tom and Brian had canceled their plans for summer jobs. The campaign became a family affair, as they prepared first for the September primary and then the November election. Francie ran the campaign from a rented office near the campus. Ruthie and the boys helped her—often long into the night—with the mailings, with the canvasing and the signs. During the day Francie scheduled the volunteers and paid help, made countless calls on her father's behalf, arranged for radio and television appearances, convinced civic club program chairmen to invite Gordon Kendall to speak to their groups.

Stella found herself involved in a constant round of rallies, teas, and luncheons with the state's Democratic faithful. Receiving lines again. She had hoped when they left United Wesleyan in Johnstown that she had stood in her last receiving line.

Gordon was happier than she had ever seen him. When he swung his feet out of bed each morning, it was with enthusiasm. He jogged at six, then ate a hearty breakfast. He walked with a spring in his step and laughed readily. He touched and hugged his children more than before. And he talked almost constantly. When he was at home, he followed Stella around the house like a five-year-old, telling about his day, of the people supporting him, of his high ideals for serving the people of his district. And he talked with Brian, Tom, and Francie. Plans. Constant plans. Another approach. Another base to cover. He even talked with Ruthie. How great it would be to live in the nation's capital. The Smithsonian. The zoo. The Cherry Blossom Festival. Mount Vernon. Boat rides on the Potomac. Stella had never seen the children and their father so close. Tom and Gordon seemed to have developed a more comfortable relationship. Tom was the most tireless worker, ever searching for more ways to help, to please his father.

Junior Bonifield reappeared in Francie's life. The likable young man had completed his first year with the Dallas Cowboys. It seemed he had a promising professional football career ahead of him. The state's newspapers had designated him the Cowboy's most valuable rookie. Obviously the young giant still adored Francie, and having the former Longhorn great in Gordon's entourage was a tremendous plus. Junior was an All-America hero—a sweet, unassuming boy who accepted adulation with a charming "ah, shucks" demeanor. Everyone in Austin and in District Twenty-four's three counties knew Junior. And liked him. Every place he and Francie went, Junior was besieged by autograph hunters, mostly small boys, but also by a surprising number of adults—men and women.

Gordon and Junior got along well. Stella understood that Gordon's special relationship with his beloved Francie was not threatened by Junior's presence in her life. Junior's kind of love required only that Francie acknowledge him. Even Junior seem to know that Gordon was the number-one man in Francie's life.

Years ago Stella had come to terms with Francie and Gordon's relationship. Father and daughter loved each other the best. Gordon needed approval from Stella, and he needed the proof of her wifely allegiance in bed, but it was Francie who made his face break into an unqualified smile. Francie returned his love in kind. The jealousy that Stella once felt had diminished and died. In fact, in many ways, she was grateful to Francie. Inadvertently, her older daughter often gave her an important gift—space. Given a choice, Gordon would rather be with Francie.

The primary was close, but Gordon, running as the establishment candidate against five others, garnered almost 40 percent, more than enough to get him in the runoff against another ordained minister—a Unitarian who was against prayer in the schools. But Austin, being a university town, had a more liberal base than Texas at large. The man had Gordon worried.

The runoff, however, was not even close. Gordon earned the right to run against the Republican candidate in November. The family had gone to the Hilton watch party confident of victory.

It was past four in the morning when they returned home, their confidence justified. The relatives had rooms at the Hilton, so it was just the six of them around the kitchen table. Stella cooked scrambled eggs and bacon. Ruthie baked a can of biscuits and opened the very last jar of Anna's orange marmalade. Stella started to stop her. No, not that jar. Stella was going to save it forever, but then, that was silly. Anna had made it to be eaten. "My mother made this," Stella said. Only Ruthie took note.

What would her mother have thought of tonight, of Gordon's election? Stella wondered as they toasted Gordon and each other in turn with hot chocolate. Her papa would have approved, but she wasn't so sure about Anna.

At ten to five Stella at last found herself in bed. She couldn't remember ever being so exhausted. Gordon was singing "Dixie" in the bathroom.

When he came out of the bathroom, Gordon went over and shut the bedroom door. The signal. Gordon closed the bedroom door only when he expected to make love. He was the victor, and he wanted his reward to complete this most special night of his life.

Stella held him, caressing his back, while he pumped up and down.

"I did it for you, Stella. I did it all for you."

Stella didn't hang up this time when the secretary answered the telephone. She identified herself and asked for Charles.

"Stella, darling, how wonderful."

Stella closed her eyes. His voice. "I guess you've heard that I'm on my way to Washington."

"Yes. I heard on the news last night. What about the work on your Ph.D.?"

"On hold, I guess. I can't research Texas women's history in Washington, D.C., but I'll do what I can when I'm back in the state. Of course, I can't attend seminars or classes. I suppose I could begin a Ph.D. in another field at another university, but it doesn't seem as important as it once did. The wind's out of my sails, Charles. I'll have two homes to keep up with and new social duties. But I'm sure it will all be exciting, and the children are so proud of their father. So am I."

"You can still teach," he said.

"It wouldn't be the same," Stella explained. "I wanted to be a professor, to work with young people the way Blanche did, to be a permanent member of a university community. The only teaching job I could get now would be teaching American history at some college to freshmen who'd be taking it only because it was required."

"You would have been teaching freshmen this year if you'd stayed in Austin."

"Yes, for a year or two, but there would have been the very real hope of something else later on."

"You've lost hope?"

Stella felt the tears stinging her eyes. He understood. "I hate feeling sorry for myself," she said.

"When can I see you?"

"I don't know. Soon, I hope. I'm not sure if my life's going to be less or more complicated now. I'm not sure of anything, except I had to hear your voice today. Are you well? Is everything the same in your life?"

"Yes, everything's the same. Don't lose hope, Stella. I can't bear it. Whatever happens, know that you are loved."

Francie hated the anonymity of New York. She hated the girls with whom she shared a small, ugly apartment, but she couldn't afford a place of her own. At the acting school there were other girls as beautiful as she and many who could act better.

She got an agent with no trouble and made a couple of commercials, but it was stupid work, and they wanted her to look like an ordinary housewife to sell cereal or soap. Francie was not interested in being ordinary. It was a hard comedown after the thrill of running her father's campaign, after the attention she was accustomed to receiving on the arm of her father and Junior Bonifield.

"How'd the audition go?" Gordon asked when Francie called.

"Not so good," Francie admitted. "They want experience. I made a couple of spots for a Newark car agency, but I don't like wearing a bunny suit for Bobby Rabbit Chevrolet–GMC. And it's not enough to pay the rent."

"How much do you need?" Gordon asked.

"Oh, Daddy, I hate for you to always be sending me money."

"Honey, parents usually subsidize their children for a while after they graduate. I'd really worry about you if I thought you wouldn't call when you need money."

"You're so good to me. No girl ever had a sweeter daddy than you. And do you have any idea how proud I am of you? When you were elected, it was the proudest day of my life. I have that picture of you hugging me election night here on my night-table. You look so handsome and happy. We both have hundreds of streamers around our neck."

"I have a copy of it on my desk in the office. Everyone wants to know who that gorgeous young woman is. My secretary says I should put a sign on the picture saying, 'She's my daughter—really.' "

"I miss you, Daddy."

"Can you come down next weekend?" Gordon asked. "There's a reception at the White House."

"The White House! I'd like that."

She hung up wondering what in the world she could wear. She wished she could buy something fabulous.

Francie hated being poor. As generous as her father was, there was never enough money. He sent her hundreds of dollars when she needed thousands. And as she looked and learned, she realized how many poor girls and guys were waiting for a break here in this cruel, dirty city while they waited tables or sold shoes. It was demeaning. Francie sold the mink coat. She was afraid her father might find out about it anyway. It was hard to go to Washington on weekends and be a congressman's daughter, then return to New York to her ugly apartment and ugly life.

Francie had once again broken off her relationship with Junior Bonifield before moving to New York. But she called him one night on a whim. He called back the next night and flew up to see her the following weekend. The maitre d' at the restaurant they went to for dinner was a Dallas Cowboy fan and recognized Junior. They got the best table. Junior's identity spread through the tiny restaurant. They were the center of attention. Francie wished she had worn a more glamorous dress.

Junior looked good. He wasn't tasteless like his father. No diamond Rolex or gold chains. When they stood naked in front of her mirror, their bodies were really quite beautiful together. And he would do anything for her. He told her so constantly.

When Junior called to tell her he had been drafted, that he was going to Vietnam, Francie flew home to marry him.

The family and relatives gathered in Austin for the small ceremony. Dub and Mary Sue arrived from Midland in a new white Cadillac. Gordon officiated at his daughter's wedding, which was held the week after Lynda Bird Johnson married Captain Charles Robb in a televised White House wedding. The two families exchanged telegrams.

Francie and Junior honeymooned on Padre Island in his parents' beachfront condo.

Three weeks after the wedding Junior was off to Vietnam. The following month Tom was arrested for taking part in an antiwar protest on the UT campus. Gordon made a series of phone calls from Washington and was able to keep his son's name out of the papers.

Brian sided with his father. "How can you protest against a war for freedom?" he demanded of his brother as he drove him home from the city jail. "Americans have been killed over there fighting for what they believe. Do their deaths mean nothing?"

"It means our government believes in sacrificial lambs. Jesus, Brian, it just goes on and on and gets no place. The United States had no business getting into another country's civil war."

"God, you're naïve," Brian said. "The line's got to be drawn. The Communists can't be allowed to eat up any more of the world."

"You can't tell people what sort of government they can have. If those people want to be Communists, then it's none of our goddamned business."

"What about the Vietnamese who don't want communism?"

"What about the people all over the world who don't want to die when this idiotic war gets to be global?"

"What if you're drafted?" Brian asked his brother.

"I'd go to prison before I'd go to that war," Tom said adamantly. "When it's all said and done, all those guys will have died for nothing. Nothing, do you hear me?"

They argued constantly—in the car on the way to the campus, during basketball in the driveway, over hamburgers at the drive-in.

When the family came to Austin for summer vacation, the brothers argued at the dinner table. Gordon got angry at Tom—and at Ruthie, who took Tom's side. Francie, of course, sided with her father and Brian. Stella would leave the table rather than be a party to such unpleasantness. She hated the war as much as Tom did, but kept her opinion to herself. It wouldn't do for the wife of a congressman to have political views differing from her husband's.

"Why don't you just agree not to discuss it?" she begged her sons. "No one's going to change anyone's mind."

Finally they gave it up. The arguing just seemed to stop one day. Both had apparently grown weary.

Washington, D.C., was a city of contrasts. Panhandlers stood in front of the Treasury Building. The classical elegance of the federal sector existed like a beautiful island in the middle of a sea of ruthless poverty and brutal ugliness.

The blacks yelled "Honky," at Stella's car. So bold they were, not at all like the shuffling blacks with downcast eyes who lived back home in New Braunfels and even in Austin. And the black students at the university certainly weren't this bold. Washington tested one's liberalism. Gordon convinced Stella that Ruthie had to go to a private school for safety's sake.

They had bought a house in gracious Georgetown not too far from where Jacqueline Kennedy owned a home. Stella was appalled at what they paid for a skinny house with half the floor space of their Austin home. Its kitchen didn't have a window. The backyard was a postage stamp. But the street was tree-lined and respectable. The house and neighborhood were befitting a congressman. Gordon insisted they could afford it. He used his inheritance from his father for the down payment.

The best part of Washington for Stella was the Smithsonian. How rare to find something that surpassed one's wildest expectations! She promised herself that she and Ruthie would explore every facet of it over the next two years.

Stella got a job in the fall teaching two sections of freshman history at George Washington University. The students were more radical than at conservative UT. She read in the student paper about their rallies, marches, and sit-ins. In the classroom, however, they lost some of their bravado. Most of them were interested and attentive. Some were surly and antagonistic, especially when they found out who her husband was. Establishment. Stella wished she could have remained anonymous.

She had bad days, but more were good. She did enjoy teaching even if it was only a required course with a prescribed syllabus. She enjoyed the preparation, the looks that sometimes came over students' faces when they were really listening. She liked the times when they asked questions and when they argued with each other. About Vietnam, of course. And whether the United States should have intervened in the Hungarian revolt. The role of the First Amendment.

But Stella was an outsider in the department. She wasn't permanent faculty, and she wasn't even a graduate teaching assistant. She was just an instructor hired from semester to semester to fill in. Her desk was in the corner of a third-floor hallway. When she went into the faculty lounge for coffee, everyone stopped talking. The congressman's wife. Teaching freshman classes for a thousand dollars a semester. Why in the world? Stella thought of trying to break down their barriers, but she didn't. She wasn't one of them. She'd fill her coffee cup and leave.

But when she was invited to return the second semester, she accepted.

Second semester she made a friend. Connie Brown was a middle-aged black woman who had a G.A. appointment and was working toward her Ph.D. Her field was black women's history. The first time Connie asked Stella to accompany her to the union for a Coke, Stella could have kissed her. She told her so.

"Pretty bad, huh."

"Yeah, poor little congressman's wife."

They had their Cokes and talked for more than an hour. Stella admitted that Gordon did not support the open housing law. Connie told about having five welfare babies before she was twenty-two, and her precarious climb up the academic ladder.

Stella liked her. Connie's sensible suit, frizzy gray hair, and no-nonsense demeanor reminded her of Blanche.

Finally Stella looked at her watch. "I need to pick my daughter up at school. But let's do this again another day."

Connie nodded and smiled. "Yes, another day. I'd like that."

Thirty-one

I t had been in June of 1962 that Mark announced over dinner, "I don't want to play ball next year." It was the first night of his summer vacation. He had just returned from Omaha where Texas A & M had played in the College World Series.

"Don't be silly," Kate told her son. "Do you want some more mashed potatoes? Freddy? Jeff? Very funny, Sara. Since when do gymnasts eat mashed potatoes?"

"Let Mark talk, Kate," Jimmy said. "He wants to tell us something."

"I've already said it," Mark said, looking down at his plate. "I don't want to play anymore. All I've ever done is play ball. Next year is my senior year. I'd like to be just a regular student, maybe bring my grade point up and apply for graduate school. Maybe law. I've been talking to Billy. We'd like to practice together someday unless he ends up running Texas Central like Aunt Effie wants or practicing in his grandfather's old law firm."

"You're just coming off a bad year," Kate said, a note of hysteria eating away at her voice. "What about wanting to play pro ball?"

"I know you've always wanted me to go on, but honestly, Mom, I've gone as far as I can go." Mark looked up at his mother now. He put down his fork and pushed his plate away. "I was a great Little Leaguer. I was All-State in high school and good enough to get a scholarship. But in college—hell, everyone on my team was a high school All-Stater. I'm up with the big guys now, and I'm really just okay. The pro scouts aren't beating a path to my door because I'm really not good enough for them. I saw dozens of players up in Omaha who have more of a chance than I do, but it's all right. I sat there and watched game after game. I played in game after game. And I realized I'm burned out. Baseball's been great, but I want something else now. I'll get a part-time job to make up for going off scholarship."

Kate looked down the table at her husband. "Well, are you going to sit there and let him throw away a year of eligibility? A year of scholarship? His future? Don't you have something to say?"

"Yeah. Good luck, son."

Jeff looked about the table. "I still want to have a pro career," he said hopefully. "Coach says I hit the ball as good as Mark."

Mark nodded. "Hell, yes, you do. Better. A mile farther. And you play basketball twice as good. You'll probably be a two-sport All-Stater."

Thirteen-year-old Freddy decided to add his bit. "Well, I'm not such a scrounge myself."

"I want to win an Olympic gold medal," eleven-year-old Sara chimed in.

"Not if you don't eat those cooked carrots, you won't," Kate grabbed the empty bread plate and went out into the kitchen.

When Jimmy found her, Kate was still crying in the pantry. "Is it that important to you?" he asked gently.

"I guess it is," she sniffed. "He *is* good enough. I know he is."

"Maybe so, Kate," Jimmy said. "But the boy doesn't want to. He's twenty years old, and he's not going to play ball for his mother anymore."

"Go to hell," Kate said, reaching for a paper napkin to blow her nose.

"I may, but first I want you to listen to me. In spite of all that crap out there at the table, Jeff and Freddy are not as good as Mark. Their coaches know it. I know it. And I think you know it. They can play ball as long as their ability and desire hold out, but you will not someday be America's first mother to have three sons playing in the World Series. You will not be interviewed on national television about the raising of America's most prominent sports family. You will not be the mother of multiple All-Americans. You will not be able to write your memoirs as the mother of the superstars. But they're good kids, Kate. Just enjoy them for that."

Kate slapped him hard across the mouth. "I hate you," she said vehemently.

Mark's only sport his senior year was intramural Ping Pong. He made the honor roll for the first time in his life and applied for law school at the University of Texas. That summer he worked on a dude ranch in Colorado. It was the first summer of his entire life he had not played ball.

Mark liked Austin better than College Station, where Texas A & M was located. College Station was plain. Austin was beautiful and full of girls. Mark even liked law school.

Sara was good. An elfin child, she resembled neither of her parents. Her hair was more blond than red. Her petite form seemed to bear no relation to her large, portly father and her broad-beamed, matronly mother.

Sara seemed to have been born for gymnastics competition. With intense gymnastics training, her lithe child's body was able to resist maturity as she won first state and regional honors. Her Polish-born coach, Leon Jonoski, wondered if the Morris girl might be his ticket to international competition. America, for all its fascination with sports, was in the 1960s a gymnastics wasteland. In Sara Morris, however, Leon saw not only athletic ability, but at this point in her life the single-mindedness of purpose that was the missing ingredient in other American girls. Leon knew that genius of any kind required the ability to turn one's back on the complete human experience and devote oneself totally to a clearly defined goal. Talent, no matter how great its magnitude, was not enough. Winners succeeded at the expense of other things. Winners were not fully developed human beings. Leon himself was that way. The child's mother, Kate, was, too. Leon did not need to be told that Kate had once competed in something herself. He and Kate Morris had transferred their own strivings onto the shoulders of the next generation. And Sara seemed willing to accept the burden.

Sara did not cry at movies. Indeed she seldom went. When the nation watched a black-clad Jacqueline Kennedy march in her husband's funeral cortege, Leon and Sara were at the practice gym as usual. She paid little attention to the riots in Watts, the war in Vietnam. Sara studied enough to get by in school. She had few friends other than fellow gymnasts. She spent more time with Leon than she did with her family.

For her mother, Sara was the last great hope. For Kate, competition was everything. First it was her own. Then her children's. Mark, however, was now in law school. Jeff and Freddy were still competing, but Jimmy— damn him—had been right. They weren't as good as their older brother. Kate did not allow herself to think of the day when Sara's days of competition would be over.

For years, Kate had had Sara up in the mornings by five and at the practice facility by five-thirty. Sara also spent her afternoons and weekends practicing. Kate carefully monitored her daughter's diet and weight, weighing Sara every morning to make sure no extra ounces had crept onto her small frame during the past twenty-four hours. Junk food was out of the question—Sara was not allowed to drink Cokes or eat french fries. If Sara minded the rigid supervision, if she minded a life without friends and normal activities, she gave no indication. It was the only life she had known since age five.

With her mother, Sara sat in front of the television and watched the '64 Olympics in which the star of the 1960 competition, the Soviets' Larissa Latynina, continued her domination of the sport with a gold in floor exercise, a silver in combined exercise, a silver in the vault, and a bronze on the uneven bars, a bronze on the balance beam. Someday the world would be watching Sara Morris compete like that. World class.

Sara was her mother's child. She was alternately pampered and threatened by Kate. She would sit quietly and brush her mother's hair or do her homework at the kitchen table while her mother cooked. Though not openly affectionate, Sara was seldom far from her mother.

With her father, Sara showed polite respect. Her father usually was in attendance at meets, and she would hug and kiss him after her victories. First, however, she would rush into her mother's arms. Her father didn't really understand gymnastics. Women's gymnastics was mostly a world of mothers and daughters. Fathers felt like alien beings trying to understand a sport that was dainty and precise, but even more they felt like outsiders in a world of women.

Without comment, Jimmy paid for the expensive coach and the travel costs for meets. He always came up with the money, not so much because of paternal responsibility as because he sensed it was all Kate had left.

After reaching 250 pounds and hypertension, Jimmy had slimmed down, started jogging, and had gotten serious about his golf again—only as an amateur, of course. But he wanted to be a good amateur. Sometimes he thought about returning to the ranks of the teaching pros but never a touring one. He was too old for that.

His marriage was comfortable but dull. Usually he and Kate talked about the kids or the house, which they were constantly enlarging or remodeling or redecorating. He owed as much money on the house now as he had when he first assumed the mortgage.

Usually he and Kate watched television from their bed until they fell asleep. Sometimes Jimmy remembered when Kate had excited him—back when her hair was curled and she wore makeup and her lean body would glisten with the sweat of passion. He now felt only affection for the faded, stout woman with the graying red ponytail. They seldom made love. It wasn't just the fat. She seemed to have lost definition and grew less Kate-like with each passing year. Jimmy missed the Kate of old with her feistiness and vigor. He hoped Sara won medals and made her mother happy. He wished there were something he could do to make her happy.

In 1966, Kate, Leon, and fifteen-year-old Sara prepared for the regional competition with an excited frenzy. After that came nationals. Leon allowed himself to dream a bit. With a little luck, Sara might earn a spot on the '68 Olympic gymnastics squad. She wouldn't win any medals this go-around, but if he kept her going four more years—maybe. Just maybe.

The first time Sara skipped an after-school practice was a shock to both her mother and her coach. The second time, they realized they had a problem. When Kate demanded that Jimmy speak to his daughter, he refused. "You can't make her practice, Kate. It doesn't work that way. It has to be something *she* wants to do."

Kate went to Leon's small, cluttered office in the back of the practice facility. "I'm worried about Sara," she said. "She seems to be distracted about something."

"Boys," Leon said. "If only she could have waited a few years."

"You've got to talk to her." Kate's voice was shrill.

"They start wanting breasts," Leon said, more to himself than to Kate, his hands hanging limply between his legs. "They want to have periods like other girls. They get tired of staying little girls. They want boyfriends and dates and chocolate milk shakes. They start wanting to be normal. I could have made Sara different—special—but now it seems she wants to be like everyone else."

It was to be left up to her alone, Kate realized. That night she went to Sara's bedroom for their talk.

A pink bedroom. Kate had gone all the way for her only daughter. The bed had a canopy, the curtains ruffles. The wallpaper was a soft peppermint stripe. The thick carpet was ivory. A collection of storybook dolls still lined the shelf above her desk. On the wall were posters showing Larissa Latynina on the balance beam and a pelvis shot of Elvis Presley.

"I'm sorry, Mom," Sara said. "I know how much it meant to you, but it's over."

"No," Kate said. "It's not over. You're weren't meant to be ordinary."

"I'm tired of it," Sara said. "I think I'd like being ordinary, and besides, *really* making it is such a long shot. I see those Russian girls and I know it. And when I look at them I wonder who's making them work so hard. Is it their mother or their government who wants trophies for the family room?"

"You ungrateful little snip," Kate spit out. She wanted to hit her. Hard. Instead, she stormed from the room.

When Jimmy asked her what happened, Kate told him to shut up. She went in the bathroom and turned on the shower to muffle her sobs. What would she do with her life now?

Leon Janoski took a job as a physical education instructor at a private girls' school in Dallas. The chances of another Sara Morris coming along were slim, and if he found one, she'd probably decide to try out for cheerleader instead of the Olympics. Sometimes he wished he'd never left Poland—but not very often. He loved American television and music. He adored hamburgers with Heinz ketchup. And if he had kids, he wanted them to be born American.

Kate gained twenty pounds and spent three months on the verge of hysteria. Real hysteria. She scared herself sometimes with visions of herself drowning in the pool. In the night when she woke up, her nightgown soaked with sweat, it seemed like a possibility. But why? Because she hadn't raised champions? How had it come to that?

Kate took stock of her life. She saw a woman whose husband stayed married to her out of habit, a woman whose children would never bring home the Olympic gold. She was fat, forty-six, and felt herself approaching a vast abyss. An ax murderer standing over her bed could not have frightened her more than an objective look at the person she had become. At last, disgusted, she joined Weight Watchers and enrolled at Texas University's Arlington branch, taking enough hours to obtain her teaching certificate. School principals, however, were not interested in hiring a still overweight, middle-aged woman who had never taught, who had never coached a team, who exuded no brash self-confidence, who did not promise to turn the program around. There were young women far more qualified.

Kate decided on another baby. It would be a reprieve. And after that? Maybe she would be too old to care.

Her gynecologist wasn't sure Kate, already showing signs of menopause, could still conceive. "My mother had a baby at forty-seven," Kate announced. She did not tell the physician that her mother's late-life baby had been born early and died.

The once lusty sexuality enjoyed by Jimmy and Kate had lessened with each passing year and finally vanished altogether, its memory an embarrassment. Sex had become relegated to the status of an infrequent bodily function. When it became necessary, it was accomplished quietly and politely only at night in a darkened bedroom.

When Kate greeted him at the door one night wearing makeup, Jimmy was surprised. He was even more surprised when she put on a new nightgown and poured him a glass of wine. The gown had a lace bodice, and her nipples showed through.

When they went to bed, she cuddled up against him.

"Hey, lady, that feels good. You got something on your mind?"

She kissed him. His body responded. Nice.

"Let's make another baby," she whispered against his neck.

Jimmy rolled away from her. "Jesus, Kate, it that what this is all about? Jesus! Not another kid!" His erection faded with his disappointment.

A baby was all Kate wanted to talk about in the weeks to come. He grew angry, but Jimmy was wise enough to understand it wasn't a child specifically that she needed. She just needed something. Poor Kate.

"They'll think we're the kid's grandparents," he argued.

"Don't you think I know that?" Kate said, her voice and body begging.

Jimmy left for a week—a business trip to California, he told Kate. The company had a chance for a big contract for weight-training equipment with the Orange County school system. After he made his presentation, he was going to call on other West Coast school systems while he was out there. They'd talk about this baby business when he came home.

He went to England.

London no longer felt like London. He wandered in and out of pubs looking for the singing, the camaraderie. He didn't find it.

The couple who now lived in the Wigginses' Gloucester house had never heard of its World War II occupants. Jimmy looked for the pharmacy where Linda had worked, but a supermarket had taken over the block. He hired a private investigator to make inquiries and went himself to West Looe in search of Linda's relatives. Then to East Looe. He couldn't

remember which had been her hometown. By week's end the investigator
had located Linda's sister. Jimmy called her, explaining he was a friend
of Linda's during the war. Where was Linda living now? In Australia with
her husband, the woman said. Linda had three children. Her husband
was a schoolteacher.

"What did you say your name was?" she asked.

Jimmy hung up.

He thought briefly about calling the woman back and asking for
Linda's phone number in Australia. But Linda had two other children.
Her baby, little Eddie, would be a man now. The sweet girl he had left
behind so reluctantly was middle-aged like he was. Like Kate. She didn't
even live in England anymore.

And he was homesick.

Back in Texas he made a deal with Kate.

"You can have your baby if I can have a bar."

"A what?" Kate asked.

"I want to sell the house, move to someplace more affordable, and
buy a bar."

"You mean like a nightclub?" Kate asked, puzzled.

"No. I mean like a local bar on the corner where bricklayers and
bus drivers stop on their way home in the evenings for a beer, where
they bring the missus on Friday night after the movies, where there's a
dart board and a television to watch football games."

"But what about your job? I can't believe you're saying this. My
God, Jimmy, all those years with that company. You're a vice president!"

"I'm a bootlicker with a fancy title. I'd rather tend bar."

"Sell our house?" Kate looked around her at the chandeliers, at the
new carpet, at the French doors onto the patio and the swimming pool
beyond. "But it's so nice. With a paddle ball court. A pool."

"When was the last time you got in that pool, Kate? Or played
paddle ball? We belong to a fancy country club that neither of us can
stand to go to. You want a baby. I want to tend bar. How about it?"

Kate stared at him. He really meant it. "I could be sneaky. If the
factory's still operational, pregnancy isn't that hard to accomplish—even
for a fat old wife."

"I know that, but you've always played fair, Kate. That's one of the
things we've always had going for us. I don't think you really want to do
that to me."

Two months before Kate's forty-seventh birthday, the test came back positive. She was not happy as much as relieved. She didn't have to face herself anymore—not for a long, long time.

She called Jimmy first, then the realtor to list the house. As soon as he hung up, Jimmy called the man who wanted to sell the Ole English Tavern, and then typed his resignation.

Effie's mouth fell open when she heard the news. But when she looked at Kate's face, she squelched whatever words of protest were about to erupt, reached across the restaurant table, and grabbed her cousin's hand. "A baby. Imagine that. Oh, Kate, honey, that's just about the most wonderful thing I've ever heard. I'm going to give you the most beautiful baby shower ever."

And Effie proposed a toast. They lifted their wine glasses as she said, "Here's to the last baby from the Behrman girls."

Kate's eyes misted over. "I love you, Effie. I don't think you've ever made anyone feel bad in your entire life."

"Oh, Kate, honey. I love you too. So much. Sometimes I think that you and Stella are the most important people in my life. Husbands go and die. Children grow and up and go off on their own. But the three of us—we'll always have each other."

"Always," Kate vowed. "Always."

Kate waited to tell Stella until her sister was home from Washington for Christmas. Stella put down her coffee cup and asked, "Is it what you want?"

Kate nodded.

"Then I'm very happy for you," Stella said. She came to kneel at Kate's side and offered her a sisterly hug. "My goodness! I thought the rest of the births would be grandchildren. Maybe we're not as old as I thought."

The remodeling of Jimmy's new tavern had to be put on hold while the entire family tackled the job of moving out of the Grand Prairie house. The children were sullen and resentful. This was *their* home too. Summer was coming, and the new house didn't even have a pool. Brian wouldn't have a room at home anymore. He lived in an apartment with two other guys, but he still wanted a room at home. They didn't understand why they were being uprooted.

"Because your father and I are shifting gears," Kate told them bluntly. "Parents have rights too."

Jimmy applauded. The children stared at him. "I never thought I'd hear those words coming from your mother's mouth," he explained. "I think I'll have them engraved on a plaque. 'Parents have rights too.' "

At first he thought Kate was going to be angry. She stood thinking about it, holding a stack of books against her round belly. But she shrugged and bent over to put the books in a carton.

Mark and Jeff lifted the bookcase she had just emptied and carried it out to the rented truck. Sara and Freddy followed with the sofa cushions.

Jimmy walked over to his wife and took her in his arms.

Her back stiffened. He could almost hear the words getting ready to be said. She had so much to do. She didn't have time for hugging. She smelled like an old goat. But she relaxed and put her head against his shoulder.

"We're going to make it, Kate." He massaged the small of her back gently.

"I wish I were beautiful," she said against his shoulder.

He pulled back and looked at her to see if she was joking. She wasn't. Her face was shiny with perspiration. Her ponytail was limp. She wasn't wearing any makeup. Her face was smudged with black newsprint from the newspapers she had been using as packing. Kate was five months pregnant, but she had actually lost weight this time—not much, but some. She had been sicker with this baby, and then with all the house hunting and preparing this one to sell—it had been a busy time.

With the extra pounds over the years, Kate's jaw had lost some of its squareness. The red of her hair had softened into gray. He remembered how she used to be. Flaming red hair. Hands on hips. Jaw thrust forward. Always challenging. Always determined. She'd had more determination than with any other woman he'd ever known.

Had he done this to her?

What would have happened if he hadn't married her? Would she have married someone else? Would she have set the world on fire? Would he have?

Or should he have been a different sort of husband? Maybe somehow he could have arranged for things to be different for her. But the war took him away, and then they were buried in babies, and he hadn't been all that happy himself. It was hard to go back and figure out what should have been. Maybe they were both exactly where they ought to be.

"No, you're not beautiful," he said, kissing her forehead. "But I've never seen you look sweeter. You'll have to settle for that."

"Did you love her a lot?"

"Who?"

"The other woman. During the war."

Jimmy was stunned. He closed his eyes and shook his head slowly back and forth. "Oh, God, Kate. Have you always known?"

She nodded.

"Oh, sweetheart, that was so long ago."

"But you went back to find her. That's what hurt. You didn't go to California on that trip, did you? You went back to England."

"I went back to sort things out."

"Did you find her?"

"I found out where she was, and I found out I didn't need to see her. I found out that I wanted to come home to you and the kids and Texas. I found out that I don't have to think about her anymore."

"Did you love her?" Kate was crying. Her nose was red.

Jimmy hurt for her. He would have given anything to have spared her this. "I cared for her," he said. "She was there. It was war. There were bombs exploding."

"Was she beautiful?"

"No, honey, she wasn't."

Thirty-two

After six months of combat Junior's request for R and R was approved. He met Francie in Honolulu. Francie found him thin, frightened, and withdrawn—no longer the football hero she married. "I've killed people, Francie. I don't think I'll ever get over it. They were people with families and kids."

When Junior reached out to her, Francie found herself responding as she never had before, and with more than a selfish need to rebuild the man she wanted to return home, to pursue their joined destinies on a football field. No one had ever needed her like that before. No man had ever wept in her arms. He was so sweet, so dear, like a lost puppy in a storm.

At first it was a game—Francie taking care of her shattered soldier boy. But in doing so, she found a part of herself she hadn't known existed. The game became real. With tenderness and compassion, Francie became the woman Junior needed her to be. She was his mother, his sister, his lover, his woman. For the first time in her life, she found herself subjugating her needs to those of another human being. His vulnerability moved her. Their lovemaking took on an intensity that overwhelmed and frightened her. They looked deep into each other's eyes while their bodies joined, while the passion flowed through their veins and consumed them.

She could not touch him enough. She would rather watch over his sleeping form than sleep herself. She bathed his body. She shaved him. She ordered his food for him and supervised his eating. She kissed his feet, knowing, even as she was doing so, that she would never do it again for him or any other man, but wanting and needing to this once.

She fretted over his thinness. "When I get you home again, I'm going to fatten you up," Francie told him. "I need Effie to teach me how to make her apple pies."

Junior knew that if he was killed when he returned to the fighting, it would be all right. Nothing could ever surpass the week he had spent with his wife in Hawaii. He worshipped Francie with a reverence that transcended anything he had ever felt before. He took out his very soul and placed it at her feet.

They fantasized about an island life with just the two of them. Lovers who needed only each other to survive. A perfect life. And when a tiny gnawing kernel of fear knotted her stomach at such a notion, Francie drank pineapple and rum and ministered to her husband's body. There was nothing she would not do with him, to him, for him. Everything was erotic, beautiful. She wished she could crawl inside of him and make love to him from the inside out.

But by week's end the kernel of doubt was heavier. She didn't know the woman who said all those words of devotion and love. By the time she gave him one last lingering farewell kiss, Francie had already begun to withdraw.

With one final wave, a great choking sadness pressed down on Francie, but at the same time a feeling of relief swept over her that bordered on euphoria. She felt as if she had been returned to herself.

On the flight home, Francie found herself looking repeatedly into her compact mirror, needing its reassurance that she had not changed, that the face in the mirror still belonged to her.

Two days after Francie's pregnancy was confirmed, two uniformed Army officers appeared at the door of her Dallas apartment. Junior was dead.

A fire in his barracks had claimed his life. Francie's grief was somewhat tainted by the fact that she was not the widow of a war hero. She felt cheated.

Dub and Mary Sue wanted to bury their son in Midland, but Francie decided on the National Cemetery at Fort Sam Houston, near San Antonio. It was a beautiful, sad place with acres and acres of row upon row of white markers. Fallen warriors. Junior was buried with full military honors complete with a bugler playing the mournful strains of "Taps." *Day is done, gone the sun, from the lakes, from the hills, from the sky. All is well, safely rest, God is nigh.*

The media were present. Junior may not have been a war hero, but he would always be remembered for his prowess on the gridiron. And he was Dub Bonifield's son. Congressman Kendall's son-in-law.

Francie was beautiful in black as she leaned on her father's arm. Gordon kept patting her hand.

Francie stared at the casket containing her husband's body. It would be buried in the ground. Her insides shriveled at the thought. She stepped forward and touched it with a gloved hand. *"Oh, Junior, I'm so sorry, baby. So sorry. I think I really loved you."*

There would never be another time for her like Hawaii. She wanted to cry. Really cry. But she'd do that later when she was alone.

Dub and Mary Sue begged Francie to live with them in Midland. She carried in her womb the only child of their only child. They longed for the baby as the damned long for salvation. Francie accepted their offer of financial aid, promised to visit them often in their mansion with its flocked wallpaper and gold-plated bathroom fixtures, but no, she didn't want to live in Midland. Instead, she gave up her Dallas apartment and moved to Washington, D.C., to make her home temporarily with her parents.

Gordon kept telling Francie she had made the right decision. At a time like this, she needed her family.

Kate's baby boy was born in April. In July Stella and Francie flew to Austin to await the birth of Francie's baby. Francie wanted her child to be born a Texan. Kate drove to Austin and met them at the airport with baby Barry. "Jimmy nicknamed him Bogey for one over par, and I'm afraid the name is sticking," Kate said as she handed her baby to Stella. "Over par or not, I'm happier with him than without him. Jimmy too."

Stella cradled her nephew and kissed his sweet face. "Well, everyone else can call you Bogey," she told the wide-eyed infant, "but to me you will be Barry. What a fine boy you are, Barry. You just keep right on making your mommy and daddy happy."

Stella held Barry as Kate drove them home. "I made Jimmy a promise," Kate said. "If Bogey does sports, it will be on his own. With the other four kids all but grown, it's kind of fun just having our little family of three. Kind of cozy and nice."

Gordon came to join Francie and Stella two weeks later, and nine months to the day after Francie had said her final farewell to Junior in Hawaii, her baby was born after only two hours of labor. She still had her makeup on when Stella joined her after the delivery.

The baby was a small but healthy boy. When the nurse marched into the waiting room to make her joyous announcement, she mistook Gordon for the baby's father.

A grandson. Gordon wept. Francie's child.

The next evening Robert Kennedy was shot in California. Gordon, Stella, and the boys kept a vigil throughout the night in front of the television set until the announcement of the senator's death finally came. Gordon wanted his grandson to be named John Robert after the Kennedy brothers. "But, Daddy," Francie said, "the Kennedys are so tragic. I want our baby to have a happy name—his own name."

Our baby. It's true, Gordon thought. He would be more than a grandfather to Francie's baby.

"I'm going to name him Timothy Kendall Bonifield," Francie said, "and I want you to be his godfather. I don't know if that's proper, but I want it anyway. Ruthie's going to be his godmother."

Back in Washington, Francie supplemented her government widow's pension and Dub's monthly checks with occasional modeling jobs. She moved into her own apartment, but her baby spent almost as much time at his grandparents' Georgetown home as he did with her.

Francie never seemed to have enough money. Her father helped her out whenever she asked, but he'd had his re-elections campaign to finance, and with two households and two sons in college, his expenses had soared. It was hard for Francie to bypass clothing that she knew would look smashing on her. She considered from time to time finding a wealthy man to marry, but other than the lack of money, she found being a widow quite useful. She was married without being married, without the stigma associated with never having married, or with being divorced. Widow-hood—especially when one had been widowed by war—brought even more respect than wifehood. And Francie was haunted by her memories of the week she spent with Junior in Hawaii. For one week she had lost herself and lived for another. It was the most poignant and the most frightening thing that had ever happened to her. She did not want to make herself that vulnerable ever again. And the image of marriage that had been projected throughout her youth was not attractive to her. Francie had no desire to repeat her mother's or Aunt Kate's life. All those chil-dren. Cooking. Cleaning. Even the more glamorous Effie cooked. Francie decided she could always remarry later if she really needed to. Right now she wanted only to live for herself and be adored by her father and Brian and her sweet baby—and even by old fat Tom. As for the other men who came along, she was quite certain they would make better lovers than they would husbands. She'd just have to figure out a way to make money on her own.

Francie loved her son. Timmie was funny and cute. His little body was cuddly and dear. She didn't like taking care of him, but she loved him.

The times she found herself in her apartment alone with her child, however, she grew restless and irritable. She snapped at him far more than he deserved. When she made him cry, Francie would experience a pang of guilt and snatch him onto her lap and soothe him with hugs and kisses. But Timmie's stools were usually loose, and she still gagged every time she changed a messy diaper. She hated spit-up on her clothing. She didn't find it amusing when Timmie peed all over her. The green snot running out of his nose during his frequent colds was disgusting. In fact, a lot about babyhood was just plain disgusting.

More modeling offers came her way, but it was department store stuff. Beneath her. She hated wearing ordinary clothing designed for ordinary people.

Francie went to New York to visit friends and check out the job situation there while Stella and Gordon took Timothy back to Austin with them the following summer.

Francie felt so free without a baby and all the accompanying paraphernalia. It was wonderful.

Tom and Brian were still living in the big house in Austin along with their elderly dog, Buster, who was seventeen and quite deaf. Tom had a job at a summer day camp for handicapped children, and Brian was a lifeguard at a city pool. The boys helped Ruthie plan the celebration for Timmie's first birthday, which included a pony ride and a new plastic swimming pool in the backyard. Stella took pictures of the four of them sitting in the kiddie pool. Brian had on goggles. Tom was holding his nose as though preparing for submersion. Ruthie was wearing a plastic innertube. Timmie was splashing excitedly.

Stella invited Dub and Mary Sue to come for the celebration and stay for the weekend. Their eyes continually filled with tears whenever they looked at their grandson. "He's the very image of Junior at one," Mary Sue said repeatedly. Timmie didn't quite know how to react to the two tearful adults who were constantly touching his hands and face. He crawled into Stella's lap whenever they came into the room.

Kate drove down from Dallas with Bogey for the party. Bogey and Timmie regarded each other solemnly. Kate and Stella took pictures of the children from two generations who were almost the same age. Kate's ponytail was gray now. She joked about being mistaken for Bogey's grandmother by grocery store checkers and the young mothers in the park.

Kate and Stella did their visiting over kitchen duty. "Are you all right?" Stella asked as they finished loading the dishwasher. They carried their second cups of coffee to the oak table with a bowl of fresh green beans to snap.

"What makes you ask?" Kate wanted to know.

"You seem different. You're quieter. Calmer. I don't know. Something."

"My life is calmer. The old nest is emptying out. I don't miss that big house and yard as much as I thought I would." Kate stared out the window. Brian and Tom were carrying the babies piggyback. Ruthie was chasing after them with a spray bottle of water. Bogey and Timmie were squealing with laughter. "I don't know what I'd do without Bogey," she said matter-of-factly.

"How's Jimmy?"

"Busy with his bar. He keeps trying to get me to come down and help him. But Sara's busy being seventeen, and it seems impractical to hire a sitter for Bogey to go be a barmaid."

"It might be kind of fun. You ought to try it," Stella said.

Kate started laughing. "But what would the girls from the Kappa house say? The Sisters of Minerva aren't supposed to be barmaids. But you're probably right. Maybe someday I'll give it a try. Jimmy's a good man. Any other man would have left me years ago."

"Kate!" Stella said, shocked. "What a horrible thing to say."

"It's true. And I would have died if Jimmy had left me. I used to think the one thing I couldn't survive was something happening to one of the children. Now I'm not so sure the worst wouldn't have been if Jimmy had left me."

"Where's my sister Kate who would take on all comers?" Stella asked. "Of course, Jimmy's not going to leave you. But if he did, you could survive anything. You'd always have your children. My goodness—*five* wonderful children. And you and Effie and I—we'll always have each other."

Kate smiled. "Well, unless he dies like poor William, I won't have to find out. If Jimmy were going to leave me, I think he would have already gone. He wouldn't have let me have another baby. Jimmy is loyal. I just wish . . ." She stopped and sipped her coffee instead.

"What do you wish?" Stella said.

Kate shook her head and laughed again. "How did we ever get into such a conversation? What do I wish? I wish I were—beloved. I wish Jimmy looked at me like Pete looks at Effie. Like William looked at Effie. But then what do I expect? I got fat and spent all my time trying to make superstars."

"Is there something you want to tell me?" Stella asked. She touched Kate's hand.

Kate shook her head. Nothing. "Push that bowl over here. Let's snap some beans."

Francie arrived from New York the afternoon of the birthday party. Brian and Tom picked her up at the airport. She was wearing her hair in a chignon and was elegant in cool beige linen. Timmie walked to his mother unsteadily on chubby little legs. Francie knelt in front of her son. "He can walk," she said in disbelief. "My God, he's walking!"

When Timmie lost his balance and sat down with a plop on his well-diapered bottom, he looked at the adult faces to see if he should cry. But as he viewed the circle of watching adults, they were all laughing, so he clapped his hands and laughed too. Bogey, who at fifteen months could walk some but still preferred crawling, crawled over to sit beside his second cousin and share his spotlight. After all, he could clap too.

Francie often went to New York, visiting friends she had made there before her marriage and taking on an occasional modeling job. Her early aversion to the city faded. She understood now that it was up to her to make things happen, that New York would not beat a path to her door. She mounted a campaign to meet the right people and be invited to the right parties. Being the daughter of a congressman helped. Being Junior Bonifield's widow did, too. In fact Francie's first lover after Timmie's birth was a New York Giant who had been a teammate of Junior's at UT. He was sweet but dull. He never talked about anything but football. She dropped him for an assistant secretary of defense, who was quite impressed with her widowhood and kept talking about her sacrifice. And the war. Even in bed he talked about the war. She didn't go out with him very long either.

Work in New York began to come her way. She was accepted by a good modeling agency. Several times a month she would leave Timmie in Washington with her parents. More and more frequently her face and form were seen at high-dollar style shows and in local commercials.

Among the men Francie met in New York was an anchor at a local television station. At his instigation, she applied for a position as an on-the-air reporter. But so did more than two hundred other people, who —Francie was sure—had all majored in broadcast journalism and had some kind of broadcasting experience. She read for the cameras but didn't really expect anything to come of it.

The following week, however, she was offered the job. Francie was thrilled and accepted at once. Her mother could take care of Timmie while she moved to New York.

Francie and Gordon were stunned when Stella refused to assume responsibility for her grandson.

It would only be for a few months—until she was settled, Francie promised. No longer than six months at the most. Just until her career was well in hand and she could afford live-in help.

Stella was unyielding.

"Do you want me to send Timmie out to Dub and Mary Sue in Midland? Is that what you want?" Francie challenged.

"I want you to be responsible for the boy yourself," Stella said, willing her voice to be calm. "I didn't pawn any of you children off on someone else to raise so I could go off and do what I wanted."

"What you wanted?" Francie scoffed. "Burying yourself in some library, reading diaries of dead people? You never did find fulfillment so you're going to prevent your daughter from having a real career."

"I'm fifty years old, Francie. I think I have earned the right to live my own life. I do not choose to take on the raising of another child."

Francie grabbed Timmie and stuffed him into his coat. When he started to cry, Francie shook him. "Shut up!" she said harshly.

When the front door slammed behind her, Gordon opened the folding doors that concealed the living room bar and poured two glasses of brandy. When Stella shook her head no, Gordon gently put the glass in her hand. Stella dutifully took a sip.

The liquid made fire in her stomach. She took another sip and waited for the ax to fall across her neck.

The grandfather's clock Gordon had inherited from his father ticked loudly from the hall. Stella had never heard it tick so loudly. She looked around the room—a tasteful room in a tasteful house, but it had never felt like home. She preferred the house in Austin with its homey kitchen and its wide front porch that reminded her of her parents' home in New Braunfels.

But here she was, not out of choice, but out of duty.

"How can you deny Francie this?" Gordon said. He was on one knee in front of her, peering into her face, his hand on her arm. His voice was low and very gentle. "I don't understand. This is a chance of a lifetime for her. Her life is just beginning, and she needs this opportunity. Poor kid. Losing her husband. Having to make it on her own."

"But my life isn't over. I can't, Gordon. I just can't. Francie's not talking about a couple of weeks. She wants me to raise the child. Please don't ask this of me. I'll forget about a Ph.D. I won't teach anymore. I'll attend every ladies' function in Washington, D.C. I'll shake a thousand hands a week. But I can't do this. My whole life has been babies, raising children. I want something else now."

Gordon got up. He walked to the fireplace and put his hands on the mantel. He just stood there, his back to her, his head bent, his body still.

Stella wondered if he was praying. Did he still do that? Maybe he was praying for the strength to deal with his difficult wife. Such a burden. She waited, cradling the brandy glass in her hands, sitting in a brocade-covered chair and listening to the clock.

When Gordon spoke, there was anguish in his voice as he asked, "What is it that you want, Stella?" He didn't turn around. "I've tried to give you everything a woman could want. I've tried hard to make you proud to be my wife. But you've never been mine—not really. I never know what you're thinking. You've always hidden inside yourself."

Gordon pulled the ottoman over in front of Stella. He sat down in front of her, put her glass on the table, and took both her hands in his. His pain was real. Stella could see that. He was wounded and confused.

"You say you'd be willing to forget about earning that degree," he went on. "Then what is the something else that you want? What is more important than your family? Help me understand. Why can't you do this for your daughter and for me? I love that little boy. He's Francie's baby. I want him to live with us and be a part of our life. Do you really want her to send him out to Midland to live with those two tasteless people who have made a shrine out of Junior's bedroom and would expect Timmie to be a football-playing replica of his father?"

Stella wondered if she was going to scream. To die. "Why can't she take him with her to New York? Other single mothers manage."

"Wouldn't you miss Timmie if he went away?" Gordon asked.

"The last time you told me you wanted a child, I had one whom you've never loved," she told him wearily.

"That's not fair. I do love Ruthie. It's just that I've never been able to feel close to her. I regret that, and I know it's made raising her hard for you. But we're not talking about a child who hasn't been conceived, a child we don't yet know. We're talking about Timmie. Can you honestly tell me that you don't love Timmie?"

"Of course, I love him," Stella said angrily. Love. It always got back to love. "Love is not the question. The question is whose life is more important. Francie's or mine?"

"Or Timmie's? Francie's not cut out to be a mother, Stella. You've always been a wonderful mother."

Stella stared at him, watched his mouth form the words.

"Do you want her to send Timmie to Midland?" Gordon asked.

Stella felt numbness settling into her bones. No, she didn't want him to go to Midland. Yes, she was a good mother. And yes, she did love Timmie. Her grandson. She loved him very much. The generation that separated them brought a purity to their relationship. Neither demanded more than devotion from the other. But now she was being asked to change that. Stella would have to erase the intervening generation and become the boy's mother. His hold on her heart would then be tainted with the burden of duty. For Stella had no illusions. She knew it was quite possible that Francie would never again take up the reins of motherhood once she was free of them. The love Francie had for her son was more that of a doting big sister than a mother. Stella knew that Francie was capable of taking her freedom at her mother's expense and never looking back.

Why did this gift of freedom come so easily to Francie? Why could there never be any for her?

But deep inside, Stella already knew the answer. Francie would feel no more than a flutter of guilt at abandoning her child. Francie lived for herself. Women like Stella never could. The guilt would overwhelm them.

Gordon was waiting for her answer. His eyes were pleading. At stake was more than the fate of a grandchild, it seemed. He would never understand her refusal. He would never forgive it. Without that gesture from her, that final pound of flesh put at the altar of their marriage, Stella would either have to leave or live the rest of her life locked in a marriage like the one her parents had endured—two lonely people remote from each other, even hating each other at times. Anna and Frederick's marriage had produced a family that took on a life of its own and demanded allegiance. It was part of an extended family that joined people together in a way no other institution came close to imitating. Family. Stella felt as though she were suffocating.

She was bound by the love she felt for her husband and her children and now her grandchild. She would always be defined by them. She would be forever the wife, the mother. The part of her that could have been something now must be carefully buried. Better that it had never been. All that had been accomplished by it was pain. She had caused her husband pain. And herself.

Perhaps Gordon was right. Perhaps it should be enough for a woman to love and be loved.

But in the same instant that she accepted the fact that she would raise yet another child, her thoughts turned to the one human being who did not define her by others.

Was it a matter of survival? Did she instinctively know that she needed something else in this life—something that belonged just to her? Thoughts of Charles softened her despair. They gave her strength. She would do what was required of her. But she would also find a moment of private joy along the way to balance out the rest.

"I want to go home for a while and have some time with the boys and Effie and Kate. Francie can manage another couple of weeks before she leaves her son." Stella's voice was flat.

"But she is supposed to start at the television station on the first," Gordon protested.

"I am going to Austin first." Stella enunciated her words very carefully. "I'm going to work in the yard and be with my sons. Ruthie will come with me. And I'm going to go shopping and have lunch with Effie and Kate. Maybe the three of us will take that trip to Mexico we've been promising ourselves for years. *You* take care of Timmie until I get back if it's so goddamned important."

"Effie, if I don't come back tonight . . ." Stella hesitated. How was she going to explain? She pushed away her lunch plate. Such a nice lunch Effie had fixed, but Stella couldn't eat. She picked up her glass of sherry instead.

"If you don't come back tonight, I'm not to worry," Effie finished for her.

Stella nodded. "I'll probably be back in an hour or so. It's an old friend. I . . ."

Effie put a finger to Stella's lips. "Hush. You don't have to explain anything to me. Poor Stella. How you must have agonized."

"Do you think I'm terrible?"

"I think you're a woman with some unfinished business. I think you've carried a torch for a long, long time and feel the years getting away from you."

"Yes. I wonder if I'm being a foolish old woman. Why now, after all these years?"

"Obviously because it's what you need to do now, and you didn't need to before," Effie said. "I've always wondered, honey—would you have married someone else if I hadn't thrust the Reverend Kendall into your life?"

Stella shook her head. "No. Marriage with . . . with this other person was out of the question, and I don't regret Gordon. I can't imagine being married to anyone else. He's the father of my children. Oh, Effie, I'm so confused. I'm not sure whether I want to do this for me or to Gordon."

Stella put her face in her hands and wept silently. Effie patted her shoulder and let her cry.

"You won't tell Kate, will you?" Stella asked.

Effie shook her head, her blue eyes solemn. No, she wouldn't tell Kate. Kate would not approve. Kate didn't believe in taking risks.

"You go and fix your face," she told Stella. "And if you don't come home, you'd better at least call me and tell me a telephone number—just in case."

Stella nodded. "In novels it just happens. You don't have to make all these sordid arrangements."

Effie smiled. "Yes, and the clothes fall magically from bodies. Zippers don't get stuck. If it doesn't feel right, Stella, just have a drink with him and come on home. I'll be here. We'll do back rubs."

Thirty-three

Charles Lasseter had been successful. His Dallas-based firm had offices in Houston and Oklahoma City. His Down's syndrome son had grown into a "twilight zone" sort of adulthood, the forever child in a man's body. Whiskers seemed an obscenity on a face that spoke in only one- and two-syllable words. His body was hairy. The penis in his trousers was large. And despite all efforts to train him otherwise, Andy frequently would take out his large penis and play with it. It and cartoons on television provided his greatest pleasures. Sometimes he would enjoy them together, fondling his beloved appendage while laughing at the antics of Bugs Bunny or Tom and Jerry.

Andy lived in a home for retarded adults. A requirement for admission to the home was sterilization: it seemed sex between the residents was not unheard of.

Andy spent two weekends a month at home with his parents. Marisa and Charles ate with him every Wednesday on guest night. Charles took Andy to sporting events. Andy especially liked to go to football games. He didn't understand the game, but he loved the color and pageantry. He still held his father's hand when they crossed the street.

Once Charles took Andy to Galveston. Andy enjoyed digging in the sand and watching the scurrying hermit crabs. He screamed, "Ho, ho, ho," like a joyous Santa Claus while he jumped up and down in the waves. Once after they had frolicked together with the waves, father and son stretched out on a blanket in the sunshine. Charles dozed off. When he woke up, Andy was gone. Charles raced up and down the beach like a madman, screaming Andy's name, shading his eyes and frantically scanning the vast emptiness of the brilliantly bright ocean. When he saw Andy come lumbering over a sand dune, his shovel and bucket in hand, Charles sank to his knees with relief. Whenever Charles thought of taking Andy back to Galveston, he remembered the absolute fear he had felt that day. Sometimes he took him to the beach at Lewisville Lake—a lake wasn't quite so frightening. And he built Andy an adult-sized sandbox in a corner of the backyard to play in when he spent weekends at home.

Charles created a trust fund assuring that there would be money to provide for Andy's care for the rest of his life.

When Marisa entered menopause, it was Charles who had suffered depression. For years Charles had dreamed of having other children. But Marisa was afraid. She remained fearful even after the advent of amniocentesis. Even with the possibility of intrauterine testing, Marisa didn't want another pregnancy. She knew she would not be able to deal with aborting such an infant even if it was diagnosed as being Down's syndrome. "That would be like saying Andy should have never been born," she explained.

Charles understood and respected her feelings, but as much as Charles loved Andy, he believed such children should never be born. Their presence in the world doomed others to life sentences. For Marisa, however, her child and others like him had become a cause célèbre. She was concerned with their rights, their care, their education. Her advocacy group had called attention to the practice in some hospitals across the state of simply letting severely handicapped infants die, and they managed to get the state's definition of an "educable child" revised.

And Marisa had her other causes. An elegant woman with unfailing good taste, she enjoyed the Dallas Ballet Society and the Dallas Museum of Art Association. She loved attending many of the city's fine arts events in expensive gowns and furs, her handsome, successful husband at her side. Her work with the Down's syndrome children was greatly admired, as was Marisa herself. Only Charles understood that beneath the poised exterior was a woman who had never really recovered from the tragedy of their son's birth. Andy bound them together in a way that nothing else could. Marisa needed Charles and her regimented life to protect her from her sadness. If she was very careful, she could be happy.

Charles wanted Marisa to be happy. He worked at her happiness, but he was fifty-six and restless. Where was the joy?

He thought of his Aunt Blanche and tried teaching—first one night class in Dallas, then as an adjunct professor at the university in Austin. He drove down for part of each week to share his knowledge with eager young students who had such high hopes for the future. He selected UT rather than some other school in Texas because of Stella. If he was in Austin, he might see her again. Part of the city was in her husband's district. They would still have a home here.

In a way, academe made Charles feel old and sad. He had no high hopes, not any longer, and teaching did not provide him as great a challenge as he had hoped for. But it was a change.

Later, when Charles looked back at the moment when he saw Stella sitting there in the anteroom of his university office, he decided it was the most memorable of his life. She was as beautiful as ever. The strands of gray in her smooth brown hair matched her wonderful eyes. Only her hands looked old.

And he wondered—in his looking back—what happened to the entourage of students who had followed him to his office with their usual post-lecture questions and arguments. When he saw her, Charles forgot all about the students. Everything else receded and there was only Stella.

He stood in the doorway.

She looked up at him, her eyes tentative.

Charles took a step forward, and she rose. They were facing each other in the small room.

He said her name. She smiled and held out her hand.

Without taking his gaze from her eyes, he lifted her hand to his lips and kissed first the back and then the palm. She was real.

"Stella," he said again. "Stella."

Her eyes were moist and loving. She was so lovely it made his chest hurt.

She had come to him. He did not know why or for how long. But the woman he had thought of daily for more than thirty years was actually standing in front of him. Stella, the only woman he had ever truly loved.

Then she was in his arms. He held her for a long time, and then his mouth covered hers. A gentle, poignant kiss. So many years between kisses. He wanted the moment to last forever.

"I love you, Stella. I've always loved you."

"And I you, my darling." Her smile was shy. "What are you doing for the next two days?"

"Only two days?"

"I'm afraid so."

He touched her hair, her cheek, her throat. Stella. Beloved Stella. The face he saw in his dreams. The name he said in his heart. The woman who had come to signify all the longing of an unfulfilled life.

He sank to his knees, his arms around her waist, his face buried against her belly, and wept. She caressed his hair, his neck, said his name. "Charles. My dearest Charles."

. . .

Charles had a spartan apartment he used when he came to Austin. He wanted to take Stella to a luxury hotel. "I'm a congressman's wife," Stella reminded him. "I can't go to public places with you." But she was disappointed when she walked into the small living room. The apartment smelled closed up. The furniture was worn and nondescript.

So it would be here without benefit of deserted beaches or windswept mountaintops or faces illuminated by firelight. Charles had insisted on going out for a bottle of wine. Stella sat alone in the plain living room and stared out the window at an apartment building across the street. Children were playing in the yard. A postman was delivering the mail at a bank of boxes. Routine.

The word for what she was about to do was an ugly one. Did love justify it? Restlessness? Resentment?

"You're having second thoughts," he said when he returned.

"What makes you say that?"

"The stricken look on your face."

Stella touched her face as though to feel its look. She rearranged the stack of *Architectural Digests* and *Times* on the coffee table. "It's more difficult than I thought it would be. I've been with the same man for twenty-eight years. And I've got stretch marks. I nursed four babies."

"I know. The bottle of wine was just an excuse," Charles admitted. "I had to call Marisa and tell her I wouldn't be home tonight. I had to lie. And I wish I jogged a little more faithfully. I wish I'd been doing fifty sit-ups a day for the last year."

"I get angry all over again because you didn't make love to me when I threw myself at you before the war," Stella said. "I had a young body then."

They stared at each other across the gold shag carpet, across the coffee table with cigarette burns. "I've thought about this for years, wanted it for years," Stella said. "But I never thought I'd have the courage. And what brought me to you finally was not love or passion but despair. I need something to soften it. Life is not what I thought it would be."

She didn't want to cry. It was stupid to cry. She was here because she wanted to be. But she felt old and used up, and this time here with this beloved man was stolen from her real life.

Charles held her. It felt nice to have his arms around her. His face was in her hair—her graying hair. His hands were lightly stroking her back. "I'm glad you're here," he said. "If you want to leave, I won't love you any less."

She lifted her face to him. "Kiss me, Charles. Please."

Stella knew she would not leave him. She would stay the two days and nights and sort out all the reasons later.

"I've always wanted you, Stella. Always loved you. *Always*. Don't make me go through my whole life without ever making love to the woman I love."

She took his hand and led him the few steps into the tiny bedroom. A plain blue comforter covered the double bed.

Stella unbuttoned his shirt and helped him slip it from his arms. Then the undershirt. The hair on his chest was half gray. There was fleshiness around his nipples and his navel—and a puckered scar across his shoulder, ugly and brutal, from the war.

He helped her out of her blouse. She turned her back to him and finished removing her clothes. Without looking at each other, they pulled back the comforter and slid under the sheet. *Why am I doing this?* Stella kept asking herself. *What difference can it possibly make?* But she felt as though she had crossed a line beyond which she could not go back. She would have this man. They would culminate this thing that had haunted them for more than thirty years, and then they would feel better or worse or just the same.

His body was not Gordon's body. Its contours felt different to her touch. He was larger, heavier, less hairy.

Stella knew there would be no rapture. Maybe another time, but not now. She felt strange being here with a different man even if it was the Charles of her dreams. She was too concerned with what he was thinking and feeling to get inside of her own self. Did he really want to kiss her breasts that long, or was he just doing it because he thought she wanted him to? Did he want her to touch his penis? Should she be aggressive or passive? The kissing was the best part.

When he entered her, she was disappointed. It felt no different. Then he raised up. "Open your eyes, Stella. Look at me."

He held her with his eyes while their bodies moved against each other. "I love you, Stella. Always. Forever and ever and ever. No, don't look away. Know that it's me and that I love you with a love that is the most holy thing I have ever felt. Do you know this? Answer me. Do you know this?"

"Yes," Stella cried out. "Oh, yes."

"Say my name, Stella. I want to hear you say my name."

Over and over she said it. The love of her youth, of her life. Charles. Her Charles.

He kissed her again, wild, hungry kisses. She felt the crescendo rising within him and realized it was happening for her too. Their bodies were no longer young, but the feelings had been waiting in a timeless limbo since their youth.

Stella cared for her grandson and for Ruthie, who was now in high school, a straight-A student and bookworm like her mother. Stella earned the reputation among the other congressional wives of being aloof—a loner.

Francie came to Washington often. Stella wondered whether she came more to see her son or her father. Francie would go with Gordon to the receptions and cocktail parties that Stella now chose to avoid. Already co-anchor of the evening news on the local NBC affiliate station in New York, Francie had acquired a patina of glamour that brought her ratings, a bevy of admiring men, and offers of higher-paying television jobs in various parts of the country. But she stayed in New York. Her station encouraged public appearances, and Francie's face had graced dozens of magazine covers. She was recognized and given the best seats in restaurants. When she and a date entered a theater, a stir of recognition went through the audience. She had become a personality. Beautiful. Talented. A congressman's daughter. And everyone knew about her widowhood, about her husband who died in Vietnam. Junior Bonifield. The football player.

Gordon attended Washington events with his glamorous daughter on his arm. He even looked younger when Francie was with him. They made a handsome couple.

Stella understood that Gordon never felt as comfortable with his wife as he did with his daughter. He and Francie admired each other enormously and had a large repertoire of private jokes, signals, shared opinions. Stella understood that Gordon saw in his daughter's eyes the man he wanted to be.

It was Francie who was in the house gallery when Gordon gave his speech against the dangers of relying too heavily on foreign oil. "Already we are far too vulnerable. An embargo from the oil-producing nations of the Middle East would cause an energy crisis in this nation and in the entire Western world." Gordon went on to encourage more favorable legislation for the petroleum industry—laws that would encourage exploration and production. "I respect evironmental issues, but at this point in our history it's better to find ways to prevent oil spills than to restrict its off-shore drilling. It's time we took off the blinders and acknowledged that without a strong oil industry, America cannot remain free and strong."

Stella read about the speech in the Austin paper. When she called to congratulate him, Francie answered the phone. "He was magnificent," Francie said. "I was so proud of him."

Stella, Ruthie, and Timmie often flew to Texas to visit Brian and Tom in Austin and Effie and Kate in Dallas.

Tom was majoring in education for lack of anything better. He was not a good student and found playing in the University of Texas Longhorn band, "the show band of the Southwest," the most pleasurable part of his college life. As a courtesy to Brian, Tom was invited to pledge his brother's fraternity, but after a few weeks he quit. Fraternity life made him uncomfortable. The two brothers continued to live together in the family home, taking care of the lawn and keeping the inside reasonably clean. Tom cooked, and Brian did the dishes. Brian's girlfriend, Cynthia, often spent the night. She and Tom were good friends. They had their love for Brian in common. The three of them cried together the night old Buster died.

Cynthia would help Tom with the cooking but never Brian with the dishes, claiming "the sight of a man doing dishes fills my female heart with joy."

The two brothers agreed on civil rights but still disagreed passionately about the war in Vietnam. For Tom it was immoral. For Brian it was a war against the evil of communism. Cynthia sided with Tom.

Stella took great pleasure in her plain, plump younger son. He was a good person.

As was Brian. As physically beautiful as Francie, Brian was a thoroughly decent human being, and so sincere, so caught up in his convictions. Encouraged by his father, he made patriotism his religion. An ROTC student at the university at a time when many young men were burning their draft cards and demonstrating against the war in Southeast Asia, Brian worked toward a commission in the Marines with a pride made greater by that of his father.

Gordon was very visible at Brian's commissioning. The state press was well represented at the campus ceremony and took many photographs of the congressman and his newly commissioned son. A university photographer took a picture of Brian with Francie and Gordon for the alumni magazine. Gordon couldn't have been more proud. Brian basked in his father's pride. His eyes glowed with it. His uniformed shoulders were squarer because of it, his chest fuller. Stella, also a UT graduate, stayed in the background with Tom and Ruthie.

"You don't like any of this, do you?" Ruthie asked her mother.

"No, I guess I don't," Stella admitted.

"I don't either. I don't want Brian to be military. I don't like that war."

"Well, don't start another argument with Brian about it. Let him have his day."

It was a glorious day. Texas in May. The campus was a riot of flowers. It had changed very little over the years. There was comfort in that, and in the university's traditions, its beauty, its accomplishments. For Stella, it was one of the most special places on earth.

Parents and relatives milled around with their uniformed sons and daughters. So young, these new Marines. So fresh of face. Eager. Naïve. How many of them would die in their uniforms? Stella wondered.

That afternoon the commencement ceremony was held on the south terrace in front of the Main Building, its tower piercing a sky of the purest blue. Kate, Jimmy, and their lively brood arrived in the latest in a long succession of station wagons—this one a blue Ford. Mark brought a girlfriend, a fellow law student from Mexico City. Jeff was studying to be a veterinarian at A & M. Freddy had just finished his freshman year, and Sara was a new high school graduate. Effie and Dr. Pete came with Billy and his wife, Barbara, in Billy's new Buick. Billy brought a movie camera.

John Petterson Elder, dean of the Harvard Law School, was the speaker. He spoke on the First Amendment, the indirect caretaker of democracy. The graduates talked among themselves. The speech was too long. Stella dozed.

Timmie sat on his mother's lap for the first part of the long ceremony. When he fell asleep, she handed him over to Stella, pointing to the wrinkles in her white linen suit. Stella woke Timmie up just before his Uncle Brian took his turn crossing in front of the podium. Timmie watched a minute, then leaned his head back against Stella's shoulder and resumed his nap.

After the ceremony Kate and Effie helped Stella serve the celebration dinner—all Brian's favorites. Chicken and dumplings. Baked apples. German potato salad. Hot rolls. Kate's homemade pickles. Effie, of course, had brought pies—an apple and a cherry. Tom and Ruthie took pictures of everyone sitting around the long table, lifting their glasses to Brian. Billy kept jumping up to take more footage with his super eight. A tablecloth crocheted years ago by Grandmother Anna covered the table. Ruthie had hung a banner on the wall that said, CONGRATULATIONS, BRIAN. WE LOVE YOU.

After dinner they gathered in the living room for the final picture taking. Billy posed the graduate in front of the fireplace with his family and aimed his movie camera. "Do something," he said. "Don't just stand there. Now let's have the graduate just with his parents. Then with his sisters."

Billy's movie taking ended with a shot of Brian and Tom. At odds politically but brothers always, they embraced for Billy's camera. They continued to hold each other after Billy had turned off the glaring lights.

Brian was sent to Vietnam. Gordon—now campaigning for a third term—took irrational comfort in the fact that their family had already lost a son-in-law to the war. He seemed to believe that gave Brian some sort of protection.

Stella called Charles before she returned to Washington in the fall. "You are the dearest thing in my world," he told her.

She left the house and went for a walk, needing to be by herself. Was Charles the dearest thing in *her* world? She thought of her four children, of her grandson, of her sister and cousin and their children. She thought of Gordon, who needed her more than all the rest. She had many dear people to love, so why did she need Charles too?

Perhaps because to Charles she was still Stella Behrman, the girl who had once dreamed and aspired and believed. Perhaps it was because she and Charles had never married.

No, Charles was not the dearest or even the most important, but the part of her that loved and needed him was the part that was most truly herself. And Charles had given her the three most perfect days of her life to treasure. Stella smiled as she remembered. She couldn't leave at the end of the second day. Effie told her not to. "God, Stella, if you feel that way, don't come home ever."

"Just one more day," Stella told her over the phone.

"I'll take care of it," Effie promised. "I'll call Tom and Ruthie and tell them you and I've got some family business in New Braunfels."

Stella went into the next room and closed the door while Charles made his call.

Then they danced around the room, twirling, laughing, two happy children. "One more day with my beloved—a gift from the gods," he said, lifting her off her feet and hugging her so hard she gasped.

They had opened another bottle of wine and drank it greedily.

Oh, God, Stella thought, had that woman really been she? Her body tingled with remembering, and she felt young. She wondered when she would see him again. Sometime. It was nice to know that. It calmed her and sustained her.

A male cardinal came swooping out of an elm tree and sat boldly on a picket fence by the sidewalk. When Stella stopped and told him good evening, he cocked his crested head and looked at her quizzically. Such a pretty bird on a pretty street in a pretty town. A pretty evening. A pretty world. Hearing Charles's voice made her feel giddy. She hugged herself. He loved her.

Stella hadn't gotten around to dealing with the morality of her affair with Charles. Affair. What a deliciously naughty word. She had never been naughty before. She was Stella, her papa's good girl. But her stern papa with his old-time religion, with his black-and-white world had nothing to do with Charles—with Gordon, yes, but not with Charles. Moral or immoral, good or bad, Stella knew she would see Charles again.

With him, she had been another person, free for a time from the boundaries of her life. Together, she and Charles had explored a vast new plane of their own sexuality, not only with their bodies but with their words. Their conversations would be about normal things, then suddenly return to how it had been, how it had felt, how they hadn't known it could feel like that. They wondered if it was like that for other people or if they alone in all the history of humankind had had such feelings.

"I've had orgasms before," Stella said, concentrating to keep a grin off her face. She was propped up in bed next to Charles, drinking the cup of tea he had brought her. "What I have with you is nothing like that. Aren't you ashamed, Charles Lasseter? You've taken this perfectly respectable fifty-year-old matron and turned her into an insatiable sex maniac."

"I'm filled with remorse," he said, taking the empty cup from her hand. "Now shut up and kiss me."

"You know, I'm in love with the skin on the tip of your tongue," Stella said. "It's soft and rough at the same time and feels so good when it rubs against my tongue."

It was true. Current went through her body with just the touch of his tongue. She would lose herself in his kisses. Endless, wet, soulful kissing that could go on forever.

The touching of love was its greatest revelation. The textures of his body fascinated her. She couldn't keep her hands still. Even when they wandered out in the kitchen to eat, she had to be near him, touching him.

The last time they made love, after the rapture of her orgasm, he withdrew himself from her and came on her belly. They had rubbed his warm, living semen into each other, a sacrament of their own making. Stella closed her eyes remembering the feel of his hand rubbing over her belly, up her waist to her breasts, rubbing his coming into her breasts, her throat. As they kissed each other's wet hands, Stella had known she was experiencing the outer reaches of her own sensuality, that no other moment would ever compare to what she was feeling at that one. She thanked God that she had not lived and died without experiencing those three passionate, erotic, glorious, loving days with Charles.

Who was she, Stella wondered, that uninhibited, sensual woman who so generously gave herself to Charles or the dutiful wife who gave of herself to her husband only what was necessary? Yet she loved them both. Gordon gave the safety of boundaries, and Charles gave her dreams. Everything in her upbringing taught her that she could not love two men, instructed her that good women didn't do that. And above all else, Stella had wanted to be good.

Her papa, who had guided her through these lessons, had loved only one woman in a lifetime. Had her papa come all over the belly of the first Anna? Had they discovered the innocence that could accompany carnal delight, the purity of holding absolutely nothing of oneself back from the other?

Stella stood in the middle of an Austin, Texas, sidewalk and watched the cardinal fly away into the still bright sky, its western reaches tinged with the first oranges and pinks of sunset. She felt as though she could fly with him. Part of her did, soaring wide and far. In her mind's eyes, she rode on his brilliantly red back the way Thumbelina in the fairy tale had flown on the back of a swallow. The higher she soared the more insignificant everything below her became, and all that was important was the soaring itself.

The other part of her turned her steps back down Atterbury Lane. She had so much packing to do, and she had promised Timmie she'd fix him a sundae and read him *The Little Engine That Could*, and she wanted to dig up some iris bulbs to take back to Washington. Next spring they would look pretty blooming in her tiny backyard. She would buy a bird-bath and put hanging baskets overflowing with petunias on the high fence.

It was a crisp, bright Saturday morning in October. Sunlight streamed through the panes of leaded glass in the front door and reflected rainbows on the wall of the entry hall in their Georgetown home. When Stella opened the door, her grandson at her side, and saw the two Marine officers standing there, their faces solemn, she knew the moment she had been dreading ever since Brian left had arrived. Her knees buckled, and she grabbed the door for support. Her body seemed to be sucking itself from within, trying to turn itself inside out.

The men removed their hats respectfully. One of them, the colonel, asked if Congressman Kendall was in.

Stella knew. There was no God, and Brian had been killed fighting for some nameless hill in a war she had never understood. The son she had borne and bathed and kissed and rocked was dead. The little boy who asked all those questions, who worried about whether grasshoppers had a heaven, was dead. The young man who towered over her and playfully mussed her hair was dead. The sons and daughters he would have fathered were dead with him.

Brian gone. Never to come home again.

"Who is it?" Gordon called from the top of the stairs.

The men waited for her to answer him.

She didn't.

"Two soldiers, Grandpa," Timmie called.

Gordon's footsteps came cautiously down the stairs. Two soldiers at his door? No, surely not, the footsteps seemed to say. Not Brian. Not my boy. It's a mistake.

Stella wanted to scream. If she could scream loud enough and long enough, these two men would go away. Then she wouldn't have to hear what they had to say. If she didn't hear, maybe it wouldn't be so. But if she screamed, she would scare Timmie.

Gordon was standing beside her. "Not my boy?" he asked, his voice begging, quavering. The voice of an old man. "No, not my boy."

Thirty-four

It would have been far easier to face the approach of her own death than to endure the knowledge of her son's. No other pain compared—not when either of her parents died, not when she lost others dear to her heart, not when she accepted once and for all that she would live her life without Charles—all paled in comparison with this. The pain was so complete, so hopeless, that Stella was not sure she could bear it. It choked and suffocated her. It clawed at her gut and squeezed the blood from her heart. Her child. Her Brian. Her son had died in a war, in pain and fear.

Stella had no choice but to bear her pain, however. Francie arrived in hysterics. Timmie came down with croup. Ruthie had nightmares and would wake screaming for Brian after seeing horrible visions on the canvas of her brain.

And Gordon was unable to dress himself for days after the Marine officers, with ribbons on their immaculate, uniformed chests, came to tell them that Second Lieutenant Brian Gordon Kendall had been killed by enemy fire near some place called Hoai Nhon.

A red-eyed Tom flew in from Texas with Effie and Kate.

Tom helped out with Timmie, reading to the sick child by the hour, rocking him to sleep, holding him far into the night because the boy's breathing was easier when he slept sitting up.

Effie and Kate moved quietly and efficiently around Stella's house doing—as women have always done—what needed to be done. And they would sit with Stella late at night with their coffee, puzzling together the meaning of sadness in their lives, reexamining the lives of the generation who went before them, with new understanding of what it was to live long years and endure what they brought.

"I remember when our baby brother died," Kate said. "I thought that was the saddest thing that ever could have happened. It wasn't. And poor Carl. Mama and Papa. But this is far worse. One of our children. Brian. Oh, my God! Brian. He was always such a good boy."

The three woman shed tears together, late at night, when the cooking and cleaning were done, when it was too late for people to stop by and pay their respects. They blew their noses until they were red and raw. Even Effie looked tired and plain. Stella couldn't remember Effie ever looking plain before.

Stella wanted Brian buried in Texas, but Gordon favored Arlington. Stella pointed out that the cemetery at Fort Sam Houston, where Francie's Junior was buried, was also a national cemetery, but when Timmie had to be hospitalized, she didn't press any further.

It took six days for the body to arrive. They met the plane. Another flag-drapped casket, Stella thought, only this time it was her son's casket being lowered out of the belly of the huge cargo plane. Stella's knees threatened to buckle, but Effie and Kate supported her. She looked over at Gordon, who was clinging to the arm of the Marine officer assigned to their family. Francie and Ruthie clung to Tom.

Stella could close her eyes and see an image of Brian inside that metal casket, his eyes closed, his head resting on the satin pillow, as beautiful in death as he was in life. Only they wouldn't be showing the body. Brian's injuries had been too grave.

Somehow her rubbery legs carried her across the expanse of concrete runway, the wind whipping at her skirt and hair. Stella stood by the casket with her three living children, her husband, her sister, and her cousin to touch the flag and cry, their impromptu ceremony seeming foolishly inadequate. She would never touch Brian again, never stroke his tan cheek or caress his dark hair, never feel his strong arms catching her up in a hug, never feast her eyes on the sight of him, never hear his voice.

Stella realized the news of Brian's death would be well reported in the Texas press. Charles would know by now. He would grieve for her, need some contact with her, want her to call. She could feel him wanting her to call. But she didn't.

Instead, Charles called her. Kate answered the phone. Her brow furrowed with a puzzled frown as she listened to someone speaking. "This isn't Stella you're speaking with," she said. "I'm her sister."

With a guarded look, she handed Stella the phone.

"Oh God, Stella, I'm sorry," Charles's voice said. "Your sister sounds like you. I . . . I just had to call and tell you how sorry I am about Brian. I guess I shouldn't have."

"Probably not," Stella said. That wasn't what he wanted her to say. He wanted her to say she was grateful he had called, that it helped to have him think of her in her pain. But she wasn't glad. She was angry. She didn't want anyone else to want something of her. She had nothing for him.

It bothered her that Charles had called Brian by name. He shouldn't be saying her son's name.

Gordon was up in the bedroom, she thought. What if he picked up the extension? No, Charles should not have called.

"I need to go," she said. "Good-bye."

"That man's in love with you," Kate said incredulously.

Stella shrugged.

"Do you love him?" Kate pressed on.

Stella rubbed her temples with her fingertips. "I don't know. Once. Not right this minute, I don't."

Kate wanted reassurance. She needed her sister to say there was nothing between her and that mysterious man on the phone.

"You're not going to do something stupid?" Kate asked.

"Of course not. Now hush up. I don't want to discuss it. Not now. Maybe never. If I do, I'll let you know."

"It's that man you saw in Dallas during the war, isn't it?" Kate demanded. "The one who stopped by our table at Neiman's with his wife? The one you went to have lunch with the next day."

"Shut up, Kate," Stella said, her half-whisper not disguising the vehemence in her voice. "Please, just leave me alone."

Charles stared at the telephone on his desk. He felt foolish and hurt. Stella had considered his call an intrusion. For days he had suffered for her, needed to tell her what he was feeling, that her pain was his pain.

But she wanted none of it.

Family separated them. Would it always? What of his dream for a someday?

But someday for them could come only through tragedy. His wife, Marisa, and Stella's husband, Gordon, would have to die before them for there ever to be a time for the two of them. How strange to need the death of two other human beings in order to find their own happiness in this world.

Yet he loved Marisa. They had so much common history now—the bittersweet experiences with their beloved Andy, the family deaths, the illnesses, the triumphs. He had shared her causes. She had been the proud wife to his accomplishments and given them meaning. Marisa had made a home for him. She was his constant.

Why did he need something else? Why did he need the dream of Stella? Far better that he dreamed of designing the ultimate structure, of endowing a worthy cause, of being a mentor to future generations of architects.

But when he closed his eyes at night, he saw Stella's face. When he drove down the highway, he fantasized her sitting beside him. When he inspected a building in progress, he imagined her at his side, wearing a hard hat, listening to his explanations.

It was her skin he longed to touch, her lips he longed to kiss, her voice he longed to hear say his name. Always. It never changed.

Charles reached for his telephone and dialed his home telephone number. At first he thought Marisa wasn't going to answer, but then there she was. A breathless hello.

"Let's get Andy tonight and have a picnic out at the lake," Charles said. "It's warm enough if we wear jackets. We can build a fire and roast marshmallows."

"What about the board meeting for Special Olympics?"

"I'd rather be with you and Andy."

Marisa was silent for a minute, weighing. "We are supposed to go out for drinks with the Simpsons afterwards, and tonight's the night they vote on next year's site. Couldn't we see Andy tomorrow night? He is coming home this weekend, you know."

"You go on to the board meeting without me. I think I'll run by the home and at least visit with him for a while, maybe take him for a walk over to the ice cream store. Perhaps I can join you later."

"How's your day?" she asked.

"Hectic. And yours?"

"Busy. Talk to you later."

Charles hung up and went back to his drafting table. He stared down at the preliminaries for another bank office building. It was hard to believe that Dallas really needed another one.

But Dallas was booming. His firm was booming. He was lucky to be part of it all.

He sat there on his high stool for a long time, his shoulders hunched over, his hands dangling between his legs.

Then he went back to his desk and called Marisa again.

"I really want to be with Andy *and* you tonight."

"Charles," she said hesitantly, "what's the matter?"

"Nothing really. I just feel lonely."

Silence. Then her voice was different. "Can you get away now?" she asked.

"No. Well, maybe. What do have in mind?"

"Why don't you go to Northpark Mall with me and buy a wedding present for Herb and Rhonda's daughter? And we can buy a new coffeepot. You pick it out this time. I'm tired of hearing you complain the coffee's never hot enough. Then we can have a drink together before we pick up Andy. I'll gather up the stuff for the picnic."

"Sounds good. I'll swing by and pick you up in thirty minutes."

When he told his secretary he was leaving for the afternoon, her eyes widened in surprise. "But what about the meeting with Mr. Heckendorn and Mr. Russell?"

"Hank and John can manage it without me."

His footsteps echoed in the parking garage. He automatically walked to his slot and slid under the wheel of his Mercedes. He sat there with his hands on the steering wheel in the half light of the dank-smelling concrete structure.

He didn't realize he was crying until he felt the tears on his cheeks.

Stella, I'm so sorry I intruded. I know you're all empty inside now. I hurt so for you. Please don't stop loving me.

He put his forehead against his hands. "Stella," he whispered. Just saying the word filled him with such longing. It pushed against the walls of his chest. There was not room inside of him for all that longing.

Brian was buried in Arlington with full military honors, something usually reserved for senior officers. But Brian was the son of a congressman and had died a hero. There was to be a medal.

Effie's husband, Dr. Pete, flew in with Billy and his wife, Barbara. Jimmy arrived with Mark, Jeff, Freddy, and Sara. Two of Gordon's cousins came from Tyler. Even Uncle Herman came. Uncle John had died the year before. Aunt Hannah was not in good health. Aunt Louise was afraid to fly, but she came to Dallas to take care of Bogey for Jimmy and Kate.

A chaplain with eagles on his shoulders presided at the service in Arlington's military chapel. Gordon had prepared a eulogy. He walked bravely to the pulpit and started to deliver it, but he was unable to read for his tears. The chaplain finished reading it for him. It was about a father's pride in a brave and noble son.

Gordon said the horse-drawn caisson that bore their son to his final resting place was the same one that had been used for President Kennedy's funeral procession. He seemed to think that was important.

The grave site was at the top of a rolling hill in the newest part of the enormous cemetery. Tom had to help Uncle Herman up the incline. From the top of the hill was a view of the Potomac, of the city, of the sprawling Pentagon. It was beautiful, Stella supposed. Everyone said it was.

There were photographers and television cameras, but they kept a respectful distance.

Three rifles fired in salute. "Taps" was played by the lone bugler. Stella thought of Carl's funeral. Years ago. Another war. And Junior's three and a half years ago in this same war. She was tired of wars and funerals.

The flag was taken from the bronze casket and folded by the honor guard, one of whom turned and presented it to Stella with a salute and a smart click of his heels.

Stella handed the flag to Francie. She wanted nothing of their flag. It was not an even trade.

When the graveside service was over, one by one Brian's family came forward to touch his casket one last time, to lean forward and kiss the cold, uncaring bronze. A final farewell. Stella was particularly touched by Kate's and Effie's grief. She watched them as they took their turn at the casket. They loved her son like their own. Tom's face was puffed and red. He spread his hands on the casket, then bent forward to plant his kiss. Ruthie, plain and gangling at fourteen, stumbled as she walked forward. Her sobs sounded like hiccups, and she sniffled loudly as she bent forward. Last was Francie, the folded American flag clutched against her breast. She caressed the casket with a white-gloved hand. "I love you, Brian," she said and pressed her lips against the metal casket.

When Francie turned to look at her mother, her face was naked and contorted. "Oh, Mother!" she said, falling into Stella's arms. "Why did he have to die?"

"I don't know," Stella said, holding her grown daughter against her breast, trying to remember the last time Francie had needed comfort from her. Not since she was a child.

After the funeral the limousines made their way to the Capitol for a ceremony in the Rotunda. Vice President Agnew was waiting there for them with the joint chiefs of staff and a sizable group of Gordon's congressional colleagues. Brian was posthumously awarded the Distinguished Service Cross. Like father, like son. Stella wondered how they had done the paperwork for the award so quickly. But red tape was probably easy to cut through for a congressman's son.

It seemed, by military standards, Brian had died well. He and his platoon had taken out a machine gun implacement, the citation related. Brian was shot by an enemy wounded after the position had been secured. How incomprehensible that Brian had died killing people, Stella thought. Her sensitive, beautiful Brian, a soldier fighting in a war—an ugly, stinking war that murdered beautiful, kind young men who enrolled in ROTC so their fathers would be proud.

After the vice president handed him the medal, Gordon tried hard to give his prepared acceptance speech in front of the cameras. But all he could do was sob something about "sacrifice" and how much Brian had loved America.

Francie wept openly at her mother's side, her nose red, her face long since devoid of any makeup, her usual aura of glamour erased by her grief. At Junior's funeral she had cried without ruining her mascara. Stella had not realized how much Francie loved her brother. She was touched by her older daughter's agony. The whole family had that in common—their love of Brian.

At home Stella took Gordon upstairs and pulled off his shoes. "You rest," she ordered. "I'll call you when we get the food set out."

Gordon reached out to her with both arms. She sat down on the bed beside him and gathered him in her arms like a child and soothed his sobbing as best she could. "Why do you lose your best?" he asked. "Why?"

Stella looked across the room to its open door. Tom was standing in the doorway and had heard his father's words.

She got Gordon some aspirin and a drink of water, then went to find Tom. He was lying face down on Timmie's bed. Stella tried to explain that his father meant Brian represented the nation's best, not their family's.

"It's okay, Mother," Tom said, rolling over and looking up at her. "I understand. Brian *was* the best. Brian and Francie. You and Dad must have run out of steam after you produced those two. Ruthie and I are kind of ordinary." Tom's eyes filled with tears. "I loved him too. He was my brother."

"My darling Tom. And he loved you. So much. I was always proud of the way my boys loved each other."

And then it was Tom's turn to be gathered into her arms. Stella tucked her arms around him and put her face against her son's chest, her only son now.

They wept together—mother and son. With Tom, Stella did not have to be strong. With Tom, she could give in to her grief. Their bodies shook against each other, holding nothing back. Beloved Brian. Life would never be the same.

Later Tom drove Stella to the hospital to check on Timmie. Her grandson was playing with his trucks inside the croup tent. Tomorrow or the day after they could take him home.

Gordon had the Distinguished Service Medal enshrined in a velvet-lined case on the mantel in the living room.

Stella avoided the room whenever possible.

With Brian dead, Gordon made a desperate effort to build a better relationship with Tom. He had never been able to communicate with his quiet, ordinary younger son, and in a sad, bittersweet way Gordon loved Tom very much.

But there had always been the nagging doubt that Tom was homosexual. Gordon was afraid he would hate Tom if he discovered this was so. He had been haunted by the fear since Tom was a small boy, and Gordon could not bear the thought of having a homosexual son.

Perhaps his fear came out of that one brief moment in a lifetime when he himself was faced with a homosexual encounter, when something deep inside him reached out and tried to claim him.

But he had been strong. He was blessedly heterosexual. Gordon gloried in making love to his wife. The wonderful normalcy of his other three children had been gratifying. Tom didn't fit in their family.

Gordon had always prided himself on his own handsome and obviously masculine good looks. But Tom was not handsome. His body was soft. Tom did not move as he should. His beard was scant, his voice too high, his chest hairless. Gordon was embarrassed by him. People had always commented about how different Tom was from his father and his brother. Gordon read between their words. They were wondering about Tom. *Was he?*

On occasion, over the years, Gordon had dreamed of the youth in Germany, of Micah, the boy with the frightened eyes and soft woman's mouth. Gordon relegated the Micah chapter of his life to just one of those wartime things—an isolated chapter that had no significance for before and after. And that one instant when he had wanted what the boy offered was an aberration—an understandable lapse by a lonely, confused man who had just survived a long and bloody war.

Gordon thought of the Jewish boy, his narrow shoulders hovering over a typewriter, his slender form carrying a tray in the mess hall, his black hair falling thickly across his white forehead. Such a sad, vulnerable-looking boy. Micah would look at him with those sad black eyes, and Gordon would see the pain of a whole race.

That one horrible moment with Micah had been the worst of the entire war for Gordon. For the longest time afterwards he broke out in a sweat just thinking about it and what would have happened if he hadn't had the presence of mind to push the boy away.

There had been times over the years when Gordon awoke from disturbing, intense dreams revolving around that long-ago night. He would need to wake Stella and make love to her to calm himself. Often his most intense orgasms came with his wife in the dark and quiet of the night.

And there was a recurring nightmare that the other Americans who had been at Dachau, who surely believed the worst about Gordon and Micah, would come forward and make public accusations. Don't vote for this man. He had sex with a little boy at Dachau after the war. Stella and Francie would hear the damning words, and they would doubt him. His darling Francie would not look at him like he was her wonderful daddy, her hero.

Micah, if he was still alive, would now be a man approaching middle life, but he still lived in Gordon's mind as a boy. Unlike his colleagues, Congressman Kendall never went on fact-finding missions to Europe. Or Israel. Rationally, he knew he would never see Micah again. But still, if he were abroad and his picture appeared in a newspaper . . .

He did not want to see Micah again. The dreams were bad enough.

Poor, dear Tom. His soft, full lips and precise cupid's bow were too pretty for a man's face.

Tom went back to Austin to finish his last semester at college. Since Brian had gone to Vietnam, he had lived alone in the Austin house. Gordon called him several times a week—strained calls. How are you? What's new? Your classes going well? Get over your cold? And Gordon wrote long chatty letters to his remaining son that said as little as the calls did.

Over spring break Gordon took Tom on a fishing trip to Canada's Victoria Island. They flew inside the Arctic Circle to a tiny settlement on Cambridge Bay. A gravel airstrip and collection of barracks made up the huge island's only permanent settlement, an American radar station that was part of the Distant Early Warning system. With a congressman on board, the American officer in charge came out to meet the plane. "Any boys from Texas up here?" Gordon asked. There was. A radio specialist from Plano. Gordon hurried off to shake hands.

The buildings were spartan and the plumbing communal. An outfitter flew small groups of men to fish one of the island's countless lakes, each day to a different one. They were all alike—crystal clear with shores barren but for the rocky tundra. The isolation made Gordon uncomfortable, and he worried the pilot might forget on which lake he had left them. What if someone got sick? A heart attack?

It was a Tuesday or Wednesday. They were with a banker from Norman, Oklahoma, and his securities-analyst son from Wall Street. The four men fished together for several hours, discussing the football rivalry between their two home states, examining the implications of Calley's conviction for the My Lai Massacre, exchanging fish stories. After eating their cache of sandwiches, Gordon and Tom wandered over to fish a tiny inlet on the other side of the lake.

"You don't really like fishing, do you?" Gordon asked as he cast out.

"I like the out-of-doors. I liked looking out the window of the plane and seeing all that vast nothingness. But I rather imagine if fish could scream, people wouldn't enjoy fishing quite so much."

"Nonsense. A fish can't feel pain," Gordon said impatiently. He had spent thousands on this trip, and Tom worried about the feelings of fish.

"How do you know that?" Tom asked.

"I just do. Common sense tells me."

They were quiet for a time, the only sound that of the water lapping against the shore.

"Have you decided about law school?" Gordon asked.

"The law school decided for me, Dad. Weeks ago. Mediocre is not their style."

"If you want to go to law school, I'll take care of it," Gordon said.

"No, I don't want it like that. I really wasn't all that hot for the idea anyway. It was just a way of putting off the inevitable decision about my future."

"I can get you a job in Washington," Gordon offered. "You could live at home. Your mother would like that. I would too."

"Washington isn't home for me, Dad. Neither is Austin anymore—not with you and Mom and Ruthie gone and Brian dead."

Brian dead. The words hung in the air between them.

Gordon wandered down the rock-strewn shoreline, needing space from Tom, needing to plan the next topic of conversation.

Tom's gasp caused him to spin around. Tom was staring down at a low embankment. Gordon rushed over to where Tom stood.

It was a skull—unmistakably human. "My God!" Gordon muttered.

"Looks like it's been there for a long time," Tom said. "We'll need to report it."

"I guess so. Although it's probably just an Eskimo."

"*Just* an Eskimo?"

"You know what I mean," Gordon said. "Just a wanderer."

"No. I think you mean it's not important because it probably isn't a white man's skull."

"Now, just what do you mean by that?" Gordon challenged.

"Nothing."

"Yes, you do. Are you calling me a racist?"

"No. More of an elitist," Tom answered. "Let's face it, Dad, you work for the Texas white, moneyed establishment."

"Don't you stand there and judge me," Gordon said, trying to keep his voice from rising. Sound carried such long distances up here in this damned emptiness. So alien it was, like the moon. "You're just a wet-nosed kid. You have no notion what the world is about, and I might remind you that you certainly have been proud enough to have a congressman as a father in the past."

"Yes. I've been very proud in the past. Now sometimes I wish you were something more ordinary."

"Well, sometimes I wish you weren't . . ."

Gordon stopped, horrified. What was he about to say? Queer? No. Naïve. Stupid. Fat. Ugly. Anything but that.

"I've joined the Peace Corps," Tom said evenly, ignoring his father's discomfort. "After graduation I'll train for a few months on some university campus. Oklahoma probably. Then I'll probably be sent to some Third World nation for a couple of years. I may stay. I can teach or clear fields or dig latrines. Whatever. Maybe I'll get rid of some of this fat you find so offensive."

"You can't do that," Gordon said, staring numbly at the skull's empty sockets where some man's eyes used to be. "It would break your mother's heart."

"No, it wouldn't. She suggested it."

Would it make any difference if he told Tom that he loved him? Gordon wondered. Or was it too late for that?

Gordon dropped his fishing rod on the rocks and stumbled over to his son. Clumsily he reached out and grabbed him. Tom was on a higher rock, making the father's head come only chest-high on the son. Awkward. Gordon hugged Tom's pudgy body. "I'm sorry, son. I wish I could do something to make things better for us. I'm so sorry."

Tom stood stiffly with his arms outstretched. Then he relaxed and put his arms around his father. They stood there, in the middle of a hundred miles of barren wilderness, locked in their first real embrace in a long, long time.

Thirty-five

Tom's graduation celebration began on a subdued note. Effie brought her pies with Dr. Pete and Billy and his wife. Kate and Jimmy arrived with their entire brood—Bogey, Sara, Freddy, Jeff, Mark and his fiancée. Mark had finished law school and had gone into practice with his cousin Billy. Jeff had a year left of his veterinarian training and planned to open a practice in New Braunfels when he graduated—farm and ranch animals. Freddy was majoring in physical education at Texas A & M. Sara had finished her freshman year at UT, her gymnast's contours fleshed out now. She was prettier and laughed a lot. The four older Morris children doted on their little brother. Bogey was plump and funny, a droll little mascot for his family.

Brian's former girlfriend Cynthia came to the house before the family left for the ceremony. She hugged Tom and gave him a present—a framed picture of the three of them—Brian, Tom, and Cynthia. It had been taken at Padre Island, on the beach. Cynthia's hair was windblown. They were laughing and waving. Brian had a Lone Star beer in his hand.

Cynthia was also graduating today, and she was newly engaged. Her fiancé was waiting in the car. This was her good-bye to all of them.

"I guess I'll always love Brian," she told Stella in parting.

"Be happy, dear. Brian would have wanted that for you," Stella said.

Conversation among the family was strained. The memory of Brian's graduation one year ago was too fresh with them. The same scene on the same campus. The same family members gathering. But there was a painful difference. There was no Brian, and any cheerfulness seemed forced. The strain between Tom and his father was apparent, and all talk of Tom's Peace Corps plans was carefully avoided. Effie took charge and saved the day from disaster. She organized the picture taking: Ruthie and Billy for the stills, Billy with his movie camera again. Effie got the men to play cards in the living room while they waited for dinner. She sent Ruthie and Freddy to the park with Bogey and Timmie. Over dinner she urged Kate to tell about the time she put the mouse in their teacher's desk drawer at Thornhill School. Soon she had Dr. Pete telling about delivering a baby during a transatlantic flight. At Effie's urging, Jimmy told about the time when, at age ten, he crawled into a cave only to come face to face with a bobcat. Stella found herself telling about how Cousin Carl saved Effie's little brother Chris from drowning in their farm pond. Effie's son Billy recalled his own graduation from the university and how the legless veteran of the Korean War carried an American flag and got a standing ovation. Effie herself told how the three cousins got caught by her father and Uncle Frederick smoking cigarettes behind the barn. "It was the only spanking I ever got in my life," she said. "My daddy cried much harder than I did."

"Lord, I've still got calluses on my rear from all the spankings I got," Kate said. "Papa wore out the razor strap on me."

Gordon told of returning home from the hospital after Tom was born and informing Francie she had a second little brother. "She thought about it for a time, then announced that she would rather have a puppy but she guessed a brother was all right."

Then, when everyone was all relaxed from food and conversation, Effie suggested Billy show the home movies he had taken last year at Brian's graduation.

Stella straightened in her chair. "No, Effie. I don't think any of us are ready to look at those yet."

"No, she's right, Mom," Tom said. "I'd like to have Brian at my graduation."

Stella looked at Ruthie, whose eyes had filled with tears at just the thought of seeing Brian in the movies, but she nodded. "Yes, I think we should see them."

Francie, holding Timmie on her lap, answered her mother's questioning gaze with a nod.

Gordon looked stricken, but he too agreed.

And so it was. Billy went out to his car and brought in the projector and screen. Everyone moved into the living room.

The lights were dimmed, and there was Brian, alive once again, smiling, clowning. Brian in his graduation gown, putting his mortarboard on Timmie. Brian receiving his diploma in front of Old Main. Brian engaging in an imaginary boxing match with Tom. Hugging his sisters.

His mother. His father. Ruthie with her Kodak taking the picture of the family gathering on the front porch. And all of them gathered around the dinner table, the room flooded with artificial illumination from Billy's flood lamps, everyone self-consciously smiling at the camera, the congratulatory banner hanging on the wall. There was Effie bringing one of her pies from the kitchen. Then, abruptly, there were Gordon and Stella with their four children in front of the fireplace. Brian shook hands with his father, kissed his mother, embraced his sisters. The movie ended ironically with the two brothers alone. Brian, who graduated last year and died. Tom, who graduated today without his brother at his side. From the edge of the screen, Ruthie handed Brian his mortarboard. He put it on Tom and pointed at his brother, mouthing words for the benefit of the camera. "He's next." Then Billy had moved in closer with his camera. There was Brian, taller, so handsome and alive, looking at his brother's face with affection and love. The brothers embraced as the film faded, flickered, and ended.

Effie even had tissues ready. She passed them out, and everyone cried and blew their noses and cried some more. Then they watched the film again, and Effie passed out more Kleenexes. The second time, they found themselves smiling through their tears. They even laughed at how silly and self-conscious they all looked, noticing whose hair was grayer and how much Timmie and Bogey had grown.

This time through, Billy stopped the projector right before the end, capturing a while longer the image of Brian and Tom. The brothers.

Tom walked up to the screen, his shadow blocking out his own image. He reached out and touched Brian, part of Brian's face now projected on his hand.

"Good-bye, old man," Tom said.

When Stella walked Effie and Dr. Pete out to the car, she thanked her cousin. "You saved the day from disaster. I don't know how you do it, but you bring out the best in us all."

"Pish posh," Effie said. "Everyone wanted it to be a good day for darlin' Tom. We just needed a little organizing."

Francie took Timmie back to New York with her. "I'm going home with Mommy," Timmie had announced proudly at breakfast the Tuesday after Tom's graduation. Stella looked at Francie's face. It was true.

For two years this little boy had been her constant companion, the focus of her life. True, she had not wanted to assume responsibility for the boy. But she had. And now Francie wanted him back.

What hurt most was how much Timmie wanted to go and be with his mother. Stella had come to think of herself as his mother and had mothered him just as she had her own children. She had experienced the joy and frustrations of motherhood anew with her grandson, and now she found she wanted to fight to keep him. She understood why Kate had fought to have one last baby. Without the prospect of a career, of the elusive "something else" in her life, Stella found she too needed to cling to motherhood. It was all she had.

"No. You can't do that," she told Francie. "You gave me Timmie. He's mine now."

"I never said I wouldn't ever want him back," Francie said.

"I readjusted my whole outlook on life to accommodate Timmie's place in it. I potty-trained him. I nursed him when he was sick. I held him in the night when he was afraid of monsters. I've earned the right to keep him. Surely you won't be so cruel and so selfish as to rip my life apart all over again."

"Selfish?" Francie said incredulously. "You're the one being selfish. Good grief, Mother, he's *my* son. I'd think you'd be happy for me that I'm successful and can provide a good home for my child. He needs to be with me."

Stella went to Gordon and begged. He sat behind the desk in his study—his father's desk from the pastor's study in Tyler.

"I'll miss him too," Gordon said, "but you can't keep her from taking what is hers, Stella."

Stella put both hands on the desk and leaned forward, her face close to his. "Do you realize the only time you ever sided against Francie was when she was in high school and wanted to go to fraternity parties? One time in twenty-seven years. It's always been you and her against whatever I wanted."

"My God, Stella, listen to yourself. Are you jealous of your own daughter? What kind of mother are you?"

"You told me two years ago that I was a good mother and that Francie wasn't cut out for motherhood, that's why I had to take Timmie. Now you tell me I'm a bad mother because I don't want to give him up. Make up your mind, Gordon. Which am I? A good mother or bad one?

Tell me. I'd like to know if I'm a failure at the only real job I've ever had."

"It was never enough for you, was it?" Gordon was speaking in anger now. He got up and walked to the window and spun around. Old hurts showed in his face, in his voice, in his trembling chin.

"Why should it have been all I wanted?" Stella knew she should stop. She was going to say things that should never be said. Don't, she told herself. She knew that words once spoken could never be called back. They would forever float around like so much flotsam, invisible evidence of the wreckage of their lives. But she could feel the words pushing against the dam, cracking it.

"You've had other things," she told him. "You have other things now. What do I have? Actually, motherhood and family were enough for a long time—as long as I had the promise of something else someday. I was all right as long as I had the knowledge that someday I could change the focus of my life, do something that challenged me and not forever be what other people wanted me to be, but you saw to it that I never had that chance. You sabotaged every opportunity I ever had, and look at me now, Gordon. I'm fifty-one years old. Where are the children I've devoted my life to? Francie and Timmie will be in New York. Tom, in order to save himself, must go live half a world away. Ruthie says she wants to graduate from high school a year early and go to college in California to try to find out if she is anything other than your *other* daughter. And Brian is dead. None of them needs me anymore. So what am I supposed to do now, Gordon? Take up needlepoint?"

"I need you, Stella," Gordon said. His shoulders were sagging. He seemed to be shrinking in front of her eyes. "I would like to think that you need me."

"Of course, I need you." Stella's voice was shrill. "I always have. But why did you have to have total devotion? Why didn't you ever want me to have something of my own? Did you think I would love you less if I had something outside of this family? You fool! Don't you see that not having it kept me from loving you more? Couldn't you see that I was suffocating?"

Of course, she was sorry. Even when he called her an ungrateful bitch. Even when he dragged out Charles Lasseter's name again and called her a whore. He told her he was divorcing her, going back to Washington without her. That she could go marry that damned architect—that's probably what she had always wanted.

Stella accepted his abuse. Unless she planned to leave, there had been no point in her bringing up her discontent now. Once maybe, but no longer. She was never going to leave Gordon. She felt more responsible for him than any of the rest, and maybe it had all happened for the best. Ruthie, for example. Stella hadn't wanted a fourth child, and now she couldn't imagine not having her, not knowing her and having her life enriched by Ruthie's presence. And even Timmie. Who was to say that wasn't for the best? Her years with him had been a joy. Yes, she should have left well enough alone. Saying all that to Gordon didn't change a thing. She should have known better. Honesty in marriage was rarely the best policy. She knew that better than she knew anything else.

When Gordon's rage had run its course, Stella comforted her husband as best she could, asked his forgiveness, blamed her behavior on being upset about Timmie.

"I'll see if I can get Francie to reconsider," Gordon offered. "Maybe he can live with us part time at least."

"No. You were right. Timmie belongs with his mother." And Gordon *was* right, Stella realized. Timmie did belong with Francie if Francie wanted him. So what did it all mean? Her own wants and needs and feelings seemed to be of no consequence, but then she herself had set the pattern years ago. Maybe it was required for a family to survive.

At the airport Stella took Timmie into the gift shop to buy him a coloring book for the airplane.

"Are you mad at me, Grandmother?" he asked.

"What for, dear?"

"For going to live with Mommy in New York?"

"No, Timmie. I'm not mad at you. Your mother needs you. And I have your grandfather to take care of, don't I?"

Timmie nodded. "I'll come to visit."

"I know, dear. You and I, we'll always be best friends."

When Timmie came into her life, Stella turned to Charles. When Timmie was taken away from her, she did the same.

Gordon went back to Washington. Ruthie followed when it came time for her school to start in September. Stella planned to stay in Austin until Tom left for his Peace Corps training. Then she would close up the house for the winter. For the first time since they moved to the house on Atterbury Lane, none of the family would be living in it.

She knew even as she was negotiating this plan with Gordon that she would call Charles.

Sometimes it amazed Stella that she still fantasized, having assumed when she was younger that the day would come, a line would be drawn across her life, and she would no longer think of things romantic. But either that was a wrong assumption or the line was drawn much later in life than she would have once imagined. She still yearned. Her yearnings were often vague—just for *something* to illuminate her life, a shimmering curtain of light to veil the harshness, to soften the pain, to diminish the sadness. Life was sad. There was no question of that. But one could hope for moments of joy along the way. Even in the very worst days after Brian's death, at some level Stella knew that she would once again come to hopefulness. And for her, Charles was part of that hope. Children came and left. Marriage was an institution, not a sacrament. Stella no longer planned a career. Perhaps a career would have made no difference after all, but it would have been nice to have had the chance to find out for herself. As a hedge against disappointment, she didn't expect much out of the future. Brian's death taught her the wisdom of that. Her comfort was the belief that there would continue to be those moments of niceness, even beauty and joy. She trusted in their coming. Family. Travel. Books. Nature. And the knowledge that Charles was out there. Maybe the real reason that her love for Charles endured was that she needed it to.

Stella no longer looked at approaching strangers hoping they were Charles. She no longer scanned faces in restaurants. When the phone rang, she simply answered it without speculating whose voice she might hear. She no longer dreamed of the unexpected. She was more calculating now. After Timmie had flown away from her, Stella went to visit Effie in Dallas. She put her suitcase in the guest room and reached for the telephone by the bed.

Mr. Lasseter was out of the office, the secretary informed Stella. He was on site, inspecting the new bank building the firm had designed out on the Central Expressway.

The building was little more than a gigantic erector set of steel girders. No walls. A sign announced it as the future home of Lone Star Bank of Commerce.

Stella crossed back over the expressway and drove down the access road and pulled up beside the other cars in the field-turned-parking lot. Standing beside her car and shading her eyes against the sun, she stared up at the bare-bones structure. He was on the third level. The man in the suit with a hard hat. Charles was looking down at her. Stella waved.

She watched as he rolled up the blueprints, handed them to one of the two men he had been talking to, and came down the exposed stairwell.

He left the metal hat on the bottom step and jumped down from the concrete foundation. He walked toward her slowly, his gaze never leaving her face.

They stared at each other across the hood of the car. She knew he was seeing her almost totally gray hair, her still slender body. He was thinner. There was a scar on his chin.

"I wondered if I'd ever see you again after that awful phone call," he said. "I hope it didn't cause you problems. And if I did, I hope you can forgive me."

"I had to deal with other things. I couldn't handle talking to you then even if there hadn't been other people around."

He walked around the car. "Would it be all right if I kissed you?" he asked.

"I have something I need to say."

He waited. The breeze blew a lock of his hair across his forehead. His hair had thinned. His forehead was crisscrossed by a maze of lines. She remembered when it had been smooth. Only yesterday. Or had it been a hundred years ago? A man in the building above them swore. Traffic noises came from the highway. A distant siren. And oddly enough, a rooster crowing.

"I need to be with you for a time, Charles. I need you to make me whole, to help me find myself again. But if you don't want me using you like that, I'll understand. It's not fair that I show up when I need you and yet don't give you the same privilege."

"Maybe you need one person in your life who doesn't ask for fairness," he said, taking her hand.

"Do you love me that much—that you expect nothing of me?"

He nodded.

"Do you still have Blanche's cottage at Galveston?"

"Yes."

"Well, I was supposed to spend a vacation with you there once, and I never got to. I figure Fate owes me that one. Would you take me sometime?"

"Is today soon enough?" he asked.

"I was hoping for tomorrow. It won't cause you a problem?"

"No. I often go to Galveston. Will you drive down with me?"

Stella nodded. Yes, she'd like that. Going someplace with him in a car.

Then he kissed her.

"The feel of you, the scent of you—oh, God, Stella, I love you more than ever."

Thirty-six

They left early the next morning and drove as far as Huntsville, where they had lunch and toured the small hospital that Charles had designed for the state penitentiary there.

Late that afternoon they crossed the causeway to Galveston Island, where Stella had lived as a bride and Blanche had died. Where the church and parsonage had once stood was now a generic motel. She had put so much of herself into that house, and it was gone.

In spite of a sprinkling of more recent buildings, much of the historic old city that had once been a thriving port retained its Victorian charm. Gingerbread was still on the fine old houses and hotels. The wide streets were still lined with palms and magnolias. Stella was glad. Texans were developing a distressing propensity for eliminating charm and erecting unimaginative, mirror-covered edifices in its stead. The cities were all beginning to look the same, but Galveston—in spite of hurricanes and fires and tourists—was still Galveston.

They stopped on the outskirts of town at a small grocery with bare wooden floors. With great seriousness, they shared every decision. Whole wheat or white bread. Whole or skim milk. Cheddar or Swiss. Orange juice or tomato. Stella started giggling. "This is so silly. Grocery shopping with you. I think in romance novels a discreet family retainer magically puts the food on the table. The lovers don't go shopping for groceries."

"I like our version better. I like shopping with you, and I want to cook it with you too. And do the dishes, make up the bed."

"Share the bed?" Stella said, with affected coquettishness.

"We'll see," Charles said with exaggerated casualness as he pretended to be more interested in selecting some pears.

She kissed him, *really* kissed him. "Oh my God," she whispered as they clung together by the fresh food bins. She could smell the cucumbers and cantaloupes and the moist, manly smell of his skin.

The grocery shopping done, they drove the last few miles out to Blanche's cottage.

The sun was setting as they drove down the rutted lane and crested the line of dunes. The cottage on its stilts was the same she remembered. Weathered to a silvery gray. Isolated. With its shutters closed, the cottage looked as if its eyes were closed, as if it were sleeping.

Stella got out of the car and walked to the dunes. With a deep breath, she gave herself back to this place from long ago. Stella looked down the beach, seeing the young woman she had been, taking an evening walk with her mentor and friend. Dear Blanche. No one had ever really challenged her after Blanche.

"She would have understood about us," Charles said softly.

"Yes. I think she was playing matchmaker when she tried to get us both here at the same time," Stella said, remembering how disappointed Blanche had been when she had to leave. And Stella had not wanted to leave. More than anything else she had wanted to see what the days with Charles would bring, but her father was ill, and she was needed at home. That was the way of life. Duty took precedence over love.

"Strange how things turn out," Charles said. "I could think of nothing but being with you. My wedding was being planned all around me, and my thoughts were here on the island with you and Blanche. I don't think I was ever so disappointed about anything in my life as when I discovered you had left."

"Would it have made a difference?" Stella wondered. "You still would have married Marisa. Maybe it was for the best."

"I'm not sure, Stella. I'd only met you that once, but I thought about you constantly. Aunt Blanche wanted me to break my engagement. She said that you and I would have at least had a chance at a different sort of marriage. I'd like to think that you would have continued your education if you'd been my wife, that you'd be a distinguished professor by now. And maybe I would have been more innovative in architecture instead of making a lot of money. But who knows? I can't imagine not having been married to Marisa, not having had Andy. They're a part of me—my family. It's just that I regret not having you in my life. I feel like I missed the best part."

"My children have been the best part," Stella said, "and the worst. I'm not sure what you would have been. I suspect if we had married, we wouldn't be here now—in love. If we had lived our lives together as two married people, the sight of you now wouldn't fill my heart."

"It's perfect here, isn't it?" Charles said, looking at the calm sea, at the vivid orange and pink sunset, at her face. She was still lovely with her wide brow, her gray eyes, her full mouth and courageous chin. Her hair was more gray than brown now, but it was still smooth and shiny.

They sat for a time, saying nothing, lost in their own reminiscences.

"We're sitting in your painting," Stella said. "Remember that painting?"

"Yes. I had the easel on the porch."

"I kept that painting for years. Then it disappeared. I missed having it around."

Charles took her hand and pulled her to her feet. They kicked off their shoes and walked on the beach in the twilight, the only people in the world.

On the way back up the beach, they gathered driftwood, which they piled on the front porch. Charles unloaded the car while Stella opened the shutters and removed the dust covers from the furniture. Little had changed.

"When I had the sofa recovered, I tried to find a fabric like the old one," Charles said as he carried a sack of groceries to the kitchen. "Marisa came down here once and wanted to redecorate. I wouldn't hear of it. I think it's the last time she came."

"Do you come often?" Stella asked.

"No. But knowing it's here is very important to me."

Stella nodded. She understood. Charles was her cabin on Galveston Island.

He laid a fire in the fireplace while Stella put away the groceries. Together they broiled fresh shrimp and fixed a salad. Stella warmed some buttered French bread in the oven. Charles opened the wine.

With a stack of Blanche's old 78s playing on the record player— "Begin the Beguine," "Night and Day," "Time on My Hands," "Body and Soul," "Georgia on My Mind"—they ate by a firelight whose glow magically seemed to fade away the years. They were young and in love. Even the scratched records sounded new.

Sometimes they would pause midsentence, struck anew with the wonder of being there alone. They would look into each other's eyes and touch hands. The cottage was filled with magic and music and love out of time.

When they went arm in arm to the bedroom, it seemed only right that the bed was floating in a pool of moonlight from the window.

They undressed in silence. Stella felt awkward even though she had come to feel comfortable with him the days they shared in Austin. But that had been two years ago. She couldn't decide if she should hang up her clothes or throw them on the chair.

She left them on the chair. She sensed him waiting for her. Stella turned. The moonlight was kind.

"It feels like the first time again," she said. "I'm not sure what I'm supposed to do."

He pulled her to him, and Stella let out a small gasp as their naked flesh touched. Oh, so good. So very good.

Two years had not diminished the passion. They kissed each other over and over. Hungry for what would come after but wanting the kisses first. And the touching. Everything was like before.

By unspoken agreement, they did not hurry. Stella was consumed with a need to kiss his body. She needed him to see and feel how completely she wanted him. She knelt beside him, feeling like a high priestess performing some erotic rite.

Over and over again they said their words of love. She couldn't say it enough times. She loved him. And he loved her. She was no longer a lovely young woman, but he remembered when she was. In his arms she felt that way again.

And when they came together, Stella wondered if she could die of tenderness. She found herself thinking of the beach, of the eternal ocean. Each wave brought her closer to fulfillment until at last she lost all definition and blended with him.

For a long time Stella hovered between sleep and wakefulness, her body satiated. It was later, perhaps deep into the night, when she woke again, instantly wanting him. He was waiting for her. It was different this time. The tenderness was put aside, and the unspent passion of a lifetime erupted.

They were hungry and wild and lusting. Their breathing was loud and ragged, their bodies covered with sweat. Their kisses were hard and demanding. Stella bit at his neck. Yes, she wanted to take a bite of him. She wanted to taste him—his saliva, his sweat, his semen. When they came, Stella cried out. Charles collapsed on top of her and wept.

Stella stared at the ceiling. My God! What if she had died and never felt anything like that? Did other people get like that? It was frightening. It was glorious and primitive and real.

Poor Gordon. Their sex had always been so careful. She had been dutiful, not lusty, but married sex needed to have limits. Without limits, there came a greater propensity for disappointment than with sex measured in careful doses.

For one week Stella stayed on Galveston Island with Charles. They saw no one else. Charles did not even call home. Marisa would call the island police if she needed him. Stella checked in with Effie every day. And she called Gordon twice, guiltily, from the little grocery store. Yes, she missed him. Yes, it would be like being newlyweds again to live with no children in the house.

Other than Stella's phone calls, they made no contact with the outside world. They talked and walked. They laughed and cried. They built sand castles and collected shells. They swam in the ocean and basked in the sun. They built fires on the beach and drank wine by moonlight. They cooked and ate meals that tasted fantastic. They listened spellbound to music that had been sung before Hitler spelled an end to innocence. They made love. Each time was different.

And they talked—like two people who had spent much of their adult life in solitary confinement. They had so much to share—the good and the bad and the sadness. Stella learned a lot about Gordon in explaining him to Charles. Her husband needed her to love him and their life together to the exclusion of all else. He thought that making her the wife of an important man would enhance her love. He didn't know her at all. He was a good man who compensated for his fears and inadequacies by becoming important.

"Are you going to teach again?" Charles asked.

"I don't know. It's too late for a Ph.D., for a career."

"Do it, Stella. A piece of a dream is better than no dream at all. I think our being here today is a testimonial to that."

The last morning Charles rolled over in bed and looked at her face. "You're leaving today, aren't you?"

"Yes. I must."

"I wanted it to last forever."

"Dearest Charles, nothing lasts forever. Nothing."

The breeze from the ocean billowed out the white curtains. The sound of the gulls greeting the morning filled the sky outside their window. Stella took a deep breath. The air. She'd miss that too.

"I could ask you to stay here with me for whatever time we have." Charles said, softly caressing her earlobe. "I would like that. I wonder if we don't deserve to spend what life we have left together."

How she loved him, Stella thought. What if her life had never been touched by his?

"Deserve?" She rolled over to face him. "What a strange word. People don't get what they deserve." She thought of Brian. Of Charles's son Andy.

"I wish there were a way."

"There are too many other people," she told him softly. "We aren't free to find a way—to think only of ourselves. All we can have are these moments right now, and if we're lucky, others like them another time. I need to believe that we will come here again."

"But what about the pain, Stella? What about the pain of being old and of knowing we won't be together tomorrow, of not knowing when we'll ever be together again? That's too hard. I used to be strong, but I'm not anymore."

She took his hand and kissed its palm. "Yes, there's pain. But there's also the sea and the gulls and the blue, blue sky and times like this. And let's face it, there are dear people we couldn't go back to if we stayed. Think of *that* pain."

He nodded. Yes, he would miss Marisa. It was true.

The drive back to Dallas was subdued. Stella watched Texas out her window and offered a history lesson or two. They had lunch at San Jacinto. She told Charles how Sam Houston secretly had the bridge over the Sims River destroyed, cutting off an escape route for his army and forcing his men to fight for their lives rather than give way to the Mexican forces. She told of Houston's romantic past, the wife in Tennessee, the legendary Cherokee wife in Oklahoma.

Charles offered comments on what he called the "folk architecture" of the region. They took a side trip so he could show her the ruins of what had once been a remarkable round barn.

"I wish I could show you my papa's barn in New Braunfels. It was special too."

History and architecture. Safe topics to get them home, when neither one of them wanted to go home.

When they reached Effie's house, she touched his lips with her fingertips. "You are the love of my life. You are the sun on the ocean and the blue in the sky. Thank you." Then she opened the car door and left him.

Stella didn't cry. Instead she went to bed and slept for almost twenty hours. When she woke up, she cried. Then she called her husband to tell him she would be coming home the next day.

Ruthie was off to college. To Berkeley, as she had planned. She looked so determined as they sat in the huge waiting area at Dulles. How brave she was, Stella thought, to go so far, someplace she had never been before, where she had no friends, no family.

And how she was going to miss her, Stella thought. Ruthie, the child she had not wanted. Such a sensible, self-contained young woman— sometimes Stella felt more like the child than the mother. Had Ruthie ever really been a child?

Stella had tried to make getting ready for college a big mother-daughter experience, but Ruthie would have none of it. "They don't dress up at Berkeley. I'd rather just wait and see what I need when I get there."

"Oh, honey, let me fuss a little, will you? A party dress? A bedspread? Desk lamp?"

Ruthie shook her head. They were sitting in the breakfast room off the kitchen. Their place. It had a window that looked out onto the narrow backyard, and the sun warmed it in the morning. The petunias were getting straggly but still offered a respectable profusion of color. "I need to get the lay of the land first, Mother. I'll get what I need out there."

"You know if you get out there and don't like it, you don't have to stay. You can always go to UT or George Washington University."

"I know," Ruthie said. "You're going to miss me, aren't you?"

Stella nodded, fighting back tears.

Ruthie grabbed her mother's hand and rubbed her cheek against it. "Well, I can tell you now—I almost changed my mind when Francie took Timmie away from you. I thought you'd at least have him when I was gone. It breaks my heart to think of you alone with just Daddy. What are you going to do with yourself, Mother?"

"Oh, I'll manage," Stella said. "There's always congressional wives stuff. Catch up on my reading. I've called the history department at GWU about being an instructor again, but I haven't heard from them yet. Sometimes they don't hire the temporaries until the last minute—after they see how enrollment goes."

Ruthie nodded. "Why don't you go back to Texas and work on your Ph.D.?"

"I've thought of that, honey. That's pretty radical, though. Your father—well, your father needs me. And I'd be so old when I finished that I don't think any institution would have me. And truly, it's not as important as it used to be. I don't have the ambition that I used to have. Maybe I'm getting lazy in my old age."

"You're not old," Ruthie said. "You have no idea how many people tell me how pretty you are."

"Really?" Stella said, pleased.

"Yeah, I don't think they can figure out how a plain Jane like me has such a pretty mom."

"That's not what they're thinking at all," Stella said. "But they might be wondering why you don't curl your hair and wear earrings. Things like that."

Stella had bought Ruthie a bedspread anyway. It had little blue flowers on it that reminded her of Texas bluebonnets. And she gave Ruthie her Grandmother Anna's volume of Emily Dickinson. Ruthie liked Emily Dickinson.

Francie and Timmie came down for the weekend to see Ruthie off. Francie had bought her sister a leather jacket at Saks.

At breakfast this morning Gordon had given her a lovely gold watch. "Good luck," he told her. "I know you'll do yourself proud."

And now they all sat here at the airport, waiting. Gordon had been to church and was still in his suit. Francie was chic in black jeans, a yellow silk blouse, high-heeled shoes. Still so beautiful. People stared. She looked like a movie star. Timmie at five looked like his father. People always thought he was older—six or seven. His hair was like Junior's, blond and curly. He sat holding Ruthie's hand. "I'll write to you as soon as I learn to write," he said. "Now tell me again, how long is it until Thanksgiving?"

"Not too long. First comes Halloween and then Thanksgiving. Until you learn how to write, why don't you color pictures for me and send them? I'll put them up in my dorm room."

Ruthie wore a T-shirt that said "A Woman's Place Is in the Constitution" with new jeans and loafers. She had a fresh permanent. It was too curly, but still it looked better than her unpermed hair. Ruthie was like Kate; she needed curls to soften her jawline. Of course, Kate hadn't had curls in years—just a ponytail.

"You've had your ears pierced!" Stella said, staring at the little gold studs in Ruthie's ears.

Ruthie blushed. "I was wondering if anyone would notice."

"I'll send you earrings," Francie said. "If there's one thing I'm over-stocked on, it's earrings. And don't you just wear studs either. When you heal up, wear outrageous ones. It's fun."

Then it was time. *I can't stand this*, Stella thought. *One by one, they have left me.*

Ruthie hugged her last. "I love you so much, Mother."

"Oh, darling Ruthie, I love you more than you'll ever know."

Stella returned to George Washington University in the fall—they had only one section for her to teach, but maybe she could have two next semester. Connie Brown was no longer there. The black woman had finished work on her Ph.D. and was teaching at a teachers college in Virginia.

More freshmen filed into Stella's classroom. They had changed in three years. These students of the seventies seemed more passive—even their clothes.

The inevitable question came the second week of class—from a girl in the third row. "Is it true you're married to a congressman?" Stella kept such a low profile; she had dared hope she might maintain her anonymity. But that was foolish. "Yes," she said. "And my son is a member of the Peace Corps in the Philippines."

"I'd heard he was killed in Vietnam," the girl said.

"That was my older son. I have—had two sons. And I have two daughters. Now I'd like to hear the lists you compiled of the events in this nation's history you consider the most important."

The girl who asked the questions was the first one who started coming to the office Stella shared with two other G.A.s. Her brother had been killed in Vietnam.

Then others started dropping by during her posted office hours with questions about her lecture or challenges to test grades. And they wanted to talk about choosing a major. What to do about an unfair professor.

458 — Judith Henry Wall

Boyfriend troubles. Homesickness. Dying parents. Stella was amazed. Mostly she listened—and mothered a bit. She had all the time in the world for them.

Stella made the first overtures of friendship toward another middle-aged female instructor. Rosemary Morrison was a professor's wife who'd stopped working on her Ph.D. when her fourth child was born with cerebral palsy.

"Someone had to take care of Johnny," Rosemary explained. "He was such a joy. We all loved him so much."

Johnny had died three years ago. He had been sixteen. Rosemary now served as an instructor when the department needed her. World history to the freshmen.

"Do you think you'll ever finish your Ph.D?" Stella asked.

Rosemary shook her head. "Most of my work was done so long ago, I can no longer apply it. Besides, I don't have the heart for it anymore."

Stella nodded. She understood.

The two women drank their morning coffee at the union rather than brave the history department faculty lounge where the professors hung out.

Stella was given two classes that second semester. Several of her first-semester students continued to drop by. It took a few weeks for any of her new students to come.

"Stella, wake up, please."

Something in Gordon's voice brought Stella instantly awake.

She rolled over in the darkness and touched him. He was sweating and clutching his arm.

"I hurt," he said.

Stella turned on the lamp and looked at his face. His skin was ashen. His eyes were closed.

Fingers of fear grabbed at her heart.

"I'm afraid," he whispered.

"It's all right. You'll be all right," she said, stroking his moist forehead. "But I think we'd better have a doctor take a look at you."

Stella called an ambulance and hurriedly put on some clothes. The taste of her dinner rose in her throat. She kept looking at the bed. Should she be doing something? Another pillow under his head? No pillows?

Take off his sweat-soaked shirt? She returned to the bed and put a cool hand on Gordon's forehead. "How're you doing?"

"Better," he said. "But I'm afraid to move. It feels like it'll hurt more if I move." He looked up at her. His lashes fluttered. "Don't leave me. Please."

"I won't. I'll ride with you to the hospital and either stay with you or bring you home, depending on what the doctor says."

The sound of sirens blared in the distance. Gordon's eyes flew open. "Oh, God, they sound so ominous."

"It sounds to me like help is on the way," Stella said. *Yes, help. Please hurry.*

It was a heart attack. Not a serious one, it appeared, but a heart attack nonetheless.

Gordon was admitted to the coronary care unit. Stella was allowed to be with him only ten minutes an hour.

In the first hours after Stella brought him to the hospital, she sat in the corridor alone, then with Francie, her mind playing out possibilities. She found herself remembering a short story she had read years ago by one of the early feminist writers—"The Story of an Hour" by Kate Chopin. It had been in an anthology of women's writings that Blanche Lasseter had once lent her. For one hour the woman in the story had mistakenly thought her husband was dead. She was grief-stricken. She had loved him—sometimes. She knew how distraught she would be to see his dear hands folded in death. She did not want him to be dead—except that his death meant she would no longer be married. Gradually as the hour progressed, the woman saw the long procession of years that would belong to her absolutely. But the report of his death had been a mistake. An hour after she had been told of his death, her husband came home. When she saw him, the shock was so great that she collapsed on the stairway and died.

Gordon's illness brought "what if" kind of thoughts to Stella's head. She didn't want to have such thoughts. She felt guilty thinking about her husband's death—as though recognizing its possibility might make it so, that if he did die, it would somehow be her fault for having acknowledged that her grief would not be complete, that she would not feel the need to throw herself on the funeral pyre. But Stella's mind kept wanting to jump on ahead, to endless summer days on Galveston Island with Charles. To Tom's home in the Philippines. She missed Tom. But for that to happen, another had to die. No, not just "another." Her husband.

Stella didn't want Gordon to die. He was the father of her children. He had been at the center of her life for far more years than he had not. Her feelings for him were so ingrained in her being that they were irreversible. She would always think of herself as his wife, and she was wise enough to know that freedom would not be without its own set of problems. Stella wanted Gordon to get better quickly so she could put her confusing thoughts to rest.

He was so afraid. Gordon needed her more than ever now. Part of her gloried in being needed by her husband, and part of her resented it. Such is the way of life. She had learned that lesson well. Seldom are things all one way or the other.

He was given a private room on the fourth day. Stella slept on a cot in his room. Francie offered to trade off with her, but Gordon wanted Stella. Stella felt foolishly pleased.

But when he was out of danger, Stella started meeting her class again. Her leaving upset Gordon. "Look, Gordon, if you were dying, I'd stay, but you're doing fine. I feel responsible for my classes. I haven't gone for a whole week."

"I miss you when you're gone," he said. "I feel better when you're here with me."

"I won't be gone long. I'll just teach the class and come right back. Francie will be here."

She brought papers to the hospital to grade while Gordon napped. At the end of the second week he went home.

Together, with the help of his physician, Stella and Gordon worked out his diet and his exercise schedule. Magazines were full of low-cholesterol diets these days. The way American women had been feeding their husbands was all wrong, it seemed. Stella prepared Gordon's low cholesterol meals and often took walks with him. They read books and newspaper articles on health-related subjects, sharing long passages with each other. They hadn't talked so much in a long time. Soon Gordon's walks became slow jogs. Then faster jogs. After a few months Stella couldn't keep up with him.

Ruthie decided not to come home for Thanksgiving, but they all had a good Christmas together. Francie couldn't get away long enough for Austin, so they stayed in Washington for the holidays. Stella missed her home in Austin, but the nation's Christmas tree was spectacular, and the one in the living room of their Georgetown home was lovely even if the family ornaments were still in the attic back in Texas. Francie, Ruthie, and Timmie decorated the tree with red bows and silver ornaments. Timmie took great care to make the icicles hang straight. Gordon went out of his way to be nice to Ruthie, asking her about her classes and insisting she go with him to pick out Stella's gift. One chilly afternoon they all made the beautiful drive along the Potomac to Mount Vernon. There were few tourists, and the attendants didn't mind answering their questions at length. Timmie was curious about everything. Stella could see him beginning to acquire a sense of what life was like before people had cars and toilets and telephones.

Christmas Day they called Tom, passing the phone around, laughing and crying and asking dumb questions about Christmas weather in the Philippines and what time it was there.

"Are you all right?" Stella asked. "*Really* all right?"

"Except for missing you," Tom said. "Your letters are wonderful. Will you call again sometime when it's just you?"

Six months after his attack, Gordon was healthier looking than before and had become a true fanatic about diet and exercise.

"I feel like a teenager," he said.

He began acting like one too. He bought clothes that were too young and wore his hair too long. He took to wearing fashionable sunglasses, and his conversation become peppered with "with-it" expressions. He bought and restored an M-G roadster. Red, of course.

And he wanted sex almost every night—and not just the perfunctory sex that had become their custom.

"I prefer to have it be more of a special occasion than an every-night occurrence," Stella protested, trying to curtail his revised interest in their sex life. The last years of her marriage, Stella had been far more concerned with avoiding sex than having it. And Gordon was usually as disinterested as she was. He wanted her to come to bed when he did— but not for sex. "I sleep better when you're here," he would tell her. "You can finish that book tomorrow." It was true. She had plenty of time in her tomorrows for reading, for preparing her lectures. The constant busyness that had been her life for all her adult years had ended rather abruptly. But she preferred to read herself to sleep. Lying in bed beside her sleeping husband and staring into the darkness was torture. Thoughts she could keep at bay during the daytime were unfettered at night. Brian. Charles and Galveston. The rest of her life.

Usually whenever Gordon wanted sex, Stella accommodated. It was much easier than dealing with the alternative. If she put him off, he wanted explanations. He would examine their sex life, their marriage, ask her if she was happy, want to know if she thought of other men. It was easier just to do it. Gordon seemed to think it was some sort of game, that if he could get her to agree to sex, she would automatically enjoy it, but then she never gave him cause to think otherwise. Sex was a duty. Like cooking. Something you might enjoy if you didn't have to do it. And now Stella was almost afraid to enjoy it. If she enjoyed it, she might think of Charles.

So Stella endured. She knew from past experience that husbands, like children, were usually going through some phase that would pass if given time. Stella waited patiently for Gordon's sports car phase to end.

Stella was writing a letter to Tom at her desk in the bedroom when the phone rang. She crossed to the bedside table to answer it.

As soon as she heard Effie's voice, Stella knew something was wrong. Her grip tightened on the telephone.

"Is Gordon home?" Effie asked.

"No. Did you want to talk to him?"

"No, I didn't want to tell you this with him standing beside you."

"Tell me what?"

"I read something in the evening paper," Effie said. "Your friend, Charles Lasseter . . ."

Stella waited. Already she knew, but she had to hear it. Her heart was pounding. It hurt. It felt as if blood would come bursting out her ears.

"Oh, Stella honey, I'm so sorry. He's dead. For a couple of months actually. I noticed his name in an article about the grand opening of the new bank building out on Central Expressway. It said the building was designed by the late Charles E. Lasseter of Lasseter and Cochran Architectural Design, Inc."

"Maybe it's a mistake," Stella said. Yes, it had to be a mistake. How could she live in a world without Charles? She had loved him since she was twenty.

Her knees wouldn't hold her. She sat on the side of the bed.

"I just called his firm to make sure," Effie said. "In December. Stella, are you all right?"

"No."

"You loved him, didn't you?"

"Yes, I loved him."

"Oh, honey, I should've flown back there to tell you. I shouldn't have called you on the phone."

"No, I have to deal with it by myself—before Gordon gets home."

"I'll come right now. Tonight."

"No, Effie, really."

"He must have been a very special man."

"Yes. Very special."

"I'm sorry, Stella."

"I have to hang up now," Stella said. "I'll call you tomorrow."

Stella stood, then sat back down again. How could he have been dead without her sensing it? He had been alive in her thoughts, yet he was dead, and she didn't know how or when. She should have felt the moment of his death. He was the man she had loved for a lifetime. She should have been with him when he breathed his last. She should have kissed his lips in death.

She didn't even know where he was buried.

Stella put her hand over her mouth to quiet the whimpering sounds she was making. *Charles. My darling.*

She felt a part of herself shriveling up and dying—a part deep inside, the secret place where Charles had lived within her and made her strong, made her feel worthy.

But even as she grieved, she looked at the clock. Gordon would be home any minute. He was already late.

Stella sucked back the whimpering and willed the tears not to flow, but they came anyway.

Tears ran down her cheeks as she looked around the room she shared with her husband of thirty-two years. It wasn't her room or his room, but their room. Gordon had a study. She didn't have a room.

By her dresser, hanging on both sides of the mirror, were assorted family pictures. Her parents standing stiffly on the porch of their ranch house. Gordon as a boy standing with his parents on the front of the parsonage in Tyler. Stella and Gordon on their wedding day. Gordon in uniform. Stella with Kate and Effie on Effie's wedding day. The children as babies. Francie's tenth birthday. The boys in their baseball uniforms. Ruthie in her Brownie uniform. The entire Behrman clan at Hannah and Herman's fiftieth anniversary. Stella and Gordon on their twenty-fifth wedding anniversary. The dear faces of those she loved. But Charles wasn't up there. She had never had a picture of Charles, and if she had one, she would have had to keep it hidden.

Stella got up from the bed and walked to the window. She stared out at the tree-lined street with all its other tasteful Georgetown residences. It was a sedate street populated with respectable people she nodded to from time to time. It had never felt like home. For one week that cottage on Galveston Island had felt more like a home to her than any place ever had before.

She walked around the room, touching things, straightening pictures that didn't need straightening, fluffing the pillows on the bed, rearranging the magazines on the bedside table. A house stayed so neat with no children around.

At her dressing table she picked up a seashell and held it to her ear. "For my love," Charles had said. "A perfect shell to remember our perfect time together." He was wearing worn jeans, a plaid shirt with its tail out. They were throwing bread in the air for the gulls to catch midflight when he suddenly stooped over to pick up the one shell that had caught his eye. The sun was so bright on the water it made her squint, so warm on her face and arms it made her drowsy. Soon they had gone back to the cottage to make love lazily and doze in each other's arms.

The shell was her only memento of Charles. Stella kissed it. "Farewell, my love," she whispered, and clutched the shell between her breasts.

When she looked in her mirror over her dresser, Stella realized she was old.

Stella sank to her knees, bending over the shell. The sobs welled up inside her. Her body shook with them. Her chest was being stabbed from the inside out. Oh, God, how it hurt.

She heard the door slam. Gordon was calling to her from downstairs. Whenever he walked in the door, he called out to see if she was there. If she wasn't at home, he would go into his study and sit there until she returned. Once she had left him a note explaining her absence, telling him to go ahead and eat without her. But the note had fallen behind the table, and he hadn't seen it. It was almost nine o'clock before Stella came home, and he was still sitting there in the study. He hadn't eaten dinner, read the paper, watched the news, or opened his mail. "I thought you'd left me," he had said.

Stella stood and wiped her face. "Up here," Stella called to him. Her voice sounded wrong. Maybe he wouldn't notice.

He would come up shortly. She would kiss his cheek and ask him if the Cartwright bill passed, then they would decide about dinner—a bite here or eat after the reception the vice president was hosting for the Texas congressional delegation.

She put the shell back on the dresser and reached for a tissue to blow her nose. She wouldn't cry anymore right now. She'd go rinse off her face and put on some makeup. For Gordon.

The knowledge that Charles was gone from her world left Stella with an emptiness that she knew would never go away. There was no promise of Charles in her tomorrows. She had needed that promise more than she had known.

She still had her family. Gordon and her three living children. Timmie. Other grandchildren yet to be born. Kate and Effie. Nieces and nephews. And behind them were her dead son, parents, aunts, uncles, generations. Family was her future and her past.

But oh, to live in a world without Charles, without the hope and dream of Charles . . .

Thirty-seven

Your presentation was great," the redheaded boy who sat behind said to her as they filed out of Latin class. Ruthie had just given her oral report. Her topic was Nero's wife, and she had delivered it in the first person. She had crawled inside Octavia's skin and described what it was like to live in decadent Rome, what it was like to be an empress and married to a madman who had his stepbrother and mother murdered. Octavia gossiped about her friends and discussed fashion and hair styles. Then she told how her husband had fallen in love with the beauteous Poppaea Sabina, how she feared her husband would soon have her murdered. The professor had been impressed and said he was going to require first person for the oral reports from now on.

"Thanks," Ruthie told the redheaded boy. "I was afraid it would seem weird, but I really got off on *being* the woman instead of just writing about her."

"Are you as serious a student as you seem, or do you go out?" he asked.

"I haven't gone out, but I'd like to," Ruthie said. Her heart started to flutter. Was he going to ask her out? She wanted him to, and she didn't want him to. What would she say if he did? What would she wear? She wished she'd washed her hair this morning. He wasn't good-looking, but neither was she. "What about you?" she asked. "You seem like a pretty serious student yourself."

"I work hard, but I'm not brilliant. You want to go to a movie or something Saturday night—if you don't have to study or something?"

"I guess so."

They walked along for a while in silence. Ruthie desperately tried to think of something to say to him besides "pretty day, isn't it?" All the days since she'd arrived in Berkeley had been pretty.

"Do you know my name?" she asked.

"Yeah, Ruthie something."

"I don't know yours."

"Greg Easterling."

"I'm Ruthie Kendall."

"Where you from?" he asked.

"Austin."

"Texas?"

"Yeah. And you?"

"Guam."

"Guam?"

"Yeah. My dad's military. Stationed there. I'm a tremendous disappointment. The only son is supposed to follow in footsteps. I came here instead of West Point. Pre-med."

"Me too," Ruthie said. "Pre-med, that is. I never planned to go to West Point." She liked walking along with this boy. They were both going to major in pre-med. That'd give them something to talk about. She liked his red hair. Her cousin Jeff had red hair. So did Aunt Kate. God, she had a date for Saturday night. A real date.

"I'm probably really dumb to admit this," Ruthie said without looking at Greg Easterling from Guam, "but I didn't date in high school."

"Me either," Greg said.

When Ruthie got back to her dorm room, she couldn't decide whom to call first, her mother or Francie. Francie could tell her what to wear, but she wanted her mom to know first.

Tom sent his parents a picture of himself, standing in a field of sugar cane on Jolo Island of the Philippine's Sulu Archipelago. His once-soft body looked lean and hard. In another picture he was with a group of students in front of a tiny school. His students were Moros tribesmen. "Absenteeism is a real problem," he wrote. "Their families earn a living from the ocean and very often take the children off on extended fishing expeditions or to dive for pearls. But when they are here, they learn. It's exciting."

A year later a third picture arrived, showing Tom with a small, pretty Filipino woman—another teacher in the school. Tom's hair was thinning. He would be bald soon.

He wrote:

I'm needed here. This out-of-the-way island is now my home. I will teach its children, and by the time you read this, I'll be married to one of its daughters. My skin is now as brown as theirs. I like it that way. When Maria and I get our house built, I want you both to visit us. And my sisters. Please.

Stella framed this snapshot and added it to the wall by her dresser. She liked the determined way her daughter-in-law smiled. "I will be happy," it seemed to say. Her next grandchild would have brown skin—a pleasing thought. She thought of the children of the Mexican laborers who had come and gone from her father's farm. Pretty little children with solemn dark eyes. What would Frederick Behrman have thought of brown-skinned descendants? Stella wondered. When Stella and Kate were little, they were allowed to play with the Mexican children. When they were older, Stella remembered how cross Papa would get if Kate went off exploring the countryside with one of the Riveras children. Would her father have been like Gordon and feigned acceptance at the union of one of his own to a brown-skinned woman? Or would he have found scripture that damned it? Stella promised herself she would go to the Philippines the instant Tom and Maria's first child arrived. She wanted a picture of herself holding that baby to put up there with her pictures. Maybe Timmie could go with her. That would be nice—Timmie in the picture too.

Maybe they could go before a baby arrived—when the house was completed.

Stella missed Tom a lot. He belonged in his new home, but she wished she could hug him once in a while and that phone calls from half a world away weren't so stiff. Sometimes she wished she lived there with him instead of here in Georgetown.

Tom loved to teach. Her son. That pleased Stella. Her teaching was important to her. She was only a lowly instructor in the GWU history department, but she did a good job.

Gordon began writing to Tom again—long rambling letters discussing everything from the national debt to indigestion. Even theology, a topic he had avoided for many years. He even confessed his doubts.

Tom's letters were short. Sometimes his wife added a note to them. Maria's notes began to increase in length, offering comments on Gordon's letters, asking his opinion, offering her own. Soon Gordon started his letters "Dear Tom and Maria." Maria's letters grew longer with Tom offering greetings at the end. Gordon eventually wrote letters to Maria that said, "Give Tom our love." Yet, he resisted visiting, seemingly content to keep his relationship with his son and daughter-in-law confined to the pages of letters.

Francie and Timmie were often with Stella and Gordon in Washington. Francie would come down to attend the official functions with her father that Stella begged off. Every six or eight weeks Stella would ride the train up to visit them in their New York apartment. The three of them would go to a Broadway matinee and out to dinner. Timmie was tall for his age and liked school "most of the time." He seemed especially good at art— like his father. He adored his mother.

"You must send your Grandmother Bonifield some of your pictures," Stella said. "She paints, you know."

Stella never quite understood why Francie had reclaimed her son. At first she thought Francie was concerned with public censorship—a mother who did not raise her own son. She was a public figure with many facets of her private life common knowledge, so perhaps fear of criticism did play a part in her decision. And Timmie returned to his mother as a well-mannered, toilet-trained child who could feed and dress himself— not the totally dependent infant who had frustrated Francie so. But Stella wondered if her daughter had taken her son back because she realized her mother no longer considered him a burden. Stella had wanted to keep Timmie with her always. Was the day that Stella found herself wanting to raise the boy the day some perversity in Francie determined this would never be so?

Francie had become her mother's nemesis. Why? Because her mother had dared to have a face and a voice? Because her mother had striven for a career and identity—the very things Francie herself strived for? It made no sense.

In a way, however, Francie was more like Blanche Lasseter than Stella had ever been herself. Blanche and Francie. Women who did not define themselves as wives and mothers. Yet the irony of ironies was that even these women wanted their own mothers to be just that—mothers. Not women who competed with their daughters for space and attention. Mothers who when they died could be remembered as saints.

But whatever the reason Francie had taken Timmie back, she and her son were getting along just fine. Francie, it seemed, had discovered she not only loved her son but enjoyed having him around. He complemented her life. The men in her life liked playing father to him. And Timmie loved his mother more than he did his grandmother. That was only natural and had nothing to do with who loved him more, but it hurt. Stella was jealous of her own daughter. Funny—Gordon had always accused her of that.

Francie was earning a reputation as a tough television journalist on the local NBC affiliate. Her interviews were insightful and often intimidating. Her goal was a network spot, but she fretted about the passing years. After thirty, her chances would diminish. Women had fewer years to make it than men.

Gordon and Francie had long conferences about his political future. He trusted her judgment, especially in public relations and media matters. Francie was ambitious for her father.

The summer after Ruthie's freshman year at Berkeley, Stella and her youngest child took what they referred to as their "trek." Using their house in Austin as home base, for most of the summer they traveled around Texas. They never drove by a historical monument without stopping. If a town had a museum, they checked it out. They stayed only in hotels built before 1940 and ate only in locally owned restaurants. They roamed through cemeteries and battlegrounds. They enjoyed the "Piny Woods" of east Texas and drove by the cotton fields of the central prairie and the rice fields of the coastal plain. They crossed grasslands and the vast nothingness of the Panhandle. They roamed the untouched seashore of Padre Island and they hiked in the untouched wilderness of Big Bend. They visited ancient Spanish missions—their favorite was the graceful San Jose Mission in San Antonio. They ate hush puppies and fried catfish. They enjoyed freshly picked fruit from the orchards in the valley of the Rio Grande and the aroma of freshly picked roses in Tyler. They talked with people in diners and service stations—just plain folks who called Stella "ma'am."

If Ruthie became bored with her mother's running history lessons, she never said so. Indeed, she asked questions that showed she listened and absorbed. She became all the students to whom Stella had never taught her beloved Texas History. Stella became for that short time the Blanche in her daughter's life, for it wasn't just historical facts they discussed. Women's history was of special interest to Ruthie. She learned about Susanna Dickenson, heroine of the Alamo. Cynthia Ann Parker, mother of Quannah Parker. Angelina Belle Eberly, heroine of the Archive War. "Lady Lucy" Holcombe Pickens, the only woman whose face appeared on Confederate money. Lizzie Johnson, cattle queen. And others whose stories were never written in books, whose names and histories Stella had discovered in archives, usually in private journals and letters. Ruthie pondered the lives of the Texas women who lived for the most part in service of others, in the shadow of their men.

"I want to be my own person," Ruthie said. They were leaning against the railing atop the lighthouse at Port Isabel, watching the fishing boats come into the harbor at twilight.

"Then don't have children," Stella said.

Ruthie was shocked. "Are you sorry you had children?"

"I didn't say that, but being 'your own person' is very difficult when you're a mother."

"People are different now. Women expect to have careers."

"Does your young man—Greg—expect his future wife to have a career?"

"Not really," Ruthie admitted. "At least not as her primary focus. He thinks women should stay home with their kids when they are little. I told him about fifty-percent parenting."

"What's that?"

"We discussed it in my women's study class, and there have been articles in that new magazine—Ms. Women and men should share parenting responsibilities when children are little—maybe both working part-time, instead of the man working full-time and the wife staying home with the kids and losing out on a career."

"That's a lovely concept, but I think it would be a rare man willing to give up that much during the early years of his career when he's trying to make his mark."

"Women have to. It's only fair."

Stella smiled. "Perhaps, but as dear cousin Effie pointed out years ago, 'Somebody has to be the mother.' And the mother is almost always the mother. Just don't think there are easy answers."

"If you had it to do all over again, would you still have gotten married and had children? And please try to forget this is your own daughter asking."

"I would never suggest to any woman that she not have children," Stella said, carefully feeling her way. "Children are the best and the worst of life. Motherhood brings the most satisfaction and the most frustration. If a woman doesn't have children, she lops off both ends of the spectrum, and that leaves only the safe, more complacent middle ground. I think most women should have children, but by doing so, they will lessen their chances of finding fulfillment in other areas—even in their marriage. Maybe I just wasn't clever enough to have both motherhood and career. Blanche Lasseter asked me once, if I had to choose, which would I take. I told her marriage and motherhood. I still feel that way."

"You shouldn't have had to choose," Ruthie said. "It's all Daddy's fault."

"It's no one's fault," Stella snapped.

"Why did you marry someone like Daddy?" Ruthie persisted. "Why didn't you marry a man who would have been proud to have another sort of wife?"

Stella considered being angry. A daughter criticizing her father made Stella very uncomfortable—still. But Gordon was the yardstick Ruthie had been given against which to measure the men who came into her life. If she married, she needed to know whether to choose a man just like her father or someone different. She had a right to ask.

"I only knew one man who might have been like that, and he was taken. But I've had a good life. I never got to pursue a career in academia, but I've loved being a mother. Most of the true joy I've had in my life has been associated with you children."

"And its great sadness," Ruthie reminded her.

"Yes. Brian. There is no sadness like losing one of your children— absolutely none. And even when you are spared this, the fear of it haunts you always. Children make you vulnerable, but in spite of the pain, I wouldn't have missed Brian for the world. Can you imagine never having known him?"

"I miss him a lot," Ruthie said. "He was so good. It's hard to accept, isn't it?"

Stella nodded. She would have to wait a few minutes before she could talk again. Both women turned and made their way down the spiral staircase. It was time to eat. They'd planned to have freshly caught Gulf shrimp, cole slaw, and Mexican beer.

Stella rethought that conversation over and over again in the days to come. She had left out something—something important but vague and hard to define. Children, marriage, career were not all there was. There was love. Or maybe adoration was a better word. Somehow Stella knew that Greg did not adore her daughter and that Ruthie would be forever torn between her husband's expectations and her own needs. That made Stella sad. But most marriages were like that, and people would always marry and have families.

Those three months of off-and-on trekking were among the most satisfying of Stella's life. The child she had not wanted had grown up to become her friend. More than any other human being, Ruthie was her link with the future. She wouldn't have missed having Ruthie for the world, either. Or Tom. Or Francie. Her children were a part of her like nothing else.

"You love Texas, don't you?" Ruthie had asked as they drove past a field of waving wheat near Woodson in Throckmorton County.

"Only because it's home. Once I would have said I loved it because of its grandeur and history and uniqueness, because of the bluebonnets in the spring and the beauty of Gulf Coast and the pride of Alamo and so many crazy-quilt reasons. But now I know the real reason it's so special to me is that it's home. It's where I was born, where my children were born, and, God willing, where I'll die."

The summer ended with a funeral. Aunt Hannah died. Once again the family gathered. Effie looked tired, even old.

In the spring they all gathered again for Uncle Herman's funeral. He had lived only eight months without his beloved Hannah. Stella thought then that Effie was sick.

"Why do I want to ask if you're sure?" Effie said. "Of course, you wouldn't tell me something like that if you weren't sure. And I think I've known for some time now—that it wasn't going to go away, that the chemotherapy wasn't working."

Pete sat beside her on the sofa in the added-on family room of Effie's Turtle Creek home, the same home she had lived in with William. The family room had been Effie's idea—to make a place where she could enjoy her second husband that didn't carry the ghost of her first. She had also combined two smaller bedrooms to make a new master bedroom and moved the personal mementos of her first marriage to trunks in the attic.

"That's the first thing everyone says," Pete said. There were tears in his eyes. "They all ask, 'Are you sure?' Then, 'Isn't there something else I can try?'"

"Poor Pete. How awful this must be for you and how you must have dreaded telling me. Why didn't you let one of the other doctors in the clinic do it instead?"

Pete laughed and shook his head in disbelief. "Only my darling Effie would worry about how *I* felt at a time like this. Would you rather I'd let someone else break the news?" he asked, wiping his eyes. "I thought about not telling you. But then that would be like lying to you, and sooner or later you would know."

"I wouldn't have wanted anyone else to tell me, and I wouldn't have liked us to lie or play games during our last months together." Effie picked up her coffee cup and stared at it, then replaced it on the glass-topped coffee table. "You've helped me live, dearest Pete. Now will you help me die? Since I have to do it, I'd like to do it well."

"It will be an honor."

Stella cried. Effie comforted her. "It's not for a while, honey. Pete says I could still have a year or so."

"But I thought you were getting better," Stella protested. "Pete seemed so certain the chemotherapy would work. Does Kate know?"

Effie nodded.

"Oh, Effie, I feel so sorry for Kate and me, having to live in a world without you."

"Yes, it's been you and Kate and me for as long as I remember. But one of us has to be first."

"Yes, but I thought we'd be old women like our mothers were."

"Me too," Effie said, nodding. "I always thought I wouldn't mind so much when we were old and ugly. We're not young, but we're not old either."

Later, as they sat in Stella's backyard on the glider and listened to the cicadas sing their evening song, they talked again.

"Are you afraid?" Stella asked.

"Yes. A lot sometimes. But other times it's less frightening than I thought it would be. I worry about Pete."

"How's he taking it?" Stella asked.

"He'll be fine for the time being. I'll need him to take care of me, and that will make him feel good—to do for me. But I worry about afterwards. You must look after him, Stella. Keep including him in family things and don't let him get lonely."

Stella laughed. "So I'm to look after Pete. Effie, do you know that before William died, he came and asked me to look after you? He didn't think you were capable of taking care of yourself. He thought you'd be lost without him."

"And I was," Effie said. "That's why I married Pete. Oh, we both know that I could have managed the business part of my life just fine, but managing isn't living. I needed to be the wife of a good man to enjoy life. That's the way I am. And I've done such a good job that I'm not sure how Pete will survive without me. I think of my poor dear papa after Mama was gone. For very selfish reasons, I've allowed Pete to make me his life. He is happy through me."

"Perhaps he'll remarry. Does that thought bother you?"

"Some," Effie admitted. "But I think he should so he'll have good meals and a social life. I wouldn't want him to love her as much as he loved me, though."

"I doubt if that's possible," Stella said.

"Maybe now Billy will finally run Texas Central," Effie said with a sigh. "Funny how important that airline got to me. I was two people. Pete's wife and a businesswoman. Strange."

The old glider squeaked as they pushed it back and forth. The air was still. Ruthie had the television on in the house. Stella recognized the theme from "Bonanza." She held out her hand and Effie took it. Back and forth the glider went. Back and forth.

"Remember the swing on your parents' front porch?" Effie asked.

"Funny, I was just thinking the same thing. This time of evening we used to go sit there and talk. You and Kate and I."

"I love you, Stella."

"I love you too, dearest Effie. Thank you for being my friend and my cousin."

They held hands and wept silently as they rocked back and forth in the squeaking glider. Two aging woman. One dying.

Stella drove with Effie back to Dallas. They went to Kate's. The three women stood in Kate's entry hall, staring at one another. Their days together were numbered. Effie opened her arms to them. "Haven't we been the luckiest three girls in the world to have each other?"

After they cried some, Effie got a bottle of wine out of Kate's refrigerator. "You go put Bogey to bed, Kate. Then I think we should get a little drunk. Or maybe a lot."

They drank the first bottle and then a second. Kate dragged out a box of snapshots she had never bothered to put in an album. "I really was pretty, wasn't I?" Effie said critically, holding up a picture of herself at age fifteen. "I wish Pete could have seen me then. You know, he's been such a dear husband. I've really been lucky. Two good men in one lifetime. Not many woman can say that. And I've always had you two. We've been good for each other, haven't we?"

Effie looked at her sister cousins, her blue-blue eyes filling again with tears. "I won't end it like William did, but you two are going to have to help me. I have a feeling that dying will be the hardest thing I've ever done. Whenever I get to feeling sorry for myself, remind me how lucky I've been."

Effie refused further chemotherapy. "What's the point if I'm going to die anyway? I'm tired of wigs. I want to grow my hair back."

"But if it might buy you some more time?" Pete said.

Effie considered her answer for several days. The possibility of a few extra weeks or months of nausea and no hair didn't seem worth it.

Her hair grew back silver and as thick as before. But even without debilitating chemotherapy, keeping her looks was a losing battle. Her flesh seemed to evaporate, leaving only skin on bones.

Stella stayed with Kate in Dallas. They spent every day with Effie, and Pete stayed with her every night.

Her breathing was labored, but Effie wanted to talk. They talked for hours on end. Effie would doze off, then waken and pick up the conversation exactly where she'd left it. New Braunfels. Their parents. Their children. And Effie talked about William.

"I remember the first time I saw him," she said. "He was the handsomest man I'd ever seen. Handsomer than John Barrymore or Clark Gable. And do you know what he said? He said I was lovely—not pretty, or a foxy lady, but lovely. And he was so courtly. Do you remember our wedding? Wasn't that a day? And my mama. She was so wise. She made my going-away dress, and my nightgown. I kept it on the first night. I loved being married to my William. And Pete. I've loved my sweet Pete. But William—he was the love of my life. Oh, God, even though I'm ugly, I wish he were here with me now."

The pain became intense. Her pancreas, the oncologist said, as though that explained things. He increased the morphine. It helped the pain but made her breathing even more labored.

The last day, Effie's mind kept wandering back to William. Pete was there. He heard. Stella hurt for him, but then he too had loved before.

"Do you remember my papa's favorite hymn?" Effie asked suddenly, grabbing Stella's hand.

"Is the pain worse? Should I call the nurse?"

Effie cried out. Her skeletal body shook with the pain. "The hymn," she gasped. "Do you remember the hymn?"

Stella tried to remember back all those years. Effie's nails dug into her flesh. A hymn. Uncle Herman sang lots of hymns. He liked to sing at church. You could always hear his voice booming over all the rest.

"I remember," Kate said from the other side of the bed.

"Sing it for me," Effie gasped.

Kate voice croaked. She had trouble making it sound like singing. As soon as Stella recognized the words, she joined in.

> "We've a story to tell to the nations that
>   shall turn their hearts to the right,
> A story of truth and mercy, a story of peace
>   and light—a story of peace and light.
> For the darkness shall turn to dawning, and
>   dawning to noonday bright,
> And Christ's great kingdom shall come on earth,
>   the kingdom of love and light."

Effie managed a smile. Then her body shuddered. Stella, Kate, Pete all held their own breath waiting for Effie's next one. There was none. Effie was dead.

Kate and Stella drove to New Braunfels for Effie's funeral as they had done so many times before for the funerals of Cousin Carl, their father, their mother, the aunts, the uncles. This time it was Effie in the casket in front of the sternly majestic altar of the Reformed Protestant Church. It was Effie, the cousin who had been a constant, whose good humor and love had supported them for a lifetime—it was Effie who was carried out to the ancient cemetery and buried among all those other Behrman dead.

The big post-funeral family dinner was held at the new home Effie's youngest brother Chris had built on the edge of town. It looked strange to see these rows of modern ranch-style homes in the town that had once been only white-frame, tin-roofed houses with big front porches where people sat of a summer's evening and visited with passing neighbors out for a stroll. Chris's brick home didn't have a front porch. Instead, it had a patio and barbecue grill in an enclosed backyard.

The meal was served, as always, by the ladies of the church. In New Braunfels they fed people well after funerals, and strangely enough, funeral food tasted wonderful. Stella found she was always hungry, although the food was eaten with an uncomfortable feeling of guilt. How could one enjoy Mrs. Zeller's truly magnificent chocolate cake when they had just put Effie in the ground? But maybe funerals were in reality more of a celebration by the living of their own survival than a tribute to the dead. At one point Stella looked over at Billy as he took a tentative bite of blueberry pie. He looked so unsure. Stella shook her head at him. "You know how your mother was about pies. Eat it."

"It's not as good as Mom's," he said.

"No pie ever will be," Stella said. "But in a way acknowledging that each time you bite into a pie will be a tribute to her. And besides, apple was her specialty, not blueberry."

"Apple was for Dad," Bill said. "For me, she made coconut cream. And fresh cherry."

Dr. Pete and Jason were the only ones who didn't eat. Pete picked at his food and kept looking around the room with the expression of a man who had accidentally gotten himself in the wrong meeting and belatedly realized he was seated among strangers. Stella wondered if he would marry again—another nice widow lady. Or would he bumble around a few years and die?

Jason sat by the window. He had not bothered to fill a plate with food. Always so frail, yet he had lived this long, hovering on the outskirts of Effie's life. Stella wondered if his wouldn't be the next funeral.

Kate's and Stella's separate families left after dinner to drive to Dallas. Gordon would catch his plane for Washington, Francie for New York, and Ruthie for Berkeley. Stella and Kate lingered. They would drive to Dallas later—alone. Stella hadn't decided whether she would stay with Kate for a while or drive immediately down to Galveston. The thought of going to Galveston gave her something to look forward to, had given her strength in the last days of Effie's dying. She would rent someplace on the beach and take long walks.

The two sisters returned to the cemetery late that afternoon. They walked arm in arm through the rows of markers, reminiscing about Effie and the others.

"I'd like to be buried here," Kate announced.

"Yes. I think I would too—here with Mama and Papa and the little brother we never saw and the one we saw only once, and with Effie and Carl and all the rest. That seems fitting for some reason—to be planted for eternity in the soil that sprang us. But I'll end up in Tyler in the Kendall plot, and you'll end up in Dallas among the Morris clan."

"Unless," Kate said with a twinkle, "we outlive our first husbands. Then we can be buried wherever we want. Pete didn't want his second wife and his first wife both buried in his family plot, and he didn't want Effie buried beside William. That's the reason she got to come here to New Braunfels."

Stella laughed. "Don't you think we're getting a little old to think about second husbands?" She looked at Kate's stout form and ponytail that no longer had any red. Even her freckles had all but gone now that she no longer spent much time outdoors. Effie had always told her they would if she'd just stay out of the sun. Stella missed them.

"And I guess when you're dead it doesn't really matter where you're buried," Stella continued. "But for some reason, I'd rather be here and not buried with another family. After far more years of being Stella Kendall than being Stella Behrman, I still feel I belong here."

They left the cemetery and drove out Hunter Road. Kate turned in at the Rosehaven drive. It was blacktop now—and circled the house. No one was home yet from town, and the house was quiet. Kate turned off the motor.

Hiram and his wife had painted it yellow with brown trim. A proper shingle roof had replaced the tin one, and a room had been added where the wide front porch used to be.

"That porch was the best part," Stella said, wishing they hadn't come. She would rather have remembered the house as it was before.

"Yeah," Kate agreed, reaching for the ignition, but a train whistled in the distance. She grinned at Stella. "Got any pennies?" she asked.

They didn't run down the hill but walked arm in arm like the matronly sisters they were.

Sitting on the same fence from long ago, the two sisters watched the train roar past. "We never did, did we?" Stella asked, after the roar died away and she held a warm pancake of a penny in her hand.

"No. We never followed any daydreams on the train. We never even rode one past Dallas. Not you or me or Effie. No glamorous lives in faraway places, and after all that talk. Hollywood. New York. Chicago. Montreal." Kate readjusted her wide hips on the narrow fence rail. "I used to fit better up here, as I recall."

"My, how we did daydream," Stella said. "Remember how Effie claimed she was going to marry the owner of the railroad so she could always ride anyplace anytime she wanted? She got airplanes instead."

"And two husbands," Kate added, "both of whom adored her. She always seemed so happy." There was a wistfulness in her words.

"Maybe she seemed that way because she was. I think Effie was born happy," Stella said, remembering the Effie of their childhood with her bouncing curls and laughing eyes.

"You know, once I saw her making out with Carl in the barn," Kate said.

Stella almost lost her balance. She grabbed at the fence. "*Cousin* Carl? All the way?"

Kate nodded with a giggle. "Behind some baled hay in an empty stall. I was looking for kittens in the loft."

"Effie had sex with *Carl?* In the barn?" Stella began to laugh. "You mean dear, dull Carl didn't die a virgin after all. Effie and Carl? How wonderfully naughty! Oh, God, I'm so glad."

Stella and Kate laughed together. The two aging sisters sat on the fence at the base of the hill, the home of their childhood at its crest, the track for the trains that fed their daydreams at its base, and laughed and hugged one another and wept.

Effie was gone. Their mingled tears and laughter seemed a far more fitting farewell to the cousin who had been like a sister to them than the tedious sermon they had endured earlier.

The love the three cousins had shared had been a simple one—unquestioning, unconditional. There would never be the three of them again.

And someday there would be just one.

Stella looked back up the hill and in her mind's eye put the porch back on the house. The big white house with the practical tin roof. She could almost hear the screen door banging closed. The happy girlish voices. The excited barking of the old black-and-white dog as he loped along beside them. Three sets of pigtails streaming behind the girls as they raced down the hill to wave at the engineer, to put their pennies on the track, to wonder about people who went places on trains.

Stella and Kate lingered for a time, sitting on the fence in their funeral dresses, their shoulders touching, silently watching the big-sky grandeur of a Texas sunset.

Why had Effie been the happiest? Stella wondered. She seemed to have orchestrated her own happiness. Or maybe it was just a matter of Effie's knowing what she needed to do to live up to others' expectations. She had spent her life basking in the approval of her men. Perhaps she had been the pleasing daughter and an adored wife and a beloved mother because she always fulfilled those men's expectations of what a daughter-wife-mother should be. Was that her secret?

If so, it had served her well. Effie had been the most contented human being Stella had ever known.

Yet as much as she had admired and loved Effie, Stella would not have wanted to be like her. Effie gave up something to be the way she was. Stella understood that women like Effie do so willingly—without a thought, really. But Stella, in spite of the unfulfilled goals, had clung to herself.

Were women like herself who had a yearning to meet life on their own terms always sentenced to be discontented?

Perhaps, but any regret Stella once may have felt had long since turned to acceptance. That was the way it was, and it no longer mattered. She had outlived discontent.

Stella's past was a jumble of memories in need of sorting. Perhaps that was the function of old age. Funny how time softened the focus of the painful memories, while the good ones were enhanced. She remembered best the good things—the Christmas morning when she and Gordon and Francie had tiptoed into the boys' room and placed a new puppy on the bed between them. Francie had to cover her mouth to keep from giggling as they watched the wiggling puppy lick awake his new buddies.

And those chilly mornings with a child coming to snuggle a small, sturdy body against the warming curve of her own while she buried her face against a dear little neck and inhaled its baby sweetness.

Her children watching with such pride while their father was sworn in as a member of the United States Congress.

Memories of two sons who became best friends, of a daughter who had become her best friend.

And Charles, with a sunburned nose and his trouser legs encrusted with wet sand, kneeling on the beach, using his architectural skills to build her the grandest sand castle in the kingdom of Texas.

And so many more. Good memories.

And if she had no memories of herself in an academic gown receiving a doctoral hood, or thrilling to the sight of her just-published book on Texas women's history, or touching a few lives the way Blanche Lasseter had touched hers—well, she had tried. But she knew the battle was over. She was too tired to strive any longer, and losing a battle brought peace as surely as winning. Stella was at peace at last.

"I love you, Kate," she said.

"I love you too, Stella."

Kate took Stella back to Chris's house to pick up her car, then headed up I-35 to Dallas. It would be a long drive, but she wanted to go home.

The light was still on in the living room when Kate pulled into the driveway. Jimmy had waited up. Kate was glad.

He met her at the door with a hug. He poured her a glass of wine and rubbed her feet.

Jimmy's hair was as gray as hers, and he had gotten fat again. He didn't play golf much anymore. Funny how he looked at the same time like the old man he was becoming and the young man she remembered.

They were grandparents now—three times over. Sara was engaged to a florist. Bogey was in second grade and was as plump as his cousin Tom had been at that age. He wasn't interested in sports. He'd rather play Dungeons and Dragons with his friends.

"We're getting old, Jimmy boy," she said, as she nestled into the curve of his arm.

"I suppose we are," he agreed. They were sitting on the sofa in the much smaller living room of the house that had been their home since Jimmy bought his bar.

"Jimmy's." He had changed the name of the bar to "Jimmy's." It wasn't as wonderful as he wanted it to be, but it satisfied him more than selling sporting goods. He got to listen now instead of doing all the talking. And he liked polishing things. The mahogany bar gleamed. The mirrors shone. The glasses sparkled. It was his own little, well-cared-for world.

Kate stayed away. She had never quite approved and still lamented losing the big house in Arlington. It would have been perfect for big family holidays, she would occasionally remind him, but she had gotten her one last baby out of their deal. And he had gotten his bar. Now Kate had to satisfy herself with grandbabies. Mark's boy was playing T-ball, and Kate never missed a game.

"Why don't you come down and be my barmaid sometimes?" Jimmy asked.

"I'm too old for such nonsense," Kate said.

"Just try it, Kate. I'd like to share it with you. Maybe we could even change the sign out front to 'Jimmy *and* Kate's.' "

She was crying now. "I thought I'd cried away all my tears over these last months. Oh, God, watching my precious, beautiful Effie become ugly and die. Watching them lower that casket into the ground. I feel like the sun has gone down forever."

"You're my sun," Jimmy said, holding her, caressing her ponytail.

"Don't start lying to me now," Kate sobbed. "Honesty was always our long suit."

"You're my sun," Jimmy repeated. "I didn't always know it, but I do now. We started out thinking we were going to be stars. We didn't skyrocket anyplace, did we? But we warm each other. We're home to each other. I'm glad you're my wife, old woman."

"Thanks," Kate said, putting her head on his shoulder. "I'm glad you're my husband, old man."

Thirty-eight

Aput-together band of high school players struck up "The Eyes of Texas" as Stella, Gordon, Timmie, and local Democratic leaders filed onto the stage. The auditorium was half full, a respectable gathering. Often there weren't more than a handful. Gordon must have a good campaign chairman in Bell County. Stella made a mental note to remind Francie to single the man out for some sort of special recognition. Barton was his name. Bill Barton. He owned the local Chevrolet dealership.

Timmie's eyes were wide. He'd never sat on a stage before. This morning he'd sat in the front row, swinging his feet back and forth and occasionally reaching up to wiggle his loose front tooth. Such a sweet, easy child. Francie had done a good job with him. Now eight years old, Timmie was well behaved—and happy.

It was Gordon's idea that Timmie sit on the stage with them at this afternoon's rally. Stella had quickly tucked his shirt into his jeans and combed his hair. She wished he at least had a belt. "Tie your shoes, honey," she had told him. "You don't want to fall over your feet."

Timmie nudged her, grinning and pointing at a large picture of his granddaddy that hung from the curtain at the back of the stage over a "Kendall for Senate" banner.

They were in Killeen. This morning they had been in Lampasas. Two hot, dusty towns north of Austin. Lampasas at least had an Old West charm about it with its rustic, turn-of-the-century buildings. Any charm in Killeen had long since vanished in the wake of pawnshops, cheap motels, taverns, and convenience stores built to accommodate the soldiers stationed at nearby Fort Hood.

The rally in Lampasas had not gone well. Only a couple dozen people showed up. The P.A. system had so much feedback Gordon became distracted and lost his train of thought. And a man in overalls stood and interrupted Gordon, asking if he really had appointed a nigger to West Point.

Timmie asked Stella about that afterwards. "I thought it wasn't nice to say 'nigger.' "

"It isn't, but that man doesn't understand that," Stella explained. "Nobody taught him otherwise when he was a little boy."

Yesterday things had gone better at Temple, where there was an afternoon coffee in the American Legion Hall with mostly women in attendance. Gordon had been at his best.

They spent the night in Salado—just the three of them. Timmie had never been to the Stage Coach Inn. He must have eaten at least a dozen warm hush puppies with butter and honey. After dinner they peered in the windows of antique shops and walked up the hill to see the ruins of an old school. Timmie asked questions. Stella liked that. She had told him how the Pony Express had once used the old inn as a relay station, and she could almost see him conjuring up images as he had stood at the top of the hill and stared down at the quaint little one-street town. She would have to take him back when the town's museum was open.

Timmie stood at rigid attention beside her as the band played a brassy "Star-Spangled Banner."

One side of a red, white, and blue banner in the back of the auditorium had come loose and was half covering the clock. Stella glanced at her watch. They were late again. Gordon was scheduling himself too tightly, and it hardly allowed time for eating or going to the bathroom. People weren't as receptive if they'd been kept waiting. She'd speak to him. Maybe she should keep his appointment book herself.

After everyone was seated, a Baptist minister in a shiny black suit gave a long invocation, instructing God to keep the country strong and to protect unborn babies from those who would rip them from their mothers' wombs.

The mayor of Killeen made the introductions, including Timmie. "Congressman Kendall's grandson." *He's my grandson too,* Stella thought. Timmie grinned self-consciously. When the mayor reminded the folks who Timmie's father was, the boy sat up a little straighter in his seat. Then the man gave an extensive introduction of Gordon, listing his long service to the state of Texas. "Ladies and gentlemen, I give you Gordon Kendall, congressman, minister of God, and the next senator from the state of Texas."

Gordon stepped to the podium. His suit was mussed from their day of travel, but he looked good. His hair was still full and much less gray than Stella's. He had kept up his jogging and looked tanned, trim, and fit. *He gets more attractive each year,* Stella thought, while she herself just got older-looking. Strange how little it bothered her. Maybe people would start thinking she was Gordon's mother. Sometimes she felt as if she were.

Stella only half listened as her husband talked, giving a localized version of the same speech she'd heard this morning. He bragged on the football prowess of the Killeen Kangaroos, congratulating their three All-State players by name. He remembered getting his shoes muddy the last time he was in this part of the state. "I know now that you never let Bell County mud dry on your shoes." This remark drew smiles. It was true. The mud around here dried like cement.

Timmie's feet were swinging. Stella touched his leg. "Count the people," she whispered, "so your granddaddy will know how many came."

Gordon asked how many in the audience had had medical bills they couldn't afford over the last year. About half raised their hands. Gordon then explained his support for national health insurance as offered in the Democratic platform.

He talked about tax reforms and his plan for job retraining centers for the out-of-work.

Next came national defense. A strong America. Everything else was rendered meaningless in the face of nuclear war.

Timmie pulled at Stella's sleeve. "Should I count the people on the stage?" he whispered.

Stella nodded. "Then we need to know how many in the audience are men and how many are women," she whispered back.

Gordon had turned to a favorite theme—America's dependence on foreign oil. "The Middle Eastern oil cartel can withhold oil and create an energy crisis like we have never seen before in this country," he warned. "Or they can glut the world with oil and destroy our domestic petroleum industry, leaving this nation impossibly vulnerable. Make no mistake about it, in 1976 the world's wheels are turned by oil. This is far more wide-sweeping than an economic issue. This, my friends, is a matter of national defense."

Stella tuned out for a while, then suddenly realized Gordon was talking about the voting irregularities that had been discovered in several counties with large black populations in the southeastern part of the state.

Black voters had been told to put their votes in separate ballot boxes—ones that were never counted. Stella sat up straighter. She hadn't heard him use this in a speech before. The segregated voting boxes had brought national attention, and the President had commented on it during a press conference. Their Philippine daughter-in-law had even sent a clipping from the Manila newspaper about the Texas voting box scandal, and had written, "This sounds more like Johannesburg than Texas."

Stella looked out at the all-white audience. They didn't want to hear it, not in this part of Texas. Gordon was calling for more than just reprimands in such cases. Poll taxes had been declared unconstitutional in 1964, he reminded them. Other Federal laws should be passed prohibiting any practices that prevent citizens from exercising their right to vote. "This is Texas, not Johannesburg," he said.

Next he called for America to spearhead a war against starvation that included free and easy birth control methods for the world's poor and a distribution of America's bounty. "How can we tolerate starving children when we have more wheat than our grain elevators will hold and obesity is one of our major health problems? Americans grow fat while others die of hunger."

Stella recognized the words. They were out of one of Maria's letters to Gordon.

A very fat woman in the front row sank lower in her seat. Stella scanned the room. Lots of overweight people.

For his conclusion Gordon asked for their vote and support in the primary. "But please don't support me just because my opponent is Hispanic. I disavow completely the 'Keep Texas Texan' signs and campaign literature that are being distributed. Joseph Gonzales is a Texan and an American. He was wounded fighting for his country in Vietnam. I ask you to vote for me because of my past service to this state in the Congress of the United States, because of my unique set of experiences and talents that make me the best-qualified man for the job."

Stella began the applause. She hurried across the stage to hug him. God, she was proud.

She joined him in shaking hands with the few people who came to the front of the auditorium. He had offended more people than he had impressed. In the cities it would be better.

This was proving to be a much tougher campaign than either Gordon or Francie had anticipated. Joseph Gonzales was a bright young attorney from San Antonio who said uncomfortable things about Texas establishment politics, who called it a corrupt plutocracy of the Anglo upper classes that had little interest in serving minorities and women, who had the support of presidential hopeful Jimmy Carter. Liberal factions would support him—no question about it. But could the women's groups, the minorities get out the vote? Stella wondered. Texas politics were changing—for the better. Gordon had too, but he was still associated in most minds with the old guard. Gordon Kendall had been Lyndon Johnson's boy. Johnson was dead now but hardly forgotten. Some Texans would vote for Gordon because of Johnson, and some would vote against him for the same reason. He was no longer conservative enough to get more than lip-service support from the state party bosses, but he wasn't liberal enough to steal votes away from Gonzales. Gordon was neither fish nor fowl. How ironic that Gordon's link with the very faction that brought him into power might spell his political downfall.

Finally after all these years of mixed feelings about Gordon's political career, Stella found herself really caring about this election—and it was probably a losing cause. She had enjoyed this campaign more than she had the others. Ruthie and Francie often accompanied them. Francie had taken a leave of absence from her television job in order to coordinate this, the most important, campaign in her father's political career.

At thirty-two, Francie was even more beautiful than before. She had made a name for herself in New York. Smart and beautiful were a good combination for television anchorwomen. There was a network opening at CBS—weekend news spots—and Francie was hopeful.

Ruthie, home for the summer after three years at Berkeley, still wore earrings, but her hair was again uncurled and usually pulled back in a no-nonsense ponytail that reminded Stella of Kate. At the rallies Francie was as often at her father's side as Stella, while Ruthie stayed in the background. Still, Ruthie worked as hard as Francie did. Her father's politics didn't embarrass her quite so much anymore.

Stella liked it when Ruthie accompanied them on their junkets about the state. Watching Texas out the window was more fun with Ruthie at her side. Stella was reminded of her and Ruthie's trek two summers ago. Ruthie cared about Texas history with its incredible mixture of heroes and villains. It was almost like being with Blanche again.

Ruthie wanted to apply for medical school. And she wanted to marry Greg Easterling and make babies with him. Could she do both? Stella didn't envy her daughter the dilemma. In her own day it had been easier. The decisions that faced the women of Stella's generation were not whether to marry but whom to marry and how many children to have. Effie always knew that. Kate had fooled herself for a time, thinking that she wouldn't marry, and Stella herself struggled. But ultimately it had already been decided.

Stella wished Ruthie had heard Gordon's speech today. She had gone with Francie to Dallas to help Jimmy, Kate, and Dr. Pete with the final arrangements for the rally there on Sunday. Stella would tell the girls about their father's speech when they got back to Austin tomorrow. Francie would be critical; such speeches didn't get votes in places like Killeen. Ruthie would be proud.

It was Ruthie who pointed out that a tight campaign would be good for Gordon. And it had been. It forced him to think through issues he had previously ignored and brought out a fighting spirit that had been dormant since Brian's death. He'd hardly campaigned at all in his last congressional race. Voters in his district didn't expect him to. First his son-in-law had been killed in Vietnam, then his son. He didn't need to campaign to get their vote. But now the excitement of a close race was good for him. He thrived on the speeches and the people and the challenge.

After the election—win or lose—Gordon had promised they could all go to the Philippines for Christmas. She and Gordon, Ruthie, Timmie, and Francie. Stella looked forward to the trip more than she had to anything in a long time. She had a second grandchild now. His name was Brian. Oh, how she ached to hold that other Brian. Her fingers had longed to touch that child ever since Tom had called to tell her of his son's birth. "I'm a father, Mom. A son. Maria and I have named him Brian."

Brian. Sweet, darling Brian. Forever young and earnest and beautiful. And now a new Brian. Stella loved him already. She didn't know if he would be smart or beautiful, but she knew he was dear. She would kiss his soft earlobes and feel the fineness of his baby hair against her cheek. She would open his tiny fingers and press her lips in his palm.

"What are you thinking about with that secret smile on your face, pretty lady?" Gordon asked as he took her arm and pointed her toward the door. Timmie came running up and took his grandfather's hand.

"About how much I want to hold Tom's baby," Stella said.

Gordon slipped his arm around her waist. "Yeah. Another Brian. I like that, and I can't wait to meet Maria. Finally. We should have gone before now."

Stella drove Gordon out to the Killeen airport. He had chartered a small plane to fly him out to West Texas, where he was going to visit Abilene tonight and Lubbock and Pampa tomorrow. A plane was best in West Texas where the towns were so far apart. Stella and Timmie were going to drive back to Austin since there was still much to do to get ready for Sunday. Stella wanted to double-check all the arrangements. Just this morning she had wondered about what the band would be wearing. Timmie needed a haircut and a new dress shirt. Did the balloon and banner people know they couldn't get into the hotel ballroom until early Sunday morning? Should they arrange a buffet for all the special guests beforehand? Gordon had invited Lady Bird Johnson, John and Nellie Connally, Governor and Mrs. Briscoe. Francie had arranged for several of the Dallas Cowboys and cheerleaders to be there. The Cowboys still remembered Junior.

After the rally the family would all go out to Kate's for dinner to celebrate Stella and Gordon's thirty-fourth wedding anniversary.

"You two going to come in?" Gordon asked as Stella parked the car in front of the one-story terminal.

"Sure. Timmie'd probably like a Coke before we start back. Right, kiddo?"

Timmie nodded. "Can I see the planes?"

They were directed across a dusty field to a small hangar, where the pilot had a panel off the side of his craft. "It'll be a few minutes," he said over his shoulder.

Gordon got three Cokes out of a machine, and he and Stella sat on a bench outside the hangar. Timmie took his and went exploring.

Gordon put his arm around Stella. "We're going to win, Stella, my love. I feel it. I know it seems uphill now, but things will shift. You'll see. Never have my speeches felt so right. I'm going to make you the wife of a United States senator—that's what I'm going to do."

He was like a boy, this husband of hers. Stella leaned over and nuzzled his neck. "I'd be very proud—win or lose. You've run a fine campaign."

Gordon looked at her. "You really mean that, don't you?"

Stella smiled and nodded. "Yes. I really mean it." He would probably lose, but she was proud of him.

Gordon leaned his head against the side of the building. The day was warm, the air heavy. Stella realized he had dozed off. Stella leaned her own head back, but she didn't sleep.

Her thoughts wandered. The Philippines. Sunday. Brian's white gravestone in Arlington. Timmie's loose tooth. Charles.

The Dallas *Morning News*, September 20, 1976:

KILLEEN (AP)—Congressman Gordon Francis Kendall was killed yesterday afternoon in a plane crash six miles west of Killeen.

Kendall, 64, was completing his fifth term as congressman from the 24th Congressional District and was a candidate for the U.S. Senate. Shortly before the accident, he had concluded a campaign appearance at the Killeen High School and was on his way to Lubbock for another campaign stop.

The plane's pilot, Jordan F. Jenson, of Killeen, was also killed in the crash. Witnesses said the plane was apparently caught in a downdraft during takeoff and did not clear power lines located a half mile south of the runway.

When told of the accident, Gov. Dolph Briscoe said, "I am shocked and saddened. Gordon Kendall was a man of God, a good American, and a great Texan. His voice has been a sane and respected one in Texas politics for almost two decades, and he will be sorely missed."

A native of Tyler, Kendall graduated from the University of Texas in 1934 and received his doctor of divinity degree from Southern Methodist University in 1938. He was an ordained minister in the United Methodist Church.

He served as a chaplain with the Forty-fifth Infantry Division in the European Theater during World War II and was awarded the Distinguished Service Cross for bravery during combat. He was among the first to enter the liberated Dachau death camp in Germany and remained there after the war to assist in the relocation of the survivors.

After the war he served at churches in Arlington and then Fort Worth. In 1953 he was named president of United Wesleyan College in Johnstown.

After serving six years on the Texas Railroad Commission, he was elected to Congress in 1965. During his tenure in the House of Representatives, he served on the Ways and Means Committee and was chairman of the Armed Services Committee.

His papers will be donated to the University of Texas Library. According to university officials, arrangements are under way for the endowment of a chair in his honor in the UT Department of Political Science.

Survivors include his wife Stella; daughters, Frances Anna Kendall Bonifield, New York City, and Ruth Alice Kendall, Berkeley, Calif.; a son, Thomas Matthew Kendall, of Jolo, Philippines; and two grandsons. Another son, Marine 2nd Lt. Brian Gordon Kendall, was killed in action during the Vietnam War and was posthumously awarded the Distinguished Service Cross.

Francie sat at her father's desk in the study of the Georgetown house. She closed the jar of rubber cement and stared down at the last page of the album she had been working on. It was finished, the final pages full of obituaries and tributes.

The movers would arrive soon to take what remained of the furniture. Francie was shipping it to New York. The rest she had sold. That's what her mother said to do. "Send family pictures and the like back to Austin. Keep what you want of the furniture. Sell the rest."

Just like that. Sell the rest. As though it weren't important.

Francie couldn't believe Stella hadn't come back to Washington at all. Francie and Timmie were the only family members at the memorial service held for Gordon in the Capitol Rotunda. It was embarrassing. Francie was angry with her mother. How dare she fly off like that! My God, her husband had just died. She had no right. She was still Mrs. Gordon Kendall and had a responsibility to her husband's memory. Francie wasn't sure she could ever forgive her. Alone, Francie had closed her father's congressional office, telling everyone who worked there how her father had appreciated them, helping the secretaries box up his papers to be sent to the University of Texas archives.

And soon the house would be empty. It would be as though the Kendalls had never lived there. Such a beautiful house. Francie liked it much better than the barny old house in Austin. This house looked as if someone important could live inside, and when her mother went off to Texas on her many visits, she and Timmie had come here weekends and stayed with Daddy.

Francie had decided to keep all the furniture from the study even though there wasn't room for it in her apartment and she would have to put it in storage. She couldn't bear to part with any of it. She and her father had spent so many hours together in the study, talking, planning, being together. It was their room.

Timmie was going to miss his grandfather. They had been such buddies. Yes, Francie thought, she and her son were going to be lonely.

Francie wondered if Ruthie would accept her invitation to come to New York and live with them. Columbia had a wonderful medical school, and Ruthie was outstanding. She could get accepted.

Francie had surprised herself in making the offer. She and Ruthie had never been that close, with more separating them than years. Ruthie was plain and quiet and serious about everything. Her politics were liberal. Until this past summer the two women had seldom done more than exchange pleasantries. The staying-in-touch aspect of their lives had always been accomplished by their mother. Letters and phone calls had not been necessary.

And now with their mother so far away, it would be up to them. They could either drift apart or work at remaining family. With each other. With Aunt Kate and Uncle Jimmy. With all those cousins. The New Braunfels people. Funerals. Weddings. Remembering the names of babies. How important was it?

Francie looked down at the leather-bound scrapbook that was full of clippings documenting her father's political career from beginning to end. *She* had been the one who cared enough to keep it. Francie touched the book lovingly.

She would keep it always along with the pictures and mementos from her father's congressional office. His college yearbooks. His files of sermons. His books. His Bible. Francie would have to be the keeper. Her mother had abdicated.

The sigh that escaped her lips was audible in the quiet room. "Daddy," she said softly, and laid her hands against the ache in her breast. Ruthie loved their mother the most, but for Francie it was—it had always been—her daddy. They had loved each other the best.

Ruthie walked through the Austin house one last time, rechecking locks on windows, closing draperies and blinds. So empty the house seemed, sad, as though it knew.

She saved the kitchen for last. This was the room that more than any other meant her mother. Daddy held court in his study, Mother in the kitchen with its varnished wooden floors and big round wooden table. This was where Mother fed them cookies and milk after school. This was where Ruthie looked first when searching for her mother to show her A papers and be praised, to tell her of aches and pains and be comforted. Fevers and good grades achieved significance through her mother. Ruthie remembered all the times she sat on the high stool and watched while her mother kneaded dough or rolled out crust. Ruthie would lick bowls and beaters. She would ask questions, confident that her mother would tell her answers or ask a question that forced Ruthie to figure out the answer for herself.

The kitchen was where Stella had coffee with Effie and Aunt Kate. And in recent years it was often Ruthie and her mother at the round table, drinking coffee or wine and talking.

Ruthie sat down at the bare table in the empty kitchen. It looked strange without the customary salt and pepper shakers and the wooden napkin holder, without a pot of ivy or fresh iris in the spring and periwinkles in the summer. The refrigerator door stood ajar, revealing its dim, empty interior. The pantry was empty too. Ruthie had cleared away even the canned goods, not knowing when any of them would come back here again—if ever.

Stella had left so quickly. Ruthie still felt angry and hurt. Ruthie needed her mother here now.

But Tom had asked Stella to return with him to Jolo. "There's a little house close to mine and Maria's," he told her. "It's not much, but we could help you fix it up. Just try it for a few months and see if you like it. You could teach, Mother. The schoolrooms have dirt floors, and the students don't wear shoes, but they're eager and thank God every day for their wonderful school. You get them when they're little and watch them grow. When I sent two boys off to the university in Manila last fall, it was one of the proudest moments in my life."

Tom had come to the funeral alone. Ruthie was disappointed. She'd have to wait until Christmas to meet her sister-in-law and brand-new nephew.

Ruthie couldn't get over the change in Tom. Her brother was almost bald, and the tropical sun had aged his skin. But he wasn't fat anymore, and he looked good—almost attractive. Being with her brother again made Ruthie realize how much she'd missed his gentle presence in her life. Ruthie had worshipped Brian, but she had been comfortable with Tom, and she realized that comfort was also love.

Now, however, Ruthie wasn't sure she still loved him. She knew she was furious with him. How dare he take their mother away! If he wanted a mother, he should have to come to her. Yes, Ruthie decided, that would have been fair—for Stella to stay in the Austin house and any time Francie and Timmie or Tom or Ruthie herself wanted to return, their mother would have been there for them—the way Grandma Behrman had always been there in the little house in New Braunfels. But Tom had taken their mother away.

The Philippines. Even as Stella told Tom she would think about it, Ruthie knew her mother would go. She could tell by the look on Stella's face. She looked almost young.

"Just for a few months," Stella told them all the day after the funeral as they sat around the table, making a meal from leftover funeral food, "to see how I get along and get used to being without your father—maybe have a fresh start. There are so many memories here. The past is . . ."

Then Stella looked off at nothing, and her eyes had filled with tears. The years crept back on her face. "Your father . . ." Stella shrugged helplessly. "I miss him," she said, and went to sit by herself on the glider in the backyard. Ruthie had started to follow her, but Kate shook her head.

With Stella out of the room, Kate had turned to Tom, her hands firmly on her wide hips. "I can't believe you would complicate your mother's life at a time like this with such a wild idea. The Philippines!"

"What would you have her do?" Tom asked his aunt.

"Come back here to live, of course. To Texas, where she belongs."

"Why? Ruthie and Francie aren't here."

"Well, I am," Kate said. "She's my sister, damn it. We have a right to grow old together. You leave her be, Tom Kendall."

Two days later Stella had flown away with Tom. She had stayed up all night the night before, packing. Clothes and books, some pictures, nothing else. "You close up the house, Ruthie," she had said. "Francie can take care of the one in Georgetown." Just like that, after a lifetime of being the mother in the kitchen.

And now Ruthie sat in the empty kitchen of the lonely house and felt like an orphan.

She looked at her watch. It was almost time to call a cab. Her suitcases were packed and sitting by the front door. There was no one here to tell her good-bye.

Ruthie had stayed here by herself for the remainder of the summer, working part-time at the student infirmary and auditing a class in history of science to fill the hours. And now it was time to fly back to California for her last year at Berkeley and to deal with Greg, who didn't want to be married to a doctor. He didn't want hired help to raise his children. Ruthie wanted both—to have children and to be a doctor. She thought it must be possible if both partners wanted it. Her mother doubted that it was; Greg insisted that it wasn't. Ruthie and Greg argued about it endlessly.

It was only a matter of time until they broke up. Ruthie knew that, but she kept hanging on, hoping he would change his mind. She wondered if it would have made a difference if she hadn't made better grades than he did, if she hadn't had a near perfect score on the national medical school admissions test. Ruthie hated Greg, and she loved him. It was all so stupid, and her mother wouldn't be here if she and Greg broke up. Her mother wouldn't be here if she and Greg stayed together. Ruthie had to face it all alone.

What if no other man ever wanted her? The fear that this might be so frightened Ruthie as much as the fear of losing Greg himself, but Ruthie refused to follow in her mother's footsteps. She had not bothered to learn how to make her Grandmother Anna's family-famous coffee cake. She hated domesticity. And yes, she would have hired help to look after any children. She had seen how boring and demanding and messy little children can be. They were not intellectually stimulating. But Ruthie did want at least to have a daughter who would grow up and someday go on a trek with her. Yes, she wanted that very much.

If she had a baby, would her mother even be there? Suddenly even that time-honored assumption seemed in jeopardy. And what if she got sick? Ruthie thought. What if she got mononucleosis like Tom when he was in high school, and Mother nursed him, made him his favorite homemade chicken noodle soup, and even read to him as if he were a little boy again? Yes, Ruthie thought indignantly, what if she got sick and needed to come back to Austin to recuperate? And was she supposed to call halfway around the world to discuss small triumphs and work through depressing funks?

Yet, in spite of the fact that Ruthie wanted her mother here, in this house, she did not want her mother's life. God, it was all so confusing.

Ruthie would apply to prestigious medical schools across the land. Greg also wanted a career in medicine, but he would have to settle for less than prestigious. Ruthie would settle for that too if she thought they would still be together when they graduated.

But whatever the school, she was going to be a doctor, and nothing was going to stop her. She was going to live her life for others in the broader way that the practice of medicine would bring, but her soul would belong to herself. She wanted meaningful challenges. She would not spend her personal life always subjugating her needs and desires to those of others.

Her mother was an intelligent and insightful woman. That knowledge had been driven forcefully home to Ruthie over the last few years as she and her mother became friends. What a waste, Ruthie had thought over and over again. All that knowledge trapped inside a woman who had spent her days scrubbing, cooking, caring for children. Ruthie would have been more comfortable never seeing that other side of her mother. Knowing it was there made the facts of Stella's life seem demeaning and unfair. Her mother's dilemma came to signify for Ruthie all that was wrong with women's lives.

But if her mother's life had been wasted, why did Ruthie already miss so much the mothering things? Why did she think how wonderful it had been to come home to this house on Atterbury Lane full of the aromas of cooking, its surfaces cared for and gleaming, her mother's presence permeating every corner of its rooms?

Now the house had no mothering smells; it was just a house. Mother herself had been the home, Ruthie realized, the place to return to, the place of comfort and caring and unchanging love.

Ruthie's warm family memories existed because her mother had made them happen. Up to this point in her life, the best part had been having a mother like Stella Kendall.

This realization made Ruthie angry. She didn't want to believe in her mother's life. She wanted only to reject—all of it—most of all the unfulfilled goals. The price her mother paid was too high.

But Ruthie was forced at least to admit that she had made them a family. There was no written record of her mother's accomplishments. When she died, the obituaries in the papers would recognize her only as the late Congressman Kendall's wife.

"God damn it, Greg Easterling," Ruthie said, staring across the room at her mother's wonderful rolltop desk. "Why can't you grow up?"

And why wasn't her mother here when she needed her?